The Walnut Mansion

Other publications by Miljenko Jergović
previously translated into English

Sarajevo Marlboro
Ruta Tannenbaum
Mama Leone

The Walnut Mansion

MILJENKO JERGOVIĆ

TRANSLATED BY STEPHEN M. DICKEY,

WITH JANJA PAVETIĆ-DICKEY

YALE UNIVERSITY PRESS ■ NEW HAVEN & LONDON

A MARGELLOS
WORLD REPUBLIC OF LETTERS BOOK

The Margellos World Republic of Letters is dedicated to making literary works from around the globe available in English through translation. It brings to the English-speaking world the work of leading poets, novelists, essayists, philosophers, and playwrights from Europe, Latin America, Africa, Asia, and the Middle East to stimulate international discourse and creative exchange.

Yale University Press books may be purchased in quantity for educational, business, or promotional use. For information, please e-mail sales.press@yale.edu (U.S. office) or sales@yaleup.co.uk (U.K. office).

Set in Electra and Nobel types by Tseng Information Systems, Inc.
Printed in the United States of America.
ISBN: 978-0-300-17927-9 (cloth; alk. paper)

Library of Congress Control Number: 2015937574
A catalogue record for this book is available from the British Library.

This paper meets the requirements of ANSI/NISO z39.48-1992 (Permanence of Paper).

10 9 8 7 6 5 4 3 2 1

CONTENTS

The Walnut Mansion, published in 2003, is the first novel by Miljenko Jergović, one of the most well-known contemporary writers in Croatia and Bosnia. He has been a major figure in a wave of "new realism" that has been predominant in the fiction of younger writers of the former Yugoslavia since the breakup of the country. But Jergović's literary artistry is hardly limited to fiction: he has authored several collections of poetry, two collections of essays, three collections of short stories, and one novella.

The Walnut Mansion won the Bosnia and Herzegovina Writers' Association Prize in 2003, and Jergović's other works have earned him numerous other awards. He received the Mak Dizdar Prize and the Goran Prize (both in 1988) for his first collection of poetry, *The Warsaw Observatory*; the Ksaver Šandor Gjalski Prize (1994) for *Sarajevo Marlboro*; the Matica Hrvatska Prize for Literature and the August Šenoa Art Prize for *Buick Rivera* (2002); the Premio Grinzane Cavour Prize (2003) for *Mama Leone* (1999); his novel *Ruta Tannenbaum* (2006) won him the Meša Selimović Award for best novel of the year in Bosnia and Herzegovina, Serbia, Croatia, and Montenegro (2007). Most recently, he received the Angelus Central European Literature Award in 2012 for the Polish translation of his novel *Srda Sings at Dusk on Pentecost*.

If one judges according to output, literary awards, and the number of translations, Jergović is one of the top two contemporary Croatian writers—the other being Dubravka Ugrešić. If Ugrešić is better known among Anglophone readers, this is due in part to the fact that Jergović has remained continually "on the ground" in Bosnia and Croatia, writing squarely for the local populations of Bosnians, Croats, and Serbs, a position that has resulted in fewer of his works being published in English translations. (Hopefully the present effort will help rectify this situation.) A further reason is that Jergović's tales are almost without exception situated within lands of the former Yugoslavia—primarily in Croatia and Bosnia. They make almost continual mention of historical and cultural particulars of the region and therefore may seem more difficult to translate and less accessible to an outside readership. (Again, it is hoped that the present work will dispel at least the latter notion.) Indeed, it is this writer's impression that Jergović is the contemporary paradigm of a Balkan/Southeast European storyteller:

he writes stories and novels replete with the charm and tragedy of the region that local and outsider alike simply can't put down.

Given his prolific *oeuvre*, Jergović can only be described as very reticent concerning the details of his own biography; he provides the following statement on his website: "Miljenko Jergović was born in 1966 in Sarajevo. He currently lives outside of Zagreb."[1] In addition to his literary activity, he works as a journalist for the *Jutarnji list* newspaper and is also a columnist for the Radio Sarajevo website and the Belgrade newspaper *Politika*. Since Jergović grew up as a Bosnian and has lived and worked for twenty years primarily in Croatia, he is probably best conditionally (and for lack of a clearly better alternative) identified as a Bosnian/Croatian writer.[2] (Note that ethnic identification has been no idle game in the former Yugoslavia and its successor states.)

Though *The Walnut Mansion* is Jergović's first novel, in its length and scope it arguably remains his most ambitious (though his latest novel, *Kin*, published in 2013, surely competes in this regard). It presents the author's vision of life in twentieth-century Yugoslavia, told through the experiences of a family from the Croatian city of Dubrovnik. In particular, it tells the story of a woman named Regina Delavale, whose life is tracked backward, from her death in 2002 as a demented ninety-seven-year-old woman to her birth in 1905. The chapters are even numbered in reverse, so that the novel begins with chapter 15 and ends with chapter 1. The focus of the novel is, in Jergović's words, a tale of "the small in the great"—the momentous events of the twentieth century share the timeline with the failed romances, petty arguments, moneymaking schemes, traffic accidents, private obsessions, bedtime stories, jokes, lies, panicked mistakes, births, and all manner of deaths of the members and acquaintances of a common Dubrovnik family.

In all, episodes from five generations of Regina's family are narrated in the novel. It includes more than fifty characters and ultimately spans a period of more than one hundred years, taking place mostly in Croatia and Bosnia. It should therefore come as no surprise that in an interview with the newspaper *Slobodna Dalmacija* in 2003 Jergović described it as an attempt at writing a "quintessential" novel.[3] But if *The Walnut Mansion* has an epic scale, its epic is not the heroism of South Slavic tradition, but (as pointed out above) an epic of small, ordinary people. And it is in particular an epic of women, as the females are the central characters that provide continuity to the story. The central theme of the novel is how these women struggle and endure amid the fallout from the misfortunes and cataclysms (most notably the Second World War) that afflicted those living in the lands of the former Yugoslavia during the twentieth century.

If the references to the history of the region seem confusing to the un-

initiated, it is for good reason. The lands of the former Yugoslavia have basically constituted a frontier zone where the cultures and legacies of the Byzantine (Orthodox), Ottoman (Islamic), and West European (Austro-Hungarian
and Italian; Catholic) imperial traditions have coexisted, competed, and also
fought throughout the modern era. Within the former Yugoslavia, Bosnia and
Herzegovina—Jergović's homeland—has been the region where the interaction
among these cultures has been the most intense and immediate.

The earliest events recounted in the novel occur in the waning years of the
Ottoman Empire (the late nineteenth century). The Ottomans had conquered
the Byzantine Empire and the medieval Serbian and Bosnian kingdoms basically by the mid-fifteenth century. The Croatian territories ceded their sover-
eignty to the Habsburg Empire in the hope of avoiding Ottoman conquest
in the early sixteenth century; this strategy worked, but at the cost of Austro-
Hungarian rule until that empire was dismantled following the First World War.
This expansion of Austrian rule into Croatia, combined with the rule of the
Adriatic coast by the Venetian Republic from the Middle Ages until Napoleon's
conquest of the latter, accounts for much of the historical context of the novel
(and Austria-Hungary is mentioned much more frequently than one might
expect in a novel about twentieth-century Yugoslavia). Further, the Treaty of
Zadar compelled Venice to accept the establishment of the independent maritime Republic of Dubrovnik in 1358. The republic existed from that year until
1808, navigating alternating periods of trade, tension, and outright warfare between the Ottomans and their Austrian and Venetian opponents. The small
Republic of Dubrovnik and thus its capital city were known for the value they
placed on freedom and their independent spirit. One can arguably see some of
that spirit in the actions of the characters in *The Walnut Mansion*. However, it
is sometimes difficult to distinguish between the independent spirit of Dubrovnik and renowned Balkan stubbornness, and some might even argue that they
are one and the same.

In the early modern era the territories of Croatia and Bosnia and Herzegovina became the locus of a static military frontier between the Austro-
Hungarian and Ottoman Empires, a situation that contributed in large part
to a frontier mentality and an ethos of resistance (to ideological commitment)
to various outside players with an interest in the area. This spirit was con-
ducive to various movements for national independence from the Ottoman
and Austro-Hungarian Empires and, as an outgrowth, the idea of a pan–South
Slavic state—Yugoslavia—in the nineteenth century. Complicating such independence movements were actions taken by Austria-Hungary to fill the power
vacuum left by the weakening Ottoman Empire, most notably the occupation

and subsequent annexation of Bosnia and Herzegovina (1878 and 1908 respectively). As mentioned above, the introduction of Austro-Hungarian rule in the wake of the Ottomans forms the immediate historical background of the novel, which, however, is encountered only at its end.

The idea of Yugoslavia gained political momentum during the First World War, and the end of the war in 1918 saw the creation of the Kingdom of the Serbs, Croats, and Slovenes, which was soon plagued by ethnic antagonisms. Royal Yugoslavia hobbled along until the Axis invaded the country in April 1941, in preparation for its attack on the Soviet Union. Hitler's conquest of Yugoslavia was followed by four years of unprecedented bloodletting, but most Yugoslav casualties were victims of their compatriots. In particular, in the fascist Independent State of Croatia Ante Pavelić's Ustashas (including both Croats and some Bosniaks) exterminated Jews, Serbs, and Roma; in eastern Bosnia, Draža Mihailović's Serbian guerillas (Chetniks) massacred large numbers of Bosniaks. Josip Broz Tito's Soviet-backed Partisans fought both the Ustashas and at times the Chetniks in their war against the Nazis. These names and terms are mentioned repeatedly in the novel.

After the Second World War, Tito and his communist Partisans took control of the country. Yugoslav communism was not as repressive as Soviet (and especially Stalinist) communism, and Tito's postwar policies soon earned him the ire of the Soviets, culminating in a tense Soviet-Yugoslav split in 1948, which was welcomed by the West. Tito then steered Yugoslavia on its own independent course, while remaining committed to socialism. His international promotion of the Non-Aligned Movement can be seen as elevating the frontier mentality of the region to the level of global political ideology. After Tito's death in 1980, it seems in retrospect only to have been a matter of time before the country broke up, as communist Yugoslavia failed badly in the economic sector and also failed (as had its interwar predecessor) to create an identity to replace the ethnic loyalties of its citizens. That time came in 1991, when Slovenia and Croatia seceded from the country, which had come under the control of the Serbian nationalist technocrat Slobodan Milošević; Bosnia and Herzegovina followed suit in 1992. Bloodletting reminiscent of the Second World War followed as well and was particularly vicious in Bosnia, a situation that led Jergović to leave Sarajevo and settle in Croatia. The outbreak of war in Croatia and the shelling of Dubrovnik by Serbian and Montenegrin forces in 1991 are mentioned in passing late in the chronological time of the novel (which is early in the story, as it is told in reverse).

If Jergović is a quintessential Balkan storyteller, his literary horizons nevertheless lie far beyond that region. In his interview with *Slobodna Dalmacija*, he revealed some noteworthy outside influences, including Zadie Smith and Jonathan Franzen, as they "prove that there is such a thing as an epic of the new millennium and that it makes sense to tackle the big themes on a scale that calls a motion picture to mind." In addition to other print influences (ranging from Fernand Braudel's theory of history to Baedeker travel guides), Jergović emphasizes the influence of film (Italian Neorealism and Fellini's *Amarcord*, as well as the work of Douglas Sirk) and music (Arab, Latin American, Roma, and the lyrics of Bosnian *sevdah* and Croatian *klapa* songs).

These self-acknowledged connections place Jergović not only in the Yugoslav cosmopolitan milieu that was open to Western influences (and one might consider a "Central European" current in Yugoslav culture), but also in the specifically Balkan (i.e., indigenously Southeast European and/or post-Ottoman) culture of the region. He is less a part of its Orthodox element.

The Walnut Mansion falls into a rich tradition of the family saga in modern world literature, and I think it is indisputably a rewarding read even for those with no knowledge of the former Yugoslavia. However, in what follows I focus mostly on aspects of the novel as they relate to the literary and political contexts of the former Yugoslavia. The novel is extremely interesting with regard to the post-Yugoslav "space" and deserves some comment in this regard.

There have been relatively few works that could count as family sagas in the literatures of Croatia, Bosnia, and Serbia. In Croatian literature, Vjenceslav Novak chronicled the fall of a noble family in Senj on the Adriatic coast in *The Last of the Stipančićes*, and Miroslav Krleža chronicled the rise and fall of the Glembaj family in eleven short stories and three plays. (One might also mention here Ivo Vojnović's *Dubrovnik Trilogy*, which, though not a family saga, narrates the demise of the Republic of Dubrovnik and the Dubrovnik nobility, which is echoed in the narrative of a Dubrovnik family in *The Walnut Mansion*.) Some important single-work representatives of the genre come from Serbian literature: Ivo Andrić's *The Woman from Sarajevo* and Mirko Kovač's *The Door of the Womb*; one might argue for the inclusion of Borisav Stanković's *The Tainted Blood*. None of these novels really covers more than two generations of a family, and in this respect *The Walnut Mansion*, with its span of five generations, appears to be unique.

As mentioned, *The Walnut Mansion* is also remarkable for its focus on female characters, as well as the prominence of female psychological narrative. Into the twentieth century most South Slavs lived in patriarchal societies, and their fiction tended to focus on male characters and values, even when criticizing a patriarchal social order (a perfect example of this is Krleža's *On the Edge of Reason*). It is interesting that some notable exceptions to the trend of dominant male characters come from Serbian literature, where the patriarchal social order has been slow in dying out. Here one can mention Stanković's *The Tainted Blood*, Miloš Crnjanski's *Migrations*, and Andrić's *The Woman from Sarajevo*. *The Walnut Mansion* differs from the first two in that Jergović is not portraying women of exceptional physical beauty (in fact, Regina's looks are barely described in the novel). It does bear a strong resemblance to *Migrations* because Regina is the prism through which the narratives of numerous male characters are viewed, just as Dafina in *Migrations* is ultimately the glue that holds the narratives of the brothers Vuk and Aranđel Isaković together.

Though *The Woman from Sarajevo* is a rather odd tale of a misanthrope, it anticipates the major theme of *The Walnut Mansion*: the effect of cataclysmic historical events on an ordinary woman. The withdrawal of the protagonist of *The Woman from Sarajevo* from society after the First World War arguably subdues this theme, whereas *The Walnut Mansion* almost continuously foregrounds the watershed events of history and their effect on Regina's life, beginning with the First World War, continuing with the Second World War and various postwar events such as the death of Josip Broz Tito. The conduct of Jergović's female characters in these events differs greatly from that of the men in their lives, who with one or two exceptions see these events as opportunities for enrichment, adventure, or revenge and almost inevitably perish, leaving their women to fend for themselves.

With this in mind, one could describe *The Walnut Mansion* as a kind of "herstory" of life in twentieth-century Yugoslavia. In one of the bloody climaxes of the novel, the narrator even directly comments on the differences between the sexes with regard to history: "Men write history with knives, and women summon it with words."

Regina's brother Luka, selling cheese at a market, makes a like-minded comment on historical greatness and the attitudes of the sexes toward it:

> The real truth of history hasn't been written down, but as there are no living witnesses, it's simplest to say that Napoleon never ate lunch or dinner like ordinary people. Instead of eating, he conquered the world. Instead of drinking, he waged war. So was Napoleon, my good people, a great man? Well, missus, you tell me: would you rather have your husband grab a rifle and shoot up the street, kill all the neighbors, and go on a war of conquest instead of lunching on those delicious mackerels you've bought?

At another point, the narrator slips in a more general comment that reveals the novel's approach to history at the end of some reflections on Bosnia as a

"Yugoslavia in miniature": "If a story about the great in the small could have been recast into a story about the small in the great, the history of our country would look very different, and we would seem more normal to those who will one day study it."

This is an important point, and it adds to the comments made above regarding the focus of the novel on the common problems of common people: a superficial familiarity with the history of the former Yugoslavia and the Balkans leaves one with the impression of a region of eternal memory and almost continual bloodletting and strife that "has produced more history than it could consume locally," as Churchill is alleged to have said. (This false impression finds one of its most extreme presentations in Robert Kaplan's *Balkan Ghosts*.) Of course, many of the characters in *The Walnut Mansion* are colorful, to say the least, but they are nevertheless *ordinary people*—people in whom most readers from anywhere ought to be able to recognize some of themselves.

The novel also makes the point, slowly, concentrically, that the edifices of an age are made small by the passing of time. Indeed, Regina's brother Bepo, living out his days in an asylum, states the idea in a fresh, prospective way:

> We believe that communism is something great and eternal. We think so because it is in proportion to us, but it won't be for our children and our children's children. The little ones can't understand the big people, just as we can't understand them. We know only that communism will seem trivial to them. They'll take a red banner between two fingers, like this, and will walk across Russia in three steps because Russia will seem small to them too, much smaller than Pelješac. You just watch children growing big and you see that there's no point in measuring the world on a scale bigger than your own life.

Russia is not the heart of the matter; one need only substitute "Russia" with "Yugoslavia" or some other cultural titan to bring the idea home. The children of today will walk over our edifices as if they were toys.

Inextricably linked with its telling of history through the eyes of ordinary people is the aforementioned reverse chronological order of the narrative. In recent years, reverse chronology has been a popular device in novels (e.g., Viktor Pelevin's *The Yellow Arrow*) and movies (e.g., *Memento, Irreversible*). Though it is often considered a postmodern technique, Jergović maintains that he employed reverse chronology simply to "follow the logic of an individual human history, the logic of memory."[4] Indeed, at one point the narrator suggests that "every whole human story starts from the end." This adherence to the logic of memory can explain the segues into the stories of peripheral characters that some reviewers have found distracting.[5] But it is precisely these digressions into the "lateral zones" of the plot that provide a fuller picture of life and enrich the historical perspective. The so-called digressions and nested narratives are far from alien to the literature of the region but recall the digressive nature of its folk epics, as well as the narrative approach of none other than Ivo Andrić (as in, for example, *The Damned Yard*).[6]

Jergović's emphasis on memory in the novel calls to mind Danilo Kiš's short story "The Encyclopedia of the Dead." In this story a woman dreams of a trip to Sweden, where in the Royal Library she finds the *Encyclopedia of the Dead*, a massive set of volumes that provides detailed chronicles of the lives of ordinary people, and reads its detailed account of her deceased father's life. She describes the *Encyclopedia* as a "treasury" of memory produced by writers who "record and value every life, every affliction, every human lifetime." These words could almost be a description of the approach to historical narrative of *The Walnut Mansion*. Likewise, the temporal structure of *The Walnut Mansion* is very reminiscent of that of the *Encyclopedia*, as described by the narrator: "Every period of time was rendered in a kind of poetic quintessence and metaphor, not always chronologically, but in a strange symbiosis of different times — past, present and future. How else can one explain a sad comment in that text, in that 'picture book' of the first five years he spent at his grandfather's in Komogovina, which reads, if I remember correctly, 'Those *would be* the best years of his life'?"

Not only does the reverse chronology of *The Walnut Mansion* produce such a "strange symbiosis of different times," but it even employs the future-in-the-past quite frequently, as in the following random example taken from early on in the novel: "That evening saw the occurrence of everything that *would lead* to the death of Regina Delavale, or crazy Manda" (my emphasis — SMD).

Thus, Kiš's description of the *Encyclopedia of the Dead* seems at the same time to be a fairly accurate outline of the narrative strategy of *The Walnut Mansion*. The *Encyclopedia of the Dead* is of course a fantasy, even within the world of Kiš's story, but the tale of Regina Delavale reads almost like a sprawling entry in the *Encyclopedia*. In any case, one cannot read *The Walnut Mansion* and come away unconvinced that Jergović is a writer who "values every life, every affliction, every human lifetime."

Jergović tips his hat to numerous writers of the lands of the former Yugoslavia, and Kiš is only one of them. (There are, by the way, other allusions to Kiš in the novel. For example, Jergović makes a passing play on Kiš's story "Last Respects," which tells of the honors bestowed upon a prostitute at her funeral. The honors are inverted in *The Walnut Mansion*: a group of prostitutes gathers to honor the memory of Luka, their spendthrift faux-client.)

I have already mentioned the focus on the effect of history on ordinary people common to *The Walnut Mansion* and Andrić's *The Woman from Sarajevo*. On a more general level (and leaving aside the reverse chronology of *The Walnut Mansion*), Jergović's narrative style shares many similarities with that of Andrić. This is not surprising, as both Andrić and Jergović were raised in Bosnia, a land where oral traditions have been strong and the people take delight in storytelling. And Jergović has certainly made no efforts to distance himself from Andrić's writing, even or especially at times when Andrić came under fire in both Croatia and Bosnia itself for his Serbian self-identification.

An important similarity is the multitude of voices in their stories. Like Andrić's prose, *The Walnut Mansion* is decidedly polyphonic: a great many voices tell stories and anecdotes that contribute to the overall depiction of life in twentieth-century Yugoslavia. And as with Andrić, though there is an omniscient narrator who does not narrate in a distinct voice, that omniscient narrator does occasionally comment directly on the plot or its themes as if actually speaking with the reader. A further feature that Jergović shares with Andrić is the frequent employment of free indirect discourse, which allows the omniscient narrator to seamlessly render the characters' thoughts.

Other writers to whom an attentive reader can find allusions are those as different as the Serb Borislav Pekić, the Croat Miroslav Krleža, and the Bosnian Meša Selimović (and there are certainly others that have escaped my attention). It thus makes no sense to try to pigeonhole Jergović as a writer who self-identifies with only one of the increasingly ethnically homogeneous enclaves that have risen out of the ashes of the former Yugoslavia. And it should be pointed out that he does not "long for [the state of] Yugoslavia; what perished had to."[7] Rather, Jergović appears to be an odd thing—a *post-Yugoslav writer*, in the literal sense of the term, and in a cultural sense, as opposed to a political one. It is doubtful that he would agree to be considered anything else. And his work, including *The Walnut Mansion*, is the richer for it.

One last point worth mentioning is that the story of Regina Delavale's life lends itself to interpretation as an allegory of the fate of Yugoslavia. Regina's rampages in the final days of her life, in which she lays waste to an entire apartment (a container of life, much as states are), seem to be a metaphor for the bloody rampages of paramilitaries that ended the state of Yugoslavia. And the reader travels back slowly to her childhood and then to her birth, when she is given a toy house carved in walnut. The little wooden house stands as a symbol of the novel's idea that the legacies left by a generation seem tiny to future generations. (Indeed, Tito's Yugoslavia was destroyed by politicians who belonged to the generation that came after its founders.) And in this way the little house in walnut can also be seen as a metaphor for the state granted to the Serbs, Croats, and Slovenes by Woodrow Wilson and the Western powers after the First World War. Thus, the reverse chronology of the novel is oddly suitable for outside readers, the majority of whom first learned about Yugoslavia at its bloody end and only slowly worked their way backward to learn the history of the country.

Notes

1. Http://www.jergovic.com/bio-bibliografija/.

2. This label should not be confused with "Bosnian Croat"—that is, a Croat born and raised in Bosnia and Herzegovina.

3. Http://arhiv.slobodnadalmacija.hr/20030716/forum01.asp. Translations of his remarks in this interview are mine.

4. Http://arhiv.slobodnadalmacija.hr/20030716/forum01.asp.

5. See, for example, the review in the July 24, 2007, issue of the *Süddeutsche Zeitung*.

6. I'm grateful to Aida Vidan for pointing these aspects out to me.

7. Http://bhknjiga.com/intervjumiljenko-jergovic-hrvati-su-sretniji-od-srba-zene -ce-im-prije-postati-europske-sobarice.html. Translation mine.

TRANSLATORS' NOTE

Like Jergović's other prose works, *The Walnut Mansion* is written in a lucid, colloquial style; the language itself presents few unusual challenges to a translator, and only a handful of small changes in content for an Anglophone readership have been necessary.

One of the biggest issues presents itself in the title. The Croatian word *dvori* has no real equivalent in English, as it refers to a specific type of house in coastal Croatia. The word is defined as "a house with several rooms of solid construction, made of stone in coastal areas, usually with a portico, a rain cistern and a storeroom." Not exactly a mansion in our current conception, but since "mansion" is defined simply as "a large, impressive house," it works best, as the kind of house in question was often larger than average homes, and a portico represents a modicum of luxury.

A greater problem for a foreign readership is the very frequent mention of various names, places, and events unfamiliar to those who are not well-versed in the history of the former Yugoslavia. On the one hand, there are far too many of these to explain in footnotes or a glossary; on the other, removing them or translating some of them descriptively would in our view make the translation anemic. Thus, we have left all such references in the text intact. Though these references may impede the comprehension of the uninitiated in places, the vast majority if not all of these names are easily found on the Internet, and the curious reader should be able to find explanations of them there in English without difficulty.

Another problem for an Anglophone readership is the names of the characters. Given that the novel has some fifty of them, most of whom have distinctly Croatian, Bosnian, or Serbian names, the task of finding suitable equivalents is impossible. In our view, transliterating these names makes them very ugly, and this is normally not the practice in the media, which simply delete any pesky diacritics (e.g., "Milosevic" in place of "Milošević"), though this is no solution either. Therefore, we have opted to keep the names in their original form, including all diacritics. The following table will demystify their pronunciation.

B/C/S	English
c	Like *ts*

č, ć	Like *ch*
dž, đ	Like *j* in *jam*
j	Like *y* in *yes*
lj	Like *ly* in *tell ya*
nj	Like *ny* in *lanyard*
š	Like *sh*
ž	Like *ge* in *rouge*

Finally, Jergović uses various words referring to Croatian and Balkan concepts that have no convenient equivalents in English. As most of these occur in one form or another in the *Oxford English Dictionary* or the *Merriam-Webster Unabridged*, we have retained them in their attested Anglicized forms. They and two frequent political terms mentioned in the introduction are defined below; the reader may refer to these definitions when these words occur. The definitions given below are based on those in the aforementioned dictionaries except that we have tailored them slightly to reflect their meaning in Croatia and the Balkans.

borek	A savory pie made of puff pastry, containing a variety of fillings such as cheese, meat, and potatoes
boza	A popular hot drink in Turkey and the Middle East, made by fermenting an infusion of millet seeds
briscola	An Italian trump card game played in the Mediterranean and Adriatic
Chetnik	A guerilla fighter in the Balkans; more specifically, a member of Serbian royalist guerillas in World War II
gusle	A bowed string musical instrument in the Balkans that usually has only one string
hodja	A teacher in a Muslim school
salep	A hot drink made by sweetening an infusion of a flour of the same name made from orchidaceous plants (cf. British *saloop*)
tekke	A dervish monastery
Ustasha	A member of a party of separatist Croats before World War II; during the war a term for officials of the fascist Independent State of Croatia
zikr	A Muslim ritual prayer recited by dervishes in which an expression of praise is continually repeated

The Walnut Mansion

XV

"Oh, Mrs. Marija, I'm a daughter, not a monster! I took care of her for thirty years. My life passed me by while I was doing that, and I didn't complain to anybody. I didn't run away, like so many children do from their parents. They run all the way to the other end of the world. And it's no wonder they do—with what passes for parents around here. But I didn't do that, and now I have the right to say something. I've been going from room to room all morning long. They sent me from the second floor to the fifth floor and back again. I don't know why they've been doing that. Would they do it if I came to report a murder? Mrs. Marija, I'm not a monster, believe me, but I did feel a load was taken off my shoulders, make no mistake about it. It was as if I had my life again. And the children had theirs again too. Can you imagine what it's like to watch your own mother turn into a monster, into a freak, into—I don't even know what to call it? She was my mother, for better or worse—it doesn't matter. I don't know whether I'm a good mother to my children, and so I won't judge her. But I loved her! I can say that, and I know very well what I'm saying. But for the last three months she hasn't been the same person. A demon got a hold of her. Now I don't believe in demons, spells, or spirits—so don't think I'm making this up. But at night we locked ourselves in the bedroom because that was the only way we dared to go to sleep. Me and my two children. In the morning I would clean up what she'd broken. I cleaned her . . . her excrement from all over the house. It was everywhere—on the walls, on the ceilings. It was terrible—you have no idea how much of it can come out of one living being. In a month everything in the house had been defiled or smashed. A big oaken cabinet, a hundred years old and weighing at least half a ton—she chopped it up one night with an axe. With one of those big axes that not even a man can lift just like that! So, Mrs. Marija, that was the ninety-seven-year-old woman that all the newspapers have been writing about yesterday and today. I understand that; they think she was some dear old granny, like one of those little old grandmas on Stradun Street. Everyone had one. A heart-rending figure, like a seal being killed or a dog in the pound. Everyone wants to tear that boy limb from limb, and they'll do it in the end! He's done for. He'll never work as a doctor again, and who knows what he'll be like when he gets out of prison? They'll convict him, I'm sure of it. But why didn't you hide him? People will kill him! Why don't you stick him in jail for now? Is it that you're expecting them to come after him and string him up like in the Wild West? That would put an end to the whole affair. Without the hassle of a trial and you getting involved in a tragedy. That's right, Mrs. Marija, this is a tragedy! But the victim isn't some ninety-seven-year-old woman—it's the young man who saved us. Me and my children! I could keep quiet because my agony is over, but I won't, even if I end up just like him. If someone needs to be torn limb from limb, you've got us; we're already used to it. Nothing can happen to us that we haven't already had to endure. There are things more terrible than death, Mrs. Marija! What a person lives through is worse. Nor is shame the worst thing in the world. There are things much worse than that, and God forbid you ever suffer them, you or anybody in your family! I won't be able to go on living if something bad happens to that young man on account of her. I can't take it; I don't care if you think I'm a monster instead of someone's child a hundred times over! But that . . . that . . . I don't know what you call it, that wasn't my mother! If I thought it was, I'd jump out of this window this instant; I'd squeeze through the bars; I just wouldn't be able to take it if something like that brought me into this world. You think I'm crazy? Oh yes, you must think I'm crazy, that I'm in shock, that what I'm telling you isn't true, and that everything will be different tomorrow, after someone has a talk with me, convinces me it's not true, explains everything to me, sends me to a psychiatrist, shoots me full of sedatives like a goose. But you're wrong! You don't know how wrong you are and how many times in the last three months I wished I could do what had to be done to save myself and my children, but I didn't have the courage. I didn't know how to do it, and today I'm sorry; I'll never forgive myself because I'm the reason why that young man's life is falling apart. That's right; I'd have killed her and my hand wouldn't have shaken at all, if only I'd known . . ."

Marija Kablar looked at this woman who wouldn't stop shouting and couldn't figure out how she'd ended up in her office, who had sent her or for what purpose. Marija Kablar was simply a police archivist and was three months away from retiring. She'd been sitting in room 407 for two and a half years, ever since the files had all been digitized, doing nothing and waiting for her time to be up. She would drink coffee and turn over a miniature hourglass. From eight in the morning to four in the afternoon she would turn it over exactly seven hundred and twelve times; she had counted on several occasions, and the number of times always came out to be seven hundred and twelve. She rarely read the newspaper or turned on the small Japanese transistor radio, so one could say that apart from coffee and the little hourglass her workday was devoid of content. In two and a half years someone had knocked on her door only about a dozen times, always by mistake, except for once when they came to check the fire extinguishers. At first she was afraid that she would be fired, but she calmed down

when she realized that they had forgotten her and would have a hard time finding her among the two hundred or so employees before her sixty-fifth birthday,
which was when she would go to the personnel department and announce that
she was retiring. That's how it goes; if she didn't remember to do it herself, they
wouldn't either and would probably let her stay on for another twenty years.
After she had divorced her husband six years earlier (when he'd run off with a
woman thirty years younger), and after all her friends and those she might meet
at the City Café had died off or moved away, all Marija Kablar was waiting for
was her pension so that she could return to Glamoč, a town she'd left a half a
century before but was still the place where she would have her peace in life, or
so she imagined. The arrival of this unknown woman upset her; she worried that
it wasn't a coincidence because the woman addressed her by name immediately; okay, her name was there on the door, but below it also said "senior archivist," so it was unlikely that there was a mistake. It was more likely that someone
had remembered her and decided to give her some trouble — if nothing else, to
remind her how she was sitting there doing nothing and still getting paid. And
just when she had only three months left to go.

"I think you've made a mistake; I don't work on cases," she said cautiously,
looking at the teary-eyed woman over her glasses. She always looked over her
glasses when she wanted to look really serious and self-confident.

"I'm not mistaken. I've been trying to say that the whole time, but nobody
will listen to me. I'm really not mistaken. I'm trying to save an innocent man.
And that's not a mistake. It's no sin. Tell me, has that really become a sin too?"
the guest asked, pressing her. She made the impression of a fairly sincere but at
the same time unbearably theatrical woman. She was either crazy or under the
spell of having found herself in a police station.

"Ma'am, I'm only an archivist. Nothing else."

"Really? Where's your archive? Show me where the archive is!"

"Did you read what it says on my door?"

"No, why would I?" the woman said, lying, and Marija Kablar began to
panic. So someone *had* sent her. That much was certain.

"Whoever sent you here to me made a mistake. Believe me . . . !"

"Pardon, do you believe in God . . . ?"

"Who do you think you are asking questions like that?!" Marija said angrily.
Now they would hang atheism around her neck, too. She couldn't figure out
what the reason was. What did they care whether she went to church or not
when they knew full well that she didn't?

"I'm nobody, that's who. And I don't believe in God, but I do believe that
what goes around comes around, every wicked thing . . ."

"Fine. So what?"

"Why won't you help me?" the woman asked. She sat there, squeezing a small glossy purse in her lap, the kind people carry to a funeral or the theater. That little detail saddened Marija somewhat. Rubber boots on an old man waiting in a line at the bank, a University of Los Angeles T-shirt on a Gypsy child begging in front of a church, a necktie on a dying man, a run in the stocking of a former British prime minister, a black glossy purse in the hands of a woman in a police station: details that moved her more than scenes of real misfortune.

"I'd help you, but it's simply not my job . . ."

"It's not anyone's job. How terrible it is that helping someone has become a job . . ."

"But, ma'am, I can't help you. It's simply not in my power . . ."

"My name is Dijana. You probably read about me in the newspapers . . ."

"I'm sorry, but I hardly ever read the newspapers . . ."

"You must have heard people talking about it. The whole town is talking about it. Some 'Dr. Mengele' in our hospital took the life of a ninety-seven-year-old lady. That's what they say."

"Believe me, I haven't heard a thing about it. Nothing at all. I try to hear as little as possible. And she was your mother? I'm sorry, missus . . . missus . . ."

"Dijana—don't you remember? You're not sorry. If you were sorry, you'd have listened to what I was saying . . ."

"But I did! You were talking and I was listening . . ."

"And did you understand anything?"

"No . . ."

"See, you didn't. You're just waiting for me to get out of here. You're putting up with me because you're polite, and unlike the others, you can't bring yourself to throw me out. . . ."

"I'm really sorry. You're right—it's wrong. Everybody needs to have people listen to them . . ."

"You're just saying that because it sounds like the thing to say."

Marija truly believed that the police should have someone whose work was simply to hear people out. Then fewer people would murder out of desperation or revenge. There should be someone, say, a psychiatrist or a priest, whose job would be to calm people down and convince them that things would get better.

"Who's the young man?" asked Marija.

"Which young man . . . ?"

"The one you were talking about. The guy who isn't guilty . . ."

"Dr. Ares Vlahović," Dijana answered, as if that name should mean something to her. Marija nodded her head mechanically, as if it did.

"And what was your relationship to him . . . ?"

"Nothing; what would it be?!" Dijana said, upset at what she seemed to be hinting at. The neighbors hadn't started gossiping yet, but they would, and she knew they would, and knew that the first thing they'd say would be that she'd been sleeping with the young doctor and was now ready to betray her own mother just to save him.

"Why do you have to be like that? Why did you think of that right off . . . ?"

"I didn't think anything. I was just asking . . ."

"Do you believe that someone's own mother, their own flesh and blood, can turn into a monster, into someone completely unrecognizable?"

"I suppose so. All kinds of things happen to people when they get old . . ."

"Well, why are you asking me about him then . . . ?"

"Do you think . . . ?"

"No, but I know what you were thinking of . . ."

"I wasn't, I'm really sorry, but I wasn't. I'm embarrassed—see how I'm blushing? I really wasn't thinking anything like that."

Marija looked at this woman and wondered whether she was crazy or whether she'd really said something she wasn't supposed to or didn't mean. It would have never occurred to her to hint at something like that. She realized that she wasn't going to be able to get Dijana off her back just like that. If Dijana walked out of the room now, Marija would retire and return to Glamoč to spend her days in a place that should be a paradise for her, but she would be continually tormented by the thought that she'd maybe insulted and turned away a woman who'd come into her office with a real problem. The first one in her thirty years of work in the police. Right after she had started working for the archives and received her official ID card and pistol (in those days there were so many pistols that they were even issued to police archivists), she expected everything to be as it was in the movies. Inspectors would come with unsolved cases from twenty years before, and she would search through registries late into the night to unlock the mysteries of murders in apparently unimportant lists, living an exciting life full of the pursuit of justice. Nothing remotely similar ever happened. Her work for the police didn't differ from work in a communal enterprise; she filed away papers that no one needed any more, and it was hardly six months before they took her pistol away. The years of cutbacks had probably begun. She didn't crave a life like those in the movies; she didn't believe she deserved it. She only had a passing thought that she might have a life like that. Afterward, she thought herself silly. She was thirty-five then and shouldn't have been girlish enough to get carried away by such things.

"What was she like before she got old?" she asked Dijana, hoping to make things right.

"I don't know any more. In any case she was normal . . ."

"You'll get over it. I can tell that you're strong."

"You're just saying that. You don't know me."

"I don't, but you can tell when a woman still has fight in her."

"So you believe in things like that?"

"I have to. Otherwise I couldn't do it . . ."

"What, you mean work for the police?"

Marija laughed, and only then did Dijana notice the years on her face; she realized that this woman wasn't in a position to do anything. That was probably why she hadn't sent her away.

"No, I didn't mean that, but get by in general, in life. Do you want me to order us some coffee? That's really the most I can do . . ."

"Fine, that's at least a start," Dijana said and hung her purse on the back of her chair. That was a sign of trust that didn't go unnoticed.

"I feel a little better now," Dijana said after a boy in a black-and-white waiter's outfit brought the coffee. She took a look at him: he was black-haired and pimply, with thin black whiskers under his nose.

"He's in his first year of waiter training," said Marija after he went out. "They send them to the police to get practice. It's easier than paying a professional . . ."

"Wow, you really sound like someone in the police! Nobody would call a waiter *a professional*," she said and laughed.

"I'm glad you're feeling better . . ."

"But you still think I'm crazy, right . . . ?"

"I'll be honest: I'm not thinking anything. I just know that you're not having an easy time of it. Nobody does if they're coming in here. Unless, of course, they're just getting a new driver's license . . ."

"I really want for you to believe me. For someone to believe me . . ."

"I do believe you, every word you're saying. Why would you lie to an old archivist? That hasn't happened yet. And it won't. I'm retiring in only three months . . ."

"You already have to retire? That can't be," Dijana lied; "you don't look that old at all . . ."

"And I'll never set foot back in this building. Take a look at that wall. There used to be shelves with files of unsolved sex crimes. They reached from the floor to the ceiling, a whole wall full of rapes. Before me some guy from Trebinje worked in here; they fired him because he read all that filth and they caught him masturbating. Can you believe it? He was pleasuring himself over the rape of a fifteen-year-old girl! I think they put me in here because I was a woman and probably wouldn't have that kind of temptation. So there you have the story of the police and my work here . . . And where are those files now . . . ? I suppose most of the cases were tossed out due to the statute of limitations. Who would keep documentation of rapes from thirty or more years ago? The archive was mostly computerized not too long ago. Since then I've been sitting here and doing nothing . . ."

"And so nobody knows about any of it any more. The train has left the station, as if none of it had ever happened . . ."

"That's right. More or less . . ."

"No, that's not right. Someone did that stuff. The rapes, I mean. And some women suffered. That stays with you your whole life . . ."

"Most of them are no longer alive . . ."

"It's still not just . . ."

"I agree, but it's all over now." Marija thought that maybe this woman had been raped. You never know when you might say something you shouldn't. That's why it's always better to make sure you speak of the bad things in life as cautiously as possible, no matter what they are. And so she probably shouldn't have said what was in those files because maybe this woman . . .

"This doctor is going to be charged with murdering my mother," Dijana said, "and what should I do now? He didn't kill her, and that person wasn't her any more."

Marija was sorry that things were getting back to where they had been at the start. She wanted Dijana to calm down but without burdening her with some-thing that—no doubt—could only be the cause of harm and mutual shame. She felt it to be an imminent danger that could only be averted if Dijana gave up on her intentions.

"It would be best to wait for the trial," she said; "the police don't give up easily. When they bite, they don't let go. My advice is to wait and not say any-thing to anybody. This is a small city, you know."

"What are you trying to say?" she asked frowning and sat up in her chair.

"That vicious stories get started easily. People are just waiting for a victim . . ."

"But I'm not the victim; the victim is a young man who will end up in jail even though he's completely innocent," said Dijana, already wondering whether she should get up and leave without saying anything because there was no point in this, talking to someone who was so insensitive she couldn't tell sandbox fights and children's games from the plight of a man, no matter who, who was completely innocent, who might suffer and pay with his life for something that could and should have been avoided if only everyone had been decent.

"If this story gets out," said Marija, trying to calm her, "then everything will be pointless. Not even a court will believe you. I've seen such situations a thousand times." She was lying; she'd never even been in a courtroom. "You tell the truth on the witness stand, and then the other side makes a lunatic out of you. The prosecution brings witnesses, usually neighbors, who say you're crazy and that you were always like that. You didn't greet them on the stairs; you tormented your own mother, who, naturally, was a wonderful woman, and so on. I'm warning you; that always ends the same way," Marija said. Her self-confidence was on the rise, and she made up a story on the fly: "A long time ago, it must be thirty years now, it happened that an old man, a retired harbor master who lived in Lapad, perished when his house caught fire. The police concluded that it was a suicide, but his daughter (who later had to emigrate to Australia) told everyone in Dubrovnik that her father hadn't killed himself but was murdered by his own son, her stepbrother, for his inheritance. And how do you think that ended? Whom did they believe? So you just wait for the trial and then tell the truth. Maybe people will be shocked, maybe they'll say all kinds of things behind your back, but at least you'll be in the clear . . ."

"Is that what you think? I don't know how I can live if I don't do something for that young man . . . ," Dijana said, and that sounded to Marija like a pretty lie told by someone who spends his whole life threatening to sacrifice himself for something. But no matter what, she wanted to avoid getting caught up in this story, especially now when the end was so near. Marija Kablar didn't think of that end as going into retirement, but as the end of a life full of misunderstandings and deceptions with which she'd never been able to cope. It all seemed instead like an endless course in a driving school. The instructors changed from time to time, shouted at her, and lost their nerves because with so many years she still couldn't learn what others did in two months. In such a life there wasn't too much suffering or sadness because it passed easily, but it passed without any kind of goal or real satisfaction. After her husband left her, she realized that she'd never loved him, but she didn't do anything because she had nothing with which to compare her love or the lack thereof. Someone else would find solitude after years of marriage to be terrible, but Marija continued to live her own life the morning after he left, as if she'd always been an old maid, with rituals that were all like the one with the hourglass. She only felt unease at the darkness and what couldn't be seen in it and at the fact that after he left, she never spoke with anyone for more than ten minutes. She began to notice who all had died, disappeared, or left town and so had decided to leave this empty place in her first month of retirement and return to Glamoč. A whole life had been definitively wasted, but she didn't regret it. She only wanted what would come afterward to be just like the time before she'd become aware that she was alive. Dijana's arrival was the first serious threat to her peace.

"Just stay calm," she said, "and don't put too much stock in anything anybody says." Dijana turned to get her purse and said, "You've helped me; you should know that you have!" And she really believed it. Marija got up and her sleeve caught the coffee cup, just enough to cause the porcelain to rattle fleetingly.

"I'm glad we met," she said and extended her hand.

"We'll surely meet again," Dijana responded, searching for something she'd forgotten on the table and underneath it. She left satisfied, though she hadn't achieved anything that she'd intended to when she'd come to the police station. She hadn't even told the story of what had happened in the municipal hospital, on account of which all charges against Dr. Vlahović should be dropped and the ongoing campaign against him in the newspapers and on the city squares should be stopped. She was satisfied that she'd gotten someone to listen to her for half an hour, no matter what she'd been saying, because that could be a new beginning for her, after which she could forget the past months, a time that at one moment had seemed to be a complete and utter catastrophe, when she'd stopped remembering what her mother had once looked like and that she'd had a mother at all.

Marija went back to waiting. She turned the hourglass over twenty more times, and one more day was over. As she started for home and took the coffee cups to put them on the radiator in front of her office, where the boy in the black-and-white outfit would pick them up, she remembered her guest once more, probably for the last time. Someone else would be interested in that story, she thought. People were too curious; that was why so many tragedies occurred in their lives. If you (and your loved ones, if you had any) didn't stick your nose where it didn't belong and only knew what you had to, many of those bad things would steer clear of you. Content with herself, she locked her office and disappeared.

XIV

The morning after crazy Manda broke the thick, milky glass on the kitchen door with her fist in one of her nightly rampages, Dijana found her lying pale in a pool of blood and excrement as if all the life in her had already drained out, and she called an ambulance. The lies and deception were over; she could no longer hide from the city what it in fact already knew—that her mother had lost her mind in her ninety-seventh year. But what a way to lose your mind: swearing and cursing the most hideous oaths and in the worst ways, wrenching the guts of those closest to her, and showing parts of herself that one doesn't even show when one's young. She would strip naked, thin as a ghost, grab herself by the nipple, and shout: "Want some milk, harbor slut? Want me to breast-feed all your bastards?" Or she would grab herself between the legs and, releasing a stream of urine, say, "Look, you dry cunt, at what a woman has!" Dijana tried to shield her children from this and even worse things as best she could. But what was worse than what was happening to their souls was that someone else might hear *crazy Manda*—as Darijan had called his grandma Regina one night. And the three of them called her that from then on, probably trying to convince themselves that she had nothing to do with the woman with whom they'd used to live. Two and a half months earlier, a little after the worst had started, Dijana had tried to get her mother committed to the municipal psychiatric ward, but that was no place for sane people, let alone the insane. Ten or so chronic cases that had been abandoned by their families had been taking up a half of the ward for years, while the other half fell to shell-shocked veterans of the war and a few sons and daughters of better houses who'd already passed through the ninth circle of drugs and had no hope of recovery and whose parents wanted to keep them out of sight. No space could be found for an aggressive, berserk old woman. There might have been in other wards, and Regina suffered from a hundred conditions anyway, but if Dijana could reconcile herself to letting psychiatrists see what her mother had turned into, letting other doctors see this had been out of the question, until that morning.

The ambulance arrived an hour after she made the call.

"What's this, does a herd of wild pigs live here?" asked a fat medic with a shaven head, unable to keep his mouth shut. Dijana tried frantically to think up some lie; she'd been busy at this since she'd called the ambulance, but she couldn't think of anything that might explain an apartment that had been completely torn apart and soiled with excrement, urine, and blood. She told Mirna and Darijan to stay in the bedroom and not to come out until crazy Manda had been taken away. It was better for the medics not to see them.

"C'mon, granny, let's go," said the bald medic and tried to pick her up by her underarms while his partner, a weedy, older man with glasses, went for her legs. But crazy Manda spun around like lightning and bit his arm. "Sweet Mother of Jesus!" he exclaimed, jumping back a couple of meters, and then yelled at Dijana, "Why don't you say something? Goddammit, get her to calm down!" Dijana was standing against a wall that was soiled with traces of filth that the old woman had smeared on it on one of the previous nights; she said nothing and looked down at the floor.

"She's not right in the head," she said finally.

"Oh really?! And we thought you just keep her here to guard the house and bite mailmen!" said the one with the gray hair. The bald one started toward crazy Manda again, approaching her this time more directly from behind, but she slipped away like a cat and flashed her teeth.

"This ain't our job; let's go!" said the one with gray hair.

"Wait, please don't go!" Dijana cried.

"Signorina, we're here to save you from a stroke or pneumonia; if you need help with that, call us, but for this you need to call someone else," said the one with the gray hair. The bald one was standing over crazy Manda and looking down at her and thinking: I'd love to kick you in the head!

She grinned at him furiously, flashing her thin, sharp yellow teeth, waiting for a chance to grab him by the balls.

Here Dijana realized whom she should be playing, resolved as she was to finish what she'd started at any price. "Take her away, please!" she said, folding her hands before the bald one.

"Where should we take her when we can't even figure out how to get a hold of her?"

"To the hospital. She'll bleed to death."

"If she hasn't already, she won't now," the gray-haired one interjected again. "Let's go, Damir, before the old bag gets you by the ass. You know there's no anti-tetanus serum in the hospital," he joked, making every effort to humiliate Dijana in any way he could. "No one will believe this when we tell them . . ."

"Would you do it for a hundred marks?" she begged the bald one.

"Not even for five hundred!" the gray-haired one said, peering back at her over his shoulder.

"Have some compassion, for God's sake!" she begged.

"C'mon, granny'll give you a piece of pussy!" said crazy Manda, suddenly enthusiastic about the idea of them taking her somewhere.

"Okay, give us each a hundred marks," said the bald one, taking pity.

"Not me, dammit!" the gray-haired one said, resisting.

"Oh yes you will, Tripun," the bald one said. "And don't you watch this!" he said to Dijana and seized the old woman by the neck with his middle finger and thumb. She wheezed.

"It hurts, doesn't it, you old hag? Well, if you bite me, I won't let go the next time," he said and grabbed her under the arm. Crazy Manda was probably too surprised to respond quickly, but since Tripun hadn't gotten her by the legs, she started stomping furiously on the parquet floor.

"Hold her, Tripun!" said the bald one, which Tripun tried to do when he figured that he'd probably stalled long enough. But since the old woman had suddenly gained strength again, he had a hard time of it, and every so often she got him in the chin or the nose.

"You're done, you old whore!" he shouted after he had finally managed to get a hold of her scrawny knees. His thumbs could feel her kneecaps scraping against the worn ends of her bones. He shuddered as if he had scratched a blackboard with his fingernails.

As they carried her down the stairs, crazy Manda howled, "Help me, people; they'll shoot me, they'll cut my throat!" But nothing could be seen except the covers of the peepholes moving; the neighbors were peering out and remembering what they saw. Dijana went a few steps behind them, in her house slippers, with a black lacquered purse over her shoulder and two hundred marks in her sweaty hand.

In the ambulance the bald one took out a syringe, and while Dijana and Tripun barely managed to hold the old woman down on the stretcher, he thrust the needle into her buttock right through her house robe: "Hey, granny, now you'll relax!" Five minutes later Regina Delavale lay motionless, like a mummified body, with a faint smile on her calm, still face, in which Dijana then saw something of her mother for the last time. When she's asleep, she's just like she used to be, she thought, certain that she would rather spend the rest of her life by the side of that sleeping body and caring for it than for crazy Manda to awaken in it once more, even for only five minutes.

Just before they arrived at the hospital, the bald one gave her one more injection. "Look, I could lose my job because of what I'm doing right now," he said. "At the reception desk you'll say you found her unconscious from blood loss. Don't you dare tell them what I did to her because I'll find you no matter where you are and rip your tongue out, got it?"

Dijana nodded.

"You must be crazy. How can you believe her?!" Tripun said and sighed. "Now let's see the money!"

Dijana held out two hundred marks for the bald one. He took only one of the notes. "Give the other one to him!" he said, pointing with his index finger as if forcing her. "Hey, I never thought I'd see the day when a woman pays me!" joked Tripun, extending his empty palm.

At the reception desk Dijana presented Regina's health record booklet and told all the necessary lies to the young female doctor, probably an intern, a beauty with big brown eyes who was equally beautiful whether she was smiling or fretting.

"Don't worry at all; everything will be all right," the doctor said, caressing her upper arm with her palm. "I'll look after her like my own grandmother!" Without warning Dijana's eyes filled with tears. She wept bitterly on the full bosom of an unfamiliar young woman who saw her own grandmother in the unconscious crazy Manda and whom Dijana had deceived like no one in her life. She wept and couldn't stop, for herself and that girl and what would happen when crazy Manda woke up and the girl realized what horror is and what a pretty, touching story can turn into.

"Forgive me, please," she sobbed, and the young doctor had no idea why she should forgive her; nor had anyone prepared her for such cases. When she'd begun working, they'd surely given her a hundred pieces of advice about how to conduct herself with patients and their families, when to lie and when to tell the truth, but they hadn't said what to do when you're holding a woman in your arms who could be your mother, whose hot tears are the strangest thing you've ever felt on your skin. Perhaps most similar to the paraffin that had run down a candle long ago on a winter night in Koločep, and she had grabbed it with her bare palm.

As she returned home with a list of things that the young doctor had written out for her to bring for crazy Manda in the afternoon—pajamas, a house robe, soap, hairpins, and a toothbrush—Dijana knew that before she set foot in the apartment, the old woman would already be awake and the shameful scheme would unravel. The whole hospital would learn the truth, that Regina Delavale hadn't fallen into a coma from blood loss but had been sedated with something so they could slip a crazy woman into the hands of the doctors. Nothing like this had ever happened before, at least she'd never heard of it, so the story would be all the more interesting and spread like wildfire until it reached the last fishwife. And then people would start spouting her name, and this would go on for years and till the end of time, outliving crazy Manda and Dijana and becoming a permanent addition to the family name, harder than the city walls and stronger than the power of a patron saint. In these parts it takes centuries for people to forget the lunatics in a family. Memories of half-witted children who died before their seventh birthday pass from generation to generation, just as generation after generation remembers whose brother raped a fourteen-year-old girl and threw her in a crevasse above Popovo Polje, or whose great-grandmother ran off with a Turk and dropped her drawers in the alleys of Izmir to put out for French traders and travelogue writers. People remember each and every bastard child born way back when this city was only a heap of rocks overlooking the sea. They've scribbled down news of events in far eastern ports, every case of gonorrhea, clap, and drip. There's no family that's been in the city for more than a generation without being accompanied by at least ten such shameful stories, against which you can defend yourself only by cultivating blights in the gardens and family trees of others and preserving the memory of their abominations and monstrosities. She knew she had to reconcile herself to that, but she wasn't ready for reconciliation. She was gripped by terror at the thought of having to respond in the same manner to anyone who might reproach her or about whom she heard that they had passed on the story and relished it. The children weren't home when she got there. They'd run out as they were wont to do, as they had been doing for months. And what would they do inside in rooms in which there was nothing to sit down on and in which you couldn't pick anything up for fear of it being soiled with filth? She stood in the middle of what had been the living room, powerless to do anything at all. A broom and a scrubbing brush couldn't clean what would have been too much for a municipal garbage truck and a pest control team: filth that you can clean only if it is someone else's. It would have been best to lock and seal that terrible place, never return there, and keep everyone out forever. Crazy Manda had succeeded in destroying everything in the house that might be considered a souvenir and that people miss when their houses burn. This apartment no longer meant anything to Dijana; it was no longer hers, only a place where she spent the night.

She was resolved not to let them send crazy Manda back to her. She would fight like a lion, walk over corpses, risk herself and her whole family, but she wasn't going to take her back, even if she had to flee the city with Mirna and Darijan and live as a subtenant and clean stairways in apartment buildings. She'd done that before and knew she could survive like that too, and the children were grown; they could fend for themselves. Anything was better than that lunatic coming back and everything starting all over again. But she had no hope of ever getting rid of her while she was alive. She found some old pajamas, grabbed Mirna's old pink kimono, which she had gotten from that Swede two years before but never wore or wanted to see; she threw some trifles into a vanity case for the beach and stuffed everything into a nylon bag. She knew that crazy Manda wouldn't need any of these things in the hospital, but that wasn't important. Dijana was doing this for herself, to convince the doctors that she wasn't a monster and cared for her mother.

She went out of the house though it was too early to go back to the hospital. She wanted a few hours to pass, for them to get a little used to crazy Manda, for her to cuss them all out and bite them all over, maybe they would find a straightjacket somewhere, because if she arrived too early, it could happen that she might have some explaining to do or—God forbid—catch the old woman while she was still sleeping. For this reason she made her way to the hospital slowly, putting one foot in front of the other and taking detours. She calculated that like this it would take her at least forty-five minutes. She stopped at every display window, looked at the colorful summer dresses, went inside shops with pots and dishes (they no longer had any in the house), smiled at the salesgirls, and constantly had the impression that she was doing this for the last time because rumors about crazy Manda would soon spread and no one would look at Dijana any more the way they did now.

"Missus, look at these; they're real royal dishes; Mrs. Simpson probably ate from them!" said a short shop assistant with a fat belly and the wrinkled face of a circus clown. She seemed as if she'd read every last romance novel ever published and had every story with a tremendously meaningful, sad ending living inside her. Here was someone who wouldn't be interested in the lunacy of Regina Delavale, Dijana thought and felt close to the midget girl, on account of which she should have said something pretty and memorable to her:

"She swam in Trsteno once, completely naked, Edward and her. My uncle saw her with his own eyes. He was a child."

The little midget girl was surprised and even thought for a moment that the woman was pulling her leg: "Do you mean Mrs. Simpson, who couldn't be queen, and so then he didn't want to be king either?"

Dijana laughed; she would have patted the midget girl on the head if only there hadn't been anyone there to see it. Her little eyes widened so sweetly, surrounded by nets of deep, Indian wrinkles. "Yes, her," Dijana said; "didn't you know that one summer—it might have been in '35, they came down here and bathed in the nude on the beach . . . ?"

"Naked?!" the midget girl exclaimed, folding her hands in astonishment.

"Yes, yes," Dijana confirmed, as if speaking of relatives they both shared.

She left the shop happy to have made someone's life better. The little salesgirl of kitchen porcelain now had something to preoccupy herself with for months.

Maybe she would go to Trsteno, skip along the cliffs by the sea, and run her hands along the rocks, hoping that Wallis Simpson's fingers had touched the same pebbles, the same fossil crab, as she bent down to kiss Edward, and one could see the red marks made by pine needles, shells, and sharp rocks on her white bottom. The less love you have in your life, Dijana thought, the more susceptible you are to such stories. As if everyone in the city except the midget girl with Mrs. Simpson's dishes had spent three quarters of their lives in love and had become completely insensitive to everyone else in this part of town.

She managed to drag her trip to the hospital out for two hours. At the entrance she inhaled deeply, as if diving into the sea in pursuit of a terrible moray eel, and went firmly forward. If the midget girl could live with herself for a whole lifetime, she could deal with this little bit of life, she thought, encouraging herself, but she had only made five marching steps when the porter stopped her.

"Where do you think you're going?" he shouted from his booth.

"I'm here to see Regina Delavale," she said, leaving out "my mother," in case word had already gotten around.

"I don't care if you're coming to see my old man; you're not getting through!"

She looked at him in surprise. Maybe there was a flu epidemic, and they weren't letting anyone in to see the patients; maybe something else was going on . . . ?

"What are you staring at?! You don't get into a hospital just like that! Yes, a hospital! You don't even get into a bar like that. First you say, 'Good day, I'm so-and-so, here's my identity card, I'm here to do such-and-such,' and then I decide whether to let you in or not. Damnation, there's got to be some order," he said, and as he spoke, he leaned first in one direction and then in the other, as if he were addressing an unseen audience or giving a public lecture about the rights and obligations of someone who's come before a porter.

"Isn't it visiting hours?" she asked.

"It most certainly isn't," he answered, giving her to understand that this very question was an insult to his office.

"When are visiting hours?"

"You can get an answer to that at the information desk," he said, making every effort to sound very official.

"Where's the information desk?"

The porter pointed behind his back. "But you can't get there unless I let you in!"

"Well, are you going to let me in?"

"We will if you are polite and ask nicely . . ."

"Excuse me? What's wrong with you?" she asked, looking at him scornfully.

She had already stopped caring whether she would get in or not. If he didn't let her in, it would be better in a way for everyone concerned. Both for Dijana, who would put off her encounter with crazy Manda until tomorrow, and for the doctors because by then the doctors would have already figured out what to do with the crazy old woman.

"C'mon then, get in there!" he said, waving with his hand like a policeman motioning a malfunctioning truck on by.

"How dare you talk to me like that?!" she said, furious.

"Beg pardon, whaddya mean?" he said, acting like he didn't know what she was talking about.

"I didn't herd sheep with you; you can't talk to me like that, you vulgar jerk . . . !"

"Excuse me, what was that . . . ?"

"What you heard, you filthy peasant; not only you but whoever let you down from the hills . . . !"

"Listen, I might change my mind," he retorted, trying to threaten her.

Instead of getting him to keep her out, she'd succeeded in intimidating the porter.

"But this is my job," he said after she passed, as if apologizing.

She didn't know where she might find crazy Manda. She went from ward to ward, down the hospital hallways that at times seemed like catacombs, so that she had to duck down to pass through the low entry into the radiology ward, where the walls were ironbound and resembled the inside of a submarine; at others they changed into labyrinths that went in circles, past glass walls behind which goggle-eyed old men were dying with tubes in their throats. She thought she'd stepped into another world or at least into another state, where the habits and rules were different than in the outside world, and that was just as hard for a living person to emerge from as it was for them to enter. A cold sweat covered her, her heart beat like crazy, and she was certain that the first cardiological patrol that came along would take her captive and stuff her into green pajamas with the hospital's emblem on suspicion of her having had a major heart attack.

After a good twenty minutes of walking, she happened upon the emergency surgery ward and in it the same young doctor as yesterday. "How is she?" she asked about crazy Manda before the young lady managed to say anything.

"I don't know what to tell you . . ."

"Did she bleed to death?"

"No, but . . ."

"Tell me what happened!" Dijana said. She was trying to appear as concerned as possible, interrupting the doctor and getting in close to her face, fearing the attack she expected from her.

"It looks like a stroke; she's been transferred to neurology . . ."

"Is she unconscious . . . ?"

"She's conscious, but she's not herself, in a manner of speaking . . ."

"What do you mean . . . ?"

"I don't know how to explain it to you. She's not really here. They had to tie her down."

Dijana began to cry again. She simply didn't know what else to do. She cried from fear and excitement or from happiness because it seemed to her that her trick had worked.

"You can talk to Onofri, the chief physician; he'll tell you more about it," the young lady said. She was a little guarded, not like she had been in the morning, though she still felt sorry for Dijana, albeit with a faint feeling of disgust. But this was definitely much better than what Dijana had expected.

She led her into a tiny office, where behind a relatively oversized desk an enormous gray-haired man was sitting. He had a large nose and a protruding lower jaw, like a giant albino bulldog. She showed her to a chair and went out quickly. Dijana sat down before the chief physician said anything. He neither greeted her nor moved at all in his black chair, which was covered with cracked vinyl. He couldn't even manage to get up. Who knows how he even gets in and out and sits down, she wondered at first, because she really couldn't figure out how even the thinnest man could pass between the wall and the desk to get to the chair, and this man was very fat.

"So," she said, more to get his attention than to break the silence.

"You must be Mrs. Delavale," he said with one of those deep, loud voices that can be heard from hilltop to hilltop, even when they whisper.

"I'm not; actually I am, I'm Mrs. Delavale's daughter," Dijana said, bumbling.

"If it's what we think it is, okay, but if it isn't, we won't be able to keep your mother in the hospital. If it's a case of brain insult, this situation won't last long, and she'll leave us. If it's something else, and you're here to tell me whether it is or isn't, then you shouldn't have brought her to us because of a slit wrist. So, I'm asking you: how has your mother been acting in recent days?"

He watched her as would someone who could see through any lie. She didn't know how to respond to him or how to gain some time.

"What is going on with her?" she asked in a fragile tone.

He looked at her, certain that this was all a lie, and said nothing for a few seconds, full as he was of experience with fraudulent patients and their families, perhaps to get her to break down, and then said, "Nothing special; I only had to evacuate half the ward, including all the nurses. You know, it's a tradition for the Sisters of Mercy to work for us, pious nuns. Not even the communists have made an issue of this. The sacrifices these sisters make for the patients and all who suffer are boundless. I've had to have them removed from the ward as long as your mother is here. What she says and does isn't for human eyes and ears. I guess you don't know anything about that, do you? If that's right, then we're dealing with a brain stroke, but a very unusual one, the kind that there hasn't been in this hospital for the thirty-five years that I've been here. I can remember that much! Otherwise such cases are known only from books. But people write all kinds of things in books, and I'm not inclined to believe every bizarre thing I read. So, to tell the truth—between you and me—I believe that your mother is in a state of chronic maniacal psychosis, or whatever psychiatrists call it, and I think it's a disgrace for you to have brought her here! Of course, I can't prove it, but even if I could, I couldn't have you prosecuted according to any law. But I'm telling you, ma'am, that it's dishonest, immoral, inhuman, both to us who work here and to the patients who are being treated in this ward and who because of your mother did not receive adequate care today. And I wonder how it was that you got her to sleep—what did you give her before you called the ambulance? Namely, this is where one could start talking about grave consequences for you. When you shot her full of sedatives, you risked killing your mother. There's a very small difference between a dose that will put a ninety-seven-year-old lady into a deep sleep and a dose that's lethal for her. Especially when dilettantes use such substances. And you, Mrs. Delavale, or whatever your name is, you're a dilettante, aren't you? But don't think you're going to get off just like that. I'm ready to testify that you attempted to murder your mother. Of course, in the event that my assumptions are correct, and something really tells me that they are, and in the event that your mother hasn't suffered an extremely bizarre brain insult, which I'm firmly convinced that she hasn't, you're not going to take us in like that. A brain insult of this kind would be a greater miracle than a monk seal appearing in the Gruž harbor. Therefore, this moment is your last chance to confess and tell me what really happened!"

When he finished, he tapped the ballpoint on the desk, as if he were holding a judge's gavel in his hand, and Dijana felt ashamed for the umpteenth time that day. All anyone cared about, so it seemed, was to humiliate her and kick her out of the way.

"You think now I'm going to get down on my knees and beg you? Is that what you think?" she said, watching him like a she-wolf about to jump on its plump and powerless prey, trapped between the wall and the black desk. Chief physician Onofri, however, didn't back down. At that moment he was seething with the hatred that had accumulated in him since he'd come to this hospital as a young doctor in the belief that he would remain there two or three years, just to get some experience, complete his internship, and get recommendations for a good specialization. But he'd ended up staying there for almost his whole life, unable to specialize in what he wanted to, walking streets that became ever more cramped as his body became ever thicker and trying to reconcile himself to the truth that he hadn't needed to study medicine to become what he was: someone who had wished in vain to get out of his hometown, to go off somewhere where he and his family were unknown and live with a view of one of the Swiss lakes. Since his wish had gone unfulfilled, he felt himself to be no different from the lowest city street sweeper. He hated his patients and their eternally concerned families, who cheated, lied, and stole and so believed they could cheat death. He hated interns, especially the young female interns who rushed through his ward (who knew how, sharing whose beds and working whose cocks) and got places where he wanted to be. He hated those who died and those who regained their health, and for a long time there hadn't been an outcome that he could be happy about. He wrote both NAD and *exitus letalis* with the same bile and without any fury. And now he had a woman before him whom he'd caught in a lie, and still he could do nothing to her.

"You're playing with me—you think you can get away with that?" he asked. "Answer me when I ask you a question!" he shouted, and Dijana tried to look him in the eye without wavering. As if a lion couldn't do anything to an antelope as long as it didn't lower its gaze. "You're a . . . ," he said, at a loss as to how to continue because no insult seemed adequate, and then said quietly, "a whore!"

"I think we're finished here," she responded calmly, then got up and went out.

"Get the hell out of here!" the chief physician shouted when she was already closing the door. His voice echoed down the hallway, which was painted in two oily shades of green, with a linoleum floor in a third shade of green.

"What did he say to you?" the young doctor asked.

"Do you really want to know? If you do, ask him. I think he'll be happy to tell you," said Dijana, and no matter how insulted she was, she felt a lot better. She was sure that they wouldn't send crazy Manda back to her. They had no way of doing it, if they didn't send her through the mail.

"His nerves are gone. Otherwise, he's a good physician, probably the best in the city. You know, that's old age for you," the young woman said, embarrassed.

"Fine, and tell me now, where's my mother?" Dijana asked coldly.

"They just brought her back to the ward . . ."

"Can I see her . . . ?"

"If you wish . . ."

"Yes, I do; why wouldn't I? Do you think anything could surprise me?"

"We had to tie her up," the young doctor said to prepare her, but the words sounded more terrible than what they were supposed to communicate.

"That's completely fine," Dijana responded.

"It's not a brain hemorrhage; her encephalogram was perfect, as with a completely healthy person."

Dijana laughed and said, "I don't doubt that a bit!"

They stood over a bed on which crazy Manda was lying on her back, without a pillow under her head, covered with a gray army blanket. Leather belts were fastened across her. She couldn't look anywhere except up at the ceiling or at a battered dresser next to the bed. She was silent, which surprised Dijana, because in the last months she would swear and shout as soon as she woke up after an afternoon nap of an hour or two.

"Hey, grandma," the young doctor called out, "look who's come to see you." But the old woman didn't move or give any sign that she could hear her. From the rhythmic and regular blinking of her eyes one could see that she was awake and completely calm. Dijana didn't know what to do. She would have liked most to turn around and leave, but that would be rude, maybe even dishonest toward the young woman who'd believed her and maybe still did. There was even a very small possibility that crazy Manda had miraculously disappeared just as she had miraculously appeared and that the bound old lady was that Regina Delavale that had disappeared one November morning, when some other woman in her body began cursing and breaking things. Dijana didn't seriously believe this, but she didn't dare do anything that she might later regret.

"Can she hear us?" she asked after ten minutes or so.

"I don't know," the doctor said and passed her palm in front of the old woman's eyes. Crazy Manda blinked.

"Maybe we should untie her," the young woman suggested. Dijana didn't want to say "yes" or "no."

"I don't know. I don't know much about this . . ."

"Do you think I do? You're her daughter; you decide," she said, and it sounded malicious.

"I can't take any more," Dijana said and went out.

She stood leaning on a wall of the hallway, her hands behind her back, and didn't know what to do. She remembered that she had forgotten the bag with things for crazy Manda somewhere, probably in the chief physician's office. And then there was a scream in the room. She ran inside and found that crazy Manda had grabbed the young doctor by the throat. Dijana grabbed her hands and tried to break her old fingers. She shouted, and then two men in white overcoats ran in. One pushed Dijana away so hard that she fell and knocked over a lamp on the nightstand. She remained lying there even though she was fully conscious and composed because she thought that if she got up, she would be blamed for the fracas, the noise that sounded like two boards hitting each other; she saw the young doctor's foot in a white wooden clog, dressed in what seemed like an orange child's sock with images of soccer balls on it.

"Are you all right?" asked one of the men in the white overcoats, helping Dijana to get up while the other tried to shove a needle in crazy Manda's behind. The young doctor was sitting on the floor, leaning against the bed. Her hands lay still, and she was gasping for air.

"I'm fine," Dijana answered, "it's not my fault."

They gave her a glass of water and took her to Dr. Vlahović, a young anesthesiologist who'd returned from his studies in Zagreb like some kind of medical celebrity, though he'd received offers from all over since he was one of the best students in the history of the school of medicine and was just as excellent in his specialization. They took him on though the hospital had no need for an anesthesiologist. The other three didn't even really have work because the surgery wards were hardly in operation, partly due to the shortage of surgeons and partly due to completely unusable equipment, so the operable patients were sent to other hospitals and cities. But they took on Dr. Vlahović readily (just as a rural soccer club would accept a young Maradona), in the belief that with him they would have an easier time procuring money for the renovation of the hospital. In the ward he did work on general or internal medicine, did nothing at all, or when the south wind would blow and Onofri was particularly impatient, he would talk with the patients and their families.

He extended his hand to Dijana and said, "Ares," but at first she didn't understand what that was supposed to mean. Only later, when she read *Dr. Ares Vlahović, Anesthesiologist* on the door to his office, would she realize that he had told her his name, something that physicians never do and that would confirm for Dijana his impeccable finesse, which she would use to explain Ares's tragic demise.

"The unfortunate woman is completely psychotic. The folksy phrase doesn't sound nice, but it's true: she's a nut! You don't need to say anything because I already know. It's clear to me that this didn't start today, and I can imagine what you've endured with her. I also know why you brought her to us. The psychiatric ward wouldn't take her, right? The problem is that no matter how much we want to—and I do, and so does Dr. Fočić, whom you met—we can't do anything for your mother in this ward. I know that this must be terrible for you, but it's a fact that the whole system will collapse because of one such case. We're no longer caring for those whom we could care for," he said in a calm and quiet tone, in which there was both understanding and cold reason.

"But I can't take her back home!" she cried out.

"Believe me, I understand that and would never try to force you to do that or try to persuade you to. We'll try to keep her here on account of the injuries on her hands as long as we can. But that won't be long. No more than two or three days. In the meantime we'll have to come up with some other solution."

That evening saw the occurrence of everything that would lead to the death of Regina Delavale, or crazy Manda. First off, a little after Dijana left for home, chief physician Onofri would burst into Dr. Vlahović's office like a fury and accost him with the question of who had authorized him to keep the psychotic old woman in the ward. Was he aware of all the regulations he was violating and how he was endangering the lives of the patients and risking the human dignity of the staff? Ares told him that for him the Hippocratic Oath was above all that, whereupon Onofri laughed cynically and pointed out that for his young colleague it was pussy that was above all else and that was the only reason he'd come back from Zagreb. He could hide the way he treated the pretty Dr. Fočić from others, but not from him. That was when Ares blew up.

"I won't stand for this!" he shouted, which Onofri understood as a challenge to a fight. He overturned the desk with his computer and lunged at his junior colleague. At that moment, to compound the tragedy, the young doctor walked in, which prevented a fist fight but served as new evidence for the chief physician's claim. What was she doing here if she wasn't on duty? And she should have left the hospital four hours ago.

After threats and insults, only some of which were returned, chief physician Onofri left the room to order the head nurse to untie Mrs. Regina Delavale because no one was to be tied up in his ward, where there were no dangerous psychiatric cases. After he did this and threatened to take the harshest disciplinary measures against the head nurse, whom he considered responsible from this moment on if the woman were tied up again, chief physician Onofri went home.

That night Dr. Vlahović four times ordered the head nurse to give Mrs. Regina Delavale an intramuscular injection with tranquilizers. Each time the ninety-seven-year-old woman had to be held down by three male nurses, two of which had to be called over from the traumatology ward. He ordered the dose to be doubled each time, but after a short respite of calm, the old woman got out of the bed and went off on another rampage. In doing so, she displayed amazing physical strength and vitality, completely inconsistent not only with her age but also her gender. When Dr. Vlahović ordered the head nurse to double the dose for the fourth time, she warned him—though as a first-rate anesthesiolo-gist he had to know (as would any first-year medical student)—that the dose was lethal. That is, it would cause death even to a young, stout male. To that Dr. Vlahović only repeated his order. Forty-five minutes later Regina Delavale was pronounced dead.

In the morning Dr. Onofri reported the incident to the police, after he'd reached the conclusion that a murder had taken place from the patient's file. He most likely also informed journalists, who went on to write about the Dr. Men-gele of our hospital, and the affair, the worst since the end of the war, shook the city overnight.

The myth of the brilliant young anesthesiologist was shattered by the very people who had created it, mostly with the same arguments, the only differ-ence being that what had yesterday been accepted as a reason for praise today was the source of the harshest rebuke. He had excelled so much in his studies because even at that time he had planned a perfect murder with medications. Calm and composure actually confirmed his callous nature, characteristic of psychopaths in white coats, of which, as we know, there have been many in history. His handsome and clean face revealed that the greatest criminals don't look like criminals at all.

Of course, no one considered the fact that Dr. Vlahović had left behind a paper trail. The patient's file had recorded the precise dosage of the sedatives, and by virtue of this the crime could not be perfect, nor should the story of his cold callousness ever been told. This and other details that contradicted the fab-rications of the press and the street were hushed up and dismissed as if this were a screenplay and not life and there was no room for anything that might unduly complicate the story or violate the conventions of its genre.

For love, the unfortunate Ares had run into difficulties from which he would have a hard time extricating himself. In particular, Dr. Onofri's crass comment concerning the affair with Dr. Fočić had a basis in reality: Vlahović would never have returned to the city if she hadn't been there. Nor, had he not been in love, would he have let himself get mixed up in the lives of people who were of no concern to him and thus condemn Regina Delavale to death, a woman whom he did not know but who was the mother of another woman whose fate had aroused such pity in his lover. It was a lie that she'd persuaded him to double the dosage to a lethal level; Dr. Fočić had left the hospital in tears long before that happened, but Ares knew what she expected of him and what she would have done if she'd found herself in the same situation. Just as she saw her own grandmother in the sleeping old woman, so she saw in crazy Manda something that had no reason for its existence other than to make the surrounding world miserable. Both the one and the other were completely understandable, made sense emotionally, and testified to the nobility of the soul with which Ares had fallen in love more than with her physical beauty. However, nothing of this could serve as an argument, either before people or before prosecutors and judges, because then law books would fill more volumes than there are in the Library of Congress, and no one except maybe God would know them so thoroughly as to be able to pass judgments in complete concord with the nature of the human soul.

All of this was clear to Dijana after she signed for receipt of the death certificate of Regina Delavale, and the tears that she cried at the cemetery, which surprised her children and satisfied her family and friends, were meant for the handsome Ares and the young doctor. The earth thudding on the black veneer of the coffin wasn't burying Dijana's mother because she'd long been dead, but it was burying those two young people who—it was no exaggeration to say— had caught her eye and with whom she'd fallen in love in a way that was not without its erotic nuances. Perhaps more than the moral act and the obligation that Ares had created with his sacrifice, what attracted Dijana to him and his young companion was their pure beauty, intensified by the meaning of their white overcoats and their babylike details, such as the orange sock with the little soccer balls on it.

She felt the murder charges against Ares to be crazy Manda's final revenge, which lent her three-month bout of insanity its ultimate criminal aspect. She departed from this world on her own account and pressing her seal on the lives of those who saw her off. In this way her ninety-seven years were continuing and would last as long as there were those whose paths she'd changed. Three people, two women and one man, would remember her as long as they lived and carry her evil inside their souls only to pass it on to others if they completely lost hope, thus making the curse of crazy Manda immortal.

After the funeral Dijana sat on the bed in her bedroom and looked at her children, confused and upset as they were, not knowing what to do or where to go now that what had filled their lives with fear and torment no longer existed. And now that it was gone, she was unable to feel any happiness.

"Well, now that's over," said Mirna and grabbed her left breast mechanically. Darijan gave a laugh; she shuddered, realizing what she'd done, and started laughing like crazy.

"Come on, stop it already!" Dijana said trying to be stern, but it didn't sound that way, nor was there actually any reason for sternness. Then she started laughing herself, uncontrollably and inconsolably, and the more she laughed, the more joy and sadness mixed within her, as seawater and fresh water mix, creating deep, powerful whirlpools in which foreigners and suicides drown and into which punctured balls, beer bottles, and plastic toy boats sink forever, the victims of neglect, indifference, or simply old age.

Mirna grabbed her left breast once more, this time deliberately, thinking that in this way she would keep up the reason for their laughter, but in fact she put an end to it.

XIII

Mirna had turned ten when her left breast grew large over the course of two months. The right one was still completely flat, like on boys of her age, but the left one was big, robust, and firm, almost like a half melon, with the nipple of a real mature woman, which protruded when it touched the cold side of the bathtub. Darijan said it was like a little prick, and so she no longer allowed him in the bathroom while she was showering. The nipple on her right breast was hardly there; it was small, light, and invisible and did not react to either warmth or coldness. She would test it every day, uncertain which side she feared more or which one confirmed in a disgusting way that something was not right with her. She knew nothing about her femininity because Dijana was convinced that the time had not come for her to be told about that. Moreover, at the time when Mirna's breast had started to grow, Dijana had just left on a trip to Cairo and would spend four crazy months crisscrossing Africa with Marko Radica, a captain on long voyages with whom she'd been head over heels in love and who'd accepted her children as his own, or so she believed. She'd left them in the care of her eighty-five-year-old mother, which scandalized the whole neighborhood, and the talk around town was that Dijana, widow of the late Vid Kraljev, had abandoned her children and run off with a black man whose member, so it was claimed by widows in headscarves, was so large that he could shake mulberries off a tree without climbing it.

Such gossip didn't bother Regina Delavale. She had already put so much behind her and had herself already badmouthed half the city, so it was okay in a way if it came back around to her. Besides, she even derived a certain amount of pleasure from the role that she'd been cast in. It was rare that women of that age became martyrs again, if only in the talk of the town, who singlehandedly cared for two small children. That seemed like another shot at youth, a third set of teeth, a miraculous rebirth, something in which every torment was sweet. She knew that her newly acquired prestige would not last long because Dijana would come back, and in the eyes of the town she would again be an old woman worth only a little more than dogs that sun themselves on the main square. But for now everyone greeted her with respect, inquired about her health and whether she needed anything, all in hopes that she would complain to them and thereby add new details to the story of the whore that had run off with the well-hung black man. But she told them that she was doing well and couldn't figure out why everyone was whining about the south wind when she didn't feel a thing.

"An old lady doesn't complain if her bones ache only if she can't get a piece of a man!" she said to the horror of those who would pass on what she said and add that there was something to it because blood was thicker than water, and it was clear who the Negro-loving whore took after.

"There are women whose pussies are so deep that none of us can fill them! And then they go looking for black men," was the expert remark of Mijo Alavanja, who was Regina's age and had been a local stud since the late '20s. His nose had fallen off after an affair with some German woman in his youth, which was the end of one career and the beginning of another. He changed from a great lover to a local wise man and expert on all things erotic and on reproduction in man and animal. He would shut himself in a stable and talk each steed, bull, and boar into jumping on a female. No one knew how he managed to accomplish this, and he jealously guarded the secret of his skill to earn large sums of money. It was also told that Mijo Alavanja even cured men of impotence in a similar way; legend has it that he managed to make some Ahma, a major in the partisans from Gacko who had lost both testicles in the Battle of the Neretva, capable of fathering children. So Mijo was a reliable source of information, and people believed what he said about some women needing a black cock for anatomical reasons. Husbands could only hope that their wives didn't number among them.

Regina didn't want to let anyone get the better of her, nor did she worry about the tale of black sexual prowess, and she was just as resolute in this as she was in her intention of exploiting the opportunity that she would never have had if Dijana hadn't gone crazy over that Marko Radica. Moreover, the children weren't a lot of work. She had to wash and iron their things, make sure that they were well dressed when they went out into the cold, and that they had something to eat. In any case there was no need to cook for them because they never even tried her chicken but naughtily wrinkled their noses and made disgusting grimaces while it was cooking in their biggest, green pot. Instead they ate their Eurocream spreads and patés, which didn't bother Regina all that much, though she couldn't understand how someone could turn down boiled chicken, when she would eat one up in two days and would still be licking her fingers, just as everyone in her family would. New customs came with new generations, and it wouldn't have surprised her if a time came when no one cooked chicken in a pot any more and everyone retched at the sight of three-toed, plucked legs sticking up out of boiling water, just as her granddaughter retched. It could be said that there was gastronomic pleasure in the fact that Dijana had left her alone with the children. She could cook chicken whenever she wanted, without her daughter's complaining that she'd forgotten that they had eaten it the day before and was cooking the same thing today.

Mirna tried to conceal from her grandmother the wonder that had grown out of her. She would call Darijan, who would wrap her upper body tightly in a wide military bandage. She wore wide shirts and fled from Regina's sight. It wasn't as bad at school as it was at home, even after the kids had started to notice that her left side was thicker than her right side and the boys were tripping over themselves to check it out with their own hands, to see if she was maybe abnormal, and she would whack them with whatever was within reach. But somehow it seemed to her that her deformation wasn't so abnormal in those surroundings. She comforted herself with the idea that that breast was still less of a stigma than faces full of fibrous acne scars, the hump on orphan Ana's back, and the water on the brain of Nazif in the first row, but when after three months of growth the melon-like bulge neared its peak, Mirna realized that it was more terrible than all pimples or any hump because it was unstoppable, fatal, and shameful. In the end that breast would grow too large and kill her like a cancer. Maybe it was cancer. She didn't know, just as she didn't know why she was overcome with shame when the bathroom mirror showed her only half of what she'd seen on the bodies of grown women on the beaches of Mljet and Korčula (on account of which her mother covered her eyes) and what she suspected was underneath her grandmother's black sweater. When she was eleven, she'd believed that women grew breasts only after childbirth and that they were the only way that one could tell whether a woman had had children or not. She imagined them to be like milk cartons that remained on the body for the rest of one's life, and as she peered at the naked women swimming on Mljet, she was certain that she would never give birth because she was disgusted at the thought of spoiled milk underneath the skin of elderly women's bodies. And now, you see, she'd grown a breast, but only one, which easily led to the conclusion that she was abnormal, a freak. And it was only a question of time when everyone, and not just Darijan, would become aware of her freakishness.

He didn't think the change in his sister was such a big deal because he'd never thought about the meaning of breasts on a woman's body. Mirna had been different from him her whole life in one detail, the one between her legs, and he thought of her enormous breast, which seemed to have been stolen from the cover of a magazine in the display of a newspaper kiosk, as an extension of that difference, something that certainly wasn't his problem, and he wasn't surprised at all by the asymmetry on her body. He even thought that it was more normal for her to grow one and not two. He would have probably become jealous of a second one because it wouldn't have meant a difference in sex but in age, and he surely would no longer have wanted to take a bath with his sister after his mother came back from Africa. Namely, Dijana would stick both of them in the tub and scrub them clean in one go, paying no heed to Regina's comments that such big children needed to take a bath alone and wash themselves. She didn't want to have to worry about whether they'd washed their ears, feet, and backs well and feel ashamed before people who would say that she didn't take care of her children. Instead, she would wash them in twenty minutes and then let them splash around in the tub, so small and naked, unaware of the difference between them and its meaning and without a single hair on their bodies. Dijana stuck to the view that her twins were the same sex until they grew pubic hair. Only then would she separate them and teach them the shame that divides the sexes. She couldn't imagine (nor had she heard of something like that happening) that her daughter would first grow one breast, far outgrowing both of Dijana's, before everything else came along.

After her breast visibly increased in size over the course of a weekend, on Monday morning Mirna told Darijan that he didn't have to bring the bandage because she wasn't going to school. She was going to stay in bed, and he should tell her teacher that she was sick. He didn't care. He packed his schoolbag, put on his shoes, and went out.

"Where's your sister?" their grandmother asked as he was leaving the apartment.

"She's off in her room; she says she's sick," he shouted to her and vanished. Regina panicked, thinking that the child really wasn't feeling well because the little star student never played hooky, and she didn't want to have to find a doctor right then. So she rushed into her room, where there was something to see. Underneath the translucent sleeping gown of her little granddaughter she could see the contour of something that made her think for a moment that she had lost her mind.

She couldn't believe her eyes! One big tit, with a nipple at the tip, stuck out as if it was mocking her age.

"Whoa, girl, what's that?" she asked.

Mirna burst into tears, seeing that her small, negligible, but nevertheless bright hope that she was carrying something quite ordinary on her had evaporated. This hope was the reason why she'd even decided to show grandma her breast, clutching herself as someone condemned to death would cling to his last possible salvation. There was no longer any way to hide what she had hidden for three months, and now, she realized that that phantasmagorical breast was more terrible than she had thought. Grandma put her hand over her mouth, which she had done only one other time in front of her: when Admiral Boško Alać had jumped from his apartment on the tenth floor and hit the ground right in front of them. The breast was something just as terrifying as the smashed head of the admiral, which had oozed a grayish-yellow substance similar to the feces that fishermen fling over the beach when they remove it from a large tuna.

"Grandma, what's wrong with me?" she asked, following her into the kitchen and wringing her hands.

"Damn you, how should I know?! But there's certainly someone who does," the old woman answered.

"Go and ask, please; ask somebody," Mirna begged her desperately.

"How can I ask?! You think I should go and say that my child has grown a tit like a cantaloupe, but only one, and ask what that might be? They'd put me in the nuthouse. No, somebody's got to come see."

The wheels started turning in Mirna's head: she'll bring people to look at her; oh no, no way. She'd rather die, as she very well might. But when? How much time did she have left until the gigantic breast pulled her down to the ground? Seven more days or seven more years? Would she stay forever locked up at home to hide her shameful deformity, until the very day the gravediggers carried her out or her growth was given its place in a jar of formaldehyde, on the morning television program, among unborn children, smokers' lungs, and the last specimens of extinct animals? She didn't think that grandma meant her any harm, but maybe there was just a little malice in her plan. Not only was she old, but an elderly something had grown on her granddaughter, and now she wanted to show it off so she might become a little younger and justify the fact that she was still alive, although every morning for years already she had called out to the black earth, and more recently to God as well, to take her and put an end to her suffering.

Who knew what Regina Delavale actually thought, but that very afternoon she called all the older women in the neighborhood to the kitchen—there were nine of them—and sat them down around the table and beside the wood stove.

"Now you'll see something," she said and went to get Mirna. They didn't say a word. The younger ones looked at each other, signaled something with frowns, and were struck with fear in the face of the strange spectacle that Regina hadn't told them anything about, though they knew that it would be something very strange, while the two oldest, wearing the perennial black headscarves of widows and eyeglasses that were always about to fall off their noses, tirelessly crocheted their white lace ornaments, as if they knew that they had little time left to live and would go straight to hell if they didn't finish their decorative tablecloths or television doilies.

"Let's go to the kitchen," said grandma.

"Please, don't," Mirna said, pulling a sheet over her shame.

"It's too late now. You have to. The women have come. They know about this," she said and pulled her out of the bed. "It's better for you to go downstairs than for me to bring them up here."

Mirna didn't resist any more, thinking that it was true and that it was all over and that her body was no longer exclusively her property because they would look at her dead body and turn her over however they each wished. She wouldn't care when she was dead, so she might as well get used to it.

Regina pushed her granddaughter ahead of her out into the kitchen. When she saw all those women, Mirna reflexively took a step back, but there was no way to leave now.

"Lift up your T-shirt," grandma ordered her, but the child couldn't move a muscle. The old woman lifted up the T-shirt with a quick movement from behind; her arms went up all by themselves, and the white fabric covered her eyes. She saw black silhouettes. The voices of her neighbors mingled with each other: "Christ almighty, the poor girl; she's half woman, half man. As if one half of her was made on one day and the other half on the next. Like this, when you cover the other half, and her face—you shouldn't look her in the face. It's good like this when you can see half her body and her head is covered. And has anything grown between her legs? Does she have any curls? How did it start? Overnight, you say? Yesterday she was the same on both sides. No she wasn't. What's wrong with you? Oh, let me feel it. Oh, it's so soft. Poor child . . ."

Mirna listened to them without moving; it seemed to her that all this was the same voice, which was sometimes deep, sometimes shrill, hoarse, and childlike, and she could have stood like that for hours, as long as they didn't lower the shirt from her face.

"Can I feel it too?" she heard someone say and immediately felt their cold fingers on her breast, squeezing it as if it weren't alive, the way they would grab a head of cabbage in the garden or snap a pod of green beans. No one had ever touched her arms, face, and body so roughly, which was proof that the strange and hateful growth wasn't something vital and precious but a torment and misery, like stones that have to be cleared from the ground where grapevines are to be planted, like heavy showers that wash away all the soil, carrying it to the sea and leaving instead of grapevines only bare rock. Breasts were a curse, whether they came in a pair or only singly, she realized.

"Cover yourself; what are you standing there for like a wooden Virgin Mary?"

Regina shouted, a little afraid that her granddaughter was enjoying having people look at her naked. Only then did Mirna awaken from her daze, in which the women could do with her what they wanted—cut her with kitchen knives and sprinkle hot ashes on her chest—she wouldn't have cried out. Terror seized her, and she ran into her room shouting like a lunatic. She threw herself onto the bed and started shaking as if electrical wires were connected to her every nerve. She didn't think anything, didn't feel anything, nor could she tell the difference between life and death. She was free of pain and only wished for everything to be over as soon as possible, no matter what it was and what the outcome would be. Only from time to time in her dull trembling would it seem to her that she felt icy, rough fingers on her breast, and she would throw herself onto the other end of the bed, trying to flee from what there was no longer any running away from because it'd happened and would thus remain.

The council in the kitchen went on for hours. Some of their neighbors believed that the devil had taken possession of the little girl, and if they drove him out, the shameful breast would shrink all on its own.

For an exorcist they suggested some Mljet hermit and defrocked priest, or some monk from Sinj, and one other man who'd done twenty years of hard labor in Zenica because he had remotely exorcized a demon from Boris Kidrič, which resulted in Kidrič's sudden death. And so the communists, as the eldest of the old women claimed while feverishly continuing her crocheting, convicted the exorcist, who was otherwise a Dominican monk and a white friar, for that voodoo magic.

But maybe it would be worth calling that hodja from Trebinje, regardless of the difference in faith and all the dangers that stemmed from that, because he'd freed more possessed children from spells in eastern Herzegovina and Podrinje than all Catholic priests together.

Regina didn't like the idea of exorcizing a demon from her granddaughter, although she'd recently begun to discover God and the church for the first time in her life. But she still didn't understand the point of exorcisms, nor could she believe that the devil slipped into people like a drunkard into his coat. She was inclined to believe that this was some inherited disorder. There was a lot of talk about such things on television, and it overlapped perfectly with what she thought about Vid Kraljev, Dijana's dead husband. She wasn't opposed to the idea that it was something inherited from Ivo Delavale, her departed husband and Mirna's grandfather. It even seemed logical that female curses were carried on the father's side of the family. There could never be as much evil in a woman as there was in her husband's or father's legacy to her.

One neighbor woman claimed that this was a medical problem and that the child should be taken to the doctor as soon as possible; there were hormone tablets, injections, and various miracles of medicine. Because that tit could kill the little girl or disfigure her for life. The doctors had to stop it from growing so the other one could catch up to its size when the time came. But she was quickly shut up, both by the other women and by Regina. It was unlikely that this was a known illness because someone would have already heard of such cases. Such girls would be seen on the street and on the beach. It was even less likely that there was a cure for such a huge tit in the hospital. And if they did take the girl to the hospital, then inside of three days the whole city would know about the deformity of the little Kraljev girl, and shame would erode the stone walls of the Delavale house.

Of course, all nine women swore not to say a word about what they'd seen. They agreed that it would be a sin against the child before God if they said anything. But in not three but only two days the whole city was already abuzz about the oddity on Old Mulberry Street. In no time the breast on the body of the ten-year-old girl grew beyond its real size and became the biggest in the long and glorious history of the city. Milk was already streaming out of it, and three long, thick black hairs grew out around the nipple. Rumor had it that doctors were coming from America to see this wonder, and the owners of an Italian circus would soon arrive as well—maybe the little girl would grow a beard too. The story of the breast was a source of entertainment for primitive and semiliterate salesgirls at the farmer's market and the fish market, just as it was for the intellectual elite—teachers and journalists as well as directors and actors in the local theater, who would gather in the City Café on Saturdays to tell jokes about the little Amazon girl and the reasons why she had appeared here of all places and now of all times, when the country's political situation was becoming ever more complicated and the threat of war was in the air.

"Maybe she'll call us to arms and lead us in the defense of these city walls?" wondered a local poet and layabout, who in the absence of talent and inspiration found all his artistic life on a corner of a table in the City Café. His quip was followed by expressions of disgust on the faces of those at the table. It was neither a good joke nor a particularly clever comment. Was there a third possibility?

Mirna was unable to pull herself together before evening. Darijan found her on the bed, shaking all over, and between sobs she gave incoherent answers to his questions. He ran to grandma and asked her what had happened.

"It's nothing for boys to worry about," she told him.

"You'll see who'll worry about what when our mother gets back," he retorted and went to his sister.

He sat at her side all night long and tried to find out what had happened, but at first she couldn't tell him, and later she didn't want to. God only knows what was going through his mind then, but her brother never found out the reason for Mirna's distress. Before he knew anything about men and women, he would ask every so often, but after he began to learn and comprehend their differences, more instinctively than consciously, he would stop mentioning that day.

One evening when Darijan was twelve years old, he saw Bergman's *Virgin Spring* and learned what the word "rape" meant. He convinced himself that on that day, while he was in school and then went out looking for doves' nests, his sister had been raped. He would believe that up until they lowered crazy Manda into her grave, and the feeling of guilt that was born while watching Bergman's scene of the father of a raped daughter thrashing himself with birch branches would never leave him. It didn't occur to him that Mirna's breakdown might have had something to do with her breast, nor did the fact that the whole city was talking about it tell him anything.

Being the only one who saw nothing monstrous in her giant breast, he had no idea that it was the source of the whole problem, which depressed him and weighed down on him for quite some time.

After that sleepless night, brother and sister slept the whole morning. Regina didn't want to wake them up because sleep was more important than school. She even took care to make as little noise as possible; she didn't take pots from the cabinet, didn't call out to her neighbors from window to window. She knew that they hadn't slept the night before. She loved those children more than her own daughter because children are guilty of nothing, but her love for them was meager, harsh, and inconstant. And that love made its appearance only when they were afflicted with some evil, when they were sick, crying, or sleeping.

Those little sparrows, death's little brother and sister, one could hardly see them breathing.

She liked to sleep a lot herself but never had enough time for sleep and felt pity for the both of them and their dreams, letting all the tenderness of her heart flood through that morning thought of her grandchildren. This happened whenever she recognized something of herself in Mirna and Darijan, the same feelings, desires, and especially fears. She would hug and shield them fervently, which always amazed Dijana. She attributed Regina's fits of affection for the grandchildren to her years, her senility or insanity, which she'd always noticed in small doses in her mother. She didn't figure out that Regina loved in her grandchildren only what she felt and knew in herself. And she couldn't have figured this out because Regina's bursts of tenderness and sweetness occurred very rarely, whereas she otherwise seemed indifferent and uninterested. Sometimes she was even unbelievably cold in situations involving her grandchildren that would have touched every other grandmother on this planet.

Living in her imploded world, Regina Delavale shared with others only what they emitted from their intact, untouched souls, as random signs of recognition. She was obsessed with what was going on inside herself, and had someone been able to enter into her heart, they would have found a woman who hadn't gotten over insults, disappointments, and years stolen in deceit. That is to say, a woman who was pushing fifty without a husband and not an old lady who was already eighty-five. This misunderstanding between body and soul, in which the former endured in conformity with its years and the latter was young in misfortune, was likely the cause of the long life of Regina Delavale. There are two natural ways to depart from this world: either you leave like most people reconciled with a lost life, or you lose your mind because the soul cannot endure the lack of reconciliation. The intensity of one's insanity in the end always determines the length of one's life.

The same afternoon Mirna told her grandma that she wasn't going to go to school any more.

"Your mother will kill you when she comes back!" the old woman said, trying to scare her, but it was no use. The girl had decided that she could never again leave the house and show her shame to the world. Besides, she didn't believe that she would live to see her mother return from her African journey. That was still around twenty days away, which seemed far too long a time to a dying girl like her. She lay on her bed and looked at the wall on which there were pictures of actors and pop singers, relics of a distant careless time that had ended a few days after her mother left on her journey, when she first noticed that the left side of her chest was bigger than the right. If her mother hadn't left, maybe everything would have been different; maybe she would have taken her to a doctor in time, done something that needed to be done; now it was too late for hope. There was no way that anyone could even her out again or halt the wild swelling of her flesh. She took pity on herself, without a father, abandoned by her mother, all alone in the world. Tears began to flow, and Mirna finally found something she recognized, a feeling that wasn't new and in which she could calm herself, for a while at least.

The next day her teacher, Klara Šeremet, a gray-haired old maid who was fanatically patient with her pupils but reputed in the city to be an eccentric, so much so that parents signed petitions with requests for her to be forced into early retirement, asked Darijan where he'd been the day before and why his sister hadn't been in school for three days now. He lied and said that his stomach had hurt and that Mirna was sick. He feverishly tried to remember what she was sick with, but it took too long for anything to come to mind.

"Your mother hasn't come back from her trip?" she asked, breaking his train of thought.

"Not yet; she'll be here soon," he answered.

"And how's your grandma?" she asked, sounding gentle and caring, not suspecting anything.

Darijan was encouraged by that; he thought that she hadn't caught his lie, as when she acted as if she didn't notice when bad pupils copied from the good ones, on account of which she was reputed to be the most stupid and by virtue of this the best teacher. "Grandma's fine; she's the only one who's not sick," he said, perhaps too cheerfully.

She nodded in approval, and just when he thought it was over and she would leave him alone, she asked suddenly, "Did you forget to tell me anything?"

"No," he answered and knew it wasn't going to end there.

It was five o'clock in the afternoon when Regina opened the door of her house for the teacher Klara Šeremet. Her face couldn't conceal a slight expression of disgust; she couldn't stand that woman. No one knew why, but Regina had been one of the women who'd spread word around town that Klara was attracted to women and that for this reason she went off to Germany during every winter break, though the teacher gave no reason for this or other wicked rumors that followed her. She went to Germany simply because she was German on her mother's side and in Hamburg had five half-brothers and half-sisters, all rich or at least well-off people who tried to persuade her to stay there. They bought her an apartment; she had a car waiting for her in the garage. But she didn't want to leave her solitude in that wicked Mediterranean city and the school that compensated for any possible shortcoming arising from her extremely lonely life. She didn't marry because she'd never even fallen in love. That didn't cause her pain; she didn't think it important, nor did she have anyone who might have brought her attention to it. Like someone who never smokes a cigarette can't imagine enjoying tobacco and so pities the victims of nicotine dependency, so Klara Šeremet pitied, quietly, without a word, all those who add someone else's difficulties to their own.

Her father, a sign maker in Mostar and later the owner of the Orion Cinema, had been condemned to death before a partisan court because for four years of war he'd received into his house Italian and German officers and had gone on outings with them on summer nights to the banks of the Neretva. Just as he'd received communist fugitives and given them what they asked for. Despite the horror of his wife Gudrun, Klara's mother, he'd also hidden a wounded partisan, Paloma Levi, in his cellar, and when she recovered somewhat, he drove her secretly in his Mercedes past all manner of patrols and sentries, all the way to Jablanica. Old Šeremet was against Hitler, but he couldn't be against decent people, regardless of their uniforms and insignias, and such people were the only ones he socialized with. Nazis were hateful as long as he saw them from afar, but whenever they came closer, before he even got to know them, he could understand that they were elegant and polite people who, if it weren't for the war, would be collecting oddly shaped stones on the banks of the Neretva or would be in the vicinity of Glavatičeva hunting for strange plants that one could not find in Germany and recording their finds.

Impetuous and gallant, he spent the war living it up, paying no heed to what was said in the town and openly scorning the Ustashas because he found no decent and cultured people among them, nor did he have any wish to get to know them. And so he managed to earn the enmity of everyone who had spent the war hungry or in fear or lost someone of their own. In actuality, he was hated by everyone he hadn't helped, and there were those to be found who would forget what he had done for them.

A few months before the liberation of Mostar, Franko Rebac, a communist since the Vukovar congress, had come and warned him to leave the town for a few days: his wife was German, he'd earned money off the Italians and Germans and had been a friend to so many of them . . .

Gajo Šeremet laughed: "My brother, who would lay a hand on me? Those are fine people."

Franko wasn't sure who Šeremet thought was fine—the fascists or the communists. He only told him, "With the fine ones comes the dross." When he left, Gudrun asked him what the word *dross* meant.

He answered, "You wouldn't believe it, but I don't know. I've been hearing about the dross since I was born, and I'll be damned if I haven't said it a thousand times myself, but to this day I haven't asked anyone what *dross* is. And you see why it's good that you're a German. You ask about things I think I know but really don't. So the first chance I get I'll ask someone with a brain to tell me what the *dross* really is."

But before he had managed to ask anyone, the partisans entered the town; he was arrested and brought before a court. And more witnesses came forward against Gajo Šeremet than against the worst murderers. Some lied, others told a truth that was no prettier than the lies, and he sat with his hands in chains, listening to the audience behind him shout out wartime slogans, and couldn't believe at all that the prosecution and the judge would not in the end see that this was a mistake. He even thought that the purpose of the trial was to frighten him because they obviously didn't like the fact that for four full years he hadn't let the war get to him or turn him into the dross that would carry out its own justice at the expense of others. He was seriously afraid for the first time when his defense attorney requested that his client be simply shot instead of hung, as the prosecution had suggested. But he kept believing that someone would come and ask, "Do you know who this man is?" And then he would go off laughing and joking to that bar under the Old Bridge and drink himself silly. Not only he but the judge, the prosecutor, and the defense attorney, and everyone else too, and he would pay the bill like a real gentleman.

His optimism seemed like a serious mental disorder, the kind that makes people become mass murderers, but in bad times an optimist only gets his own head put on the block. When they led him out against the wall and blindfolded him with a black kerchief, Gajo Šeremet soiled his pants in an instant.

"Whoa, get a whiff of this traitor's perfume!" was the last thing that Klara's father heard, but fortunately he didn't feel a thing when he collapsed in the mud and filth from which he had tried so hard to set himself apart.

Klara's mother was taken off to a camp for ethnic Germans somewhere in Slavonia, but at the last moment she managed to foist her three-year-old daughter on Aunt Tereza, Gajo's older sister and the wife of Pero Domanović, a partisan commander who died in the fight for Mostar. Tereza raised Klara, trying unsuccessfully for years to return the child to her mother, who would see her again only twelve years later. But by that time everything had already been decided; fate had assigned each of them their place under the stars, and Klara wasn't about to move to Germany. Every winter she would go to Hamburg, feel that her brothers, sisters, and relatives were her own flesh and blood, but nothing more. After her Aunt Tereza died at the end of her studies, she continued on her own, without love and marriage, happy in fact.

"I'd like to see Mirna," said the teacher, the first to speak.

"Well, I really don't know," Regina said and moved aside so that Klara could pass, although she hadn't invited her in and didn't intend to do so.

"Is she sick?"

"I don't know."

"Fine, then take me to her."

"Why?" the old woman asked, squinting warily at her opponent. She tried to get her to go away, even if her grandchildren would be the worse for it, but without openly turning her away and slamming the door in her face because that wasn't done in good houses. No one knew why it wasn't done, but there you go; that was the custom, and one might as well follow it.

"I'll see her because I'm her teacher," Klara responded, used to all the local customs. And then she started for the wooden staircase that led upstairs.

"Wait, the girl isn't well," Regina said, coming after her.

"Which door is it?"

The old woman pointed at Mirna's and Darijan's room.

"Thank you very much. You're no longer needed."

The girl would have sooner expected to see the wicked witch from Hansel and Gretel in her room than her teacher. She pulled the bedsheet over her head and quickly curled up, like a hedgehog. She was going to stay that way no matter what the teacher tried because she would have to give up sooner or later and go away. Klara sat down on the bed, put her hand on the heaving white mound, and said nothing for a little while, as if she were unsure what to say or how to begin.

"Whatever happened, I don't think it could have been that bad," she said and fell silent again. "You haven't missed anything important, and no one is unhappy with you. Do you hear me? Okay, you don't have to say anything. I came because I was worried about you. Nothing else is important. Are you maybe sick? If you were, you wouldn't be hiding. But that's all right; we all feel like hiding once in a while. You can't always do what everyone wants you to. I can't do that either, and then I hide, and other people either notice or don't notice. Those who love you and happen to be near notice. Mirna, are you listening to me? Of course you are; I'm really stupid, how wouldn't you be? Does something hurt? If the answer is yes, just move your leg. Are you having a problem in school? Has someone hurt you? Did something else happen?"

Mirna straightened her right leg just a little.

"Is it something awful?"

She straightened it all the way out, so that it stuck out from beneath the sheet.

"Did someone say something to you?"

"No," Mirna spoke.

Her teacher gave a deep sigh and patted the body under the sheet.

"I can't show you," the girl said.

"What?" Klara asked, beginning to sense what awful kinds of things a ten-year-old girl wouldn't be able to show anyone.

"Fine; you don't need to tell me. And you don't need to show me now. But I'll tell you something: nothing that you could show me will seem as awful to me as it does to you. I already told you that, right? Yes, I'm repeating myself. You know, when I was younger, and not much younger than I am now, I hid from people. Not from my pupils, but from my friends, people who liked me. I always did that when I was out of sorts and didn't know why, and I was afraid that I would lose them if I let them see me like that. Today it seems funny to me, how I was, but the fear that I experienced still isn't funny to me. If you don't want to tell me what's wrong, I'll respect that and leave. You don't have to come to school tomorrow, or the day after, but you can't stay here forever. You'll have to come out sooner or later. No one will force you to; you just won't be able to go on like this. Now think about what will be easier for you: to get it over with now or to leave it for another day. Either is okay. But I think you think it's better to get it over with now. Listen—I think that, but I'm not saying you have to think so too. Do you want me to leave now?"

Mirna didn't answer. If she told her teacher to leave, she would spare herself more shame and would be left alone. The latter didn't seem like such a good idea any more.

"Move your leg if you want me to stay!"

"Stay," she whispered.

Then they both sank into a silence that lasted for a long while. Mirna knew that her teacher would stay as long as she wanted her to, and Klara was no longer in a hurry to go anywhere. She listened to that child's breathing and felt unusually useful. This was what she most often expected of herself and was the reason why she couldn't imagine living in Germany or taking retirement—she felt useful! This feeling had been accompanying her all her life, without there being any real reason for it—just as there wasn't for many other things. Klara Šeremet had simply been born that way, and it was only her eccentricity that made people make up causes and hidden and shameful reasons, although when she was alone with herself and under the heavens, which in the end determine all miracles, she was a very ordinary woman.

"You won't hate me?" It was already very late when Klara heard a voice from under the sheet, and the room was already sinking into darkness.

"For God's sake, Mirna, I won't."

At first her head came out from under the sheet.

"It's dark," said Klara.

"Don't turn on the light," the girl said and pulled the sheet off herself.

"Do you see anything?"

"Well, it's dark . . ."

"Here, something has grown on me . . ."

"Where?" Klara asked, biting her tongue. "Oh, so that's the problem! Your mother didn't tell you anything about that? Fine; of course she didn't because she hasn't had time. Nobody ever knows when it'll happen. Women's breasts start growing at different times, when we're between ten and fourteen years old; it depends, but this is normal . . ."

"But only one is growing on me. It's enormous . . ."

"What do you mean, only one? Of course, they don't grow equally fast."

"No, the other one isn't there at all."

"Are you sure?"

"Yes, it's not there . . ."

"Do you know what, Mirna, that's probably normal too . . ."

"What do you mean — normal?"

"It's nothing to get upset about. The other one will grow too."

"Just like it's supposed to?"

"Of course. You must have seen women on the beach . . ."

"I have, but . . . ," Mirna said and stopped.

She wasn't sure what to believe. It seemed impossible that there was something that happened to every girl that she knew nothing about.

"Soon other things will start happening to you, things that aren't abnormal or anything to get upset about, but your mother will tell you about them when she gets back. You won't have to ask her anything. She'll tell you herself as soon as she sees you."

Klara was starting to feel a little uncomfortable. In the darkness of the room, in which the only light came from the starry sky, she was sitting with a girl and was unable to tell her something that was so simple to say but for some reason wasn't said just like that, especially to a child to whom one had not given birth.

"But I don't think I want to go to school now," the girl said when her teacher had already gotten up. "There's simply no way I'm going to do that."

"Why don't you want to go? What's happening to you now will soon happen to other girls. What would happen if all girls stopped leaving the house as soon as they start turning into women?"

"But there's only one and it's huge. Everyone can see it."

"So what if everyone can see it? Get some sleep and we'll see you tomorrow. Be happy that everything is okay."

"What were you doing so long in her room?" asked Regina, who'd been waiting for her outside the door. Klara thought it would be good to tell that old hag everything she had coming and a lot more, but she didn't say anything except good-bye when she was at the door. And even that was too much in a way.

"God forbid I ever set eyes on you again, you fucking cunt," mumbled Regina after she slammed the door behind the teacher.

She was furious; a spider would have died from poisoning if it bit her. It was as if someone had defiled her house and poisoned the air that she breathed. She sat down by the hot stove, popped her knuckles, and cursed everyone to herself in order: her daughter, who was whoring around who knew where and with whom — and it wouldn't be a surprise if it were some black man, and her children, who hadn't even really hatched yet but were already adding to the family shame, picking up where their parents had left off. She cursed herself because she'd been tricked again, which always happened, and someone again expected her to feel guilty. But as far as she was concerned, Regina Delavale wasn't guilty of anything. Others would have known that she wasn't guilty if they had lived her life, day in, day out, year in, year out, or at least heard her story from someone. They wouldn't hear it from her. She would stay as silent as a tomb and put up with everything as long as she could, and when she couldn't go on any more, then her dead mouth would swallow it.

"Get the hell out of here, you whore's bastard!" she yelled at Darijan when he came into the kitchen for bread and Eurocream. He tiptoed out as if fleeing a cage of lions in a nightmare.

Mirna obeyed her teacher and went to school the next morning. She put on the biggest shirt that Darijan had and Dijana's raincoat over that, but out on the street there wasn't a pair of eyes that didn't stare at her. Women dressed in black whispered to one another and pointed at the girl; men in the City Café put their newspapers down on their tables and watched her pass by; groups of children laughed. She was sure that it wasn't because her breast was noticeable now—they couldn't even see it; rather, grandma's lady friends had spread the story, and the story would grow until everyone stared at her. The more people there were that looked at her like that, the fewer there were that didn't see her. That was good in a way. Darijan walked a few steps behind her and didn't raise his eyes from the street. They looked like city paupers who would only be pitied by the author of all those fairy tales, but he was far, far to the north and had been dead for a long time.

Strangely, it was her schoolmates who were least interested in her breast. After she took off the raincoat, they all took a good look at the bulge under her shirt, as if on command, and were immediately disappointed because after listening to the stories of the adults, they'd believed it to be much bigger. Afterward they were ready to forget that tit. When you're little and you measure life in days and not years, you often see a miracle happen, but more often you're disappointed and convinced that there wasn't any miracle.

Boris Werber, the son of a couple of painters who'd moved from Zagreb the year before, reacted more excitedly but only because the story of the little Amazon hadn't reached his parents. "Look at her titty!" he exclaimed and grabbed Mirna, whereupon Darijan lunged at him and a fight ensued that left the little Werber with a cut over his eye. When the teacher came into the room, there was blood all over the place, and Boris was howling as if someone were skinning him alive.

The principal showed up too: "Who was fighting?" he asked. He grabbed Darijan by the ear and hauled him off to his office. The teacher ran after them but stopped and turned on a dime like a basketball player starting back down the court and ran back to the bloodied Boris. Then all hell broke loose, but it didn't have any lasting consequences or, as was the custom, create new problems in the staff room and lead to enmity among the families of pupils that were still somehow on good terms. They took little Werber to the health clinic, where he received stitches on the cut over his eye; Klara ran back and forth between his frenzied parents and the principal, who had to have the background of the episode explained to him as well as the reason why Darijan's parents couldn't come to the school the next day so that everything could be resolved according to some pedagogical ideal.

The next day Tobias Werber, Boris's father, came to the classroom. "It's good that you protect your sister, but don't kill a friend," he said to Darijan. "And you, now you know what will happen to you if you don't act like a gentleman with the ladies," he said, turning to his son. And everyone was proud: Mirna was proud of her brother because he had defended her; the principal was proud of the teacher because she knew things about her pupils that their parents didn't; Boris Werber was proud of his father because the general consensus was that he was a big man, unlike most fathers. Darijan alone didn't have anyone to be proud of. After the bloody duel Mirna's breast was no longer the talk of the classroom, but it would be the talk of the town up until Dijana returned from Africa, which was when the war began. While she was unpacking her bags, explosions began to reverberate. Since she hadn't heard a word about the news at home for four full months, she had no idea what was going on and ran in a panic into the kitchen, where Regina was putting the plates into the cupboard.

"Mother, what's that?" she asked, and her mother laughed furiously, as if she had expected just such a question.

"Nothing; soon they'll come and slaughter both of us like pigs! They won't ask which one of us is a pig and which isn't."

These words shocked Dijana more than the explosions did. No matter how she could be, the old lady had never talked like that.

"Mother, what's wrong with you?"

"You're asking me what's wrong with me, you're asking *me* that! There are your two children; ask them to tell you! Take a look at your little girl if you're a mother, and then ask me something."

"And what should I look at on her? You mean her tit? So I should look at that?! If I'd known what you're like, I'd never have gone."

"And it would have been better if you hadn't."

"Get lost, you old cactus; you've ruined my life. My every day is bitter because of you."

And so, while shells were falling around in the city, the two of them argued and scuffled, and for the first time they showed no mercy to each other, nor was there anything that they remembered about each other and didn't say as soon as it occurred to them. That fight wouldn't be forgotten. They were each a millstone around the other's neck in life, like two uninvited guests in the same house that suddenly didn't belong to anyone. They preyed on one another even when they spent days together in complete silence because at any moment it was clear who was thinking what.

"You sure got your fill sucking black cock, you Gruž slut!" the old woman said just when Darijan came into the kitchen.

"The siren is sounding. That means we have to get down into the shelter," he said calmly and went out.

The following month, which was as long as the war lasted in Dubrovnik, would be the most difficult in Dijana's life, worse than the three months she spent with crazy Manda. Her son and especially her daughter rejected her and treated her like a stranger. They didn't forgive her for being away, but she didn't know why because no one had told her what had been going on with Mirna's left breast, nor would she ever learn about the gathering of the old crows in the kitchen, which culminated in something that was almost like a rape. She was unable to bear the scorn in her children's eyes or their sudden cruelty, which was even greater for Regina than for her.

Their relations would improve a little only on the twenty-third day of the fighting. While they were in the shelter an incendiary shell hit their house and it burned to the ground, leaving nothing to serve as a remembrance of their previous life. When the fighting suddenly ended, just as suddenly as it had begun for her, Dijana would feel naked and barefoot, with the three of them to worry about. Then it was duty and not love that tied her to her mother and children, which she knew herself because not a day would pass without her thinking that if it weren't for them, she would go off to Cairo and board an ocean liner with Marko, the only person who had made her happy, work as a cook or maid, and finally find what she was looking for in life.

Years would pass before she would feel something for Mirna and Darijan that she could confess to others. In the meantime she would experience them as a widow's inheritance, something that resembled most the black dress that wives of seafarers and fishermen would put on and never take off again.

Apart from that blaze in which the family memorabilia burned up, none of the four of them felt the war. The topic that would set the tone of life of the city for years to come didn't concern them because it was smaller and less tempestuous than the episodes of their familial discord, which would continue to the end of Regina's life, when Dijana was already slowly entering the beginnings of old age. After the gathering of the neighbor women to see her granddaughter's breast, Regina would behave like a murderer who was hiding from the police and simultaneously trying to think of an alibi, a new one every day. She would

find people to blame for what she had done all over the place, most often in Dijana, who was incapable of being a real mother because her female organ was
stronger than her soul. Then she found the culprit in Mirna, who had struck the
same roots and at ten was already a little slut, on account of which she had to
be physically marked as well. She also found a culprit in Klara, whose eccentricity rubbed off on her pupils. And she also blamed all who could have been
connected to the monstrous appearances in the Delavale family. For example,
after a few months she remembered that right before the swelling of her breast,
the little girl had been vaccinated against tetanus. There must have been something in that vaccine. Someone was conducting experiments on the children,
and that was the reason for her granddaughter's suffering. This discovery didn't
put her in a rage but put her in a state of deep depression. And the depression
would last until the next alibi was found. In that experiment, Regina Delavale
saw something that created a bond between two fates and tragedies of life, that
of her and that of the girl, realizing for the umpteenth time that in this world
one is condemned to suffering, misery, and shame once one is born a girl.

Mirna's maturation occurred out of order and beyond the rules according
to which children had been entering the world of adults since there had been
people. At first she was continually hateful toward her mother, indirectly blam-
ing her for what had happened to her; this was followed by a long period of indifference, until they both grew accustomed to that as some kind of natural
relationship, which obligated neither of them to anything. Thus a wide space
of freedom opened up before her, which she would use as long as there was
anything to use.

It wasn't three days after her first cigarette and she was already smoking in
front of Dijana; she would go through boyfriends as if they were on a conveyor
belt, especially in the summertime, and scandalize the city with licentious behavior on beaches and in parks. Right until the day when she would have a two-
month sailing adventure around the Kornati Islands with a Swede named Max,
a forty-year-old sailing enthusiast and owner of a huge yacht who was spending his immense family fortune sailing warm seas the year round. Max's love
would be expressed in tens of thousands of dollars that he managed to spend in
Adriatic restaurants, nightclubs, casinos, and other places where one can spend
as much money as it takes to spend one's way into becoming everything one
couldn't be in life.

That went on until the morning they were sitting in a café on the Šibenik
waterfront and Mirna told him that she was pregnant. He jumped up with
joy, poured champagne down the throats of all the guests on the café terrace,
bought drinks for the whole waterfront, ran off somewhere, and returned with

a beautiful pink kimono, told Mirna to wait for him for ten more minutes so he could just go to the bank for money, and then set sail, never to show his face again, probably feverishly wondering whether he had maybe already given that girl his address and telephone number in Malmo because if he had, problems would arise that he would be unable to solve. Mirna waited for Max until nightfall, and then without a kuna in her pocket she went out on the highway and waited for someone to stop and drive her in the direction of Dubrovnik. With the pink kimono and her identity card in her pocket, without anything that would remind her of what had been happening to her in the last two months except what she was carrying in her belly, she felt like those refugees whom someone kicked out of their beds at three in the morning and thrust thousands of miles from their homes. The abortion was performed in the same hospital in which crazy Manda would meet her end.

After Dijana returned from Africa, Darijan withdrew into himself. He hid from his mother's and his grandmother's quarrels, fled from Mirna, to whom his debt grew from day to day, until in the end he was ready to leave and never come back to the charred remains of the family house. Up to the time of Regina's death he wouldn't do this for the simple reason that there hadn't yet been a good occasion for him to go off somewhere.

Klara the teacher had on several occasions during the last year she was the homeroom teacher for the twins attempted to tell Dijana something about what had happened during her journey to Africa, but she gave up in the end, as she was rebuffed in the most vulgar way, with open allusions to her sexual preferences. In a surfeit of rage that she could not express in her own home, Dijana used fragments of Regina's insane fantasies about the teacher's stay in Mirna's room and thus calmed her conscience and preserved a pure remembrance of Marko Radica, who was nevertheless most important to her.

"If you stay, I know she'll curse you, but you'll have me until I die," he told her on their last night in Cairo. She lay with her head on his breast, wept bitterly, and in fits of rage worthy of an American movie actress, she plucked hair from his chest. By morning she hadn't responded to his offer; nor did he repeat it. He knew that something like that was impossible because she wouldn't leave her children and go with him, just as he wasn't going to return to his city. They'd met ten years too late, and that couldn't be helped. She would live far from him, waiting for postcards from Singapore, Hong Kong, and Liverpool, until one day they stopped coming and the fire in her died out.

Six months after that month of war, Mirna's right breast grew to the size of her left one. But that, like her first day of menstruation, wasn't of interest to anyone.

XII

"I thought you were smarter than that," Dijana's mother told her the day it became definitively clear that her period wasn't late and that Vid had sowed his unwanted seed, which was now swelling and from which in all likelihood a life would be born. And from that, love between a man and a woman.

"That's all you have to say?" she asked Regina.

"Everything will be all right," the old woman answered laconically, with no intention of going into the problems that were developing in Dijana's head in any detail.

"Mother, what should I do?"

"Nothing, child; everything will happen naturally since it began like that . . ."

"Mother, I don't have much time to decide," she wrung her hands, expecting to receive some kind of approval or for Regina to take responsibility for the decision that she couldn't make herself.

"And what are you talking about, please? Killing what's growing inside your tummy? You can; no one's keeping you from doing it. But you won't feel better then. I'm telling you you won't," Regina said, with no desire to encourage or comfort her because no one had comforted her when at thirty-eight she had given birth to Dijana.

"I don't know whether I love him," her daughter said, trying once again.

"As if one can know that," her mother responded. She put on her slippers and went out into the garden to see how the seeds she had planted were coming up.

It was late April 1980, and the city was quieter than usual. All one could hear on the square was the clicking of cameras and the clamor of German, English, and Italian kids. The locals kept quiet in accordance with a long, public ceremony that had begun around New Year's, when the leg of their state's president for life, and the most beloved person in the meager and bloody history of romance among the Balkan peoples and nations, had been amputated in a hospital in Ljubljana. Every day an unnamed medical advisory council issued brief reports containing upbeat and encouraging news about his imminent recovery, which in fact sent word of his impending death. No one dared mention it out loud or even in a whisper because such an outcome was socially unacceptable. It wasn't only political reasons that forbade the country's eldest son from dying, but something else that was planted much more deeply in the collective and in each of its members. The life that was fading in Ljubljana was an archetype that had been handed down to the people regardless of whether they belonged to the majority, who were blindly in love with the state and all its written rules and customs, or to the barely visible minority, who hated that same state, who responded to it in kind or with worse measures. That man was something much larger than a father or a king and more real than God. He was irreplaceable, both on the throne and in the minds of his subjects. The fact that he'd been elected as president for life a few years earlier wasn't so much a sign of his absolutism as it was of the sincerest wish and desire of the majority of the citizens. Limiting the mandate of such a man was just as unimaginable as putting one's aging parents in an old folks' home. Yes, people did do that, but not in good homes and not in Yugoslavia.

In all the churches of the city people said heartfelt prayers for his recovery, urging the Almighty to make allowances for one atheist, and God was already supposed to know why he should act on their request. In creating man, God had also created competition for himself. If he didn't listen to the prayers for Tito's recovery, he would soon see for himself what kind of monsters his most perfect creations could turn into.

Dijana's pregnancy had thus come at a time when no decision that men could make about themselves and their lives could seem more important than what was happening in the Ljubljana medical center. Even then someone probably knew that this was all an illusion and that everyone wouldn't die with the eighty-eight-year-old patient, but in the reports of his critical condition Dijana found a good reason not to decide anything concerning the life that was growing inside of her. She had neither accepted it as her own nor rejected it but was simply waiting: the nightly news on television, the morning paper, months of pregnancy and months of illness, and the moment when it would be too late for any decision and the new life would have to be accepted as a gift from providence.

The May Day briefing of the medical council quit hiding the truth. The captains of the ship admitted it was sinking, and they made that admission to everyone in the form of a terse, lucid sentence that did not mention death but that, in contrast to the sentences of the previous statements, which had all been stylistically eloquent, was devoid of hope. Instead of a comma—the punctuation mark dearest to the heart that relativizes the meaning of every misfortune—there came a period, the finality of which was beyond doubt due to the very structure of the obituary from the president's physicians. It was just a matter of when, on which day, and at what time of the day the life support monitors would be turned off in the Ljubljana hospital and how the news would be announced that the man whose undoubted immortality had been sung in hundreds of thousands of verses—more than had been any other subject in their language—was dead.

On that Thursday, all day long, Dijana sat in front of the television. Behind her an old Avala radio set was also turned on. A newspaper was spread out on the table, and she was crying and couldn't stop even when Regina came in the room and went out again, comforting, scolding, and hugging her and then giving up. Regina kept telling her how beautiful it was to give birth to a child and that it was her last chance to do it because her biological clock was ticking. And she told her that she could also abort it. There was no shame in that, and life without children had its advantages. Then she offered to raise her children for her—she would probably live a while longer; people in her family lived to a ripe old age. Then she suggested that they go to the hospital, to pay the doctors for an abortion under full anesthesia . . .

She offered Dijana everything that otherwise she wasn't ready to offer and didn't even occur to her as a possibility, only to get her to stop crying and calm down. She did this because she was afraid that her daughter might be getting one of those hysterias of pregnancy that would grow and develop until it completely dimmed Dijana's consciousness and extinguished all her senses. And then she would be beyond the point of no return. She sensed how difficult it was to come back from a state of mental confusion full of hallucinated images and voices, when there's no longer any space in your heart or mind, where you are what you really are, because everything you see and feel is a warped perception or an alien thought. Most terrible is the fact that that world is incomparably more convincing than any reality. Reality is pale and ambiguous, but insanity is powerful and true. There's no greater truth than insanity.

However, all Regina's attempts were in vain. Not even slaps and threats to throw herself under a bus if Dijana didn't stop could help. Dijana wept for Tito and was impervious to any thought that didn't have to do with him. Nothing Regina could say on that May Day could compete with him.

Later she would remember her mother's words and offers—not without a guilty conscience—as one of Regina's rare acts of motherly heroism, and in any case her last. She would wonder how that heroism vanished and where it had come from in the first place. But she wouldn't find the answer, although it was clear and could be found in stories from Regina's past, which were not unknown to her. She would likewise wonder about the real reasons for her May Day despair and conclude that she'd been more sensitive than others because of her pregnancy, which was why she'd wept bitterly, enough for the whole town and half the country. In any case, she rejected the idea—which would surface in the first years of Mirna's and Darijan's lives—that the birth of her children (or rather her failure to make the other decision) had been determined by the death of Josip Broz Tito.

Finally, around ten o'clock, sleep swallowed Dijana's tears, and the next morning she awoke with a painful case of pinkeye and in a state of depression. Her first thought was that her life, just like the life that was growing in her womb, brought nothing but suffering and that fear was the only real reason why she hadn't killed herself ages ago. The next thing she realized was that on that morning she felt none of that fear. When a person is truly miserable, he ceases being afraid, and according to her own assessment Dijana was truly miserable on that second of May in 1980 and concluded that this was something to be exploited.

She went into the bathroom, filled the bathtub with warm water, and took Vid's razor blades from the shelves behind the mirror. She lay down in the tub and decided to wait for her body to get used to the temperature of the water. In some movie she'd seen that this was how it was done. Not long after, her knees began to hurt. She'd dreamed for years of buying a large bathtub in which she would be able to stretch out and relax.

And then all at once she had to pee. In the last few weeks she'd been peeing every half hour. She didn't know whether this was somehow connected to being pregnant or whether she had an infected bladder. She thought about getting up and going over to the toilet bowl, but she got cold at the mere thought of getting out of the water and stepping on the cold tiles with her bare feet. She realized that it didn't matter at all whether she peed in the bathtub if she was only going to slit her wrists afterward anyway. She let water mix with water and took a little pleasure in her empty bladder and the mild shudder that comes when one finally pees after a long wait. She stretched her legs out over the edge of the tub, and the pain in her knees gave way to a new feeling of comfort.

When enough time had passed for the tips of her fingers to shrivel, she remembered the razor blades. She grabbed the little packet, began to open it up, and all of a sudden she felt sorry about interrupting all of this. Why should she cut short the moments of her pleasure on account of a life that had no meaning? Everything was good now, and she could end the suffering easily when it appeared again. And she knew that it would, but that didn't make her unhappy. How could she be unhappy when everything she saw and heard now was so nice? Except her legs, which were before her eyes. They too would have been pretty if it weren't for the hairs all over them. They had grown since last autumn and now resembled those ugly and greasy hanks of hair that bald men comb across their heads. If she put her legs down in the tub, she wouldn't see them, but then the pain in her knees would come back. She stretched up and took Vid's razor out from behind the mirror. She unwrapped a razor blade and put it into the razor. She stopped, hesitated a little, and took Vid's shaving cream. On this occasion that seemed more elegant than ordinary soap. She sprayed her left shin. The thick foam looked like snow and smelled like pine trees. Men shave every day and that thought never occurs to them. Too bad, because it's nice. Snow that smells like pine in a can of shaving cream. She spread the shaving cream along her legs and drew the razor from her foot toward her knee. White and clean skin was exposed, without a single blemish or any blood. She sincerely admired her left leg, as if it belonged to someone else or as if it weren't a leg at all but, like the snow with the scent of pine, the work of a good magician. She carefully passed the razor along her leg and watched it become younger and younger. Then she began shaving her right leg, which became just as beautiful, but Dijana was still disappointed. People get used to things quickly, and there's no beauty that won't disappoint you a little the second time you see it.

After she finished shaving her right lower leg, she took a look at her arms. Little black hairs had also grown on them, it was true, not like on her legs, but these were also worth some effort and pleasure. She shaved her left forearm and then cut herself a little on her right. But it wasn't anything terrible. The pleasure was stronger than the blood.

Then she gave a deep sigh; would this be the end of an adventure that had brought only happiness? She wanted to prolong the journey through the newly discovered white spaces at any price. With the tip of her big toe she pulled out the plug. The water drained out of the tub, quietly at first, and then with a gurgling sound. When half of it had drained out, Dijana again reached toward the mirror and took the little nail scissors. She sat in the empty tub and for the first time in her life cut her pubic hair, which, as they say, covers one's shame.

Her heart beat from excitement, and she felt as if she weren't yet fifteen years old. Too bad you can't remember many things you might do for the first time in your life and that aren't suicide, she thought. She shook the can of shaving cream, sighed deeply again, closed her eyes, and pressed the lever. Although the foam was soft and light and she would hardly have felt it on her arms and legs, the very touch of it shocked Dijana. The hairs evidently protected the delicate sense of touch of that part of the body. Slowly, with a great deal of attention, pleasure, and caution, she drew the razor across her mons veneris and the neighboring depressions, hillocks, and volcanoes, trying to take as long as possible and, when the end came, to know well that she had thought about the end long enough not to yearn for it.

With virginal fear she lowered her fingers and then her palm onto her mons veneris. That was the sweetest touch of a body that she'd ever felt because it was simultaneously hers and someone else's. Then, without much worry, she remembered Vid and the fact that she would somehow have to explain this change to him when he returned from his trip through Bosnia. He'd departed ten days before, at a time when the briefings by the medical council had been full of optimism, and she still hadn't known that she was pregnant. Thinking of that meant a return to life outside the bathtub, a return that had ceased to be chronically depressing and had become healthily malicious.

Vid was supposed to come back late Sunday night with finished photographs of Banja Vrućica near Teslić, which together with pictures and texts on ten or so other spas for rheumatic diseases in Bosnia were to be part of a guidebook for the Adriatic. It would be published in ten European languages and would be used to attract aging, gouty, and tubercular tourists (especially rich ones) to special two-part packages: first, two weeks of therapy in one of the Bosnian spas, whereupon they would leave for a week of sea adventures. Banja Vrućica was the sixth or seventh place in which over the last year Vid Kraljev had stayed for three weeks as an assistant photographer to Petar Pardžik, the famed Belgrade artistic and personal photographer of all Yugoslav rulers from Petar I Karađorđević the Unifier to Marshal Tito. He'd taken on this project at a request and on an order from the highest leaders of the Bosnian Communist Party, who were convinced that Pardžik was the only one who could photograph those spas and hospitals so that they would look attractive to Krauts. And maybe he would lend them some of the old Habsburg imperial and royal charm and produce portraits of the buildings that made them look almost like marshals and field marshals. Kraljev had been assigned to him as the most promising young Yugoslav photographer, the winner of federal photography competitions, to which he had submitted some enlarged photographs of sea crabs whose legs and pincers looked like menacing science fiction abstractions or towers and giant fossils. But special significance, which was probably even crucial for Kraljev's fame, was lent to all this by the fact that he titled all his photographs with names and key places from the war of national liberation and the socialist revolution, such as *The Battle for the Wounded* or *Shots from Ljubo's Grave*. But Pardžik didn't need an assistant, and Vid Kraljev couldn't ever be one to anybody. The old man spent whole days complaining of his illnesses and going through brightly colored pills on his palm, rearranging them and dividing them up, lining them up into colorful rows, and developing a theory according to which it wasn't good for heart pills to be blue and bladder and prostate pills to be green.

"Someone must have taken this into account," he said. "It would be hard for someone to believe that a green pill would make them pee. That's like reducing a fever with red pills. Damn, they could only cure people with Daltonism! It's like graphic artists are condemned to die as soon as they fall ill! Haven't you thought about that? Of course not; I'm not surprised. You're young. Your time to think about it will come."

That's how the old master philosophized as Vid lugged cameras and tripods behind him. Loaded up like a mule, he thought about simply strolling off some afternoon during Pardžik's break and going to the bus station, buying a ticket, and leaving the old man alone to occupy himself with the only thing that interested him, for which he needed neither cameras nor tripods. He would have done that on the first trip, when they were supposed to photograph the spa in Kladanj, but he was afraid that in the best case his desertion would get him banned from exhibitions, if they didn't simply arrest him for sabotage.

Every other day Comrade Fejzić called from the Bosnian Central Committee and inquired about how the work was going. Pardžik left the conversations with him to Vid. And he lied, saying that at that moment Comrade Petar was touring the locations, waiting for the morning or afternoon light to illuminate the building, or he would think up something unbelievably stupid—say, that the old man was carrying out a technical inspection of the lenses or that he was coordinating the plan and the alternative plan, which made Fejzić particularly enthusiastic.

"Keep up the good work," he would say. "The working people and citizens of Bosnia and Herzegovina will be grateful to you."

At first Vid thought that Fejzić was bullshitting them, but then he realized with horror that the man was deadly serious and that the gratitude of the working people and citizens was really a kind of threat about what would happen if the work weren't completed in the best manner possible. And that threat concerned him alone, and not Petar Pardžik, the respected artist and hero of socialist labor who was already above suspicion because of his age and prior achievements, whereas Vid, a youngish forty-year-old assistant, still had to prove himself and might very well die trying.

"Why don't you quit?" he asked Pardžik after he had spent the sixth day walking hunched over because he had pinched a nerve between two vertebrae.

"Quit what, my dear man? This isn't work that you just quit! You'd better understand that while there's still time. When you photograph some bigwig for the first time, you think you've torn a star from the sky. Do you know what an honor it was for me in 1913 when I was invited to the Royal Palace to photograph His Majesty Petar? And I had no idea what it meant. I got out of the poorhouse for the rest of my life, and they fucked me good. Both at the same time. I've always been able to wear nice suits, I could afford the best restaurants, I went to Paris every year and was never broke, but I couldn't ever turn them down after I photographed the first one. What would have happened to me if I had said 'No' when they asked me to take the first pictures of Aleksandar Karađorđević as the new king? I'd have ended up doing hard labor, my good man! Or if afterward I'd refused to photograph General Pero Živković, his family, and their dog? God, I even had to take portraits of that idiot's dog. Please, taking pictures of dogs is the worst humiliation a photographer can suffer because you have to make an unbelievable fool of yourself to get a dog to pose for you. It's hard to be a fool and be famous. It's better to be just a fool. Later I photographed General Nedić, and Dimitrije Ljotić and the Germans, and I would have taken Uncle Draža's picture if I hadn't hidden from his agents. God, why would I go to Ravna Gora just to get killed on the way? Oh, if they'd kept me there a few years! And I knew that Draža didn't have a chance and wouldn't come around and ask, 'Well now, Pero, why didn't you want to take my picture? Am I really the only ugly one around here, goddammit?' Uncle Draža was naïve, but I'd better be quiet about that. Well, and then it was '45. Could I refuse Tito? I could have; of course, then I'd have been able to choose whether to be hanged or shot. It's just that his little toadies reproduced like amoebas. Six republics, at least twenty Tito wannabees in each republic, so my job was to make my way from Triglav to Đevđelija and take pictures of everyone. Fuck them! And the very next year they're replaced, and I have to take pictures of the new ones. Don't think I'm for the king; I don't give a fuck about him or the monarchy, but then it was clear how many there were who could come tell Petar Pardžik, 'Hey, Pero, come take a picture of this genius!' Besides the king there was only the head of the government and Prince Paul and maybe someone else in extraordinary circumstances. But under Tito they were countless. In '50-something they ordered me to photograph our soccer team that beat the Russians in Finland. Krcun, the minister of the police, came and ordered me to do it, and I said to him: How can I photograph a bunch of clods kicking a ball back and forth across a field, who live out their lives doing nothing? And do you know what Krcun said to me? He said, 'Well now, comrade, would you photograph the Russians if they'd won?' What could I do? I photographed them too. If I hadn't, I'd have ended up on Goli Otok. And the same thing now. They got me out of bed to photograph this Bosnian shit, and I just said, 'Yessir!' But you didn't have to. If you'd said you don't know how, that you don't have enough experience, that you're stupid or a jerk, they'd leave you alone and wouldn't ever call you again. But now it's all over. You're in the machine, and there's no way out. But it'll be easier for you when the greenbacks rustle under your nose. Then you'll forget and you won't know what you did, until they call you up the next time. And then you'll suffer some again. First the pleasure and then the pain. That's the way this work is. That's the way life is. First the pleasure and then the pain. Only I don't have time for pleasure any more.

There you have it. I won't have time to spend my money. I got screwed early in the game! But Uncle Pero will show them something from the grave! When they drive me on a caisson down the Boulevard of Titans, I'll know that it's over. No more 'Take a picture of this guy, take a picture of that guy.'"

And so Vid had been lugging the equipment from one end of the spa to another for days, listening to Pardžik's stories about the distant past and his laments over pills, without the old photographer taking a single picture. Only on the day before they left or the day they were traveling would Petar Pardžik take about twenty hasty shots without any special preparations and regardless of the angle of the morning or afternoon shadows, without even switching cameras or lenses. Later the comrades on the committees and tourist associations would admire his genius, and the newspapers would run reviews of those photographs in their culture sections, which were written by eminent Yugoslav authorities on artistic photography, art historians, and university professors of esthetics, although those photographs differed in no way from dilettantish photographs taken by rheumatic retirees passing the time between therapies in the spas. It had been a long time since the old man had actually been a photographer, and he'd had enough of art since the time he'd photographed General Pero Živković. He knew all this and wasn't afraid of others finding it out too. He showed Vid Kraljev what the passions of youth turn into and what happens to artists who gain the admiration of kings. It could even be said that there was an unusual relish in Pardžik's disclosure of all of this. He had no interest in teaching the young, forty-year-old man about life; he wouldn't have done it if Vid had been half as old, nor was it important to him that Vid avoid his fate. He made his confession only as a small act of vengeance on everyone, from Petar I the Unifier to Marshal Tito, including his own positive critics, who took away his belief that photography was a miracle because it showed the naked truth of the eye.

"We could do something today," he told Vid over breakfast in Banja Vrućica, early in the morning on Sunday, the fourth of May, 1980.

"It's not that we could—we have to," Vid answered nervously.

"And why would anyone, if you'll excuse me, have to do anything but die?" Pardžik asked, taking a pinch of salt and entertaining himself as he imagined a Siberian snowstorm hitting the top of his hardboiled egg. He was salting it for the third time, and the scene was magnificent.

"You'll die if you salt things so much," Vid said caustically, already on the verge of losing his temper because they were traveling that day and Pardžik still hadn't photographed anything.

"Who says I'm going to eat this egg? Ha, I'm not! Pera Pardžik doesn't eat what he admires. You know, I admire this egg here. Not just any egg, but *this* one. That means I'm an artist. Artists can tell one egg from another. You, if you're nervous, can go ahead and take a walk and look at the women. Maybe a young one will catch your eye. Leave *me* alone. When I'm ready, I'll find you. If I'm ready. The little time I have left I want to spend as I see fit, and I advise you to do the same. There's nowhere to hurry off to. Believe me. Nowhere."

He spoke with his head lowered all the way down to the tabletop, so he could get the best view possible of the salt falling onto the egg and the patterns the crystals were forming. He wasn't quite satisfied because his thumb, index finger, and middle finger hadn't completely mastered the technique of a salt blizzard, and it all resembled somewhat the way artificial snow fell in American movies of the '40s. But he was certain that he would succeed in the end and get the egg perfectly salted that day. Rage and pity mingled within Vid. Without caring if everyone in the dining hall was gazing at him, the old man, his cheek propped on the table and his right hand raised high to release the salt, reminded one of a child at play, unaware that if he continued what he was doing, he might get a slap.

"Okay, so we still don't know when we're going to take the photos?" Vid asked.

"Bull's-eye! You got it, my young colleague. We still don't know anything," Pardžik said, trying to spread drifts and accumulations of salt on the egg.

"Fine; I'm going to go read the newspaper," Vid said, rose from the table, and started toward the television lounge. Then he changed his mind and decided at first to go to the reception desk, to call Dijana and tell her that he had no idea when they were going to leave Banja Vrućica but that it wasn't likely that they would arrive before the next day. These last days she'd sounded strange when they talked on the phone. And he couldn't get that out of his head. He wasn't sure about whether she really loved him in the first place, and these Bosnian trips, he thought, were only helping to cool what in Dijana had never been as hot as what was in him. He'd been crawling after her for almost twenty years, and each spring and fall he proposed to her. He was her friend and someone whom she didn't call on the phone and avoided in the city. He'd changed jobs and professions for Dijana, and in the end stayed with photography. Either because she really liked artists or because she was already slowly entering that phase of life when it didn't matter what her men did.

She'd rushed into his arms in the late summer of 1978, after a season she'd spent bedridden with pneumonia and that low-grade fever that they say is in some cases a symptom of insanity but in three months will drive even the most normal woman insane. She was dead tired. He took her out for a first stroll. She was continually sweating and her every muscle ached. Half an hour later she begged Vid to take her back home, grabbed him under the arm and clung to him, and realized that there were no real reasons for having rejected him all those years because in any case the most important thing in life was to have someone who will take you and put you in bed when you're ill and you can't do it on your own.

They got married just before New Year's in 1979, whereupon Vid tried in every way to persuade her to have children. It was getting late for her, and she would soon be sorry if she didn't take this last chance. But in fact he didn't have his heart set on being a father. Rather, he needed something that would forever solidify their union and awaken true love in Dijana. As he would reflect on his fatherhood, he always imagined her looking at him. He saw Dijana watching him from the side as he taught his son how to walk; she was there as he changed his daughter's diapers; she watched father and son on their first fishing trip from a rock, then how he taught the little boy to row a boat, the little girl to braid her hair, and when he took her to school by the hand . . . None of Vid's images of fatherhood were without her, nor was there anything that he imagined about his unborn children that remained only between him and them. All he really thought about in 1979 and 1980 was his obsessive vision of a son and daughter, which he intended to use to buy Dijana's love. He was unable to do this with subtlety, charming his wife and winning her over with small deceits, but hit her over the head with it, always with the same words and arguments, whereby he actually lost her good will and Dijana started avoiding him again, in a smaller space to be sure, just as she had been running away from him for the last twenty years. She gave a sigh of relief when he would go off on a trip and was gone for a long time.

He dialed her number a dozen times but didn't get a connection. Only when he began nervously hitting the telephone did the fat woman at the reception desk, who'd been there the whole time and stared at him while he was trying to make the call, hiss through her teeth:

"The lines are down. Can't you see that? They've been down all morning."

He went to the television lounge; retirees were watching *Allow Us a Word.* The winner of the *Exemplary Soldier Karlo Papec* pin said that he only had one wish—for the speedy recovery of Comrade Tito. The retirees nodded to that, and lieutenant Musadik Borović added that Karlo was a good comrade, "always ready to help those who don't catch on quickly, and that's why he received the most prized military award."

"You see?!" said an old man with thick glasses who was sitting closest to the television, almost touching the screen with his nose, whereupon an old man wearing a wool cap and a Salonika mustache remarked:

"I can't see anything with your head in the way!"

Vid took a newspaper that was on a little table behind the television, sat down in an armchair in the corner, and opened the sports section. In Split there had been a championship match between the Hajduk and Red Star teams. He read the announced lineups, trying to calm his nerves, but it didn't work. Soccer can prevent a nervous breakdown, but only if things haven't gotten way out of hand. And this time they really had. It seemed to him that Petar Pardžik was rapidly losing his mind; the thing with the egg was completely new, something that hadn't happened on their trips before.

Vid was terrified that this would continue, that the old man would go completely crazy before the project was finished, and Comrade Fejzić would lay all the blame on him or force him to finish Pardžik's work on his own, after which he would also take over the title of court photographer according to the dynastic laws. He would constantly be away from home, Dijana would find a lover if she hadn't already, or the idiocy of old age would produce other problems that he couldn't even suspect now, but of which there wouldn't be fewer than those that were now on his mind. Then he read once more the names of the players for Hajduk and Red Star who would run out on the Poljud field, folded the newspaper, and started reading the headlines. Comrade Tito's condition continued to be critical, the Ljubljana council reported. Vid Kraljev was probably one of the very few Yugoslavs who had bigger and more important problems than that.

As Pardžik didn't appear and Vid's nervousness only increased, at lunchtime he decided to go look for him and suggest that he go ahead and take those twenty photographs of the spa himself, if the master was indisposed or had no inspiration, so they could leave before dark. He found him snoring in his room, probably exhausted from salting the egg. He roused him, ready for an argument even if it cost him his career as an artistic photographer. However, Pardžik jumped right out of bed.

"You're right, you're absolutely right," he repeated in answer to Vid's complaints. "Here, I'll be ready in ten minutes," he said and started fumbling about in his room, completely forgetting about his rheumatism, gout, and age. After his afternoon nap his unease due to the fact that he had put the young man in a difficult position was now suddenly more important than any illness. Vid furiously grabbed the equipment and loaded himself up with a whole museum of antique technology because Pardžik had stubbornly refused to replace his thirty- and fifty-year-old cameras with new, technically up-to-date ones that were also easier to carry, maintaining that they weren't any better but in fact worse and less reliable, serving only to enable any idiot to do photography.

Vid hurried three paces ahead of him, and the old man hurried after him and tried to get into his good graces. "I'm really sorry. But you know what an old man's brain is like. What you excrete from your bowels every morning, that's what I've got in my head! Out in the country around Negotin they're right when they take an old man out into the woods, lean a flatbread on his head, and — bam! — hit it with the butt of an axe. 'I didn't kill you, the bread did!' Well, they should have done that to me a long time ago. Believe me. Oh, God, I feel so bad about having gotten this man into a situation like this. Just wait a bit; I'll have everything finished in half an hour. You just put all the equipment on that rise over there, and I'll do everything else. Go to the hotel, get some rest; I know you're tired of me. Do you have any more money? If you don't, I do. Just go have a cup of coffee and calm down. Oh, Petar, black Petar, what have you done, where's your shame . . . ?"

Vid stopped, dropped what he was carrying in his hands, and said, "Stop it already! What, do you think this is my life or something? Well, it's not, and I'm not interested in what you've got to say. I couldn't care less whether you feel bad, and I'd ask you to be quiet. You know, I'd just like to hear birds chirping or a bear, anything but you."

The eighty-five-year-old court photographer looked sadly at Vid, and his eyes filled with tears: "Whatever you say; just don't be angry at me."

After this Petar Pardžik wouldn't utter a word, up until four o'clock, when he snapped the last photograph. All the while Vid was sitting on a tree stump, ten or so meters from the old man, smoking cigarette after cigarette and trying without success to calm down. Nothing was going right for him, and in fact the pranks that the old man had been playing that morning were the least of the worries that had put him in that state. He was thinking about Dijana, her stubborn refusal to give him a child, and his own misery, which had begun the day he fell head over heels in love with that eighteen-year-old prep school student and decided never to stop loving her. He couldn't have loved her all twenty of those years. It's more likely that his irrational hardheadedness had kept him from listening to his own heart, unless it too was stubborn and stupid, creating feelings from all manner of things that had nothing to do with them. He'd sat for months on the toilet with the lid closed and poked holes in packages of condoms in the belief that his love would pass through the hole in the rubber membrane. And while doing this, he'd always felt just as wretched, but at least he thought that he was doing it for some high and noble reasons. And now he was just miserable and nothing else. That misery was the kind on account of which he might kill someone since he didn't have the courage to kill himself. It was twenty to five when Pardžik and Kraljev got into the white Golf that the Bosnian Central Committee had put at their disposal until the project *A Healthy Guest Is a Rested Guest* was finished.

"I'm sorry again," said the old man.

"It's all right," Vid answered; "you're not to blame for all the stuff that's been getting bottled up in me."

As they drove out of the parking lot, a woman ran out of the spa with her head in her hands, and her face showed that she had been sobbing hysterically.

"It seems we've got a fatality in therapy," Vid commented.

"It's good we left in time," the old man responded and then thought how he'd said something stupid again—because what could they have to do with someone who'd expired trying to use medicinal baths to treat something untreatable, a heart that had reached the end of the line and should have been cared for when that person had been young and healthy? He imagined an old man lying at the bottom of a swimming pool, whose gaze was locked onto the blue ceiling tiles while between his cyanotic, bluish-purple lips there was only bonaccia, that unnatural peace that sows panic among the living, on account of which they had invented God and the conviction that under the heavens there exists something more precious than a sigh passing between one's lips. Soon that'll be me, he thought and wanted to say it aloud, but then he changed his mind because he had already tortured the young man enough today.

The road to Zenica was eerily empty. Apart from police cars and an occasional military truck there was almost no one out on the road, which was strange, especially at the end of a long weekend that had begun with May Day and lasted for four days. One would have expected for people to be returning from their vacations, for students to be on their way to Zenica and Sarajevo, because the next day they all had to go to work or classes. Darkness was falling, televisions were glowing through the windows of the houses along the road, the afterglow of the sun was sinking behind the mountains, and Petar Pardžik was drifting off to sleep. Vid would glance at him from the corner of his eye; the master photographer was sliding and pitching back and forth in the car as they drove down the curves on the road. He's so old, he thought, but since there was no continuation of that thought and Petar's age didn't touch Vid the way anything living or precious did that was near its beginning or end, Vid moved on to something else, a topic that would occupy his thoughts more and more during the drive.

When someone is driving at night, if he's alone or the only one awake in the car, it's important to find something to think about. Then the drive becomes a pleasure, and he sinks into melancholy and mild sorrow, which he later remembers as a time free from care. People who don't like to drive or hate being alone in a car are actually not in a condition to let one thought travel through their mind freely, without interruption. Vid had started from the Hajduk–Red Star match, which was already long over, but he didn't know who'd won. If the old man hadn't been sleeping beside him, he would have switched on the radio, but he couldn't do that now because Pardžik would have thought that he was paying him back and would have probably again given him that look of an abandoned salamander, which had made him feel sorry in spite of all of his anger at him. At that moment he knew that Pardžik would die, in a year or two or five, and that when he read the news in the morning paper, he would remember that look of his as they'd climbed up the hill and would feel guilty. He wanted to do something nice, to cheer up the old man, whenever the time came, of course.

Instead of turning on the radio, he began to turn over in his mind all the matches that he could remember between Hajduk and Red Star over a long period of thirty or so years, during which there had been a dozen generations of soccer players. They came and went; talented players were born only to collapse in the face of their initial success; the greatest players wore the number 9 or 10 on their jerseys, Jurica Jerković for Hajduk and Jovan Aćimović for Red Star. Then there were farewell matches, bouquets of roses, crystal and silver cups, tears and chants. Džajić, who was good at moving up along the left wing and the greatest player that Vid had seen in his life. The Hajduk goalie Mešković, who suffered from night-blindness and played poorly in nighttime matches. The finale of the Tito Cup, with the president's emissaries in the VIP seats, tears of joy, the oldest player kissing the cup, the speaker repeating his words ten times—the most precious trophy, the second-string players who went into the game from the bench in the last ten minutes of the game—Mijač, Matković, Dramičanin, Boško Kajganić . . .

Athletic careers are like human lives, with births and deaths, only they don't last as long as life, so that a whole century fits into thirty years, and one can think about it while he's driving like this through the night, on the empty roads alongside the Bosna and Vrbas Rivers, past little Bosnian villages, none of which have more than twenty or so houses and a mosque at the base of a hill. When he drove, he always had the same feeling, no matter what he was thinking about: the people who lived behind those windows built their houses at a safe distance from one another, so that they could breathe the same air and be friends to one another, and not as on the coast, where houses are piled up on top of one another, anyone can peer into his neighbors' bedroom, and there's no place except the sea where you can escape others' eyes. This was why the Dalmatians were seafarers and it wasn't hard for them to leave their towns and cities for years, leaving for Australia and New Zealand and never returning. Whereas the Bosnians stayed where they were; they didn't change for centuries and provoked mild disdain in the eyes of others, sometimes even open hatred, because they were stupid and backward people who never saw the world and going twenty kilometers from their homes was too far—that is, going far enough to where they couldn't see the roofs of their houses. They didn't care whether they were in another district or on the other end of the world; all they ever wanted was to return home. They were happy because they were far enough away from one another.

Even in soccer stadiums they didn't all cheer together but shouted out jeers to the opposing players individually, told jokes, mocked bowlegged forwards and a center half with a low forehead, but you always knew who said what, and for every word said a hundred years and a thousand matches ago, you knew whose it was and who'd said it first.

If he'd lived there, he wouldn't have photographed crabs but hundreds of old slippers and worn-out shoes arranged on concrete landings in front of Bosnian houses. One would think that there are as many Bosnians as Chinese, but this is only because old shoes are never thrown out but are left out in front of the front door so they'll be easy to find when one goes out into the yard or to the store across the street.

As his thoughts strayed from soccer players to Bosnians and the bluish lights in their windows, Vid Kraljev saw a policeman holding up an illuminated stop sign. He slowed down and pulled off onto the gravel shoulder of the road. Pardžik opened his eyes and didn't know where he was. Vid rolled down the window, and the swarthy, mustached policeman bent down toward him, opened his mouth to say something, and then swallowed it.

"What happened?" Vid asked.

"Nothing, just please drive carefully," the policeman said through his teeth as tears streamed down his cheeks.

"Yes, of course, it's dark," he answered confusedly, and they drove on.

"Everyone's gone crazy today," he said and looked at Pardžik, who gave a melancholy smile.

"He thought we know, but you see, we don't know a thing . . ."

"What are you talking about . . . ?"

"I'm not completely sure, my boy, but I think my last king and emperor has died."

Only then did it hit Vid, and something shot through his knees. All these months he hadn't had time to think about what would happen if Tito died, but he must have sensed, the way one does the night before a sirocco, that everyone was thinking about it.

"Oh, no, it can't be!" he exclaimed with the sincerity of a housewife at market.

"You think it's impossible? Of course, I thought the same when they killed King Aleksandar. I photographed the arrival of his dead body at the Split quay. And you know what I captured in my photographs? Fear! Nothing else. Only fear. People were crying but were actually only afraid, just as this policeman is afraid. He wanted us to help him; that's what he really wanted. You should have gotten out of the car, hugged him, and said, 'Hey, whiskers, everything'll be okay!' And then he'd tell you that he has a wife and three kids but that Tito means more to him than they do. And do you know what the strangest thing is? He really thinks that. He'd let his kids perish just so Tito would live. Only later would he realize that he hadn't done it out of love but out of fear, and then he'd lose his mind. You see, that's the way it is. And don't say now, 'Forget old Petar; he doesn't know what he's talking about,' because I really do know about this. It's been verified many times. People are strange and become savages easily. Yes, my young colleague, Tito has died, my last king! I'm not afraid; I'm just sad. And that's because he's my last. It's an accident that he's died and not me. That's about the size of it, and it's up to you to find your way. You're young and you'll live to see more such nights."

Vid wanted to believe that what Pardžik said was just a continuation of the idiocy he'd displayed that morning, but it didn't help. He turned on the radio. There was some somber music playing, filled with dark strings and the distant echoes of large theater drums. He changed the channel, but each was playing the same requiem. Only on one, through the crackling ebb and flow of electromagnetic waves that bounded across the mountains of Bosnia, did he hear a distant female voice babbling something in Italian.

"See, I was right," said Petar Pardžik, and those were the last words uttered in the official white Volkswagen Golf of the Commission for Information of the Bosnian and Herzegovinian Central Committee.

Either the car hit a gasoline slick on the road or it spun out of control because of a pothole; it was never established because the police investigation was conducted very hastily, which was justified by the objective circumstances and the confusion on account of the death of Marshal Tito. To make a long story short, the Golf slid into the other lane, in which at that moment a bus was heading from Zenica to Teslić. The driver, Stipo Valjan, was unable to brake in time and struck the passenger's side of the car; the bus pushed the Golf around twenty meters before it stopped. Stipo Valjan's head smashed into the windshield, and for a minute or two he was unconscious. Then he got out, his head bleeding, all alone, because he wasn't driving a single passenger. He'd asked the station chief whether he was going to cancel the buses and was told that at this moment it was most important for the buses to run normally and to be on time, as if it should be the holy duty of every working man and citizen to honor the memory of their greatest son. And how are memories honored? By honoring the deeds of great men for the living.

This country was thus born from memories, and that was the reason why Stipo Valjan happened to be driving his empty bus toward Teslić.

All bloodied, he staggered up to the driver of the Golf, who was sitting pinned amid crushed metal, parts of which had passed through his belly and his left thigh. Yet it didn't seem that he was injured but that as if by some miracle the metal had sprouted from him in those places, just as isolated pines grow out of cliffs above the Neretva canyon, amid bare rock, without any soil at all. The driver of the Golf smiled at the guy with the bloodied head as if he were someone he knew but hadn't seen for a long time, then opened his mouth to ask if it were true that the President was dead, but his lips didn't move. There was no sound in his throat; his lower jaw seemed to be riveted to his head. Vid was truly surprised by all this, and that was the last thing that happened before he breathed his last.

Half an hour later the police and an ambulance arrived. Stipo Valjan would spend three days in the Zenica hospital and would be summoned to the State Security Service in Sarajevo to give a statement because all accidents in which party or state automobiles were involved had to be investigated by the service. After he spent the whole of May on sick leave, he was already driving his old route again on the first of June. His head would ache when the weather changed, but that, along with Vid Kraljev's meek smile, was the only aftereffect of the accident.

That smile came to him in dreams and calmed him for years, and the unfortunate driver couldn't figure out what kind of spirits were visiting him and what heartless man lived within him for that terrible event to be remembered only positively and through the tender smile of a man.

It took three workers of the Zenica railway service all night using blowtorches to remove what remained of the famed Yugoslav photographer, probably the greatest after Skrigin, Dabac, and Afrić, and his promising assistant, whose few but exceptional works, as it said in the obituaries, had created one of the more memorable branches of Yugoslav modernism and experimental photography. The police had roused the workers from their sleep and brought them there still sluggish and hung over to do a job for which otherwise one would have had to wait until a special team from Sarajevo arrived the next morning. There would have been an interrepublican scandal had people from the Belgrade Academy of the Arts arrived before the body of Petar Pardžik, their emeritus professor and long-serving dean, had been extricated from the wreckage, and so the three railway workers had to do what they'd never had to do before, under the supervision of the same mustached policeman. They sighed and complained without saying a word, and through the night three acetylene torches glowed and threw sparks. Their blue light seemed to be the same as that cast by the televisions, which for the first time in the history of Bosnian roads cast their glow right until morning.

At one in the morning the phone rang in Regina Delavale's kitchen. She

heard it through the walls in her sleep and waited for it to stop. It would stop
for a few seconds and then started ringing again. The on-duty inspector in the
Maglaj police station probably dialed the number he'd been sent from Sarajevo
and let it ring for the full twelve rings each time before an elderly female voice
spoke on the other end.

"Maglaj police station on the line. Is this the number of Dijana Kraljev?"

Regina froze with fear; it even occurred to her to say that they had called the
wrong number because the militia had no reason to call Dijana.

"It is," she said nevertheless.

"Are you her?" the voice asked, leaving no possibility for her to refrain from
answering or lie.

"I'm her mother," she admitted.

"I'm obliged to inform you that your son-in-law Vid Kraljev was involved in
a traffic accident on the Tešanj-Zenica road and that he died from his injuries
at the scene."

Regina held the receiver and said nothing. If she didn't say anything, maybe
what she was hearing hadn't happened.

"Are you on the line? Did you hear me?" the voice asked without changing
its tone.

"I'm on the line," Regina answered.

"Then please accept my condolences," the voice said and hung up.

Regina sat down on a kitchen chair and put her elbows, which someone had
just filled with lead, on the table. She didn't know what to do now. She'd been
alive for seventy-five years and had never faced anything like this. Maybe she
should have a cry and then go like that to Dijana—but how should she wake
her? By shouting in front of her bedroom door or by going in quietly and calling
her, shaking her shoulder? She didn't know how she would do it, and though
any other woman in her place would have simply despaired and made a racket
from pure sorrow or unease at having something like this happen to her, she sat
there, staring at three kitchen rags hanging on hooks and repeating, "Ah, poor
Vid, poor child . . ."

It couldn't be said that she really meant it when she spoke those words, but
they seemed to her to be the most suitable for the situation she found herself
in. In fact she would have preferred to lie back down in bed and think about
what she'd heard only in the morning, but she couldn't do something like that.

She sat down on the foot of Dijana's bed, and before she touched her, her
daughter woke up.

"Vid's dead," was all she said.

"Not Vid, Mother, but Comrade Tito," Dijana said softly without moving.

"Vid. He died in Bosnia. It's Vid, Dijana, him. They just informed us."

Dijana sat up straight with the movements of a mechanical doll; she looked at her mother and couldn't understand what she was saying: "Who informed us . . . ?"

"The Bosnian police."

"How do they know that?" she asked, watching Regina dully, thinking that she was making something up. Her bad side was doing this; she didn't like Vid, just as she didn't like any of Dijana's other young men and not a single man who approached their house.

"There was an accident and Vid is dead now. That's what's happened, my child," Regina said in a serious tone, with language that she otherwise didn't speak, and it sounded like the words of a television anchor.

"Oh, Mother!" Dijana said, reaching out with her arms and grabbing the old woman firmly. She didn't let go of her for a long time and didn't think anything, except that she'd forgotten or lost something, but she couldn't remember what it was at all. Like her keys when she was looking for change in her purse.

Vid was buried on the sixth of May, in the old cemetery above the city, amid gray stones with the names of long dead families. His grave, seen from afar, was a single oasis of flowers and greenery amid the gray, waterless stone wasteland.

Dijana stood between Vid's older brothers. There were six of them, all dressed in the same black suits and ties; they looked like teary-eyed Neapolitan weapons smugglers, and only the dandruff on their collars contradicted this impression, turning them into what they were. She was the only one who wasn't weeping; she clutched a bouquet of roses and felt a prickling between her legs, as when Vid hadn't shaved for two days and went down on her in the middle of the night, ignoring Dijana's giggling, which came from an inner feeling of unease that awoke whenever he did things that surpassed her love. What she'd done a few days before and would excite her as soon as she thought of it, she felt to be the first act in a story that had to end in a graveyard. The poor guy; he'd have been so surprised, she thought, to see her or feel her shaved mons under his fingers, certainly more so than if she'd said that she were pregnant, and who knows what would have happened further and how Vid's head would have reconciled motherhood and those other things that one imagines more than talks about.

Her thoughts fled from the place where she was; she tried not to look over at Regina, who was standing alongside Vid's mother, Aunt Nusreta, holding her by the arm, comforting her as she wept and sobbing as soon as she stopped. She treated her like her best friend, like a cousin in need, although she openly scorned her, both for her "Turkish" name and behavior, which with its gentleness and discretion rubbed Regina the wrong way, and for the fact that she'd given birth to seven sons and raised them, which offended Regina to her marrow and led her to spend hours analyzing Nusreta's physical makeup and the organs through which so many children had passed. And if Vid were at home, she made subtle jibes concerning his mother, convinced that he didn't understand them. Dijana made a horrible scene on several occasions when this had happened, trying to shame her or force her to shut up, but it was futile because Nusreta was one of Regina's obsessive subjects, on account of which she developed a whole theory about Muslim child-bearing women, based on something that she'd read in the newspaper or seen on television, in which people with Muslim names and surnames usually appeared in the roles of brutal warriors and their primitive women made up for their defeats in wars by procreation. But during the burial ceremony she hugged Nusreta as if she were one of her own, in order to find a place for herself as well in that festival of sadness.

After the procession the column went to the Hotel Otrant, where Vid's brothers had already reserved a long ceremonial table because going straight home from a cemetery brought bad luck.

Death should be left at some wayside place, best in a tavern, where, intoxicated with alcohol, it will approach someone else and leave the mourning family in peace for a while. They reserved the head of the table for Dijana, where she was again surrounded by Vid's brothers, who addressed her exclusively as "our bride" and saw in her their eternal widow, whom they would honor and care for right until she remarried, whereupon she would become their greatest enemy — she who'd spat on the grave of her dearest and broken a vow that was measured only by her life. She felt that and wanted to run home as soon as she could, but she couldn't because they were making posthumous toasts to her Vid, one after another. They would pour half a glass of stiff grape brandy onto the hotel's green carpeting — the custom was to give the dead soul a drink — and they would down the other half in one draught, both the men and the women, the young and the old. Nusreta did the same and with her, of course, Regina, who after the fifth brandy was already so drunk that she got up, raised her arms to quiet the people, and said:

"I'll tell you something that not even the deceased Vid knew but should have found out yesterday, poor child; God have mercy on his soul. The bride is with child. Dijana is carrying Vid's child!"

She shouted out the last words and collapsed in her chair. The six brothers stared at their widow, and she lowered her eyes, hoping the earth under her would open up.

Petar Pardžik was buried a day later, on the Boulevard of Great Men in Belgrade, with twelve-gun salutes and a military orchestra and in the attendance of

the Yugoslav cultural and public elite. There were few politicians, probably because they were saving themselves for Marshal Tito's funeral two days later, but
a high party delegation arrived from Sarajevo, headed by Comrade Fejzić, who
said of the last and unfinished work of the great photographer and activist, "He
was consumed in flames and gave his life for art and the ideals of the working
class, and for generations to come no one should forget Petar Pardžik and all
those named and unnamed men who gave their lives to lay the foundations of
our socialist order at Sutjeska and the Neretva, Kozara, and Romanija."

After Fejzić spoke, Pardžik's friends, art critics, and professors each said a
few words, and then his body was lowered into the grave accompanied by the
sounds of the *Internationale*.

However, this death was hardly mentioned in the newspapers and on television because it was difficult to find space for any grief other than that greatest
sorrow, and it might have even looked suspicious if Pardžik's passing were met
with an overly strong expression of grief. But the prize for a lifetime achieve-
ment in artistic photography was named after him and would bear his name
after the fall of communism and the breakup of Yugoslavia. That was fair in a
way because Pardžik had bestowed equal honor on all rulers, states, and political systems and would have shown the same respect for those whose time he did
not have the fortune to live to see.

After the procession it was decided to give a monetary award to the widow
of the master's faithful and final assistant, in the amount of an average yearly
Yugoslav salary.

On the day of Tito's funeral, while sirens wailed outside and the sounds of
Lenin's March and television sets could be heard through open windows in the
neighborhood, Regina and Dijana sat in front of a television that was sealed
and wrapped in blue packing paper. Namely, her mother had called an official
from the municipality and in spite of Dijana's objections had had him seal the
television during the period of mourning in the family, as was the local custom.
She did this so there wouldn't be any stories of Regina Delavale singing and
dancing instead of mourning her son-in-law. No matter how attached she was
to television and how little she was concerned about the gossip in the city and
the neighborhood, Regina wanted in no way to be denied anything that brought
grief to the household. Dressed strictly in black and with a kerchief around her
head, she went out, she accepted condolences from friends and strangers alike
and told for the hundredth time about the circumstances of the traffic accident in which Vid had died. "After they heard that Tito had died, they hurried
home to see their loved ones, as would anyone else, and so you see, fate's a tricky
vixen; you never know which curve is hiding your grave," she said and nodded,

as big-butted women at the fish market clucked their tongues and offered her their fresh sepiolas, which had been pulled from the sea that very morning—she should take some home to her pregnant daughter, that unfortunate girl who was carrying the child of a dead man in her womb.

For some reason people were quite excited by the fact that the woman was going to give birth to a child for a man who no longer existed; it was something like a calf with two heads, a black man with an elephant's head, or similar circus attractions. Giving birth to the child of a dead father seemed to the street to be more interesting than having a stillborn child. Although this was not the first time this had happened in the city (there'd been similar cases now and then over the last fifty years, as far as the streets could remember and revive old news) but it was evident that it would be just as strange even if it happened every year. The child in Dijana's womb (and until the day of birth no one would have any idea that there were even two) was for the city something that was at the same time both a bastard child and an immaculately conceived little Jesus. That's how it was, though there were no real reasons for it, nor had they ever existed.

Dijana wouldn't forgive her mother for having told everyone about her pregnancy. At first she wouldn't even talk to her, and then she would open her mouth only when she had to or when other noises became too much for her to take in their silence. She didn't feel like leaving the house. She'd received seven days off from work due to a death in the family and had no one to whom she could tell the truth about Vid and about that seed of his that now kept growing in her. She felt dull and the only thing that kept her going was her fear of falling into depression and despair again or falling into some heretofore unknown form of despair. And so she sat in her armchair, listening to the sounds of the great funeral in Belgrade, which came with a breeze and the scent of the sea and pine trees, the distant barking of dogs, and cries of seagulls fighting somewhere down below over some fish innards and rotten animal parts that the sea had brought from who knows where. Regina sat beside her, furiously crocheting on some embroidery that would hem a ceremonial white tablecloth because her daughter was behaving like an ass, just pouting and trudging from the armchair to the toilet and back again. And Tito's funeral was going on, without her seeing anything.

She would crochet like that until the late afternoon, when she would leave the house without a word, knock on the window of her neighbor Tereza, and tell her that she couldn't take it and that she needed someone. And then on Tereza's television she would see the Zambian president Kenneth Kaunda standing over the white marble grave and wiping tears from his eyes with a large kerchief on the end of his little finger. That enormous black man with a kerchief the size of a café tablecloth awoke a sudden television sadness in these neighbors.

They looked at the screen as if it happened to be showing a series about a family tragedy in the American south. They turned to one another when Kaunda plunged his face into the kerchief. His shoulders shook as if a herd of antelope were galloping across them. They looked each other in the eyes and still deeper, into their pupils, and at the same moment they burst into tears.

"Oh, the poor man; he made such a journey to find his friend dead."

Dijana would sit a while longer in front of the sealed television set, and then everything boiled up inside of her. She took the scissors, cut the seals away, cut up the blue paper, turned on the Niš Electronics Ambassador, and came in at the moment when a Kakanj miner came out of a shaft and told how the Marshal was for him a light, the earth, water, and the air he breathed, and two tears left pure white trails down his sooty face. She nestled herself in the armchair, curled up her legs under herself, and was happy because she was returning to the community of the sad, which was in any case more pleasant than the confused loneliness that issued from everything she could think of. She pitied Vid as we pity mutts we pass by on rainy days, with full awareness that we could make them happy for life if we only took them home. She could have been his Madonna, and everything would have been nice and simple for both of them; they would have stayed together to the end, without Vid ever betraying her. Because if he'd waited on her for twenty years, he would have lived out the remaining twenty or forty as a reward and providence, the finger of divine fate that confirms that persistence in desires makes sense. He would have solved all her future problems, she thought, because each of them was simpler than what had begun it all, and that one was that she didn't love him and never could have. She could have done what she wanted, cheated on him, acted viciously and haughtily, lived her own life, and left him to worry about everything that was both of theirs or was the price for such a life. He would have done everything and wouldn't ever have rebuked her. So it seemed to her now that Vid was no longer there, and she felt relieved because of this.

The general secretary of the Communist Party of Italy said that the world workers' movement had lost one of its greatest leaders and visionaries: "Today nothing can fill our devastated souls!" The bit about devastated souls particularly touched Dijana. She pulled a wadded tissue out of her sleeve and wiped her nose with it.

When in the latter months of her term, when the time for an abortion had long since passed, she thought about the moment when she'd conceived; images of the two funerals kept coming back to her, one live and one televised. She was unable to begin the tale of her child in any other way, a child with whom she would spend the rest of her life and never be free again. The time when the doctor had told her that she was pregnant seemed so murky, and the act between her and Vid, when the biological causes of what she would attribute to later events had come into existence, was in her memory completely unbelievable. She remembered Vid turning his back to her as he put on the condom; he always did that, as if it were the most shameful part of sex; she clearly saw his vertebrae catching the dim light. She saw the moment before he entered her, when she grabbed him by the cock as she always did. Then he gave a deep sigh, and she actually checked whether he had put on the condom well or was trying to trick her so his semen would, as if by accident, pour into her. The condom was always on right, so how did what happened happen? This was a mystery to Dijana, something that would remain unanswered. And so twenty years later, when Mirna asked her where she and her brother had been conceived, she would stutter trying to think up some lie because the actual truth, or so it seemed to Dijana, didn't even exist.

That summer the Olympics were held in Moscow, and she sat in front of the television for days on end, gobbled down unbelievable amounts of potato chips, and watched every last bit of live coverage and reports from the strangest competitions, including the steeplechases and lawn hockey. She vainly cheered for the Indian hockey team, in which all the players were surnamed Singh, so Dijana imagined that they all belonged to some big, happy family in which there were so many brothers and relatives that they didn't even know each other that well—they met each other on the street and passed each other by like strangers, and no one could pester any of the others with his personal problems. That was the only way, she thought, that you could have a happy family. Hundreds of them under the same roof, and all they had in common was that they all played lawn hockey. Her palms sweated as the Singh family tried to break through the granite defense of the Pakistani team and almost didn't notice her belly growing bigger with each day, and in the folds of her first wrinkles there were now little pockets of fat, which would soon change Dijana's physiognomy and in a matter of months change her from a young and pretty woman into a middle-aged postal official whom the perennial tourists would no longer recognize. What she blamed on her pregnancy and hormonal imbalance had more to do with the potato chips and the Olympics, which postponed Dijana's fits of depression and beat back any thought of the fact that she should do something with her life.

In the swimming competitions she took notice of Darjan Petrič, a sixteen-year-old Slovene with the face of a boy and the body of a man from one's dreams, and she decided that if she had a boy, she'd name him Darijan. Years later she realized that she hadn't even done that right and had thrown in an extra *i* that had appeared in his name in Cyrillic at the top of the television screen because someone in the Soviet television service had erroneously transcribed Petrič's name.

Seeing what her daughter was turning into, Regina washed her hands of trying to tear her away from the television. Here and there she would gripe about what was going to happen when the municipal inspection discovered that she'd broken the official seal on the television set and crushed the wax red star, thereby dishonoring both the state and her deceased husband. Dijana said nothing in response but continued munching on potato chips and watching the quarterfinals of the handball tournament, and so her mom would go off into the kitchen or to the neighbors, whom she told that her daughter was already half-mad for lack of a man and that she was afraid of something terrible happening to her. But of course she wasn't afraid but needed something that would make her the center of attention, which was greater and more important than the ills of old age and the problems of meager pensions, the only things her women friends talked about.

But it seems that her imagination summoned the devil. Two days after the Olympics were over, Dijana got in a tub of hot water and tried to slit her wrists. She ran into the kitchen completely naked, firmly gripping her left wrist, which was flowing with dark, red blood. Regina nearly fainted because of the blood and because she didn't see a thick fleece under her daughter's round belly. Her freshly shaved mons veneris with its pinkish canyon gleamed like the city's towers in the August sun. That was Dijana's last attack of nerves that was properly hushed up because Regina didn't say anything even to their immediate neighbors. The laceration was sewed up in the emergency room, where Dijana received a referral for a psychiatrist. She didn't go since she had no idea what she would say to anyone, let alone a stranger, about herself.

With the arrival of autumn she calmed completely and no longer even spent days sitting in front of the television. She was reconciling herself to her fate and waiting for the birth of her child, having succeeded in convincing herself that when that happened, her life would take such a path that she would be like one of the Singhs who didn't have to think about one another. She only got upset when every few weeks one of Vid's brothers would come by to ask her if she needed anything and whose arrival would remind her to whose lifelong loyalty she had sworn herself, but that would happen less and less frequently as the days of mourning passed on and they began to realize what kind of woman from hell their Vid had run off after. They stopped all contact with the Delavale house after Dijana said in response to a suggestion by one of them that she name the child Vid or Vida that it was out of the question, not in the least because she thought it was an ugly name in both its male and female versions, but more importantly because it would remind her for the rest of her life of someone who was dead and might put a curse on her child so that it might suffer its father's fate.

After that the six Kraljev men never darkened their doorstep; Nusreta would only call occasionally, asking how she was feeling, whether she wanted anything or would like her to send some oranges from their garden. But Dijana's pregnant state didn't produce any special wishes, nor did it awaken any desire for certain foods, as is often the case, or at least fruit, which would let a woman divine the character of her child in its future life. If an expecting woman obsessively asked for strawberries, then she was probably going to have a daughter, but if she had a boy, he would have a number of birthmarks all over his body, pale skin, and effeminate movements. If she wanted lemons and oranges, she was going to have a son who'd be loved by everyone, always ready for fun and jokes, and would have it easy in life, or a daughter whose beauty would be unbearable for her competition. But if the woman wanted red meat, she was going to have sickly children who wouldn't be distinguished by anything else or be bestowed with special talents or beauty, but not curses either . . . Thus, it was known what every expecting mother's wish meant, and so those who were well intentioned and those not so well intentioned were just waiting to hear what she would say and would jump to fulfill her every wish, no matter what it was or what it meant, convinced that they were the couriers of a fate that was already written down and couldn't be changed. Dijana, however, was a mystery. Although she ate beyond any measure, she didn't care what she ate. When Nusreta would ask, "Don't you want some oranges, girl?" she would only laugh and say for the hundredth time that she didn't.

She gave birth on the twenty-first of December. At first Mirna came into the world easily and quickly, and then Dr. Žižić shouted, "There's one more!"

Dijana howled both from the pain and because she had reconciled herself to having her dead Vid's child but not his twins. Darijan took much longer to come out, as if he'd burrowed into his mother's womb, clutching her uterus with his little claws, not wanting to come out at all.

He was born just as the radio broadcast two twelve-gun artillery salutes fired inside the capital, Belgrade, and two six-gun salutes in the capitals of the socialist republics, which marked Army Day in memory of the day, thirty-nine years before, when Comrade Tito had organized the First Proletarian Brigade in the small Bosnian town of Rudo. The speaker pointed out that this was the first time that they were marking this date without their greatest son and glorious military leader, and Dijana was finally able to breathe.

The news that the newborns were twins, a boy and a girl, spread through the hospital, and this information likewise had to be a sign that needed only to be read so we would know what fate was telling us through its little emissaries, the condottieri of a new age, in the face of whom everyone felt fear and wanted to allay it in every way.

"Well, now I can relax," Regina whispered over their wall to her neighbor Emilija, who happened to be weeding dead marigolds from her frozen garden so they wouldn't come up in the spring.

Her warty face smiled bitterly: "Well, it's good that you're relaxing too!"

As Regina went down the steps of the hillside lane, she heard Emilija repeating, "Well, my Regina, oh, my Regina . . ." For every uprooted marigold stalk she would say *Oh, my Regina* once, and there were so many dead marigolds that she was still repeating her formula when Regina was long gone and could no longer hear her.

She went on repeating it for a full forty minutes, when she lay down among the marigolds, taking care not to crush any of them, and died.

XI

Dijana ran away from home for the first time when she was twenty-five. If one can really call what she did running away and if at that age, regardless of the circumstances, you aren't in control of your own life.

She packed her things while Regina was out and left a note on the table saying that she was going to leave with the one she loved, that she was ready to sacrifice everything to be with him, and so was doing just that. She pushed her bags and suitcases through the bathroom window so the neighbors wouldn't see and her mother wouldn't find out about it before she got back home. She left the house as if she were only stepping out into the garden, then grabbed her luggage, which had crushed a whole patch of green onions, and threw it over the stone wall, where a taxi was already waiting.

Unfortunately, that was the first and last romantic episode in Dijana's flight from home. Everything that would happen over the next nine months was more like those dark French films that were in fashion in those years than it was the escape from home and love story that she had been imagining.

Dijana sat in the bus station waiting room. She looked through a glass door and watched swimmers in a swimming pool that had been built on that spot according to someone's crazy idea of good architecture, and it occurred to her how easy it was to act rashly. She scolded herself for not having known that earlier. Heartfelt desires confuse people, especially if they desire something that's easy to get provided they give up something else. Now, for example, people about to leave on trips were watching the swimmers with longing in their hearts. The swimmers, on the other hand, watched the travelers and longed to be going on a trip. Dijana believed she had risen above those travelers and swimmers. She was going to a city she had never seen before, to be with a man she loved, though she knew almost nothing about him. But she wasn't worried about that either. Love isn't a crime and doesn't depend on dossiers full of all kinds of data and facts that pigeonhole someone in one way or another. You fall in love and that's it, she thought, and nobody, least of all Regina, was going to tell her she was wrong.

She left the platform, which was bathed in sunlight, and the city, whose painful August glare was one of the reasons the tourists needed to see it only once to remember it their entire lives. And there was only one tiny cloud over her joyous mood. She had forgotten her sunglasses on the shoe cabinet.

Eight hours later, the bus was making its way into Sarajevo through fog and deep snow. The driver had to force the men out into the cold several times. In short-sleeve T-shirts, almost barefoot, they pushed the vehicle through snowdrifts. They cursed in the name of God and the Virgin Mary, cursing both meteorologists and Bosnia itself, a small country that seemed like it ought to be close to the sea but had by some mistake actually been planted at the North Pole. Only the night before the news on the television had said that Yugoslavia would wake up to a sunny morning—a wonderful opportunity to take advantage of the charm of late summer and head for the beaches, rivers, and lakes to relax after another day of hard work.

That was exactly what Kamenko Katić, the preeminent weather expert, said as pictures of empty Adriatic beaches drifted across the screen, showing only a few swimmers sporting looks typical of the 1960s.

One male swimmer, whose long hair came down over his eyes and whose sideburns were shaped like little battleaxes, looked like a cross between a guest worker and a street revolutionary. With eyebrows plucked in the shape of thin crescent moons and a rubber swim cap to protect her cold perm from seawater, a female swimmer looked like Brigitte Bardot's East European sister. Watching them smile into the camera, full of optimism and faith in a better future, Dijana couldn't but believe Kamenko's words.

As the bus passed through Hadžići and Tarčin and slipped into a pall of lead-gray Sarajevo fog, Dijana shivered in nothing but a light shirt because all her sweaters and her only winter coat were in the luggage compartment below. What she could see through the window frightened her: shadows of highrises; a long row of military barracks, conscripts standing guard; streets along which fathers pulled their children on sleds; tall, slim minarets likely to puzzle those who saw them the first time and didn't know what to do when passing by them—whether they should do anything other than what they did or didn't do when standing under a church tower.

Such thoughts probably wouldn't have bothered her if the weather forecast hadn't been so completely wrong and if she hadn't felt that she was outside the region mentioned by Kamenko Katić, far away from the country where she felt secure. There was none of Yugoslavia in Sarajevo, though the television and the newspapers always said that the city was a "Yugoslavia in miniature."

Dijana didn't understand the point of this ideological trick, which might not have seemed like a trick by those who weren't arriving there in the late summer from the sunny south, and the way in which she thought about it was pretty much in line with the spirit of the time. If Sarajevo was indeed a "Yugoslavia in miniature" and if the whole of Bosnia was given the same label whenever needed, then why did Yugoslavia never—not even in the boldest party metaphors—become a "big Sarajevo" or a "big Bosnia"? Was it because ideological metaphors don't obey the principles of formal logic or because a metaphor in the opposite direction wouldn't have had enough appeal?

The real reason doesn't matter here. If a story about the great in the small could have been recast into a story about the small in the great, the history of our country would look very different, and we would seem more normal to those who will one day study it. But Dijana didn't spend even five minutes of her life thinking about it.

Outside the bus she was greeted by a winter like she had never experienced and the heavy smell of burning coal, which she would never get used to but would stay with her for all her life as the dominant sensory memory of her months in Sarajevo. That smell would also bring her thoughts back to the city and the first time she left home, as an unmistakable harbinger or a symptom of a bad mood. She kept trying to push through the crowd to the conductor handing out the luggage so she could slip on her coat as quickly as possible, but other passengers were stronger or quicker on their feet, so she ended up being one of the last ones in line.

"You're almost naked, girl!" said a man with a mustache wearing a blue Centrotrans smock. "And look how many bags you have, you crazy woman," he added in disbelief as he handed her bag number four and she pointed to yet another large suitcase.

She was barely able to move all her luggage off the platform and carry it into the grimy bar at the station while fighting off a bunch of Gypsy children demanding money. When she finally sank down into a squeaky wooden chair and opened her suitcase, which was crammed full, its contents sprang out on the muddy floor. She somehow managed to get a hold of her coat, so she tried to put everything else back into the suitcase and shut it again. From a corner the bloodshot eyes of the station drunkards watched her mutely. They were clearly not used to seeing female passengers like her. With her hair disheveled and wearing only a summer dress under a heavy winter coat, she climbed onto the suitcase and began jumping on it until a waitress came up to her and said "Hold on, girl! What do you think you're doing?"

The waitress then pushed down on the suitcase with her big, fat hands, the locks clicked and everything was as it should be again. The waitress flashed her a big smile and said, "Everything will be all right." Dijana wondered what in the hell she must look like if a woman she didn't know was telling her that.

She ordered a glass of juice and waited for Gabriel to come get her. Although her bus had arrived forty minutes after schedule, he wasn't there.

Meanwhile, Regina became frantic when she returned home. After reading

Dijana's note, she ran over to Bartol Čurlin's house, who at that time, in 1969, was the only person in the neighborhood who owned a telephone because he worked for the municipality. He was a bachelor, good-natured and quiet, so people came to his house as if it were a public telephone booth.

"The slut's run off! Call the police!" Regina yelled all the way from the yard. Bartol grabbed her by the hands and tried to calm her down so that she could explain what had happened, but Regina struggled against him as if possessed by the devil or as if he were trying to hurt her. "She'll piss away all the milk she sucked from my tits!" Regina screamed, at which point Bartol simply gave up. "There's the phone," he said and stood by the door as if ready to run out of his own house at the first sign of danger.

Regina called the police, told them that her daughter had run away from home or had perhaps been kidnapped by someone, and when the voice on the other end of the line asked how old the child was, she said—seventeen! They told her to wait three days and call again because if her daughter didn't appear within that time—and she most probably would—it was only then that a search warrant for her could be issued. On hearing this, her mother sobbed a little, swore a little, but in the end promised to call again in three days.

As Bartol listened to the conversation, he rolled his eyes and raised his eyebrows in disbelief. When Regina hung up, he only asked, "Since when is Dijana seventeen years old?!" Regina didn't even look at him and instead ran out of the house, yelling, "How should the police know how old the slut is?!"

She spent the whole day searching the house for any clues Dijana might have left, rummaging through drawers and closets, furious because she knew with whom she was and where she'd gone. At first she thought her daughter was hiding somewhere in the city, in the house of one of her lovers, who in Regina's imagination numbered into the hundreds.

Some she knew by name; others she remembered only because they would turn around and make catcalls when Dijana passed them on the street, while she responded with a lascivious shake of her tail and words that convinced her mother that she'd slept with all of them. In her head Regina kept a whole catalogue of bastards, losers, and blockheads; sailors with the clap; whoremongers, robbers, and taciturn Turks who had descended into the city from Gacko and Trebinje; sons of the houses of washed-up Dubrovnik gentry where syphilis was passed down from generation to generation; muddy workers whose members were thicker than the telephone cable they had been laying in a ditch in front of her house for more than six months, peeking under Dijana's skirt the whole time; harbor pimps and bisexuals who forced themselves upon men and women in rusty train cars in switching yards; students with nervous disorders and young widowers; priests with translucent skin who pressed the locks of seven-year-old angels between their pink, sweaty fingers; Turkish truck drivers who would pay a hundred dinars to shove their circumcised members into the mouth of any woman who was willing; math teachers with reading glasses; aging mongoloids with cucumbers protruding from their rear ends; insatiable old men who, if there were such a thing as divine justice, would have been dead ages ago . . .

There was an entire male world in Regina's head, picturesque as Godard's Paris, in which every man's ultimate goal was to spray his semen wherever he went, and, if possible, inside her child. She hated them with every bit of strength in her big heart. However, if someone told her she'd gone too far because it wasn't normal to call one's own daughter a slut or anyone who eyed her a maniac, she acted like her hatred was the highest and holiest form of motherly love. When it came to sex, she felt extremely protective, although her feelings toward the one she was protecting didn't differ very much from her attitude toward Dijana's real and imaginary men. The girl reminded her of the tragedy of her own life and therefore had to be punished. In her dreams, at least.

She dreamed of finding her in the parks and by the harbor cranes with males panting on top of her. Once in a while she recognized them in her dreams, but they were also often unknown, imaginary men, monsters with the faces and bodies of various animals, freaks with eight pairs of hands or feet, hairy were-wolves, and giant lobsters pinching Dijana's thighs and leaving behind marks that did not bleed but oozed something yellow and slimy.

Regina threw them off of her child with such fury that they would fly directly into the sea or even farther. They slammed against the rocks of distant islands or went straight up into the sky with a scream. And then, as in every one of her dreams, she would start beating Dijana. She would punch and kick her, but Dijana wouldn't make a sound. The blows would glance off her body as if Regina were hitting an inflatable mattress. Completely exhausted from this, Regina became so desperate that she would break out in tears and wake up covered in sweat.

Regina soon realized that her daughter wasn't hiding in the city because it wouldn't make any sense; she must have run somewhere far away. But how far? To another city or to another country? Or had she boarded a ship with one of the sailors so that now no one could know on which corner of the earth she would set foot on land again? Regina ran into the living room, and, of course, Dijana's passport was missing from the drawer under the television. In three days, the time needed by the police to start a search and launch an investigation, Dijana's ship would have long sailed through the Strait of Otranto and disappeared amid pirates and sharks.

So Regina decided to call the police again. But Bartol wasn't at home or didn't want to open the door, and she ran straight to the station.

"My child has been kidnapped!" she yelled at the officer on duty.

"Your grandson or granddaughter?" asked the dark-skinned policeman with a low forehead and knitted eyebrows.

"What do you mean my grandson?—my own child! She plopped right out of me!" Regina answered, making a downward motion in front of her abdomen as if a child had actually plopped out of her without her noticing while she was strangling conger eels and mullets at the fishmonger's and someone had run off with her.

"What're you talking about, old woman; how old is the child?" the policeman frowned. "I'm not an old woman, you ass!" Regina said, bringing her face closer to his.

He stepped back and reached down to his hip as if to pull out his baton. "You'd better watch your language when speaking to an officer!"

At this Regina withdrew a little and then asked him, "Is this the way to treat a mother? What would your mother say if she heard you now?"

The policeman scratched his forehead with the nail of his pinky; that was obviously what he did when he didn't know what to say. Perhaps the old woman actually did have a small child; you never know for sure with women; some look like they are thirty while in fact they are seventy; this one looked like she was over sixty but might have been only forty.

He took a notepad from a drawer, opened it in the middle, and spat on the tip of his pen: "Name, sex, and date of birth of the child, date and hour of her disappearance, persons suspected of participating in the criminal act," he recited in one breath. So Regina sat down and began to tell every lie that she believed would sound good in a policeman's ear. That she'd already received anonymous letters and warnings, that her daughter had been followed by suspicious-looking men who were clearly not locals, that she'd heard about a man who had arrived from Australia whose pops had been an Ustasha butcher in Popovo Polje and who might have come back to seek revenge. And could anyone think of a better act of revenge than kidnapping children to be exchanged later for criminals who were rotting in prisons somewhere, maybe even for that Miljenko Hrkač, who'd planted a bomb at a cinema in Belgrade the year before and was currently on trial . . .

The officer on duty carefully wrote down everything Regina told him. "All right, miss, we'll look into it!" he interrupted her at one point. Regina wanted to add a few other things, but the officer was already hurrying down the hallway and she couldn't catch up.

She went home thinking that nothing would come of it because the people's police force didn't take care of simple folk like her, only of party members and their children. However, after less than an hour, two men wearing civilian clothes knocked on her door.

"Comrade Regina Delavale?" the older one asked after flashing his wallet with his police ID in front of her nose. "We have orders to take you into custody!" Regina tried to close the door, but the other one had already wedged his foot in the doorway and grabbed her by the collar. There was a clinking sound made by a button that fell on the tiles in the hallway.

"It's better for you, old woman, not to resist!" the one in charge told her, but by then things had reached a boiling point inside her. She could feel bile rising in her mouth, except that she didn't know what to tell them or what one could say to people who, instead of finding runaway children, arrest their mothers. So she simply spat into the face of the man holding her.

The next thing she felt was a flash of light in her eyes and head, as if the tip of her nose had been struck by lightning, and her hands were already in handcuffs.

As one could have expected, the entire neighborhood was assembled at the windows and under the awnings when Regina Delavale was led down the stairs in handcuffs and with a bloody nose and was put into a Fiat 1300 with police markings.

Before hearing her version of the story next day, Regina's neighbors were firmly convinced that she'd crossed some political line. Either that or she'd cursed Josip Broz Tito or the Communist Party at the marketplace; maybe they'd found some papers in her house, or that Ustasha brother of hers was still alive and she'd been hiding him up in the attic while he was planning sabotage operations. They went to see old Tere Kalabrežova, the widow of an Austro-Hungarian colonel who was deaf and blind and would soon turn one hundred but who had the most complete and fairly reliable data on every family living in the city. Some fifteen of them, both women and men, gathered around Tere's bed to find out about all the Ustashas of the Delavale and Sikirić families—the latter being Regina's maiden name. But Tere couldn't remember any living traitors to the country among all of Regina's relatives. She had no living cousins or uncles, her brothers were dead except for the one who lived in Trieste, and he wasn't suspected of anything. There were two or three suspicious members of the late Ivo Delavale's family, all distant relatives, but none of them were said to have survived the war.

"It seems she's losing it," said Mile Milun, disappointed like the rest of them because they hadn't learned the real reason why they'd come for Regina. The story about Ustashas and saboteurs had been a favorite for several years, and despite the fact that no one had seen a living Ustasha or any of those who harbored them, everyone awaited a possible encounter with nervous excitement.

Two inspectors questioned Regina in turns. While the first one comforted her, telling her he also had a caring mother like her, the other threatened her with eight years in prison, the exact number of years she had subtracted from her daughter's age.

"Who talked you into it and why? Who did you talk to before you arrived at the police station? Who all knows that your daughter has left home?"

They repeated the same questions over and over again, and she answered one thing one time and another thing another time; she would tell a little of the truth before returning to her lies, which, at least in the eyes of the police, made no sense whatsoever.

They kept up the pressure on her in the same manner until the morning, when the station chief appeared and ordered them to let the old woman go: "Can't you see she's crazy?!" Regina went back home, broken and helpless. After she pulled herself together somewhat, she realized what her choice was. She could give up on herself and her life or find Dijana no matter what it took. She'd already shamed herself too much in front of everyone in the city to give up now.

Gabriel showed up three hours after her bus had arrived, when Dijana had already begun to lose hope, finishing her fourth glass of juice in the bar of the bus station in a city where she didn't know a single address or telephone number except his. She tried calling from a phone booth a few times, but he didn't answer.

"Oh, my dear, that's men for you!" the waitress said with pity, while the four drunks with the purplish faces giggled at the end of the bar. Dijana's shoes had soaked through as soon as she stepped onto the platform. At first her feet were cold, but then her toes started to itch unbearably. When she rubbed them against each other, the itching turned to pain, and then the pain itself would start to itch. She'd never felt this before; had she maybe picked up an infection, a fungus, some hideous skin disease? She tried to imagine what her toes looked like, what color they were, and whether the skin on them was peeling off. Then she couldn't take it any more and took off her shoes and stockings; her toes seemed normal, just a little bluish, with black dirt around the nails, equally itchy and tender.

And just when she was scratching them and smelling the palms of her hands—carefully, so the waitress and the drunks wouldn't notice—Gabriel came in. A young man and woman were behind him, grinning broadly. She quickly pulled on her wet stockings and shoes and jumped up into his arms.

"Hey, Dijana, what's up, girl?" he asked, as if he weren't late at all. There had in fact been a misunderstanding: he'd thought that she was arriving on the bus from Budva, which always arrived two hours later and was just now pulling into the station. They started to panic when Dijana didn't come out of the bus, but here she was, waiting for them in the station's bar!

"This is my friend Musa and his girlfriend Goga," he said. Musa seemed to be much younger than Gabriel. He had long, blond hair and a nice-looking bare face that had never been touched by a razor. He looked like a high school student from those prewar wanted posters for communists. She was an unattractive, plump girl who was obviously trying to look like Janis Joplin. And she was fairly successful at it, no joke. In striped bell-bottom jeans that dragged in the snow and made it impossible to tell whether she had any shoes on, Goga was a marvel for Sarajevo. They hadn't gone a hundred meters from the station when people started harassing her. A taxi driver shouted, "Take a bath, girl!" from a gray Opel Rekord, probably unhappy that they didn't want him to drive them into the city.

"Man, look at her!" said one Gypsy to another.

"Get a load of this; the American pussy is finally here!" said a balding man with a mustache, absently but still fairly loudly, from the entrance to the Tripoli Grill.

But since the three of them didn't show at all that they'd heard any of this, Dijana realized that it was a common occurrence and that these catcalls differed from those in Mediterranean cities only in the degree of candor and kind of insult. At first she thought she wouldn't have a problem with this manner of communication.

The trolley took them to the old central market district, and then, dragging all of Dijana's luggage behind them, they began an uphill ascent along steep lanes and alleys that went on for more than half an hour. Every few meters she would slip and fall. Bags flew in all directions, and Gabriel would lift her up with a smile. Sweat was streaming down her face, and Dijana couldn't figure out how the three of them could be so cheerful and laid back. It was as if something else were happening to them, as if they enjoyed climbing uphill like this. She hadn't spoken ten sentences since she'd arrived in the city, but she already realized that nothing she might say would express a feeling that she could share with them. She was wet, dirty, and exhausted when she entered Gabriel's house. The first thing she did was take off her shoes.

"Come here for a minute," he said, calling her over to the window. "Take a look; this is why I climb up here every day!" Somewhere far below—farther than Dubrovnik looks from atop the Srđ fortress—there was a city, buried in snow and smog. Lights blinked in the windows of buildings and high-rises; on top of one of them was the blue neon sign of a Slovenian TV station. Lombardy poplars rose up, their top halves white with snow, their bottom halves still green; on all sides the horizon seemed to be at the same level as the window where she was standing.

"It's really pretty," she lied, realizing at the same time that this might be the most beautiful and important view in the world for someone if they'd seen it every day since birth and then suddenly lost it.

"A little brandy to warm us up," said Musa, bringing a bottle from the kitchen. A fire was burning hot and bright in a coal stove in the corner. It produced the same odor that permeated the entire city. So this was the price that Sarajevans had to pay to fight off the cold and warm their homes. Dijana was sitting on a divan; she'd folded her legs beneath her, the way she had seen it done. She thought the brandy smelled like medicinal alcohol; her head was getting foggy, and she could feel herself sinking. She leaned on Gabriel's shoulder and then sank onto his lap.

She fell asleep. She didn't hear anything else, except the occasional sounds of a quiet and distant conversation in which familiar words were pronounced in a strange way, creating the impression that they were spoken by people who never stopped joking. Vowels were rare in that conversation, remaining mostly in the throat of the speaker. However, the vowels that could be heard were long and drawn out, almost endless. They were an expression of intimacy but might seem to be mockery to anyone outside the closed circle.

Dijana had met Gabriel the previous autumn. He'd come to the city as a tour guide for a group of Austrian pensioners who wanted first to see where Archduke Franz Ferdinand had been assassinated and then the cultural and historical sights of the most beautiful city on the Yugoslav coast of the Adriatic. But as a perforated appendix had sent the driver of the Bosnatours bus to the hospital, Gabriel had to be both their guide and driver. This was his first time driving a bus since the army and the first time ever on such a long route. Everything went fine except that for some reason he missed the turn for Dubrovnik. Instead of returning to the main road, he tried to find a shortcut by maneuvering the bus through the narrow streets, eventually getting stuck right in front of the entrance to Dijana's house, at the end of a street ending in a flight of stairs.

From the kitchen, the mother and daughter heard an engine raging right on the other side of the wall. Then they heard panicked male and female voices, German vowels and Bosnian curses. They'd come out of the house right when the bus scraped the stone wall of their house. Regina stopped in her tracks, staring with her mouth agape at the metal monstrosity that had never before appeared on this street, which was rarely used by anyone on foot, let alone in a small car. After starting forward and backward several times, scraping the wall even more, Gabriel turned off the engine and got out of the bus. Thin as he was, he barely managed to slip between the wall and the door. Paying no attention to the two women standing just a few steps away, of which the older one was already clasping her hands together as if in prayer, he walked back and forth nervously like a hamster in a cage, trying to come up with a solution.

Dijana thought he looked funny, with his beard and long hair, wearing an ugly suit with a Bosnatours emblem on the breast pocket. But he would have looked just as strange if she'd seen him in normal circumstances. Then he peeked back into the bus and said something, after which the old men and women all hurried toward the exit. Three thin ones managed to pull through somehow, but then it was the turn of a slightly overweight lady who couldn't get through no matter what. She became frightened and tried as hard as she could until she got completely stuck, unable to move either way. She began to cry for help and shout, and by that time all of the neighbors had gathered around. As shocked as Regina, they simply stood there, watching this wonder of a bus. Only when Gabriel began to push the overweight lady back into the vehicle because he couldn't get her out did Bartol speak: "Young man, young man, push a little to the left, to the left, yes, that's right, yeah . . ."

He got the old woman back in the bus, but this only increased the panicked rush of the passengers to be evacuated. Everyone, male and female alike, headed for the door. Some did so probably because they thought themselves thinner than others, the rest because fear had robbed them of their sense and they thought this bus would be their Titanic then and there, in the middle of Yugoslavia, the land of communists and partisans and those who'd killed their archduke. So they trampled each other, elbows and knees gouging the bodies of those next to them, the ladies clawing at the windows with their fingernails. It was up to the onlookers to decide whether they were watching a tragedy or a comedy and whether to laugh or offer help. Gabriel was trying to soothe the distraught elderly tourists, begging them to calm down and kicking all those who were trying to push their fat bellies out, only to explode in the end: "Why don't you all go fuck yourselves?!"

He waved his hand angrily and walked away from the bus. It was obvious that he didn't know what to do—he started down the stairs, then came back and stopped again.

Dijana believed that she'd never seen a stranger and more endearing man in her life. Soon neither she nor the other onlookers cared about what happened to the Austrian pensioners. They didn't seem like real people but were more like characters in a movie or a circus that had ended up putting on a performance in front of their houses. They watched them silently pushing, shouting and weeping, falling on the seats, and tussling with one another. They could have even died like that, suffocated from poison gas and decomposed from chemical weapons; it wouldn't have mattered.

Before Bartol called in the police to try to control the situation, seven of the Austrians managed to get out of the bus. The locals gave them water and wine to drink, brought chairs out into the yard, and revived German vocabulary from their school years, until the foreigners finally turned their gazes from their trapped countrymen and took their smiling place in the free world. When they remembered their comrades, they did it without a great deal of understanding for the situation in which they had found themselves a little earlier and tried to calm them with words of comfort that they obviously didn't mean.

Gabriel kept pacing back and forth and swearing, certain that his career as a tour guide was over, and figured that he'd be lucky if he didn't have to pay for the damage to the bus out of his own pocket. He passed by Dijana, who followed him back and forth with her eyes, enchanted by the appearance of this stranger. He was like Tarzan in New York, completely out of place anywhere but in passageways hidden deep in the jungle. Regina, of course, noticed the look she gave him and was not at all happy about it.

The police first registered the case, and then there began a long consultation about what to do from there. They managed to get two more of the thinner old women out of the bus. An ambulance also arrived because one of them had also suffered a heart attack. People from all over that part of town gathered around. The police tried unsuccessfully to clear the area, and people pushed their way to wherever they could get the best view of what was going on inside the bus. Some children climbed onto the surrounding rooftops. Bartol warned them to get down because they might break the roof tiles, and then a tow truck arrived. The driver squeezed back into the bus to ovations from the crowd and tried to back it out of the jam, but he couldn't do anything except smash the left headlight and further scrape the side of the bus against the wall of Regina's house. Whenever the metal started scraping against the rock, Gabriel would grimace as if someone were running a razor over his fingernails.

"Do you want me to bring you a brandy?" Dijana asked him.

"How about a pistol so I can shoot myself?" he responded without taking his eyes off the bus. He himself was slowly turning into a battered and rusted wreck.

"Wouldn't a little brandy still be better?" she insisted. And then Gabriel finally took a good look at her. She wasn't that pretty, but there was something intimate in the way she spoke to him and looked at him, something he usually attained with women only after months of laboring and waiting on them, if at all.

"Hey, girl, you saved my life," he said when he took a slurp of brandy from the glass, and Dijana laughed as if he'd said something very witty and took him by the hand. That touch was somehow excessive.

The bus with the captive Austrian pensioners remained there overnight. The people went home, the nine rescued tourists were put up in a hotel, and Gabriel, like a real sea captain, decided to wait out the morning on the steps, so that the unfortunate elderly tourists would see that he hadn't abandoned them. Around nine, after Regina had already fallen asleep, Dijana sneaked out of the house with a plate of beans and a piece of bread and spent the night out on the steps with Gabriel. There wasn't much space, their sides touched, and so words flowed more quickly and closely than they usually do between a man and a woman who've just met. They chatted about anything and everything, only not about themselves.

He told stories about his father Mijo and his card partner Žućo, who had a strange ability: an hour after eating two plates of beans, he could fart the song *When I Left for Bentbaša* from start to finish.

Gabriel spoke of breaking wind cheerfully and without any shame or the usual excuses, as if that were something one obviously had to tell a girl when he met her. What girl wouldn't be fascinated by explanations of how one gets the low notes and what one had to do to get the large intestine to produce a high C, which, as Gabriel said, came out of that instrument in a much more pure form than from a clarinet or saxophone. It was also very important for the beans not to have too much roux in them and that they be cooked with dried and not raw meat. Roux and raw meat decreased the melodiousness and increased the odor of farts.

Then he told about Hurem, another friend of his father's, whose nickname was Cathead. Why Cathead? Because when he had an erection his glans was the size of a cat's head, so big it couldn't fit into a jam jar. When women saw that, they fled as fast as their legs could carry them.

Dijana's head spun from such stories, which would have been disgusting if she'd heard them from anyone else or if they'd been told in a different way. However, they attracted her to Gabriel instead of making her repulsed by him.

When dawn came, Dijana was already prepared to follow that man to the ends of the earth, certain that whatever might happen to her with him would be different from everything else she'd experienced with men. Men had come like princes and gone like villains; at first they were head over heels in love, and then they would tell her that they were leaving her because she was too good for them and they didn't deserve her. Never did it happen that a man left her saying that she was a stupid cow; rather, they all left claiming they were jerks and would regret it for the rest of their lives. But this man sitting beside her and telling her how the prostitutes in some Doboj brothel had beaten up his father because he discovered that he'd forgotten his wallet only after being serviced — he was surely no prince and wouldn't exit her life like a deserter.

For his part, Gabriel was happy that he'd met a woman who could listen to the story about Žućo farting without feeling obligated to react with expressions of disgust but laughed like any normal person should. He didn't like the fact that most women acted as if they had never pooted in their lives but only blew on dandelions and spread the scent of roses around themselves. If they couldn't tell the truth about that, they'd lie about everything else too.

In the morning a rescue team from the city's traffic department arrived with a special vehicle that towed the Bosnatours bus out of its predicament with a winch and steel cables. The tourists were freed and flew that very day back to Vienna and never even considered going back to Yugoslavia. Meho Obučina, director of the Sarajevo branch of Bosnatours, told Gabriel to keep out of his sight and to forget about ever getting another job in a Yugoslav tourist agency; he'd better get a job in the city garbage service because he didn't have a future in any other profession! Gabriel told Meho to go get fucked and slammed down the telephone receiver.

"Calm down, Gabriel, please," Dijana said, hugging him. "How can I calm down, damn his eyes? — I'll tear him apart when I get a hold of him!" Gabriel shouted, and everyone in the post office looked to see what kind of maniac Mrs. Delavale's daughter was mixed up with.

They spent the next ten days frolicking in hidden inlets and Vid's house. Namely, Dijana had asked Vid to rent out a room to a guy from Sarajevo who was down on his luck; he had no money now, but she vouched for the fact that he would send him the money as soon as he got home.

"And what's he to you?" Vid asked.

"Nothing, what would he be? He's someone in need of help, and in this town there's no one to expect that from," she answered reproachfully.

Those first days they tried to keep Vid from noticing what had begun between them, but then one Friday he returned home from work earlier than usual and found them fucking in the middle of the kitchen. She was bent over the table on which she'd just been cleaning mackerels that were now knocked all over it; she still had the knife in her hand and fish scales in the corner of her mouth, and he was slamming into her raised white behind, covered in sweat and with the look of a tiger.

Vid stopped in his tracks and didn't know whether he should say or do anything before he got out of there.

"Those are mackerel, right?" he asked idiotically. Dijana stared at him with a foggy gaze and gripped the knife, and he thought she looked like a cow that was going to slaughter itself. The man behind her kept on thrusting into her, his eyes closed; he hadn't heard Vid and was unaware that someone had come in.

"Mackerel, huh?" he asked again, but she didn't answer. But she surely had heard him. She must have.

That was without doubt the moment when Vid was closest to forgetting her forever and giving up on what would last for eleven more years before Dijana finally became his. Maybe then he would have left her if he'd had the strength to kick the guy from Sarajevo out of his house. But he didn't know how to do that, and he wouldn't have known how in a less delicate situation, all the more so because at that moment he found justification for him. The guy was nice and witty; he hadn't arrived on false pretenses; he hadn't lied about anything and most likely had no idea what he was getting himself into. It would have been stupid to tell him now that he couldn't stay here any longer. Why should he kick him out? Because on the middle of Vid's kitchen table he was screwing a girl that he evidently liked? It would have been petty to tell him to go.

For the next two days Gabriel tried to find a way to talk to him one-on-one and explain everything to him, but Vid stubbornly avoided him, more and more ashamed.

"I'm so embarrassed I could kill myself, but I love her!" the guy from Sarajevo told him when they were alone together for a minute.

"No doubt," Vid answered, and the words came out of his constricted throat like grains of rice from the windpipe of a child that has swallowed the wrong way.

It was only because she hadn't let herself be seen too much on the square with her new lover that Dijana managed to hide Gabriel from Regina. Her mother, of course, suspected that something had happened between her and that Bosnian, but this was just one of several dozen suspicions of the same or greater intensity, and so it never occurred to her that Dijana had fled to Sarajevo and that Vid's house had been the scene of an incident that, if such things could be measured in cubic meters and register tons, surpassed her previous affairs. But Regina would nevertheless go to Vid, for she knew that he might, for obvious reasons, know the most about the disappearance of her daughter and believed that he would tell her everything so he might shorten his path to Dijana's heart.

"I know what she means to you," Regina began. "And you know how a mother's heart is; nothing can deceive it. Dijana is my child, my bones, my veins," she continued, grabbing herself by her left tit, so he could see what a heart was. "And I'd like her to be with you; I know how good you'd be to her. You wouldn't even look at her crossways, right? Oh, you see how a mother knows! But a devil has gotten into her, and she doesn't know what's good for her. That's what women are like, my dear. Like those moths that fly up to a light bulb and burn their wings, and afterward everyone says, 'Look at the slut!' But my Dijana's no slut. She's something else; she has a heart this big, but she doesn't know how to get to it. That's the hardest thing for her. Women, Vid, aren't made of one gut. A woman has many different guts. And Dijana's a woman. She's not a child; I do know that. And her heart, woe to me her mother, isn't of just one gut either. It's got more, Vid; only those other guts lead to depravity and search out depravity. Her guts have an itch because they're looking for a man, looking for depravity, and she now feels like doing depraved things. But she doesn't know it! I'll split in two; my head will explode like a melon if I don't help her now. And how can I, poor me? A widow without anyone to help me and lend me a hand. It would be different if her father were alive. Daughters need fathers, my dear Vid! Only a man's hand can put every gut in its place, so that she thinks with her head and feels with her heart instead of—God forgive me—both with her ass! There's no other way to put it. So I'm asking you now, my dear Vid, my child, mother's little angel, to help me and tell me if you know anything. And I know that you know and that your heart is leading you to my Dijana. Where is she now? Tell me, Vid."

He looked at the old woman and knew that she couldn't stand the sight of him. She hated the other men who hung around her daughter and hated and scorned him too, as heartless women don't pity and scorn men who've been rejected. He could tell her where Dijana was now; he assumed she was in Sarajevo and that her love for the long-haired bus driver hadn't left her. Another reason why he knew this was because she'd driven him away and avoided him all these months, as she always did when she was in love. He might even manage to keep Dijana from ever finding out that he was the one who'd given her away: by not telling Regina what he thought, but indirectly by reminding her in a way of that day when the bus had gotten stuck in front of their house and Dijana had stayed out until sunrise keeping the Bosnian guy company on the steps.

But the thought that in doing so he'd help the old woman, whose imagination was more disgusting than a table full of mackerel, made him just shrug his shoulders, nod, and say a few comforting and soothing words of the aged.

"I'm sure she'll come back," he said; "I can feel it, believe me."

Regina, naturally, didn't believe him, but she didn't show it. Instead she patted him on the cheek.

"Someday you'll be my son-in-law!" she said. Vid blushed and lowered his eyes and then suddenly raised his head because he thought the old woman would think he wanted to cry. Of course he didn't feel like crying. Rather, his stomach was turning, and he could hardly wait for her to go away.

She waved to him as she went down through the garden in the darkness, in which no crickets were chirping though the night was hot, worse than any summer night. Nature had been turned upside down, and the seasons had started to change places as in a game of musical chairs. Would eternal summer take hold or would it be winter forever?—No one knew yet. But lately people had begun talking about why the seasons weren't as they'd been before. Almond trees bloomed in December, and frost would kill them during Christmas; the hills above the sea were white with snow in May, and then two days later a Saharan heat-wave hit . . . Older people saw Lucifer's hand in this—when he came down to earth everything would burn or freeze—whereas the younger ones and those with schooling believed that everything was the fault of nuclear tests on the Bikini atoll and in the Nevada desert. But everyone agreed that it couldn't last long. Either the world would come to its senses or judgment day was coming.

In the Belgrade newspaper *Politika* a Soviet meteorologist announced that "if the Americans continue detonating bombs, planet Earth will cease to exist in its present form by the year two thousand." Instead of being frightened, judging from the letters to the editor, the readership was comforted.

"By the beginning of the twenty-first century there will be colonies of humans on the planet Venus. Those who survive the explosion will abandon Earth as a great garbage dump," wrote Aleksej Navadin, an amateur futurologist from Sombor.

It was already past midnight when Dijana woke up, in the middle of Sarajevo, with her head in Gabriel's lap. He wasn't moving because he didn't want to wake her up. Since Goga and Musa had gone, he'd been sitting in the dark, smoking and wondering whether he wanted this of all things: for his seaside girl to move in with him and move his life from one phase to another. That was in any case better than its getting off track but not so good that he wouldn't be afraid now. It was true that for months he had been inviting Dijana to come to Sarajevo. But he'd done that because she wouldn't stop complaining about her mother and telling him about monstrous daily episodes that he didn't quite believe—what mother would behave like that toward her own child, especially a daughter? And after she told him about her day on the telephone, it was normal for him to invite her to come to him. He'd invited others like that and knew that they wouldn't come. This kind of invitation doesn't have its own name, but everyone knows about such invitations and understands that they serve to ease the spirit of the person you invite. Who would think that such an invitation is really an invitation?

Dijana didn't think that either up until three weeks before, when she said, "Fine; I'm coming; we'll live together and be happy!" It sounded as if it were copied out of a romance novel.

It didn't occur to Gabriel to think about what he'd said or to ask himself whether or not he wanted what he had suggested. He simply didn't know what to do with her, and all of a sudden everything having to do with Dijana had become a problem. From the fact that she would live there and he wouldn't be alone in his house or be able to keep his habits, including pissing in the kitchen sink, which he'd suddenly become so fond of, to the problem of her walking the streets of this city, which wasn't anything like what he had told her and in which she couldn't lead the life to which she was accustomed. He felt so stupid, and all that occurred to him were stupidities. He was afraid.

"You woke up," he said in the darkness when he thought she'd opened her eyes.

"Everything hurts," she moaned, "and I think I've got a fever."

"You have a what?"

"A temperature. I've gotten sick."

"C'mon. How could you've gotten sick? You were asleep, and you woke up. You want me to turn on the light?" he asked and put her head down on the divan. Dijana covered her eyes with her palms, expecting a flash of light.

"Everything will be all right, believe me," he said as she squinted at him through her fingers. He didn't sound convincing. She sat up and put her palm on her forehead.

"I'm burning up," she said. He grabbed her by the forearm and touched his lips to her cheek: she was shivering like a freshly awakened bat. Nothing more than that. At least that could be considered comforting.

By sunrise Gabriel had told Dijana everything that he hadn't said a word about since they'd met. Not once did he mention his father Mijo, or Žućo the farter, but as if afflicted by a strange mental disorder, he said all the worst things about himself that he could remember. At first she dismissed this and tried to get a word in, but then she just played with an empty brandy glass and used the wet bottom of the glass to trap grains of coal dust on the veneer of the tabletop. She listened to him and wondered what had happened to Gabriel's cheer and whether there had even been that night when she'd kissed him in the ear while he imagined funeral services for the passengers who perished in his motor-coach Titanic, pondering out loud the words that relatives and priests would use in speaking about them in the cemetery. She now had someone else before her who only looked like that guy but whose every facial feature said the opposite and was a different sign. With such a big nose and long hair, with a goatlike beard in which every whisker grew in a different direction, he'd looked like Don Quixote at the time. But now he was nothing other than the black bird that medieval plague doctors would disguise themselves as.

"I'm just a shit of a man; I'm constantly saying that things are fine and dandy when they're fucked up. When you know me better, you see how bad they are. I just try to figure out how to get away. No matter what I've done or where I've been, it's always been the same. As long as there's something to eat and drink, I'm good, but as soon as it's about something more, I'm useless. Kill me, but I can't! Do you have any idea what all I've done in my life, I mean, what jobs I've done? We met when I was a tour guide, and that was my best job. When I was little, I learned German because my grandma was a Kraut, so I led the old folks around, and thank God no one thought twice about what I was telling them. This mosque is older than the pyramids in Egypt, Hitler stayed in this hotel when he was in Kladanj, and according to local tradition this water heals members of your family. You drink your fill, and your uncle in Hanover or your aunt in Chicago is well again. And it's true: I enjoyed that job because the little old ladies gaped at me as if they expected Soyuz 5 to fly into their mouths and believed everything I said, and I didn't give a shit. I could bullshit them as much as I wanted and think—wow, look at all those old apes, fuck them; they should be buried while they can still walk so the gravediggers won't have to bother carrying their coffins around. You understand, Dijana? That's me, and not what you think I am. Now I'm working in the National Theater as a joiner. I hammer in nails, and that's my whole job. You know when a nail comes out on the other side and a carpenter hammers it into the wood so nobody will cut themselves on it? Well, I can't be bothered. I don't give a shit if the third herald in Hamlet bloodies himself on a nail in the middle of the performance. Or maybe I relish the thought of him hurting himself; I dunno. I should have told you all this before, but I fucked you over too, like I fuck over everybody. And now I'm sorry. Now it's all there for you to see, to hell with it."

He spoke and swigged brandy from the bottle until he started drifting off to sleep. "I'll stay here; you can go into the room. You can find a duvet and pillow in there. Sorry, Dijana."

She turned out the light, grabbed her suitcase in the hallway, and opened doors one after another until she finally came to the bedroom. On the wall above the bare double bed hung a large wooden crucifix with a contorted Christ that had two semiprecious stones instead of eyes and looked so awful that she had to take it down from the wall. She shoved it under the bed and was going to put it back up in the morning before Gabriel woke up. A black, dusty outline of the cross was left on the wall, and it seemed to Dijana that no one had moved that crucifix for at least twenty years. In a huge oak cabinet she found hundreds of sheets, pillowcases, and duvet covers piled in several neat rows. She was surprised by their firmness. The linens had been starched so much that they seemed to be made of cardboard. They smelled of dampness, naphthalene, and dust. She somehow drew a sheet over the bed, put covers on a pillow and a duvet, took her nightgown from her suitcase, and went off in search of the bathroom. She found it at the end of the hallway, behind the sixth door. In the darkness she couldn't guess what was in the other five rooms, and she didn't want to turn on the light because she was afraid of seeing something like the contorted Jesus.

Her shock was probably not only due to the fact that the Savior in Gabriel's bedroom had a face from horror movies, but also because when she had imagined Sarajevo and tried in advance to get used to the idea of life in that city, she had expected the Turks Regina spoke of, Muslims who were completely unknown to her, saccharine looks and greetings from Vid's mother Nusreta, whom at first she believed wanted her for a daughter-in-law, only to realize later that Auntie Nusreta greeted everyone like that and believed that a caring smile for everyone and everything was a sign of decency and a good upbringing. With such smiles you ease in others what you want them to ease in you. Nusreta didn't stop doing that, though she'd lived for a long time among people who never returned the favor because it wasn't their custom. But in its soul the Orient doesn't envisage life from one day to the next. The fanaticism of Islam consists of doing your own thing without hoping for a reward and all for some distant future (which perhaps is not located concretely in time) when someone will finally answer you.

To Dijana it really seemed that even Gabriel, despite his name and regardless of the fact that he'd crossed himself and kneeled when she'd taken him into the cathedral, was like someone of that world of mosques, baklava, and shades of Lawrence of Arabia, which, apart from those television shows with Zaim Imamović, Nada Mamula, and Rejhan Demirdžić, was her first vision of that imagined Sarajevo.

The crucifix with the terrible Christ contrasted with the oriental world but also differed from the Christian bliss and gold to which she was accustomed in her city and smashed her first illusion of the attraction of this adventure in the unknown. The grimacing Christ with the glassy blue eyes would remain a deep memory of Sarajevo, second only to the stench of coal smoke.

The bathroom was a large, cold room, with an antique bathtub and a toilet bowl decorated with blue and pink climbing roses. Oily, yellowish paint was peeling from the walls, and there was no warm water in the boiler. And the cold water was so icy that Dijana jerked her palm away because she thought it was hot water. She stood in the middle of the bathroom, saw her own breath as if she were on the street and not in a house, and didn't know what to do. She'd never gone to bed more dirty in her life.

She shot up from her sleep as if she'd been torn out of it by a garbage truck, her heart pounding, and at the first moment she didn't know where she was. When she collected herself, she pulled on her damp shoes and went to get the rest of her luggage. She opened up the suitcase and each bag in the middle of the room and tried on the things that she was going to wear. She returned the crucifix to its place (Christ didn't look any more docile in the daylight), started for the bathroom, and then changed her mind. There was certainly still no hot water; she dressed herself as warmly as she could and went to find Gabriel. However, he wasn't there, and as his shoes and jacket were missing, she realized that he'd gone out. She again looked out through the window at the snow-covered city, and it seemed smaller to her than it had the day before. It was a sunny day, with no fog or clouds. One could hear noise in the gutters. The snow would melt quickly. This was probably the order of things at this time of year, she thought crossly. Before she managed to sit down, she heard a key in the door.

"Dijanaaa, look who's hoooome!" Gabriel said with the voice of a child; "look what I brought youuuuuuu!" He put a canvas bag full of hot flatbreads down on the table and took two yogurts out of his jacket pocket.

If thirty years later someone had asked Dijana when she'd had the best meal in her life, she would have remembered that day and her first flatbread. There are certainly differences between one kind of bread and another, but they aren't big enough for different kinds of bread to be known by their names instead of just their color and the kind of flour. This flatbread was also bread, but it had earned its different name.

Dijana would know everything in this city that she came to love by its taste. Her other senses would be shocked and disgusted, but her palate would remember those nine months in Sarajevo with nostalgia.

After she had almost perished because she had lied to the police about Dijana's age, and after she hadn't learned anything from Vid, Regina left by bus to Nikšić, to the place of one Nikola Radonjić. He was a former partisan colonel who'd done hard labor for fifteen years because he'd murdered his father- and mother-in-law. A rumor spread along the Adriatic coast and in Montenegro to the effect that he solved cases that the police weren't in a position to solve. He could find stolen family gold, chased fleeing debtors around Italy, caught and if necessary liquidated known and unknown murderers and rapists. Legends of the Colonel reached the ears of the secret police and the police, but in that year of 1969 they hadn't yet gotten mixed up in his life. Either they had an arrangement with him, or he was doing dirty jobs for the government.

In fact, the Colonel was the first and only private investigator in Yugoslavia. Only he didn't have the name of a firm on his door, nor did he give interviews for the newspapers or television.

Regina had gotten his telephone number from Ivka Karabogdanuša, a café singer (and some said a prostitute as well). An Albanian had thrown acid in her face out of revenge because the café owner had cheated him at cards. The Colonel found the Albanian in Milan and brought his passport and both ears packed in a jewelry box to Ivka.

"Here, take a look if you don't believe me," she said and opened it before Regina's eyes. "I didn't even ask what else he did to him. This is enough for me," Ivka Karabogdanuša said, hiding the burned half of her face with curls of her enormous blond wig. Two shriveled ears, which stank of an altar suffused with incense, were enough to calm Regina and convince her that the Colonel would solve her case successfully too.

When she called him, a female voice came on the phone and told her that Comrade Radonjić's first available appointment that day was at ten in the evening, and the next one was in fourteen days. It would turn out that this was a lie and that the Colonel's secretary always said the same thing, on account of which people from all over hurried to catch buses and trains, fascinated by him even before they saw him. People always want to see people who don't have time.

Regina told the driver of the green Moskvić taxi to drive to number eleven Sava Kovačević St.

"And you, lady, you're going straight to the Colonel!" he said immediately. "What trouble brings you to him?" he asked.

"It's not important," she responded sharply.

"Hah, you know whether it's important or not, but it's better for you if it's important. You can count on a look from him costing you a million. If you were a young woman, it would cost less, and it might be possible to pay in other ways too, but as it is, I don't know at all," the taxi driver joked, evidently unhappy because she didn't want to tell him what kind of trouble had brought her there.

She rang at the gate of a stone house with small windows that looked like a bunker. Two furious dogs with curly hair ran up and began foaming through the bars, and then he appeared. Tall and upright, he went toward the gate with an old military coat thrown over his shoulder, wide trousers tucked into high officer's boots, and an unbuttoned white shirt. Regina didn't think that she'd ever seen a more handsome man in all her life. He shooed the dogs away and let her into the yard. She introduced herself immediately. "The Colonel," he said, without extending his hand. They passed through a dark hallway to a room with a large office desk and a high, wooden armchair with two eagles carved at the top. He sat down and pointed to a round piano stool on the other side of the desk. The only light in the room was a small night lamp with a forty-watt bulb, facing away from him, so that throughout the conversation the Colonel's face was in complete darkness.

She told him about her case, mostly telling the truth.

"And you have no trace of her at all, and you don't know who might know more?" he asked and then wrote down the names of all of Dijana's male and female friends, everyone whom she'd seen and gone off to see and Regina could remember.

"The fact that you yourself haven't found anything makes this more expensive," he said. "Besides, you haven't said what you want from me. I don't know what else I could do, except find out your daughter's whereabouts . . ."

"But couldn't you get her to come back?"

"How? I'm not God. You don't even know who she's with now. I might be able to give him a scare, and if he's some robber turn him into the authorities or something like that, but what can we do if he's not?"

"Well, you investigate . . ."

"So, you want me to find out where your daughter is, who her man is, and whether he's wanted for something and if so, whether to do anything about it? If that's what you want, the whole thing'll cost you around a million and a half dinars, calculated in old dinars, while only finding out where the girl is would come to a hundred and fifty thousand. And if you decide on that, you'll have to keep working on your own because I only take on finalized jobs. You need to tell me now what you want, and that's what I'll do. There can't be any additional requests later."

"Fine; I'll pay for everything."

"But I don't guarantee that the girl will come back. I only guarantee that you'll know everything about him and her. And there'll only be more if I get anything on him. And one more thing! You give me half the money in seven days and the other half when the work is done," the Colonel finished.

He rose, and that was a signal that the meeting was over and that he was done asking questions.

The very next day Regina put out word that she needed urgently to sell a house with an olive grove in Kuna on the island of Pelješac for a million and a half dinars. Since the offer was incredibly good because the house was worth at least three million, a buyer with cash turned up immediately, and so because of Dijana's first attempt to run away from home the Delavale vacation home, which had been passed down in the family for seven generations, was lost, though it had never occurred to any of them to sell it even in the hardest of times.

The Colonel sent a courier from Nikšić for the down payment, and all Regina had to do was wait, worry, and seek new reasons why her daughter had run away from home. But every one of them nevertheless got back to the sick Delavale lineage, which should have been eradicated long ago, in any case before she'd taken up with Ivo, thus sparing the world from an incurable human defect that only increased with each generation. She tried in vain to salvage what Dijana had inherited from her and taken from the Sikirić family, but there was no chance of that happening. She took after her father in every way because filth is always stronger than men, evil stronger than good, upside-down stronger than right-side-up, and the world will collapse the day when every good lineage is wiped out by some Delavales and there's no longer a single mother who hasn't given birth to a wicked child.

The Colonel was counting the money and getting ready for the search when Gabriel succeeded in persuading Dijana to go with him to the theater. He didn't want to leave her alone at home because she was afraid of anything and everything and said that there was maybe a decomposing corpse underneath a pile of his uncle's books, which blocked the way into one of the rooms, since there was such a stench; she took the crucifix down from the wall, demanded that the light be on in the hallway all night long, and looked into rooms into which he'd never entered. And she didn't know what to do in the city and acted more like a rude foreigner than all the Krauts and Austrians whom he'd shown around. Today he would have left her in the care of Musa and Goga, but they'd tricked him and gone off to a birthday party on Mt. Jahorina. That was better than showing a little Dalmatian girl around Sarajevo when they had no idea what to show her.

He left Dijana to wait for him in the theater café while he finished arranging the props, and at half past seven he was going to take her into the performance. She drank an orange soda called Oro, which was bottled in the Tališ plant in Maribor, which was the domestic competition for Coca-Cola, that dark American miracle that had been spreading throughout Yugoslavia (the first communist country to drink Coca-Cola) since the previous year. That fact filled people with pride, and so anyone who thought much of himself didn't drink Oro or Cocta. Dijana, however, didn't care. She sat alone at a table, and in the corner of the café a group of people, probably students from down south, were singing *I'm Going Away, My Fay* . . . in parts.

Gabriel carried risers from one end of the stage to another and panted as if he were about to give up the ghost, until Meho Pezer lost his cool and started shouting at him: "Listen, you horse's ass, if you keep breathing like that, I'm going home, and you can fucking go explain everything to the manager and the director! I'm supposed to be on sick leave and instead of saying thanks for coming, you keep making an ass of yourself. What do you want? To act? Is that maybe what you'd like? That's okay, pal, you just act and let me live my life."

Gabriel put down his end of the riser. "Wait, let me explain!" he said trying to get him to calm down.

"Well out with it; whaddya got to tell me?!" Meho said and slammed his end of the riser down so that the sound echoed through the theater.

"It looks like I'm married. I didn't want it, but it looks like that's what's happened," he answered.

"What was that?" Meho Pezer asked in surprise. He'd been married for fifty some-odd years, and two of his nine children were already retired. But he wasn't yet seventy.

"That's what's happened. This girl moved in with me."

"What girl?"

"A girl from the coast."

"I didn't know about her. But why did you let her move in?"

"Well, you see, that's the problem. I didn't let her; I invited her."

"Great, and what do you want now? You invited her, she came; nothing better! Now you can have kids."

"It's not quite like that."

"Well, how is it, for God's sake?"

"I didn't really think she'd move in."

"Oh, I didn't think my Fazila would get married to a Pezer when I asked her, but you see—she did, and now I put up with it!" Meho said and laughed. He was already in a better mood, although he acted like he didn't understand anything.

"Meho, I can't get married," Gabriel said, his voice quivering.

"Why not? You like men? If that's the reason, get away from me. And now lift that thing; Hamlet won't have anywhere to fuck with Ophelia."

Gabriel's confession ended here, but the next day half the theater would know about his unhappy romance. Meho, of course, knew very well what was going on, understood everything, and told whoever needed to hear it, pitying the unhappy young man. This only secured Gabriel respect among the acting community, which took open pleasure in its tragic love stories, failing marriages, fictitious nervous breakdowns, and other emotional occasions for the consumption of large quantities of alcohol.

It was the fact that as a stagehand and assistant decorator Gabriel had acquired something that was considered to be the mark of a high caste that led Viktor Barilla, the director of *Hamlet,* to give him a minor role as the second herald after the old Jozef Černi ended up in the hospital due to a stroke. Thus Gabriel became one of the actors, which from his point of view was the only good thing in connection with his nine-month common-law marriage to Dijana Delavale.

They went to the seventh row of the orchestra and sat down in seats ten and eleven, which were permanently reserved for members of the party or state delegations from non-aligned countries that arrived in the city on a daily basis to conclude trade agreements for arms and petroleum, in case one of them wished to see a stage performance outside of protocol. Since this had never happened, the two best seats in the seventh row were always given to stagehands, but they didn't use them either, unless one of the younger ones had found a girl who was open to being charmed with courtship in a theater.

Hamlet was mind-numbingly boring. It dragged on and on in complete harmony with the fact that it was directed by a man who'd done the same job in the same theater twenty-five years before when he was young, brave, and full of potential, under the Ustashas and the German occupation. And this performance in 1969 was supposed to be a kind of quiet rehabilitation for him, after his having been forbidden to work in Sarajevo for a quarter of a century.

As with every other rehabilitation in those years, this too presupposed an act of repentance, humility, and complete discretion, to which Barilla kept so successfully that this performance was completely unwatchable for anyone, which again wasn't a reason for him not to win the praise of newspaper critics or to be invited to participate in several Yugoslav and foreign festivals. No one, apart from the secret police and the comrades in the Committee for Work with Ideas in the Central Committee, remembered Barilla's wartime productions and his errant youth before packed auditoriums whose applause at the premieres was orchestrated by Mile Budak, the minister of religion of the Independent State of Croatia. Nor was there an actor in the 1969 staging of *Hamlet* who knew why the maestro was so indisposed, why he didn't say a word at the rehearsals, and gave only one instruction to the actors: "Tone it down a little; you're not at a demonstration!"

The problem that came between a theater director and the government was solved at the expense of the audience, who understood nothing, least of all why it was suddenly supposed to be bored to tears at a performance directed by someone who'd received acclaim in Zagreb and Belgrade and who bore the honorary title of the "Nestor" of Yugoslav theater. The audiences didn't know— not because they didn't want to but because they weren't told—that the great

Viktor Barilla was in Sarajevo to remedy something that couldn't be remedied, his own past and the past of that city. But worst of all was that he wasn't the only one involved in this project.

People came to Sarajevo from Zagreb and Belgrade mainly to atone for their sins. While a few were punished for a lack of talent and—after being rejected in the theaters of the eastern and western metropolises—went to Bosnia, others, such as Barilla—as the greatest names of Yugoslav arts—went to Sarajevo to atone for sins that had been bequeathed to them by Ante Pavelić, Milan Nedić, or Stalin. Few of those who atoned for such sins with an awareness of their own creative dignity and name would be remembered. In Sarajevo they usually directed and acted blindly, as if before a morgue or a commemorative grave full of the frightening skulls of murdered victims. And the audience was left equally confused and more and more convinced that it was the city itself that oozed boredom and not the motives of those who came there.

But that's no reason to be too hard on Viktor Barilla! In contrast to others, he didn't go to Sarajevo because of some humiliation in Zagreb or Belgrade. He'd been celebrated in those cities, and avant-garde theatrical styles had been named after him. He taught in theater departments and was the aspiration of the finest intellectuals, and people from party committees bowed down to the black earth before him. However, in his twilight years he decided to try to resolve his misunderstanding with a city to which he didn't need to go because apart from two stints of directing during the Independent State of Croatia, nothing tied him to Sarajevo. He wanted to die reconciled with that city, which is perhaps worthy of some respect. No matter how futile his effort was . . .

They both dozed on and off for three and a half hours, touching each other in rhythm to the king's long monologues.

"Hey, look, that's the head of Piro Trola," he said and poked Dijana with his elbow during Hamlet's chat with the skull.

"Whose head?" she asked, not understanding what he was trying to show her.

"Piro Trola, the city fool. He didn't have any family, and when he died, they didn't bury him but cut him up for use by the School of Medicine. The theater loaned the head. I suggested that we put Piro Trola on the poster, among the names of the cast, but they didn't listen to me. I don't know why; his head has been on the stage longer than those of the people whose names are on the posters."

For the rest of the scene Dijana stared at that skull, which looked like every other skull but was more terrible than any better-looking, anonymous, decomposing corpse because it had a first and last name. Her stomach turned at the thought that it had been a living person, that Gabriel had known him and was now happy to see him up on the stage, and it didn't occur to him that he had a similar such skull, which someone might skin tomorrow and declare to be for the stage props.

"You're really weird," she said and left to go pee. In the darkness she tripped over the feet of high school students who'd been brought to the performance.

That evening they had their first fight. Actually, Dijana had never before quarreled so seriously and bitterly with anyone other than her mother. She told him she couldn't believe that such Neanderthals existed.

"What would you do if you knew they were going to carry your head into the theater?"

"I wouldn't give a shit. That's what I'd do . . ."

"Can you say a single sentence without a *shit* or a *fuck*?"

"Can you shut up, or do you want me to slap your face so you can hear some music?"

"Gabriel!"

"Yes, dear?! Please, please dear!" he shouted, stepping into her face and swinging his huge hands.

"I'm not afraid of you," she continued in a softer tone. "You're mistaken if you think I'm afraid of you. Only cowards shout like that. You're a coward. You shit your pants because I came. Ain't that true, Gabriel?—You shit your pants? But why did you invite me? Because it sounded nice, huh?! You hoped you could play a knight in shining armor, but mostly, you know, from afar. You're such a shit. Let me tell you, you're such a shit."

She was trying to provoke him, just as she would do if she knew it were the end. She wanted to do everything to make sure she would never again hear some guy telling her he didn't deserve her. But instead of completely blowing his top, Gabriel stopped, muttered something, and burst into tears like an actor in a bad Indian film a little before the girls' choir starts singing an ode to the Brahmaputra. And no matter how furious she was and ready to run out of the house without a dinar in her pocket or anywhere to go, Dijana didn't know what to do. She stood in the middle of the room, her fists clenched and her feet apart, and panted like a bull when the toreador runs out of the arena.

Such fights would be repeated at least once a week, with slight variations in the insults and the particular bone of contention, and they were always about something that had to do with both Gabriel and the city to which she'd come. It seemed to Dijana that everything bad and ugly that she'd experienced in Sarajevo lived in his person, as if he were infected with all the illnesses one could catch out on the street. She raged because he'd deceived her and won her over with pretty words and a charm that lasted until she settled into his world and then disappeared like the glittering on lake water on a sunny morning. She attacked him and tried to chase Sarajevo out of Gabriel since she still wasn't ready to chase herself out of Sarajevo.

In the end he would burst into tears or run out of the house, leaving her on her own all night long to wander among the rooms full of heaped furniture and rolled carpets, piles of German books, and prewar newspapers, nothing but posthumous remains that, like Piro Trola's skull, were crassly put on public display.

She didn't learn very much about the life of that house or Gabriel's Uncle Bruno Ekert and Aunt Fanika because that was one of the few things—actually the only one—about which Gabriel didn't talk at length. Instead, he would slip out of that topic and hurry into tales that were often more painful and terrible than that of his uncle could have been, at least in Dijana's opinion.

Basically, she knew that in 1945 Bruno Ekert had been sentenced to death for collaborating with the occupier—what kind of collaboration he wouldn't tell her. Then his sentence was commuted to twenty years of hard labor and the confiscation of his entire property, which, due to an administrative error, was never carried out but also not retracted, so that this was and wasn't Gabriel's house. His Aunt Fanika committed suicide five years later by drinking essence, so from 1951 until six years earlier, when Gabriel had moved in, no one had lived in the house, nor had anyone entered it. Bruno Ekert hung himself in the Zenica prison on the twenty-eighth of May, 1966, two days before his sentence ended and he was to be released.

That was all that she managed to get out of Gabriel. He shut up and blushed when it came to the other part of the story, as if he were awkwardly hiding some incurable family disease. Leaving her in the middle of the night alone in the dead house of two suicides, Gabriel punished Dijana in the worst way.

If they weren't at home arguing and fighting or at Goga's and Musa's parties, which lasted all night long, complete with the music of Janis Joplin and Bob Dylan and Afghan hashish, Gabriel and Dijana spent their time in the national theater. In four and a half months they saw all the plays, operas, and ballets several times. They even saw Branislav Nušić's *A Suspicious Person* seven times. The only thing they avoided was Barilla's *Hamlet*, which, however, was performed twice weekly, though the audience grew smaller and smaller after all the elementary and high school kids had come, as well as those on school excursions from Tuzla and Zenica, who on an instruction from the republican secretary of science, education, and culture were required to see precisely this performance. When Gabriel began to play the second herald instead of the ill Černi, Dijana would wait for him in the Theater Café.

The trips to the theater were for both him and her the best way to kill time in the evening. She didn't have to go hopping from one Sarajevo café to another and listen to everyone who noticed that she wasn't a local tell her that there was nowhere in the world where one could have a better time than in Sarajevo because nowhere were there people like those in Sarajevo, and he didn't have to sit in fear of her looks and comments that tore his city apart.

Apart from this, as soon as he went out somewhere with her, all kinds of crap would happen that he'd never experienced before. Either out of the clear blue sky people would knife each other before Dijana's eyes, or the waiter in the Morića Inn would trip in a doorway and spill a bowl of hot stew on Dijana's head, or it would happen, as in a legend that everyone had heard but no one had ever seen in real life, that in the middle of the market square some bumpkin with a shaved head would come up to them and force Gabriel to buy a brick for five hundred dinars. With each new day reality would bear out Dijana's newly acquired biases, and there was no help but to take refuge in the theater.

If Sarajevo were the city that she saw and experienced every day, no one would have lived there, Gabriel thought, reconciled to the fact that there was no place in the world that he could share with Dijana that would be the same for both of them.

And then there was that tragic Friday and the premiere of *Nikola Šubić Zrinski*. It was never clear whose idea it was or why the national opera of the Croats, in which the protagonist dies fighting the Turks, would be performed in Sarajevo, that bastion of "brotherhood and unity" and communist orthodoxy, but rumor had it that this was done on a directive from the supreme leadership of the party, as part of a broader effort to win over the Croats in western Herzegovina, an area that had lived under a kind of martial law for twenty some-odd years, under a stigma because of its mass collaboration with the Ustashas in the Second World War. Children can't be guilty for what their fathers and grandfathers did—this was the new party slogan. But people also pointed out that then that opera should be performed in Lištica or Ljubuški, because what did Sarajevo have to do with the Ustashas and why would those injustices be corrected by the story of a Croatian lord who fought the Turks?

It wasn't that Sarajevo pined for the Ottoman Empire and the time of the sultans; no one remembered any of that, but they hadn't ever liked the whole bit about fighting and pursuing the Turks. They had an instinctive feeling that all those folk songs and tales, in which some Jovan and Ivo were killed by some Sulejman, nevertheless in a roundabout way had something to do with them and any Bosnian who had a Turkish name. If nothing else, it seemed that Bosnians didn't have a right to their heroic legends because they hadn't fought against

Ottoman despotism, about which one learned in school that it had lasted for five centuries, though the calendar showed that it was only four centuries. So at that time it had barely been five centuries since the Turks had come to Bosnia — but how many years had it been since they'd already been gone?! So many that only the cobblestones remembered a Turkish foot stepping on them. Over in the cemetery in the city center a public toilet was opened so the people would know that not even the dead have the same rights. It would never happen that the smell of shit would waft over Catholic or Orthodox graves, though they contained people who had died at the same time as those who were now bathing in shit.

The market district was softly abuzz with talk, and the Muslim men watched what they said in front of their Catholic and Orthodox neighbors for the first time in a long while because they felt that this opera was a serious thing, on account of which you could lose your life or be sent to do hard labor, though none of these people from the three groups had ever in their lives set foot in the National Theater.

But the Catholics in the market district, who were in the minority (there might be one or two among the clockmakers, cobblers, and tailors) were damned if they weren't getting ready to go to their first opera. And they weren't hush-hush about it but called out from their storefronts that they were going to buy tickets, the next day if possible.

No one knew whether they were fooling around or really meant it, nor did anyone ask, because it's better not to open your mouth about things you'd rather not get asked about. But it was quite possible that a few of them bought tickets and set off that evening for Ivan Zajc's opera *Nikola Šubić Zrinski*.

By half past six there was a large crowd of people in front of the National Theater. While some looked as if they'd gone to the opera — tall old men with railroaders' mustaches, leading their little old ladies under the arm who'd just taken their heads out from under hair driers and whose coiffures shone blue with dye like foaming groundswells — the majority of them didn't look as if they were going to the theater.

Guys with big heads scowled like villains in partisan movies and kept looking back and forth over the crowd, just as if they had cameras instead of eyes and were shooting film. Students came from provincial universities, in mended navy blue or black suits, the kind people buy once in their lives in Kakanj or Doboj for funerals and weddings. They kept to themselves in a few groups and cast glances full of spite at the fatheads. There were also paupers from the Sarajevo basin and Stup, in muddy rubber galoshes; some milkmaids from Ilijaš; and two or three old women in threadbare, stained suits wearing too much makeup and hats. One of them wore a large silver cross around her neck and every so often pulled it out of her blouse because it kept falling in.

The atmosphere, at least from the point of view of someone not from Sarajevo, was as in one of De Sica's films, but for anyone who was born there or knew the city, it was a place to be avoided. Namely, there was a feeling of danger that you recognized even if you'd never experienced it and had no idea what it actually meant. And the majority of the people had no experience with such danger because years would pass—ten, fifteen, or twenty years—before something similar would happen again. Although the older generations, those from the market district and the city center, knew well that such things always come, like earthquakes, fires, and blizzards. They were impossible to avoid, but you should try to get as far away from them as possible because they were surely going to do someone in, and someone would surely get carried away by his crazy head or crazier heart, let his tongue wag, and the result would be something that would keep the city in fear for years or in the conviction that they were the worst people on earth because a quiet life meant less to them than five minutes of insanity.

And then, of course, what could be expected and what must have been known by whoever decided to stage *Nikola Šubić Zrinski* in Sarajevo? A group of students, there might have been seven or eight of them, formed a circle, joined arms, and sang the aria *To Battle, To Battle*. They sang as loudly as they could and sang fairly well, except that they turned Zajc's hymn into something of their own that had echoes of Vlašić, Zvijezda, and Vranica, the howling of wolves and the yell of someone falling into an abyss on the far side of a mountain. Their voices knew nothing of the romantic longing in the songs of the market district; their longing was stronger, harder, and more menacing. Mountain despair and the tragedy of the villages whence they'd come: villages that had lived or died by the sword. And they would probably do both! Slaughter is always forgiven in these parts but never forgotten. And every forgiveness has its expiration date. Some are forgiven for ten, others for fifty or a hundred years, but no one remembers anything, any crime, ever having been forgiven for all time.

If an opera buff had been in front of the National Theater in Sarajevo in 1969 and heard those highlanders singing *To Battle, To Battle*, he'd have said that Zajc's aria had never sounded better. Instead of a provincial imitation based on a European model from the nineteenth century, the voice of the people had made itself heard. That wild Balkan folklore that deserved its own Béla Bartók but never got him. But such a figure would have listened to those students who'd decided to die and made some musicological observations. In a few seconds people began to move away from the circle of singers; soon no one was within fifty meters of them, and then, when the area had been emptied, the fatheads scowled, there were certainly thirty of them, and moved in on the singers, surrounded them, and simply swallowed them up.

People swore that they didn't see them being taken away, and there wasn't any reason not to believe them because they tried not to see anything, but two days later in the Belgrade *Večernje novosti* there was an article about a "nationalist incident in front of the National Theater in Sarajevo." The people didn't need newspapers because they already knew everything. The premiere was staged without disturbance, with an applause that lasted just long enough for no one to look suspicious.

At the time of the incident Gabriel was setting the stage, and Dijana was in the theater buffet talking to Katarina Katzer, a promising young ballerina to whom she sometimes would complain about life in Sarajevo and with whom she found understanding because Katarina, surely for some other reasons about which one doesn't speak in polite society, didn't think this was the nicest place on earth either. To the end of the performance, not one of them had any idea what was going on in front of the theater.

The next day at nine in the morning a black Citroen stopped in front of Gabriel's house. Two inspectors in civilian dress got out, went in, and took Gabriel away for an interview at the State Security Service. And in no less than the offices of the secret police that dealt with cases of counterrevolutionary and hostile activity. Dijana wanted to go with him.

"Comrade, no one has asked to see you; when they do, we'll come for you too!" said one of them, a stout blond guy, rebuffing her.

She stayed behind in the house and waited until she completely lost her nerve and went looking for someone to spend time with until Gabriel came back. She called Goga and Musa, but they didn't answer, and then she walked over to Katarina's place, told her what had happened, and Katarina didn't think it was strange at all, as if she'd expected such things to start happening there as well, and went back home with Dijana to wait for Gabriel.

"I have no idea what happened outside the theater," he told Inspector Jere Vidošević, a dark-skinned man with a Stalinesque mustache, before the man asked him anything.

"How do you know that's why we called you?" he said and gave him a dirty look, writing something down at the same time.

"I don't know, but I suppose that's why. Why would you call me in otherwise?" Gabriel asked. He still wasn't too worried.

"To have a talk, like citizens talk with official services. Conscientious citizens. Those who have nothing to hide. Right? Why would an honest man worry when we call him in? That would be just like me going into the theater and worrying whether someone was going to kill me with one of those, whaddya call 'em, fake pistols. But hey, Mack, a pistol can be real. You and I both know that," Jere said full of affectation, as if he were acting the part of Kočić's David Štrpac.

"What kind of pistol? I don't get it," Gabriel said, confused.

"I don't understand. That's how you say it: *I don't understand.* You work in the theater, but you talk like a bum. Don't let Comrade Barilla hear you. Or is he a gentleman? Huh, tell me—is Barilla a comrade or a gentleman? So I can know what to call him when he comes over for coffee. We know that he took you on as an actor. The second herald, hah! And he took you of all people! 'You know, he's a joiner, but he's got talent!' Oh yeah, those guys in acting schools don't know what they're doing, but the famed director does, ain't that so?"

Gabriel thought that they had summoned him there to find out why Barilla had taken him for the performance and that made him angry: "I didn't ask them to give me a part. He did that because none of the actors would take such a small role . . ."

"That's right; that's what I'm saying! And then he gave it to you. He knows what he's doing," Jere said, continuing the same tone.

"Why didn't you call him in and ask him?"

"So you'd like to tell me how to do my job? You know, that wouldn't help you because as soon as someone starts poking their nose into my job, I get this stabbing pain in this side of my head. You know, it was right here that I took an Ustasha bullet in '49, when I was chasing holdouts in Herzegovina. I haven't had any serious consequences from it, except that I fucking lose it when someone tells me how to do my job or when, God forbid, someone in this chair starts bullshitting me. Then, my dear, good, and honest Gabriel, I get really fucked up. And when I'm fucked up, then I take this hand here, grab the guy's head with it, and slam it into that safe over there a little. Just to calm down. Turn around and look at it; it's behind you. Hey, turn around when I tell you to and look at the safe! Oh, and then I smash your head into the safe until my head clears and my sequela subsides. Only that tends to take a while, and then fuck it; you just hope your head is hard. If it's hard, you live, but you walk around like an idiot without knowing what you used to have inside it. If it's soft, well then you can kiss your ass good-bye along with the state, the party, and Inspector Jere Vidoše-vić! Your head, Gabriel, as far as we know, isn't Bosnian. Gabriel Ekert—I can tell you right away—that means a soft head, so it's better for us not to try it out. Right? Ekert's not a Bosnian surname. It's a Kraut one. Beg pardon—German! I hope you're not offended. You aren't, are you? We know your father, Mijo, a cheerful little man, right, but dammit, you tell me: did your old man have a brother?"

Faced with this question, Gabriel broke and started stuttering, and in a sec-

ond the innocent man who had ended up there by mistake became a wrong-
doer who was covering up his crime. It didn't matter what he'd done or whether
he'd done anything that might give him reason to be afraid of the police. Guilt
is proven not about the innocent but the guilty, that is to say, those who are pronounced guilty and start feeling guilty. As soon as you feel guilty, you also start
acting guilty. This is why there's no police force better than a communist one
because it never happens that they let an innocent man through the exit door.
All are guilty; it's just that some are punished and others forgiven. From that
place it was easy to send someone to do hard labor because there was no one
who hadn't at least once said something that was punishable with five years of
prison. And if such a just man ever turned up, he'd heard someone say something and didn't report him.

"What's wrong? Is your tongue tied? Oh, what I don't see in this job! A man
comes into my office healthy, whole, and sane, and an actor too. He says hello
and asks how I'm doing properly. Look at him—he's full of himself. He has
things to be full of. It's not a joke that the last row in the theater hears you when
you whisper. And then all of a sudden, it's like he's thunderstruck. Maybe he's
sick? Want me to bring you some sugar and water? No? Then what, so to speak,
the fuck is your problem?"

Gabriel sighed heavily, and then started talking before Jere managed to comment on that sigh:

"Yes, I had an uncle. He died in prison. I never saw him . . ."

"What a shame! You never went to visit him! If he was guilty before the state
and the people, if he stole and killed, it's still not proper for his kin to renounce
him," the inspector continued.

"He didn't kill!" Gabriel objected. Jere suddenly grew serious and frowned,
and on the left side of his brow a hole suddenly opened up; a piece of bone was
missing under his skin and one could see his brain pulsating. He leaned over the
table, almost right up to Gabriel, as if he were going to pounce on him or hit him
in the face: "And how do you know, effendi, that Bruno Ekert didn't kill? Now
you'll tell me who told you that so we can ask him about his health a little . . ."

"No one told me," Gabriel whispered.

His knees shook and every muscle on his face was twitching. He expected to
get hit and wanted it to happen as soon as possible, for Jere Vidošević to take
him down and for what had to happen to happen. Just so it would all be over as
soon as possible.

"Aha! So tell me like that so I understand you! So I won't wonder to myself,
what's this guy talking about, have magpies swallowed my brains, or is he a total
asshole? You should've told me up front that the Ustashas didn't slaughter and

kill, that there wasn't any Jasenovac, that they didn't leave a million some-odd dead people behind. People or Serbs and Jews. Oh, beg pardon, if you please! You all say Yids, right? Yids! No entry for Yids and dogs! Is that what they say, you dog's führer, or did we make that up too? Talk, you son of a bitch; isn't that what they say?!" Jere Vidošević howled, and Gabriel kept himself together as best he could, his gaze fixed on the sharp edge of the black office desk.

He was feverishly wondering what he was supposed to do now. Keep quiet or say something? If he kept quiet, this man would beat him on the spot because he was provoking him, but if he said he always said Jews and not Yids, what the hell did that have to do with anything? And he would look like he was talking shit.

But at that moment an elderly little fat man in a gray suit ran into the office: "What's going on, Jere, what happened? Come here, c'mon, relax a little; Fazila's brought kebabs . . ."

And before Gabriel raised his head, the little fat guy was already sitting in Vidošević's seat, and Jere had vanished from the room.

"Forget him, man; he's crazy. Someday he'll kill someone. I tell him, 'Jere, poor Jere, retire, relax, take care of your apiaries; this isn't for you. The fool; he's got more years of service than years of being alive, when you count his time as a partisan and his ten years of chasing Ustashas around Herzegovina. But he won't retire! Be that as it may, tell me, boy, did you see anything yesterday outside the theater? We can be done in ten minutes. Ugh, damn it, how uncultured of me; I didn't introduce myself, and that's proper according to the rules of the service and ordinary customs. Martin Barnjak," the inspector said and extended his hand. That hand was small, like a child's, and somehow all round, with a wedding band that had been put on long, long ago, when the finger was thinner. Gabriel accepted that hand like the greatest gift he could have been given.

"I didn't see anything. I was setting up the stage scenery. I went into the theater at four in the afternoon, and at that time there was no one outside . . ."

"Great. We knew that already, but we're just following procedure. You have to get a statement, regardless of the fact that it's clearly stupid, both to you and to the person you're asking. But what the hell, those are the rules of the service. Now did anyone tell you later what those guys were singing in front of the theater? I'm just asking; I'd like to know . . ."

"The aria *To Battle, To Battle*. It's from the opera."

"I know, I know; I saw *Zrinski* when I was in Zagreb. I'll see it here too, to see which version is better, ours or the Zagreb version. Oh, as it happened, the young rabble were singing to try out their voices. And what do you think, frankly speaking, why did they sing that song and not some other?" asked Barnjak, who, both because of the idiotic smile that didn't leave his face and the way in which he asked questions, reminded Gabriel of an annoying uncle who comes to visit once a year when you're little, usually for your birthday, gives you a plastic train as a gift, and won't let you be until he leaves. He holds you on his knee, grabs you by the cheeks, and asks whether you love him more than your father and whether you have a girlfriend.

"Really, I don't know why they were singing *To Battle, To Battle*," he said.

"Right; what an idiot I am! How would you know?!" Barnjak scratched his bald spot in confusion.

"But what would you've had to say about that song if you'd been out in front of the theater?"

"What would I have had to say? Nothing—what would I have to say? People sing what they're going to hear in the opera. Seems normal to me," Gabriel said, as Dijana returned to his thoughts, the fact that she was left alone in the house and was certainly pissed that he wasn't there or rummaging through the rooms that no one went into.

"Normal, n-o-r-m-a-l!" Barnjak repeated to get the spelling right as he wrote it down. "Fine; if that's normal to you, then it's normal for me too," he said and left the office.

Gabriel sat for half an hour in his seat and didn't budge so as not to spoil anything before Inspector Jere came back. But instead of him a guy in a uniform appeared. Gabriel jumped up.

"Turn around and put your hands behind your back!" the policeman yelled.

Three minutes later Gabriel was in a room without windows, between walls painted with a greasy green paint, in handcuffs that wouldn't be removed from him until the next day, when despite the fact that it was Sunday and no one was working, he was led before a police magistrate and was sentenced to sixty days imprisonment because he'd supported the singing of nationalist songs in front of the National Theater in Sarajevo and expressed regret that he was unable to sing along.

And so Gabriel suffered on account of *Zrinski*. That was the year he'd first complained that he'd been born in this backwater and not in America, from where even in Sarajevo people had been hearing the first rumors of a festival on the private farm of one Max Yasgur, in a place called Woodstock, where one generation won the right to renounce the history of its parents that had been written up for it, to renounce the state, the flag, the law, and everything else that no one could live with any longer. Gabriel too believed for a short time that he would be protected by that Woodstock, if only because he'd heard of it and gotten drunk at Goga's and Musa's place to songs that had been played there.

And they had about as much to do with the aria *To Battle, To Battle* as he did with his Uncle Bruno.

His hope died out, as do all hopes and beliefs that you can be outside the world and escape the troubles that started on their paths before you were born and before anyone or anything besides those troubles reckoned with the possibility that you would one day be there. As he squatted in his green cell, all of Gabriel's problems came down to one. Actually two: pissing and shitting. The one and the other urge seized him, and he stopped thinking about other urges.

Dijana spent the night with Katarina Katzer without managing to get a word in edgewise or think about herself and Gabriel very much. Katarina told her about her whole life, packed full of dead aunts and curses that a Galician priest had cast on the Katzers two hundred years before, because of which every male member of the family loved men. With time the curses deepened, and the Katzer women started loving women. This curse was the downfall of her great-grandfather, her grandfather, and her father and all five of her father's sisters, who all killed themselves in turn in Vienna because of some actresses and ballerinas. Every two years one of them would stick her head into an oven and turn on the gas, and her relatives in Sarajevo would go to the funeral.

Katarina didn't say anything about whether that Galician curse had affected her. But Dijana cautiously moved away whenever in the fervor of her story Katarina reached for her hand. Dijana laughed and cried at the unbelievable confessions of a Sarajevo ballerina, in which there were certainly lies and a strange delirium that drove the girl to talk without end and caused her to talk faster than she could think, so that she would fly back and forth between different times and would no longer know where she was or in which character.

Then she would stop for a moment, look up at the ceiling, frightened that it was going to collapse, and instead of finishing the story she'd begun, she'd begin another. About the Moscow ballet school and about how when she was eighteen she'd stopped menstruating, but she wasn't worried about it because she would start again when she broke her leg one day, the same month that her dancing career would come to an end. Horses and ballerinas break their legs only once, the difference being that horses are shot but ballerinas are given pensions so they can have something to spend on their youth. Katarina knew that she was going to break her leg; she'd had the same dream several times and knew exactly where it would happen. But she didn't know when. Nor was it important: six of one, half a dozen of the other. Menstruation would replace *Swan Lake*.

At about six Dijana put her in the bed under the crucifix, and Katarina fell asleep in mid-sentence. Dijana went back into the living room, lay down on the divan, watched the flames in the stove until she dropped off. At eight a police car stopped in front of the house, and the same policeman who'd led Gabriel away rang the doorbell until he woke Dijana and handed her a summons for an interview in the State Security Service, where she was supposed to come on Monday at ten. She asked him where her boyfriend was; he said that he didn't know but that he was sure he was safe.

Only a day later did Dijana learn that Gabriel had been sentenced to sixty days in prison and that he was in the central prison, which bore the name Miljacka, a small river in the city that absorbed all the Sarajevo sewage and thus stank even in winter. At the police station they asked Dijana the usual questions about the man with whom she was living, where she'd met him and how, whether he'd said what his uncle had been during the Second World War, and what her thoughts on that were. With whom they socialized and whom they saw, what they talked about, and which films they watched. And when the inspector asked her when they had made love for the first time, she answered that it wasn't his business, whereupon he only laughed and went on to something else.

"Stop by from time to time," he said when they parted, "especially if you notice something suspicious. You have to develop a culture of security. You've seen yourself how theater culture ends up."

After she saw Gabriel despondent for the first time, and with his head shaved bare — "I had to sign that I was getting my hair cut on my own volition; they say it's because of lice," he said — Dijana suddenly forgot what had happened between them since she'd moved in. She was resolved to be a support for this man, regardless of what would happen, because they'd told him that this wasn't the end and that there would be criminal charges, pursuant to Article 114 of the Law on Criminal Procedure, for counterrevolutionary activity and violation of the constitutional order of the SFRY. She was prepared for everything and not for a moment in the next two months did she waver. Nothing was more important to her than her Gabriel being released and coming home to peace and family harmony.

That time, no matter how hard it was and no matter how ugly those few people she'd met, including Goga and Musa, showed themselves to be, was the time of the greatest love in Dijana's life. The greatest up until the tragically late appearance of Marko Radica. She loved Gabriel because he was suffering, and she considered that suffering to be some kind of emotional debt, and she loved him because he wasn't there next to her and she could imagine him as he'd never been, like Joan of Arc in that silent movie, her head shaved and her eyes full of suffering, stripped of all masculinity.

She tried to call Goga and Musa for days on end, thinking that she might find some work through them, because there was no money in the house, and in the theater they wouldn't hear of giving Gabriel's pay to her. Goga and Musa didn't answer the phone, nor did they open the door when she would ring. She knew that they were home and didn't want to let her in. The light was on the fifth story of the building on King Tomislav Street, and one could hear Bob Dylan's voice all the way out on the street. She didn't give up because she simply didn't know whom else to approach to get help. After a week of passing by their place trying to get a hold of them and after she'd borrowed money from Katarina for the third time, she sat down on a bench across the street from their entrance. Sooner or later one of them would go outside. Not ten minutes had passed before Goga appeared.

But before Dijana managed to open her mouth, the girl opened fire: "I don't know what you want from us! Leave us alone from now on, goddammit! I don't know who you are or what the hell he thought he was doing getting thrown in jail! He didn't ask us when he did what he did, and don't go dragging us into your stories. And I'd advise you as a comrade not to mess around our house any more. You're just lucky I found you. Musa would rip out your cunt if he saw you! Beware of him! The Chetniks cut the skin off his grandfather's back while he was still alive, and he doesn't like all your stunts with the singing. Now you know, and you can get the hell out of here, and don't greet me on the street if you see me."

Without saying a thing, Dijana turned on a dime, like a soldier in Chaplin's movie, and left, eased of one worry in life.

She kept taking the crucifix down in the evening and putting it up again in the morning. Gabriel told her a hundred times not to put it back up. If she didn't like it, then it didn't need to be on the wall because in this house everything was in some accidental order and arrangement anyway, and he didn't feel like starting a job that would never end, and this was why he lived in the disorder that he'd inherited from his deceased aunt. But she hadn't listened to him and stubbornly returned the crucifix to the wall. That was a kind of ritual that she clung to, and it made life easier. If on the first day she'd moved the bucket with coal somewhere else, she would have repeated that every day, but since she'd been tired from the trip and frightened of the contorted Christ, she moved it. And so, while she prepared the crucifix for sleep, sure that there was no one left who might help her find work, it occurred to Dijana to go to church the following day, to tell everything to a priest and ask him to find her some work. She didn't really know why people in the church would be more compassionate about Gabriel's agony. And how could she when she'd grown up among nothing but atheists and pagans, because in the whole neighborhood barely two old women went to mass. But when there had been reason to really make someone's life hell, usually some uncle would be found who'd been a priest and had fled to Argentina with the Ustashas, and Dijana had a hunch that it might be possible to find room in the church for the avuncular sins of Gabriel's soul.

Father Antun was a tall and thin young man, maybe younger than Dijana. He met her in the parish palace, dressed in a black suit with a collar that squeezed his neck, and he continually pulled on it with his index finger, as do people who are unused to neckties.

"You've been here for half a year, yet you haven't come to church and waited for your problems to bring you here. It's fine this way too. Many have turned to the church because troubles forced them to. But there's a long way from turning to the church to converting! No matter; the majority crosses it and returns to belief in the Lord. And your poor victim, with whom you live outside of marriage, did he go to church? You don't know?! Of course, if you didn't go yourself, how could you know about him? It doesn't matter. The largest church that exists is the human heart. Faith is in the heart and not in walls. Walls come and go. You'd like for the church to help you out with some everyday things, right? One has to live on something, that's clear. But how can the church help you if it can't help itself? People say, 'The Lord will provide!' The Lord provides, but he can't provide more than the people take. That's how it is, you poor woman. I can't chase you from the doorstep, but to tell the truth, I don't know how I could help you. Here, you can have the leftovers from lunch. You can eat just as we do! No more, no less. But I'm afraid that even that won't be enough. You have to help that unfortunate friend of yours. He's yours, although you live together, God forgive me, like animals. Go at least to the city hall and get married, if you won't do it before the Lord. Look, maybe you could clean stairs at the seminary. I can ask, if you don't consider it beneath you to do that. But no work should be beneath a child of God. You didn't tell me: have you received any of the holy sacraments? Oh, Mary in Heaven, what kind of world do we live in? Okay, I'll ask around about work."

Father Antun asked around, which Dijana would never forget. Although it would be an exaggeration to say that she remembered him with gratitude. She cleaned stairs every other day, until the end of her stay in Sarajevo. They paid her little, much less than they'd have paid a full-time cleaning lady, but at least they paid her on time; every other Friday at five in the afternoon she would knock on the door of the office of the lay priest Branko Zidarić, the business manager and director of the seminary, and he would give her an envelope with money in it, always sending her off with the same words: "May the Lord help you, and don't spend too much!"

Maybe finding help in a church when there was none else around would have awakened faith in some people, but in Dijana's case something like that wasn't possible. She passed by crucifixes, religious paintings and chapels, young seminary students with fervent eyes, and professors in habits who watched her go with fatherly smiles with the same indifference with which she'd listened to Father Antun's words of condescension and scorn.

She was only grateful to the contorted Christ with the blue eyes, which had given her the idea that had saved her and which would be the main character in her nightmares after she left the city. She would dream of it taking her back to Sarajevo without her being able to resist.

What it was that Colonel Nikola Radonjić actually investigated, with whom he spoke, and who told him that Dijana had fled to Sarajevo would remain a secret of his detective work (Vid certainly hadn't because he didn't even go to his place), but the day after Gabriel was released from prison the Colonel appeared in Sarajevo. He rented a room in the Hotel Europe, told the receptionist that he was staying for three days and not to tell anyone who tried to phone him or otherwise get a hold of him that he'd stayed there. The receptionist, Halid Lizdo, thought these demands to be suspicious, of course. He called whomever he was supposed to call, but they told him, probably after checking, to do what the Colonel ordered. Lizdo concluded that some bigwig was in room 112 and told the cleaning ladies to be doubly careful around that guest. If in other rooms there were two towels each, in room 112 there should be four; if they replaced bars of soap every two days, in that room they were to do it every day; and if they cleaned other rooms only in the morning, this one needed to be cleaned in the morning and in the evening. Just as they did for guests sent by the Central Committee and the presidency.

But instead of it pleasing the Colonel, he was suspicious when he returned in the evening to find his bed made. Who knows whom he suspected and of what and to whom he was indebted, but that was enough for him to change his plans. So instead of taking care of the case of Dijana Delavale and her lover in three days, he decided to do it immediately. It was past midnight when he found the door to Gabriel's house. He banged on it resolutely like the police and yelled, "Open up! Police!"

Gabriel jumped out of bed, stopped in the doorway, and shook as if he were having an epileptic seizure. Thin as he was, weighing forty pounds less than he had when he went into prison—and even then he hadn't been fat—he looked like a mental patient who was being taken away for electroshock treatment. This was too much for Dijana: she wasn't going to let them take him away from her even if they killed her or sent both of them to do hard labor.

"Open up or we'll knock down the door!" the Colonel bawled.

She ran into the kitchen and grabbed a rusty butcher's knife that was hanging under the cupboard and probably hadn't been touched since the time of the Munich Agreement.

"Dijana, don't! Please!" Gabriel pleaded, shaking.

The Colonel slammed into the door, and pieces of plaster fell from above the doorframe. She stood by the door and raised the butcher's knife, determined to split the head of whoever came through the doorway. It was probably that image, which promised something worse than the worst imaginable, that made Gabriel come to, clear his head, run up to the door, take the butcher's knife away from Dijana, and open the door.

"Oh, you see a Winnetou! Yeah, and whatcha gonna do with that tomahawk? Come at the people's police?" the Colonel said in Montenegrin, probably banking on the general opinion that the Montenegrin police were the craziest ever.

"What do you want from him?" Dijana yelled.

"So the girl is leading the dance, huh? Ain't that right, mister hero? Get some clothes on! Look at him, in pajamas like an old woman! . . ."

"You're not taking him anywhere!" said Dijana and stood in front of Gabriel.

"Okay, fine. Then we can do it here," said the Colonel and pulled out a Colt.

Dijana gaped in shock because this was the first time she'd seen a revolver; it seemed larger than in the movies, and it had never occurred to her that they might kill Gabriel. He dropped the butcher's knife. Dijana began to cry, standing motionless half a yard away from the man with the cowboy pistol; she sobbed loudly and inconsolably, like Cinderella when she was left alone.

"That's more like it; now you're acting like a real girl. Move it!" he said, forcing them into the living room and setting them down on the couch beside one another. He stopped and looked through the window, lost in thought:

"What a pretty city; the man who's seen it is lucky. Why would you want to bring down socialism in a town like this? If you tried to do it in Nikšić, I'd understand! Maybe I'd give you a hand, help you out like when one neighbor helps the other slaughter sheep. But trying to bring down socialism here?! Damn, that's too much. In Nikšić you'd get a bullet in the forehead and that's it, but in Bosnia the people are different. Soft. So they have to call me to finish the job with guys like you."

Gabriel felt himself getting warm around his groin, and the warmth spread and went down, until he felt that where he was sitting was wet. Dijana sobbed and tried to say something, but nothing came out of her mouth.

"Want this tablet?" the Colonel asked, pulling a vial out of his pocket, "to take yourself? You won't suffer. Ten minutes and your heart stops. Or I can shoot you. You got a toilet here, some kind of bathtub? It's best there. I don't like to soil people's homes. I only shoot people in the head, and the brains and blood won't come out even with a month of cleaning, and I can see that your girl isn't much for work; she'd just wail and snivel. That's why I like to do it in the tub. You sit down like you're going to take a bath, close your eyes. and that's it. It's easier than getting circumcised when you're a Muslim! Let's get it over with, so I can get home for dinner! And your girl here surely has work to do, so let's not hold her up," he said, poking Gabriel in the shoulder with the Colt.

"You're not the police," said Dijana.

"As if it matters. You can check who I am when I'm finished," the Colonel explained.

"Please don't kill him," she said, folding her hands; "he's not what you think he is . . ."

"Girl, I don't think; I do. If I'd thought in my life, I'd never have achieved what I have."

"Don't kill him!"

"Why? Try and tell me why! You left your old mother to die from worry and sorrow and ran off with this enemy of the people. You see, girl, I'd kill him even if it weren't my job. Because my stupid head can't fathom how somebody can do what you've done to your mother."

"I didn't want to . . ."

"Didn't want to what, you harbor whore?!" the Colonel roared so loud that the house shook.

"Don't kill him," she begged.

"Now you listen to me," the Colonel said softly, walking from one end of the room to another; "you've got twenty-four hours to get out of Sarajevo. Pack your crap and go back to where you came from. I can see whether there's any chance of us sparing this guy's life, but I won't guarantee anything! But if you don't do what I say and I find you here tomorrow, I'll blow his brains out on the spot and you'll go off to hard labor. And you'll be older than your old lady when you get out. And don't think of calling him on the phone because we'll know about it! Or, God forbid, to try to meet him anywhere! Don't come back to Sarajevo, and he won't be going to the seaside soon. There you have it, girl; that's what I can offer you now, and the Federal Secretariat will decide what to do with you, boy."

It was noon, a cool day in May, when Dijana left for home from the same platform where she'd arrived nine months before, with the same suitcase and five bags. She left Gabriel without a kiss, convinced that this was all some kind of lie, that someone was dreaming all of this, and she was just a character in someone's nightmare.

She never saw him again, nor did she ever ask anyone about him, and she passed through Sarajevo only once more, in a train that was headed for Belgrade. She knew that they hadn't killed Gabriel, and with time she realized that that guy who'd separated them had done her a favor, no matter who he was or how crazy.

On the twenty-first of February in 1975 Dijana would hold the Belgrade daily *Politika*, waiting on a young man with whom she'd run away in the Vuk's Inn restaurant. But she would skip the page with the obituaries because she was still young enough not to read the names of the dead. She'd flip through *Politika* and wouldn't see a familiar face, which she would doubtless have recognized. The caption under his photograph read as follows: "On the nineteenth of February the heroic heart of Colonel Nikola Radonjić, a recipient of the *Partisan 1941* and *Heroes of Socialist Labor* decorations, stopped beating. He tragically died on assignment, and his friends and colleagues wish to express their admiration and praise for the man." Dijana's Belgrade episode was less important than that obituary and everything that had preceded it.

Every year, when autumn arrived, she left home, leaving her mother a note saying that she'd found the love of her life and would never be returning home. But she came back in three days or three months; the duration of the escape wasn't important because Regina knew that Dijana always came back and that there was no need to get the Colonel and sell olive groves and vineyards. Eternal love was a calendrical phenomenon and lasted no longer than a season. That was in the Delavale lineage, and it's no different anywhere where there are men and women who fall fatally in love.

At the swimming pool by the bus station the first bathers exposed their pale winter skin to the sun. In Sarajevo, as soon as spring arrives women bring their carpets outside, spread them out on the asphalt, kneel, and scrub the accumulated filth. If a car comes along, they run onto the sidewalk and curse the driver who ruined their efforts. Dijana saw no difference between those women and the people at the swimming pool. All of them laid out what was most valuable to them when the sun warmed up, and the cycles of nature began anew. Hers consisted in returning to what she couldn't escape from, no matter how far and long she ran. In her first attempt there had still been faith and hope, or she still simply hadn't known what she would feel up to the time her mother died. A power stronger than love was needed to tear out the roots that held her to Regina. And she didn't have that strength within her, nor did she know where to find it beyond her.

Regina met her daughter's return feigning complete indifference. She helped Dijana carry her things inside; babbled about how everything in the house had broken, burst, and fallen apart since she'd left; showed her the new washing machine, which, unlike the old one, did everything itself and you didn't have to start it again every half hour. Naturally, she didn't tell her that she'd bought it because the Colonel had lowered the price of his investigation by two hundred thousand dinars. She didn't mention that she'd sold the Delavale villa. But not because she wanted to hide it. The washing machine was more important. In this Regina didn't differ from the majority of Yugoslav women who thought that the change from semi-automatic washing machines to those that had a built-in programmer was the greatest social advance since the Second World War.

Dijana would discover on her own that there was no longer a Delavale villa, two months later, when she was traveling with Vid around Pelješac, where he was negotiating the purchase of the autumn harvest for a vintner in Cavtat, and when in the evening they went to spend the night in the family vacation home and saw that the lock had been changed and the stone inscription had been chiseled away.

Regina didn't ask her daughter a single question about what she'd done or where she'd been for nine months, nor did Dijana want to talk about it. It seemed suspicious to her that her mother knew that Sarajevo was involved. She spoke of the time before and after her return from Sarajevo. But since her suspicion didn't manage to lead anywhere and Dijana didn't know how to act on it, it was never a flash point between them. Even if she suspected that Regina had played a role in the story, which was really hard to believe, she had no reason to occupy herself with that, especially in the first two or three days after she returned, while her mother was still quite discreet and, counter to her nature, didn't poke her nose into her life or make comments when a man greeted her on the street.

Regina's behavior would change suddenly and return to its old ways after the death of Uncle Luka, her youngest and last living brother, who had come back from Trieste a week after Dijana, where he'd lived for the last sixteen years, to die in his country and home city. They carried him on a stretcher from the ambulance and into the house. A nurse came with him, an Italian named Patricia. They laid him down in the guest room, on a bed on which no one had slept in years and which had never seen a guest and was only called the *guest bed* by habit. Luka laughed and joked about his illness. Regina hugged him and skipped all around, younger and prettier than Dijana could remember her.

For the first time in a long time she didn't hide from her mother in the house but sat by the side of Uncle Luka's bed and enjoyed herself. This was how she was on that Saturday evening. Had the sourest grumps and the most miserable wretch alive found themselves in the Delavale house, they would have split their sides laughing with that mother, daughter, and Trieste nurse by the side of a man who'd seemingly lived his whole life only for his final day, when he would make the whole world laugh. Regina and Dijana went to bed at about midnight, and with the first light Uncle Luka was dead.

"All the city's whores came to his funeral," said Regina, "as if he too were a Delavale! And maybe he was; the devil knows who sent the lot of you out into the world."

It was then that Dijana knew that peace in the house had come to an end. All it took was for something else to happen that was more important than her return. That happened to be Luka's death. Though it was true that whores had come to his funeral and that they'd wept and covered the grave of his cheerful soul with flowers. That didn't surprise anyone, not even the priest who conducted the service saw anything that would disturb the solemn moment when Luka passed from earthly to eternal life:

"'The Lord has a scale with which he weighs all the sins of the deceased, and we can only send our brother Luka Sikirić to him. He made our time in this valley of sorrow more cheerful, and there isn't a one among us whom he didn't make laugh at least once, by pure cheer and without malice."

X

On the fifth of March, 1953, the strongest bora of that winter began to blow. Sometime around ten in the morning it came out of nowhere and caught everyone off guard. It blew away sheets that were hung to dry in front of houses, carried them over rooftops, down streets, and through squares. It cast them far out over the sea, spun them high into the air, as if it weren't a bora but some unknown weather coming from the north and east that had never blown there before to uproot and smash everything in its path. Women came out of their houses and ran through the city like lunatics, trying to catch their sheets, but they hardly got a one. And if they did, the bora tore it out of the woman's hands, carried it upward to the sky, and hurled it out over the sea. Had any of the women stubbornly held on to their sheets, it would have carried them up into the sky as well. It was fortunate that this wasn't a city like those in eastern Poland or Russia and that the people, no matter how crazy, still clung to the land because otherwise the March bora would have hurled them into the sky in all directions so that not even God would have been able to sort them out according to their faith or lack of it or the gravity of their sins. They ran into their houses and waited between stone walls for the storm to pass.

Regina was home alone. She'd packed Dijana off to school early that morning, when no one knew yet what kind of storm was approaching. Dijana went off in light clothing, dressed for the way the weather had been the day before. Regina told her to take her raincoat just in case, but she didn't want to. The other kids laughed at her, told her that her raincoat had been her dead father's, which was true, but Regina had worked her hands raw patching and shortening it. It was true that it was a little wide for her and she had to turn the sleeves up three times, but Regina didn't want to take it in any more or shorten the sleeves, as if it weren't a raincoat but a ball dress and as if it weren't for a child but a bride! But no! Dijana said the raincoat was too wide! Other kids laughed at her! As if it mattered that they laughed. You laugh at them, her mother told her a hundred times, whereupon the little girl would start pounding the table with her hands, shouting, and pulling out her hair.

"Don't pull out your hair," she said. "Don't pull out your hair," she said again. "Don't pull out your hair; I'm telling you for the last time," she told Dijana after she had stubbornly refused to wear the raincoat all winter. She wouldn't put it on even when it was raining, or she would take it off as soon as she went outside and throw it over the wall into the garden. And Regina would spank her when she came home from school with a cold and a fever. One day she'd get pneumonia. Who would take her to the doctor then, fret over her at night because there was no medicine in the city and people died from pneumonia more than from anything else?

But nothing helped—neither gentle words nor spankings, not even pointing out that she'd spent half the school year sick in bed. She could have still somehow dealt with that, but whenever the girl started pulling out her hair and whole tufts flew around the kitchen, Regina felt she was on the verge of a nervous breakdown. The child was doing what grown women did when they got into swearing matches with their husbands, who then threw them out of the house and they ran around their yards like lunatics, pulling out their hair. What they really wanted to do was kill themselves, but they didn't know how or what to do it with, and their fear exceeded their hysteria. Or what prostitutes did when sailors ran off without having paid—they pulled their hair out in front of the whole world, as if everyone should rise up because prostitutes hadn't been paid for fucking, as if their cunts were a public good that everyone should be concerned about like highways, factories, or municipal buildings. As if the party had expropriated and nationalized their cunts and everyone who wasn't an enemy of communism had to care whether English sailors had paid for fucking our prostitutes! That's exactly how Dijana would pull out her hair when her mother ordered her to put on the raincoat and told her that if someone laughed at her she should laugh back at them.

"Don't pull out your hair; I'm telling you for the last time!" she said after the girl looked her directly in the eye, grabbed a lock with her right hand, and tore it out with one pull, as if Lucifer himself were giving her strength.

Fine; Regina responded calmly and went down to the cellar. Among Ivo's tools that lay strewn about, tangled long lines and large fishing rods for scabbard fish, she found a tin of American glue. Ivo had brought it from one of his last prewar sea voyages. That glue was amazing; they'd never seen anything like it. You didn't need pegs and jugs because that glue glued everything. She opened the tin with a mason's trowel and took out a glob of the syrupy yellow substance with it. It dribbled down after her as she went through the house, but Regina couldn't have cared less. She'd decided to teach that child a lesson, no matter what the price. If she wasn't going to live honestly, better not live at all.

In the meantime Dijana had already calmed down; she was rummaging through her school bag, thinking that her mother had given up and gone about her business and that she was now free to go to school without the raincoat.

At the last moment she saw Regina cocking her arm back and tried to move away and was surprised when it wasn't her hand that hit her head but something soft and moist.

"Now pull your hair, you animal!" her mother yelled.

Dijana grabbed her head, and her hand stuck to it. In a moment she was seized by a terrible fear and reflexively reached up with her other hand, which also got stuck.

Regina led her down the street with her hands on her head like a prisoner of war. Actually she carried her by the collar more than Dijana walked by herself. Her daughter didn't know what she'd done and screamed in a voice that was more animal than human. She felt her palms fusing to her head. She was turning into a powerless monster with no will or strength of its own, left completely to Regina's mercy. It seemed her hands weren't glued to her head but had grown out of it and into her shoulders. Everything had been inverted, changed into a horror worse than any nightmare, and she didn't know how or why or what power there was in her mother that could reshape her and turn her into something no one had ever seen before.

"Oh, Mary, Mother of God, what's this?!" Šime the barber asked and folded his hands when Regina carried Dijana into his shop.

"She stuck her head where it doesn't belong, that's what," answered her mother calmly. The barber approached Dijana cautiously, as if he were afraid she would bite him, and looked at her from all sides, taking care not to touch her.

"And now you've brought her to me, huh? This isn't my line. I cut people's hair and shave them; I don't know what to do about this," he said, stalling and assuming an affectation.

From one of the chairs the school principal, Kosta Najdanović, whose face was soaped for shaving, watched in amazement. He was one of those people whom years of experience with children in the city had taught not to be surprised at anything. Had people started walking on the surface of the sea, had soldiers and policemen grown wings on their backs, and had children started riding to school on hogs, Principal Najdanović wouldn't have been surprised in the least. Or at least he would have pretended he weren't, in the belief that it was the only way to preserve his authority among the schoolchildren and their parents. But when he saw Dijana with her hands on her head, crying and anguished, not even he could pretend that he was witnessing something that perhaps didn't fit in with a healthy upbringing and good behavior but wasn't unknown to him. At first he didn't recognize the pupil from his school.

"Šime, for God's sake, help the child. I'll shave myself," said Kosta Najdanović, pulling himself together. He picked up the razor and began shaving himself. He was in a hurry to get to the school because there was going to be a session of the teacher's council on the occasion of the departure of the school's relay team, which as a part of the Youth Relay would present a baton to Tito on his birthday. Kosta, like any old man, didn't like to be late and was a little afraid that he might get the blame if the relay didn't go as planned. He'd moved to the city from Nevesinje and was rather suspect, like every newcomer.

And while he shaved quickly, passing around his nose and ears, and while he ran out of the shop not forgetting to pay, if only for the soaping since he'd done the shaving himself, the barber tried to unstick Dijana's hands with rubbing alcohol. But not only did it not work, but the skin on her head began to burn, and she droned like a ship's horn when it goes into a harbor. She was already hoarse, but her wailing could be heard through the walls, and people from outside started coming inside the shop to see what was going on. When someone came in, they would say, "Goodness gracious!" or "Poor child; what do you think you're doing to her?!" Then they would turn around and walk out.

This frustrated Regina so much that she tried to get Šime to close and lock the shop, which was the furthest thing from his mind. Because how can you close a city barbershop in the middle of the day without its causing a scene or making people angry so that they go off to your competition? He'd already been having big problems since that ass-kissing Hurem from Trebinje had opened up a third barber shop in the city, even though Šime's and Andrija's shops were more than plenty, and the city had never had three barber shops in the thousand years of its history.

And so people went in and out, until Roko Ronson appeared, a mechanic and ship's engineer who lived above the shop and had probably been drawn down by Dijana's racket.

"Hold on; I'll bring something that'll remove any glue or cement," Ronson said and came back with a bottle of thinner or something similar.

Half an hour later, after much anguish and waiting, Dijana had her hands again, but instead of hair all she saw in the mirror was a disgusting, dirty clump of a hairball, like the clump of hemp fiber that Uncle Luka used to wipe his boat motor.

"What do we do now?" Šime asked. "Well, girl, I'm afraid you're going to be bald a while like me!" Roko Ronson said and laughed.

Dijana lost her will and the power to resist; she yielded to fate and the barber's hands. At first he took a pair of the large scissors barbers have and cut off the clump of hair and glue and then took a pair of clippers and slowly removed the hair that remained. Every so often he would oil the teeth of the clippers, study his work in the mirror, and continue working, satisfied because he could finally again do what he was trained to do and what all barbers usually did. Šime was indeed convinced that he was the only one people came to with such crazy problems and that he'd spent half of his career dealing with people's idiocy and not haircuts. And that career had been going on for a long time because he'd been in this barbershop since 1925, at first as an apprentice to the deceased Karlo Karakuna, and then as his employee. When the master barber became feeble, he left the shop and everything in it to him on condition that he take care of him until he died. And he had taken better care of the barber than his own father and wept more at his funeral than he had at his father's.

After he shaved the last of Dijana's hair, he cheerfully slapped the girl on the back of her head.

"There you go; now you look just like a boy!" he said, brushed off her bald head with a feather brush, and put baby cream on her skin. "Hey, Uncle Šime will give you the Nivea for free! There's usually a special charge for that!" he said, trying to cheer up the child somehow.

She stared at the mirror, motionless and aghast, and saw someone there who did resemble her but wasn't her and couldn't be her because it had large, terrible eyes and two eyebrows like black crescent moons, above which red-gray skin rose like on the heads of Gypsies and rachitic Bosnian children who were brought every summer in trucks to the front of the Villa Magnolia to relax and, as their teacher put it, have the sea and fresh air full of the scent of pines boost their blood count and strengthen their bones.

"Those are your comrades," she explained to the class, "who will build our homeland and socialism with you!"

The pupils listened as if what she were saying was the silliest thing on the face of the earth or she were trying to tell them a lie that no two-year-old would believe. The boys in the back rows couldn't contain their giggles because how could they believe that their teacher was in her right mind when she tried to convince them that they were no different from those bald Bosnian monkeys with the aquamarine eyes and the huge heads? They were there, were normal, had hair, and spoke like people speak. They would have sooner believed it if the teacher told them that the goat munching leaves and almonds behind the school was actually an elephant than agree to be the same as Bosnians. The latter were ugly, warty, and dirty, no matter how much they bathed in the sea.

"Tito loves you and them the same!" the teacher said, making her last argument, which wasn't any more convincing, but not even the bravest in the classroom would laugh at that.

Dijana was looking at one of those Bosnians right now, one who blinked when she blinked. He moved his nose, bit his lip, and did everything that she did. She was ashamed because the little Bosnian she was looking at was her. That shame was greater than her hatred for her mother, the horror at her hands being stuck to her head, her fear of the dark, her rage at being made fun of in school, or her sorrow and melancholy and everything else she thought and felt. There was no longer anything in the world that she was stronger than and that she might stand up against. As soon as she went outside—she knew well—everyone would look at her as they looked at those anemic and brittle-boned creatures that were brought to the villas of local landowners, which were where the history and culture of the city had been born. The partisans humiliated that culture in the most horrible way, showing the people of the city in no uncertain terms that they placed more importance on some rachitic children from the midst of Turkish cities than the civilized customs of these city walls. It was as if they'd let swine in to root around in the villas of our noblemen! Dijana wasn't aware of the essence of that humiliation, but she understood its significance well. She walked behind her mother with her head bowed; the breeze that blew softly on her skin reminded her that she was naked and condemned to be another.

She went to school with a hat pulled down over her head, and when the teacher told her to take it off, asking how she could be so uncouth as to sit in the classroom with a hat on, Dijana burst into tears, thrust her face into her palms, so miserable and helpless that those in the back rows started to giggle again.

Vlaho Andrijić, a star student in the first row, said: "Comrade, she won't take her hat off because Šime shaved her bald!"

At this point the whole class burst into laughter, and as the teacher hadn't realized what this was all about or who Šime was and what had happened, she thought that Vlaho was smarting off again, which was a habit of his anyway, and grabbed him by a lock of hair above his ear. He wailed, and she sent him to the corner as punishment.

"And now you get that hat off!" she shouted in a strict tone, proud of the fact that a deathly silence had come over the classroom. Dijana didn't answer. She was hiding her face and crawling along the school bench. The teacher approached her with a firm stride—oh how well things were going today!—and grabbed the hat. Dijana covered her head with her hands; her little palms could hardly cover the shameful spot, and she froze like a statue. The teacher was befuddled; she didn't know what to say (it was terrible to be at a loss for words in front of thirty living mouths) and then regretted bitterly what she'd done. She succeeded so rarely in imposing her authority, and when she had, now this of all things had to happen. She squatted down by Dijana's bench; tears were dripping on the black wooden floor.

"I'm sorry, child," she whispered. Then she got up, clapped her hands twice and said, "We're going outside; PE is next!"

Everyone forgot the bald sensation in a moment. "Hurray!" shouted the gigglers in the back rows, and the classroom emptied as quickly as a fire station does when a fire breaks out. Only three remained in the room: the teacher, Dijana, and Vlaho, who continued to smart off. If he was being punished, well, he might as well be punished for something!

"Andrijić, get outside!"

She asked Dijana what had happened—was she being punished for something at home, or had she gotten lice? But the girl didn't say anything: "Comrade, don't! Comrade, don't! Comrade, don't!" was her response to each question.

Well, not two weeks had passed before Dijana went off to school without the raincoat again! And in such bad weather to boot! Regina no longer knew what to do or how to bring her to her senses. There had been ten days of peace in the house; she hadn't resisted anything, hadn't dug in her heels about anything, and then everything started all over again. It was shameful to think, let alone say it, but Regina would have liked most to beat her with a rolling pin until she broke the devil in her. If the devil could be broken at all and if he hadn't crawled too far down inside her. She would kill her only to make a woman of her, Regina thought in a rage as the bora outside grew stronger and stronger. The roofs of the houses distended, the beams in the garrets creaked, the crown of the old mulberry tree vanished, the one that had always been visible from the window, over behind the house toward the city center. That's how easy it is for people to end up alone, she thought. You can't leave the house or call out to anyone; the bora carries you away as soon as you poke your nose outside. And it was the same for everyone. Only some were at home with their families, and she was all alone and might die now without anyone knowing or caring. Every house in the city was like an island. There are two kinds of islands—those that have been settled and the barren ones. On the barren ones there isn't a living soul, and the settled ones are full of people. Regina was the only one who was on an island that didn't belong to either kind and was living alone when she didn't care for solitude. And the minute she felt good on her own, everyone was crowding around her, she thought, feeling sorry for herself. She would have shed tears if only there had been a man to take them into his soul. She was still under fifty; she had a small child and nothing but death to look forward to.

She pulled a kerchief out of the dresser that smelled of starch and lavender and sighed a little. "O God, woe is me," she said as if someone were listening.

It wasn't long before lightning started outside, and thunder could already be heard from the far side of the hill, although out at sea the horizon was in sunlight and it seemed that there wasn't even any wind blowing out there. Whoever wasn't preoccupied with themselves and their miseries, real and imagined, had to feel fear. Nature was all topsy-turvy, and that fifth of March would be remembered and retold as a day when a bora blew unlike any other and brought rain from parts of the world that never sent rain this way. Or maybe it wasn't like that because clouds have always come from every corner of the sky and winds have swept through wherever they could pass, but the fifth of March, 1953, had to be remembered for something that had never happened before. People had to invent a story about it.

Regina thought she heard someone knocking on the door. It was probably some shutters that had torn open and were now banging in the wind. A few moments later there was the same noise again. So it wasn't the bora, but if it wasn't, what was it then? No one went out for a walk in such weather, and if some trouble had put someone outside and sent him to her door, it was better not to open up for such a visitor. They could go somewhere else. To Bartol—he was a good man. And he had connections that always came in handy. Fear took hold of her; she didn't know of what, but she felt as if it was late at night and she was stuck out in the mountains. Still, curiosity drove her to tiptoe over to the door, ready to jump back in a flash if someone burst in. And there was knocking again. A male fist; there was no doubt.

"Open up, dammit, woman; I know you're in there!" Luka shouted, trying to be heard above the wind, and she finally heard him.

"You're crazy! Do you know how afraid I was?!" she said, and he hurried past her into the house, soaked, bedraggled, and coatless.

"We were playing cards and that Špiro says, 'Let's listen to the news from Radio London!'

'Ah, now that you're losing you feel like listening to the news. Why didn't we do that when you were winning?' I say to him. He turns on the radio, and you know what?! You don't—how could you when you only listen to Radio Zagreb? They say Stalin is dead! Wow, imagine that; Stalin's dead! They say the news comes from unofficial sources but that the Presidium of the Supreme Soviet has made an announcement. So he's dead!" he said without taking a breath, as if he were afraid that she would interrupt him and say it wasn't true, that he was only fantasizing, and that Radio London was lying like everyone else, and the only question was where you lived and whose lies you became accustomed to living by.

Luka had become accustomed to living by the news of Radio London and not the news of Radio Zagreb, Belgrade, or Moscow (when it had still been a time for Radio Moscow). He had hated Stalin even before the resolution of the Informburo, a time when unflattering words about him could cost you your head.

But Luka didn't watch what he said, nor did the city spies take what he was saying seriously. He rambled on, and Regina told him, "Don't; be quiet; you'll catch the devil's ear and disappear into the night; we'll all suffer because of you . . ."

She told him to remember how Bepo, their older brother, had ended up in a nuthouse. She asked him if he knew what might happen if those who didn't already know heard the news that their second oldest brother, Đovani, hadn't gone to Australia never to be heard from again but had changed his name to Jovan and gone off with Draža Mihailović to Ravna Gora and—as rumor had it—killed and murdered? If anyone found out about that, then everyone would know why Luka was saying such things about Comrade Stalin, and he wouldn't need a court or a prosecutor. After the Cominform Resolution, when it seemed that Luka had finally found his place, he went around the city telling every partisan and party member to his face that he'd known who and what Stalin was long ago, when others were praising him to the high heavens and putting him above Tito. And he'd repeated to everyone word for word the phrases they'd spoken in Stalin's honor.

People didn't like it at all. Either someone had reported that he was talking too much bullshit, or maybe he'd reminded someone in the security agency or the secret police when and where they'd praised Stalin, but one morning they came for Luka and led him away for questioning.

Different investigators came and went; in the nine hours of questioning seven or eight of them each came in and asked him only one thing: "Why, Comrade Sikirić, did you attack Stalin before the summer of 1948, and what were your reasons for doing so?"

To each of them he impudently answered that the reason behind everything he said was common sense and that he didn't understand what reasons others had had before the Cominform Resolution. This went on until he gave this answer to a one-armed Slovene, whom he didn't recognize though he'd seen him around the city and couldn't have forgotten him or confused him with someone else. That Slovene, with his hair combed back and his thick, tangled mustache, looked like one of those members of the Central Committee of the All-Union Communist Party of Bolsheviks who had Georgian, Armenian, or Caucasian surnames, who would without doubt be condemned to death for treason and Hitlerian-Churchillian espionage but still declare their love for Stalin in front of a firing squad. After the war the city had become full of broods of all kinds of characters who bore a natural resemblance to minor characters in the novels of Maxim Gorky and Nikolay Ostrovsky or did everything in their power to become like them, just as normal people sometimes wish to look like James Stewart. But none of them looked like their idols quite as much as that one-armed man with the mustache did. His resemblance was so close, it seemed that he looked like his idol more than the latter looked like himself.

"So, Comrade Sikirić," the Slovene began after Luka had recited to him his answer about his reason being common sense, "you knew that Stalin was a fool and a traitor while others had no idea. But, you see, I lost my arm for Comrade Stalin. It was an honor for me to liberate Belgrade with the heroes of the Red Army, and I was sure that he was watching me from somewhere. The great leader of the world proletariat! I didn't let out a peep when my arm was torn off. I'd have been ashamed in front of Comrade Stalin! And during that time you were hiding under women's skirts and speaking against him and thought we were all idiots. You're still not ashamed. Sikirić, I don't know you, but I do know that you're a worm and that I should squash you under my boot and walk away. You think you've gotten out of this? Well, you haven't! You think that your cause has won? Well, it hasn't, and it never will! Someone has to flush turds like you down the toilet! No one gave *you* the right to insult Stalin!"

Luka's smile went cold. He regretted that he hadn't listened to the voice telling him to avoid this man and try to be invisible in his presence, as he'd done whenever he met him on the street.

"We loved him. All of us! Every honest citizen of Yugoslavia, every antifascist, every man in this city who wasn't a local traitor, an Ustasha, a Chetnik, or a White Guardsman. Or a worm like you, Sikirić! How is it that you don't know what you're doing when you call out honest men, antifascists and partisans whose boots scum like you aren't worthy of cleaning? You're not worthy of cleaning our boots. And you dare to speak against Stalin! We shot anyone who would say a word against him. Every honest man pulled the trigger. And now we'll shoot those who were against Stalin before his betrayal!"

"This guy is crazy," thought Luka and started trying to figure out how to call someone in to save him because this idiot might really pull out a pistol and shoot him like a dog.

"If we bowed down before people like you, we'd be spitting on the war against fascism, on our dead comrades from Granada to Vladivostok, on the battles for Mt. Kozara and the River Neretva, on dead mothers and children; we'd be spitting on our youth. And, Sikirić, we're not going to do that! We won't for the sake of ourselves. Are we to become slaves and you a saint? You filth; do you think Hitler would have lost the war if it hadn't been for Stalin and the glorious Red

Army? Who'd have beaten the Germans? Maybe the Americans, or the English, the handful of them that dared to strike at the fascists? The only thing they did was drop atomic bombs and burn undefended cities. Boy, that was their war against Hitler, but the Red Army bled. And we bled under the same banner! And no one else. You see this arm?! I'll take it and slit your throat after I shit in your mouth and make you lick my ass if I ever get word that you've told anyone you're against Stalin or if I hear that you've let that name cross your lips again. Now get the hell out of here and make sure I never see you again as long as I live."

Luka realized then that this wasn't a country in which he wanted to grow old and that the people whom he passed on the street weren't worth being afraid of. They asked Luka whether his belly ached, why he was frowning when he'd never done so before — had someone he knew died? And he only thought how nice it would be if they never saw his face again. The Slovene, in fact, was right. Everyone loved Stalin, and even today when they no longer loved him, they couldn't forgive Luka for badmouthing Stalin. Their God had fallen from the heavens like a meteor. He no longer existed, and no one prayed to him any more. But the crime of godlessness didn't thereby become less grave. If they weren't telling him this, they certainly thought it. What else would they think?

There are few reasons in the world why good, intelligent people would agree to publicly humiliate themselves, but the fact that someone else had been against Stalin and he turned out to be right certainly wasn't one of those reasons. His jokes at Stalin's expense could be forgiven, but reminders of those jokes couldn't be. If the whole world admires a murderer, it takes great courage to stand in the middle of a city square and tell people they are wrong, but when the people's admiration passes, it's crazy to remind them that they had worshipped a murderer. They would kill you with all the passion of self-denial that is always greater than real love or hate because it was actually the sum of the equation. Yesterday's love for a dictator and today's hatred combine to produce the most powerful human passion, which no physical or spiritual power can resist. There was no moral institute or institution, no church or party, that could stand in the way of idiots who wanted to remind someone that they'd been against Stalin even before. That was because everyone, good and bad, had been on the side of Stalin. Idiots who didn't realize this were fated to have the sky come crashing down around them.

However, it was true that if the Red Army hadn't sent its soldiers to their deaths, Hitler would have won the war. America and England were only a nice decoration, a fine humanistic decoration on millions of Stalin's dead soldiers.

When Radio London broadcast the news of Stalin's death, Luka left the card

game and his card buddies; he didn't put on his coat because it seemed un-
necessary to him on this occasion—what could a bora and a storm do to him
when Stalin was no more! He went to his sister because she was the only one to
whom he could express his joy freely, without his stomach constricting or feeling nauseous if she were happy too. In any case, she didn't care. Her life took its
course with or without Stalin.

"He's dead and gone," she said. "And you're going to catch pneumonia!"

Luka was looking for the bottle of brandy that was in the cupboard, behind
the pots and plates. Regina would always hide it in a different place so that it
wouldn't be drunk up so fast and because it irritated her that any time a man
came into her house, all he did was look for the brandy.

"C'mon, dammit, give me the bottle; Stalin's dead!" he said after he couldn't
even find it under the sink. He needed brandy to convince himself that Joseph
Vissarionovich was no more.

Around five in the afternoon the bora stopped blowing all of a sudden; everyone came out of their houses and inspected the broken limbs of mulberry and
fig trees, pushed at tiles that had fallen from their roofs with the tips of their
shoes. They did it carefully, as if they were bombs that might go off.

Though most of the city was left without power and there were only a few
who could hear the news of Radio London, everyone knew that Stalin was dead.
But no one talked about it. If someone wanted to check to see whether his
neighbor knew about it, he would simply flash his eyes and make a face. The
answer was the same. That initial expression was passed from face to face until
everyone in the city had given and answered the question about Stalin's death
with their eyes and nose. No Parisian master pantomimist could have taught
so many different people to do the same thing at the same time. It happened
after the great bora on the fifth of March, 1953, continued for an afternoon, and
that expression was then lost, vanished forever or until the death of some new
Stalin. Not until Radio Zagreb and Radio Belgrade broadcast the news, stress-
ing who and what Stalin had been for the peoples of socialist Yugoslavia, did the
people dare to start talking about it. And after everything that had happened,
who could know in advance what attitude to take toward Stalin's death? It was
better to hear what Tito and the party had to say first and only then say that
Stalin should go fuck himself.

As soon as the bora quieted down, the teacher let her pupils go home. They'd
stayed three or four hours after school, but that was better than having furious
parents coming the next day. Dijana pulled the hat down over her head and ran
home, convinced that her mother wouldn't believe her when she told her that
the teacher had kept them after school. She also wanted to hurry home because

children started picking on her as soon as she left school. Someone would take the hat off her head and they would throw it to each other in the schoolyard; she ran from one to the other, but the hat was already with someone else. The whole school was in on the game, and there was no help until one of the instructors or teachers showed up and the kids scattered and Dijana finally managed to grab her hat. She didn't have another one, and she knew that her mother wouldn't care if they stole her hat. She'd say, "Steal theirs!"

She ran around the schoolyard for hours like a chicken with its head cut off, horrified by the mere thought of having to go without a hat before her hair grew back. Of course, her persistence only provoked the children, and a game called "Baldy Delavale" gained unusual popularity in the school. It even became more popular than their favorite pastime of catching a cat, hurling it into the sea, and throwing rocks at it when it tried to get out of the water.

She came home, and Uncle Luka was dead drunk. He was singing a Russian song and tugging on Regina to try to get her to sing along. She was cooking and hitting him with a wooden spoon on the ends of his fingers. Uncle Luka would cry out and say that no sacrifice for the revolution was too great. He kept singing, then tugged at the hem of her skirt and got it on the ends of his fingers, cried out, and enjoyed it. Regina was tittering and tried to yell in a strict tone for him to settle down, but she was enjoying these antics. She didn't ask Dijana anything and said only, "In a few minutes lunch will be ready, lunch or dinner, who knows on a crazy day like this." And then she would swat Luka's fingers again.

Dijana loved him as others did, but her uncle was to her what her father and mother couldn't be. Whenever they asked her what she was going to be when she grew up, she said—"Uncle Luka!" And then everyone would look at one another in awkward silence because Luka had just one flaw. No one had rubbed it in his face, though everyone always had it on their mind, and that was that he'd never done anything with his life; he had no job or profession. He had graduated from the prep school with excellent grades; people said that he was really talented in math and that he should go to the university, but then the war came and nothing came of studying at the university. And if there hadn't been a war, it was unlikely that he would have ever gotten a degree because there were so many interesting things in life besides being a serious and respected man. Since he'd graduated from the prep school, he could get a job of course, but why should he spend days on end in a legal firm, a municipal office, or some other, worse place and throw his life away like that? He could play cards and chess, talk with children and the elderly, and cheer up people whose lives were dragging them down and might never laugh if it weren't for him. For him there was nothing greater or more beautiful than seeing people laugh at what he said.

When Dijana was born, he stood over her cradle for two months, making faces and sticking out his tongue. The women tried to no avail to explain to him that the child couldn't see him and wasn't amused by his jokes. He didn't believe those old wives' tales, nor would he ever have believed in them even if he'd heard them from the smartest man in the world because it wasn't possible that there was a single person, whether two days or two hundred years old, who wouldn't laugh. After the two-month-old baby finally laughed, Luka wept tears of joy. He put Dijana on his lap and said, "My dear child, my little dove, my pretty flower." He cried and everyone was astonished that she didn't burst into tears. And she would howl as soon as others put her on their lap or said something to her instead of merely being quiet and breathing.

And so, instead of working, Luka stole time. True, many others in his generation did the same thing. If during the war someone hadn't joined the Ustashas or the partisans but had hidden out, forging documents, cheating the state and the people, usually that person didn't bust his ass trying to get a job after the war either. People probably figured that whoever was able to cheat the military and avoid making a sacrifice for the homeland would in the end cheat life too. The city folk scorned such young men and often even openly hated them. Not infrequently there were reports to the Ustasha police, and later to the partisan authorities, that some deserter was being hidden in a cellar or that someone's papers certifying that he was unfit for military service should be checked. Deserters fared worse among the people than criminals or enemy sympathizers. Informants were the same in both regimes and fared better when power changed hands or the government changed than those who turned in Ustashas to the royal authorities or reported some hidden communist to the Ustashas. No one considered it a crime to turn someone in if he'd tried to save his ass from the jaws of historical imperatives: while young men were shedding their blood in Stalingrad and defending Croatia's border on the Drina (or liberating Belgrade and holding the Srem Front and laying the foundations of a new Yugoslavia), and the elderly feared that they might starve or the British or Germans would bomb the city to cinders, shirking one's military duty was an insult of the worst kind.

The only one who was allowed to do this was Luka. People needed someone to make them laugh. But it was still awful to hear Dijana as a tiny little girl say that when she grew up she wanted to be Uncle Luka.

At around eight he decided that he was going to celebrate Stalin's death with anyone who was celebrating. Regina tried to hold him back, in vain. She told him that it was late and that he'd had too much to drink, but if he wanted more — here was another bottle, and he could do whatever the hell he wanted as long as he stayed right where he was. He wanted to be with people; the brandy had the effect of making him forget what their happiness was made of and what had made them happy in times past. He went out, and Regina barely managed to put Ivo's coat over him, telling him that he shouldn't because in his heart he had been warmed by the hot stove of the revolution. The next day he couldn't remember what had happened after that. He woke up in a ditch along a road leading to villages up in the mountains, beat up, with broken bones and soiled with excrement. Whoever had beaten him had taken care to disfigure his face as much as possible. With a smashed nose that had bone and cartilage protruding from it, with his upper jaw bones broken and eyes he couldn't open, Luka Sikirić was unrecognizable. They took him to the city hospital, where doctors patched up what could be patched and reset the bones that could be reset and said that all one could do was wait. If he survived to the next day, his chances of pulling through were good.

"Stalin came for his head!" a whisper went around the square. People shook their heads worriedly—like a field of dandelions in the wind—and everyone felt sorry. Those who didn't shook their heads even more.

As he lay in the hospital, Luka was convinced that this had all been arranged by the Slovene investigator and that it was the secret police that had beaten him. Months later he would realize that it could have been the work of any of those whom he'd reminded of how they'd praised Stalin or those who knew that he had something to remind them of. It took him three weeks to get out of bed. He was unsure on his feet, and his face didn't resemble the face he'd had before. The problem wasn't so much the scars but how much his expression had changed. In place of a cheerful and youthful thirty-year-old who could pass as a high school senior to girls in Metković and Mostar, the mirror showed a middle-aged man with cloudy and expressionless eyes, a high forehead, and a flattened nose. The only living things left on that head were two rather floppy ears. But not even these could be funny to anyone any more.

But Luka had been frightened to death by something else. In the mirror he saw the face of his oldest brother, Bepo, who'd gone crazy after returning from the war and died in Sarajevo's Jagomir sanatorium. Bepo had never resembled him. People said that Bepo, compared to his brothers and Regina, seemed not to have come from the same father and mother. Luka thought that maybe this was a sign that he would meet the same end if he remained there, in that rotten city and crazy country.

So he decided to flee Yugoslavia. He wouldn't request a passport because he would never get one, and if he did, he would be suspect. Rather, he would flee like one fled across state borders, along with wolves and bears, robbers, crimi-

nals, industrialists, and prostitutes, degenerates who fled justice and the same
degenerates who were convinced that they were following capital. It didn't matter with whom they grouped him because as soon as you emigrated, you loaded
your head with the sins of all those who'd done the same thing any time, anywhere.

For a month he collected his strength and money. The square was amazed
at how serious Luka had become. And he was better off that way because you
couldn't live from revelry alone! One should think hard about life; wine doesn't
like being stirred up, but one should rack one's brains, or so the retirees said
as they strolled along Porporela beach. Through some harbor prostitutes Luka
met an American sailor named Oliver Reed. He never forgot his name, and
that sailor offered him a job that consisted of the following: he would take three
packages that he had on his ship to Jablanica and give them to a man there.
That man would give Luka money that he would give to Reed, and that was
the whole job!

"What's in the packages?" he asked the American.

"That's not your problem," he told him.

"Fine; if it's not my problem, then no job," Luka said in a conciliatory tone,
thinking more about how to get his hand up Renata's skirt—she was the youngest and most exclusive prostitute—while she squealed and moved away from
him bit by bit.

"The pay is three thousand dollars," Oliver said, knowing that Luka had
never seen that much money in all his life. After the war three thousand dollars
could buy everything that the state still hadn't nationalized—houses, vineyards,
fields—and you would still have some left over.

"I'm not in a position to agree to do that. And I don't know what the situation would have to be for me to agree to your offer," he said. And since he hadn't
succeeded in getting his hand between Renata's legs, he grabbed her by the tit,
whereupon she slapped him.

"Boy, that costs money; watch out!" the American said, laughing. "Look, I
can offer you four thousand, but that's my last offer."

Luka looked at him in disbelief: "Four thousand dollars! I'm in even less of
a position to put my head on the block for four thousand. Tell me what's in the
boxes, and we can make a deal. But, you know, if it's weapons or propaganda
materials, count me out."

No matter how indifferent he was toward Tito and the party, Luka had no intention of passing flyers and guns to some Chetniks or Ustashas just because the
Americans thought they'd fucked up by helping out the partisans. Moreover, he
didn't even believe that they'd fucked up. Or at least they hadn't fucked us up

because if someone else had come along instead of the communists in 1945, it wouldn't be people that were missing but whole nationalities, and who knows when the war would have ended.

"It's not guns or propaganda," the American said; "it's medicine, penicillin, so children won't die from the most common colds, which the communists will use for their own propaganda purposes." Oliver turned serious before he mentioned the communists.

"And that's why you decided to smuggle penicillin. I have to tell you that you're a lunatic. But fine, okay, I agree! I'll take that to Jablanica and take your four thousand dollars." But Luka's extended hand hung in the air.

"Three thousand, because I told you what you're carrying," said the American.

"Forget it!" said Luka and got up, offended and resolved not even to agree to four thousand now. Reed dragged him around the square for a while, refusing to let him go, telling him that in San Pedro he had a wife and sick child and had to do what he was doing.

"Then take your penicillin and give it to *him!*"

Reed asked him if he didn't feel sorry for the people he could save and whether he'd thought about what he could do in life with four thousand dollars. He said he'd told him three thousand because he thought that people in Yugoslavia loved to haggle, and now he was apologizing and begging him on his knees to accept the job.

While Luka was on his way to Trebinje and farther on to Mostar and Jablanica, driving a van borrowed from the Dupin swimming club, a riddled piece of Italian junk captured in the war, two things weren't clear to him and he tried feverishly to figure them out. First, why had the sailor picked him of all people for this job? Second, what made him think that he was going to bring him the money when he could drive off in any direction with all the money in his pocket and let the American eat his dust?

There were no checkpoints along the way to stop him. The roads were empty. All around were burned villages and a bridge that Tito had blown up to save the wounded rested peacefully in the green waters of the Neretva. Close-cropped Bosnian children tumbled around in the dust; small, stubby horses pulled beams out of a ditch while a peasant in an army blouse lashed them savagely with a whip; a butcher led two lambs to slaughter.

Women dressed in shalwars and wearing kerchiefs around their heads stood with folded arms, watching the van pass in the belief that it was a sign that something was being done so that things would be better for them all and that if not people, then dear Allah would provide food and drink for this grateful and beautiful little country. The van connected two distant places that they had never been to, but they believed that in those places everything important was being decided and thus that people who covered such distances were important too. In those months, angels of all three faiths raced every sunny day from one horizon to the other.

In Jablanica at the prearranged location—in the Edhem Pivac café—he was awaited by a very fat young man who wore a good-natured expression on his face and had extraordinarily pretty eyes, the kind that seem like puppy's eyes and you believe them even when they lie to you. He said his name was Orhan Velić, but Luka didn't put any stock in that, just to be on the safe side. They exchanged the goods behind the café. Orhan checked the contents of the boxes, and Luka counted up the ten thousand dollars.

"Why are you doing this?" Luka couldn't help asking as they parted.

Orhan laughed and said, "If I told you it's because I'm a good person, would you believe me?" He turned around and waddled away along a row of poplars, on which black and green death notices were pinned, one next to another.

Luka stood glued to the spot, watching him until he disappeared between two poplars. He remembered the man with the dog's eyes later, on the day of his great death-bed joy. "If he'd been a dog, he'd certainly have succeeded in life. As he was a man, they certainly beat him like a dog," he said as Regina, Dijana, and the nurse Patricia, who didn't even know Croatian, split their sides laughing. Then, in the spring of 1969, Luka Sikirić, settling his accounts, thought that he had only once been at a loss in life. People laughed even when he said something serious or sad. But he wasn't sorry, and he laughed along with them, over the unknown grave of the pretty-eyed Orhan Velić.

As Luka gave him his six thousand dollars, the American jumped for joy and started hugging and kissing him. Luka couldn't understand any of this. And it's better that he didn't because in Jablanica he'd given Velić phony penicillin that the Sarajevo underground bought up, after Reed's deal with Albanians had fallen through at the last moment and after which he could choose either to throw the boxes into the sea or attempt something that had little chance of success. First, to find someone who would deliver the phony penicillin to Orhan Velić, which from his position on a moored American ship seemed impossible, and then to make sure that Orhan gave the money to the courier instead of killing him because if he'd killed him, no one would have come after him for it, and he'd have had ten thousand dollars that he could have then passed on to his own people. And finally, the guy that Velić gave the money to had to be honest enough to bring it back to him. When he'd offered Luka three and then four thousand dollars as a fee, he was already sure that his deal was ruined. He tried it with him in the crazy belief of pioneers in the Wild West who didn't quit as long as there was even a glimmer of hope for success. It was true that Oliver Reed wasn't risking anything, apart from the life of an unknown man whom fate had determined would pay someone else's bill.

And so the next winter people who'd been treated with phony penicillin died throughout Bosnia, hoping until the end that they would get better because they were taking American medicine. Maybe they would have lived if it hadn't been for Luka Sikirić, just as Luka might not have survived if Orhan Velić hadn't thought he was a nice guy. Luka didn't look like a smuggler or a criminal at all to him—it was obvious he liked the way Luka looked.

On the night before his escape to Italy, Luka Sikirić assembled all the harbor prostitutes in the abandoned shipyard. There was eating and drinking until dawn; whether anything else went on is hard to say, but it's unlikely that it did. Luka was the only man among the thirty of them and wasn't in good repute with women. Once a year he would lie on one to see whether anything had changed, or he would slip his hand under the skirt of one of them in front of other men to show how good he was with the prostitutes. And that was all. When they parted, he gave each of them enough money so they wouldn't have to do anything for a month except live like queens, and then he left. Maybe everyone else would have thought that Luka Sikirić was crazy, but the prostitutes, to the very last one, were sure that he was an angel. Sixteen years later every one of them who was still alive came to his funeral. Younger ones came too because of those good old days that they had never experienced. It was comforting to know that there were such days once and that people and angels existed that gave prostitutes money, smoked and drank with them, without asking for anything in return.

At seven in the morning Luka came by drunk to say good-bye to Regina and Dijana. The little girl had just gotten out of bed and was getting ready for school, and his sister was sitting beside the stove and shelling beans.

"I'm going, and we might never see each other again," he said.

"Don't talk shit while you're drunk!" Regina responded calmly.

He lifted Dijana up into the air. "Dijana, sweetheart . . . ," he said but didn't know what else to say. "Don't give up, sweetie!" he said, left a thousand dollars on the table, and left.

He didn't say "farewell" or "good-bye," and Regina sighed: that damned brandy would kill him. Only when she was done with the beans and got up did she see the money. She nearly fainted; she knew well how much a thousand dollars was worth. Dear departed Ivo wouldn't have earned that much in six months of voyaging. She was seized with panic. She ran outside to look for her brother, but she was smart enough not to tell anyone about the American money because if she had, Luka would have been arrested before he reached Gorica. "He's gone off to hang himself, woe to me, mama!" she cried, running around the yard, and raised the neighbors to search for him. They looked into each attic, searched for him in hidden inlets and parks, and when he didn't turn up for two days, they reported his disappearance to the police.

A month later a postcard arrived from Milan that read: "I'm well and healthy. I don't talk shit while I'm drunk. And I won't give up. Yours, Stijepo Bobek!"

He was afraid that they would be accused of some misdeeds if he signed his name, and so he put the name of a popular soccer player, one of the members of the team that had beaten the Russians at the Olympics in Finland. He knew that both of them would know who had written them and would be glad to read what he'd written. In a few months he'd spent the money he still had on Milanese hotels and socializing with the strange people whom misfortune had brought there from all corners of the earth. There were Russian dukes and professors of mathematics, who in 1918 had come in coats into which hundreds of ducats had been sewn, with pockets full of diamonds, and with a sorrow that spent all their wealth in a minute, so that they were reduced to begging and rummaging through garbage bins in the area. There were renegade members of the Comintern, who in '30-something had managed to save their skins from Stalin and had already been hiding there for twenty years either from Mussolini, the Italian partisans and communists, or from themselves because apart from the revolution they had no other work. In Milan there were gentlemen from Zagreb and Belgrade who'd fled in 1941 from the Germans, Nedić's men, the Ustashas, or the mobilizations, or in 1945 from the communists and their lust for revenge. There were Jews of every kind: German Jews, Polish Jews, Zagreb Jews, Hungarian Jews, Romanian Jews, and those happy-go-lucky ones—the Bosnian Jews, who were constantly pulling someone's leg, telling vulgar jokes and anecdotes. But when they gathered among themselves in a corner of the railway station or in the barracks for collective accommodation, they spoke sadly in a strange language that was and wasn't Spanish and would then break into a melancholy Bosnian song that was nice to listen to but made you lose your will to live. There was also a Chetnik rabble in Milan that moved among two or three taverns owned by Italians with surnames ending in -*ić*, where they blathered on about international politics and the intentions of King Peter—"a thug and not a king, the fucking bastard!" They fell into bouts of depression because they realized that Peter didn't have anything in mind and would drink themselves blind drunk and shout so loudly that the sky over Italy would shake, and the police would draw a wide berth around them. But Luka would sit with them too, treat them to drinks, and try to explain to them in a roundabout way that they were all brothers because they spoke the same language, to which they would nod in agreement. But after that he would tell them that the Bosnian Muslims were their brothers and even the communists too.

"You're a good person but also a complete idiot," they would say and look at him with pity in their eyes, convinced that one day he would pay with his head for telling people things they didn't want to hear. What he said sounded good in church or on one's deathbed but couldn't be true in real life. If such truths existed, the whole world would have burned in hell after the last war.

There were also poor Ustashas in Milan. They hurried along the facades as if they'd sold their own shadows and were ashamed that people might notice. They had the eyes of wild deer, and all of them introduced themselves as engineers, old Zagreb nobility, or Travnik beys. But they weren't any of those. They needed something to hold on to and for which the world would take pity on them. But they realized bitterly that no one would take pity on them of all people because there were no sins that were greater and more despicable than theirs. No matter how much he'd seen who the Ustashas were and what they'd done in and around Dubrovnik during the war, Luka couldn't believe that these men were the same people. "The eyes of a swine or a man who hunted Serbs and Jews to slake his thirst for blood, those eyes never turn into the eyes of a doe," he thought and offered them help. But they fled, convinced that he was a provocateur, an agent of the secret police, that he would blow out their brains on the spot or cram them into trucks and take them to Yugoslavia, where he would sic Serbian and Jewish dogs on them. In Milan there were two or three Catholic priests, Croats who'd been sent from Rome, who gathered up those big-eyed ne'er-do-wells, hid them in monasteries, and provided them with papers for countries across the ocean. Luka even tried to make contact with them. They would smile at him condescendingly and in their nasal bishops' tones bless the moment that Luka would move on and leave them in peace.

There were people of all kinds in Milan in 1953. If anyone had filmed it, it would have been one of the sadder films. So many people who had nothing except what they carried in their hearts and heads and had no place to call their own.

It wasn't until Luka spent his last dollar that he felt that he belonged to the world of those people, and he began to be wearied by the thought that he was far away from the place he called home. He listened to nostalgic stories of cities and homelands—Chełmno, Kraków, Vukovar, Prague, Budapest, Warsaw, Chernopol'ye, Bitola, Zagreb, Belgrade, Split, Sarajevo, Skoplje, Koprivnica, Subotica, Travnik, Vienna, Banja Luka, Odessa, Mostar, Talinn, Bucharest, and Dubrovnik. He listened to one man's lament for his city and was surprised to find that he didn't feel sorrow. That man, whose name was Moritz Ferrara, had fled Dubrovnik in 1943 to save his skin from his neighbors, to whom state law gave the opportunity to consider everything that had been his to be theirs, including his life. Ten years later Moritz was ready to forgive them for everything if only they would let him come back and act as if nothing had happened. But he knew it wasn't possible because he wasn't the one who was given the right to forgive; rather his neighbors were supposed to forgive him because he'd put them in the difficult situation of having to persecute him, only for world history to be shaken up later. New laws were passed that declared the old ones to be criminal, and those who'd carried them out — that is to say, Moritz's neighbors — to be criminals. As if those people had ever made any kind of laws or opposed them. If it hadn't been for him, they wouldn't have been living in fear then, and even if they forgave him for everything else, they couldn't forgive him for that fear. Moritz Ferrara would die from an illness that had no name but could be most accurately described as a tumor of the soul. His homeland would grow inside of him, until it sucked in all his vital fluids, softened his bones, and killed him in the end, either in Milan or in some other city.

Luka didn't believe that he would ever come down with that illness. His reasons for leaving were almost inconsequential in comparison to those of Moritz Ferrara. He was simply different from those among whom he'd lived, and he couldn't change, or he arrogantly thought that he might be bypassed by the stupidity that had made blood flow in rivers and on account of which everyone felt guilty afterward.

Thus, something existed that was more important for him than his homeland, so it was logical that he never fell ill because of it. Maybe he wouldn't have even fallen ill or the illness would have been delayed longer if he hadn't been so spendthrift or if he'd had more American dollars. But on the day when he first thought that he should save his money for later instead of feeding a bunch of washouts in the first tavern he entered, Luka was close to the realization that Milan wasn't a place where he wanted to spend the rest of his life. And when he held the first lira that he'd earned in his hand, after he'd had a role as an extra in a film about a pauper who ran after the rays of the sun and flew off into the sky in the end, he could already understand the endless sorrow of Moritz Ferrara and the railway-station history of the Jewish simpletons from Chełmno and the reasons why the Russian aristocrats spent all their ducats and diamonds instead of investing them in something and living the same life they'd lived in Moscow and Petrograd. As soon as you can't go back to where you came from, you begin the life in railway lobbies; everything is temporary and you have no reason to plan anything or start anything anew because you're waiting for your train, and nothing can be important besides waiting and chatting with others who are waiting. That train will never come, as everyone who has ever waited for it knows, but you don't think about that until you spend your last ducat, diamond, and dollar.

After his first year in Milan, when he was already living the life of a European railway bum and singing the sad love songs of his homeland, Luka decided to move to Trieste. They tried to dissuade him and warned him that that city was half in Yugoslavia and was teeming with Tito's agents. Abductions and murders were common, and the Italians and Americans were fairly indifferent to them. It might happen that he would fall asleep in Trieste and wake up in the Zenica prison. And it wasn't likely that he would find work in Trieste. The locals there lived badly. And there were many Istrians who had the right to live there and didn't look kindly on Yugoslav emigrants if they were Slavs . . .

But nothing could dissuade him. Or he was a little attracted by what they were trying to frighten him with. Trieste was closer. It didn't matter what it was closer to, but it was closer and by virtue of this fact it was more his. He went there with an unmuddled feeling that life could and had to be happiness, cheer, and idleness and that only obscurantists, those who were hard on themselves and those around them, seriously planned every step they took and were deathly afraid of not having anything to live on. It was only natural that they ended up destitute and died of hunger. If someone never thought of poverty, it was most likely that they wouldn't become poor—Luka Sikirić was convinced of this, and in his case it turned out to be true.

On his very first day in Trieste he met both the State Security Service agents and those who were hiding from them. The Yugoslav spies, secret agents, and cutthroats drank in one bar, seemingly incognito, and in another, a few hundred meters away, there were gatherings, just as incognito, of deserters, losers, tax officials, distrainers of defunct states, and the commanders of Quisling armies, but most of all there were those who simply bet on the wrong side. This they'd done too publicly, so after losing in the betting office of history, they took to their heels. Those in the first bar spoke about those in the second as if they were a gang that needed to be taken out, while those in the second bar spoke about those in the first as if they were a gang that would be taken out by the English, Americans, and the free world as soon as they pulled themselves together and realized that Tito had screwed them over in 1945. The phrase "the free world" was used by those who were not free, more as the name and surname of a fairy tale hero than as a political label or a literary metaphor. When they said "the free world," it seemed as if those people saw clearly the shape of the nose, the eye color, and the high brow of its imaginary prince.

None of them, neither the pursuers nor the pursued, were in any particular hurry. The bosses of the spies and agents had evidently given them no deadlines for finishing all their work, and they would rather drag out these jobs than get new ones, while their victims continued to believe that it was a matter of days until the Allies would take out Tito and the communists and they would return home. True, something always happened to delay American action in Yugoslavia. At first the tensions with the Russians were too great because Harry Truman wasn't as smart as his predecessor. Then there was the unfortunate war in Korea that prevented them from moving on Yugoslavia. And Stalin's death didn't come at the best time either . . .

Luka started dropping in at both bars right away. He told everyone who he was and where he'd come from and why he'd fled Yugoslavia. And everyone, of course, was sure that he was lying. A quiet suspicion arose among the agents that he was actually a high-ranking officer and that he'd been sent from Belgrade to check up on them, whereas the fugitives were sure that Luka was a secret policeman and that he'd been sent from the other bar to infiltrate them and acquire as much reliable information as possible. However, both sides were mystified about why he didn't ever ask any questions or start political discussions but told jokes, fooled around, pulled people's legs, and hid corkscrews from waiters.

"He's a fucking dope!" said Raško Pribojac a.k.a. Šajkača, the main figure in the agents' bar.

"He's not stupid, but he's not all there either," remarked Husref-beg Urumlić, the clearest thinker among the fugitives, who had been a communist before the war and an Ustasha official in Janja during the war.

"Should we give him a scare?" asked Lojze Bohinjc, the youngest and most ambitious among the spies.

"I'd like to knock some sense into him—beat on his kidneys, toss him into a canal, and then see how he recovers!" said Rudolf Zovko, the only Ustasha officer in the fugitives' bar.

"Let the idiot be," said Šajkača dismissively.

"God protects idiots," said Husref-beg.

But Luka Sikirić realized soon enough that no one in the two bars laughed or had any fun and that it was impossible to get those people to warm up or at least get them to say something about something that didn't have anything to do with the war and politics. He saw that the time he spent among them only depressed him and that he shared nothing with them apart from the language they spoke. Everything else was all too familiar to him but odd and hateful as only your own world can be hateful and odd. And so he quit going to the agents' and the fugitives' bars, without anyone even noticing that he wasn't there.

He found a job selling cheese in the city market. He worked for an old peasant, a Slovene by origin, who had a goat farm in the Italian Karst and was on the verge of financial ruin because middlemen were swindling him, taking cheese, and never showing their faces again. And he was a strange character himself, one of those highlanders who become distrustful and paranoid after years of living alone and are suspicious if they see someone on the neighboring hill, let alone the market middlemen.

"You've got a nice watch. How old is it?" he asked Luka after two hours of sizing him up, and Luka decided he wanted to leave and looked at his watch to find a pretext for being in a hurry.

"About a hundred years old. Maybe even more," he answered.

"Is it worth a lot?" the peasant asked, his interest growing.

"I don't know. It's valuable to me because it was my grandfather's," Luka said.

"Did you love your grandfather?" the old man asked, continuing to pester him.

Luka wasn't sure what he wanted. He started fidgeting and getting nervous. "I loved him. Why would I keep the watch if I didn't? I'd have sold it by now."

The peasant lit up, jumped from his chair, and extended his hand. Luka took it, still sitting, very confused in his soul.

"We've got a deal," shouted the peasant, "I'll give you cheese, and you give me the watch as security that you won't cheat me! I'll give it back to you when you bring me the money from the cheese."

Luka took out the watch without a word and held it out to the peasant. He didn't do it because he was dead set on getting this job. He liked the story; he would certainly tell it to someone later in life. Besides, it would have been stupid to disappoint the old man, who was so happy about his perfect idea.

The job selling cheese was, to tell the truth, the first job that Luka had had in his life. But instead of being a miserable burden to him, it turned out that his daily trip to the market wasn't any different than going to a café, except that the people who came to the market were more interesting.

The sellers came to the market at five in the morning, to occupy the counters and sell their goods as soon as possible, but Luka came at nine, unfolded a camping table, stacked as many cheeses as would fit on it, and then began his show. Either he would shout out the names of all the cheeses he'd ever heard of, or he would tell jokes and funny stories in Croatian about famous generals and dictators, and the old Italian ladies would stop and look at him as at the ninth wonder of the world.

"And Napoleon, my good people, Napoleon couldn't eat or drink very much. He had a bad stomach or had a nervous disorder or God hadn't given him enough enzymes and acid to digest food without problems. The real truth of history hasn't been written down, but as there are no living witnesses, it's simplest to say that Napoleon never ate lunch or dinner like ordinary people. Instead of eating, he conquered the world. Instead of drinking, he waged war. So was Napoleon, my good people, a great man? Well, missus, you tell me: Would you rather have your husband grab a rifle and shoot up the street, kill all the neighbors, and go on a war of conquest instead of lunching on those delicious mackerels you bought?"

The lady smiled, raised her eyebrows, and shrugged her shoulders. Maybe because she didn't understand him, though the majority of people in Trieste knew Slovene or Croatian, or maybe because one wasn't supposed to answer such questions so as not to take time away from the continuation of the story.

"Of course you wouldn't! You'll fry him up some mackerels, whip up a marinade for him, feed him and give him something to drink, and then you'll both lie down for a little while after lunch, listen to the gulls wrangle over fish heads, smell the pines, and think about how nice life is. But it wasn't nice for Napoleon! Napoleon was unhappy. He couldn't eat or drink, and everything life had given him could be measured in millions of decares of other people's land and the millions of lives of his soldiers. Napoleon wasn't a great man!" he yelled as he finished with his index finger raised high. He held it in the air for a few moments, and then in a softer and calmer tone he would say, "My good people, this cheese is excellent; I eat it every evening, and I'm still not tired of it; please buy some!"

The people who had gathered around would buy Luka's cheese as if bewitched, and by around ten everything was sold out. Soon it started happening that some of the people wouldn't be able to get their cheese, and so he would have to apologize to the women and cheer them up with new stories. He already spoke Italian like a native, but he would always tell his culinary jokes and stories about generals and dictators in Croatian. It seemed more suited to him: not every language is suited to every foolishness.

After he finished work at the market, he went to the old man and gave him the money. He would pull out the watch from a wooden box and put it in front of Luka, go off to get more baskets full of cheeses, and when Luka took them, the old man would take the watch back, lock it up in the box, and always repeat the same thing: "You give me liras, I give you the watch!"

They'd already been working together like this for a year, the herd of goats had doubled in size, and the old man had found five more workers for the farm so he could produce as much cheese as Luka needed, but he would always put the watch back in the box. There was nothing bad about this, or Luka couldn't see anything bad about it. It was funny and in some way special, as children's stories are special in which crazy kings, hermits, and elves do things that no one in the world can understand but which in the end save the world.

"Do you really still not trust me?" he asked the old man after he'd rented a van because the demand for his cheese had become too great for Luka to carry it in baskets.

The old man blushed, lowered his gaze, and started scratching a splinter off the table, like a pupil that didn't know an answer.

"It doesn't matter, it really doesn't matter!" Luka said, sorry that he'd made the old man feel awkward.

"I trust you. And I did after the first time when you didn't cheat me. I wanted to give you the watch back, but then I thought that something would take a bad turn if I gave it back. I didn't think you would cheat me but that something else would happen: there would be an epidemic, the whole herd would die, lightning would strike, my heart would give out. And that's how it was every time. I'd give you the watch back; I feel awful about taking it; I could die of shame, but the more I feel ashamed, the more I fear that something bad might happen."

And so the watch stayed with the old man. Luka didn't take it back even after the man opened his first shop in Trieste and started selling cheeses from all over Italy and France, not even after he opened shops like it in Bologna and Milan. Among the most famed cheeses of Europe, a place of honor was always reserved for the goat cheese from Kras, "The Cheese with a Story." Everyone who bought it received a booklet of Luka's tales, which had been compiled by a local journalist. The booklet told about the evils inflicted on the world by people who didn't enjoy food.

Luka Sikirić acquired a great amount of money and again lived the life of someone who didn't have to do anything, but at least once a week he went to Kras. The old man placed the watch on the table, Luka got out the money, the maid brought two baskets with cheese, and everything was supposed to be like that first time. But there was nevertheless a feeling that this was a game that lengthens your life and reminds you of good times. People become aware of the beauty of such times only after they pass.

"All of this is killing me," he complained to the old man, who said nothing and felt as he had when the middlemen had swindled him, taking his cheese and vanishing, except that he no longer had anyone to be angry at, nor could anyone understand where the deceit was and what it was that tormented these two men, who, doing only what they'd wanted in life, had reached the end. The end didn't make them happy.

In the summer of 1968 the old man turned eighty-five, and Luka Sikirić

was told in a Paris cancer clinic that he had three months to live. He strolled
down streets where children played war. They turned over cars, smashed display windows, pulled granite cobblestones from the street, and hurled them at
the police, shouting their revolutionary slogans. The policemen shot tear gas
at them and swung their batons, and many of them ended up in the hospital
with bloody heads. They were forbidden from shooting at the children. The
parents, against whom the revolution was started, forbade it. The stupid cops'
brains couldn't comprehend this as the nurses tended to their wounds, and not
even the most intelligent people would have comprehended this were it not for
books, movies, and especially philosophical treatises that would turn 1968 into
a significant historical event, more important than all the wars fought in French
colonial Africa and maybe more important than the war in Vietnam, in which
thousands and millions, mainly nameless slant-eyed primates, were being killed
in the name of the same ideals against which the children of Europe had risen
up. No answer would ever be given to the question of how a revolution, in which
the counterrevolutionaries were not allowed to shoot, could be such an important historical event, but its meaning would finally be known in ten or fifteen
years, when the children in the streets of Paris had grown up into replicas of
their fathers.

As in an educational documentary film, in which sailors from Kronstadt
moved past, the Aurora and Winter Palace were stormed, Rosa and Karl gave
fiery oratories and fled in the face of enraged veterans of 1914, Mao called on
his fighters to go on the Long March, the Khmer Rouge turned temples into
schools in which the pupils taught the teachers, Stalin said "No" to Tito and
Tito said "No" to Stalin, and it wasn't Maxim Gorky but an ugly little man
with spectacles who was leading the children. The difference between him
and Gorky was actually the difference between a game and a real revolution.
Gorky's revolution had been bloody and powerful, and it was no wonder that
people had fallen in love with Maxim's mustache and his gray, dull novellas,
but the game was ugly and miserable because not even the children, no matter
how carried away and furious they were, had counted on their little street party
to change the world. They had only wanted to live out a few romantic moments
that had been denied to them because they'd been born too late. And in the
West, which had never had the Red October Revolution! That was a time of
longing for the East, both European and Asian, for a history that was so attractive when it happened to others, and even more attractive if it was turned into a
performance and games in the street.

As Luka watched them rush at De Gaulle's cops and challenge the operatic
power of a wise old general, he knew that they would come home sweaty and

dazed from tear gas and that when they grew up, they would remember with fondness the day when the streets of Paris looked like an advanced Leninist kindergarten. That was probably the most important difference between a revolution and a party with a revolutionary theme. Whereas no one at all remembers a revolution with warmth in their hearts, not even those who never renounced it, not even that Slovene who lost his arm in a Red Army assault, revolutionary parties are remembered as the most beautiful moments in human history.

In the end, war memorials aren't worth anything, whereas memorials of 1968 and invitations to the red party can later be shown to one's grandchildren, who then think how their grandfathers have turned into such conservative monsters in the meantime.

On the train to Trieste he tried to make peace with the thought of the coming end. Instead of despair and mortal fear, which someone else in his position might have felt, Luka was tormented only by disbelief. No matter how hard he tried to convince himself that he was dying, something inside him said that it wasn't possible. Death is a cinematic illusion in which people either believe or don't believe, except you don't have to go to the movies if you don't believe that those moving pictures are life and you'll die one way or another. Luka wanted some awareness of it because he wasn't a squid or a moth! But it simply didn't come. The idea of nonexistence ran contrary to common sense. The scenes that passed along the railway track, the smells of the people who got on and off at the stations, their voices and exclamations, the way they looked at him without sorrow or fear, unconcerned with whether they would ever see him again—all this couldn't disappear just like that, in three months, ninety days, two thousand hours. If he was there and so present and himself a part of that presence, no less alive than the handle on the door of the compartment, the flies on the dirty blue curtain, the Italian conductor who asked him how he managed to get out of Paris alive, the old leather conductor's pouch that the man had worn during the reign of Mussolini—he or his colleague who was long retired, in retirement, or in the Trieste cemetery among merchants and sea captains.

Luka didn't want to be buried there, just one more foreigner whose unknown fate would be the subject of pity for pairs of imaginative young lovers. He would be buried in his city, in a cemetery full of familiar faces, where someone might be your relative or enemy, and where nothing is indifferent to anything else. It was nice and soothing to live on the other side of the world, or at least a thousand miles away from his hometown, but being buried in a foreign land was a misfortune. Every man should be buried where he was born or where he learned to speak and whence he decided to leave. As soon as he felt that the end was near, he would make arrangements to be taken back across the border, even if he had to pay the customs officials and the police, and to be driven to his sister's place so that he could await what he couldn't believe in and with which it was actually easy to reconcile himself.

Instead of three months, which was what they promised him, he lived for more than a year. Without great suffering or pain, growing thinner from day to day and frightening others more than himself, Luka kept on going, along with his daily rituals. And he continued going to the old man in Kras once a week, taking out the money, looking at the watch, and carrying off two baskets of cheese. Up until the day when he could no longer lift them.

"Franc, I think the time has come for you to give me back my watch," he said. The old man burst into sobs, begged him not to go, to stay a little longer, told him that it was bad weather and the sirocco was blowing. And as soon as the sirocco starts blowing, people lose their strength and it doesn't matter how old they are or what they are sick with. Luka tried to console him, tried to get him to laugh, but it didn't help—what had held together for eighty-five years fell apart before his very eyes in a matter of minutes. There was no longer the coarseness of which the peasant had been so proud because it kept him from hunger, people, and wars as he had moved his goats between two front lines, not yielding even in 1916, when the children of two feuding kings died in the battles of the River Soča and Mt. Meletta, and when he had to keep his animals from grazing on bloody grass and getting used to the taste of human flesh, because if they had, they would then only have eaten such grass, and he wouldn't have been able to keep them from a wicked habit, one that turned monkeys into humans—a taste for blood that would make a beast of any living creature. He realized then that the only creatures that didn't feed on flesh and blood were those that chance had kept from ever picking up the scent. But if the wars continued and if a few other peoples bled to death in little mountain streams, then there would no longer be any creatures that grazed on leaves and grass; sheep would slaughter and be slaughtered, and no one would make cheese from their milk. A man has to be hard and tough if he's not to lose his mind amid dead regiments and divisions and devour himself along with his goats that feed on the corpses of those who believed in their kings.

He didn't leave Kras, not even during the most heated battles in the First World War. He didn't think of leaving thirty years later, when it wasn't clear where the border between Italy and Tito's state would run and people tried to frighten him with the idea that the communists would take away his goats. What would the communists do with his goats? Attack Berlin and Budapest, hunt down the bourgeoisie, and demolish churches? Goats were no use for such things, nor were goatherds. So it didn't matter where the border ran and what colors would be on his flag. Neither the one king nor the other was to be believed, and their jobs mattered to men only in time of war, and he had to keep an eye on his goats so they wouldn't eat leaves soiled with human brains or bloodstained grass.

Such was the old man's belief, and since it differed from what others believed in, he kept people at arm's length. Up until that funny Dalmatian came along, took his cheese, left his watch as security, and created a bond between them forever. He sold cheese in a way that no one had ever used to sell anything and made up things that weren't in cheese, or maybe they were, but no one had known about them before. Cheese probably isn't just cheese, the old man thought, and was happy that there was something outside the world of goats that one should fight for. If it hadn't been for Luka Sikirić, he would never have arrived at that himself. The fact that he now wanted to take his watch and disappear forever hit the old man harder than if some great, unreal thunderbolt struck and killed all of his one thousand two hundred goats in an instant. The idea of his own death seemed much easier for him to take. You can't be such a softy that you wail about the fact that you'll be gone.

In the end Luka had to leave his watch with the old man and promise that he would come to see him again. This lie wasn't hard for him to tell. The old man had bewildered and frightened him because there was no way Luka could get him to laugh, fool what was left of the child in him, and lead him across the river to see that the other side was also just a riverbank and that one shouldn't get upset when it's time to go. As they parted, the old man came out of his house, which he hadn't ever done before because he would start going about his work as soon as he locked the box. He waved from the stone doorstep until Luka's car disappeared around the corner.

The same day Luka planned out his last journey. He telephoned the Yugoslav ambassador in Rome to inquire about his status. Two hours later the ambassador informed him that he wasn't wanted, nor were there any special reasons why he should be afraid to return home. He even offered him a Yugoslav passport to assure him that he was not the subject of any proceedings in the country.

"A lot has changed in the last fifteen years," the ambassador said. Luka didn't answer him, but he would have liked to tell him that things change in fifteen days, let alone fifteen years, and there was no country and embassy at any time that hadn't always said that things were now better, that there was more freedom and the laws more reasonable than fifteen years before. The problem was only that freedom never seemed to increase or the laws to weaken enough for a man not to have to inquire if he was still guilty of something before those from whom he'd fled.

Besides, Luka didn't completely believe the ambassador. He decided to pay
off the customs officials just in case, send some gift packages of cheese to Marshal Tito in Belgrade and a wheel of parmesan the size of a tractor tire both to
the municipality of Dubrovnik and the city commission. If they all accepted
their cheese, that would be a sign that they were really not unhappy with him,
he thought naïvely, and waited for days for the arrival of the signed delivery
slips showing that the gifts had been received. And they arrived two days after
he could no longer get out of bed. He traveled in an ambulance, entertaining
nurse Patricia, carefree, happy, and truly convinced that he'd bought his freedom with the cheese. The customs officers wouldn't accept any money, nor did
they understand why he was offering any, but they held him up for hours at the
border and tried to check which service these travelers had gotten into trouble
with and were now trying to buy their way past the customs officials. But the
driver, Patricia, and the Italian citizen Luka Sikirić were all as innocent as newborn babies. Up until the collapse of the Yugoslav government, at the Opićina
border crossing generations of customs officials passed on the story of some ill
man who had offered a large sum of money to enter Yugoslavia although his
papers were valid and he wasn't wanted by any police force in this world. Maybe
even today some grandpa tells his grandchildren softly, so no one will hear him,
about what a country that was, that people even offered to pay gold for things
that it offered for free and that they were entitled to according to the law.

Luka died in his sleep, tired and happy because he'd spent a day with those
dear to him. Patricia didn't have to close his eyelids. She lowered his hand back
down on the pillow and pulled a piece of paper out of her pocket that he'd given
to her when they were starting out on their trip.

"If I die in the middle of the night, go ahead and go to my sister and wake her
up. She's a light sleeper, and she'll be awake as soon as you enter her room. If
that doesn't happen, that'll mean she's died before me, and our plan has come
to nothing. Well, since that's not likely, then you'll bow down to her and sing
O tu che in seno agli angeli. That was her favorite song, and she'll be touched
that I remembered. But don't be too serious. You can wave your arms about,
dance a little, so it's cheery. And it can't go on for too long, or she'll get angry and
chase you out. When it's over, lean down again and say, 'Luka's dead.' Tell her
just like that, not in Italian because she might act like she doesn't understand
you. C'mon, repeat after me: 'Luka's dead, Luka's dead!' Good, but I'll write it
down so you don't forget how to say it."

Before she went into Regina's room, she took a look at the piece of paper,
drew a breath, and started singing, loudly, as Luka had said. She didn't exactly
sound like Mario Lanza, but no one besides him has ever sung *O tu che in seno*

agli angeli properly, along with the crackling of a worn-out record album and at a tempo slightly accelerated at seventy eight revolutions per minute, in the spirit of the last era in which artists weren't people but puppets on the strings of the universe, and there wasn't the slightest difference among Mario Lanza, Enrico Caruso, Rudolf Valentino, and Charlie Chaplin. Luka Sikirić was Chaplin in the lives of those he had entertained and thus proved that when the angels of silent film and wind-up gramophones disappeared, they left the world without something that was more important than technological progress and the need for pictures to be more accurate than reality.

But in 1969 it was already too late to mourn for angels. Nurse Patricia sang their song as best she could, along with choreography that she'd seen in one of Fred Astaire's movies, which might not have been what Mario Lanza was trying to achieve, but it would have brought joy to anyone who treasures all the past and isn't concerned with the disparities among decades. Fred and Mario were equally removed from the twenty-three-year-old Patricia; she knew nothing about them except that they belonged to the world of her aunts and uncles, in which it was customary to stress one's every inclination with tears. They cried during television comedies; they cried as soon as they heard a song they liked on the radio; it was enough to say the name Verdi for the men and women in the family to take their handkerchiefs out of their pockets; they even cried if someone mentioned the name of a shoe polish that people had used thirty years before.

She'd never understood those tears or why people cried when they weren't unhappy or what that sorrow was that people enjoyed more than any kind of happiness. They were fretful and irritable, all those uncles and aunts, as soon as the conversation turned to something that was still alive and in existence and for which they would, or so Patricia thought, shed tears like that at some later date.

When Fanelli, the head doctor, had assembled his nurses and asked them who knew how to sing, and when three of them responded that they did, and when he then called them into his office for auditions, Patricia thought that the old guy had lost his mind, which was evidently a common occurrence in that generation. Like many of her aunts and uncles, he must have felt like summoning his youth with the singing, but as soon as he chose her, folded his hands, and said, "Wow, that's really beautiful!" she began to get seriously worried that he had some dishonorable intentions in all of this. But then he went on: "A patient of ours for some years now, Mr. Sikirić, otherwise a wonderful person, a cheese merchant, but what cheese it was! I've been all around France and Holland, and I know cheese; I can vouch that I've never seen such a selection of cheese anywhere. Well, Mr. Sikirić's carcinoma is in its terminal phase. I told him 'Luka, we're friends; I don't want to lie to you.' And he says, 'My dear Fanelli, is there a friendship in which no lies are told? — You only tell the truth to taxpayers and women you don't love!' Okay, I won't go on about that. You're young, you're not interested in that stuff, and it's not nice to tell about your personal secrets, though I'd like to. You know, Luka is a very witty man, but fine; that's not what this is about. Rather, he wants to die in his city, on the other side of the Adriatic, and he asked me to pick out a nurse who can sing well to accompany him on his trip. He didn't tell me why he needs a singer, but I have no doubt that it's something very good. You, Patricia, are ideal for this. You know your work, you're beautiful, and you sing well. This isn't just work but something more important than work. You'll see! You'll never forget Luka."

Patricia's knees almost gave out from fear. She believed that the last wish of a dying patient could only be something erotic in nature. He certainly wasn't interested in her only to burst into tears in the end, and if it weren't that, why would he want a pretty young singer? She didn't dare say "no" to Fanelli, but she was prepared to quit her job if the patient that she was accompanying crossed the line. Which line? Well, the one that she would draw.

For two days she thought about where that line should be, and the more she thought about it, the greater her confusion became. At first she decided firmly that she wouldn't allow the man to touch her. She would satisfy him in everything that didn't require touching him. Maybe he wanted her to perform some deathbed striptease to a dirty song. Was it okay to agree to that? Of course not. There was no difference between stripping for money and sex for money. So he could forget the striptease! It was amazing how lowlifes remained lowlifes in their final hour.

But what if she liked him? What if he was a lovable and precious guy, just the type she'd been dreaming of? What if he was the type that she would fall in love with if she met him in different circumstances and by a happier twist of fate? Why wouldn't she strip for someone like that? Because it was a matter of principles that you dared not abandon. Yes, but you regret having acted on such principles more often than you do if you've given them up. She decided that she would strip if it turned out that Luka was her type of man. But what if he wanted more than that? If he tried to get more than that, then he certainly wasn't her type. As a rule that was true, but rules were the same as principles. Those two words kind of had the same meaning but just sounded a little different to her, so if one could have regrets because of principles, one could also have regrets because of rules. In the end she decided to act depending on the situation, but with that her fear of meeting Luka Sikirić was not lessened. "Am I a whore now?" she wondered as she packed her suitcase.

After only half an hour of traveling together with that male skeleton, whose skin had an unhealthy reddish-gray hue and had become as thin as tracing paper from his illness, on whose face the only living things were his eyes and scars, whereas everything else on his body looked like an artificial corpse, Patricia could tell that he was just her type of man. He might have looked different, been less alive, with open, putrescent sores and macerated lesions; he could have stunk and had the head of a brontosaurus and wooden pegs instead of hands, but Luka would still have been the same, the one that she'd wanted, thinking that such men existed only in her imagination. Where else were there funny princes who found all the reasons for their happiness in their princesses and thought only of entertaining them?

She decided to agree to do anything Luka might want and was disappointed when she realized that she'd been chosen for something that was supposed to happen only after he was dead. This would pain her for years, and for years she would want someone to whom she could tell how she'd wanted to strip and sing in front of the man of her life when she'd met him in the last days of his. The man who didn't think that strange would be her husband. And there was no chance of her getting married to anyone who didn't understand her love story or thought that it was perverse, that she was led by dark desires. Patricia's desires were as innocent as Luka Sikirić had been innocent.

She sang his last wish as it grew light outside, as hung-over men hauled empty crates from one end of the market to the other, small wooden boats sailed out to sea, birds and cats awoke, and a woman in a nightgown curled up against the wall at the head of her bed, as if she were unsure whether she was dreaming. Tears streamed down her face even before Patricia said, "Luka's dead." Because she'd realized what had happened or because she too was like Patricia's aunts and uncles.

That was how Regina lost her last brother.

IX

"Comrade, when did your child die?" asked a bowlegged midget who was hurrying after Regina. He could have been sixty, but she wouldn't have been surprised if he'd been only thirty. Among lunatics and ne'er-do-wells, whom God endowed with the intelligence of a five-year-old, it wasn't always easy to tell who was how old. Their time flowed differently than it did for everyone else: for some of them it was quicker, for others it was slower, but never as it was for the people who considered themselves normal. That was the most obvious difference between the sane and insane. If not the only difference that was completely reliable.

"Comrade, what did your child die from?" the midget persisted, and as soon as she turned around to chase him off, he ran and hid behind a tree. He came back when she started walking again, keeping two steps behind her and asking another question: "Comrade, does your heart ache? You carried your child under your heart, and now it's empty there." She grabbed a rock and threw it at him to scare him. He jumped and squealed like a little dog when someone steps on its tail, though the rock missed him by three meters.

"Comrade, take me; I'll be a good child. No mother gave birth to me; I came from the war. Take me; I'm war booty," he said, offering himself.

Regina tried to ignore him. Fortunately the road to Jagomir was empty, and no one saw the woman in black and the bald little monkey chasing her, because an onlooker would have surely laughed, made some smart-aleck remark, or grabbed the midget and beaten him up, convinced that he was doing it to protect normal people from lunatics.

The midget gave up only when they arrived at the gate of the insane asylum, an old Austro-Hungarian building shaded by oak trees that had been planted long ago in the belief that the eyes of the insane would rest and calm down under their thick, green crowns, which in the meantime had turned into a jungle just as wild and unkempt as their souls.

"I'm not going in there. The people in there are crazy. You're crazy too!" he said, frightened and disappointed.

He'd probably already been inside, or maybe his family had threatened to send him to the insane asylum if he didn't behave.

On the grounds men in gray pajamas were standing or walking around slowly. Some wore tattered partisan overcoats over their pajamas. One of them had an officer's belt drawn tight around him; he was evidently proud of it because he tightened it as much as he could and waddled around like a goose.

When she went through the gate, all of them fixed their eyes on her. They didn't try to come closer; each of them watched her from where he was, wherever he happened to be when she came, no matter whether he was only five or fifty meters distant.

Those who were further away might have envied those who were closer but didn't try to get a better spot. Regina felt awkward in front of their hundred big, languid eyes. Especially because the eyes of her Bepo might be among them.

She'd come to Sarajevo at the request of Dr. Hoffman; he'd informed her that Bepo Sikirić had been refusing to eat for six days and might change his decision never to eat again if his sister came to see him. He hadn't seen her since December 1945, when he'd been transferred from the Tuzla barracks, first to the psychiatric ward of the local city hospital, and three weeks later to the Jagomir insane asylum in Sarajevo, the oldest clinic of its kind in Bosnia. It had been established during the reign of Franz Joseph, which was when Franz Hoffman had come as a young doctor from Vienna. Regina had never visited her brother because she was afraid of seeing him crazy. She shuddered at the thought of entering an insane asylum because she thought that in such a place she would go nuts herself. If any illness was contagious, it was losing your mind. It didn't matter that books said otherwise. The plague and cholera passed from body to body, just as pollen passed from plant to plant, if the wind and temperature were right and if a body's resistance had already been lowered and it was susceptible to viruses and bacteria. And insanity spread with the terrifying logic of the elements. Reason was weak in the face of all forms of insanity because reason was the exception and not the cosmic rule. The path to insanity was a return to the logic of cliffs and rocks, amoebae, brackens, and all life that wasn't human. She walked through the grounds certain that the plague was slowly overcoming her, but she had no choice. She couldn't just let Bepo die of hunger like that.

In front of the entrance there was a young man sitting on a stool wearing blue work overalls. He was sharpening pencils with a large hunting knife and putting them in a little metal box. When he saw Regina, he got up. She took a step back from the knife, and the young man smiled and said, "Don't worry. I work here. I'm Hamdija."

He took the knife in his other hand and extended his right hand. He was over six feet tall, and his hand was the size of an oar, warm and soft. "Dr. Hoffman is waiting for you. He asked me three times whether you'd arrived. You know how it is—an old man, old school from Vienna."

"This guy surely beats them," Regina thought, "but he acts proper when families come because they might report him."

He led her through dark, windowless corridors; there was only one light bulb burning in each of them; the paint was peeling and coming off the walls in big flakes. "So this is what my Bepo fought for?" she wondered.

"We have patients that have been here for more than fifty years, but most of them are old partisans," Hamdija began, speaking in the tone of a tour guide. Regina thought that this was a place where they could read everyone's mind.

"We have two colonels, a few majors, some captains, company commanders, political commissars, and one national hero. Most of them went through the battles of Sutjeska and the Neretva. Four years in the woods, and then in their first three months of freedom they all had nervous breakdowns. They fell apart so much that no one can put them back together again. It's terrible, ma'am."

She was taken aback that Hamdija called her "ma'am." That wasn't forbidden, but it was a sign, and a dangerous one. People only said "ma'am" or "mister" if they were making a threat or working out some kind of plot with someone. Maybe they wanted to poison Bepo and intended to get her involved.

"Damn, sometimes I feel guilty before these people. Dr. Hoffman tells me that isn't good, but there's no helping it. That's how it is. How could I be right if I'm the only one who's normal among all these men who fought for this country? I didn't fight because I was still in school, and now it's me who's healthy and all of them who are sick. Oh, ma'am, if you stayed here a little longer you'd know that one can't rightly say who's crazy and who's normal," he said as they passed from one corridor to another for the third time already, walking through labyrinths and catacombs in which they didn't meet a soul.

"Don't worry about me; I say all kinds of crap," he said dismissively when he noticed how Regina was looking at him.

Franz Hoffman was seventy-five and looked good for his age. He had curly gray hair, a mustache in which every whisker went in a different direction and so looked as if he had purposely tussled it. He looked like the Serbian poet Laza Kostić in the one photograph that was reproduced in school textbooks and encyclopedias during the Kingdom of Yugoslavia. He jumped up when they entered the room and kissed Regina's hand. That frightened her even more. No one had showed the fairer sex that honor in at least fifteen years.

"Sit down, please, sit down! Hamdija, boy, make the lady some coffee," the old man said, fussing about as if guests were arriving for the first time in years. "How was your trip?"

Regina nodded—*good*, but she couldn't bring herself to say it. She thought that anything she might say would come out wrong and would do her and Bepo some harm. What kind of harm, she didn't know, nor could she know in such a place, among these people.

"Yes, it's far, really far away. I haven't been to Dubrovnik since '23. But the city is beautiful, especially when you're a young man, and then later you remember it and don't know which was more beautiful—your bygone youth or the city," Hoffman said, trying to calm down and win the good will of a woman who, he was sure, held his life in her hands. But instead of making a nice remark, what he said came out garbled and idiotic, so he laughed and tapped himself on the forehead with his fingertips. That didn't change anything either. She kept her hands in her lap and looked at him as if she didn't understand the meaning of his existence in the world.

After the patient Bepo Sikirić had refused his food for the first time and stated that he'd eaten what there was to eat in life and had no intention of continuing to eat the ground bones of his dead comrades baked into bread (because enemies of the people and wartime speculators cut corners to save flour), Dr. Hoffman spent the night tossing and turning in his bed and thinking about what might happen if a colonel in Tito's army starved to death, someone who was also a veteran of the Spanish Civil War and a revolutionary. How would he convince the secret police, the State Security Service (and who knew whom else) that he wasn't to blame for his death? They would take him out in front of the wall of the asylum, where he'd worked for more than fifty years, and shoot him before he could get a word in. And he'd be lucky if they didn't torture him before they shot him. After the patient had refused his food the next day and then refused it for three more days, Franz Hoffman wrote a last will. He also told his Tidža, with whom he'd lived since 1907, when they'd gotten married in St. Stephen's Cathedral in Vienna and she'd converted to Catholicism and taken the name Margaret (people in Sarajevo didn't know anything about this and continued calling her Tidža), that he had a feeling that he'd been pushed up against a wall, both in reality and metaphorically. And that this time there was no chance of escape. Tidža mumbled something, took a rolling pin, and started vigorously rolling out a layer of dough, stretching it to the point where it was paper thin. But unlike his life, it would never tear. And for years he'd been waiting for Tidža to make a mistake and for the dough to get a hole so she would have to start rolling it out all over again, until finally he realized that there was no chance of her making that mistake.

"They'll kill me, my dear," he said, trying to make her understand that this time it was serious.

"Oh, Franz, people talk about all sorts of things, and you talk about how someone's going to kill you. You've been doing it for twenty years now. First it was Hitler who was going to kill you because you went to Vienna to study with Freud and because people saw you reading his books in cafés, then the Ustashas wanted to kill you when you wouldn't show them the papers that told what religion the patients were, and then the partisans wanted to kill you because you're a Kraut and because you went to the Ustasha and German celebrations at Christmas and Bayram. Oh, if I only knew who wants to kill you now! But for God's sake, don't tell me! I'll sleep easier. And when will you come to your senses for once? Who might kill me? And who would deal with all the crazies if it weren't for you? People aren't stupid. They pray for you to live as long as possible. If you die, the crazies will be walking around the market squares, and then nothing will help at all, not socialism, not Truman's eggs," Tidža said, and he realized that there was nothing he could say to convince her that his life depended on Bepo Sikirić's.

He breathed a little more easily when he and Regina talked on the phone and she agreed to come and talk to her brother. He thought she wouldn't, that there was no chance of that woman overcoming the reasons why she'd never visited him before. He didn't know what those reasons were, nor was he particularly interested. The reasons why relatives didn't come to visit patients were always the same and didn't differ that much from the reasons why others came to visit every week and inquired when their relatives would recover. Both kinds of people were irrational. The former, because they believed that their fathers and sons were already dead. But they weren't—they were all too alive. God knew how much longer they would live, and they were often very concerned about someone coming and visiting them. And those who came to visit were irrational because they thought it was simply a matter of days before their sons and fathers would get right in the head. As if their heads were full of water and all one had to do was wait for the sludge to settle on the bottom. But the fact that Regina nevertheless said she would come was the first good sign in a long series of bad signs that had combined in recent days to lower a gravestone over the head of Dr. Hoffman.

Hamdija came in with their coffees. On three copper trays were three small copper pots, each with a lid that had a crescent moon and a star, as atop minarets on postcards. Golden floral decorations were painted on the coffee cups, and in each little sugar dish were two cubes of sugar.

"Prewar coppersmith work," Hoffman said, full of pride, as if he had hammered out the pots himself. "My sister sends the sugar from Vienna. It's not easy to find it there either, but she manages. I won't drink coffee unless it's got sugar in cubes," he continued and dipped a cube into his coffee as a demonstration. A brown color spread through the white of the sugar.

"A pity," she thought as she watched the crystals melt and disappear. A sweet taste on the palate wasn't something that could take the place of the beautiful, symmetrical cube, the product of Viennese masters and international smugglers, and it was more of a rarity and a wonder than ancient statues, cathedrals, and the stone arches in the atrium of the Franciscan monastery and everything else created by human hands that had survived the war. She plopped in both her cubes quickly and pushed them down with the little silver spoon so that they wouldn't dissolve slowly but would disappear at once.

"Will he recognize me?" Regina asked.

"Of course. He hasn't forgotten anyone. He thinks the same things about people that he did when he was healthy. It's just that his attitude toward himself and life is a little different," Hoffman said, and it seemed to him that she might think that was a reproach for her not having come all these years, "but he lives in a different world, on a different planet, not on ours. On some Saturn because it's easier for him. It seems to me that it's easier for him, although I know as much about it as you do. That is—nothing!" he said, trying to look at her as a co-conspirator and hoping that this might open her up so she would do something to persuade her brother to start eating. Though she was dressed in black, she looked to him as if she were under forty and was, at least in the eyes of Dr. Hoffman, very pretty. She had pale skin and a regular face, which was a rarity among Mediterranean women, and she looked like an actress in Fritz Lang's silent movie. He couldn't remember the name of the movie or the name of the actress, but the whole world revolved around her, and men took care not to get shot and to come back from every war for her.

"Do you want to see him?" he asked after Regina had drunk the last of her coffee. She shrugged her shoulders and looked at the floor.

"Don't be afraid; I'll come with you," Hamdija said in encouragement.

"What would she be afraid of, I beg your pardon!" Hoffman snapped, feigning indignation.

Bepo was alone in his room. He sat on an army bunk and was looking at the wall on which there were two photographs: one of Vladimir Ilich Lenin delivering a speech to workers and another of the Arc de Triomphe in Paris.

"You came!" he said, astonished. "Hamdija, this is my sister, my only sister! Oh, I'm really crazy; you must have already met," he said and hugged Regina.

"I'll leave you two alone," said the young man.

Regina felt a flush of unexpected joy because Bepo wasn't like she thought he would be. For years she'd looked away when she ran into a retarded child or one of the city's four oddballs. Regina saw her brother in every grimacing visage, in people who were very drunk, or in market sellers when they blew up because a customer had cheated them. Their distorted faces, warped with hatred and fear, were the closest thing to insanity that she could think of.

The last time she had seen him healthy was when he'd received three days' leave after the liberation of Belgrade. At that time there wasn't anything noticeably different about him, no signs of the war. He wasn't even worn out; he looked as if he were coming home from vacation, all tanned and muscular, better looking than he had been before. He laughed a lot and took an interest in everything. He walked around the house and looked over everything he was going to repair and patch up after the war was over.

"Just a few more months and you'll have me home," he said when they said good-bye, and every evening Regina had only one thought: Don't let the last bullet hit him; don't let him fall in the last battle; don't let him be like that soldier in the story who died because a general spent three more seconds signing the cease-fire because he had a surname with seventeen and not seven letters or because the pen ran out of ink. Or the courier got to drinking in a village tavern and arrived late with news of the end of the war.

When they sent word that Bepo was in the hospital because of an attack of nerves, she thought that it couldn't be anything serious. If he was alive and well and nothing hurt, he would have to be okay in the end. His soul wasn't yet an open wound that would bleed him to death. All the lunatics in Regina's life had been lunatics from birth or lunatics because they just wanted to be that way. But Bepo had been born the most ordinary man under the stars.

But after he'd been transferred to the Sarajevo asylum and after his revolver, service booklet, and decorations had been delivered to her at home, she realized that something bad was happening. Only the dead are stripped of their weapons and decorations, and only then are sisters asked whether they need any help. The army had to care for the families of dead comrades; yet her Bepo hadn't been killed—he was going through something else. She didn't know what, but it was certainly terrible if they were awarding him with posthumous honors.

Thus she developed her story about sane people and normal people, which might have had little to do with what was written in books but was true. Truth is everything one believes in, and it's easy for there to be truth in the idea that insanity is more contagious than the plague or cholera.

That was death without a grave, she concluded after she'd thought about it for days and changed her mind about whether she would go to see Bepo in Jagomir. Insanity was contagious. She realized this when her life began to change only because she knew where her brother was. And it changed by virtue of the fact that a difference arose between what she saw and heard and what was real. Maybe not even anything that was happening to her or anything that had remained when Ivo died was what it was, but what it wasn't. The difference between "is" and "isn't" lies in the decision for something to be or not to be.

She would look at Dijana, her little girl, and wonder whether the problem lay in the name she bore or in the life that had begun within her. And she didn't love her with the love that she'd imagined when she was carrying her or as she listened to other mothers talk about what it meant to have a child.

"They told me you're not eating," she began as soon as they sat down on the bed.

"How's the girl? I'm sorry I haven't seen her," he said, acting as if he hadn't heard.

"She's fine. Getting bigger every day," she said; it was the first thing that came to mind.

"If she takes after Ivo, she'll be tall. Taller than you by a head, and maybe taller than her uncles. That's right. We grew taller than our papas and mamas, and they were taller than our grandpas and grandmas. In three hundred years men will be like cypress trees, and women like poplars. They'll marvel at the little houses we lived in. They'll laugh at us, but we won't care because we won't be around any more," he said, cracking his knuckles until the joints stopped popping. Then he stopped.

"Bepo, why aren't you eating?" Regina asked.

"We don't leave much of any value to our children. To our children or future generations. No matter how we might think we're leaving them a lot, no matter how much we've sacrificed, it won't mean anything to them. A little world that you can't move into. It's as if we'd inherited the little we have from ants. In America there are anthills that are a hundred times bigger than ours, but they're still not big enough for people to live in," he said and waved his hands. Then he made anthills in the air with his palms, left just enough space for an ant between his index finger and thumb, and used his palms to show the difference between the large ones and small ones.

"You'll die on me from hunger," Regina interjected as soon as he ran out of things to say and show.

"We believe that communism is something great and eternal. We think so because it is in proportion to us, but it won't be for our children and our children's children. The little ones can't understand the big people, just as we can't understand them. We know only that communism will seem trivial to them. They'll take a red banner between two fingers, like this, and will walk across Russia in three steps because Russia will seem small to them too, much smaller than Pelješac. You just watch children growing big, and you see that there's no point in measuring the world on a scale bigger than your own life. I've come to understand that!" he said raising his voice and lifting his finger above his head. That was the gesture of a strict teacher, an attempt at being funny.

"Bepo," she said, grabbing him by the hand, "what's wrong, dear Bepo?" she asked and started crying.

"That won't help you at all," he snapped at her in disgust; "how can you ask me that and cry? If you're going to cry, ask something else!"

She hurriedly wiped away her tears with her sleeve: "Here, I'm not crying any more. What's wrong with you? Tell me," she said, trying to smile.

"Oh, that's better! And not so I think I've stolen an apple. Nothing's wrong with me. Every morning Dr. Hoffman brings me *Politika* and *Oslobođenje*, and I see that nothing can be done with the world. Take a look, a cease-fire has been signed between India and Pakistan. They were fighting over Kashmir, and it really seems to me that Kashmir is their Bosnia. I imagine it has a lot of sheep, green mountains with snowy peaks. Why else would they fight over it? The only thing I can't understand is what's going on with Berlin. Stalin won't let the English enter the city via the railways and roads, so the English fly in and out more than a thousand times a day in airplanes. As if the Russians couldn't shoot down their airplanes. It really seems to me that the Allies are spiting them.

He showed how airplanes take off and land and did it so well that his hands almost seemed to turn into big military transport planes.

"And you're acting out of spite!" she said.

"Why do you think so?" he asked, saddened.

"Because you're not eating, Bepo. You'll die if you don't eat."

"Mother in Heaven, you're treating me like a child. 'You'll die if you don't eat, you'll die if you don't eat.' I'm sure you talk to Dijana like that. Do you think I'm a child just because I'm in a mental hospital?"

"I don't think so. I just think you're acting out of spite."

"Hamdija certainly told you that. He's a good, simple-minded boy. Hoffman wouldn't talk such nonsense. The boy doesn't know what life is."

"They're both worried about you. You'll die."

"Of course I'll die. Everyone dies, right, don't they? They die no matter what."

"Why aren't you eating?"

"You wouldn't believe me if I told you. If I could tell you at all. But I can't! That's between me and the movement. Once you get into it, there's no getting out. But I don't regret a day of it. I'm only sorry about Spain and Granada. Spain will never again be what we dreamed it would be. It'll be too small for our children, and they'll toss it aside like a toy. We're the last who knew how beautiful it was. And how big it was."

"Are you going to eat?"

"Regina, you're stubborn as a mule. You didn't used to be like that."

"Are you ever going to eat again?"

"You're crying again! Have you lost your nerves? Watch out; that's how it starts. Ask Hoffman if you don't believe me. No, I'm not a child, and you don't have to pester me. Or are you trying to help me? I'm beyond help. I ate my share of bread, and I don't need any more."

Regina jumped up, grabbed her chin, which was quivering uncontrollably, and ran out of Bepo's room, straight into Hamdija's arms. He led her without a word down corridors full of empty echoes, in which her sobs sounded like the grating noises of a cabinet being pushed from one end of an empty parlor to another.

He placed a glass of sugar water in front of her. Dr. Hoffman pointed over to the cabinet with his eyes, and Hamdija took out a bottle and two brandy glasses. Regina tried with all her might to keep a straight face so she wouldn't burst into a sobbing mess.

"Have a drink, ma'am; unfortunately we haven't come up with a better medicine than brandy!"

Hoffman downed the brandy that Hamdija poured for him and shook like a shaggy dog coming out of a lake. His every hair stood on end, more from fear than anything else, because he knew that Bepo Sikirić wasn't going to be dissuaded. And that was Hoffman's choice: either he could wait for them to put him up against the wall, or he could pass judgment on himself.

It occurred to him to give himself an injection of morphium; there's no nicer way to die than with morphium, if any death can be nice. The older he got, the more he wanted to live, and the fewer reasons he had to die. At one time he'd been ready to die for his emperor and king and flew into such a rage at those who'd killed Archduke Franz Ferdinand at the Latin Bridge that the next day he enlisted as a volunteer in case Vienna decided to punish Serbia militarily, but his enlistment papers got lost somewhere and no one called him up for the army when war was finally declared. They probably figured that a psychiatrist wouldn't be much use on the front or might even damage the combat morale of the regiment.

Soldiers don't think about their souls, nor do officers think about the mental health of their soldiers because if they thought about such things, no one would ever fight wars.

Well, it wasn't just the assassination in Sarajevo that had inspired Franz Hoffman to die for a higher cause! Four years later, when the empire went to hell, Bosnia was in the grips of hunger and misery, and anyone with a Kraut name and surname was looking to pack up his things and leave for Vienna, he slammed his fist down on the table: "One doesn't abandon a people who have accepted and fed you! No, not when the people have got it bad." He turned around, and without saying anything else, he left the meeting that Professor Ernst Erlich, the retired director of the Land Bank, had convened at his villa at Vrelo Bosne; this meeting was supposed to decide on an SOS letter that they were going to send to Vienna asking the royal palace not to forget its sons and daughters imprisoned in the Turkish provinces, not even in those times, which posed the greatest difficulties for the people and the crown. He never saw most of the people at Erlich's villa again, and he hardly ever greeted those who stayed in Sarajevo.

He no longer wanted to have anything to do with Austria, the Austrians, or his German roots. A new state was being created, a great kingdom of the South Slavs, in which Hoffman had decided to be a Slav by his own choice. A few days after Serbian troops entered Sarajevo, he heroically stepped into the local registrar's office and asked a scowling Serbian officer to Slavicize his name and surname on the spot. But since the latter was only half-literate or at least fairly sloppy, he simply entered the name Franz Hoffman in Cyrillic script. Thus he became only half Yugoslav, whereas half of him remained what he'd been before. But that didn't bother him: "If our King Petar the Unifier ever needs a good warrior, you can always find me in the sanatorium for the mentally ill in Jagomir!" he shouted, stepping right into the face of the officer. He thought that was necessary and that shouting was a Serbian folk custom because all the Serbs he'd seen in recent days had been hollering at the top of their lungs. Hoffman didn't connect that with the fact that every one of them was in uniform and that he'd never seen a Serb in civilian dress because before the war they'd only seldom crossed the Drina and came to Sarajevo only very rarely. Or maybe he'd seen those people, but didn't know they were from Serbia. Somehow he thought that they had to be very different, cockier than Bosnians.

"Who the fuck do you think you're talking to, you shit; you want me to tie your ears in knots?" the officer replied in an even louder voice. Hoffman ran out of the office and couldn't understand why the officer had gotten angry at him.

It was a good time; one's soul didn't cramp up from hardship, and there were so many things to be happy about and for which it paid to have courage. Afterward there wasn't a single one. Whether this was because people were getting older or because the times were topsy-turvy, this was something that Franz Hoffman often wondered about.

And the worst of times—times of mental unrest, depression, and dyslexia— began for him on the twenty-eighth of February, 1933. He was sitting in the café of the Hotel Europa; outside it was snowing. In the corner someone was playing Mozart on the piano. It was approaching noon and the regular patrons were already starting to go home for lunch when Hoffman opened the Belgrade *Politika* and on the third page read the following headline: "Reichstag Burns to Ashes and Cinders! Chancellor Hitler Accuses Communists and Social-Democrats!" There had been even worse news that he'd read in the newspaper, but none had ever worried him like this. A heavy stone, like those used to press sauerkraut in crocks, fell on his stomach. He began to gasp and couldn't get enough air. "This is panic," he thought, "female hysteria, or arrhythmia." He checked his pulse; his heart was beating powerfully and regularly. He folded the newspaper and looked at the wall for a few minutes.

"Are you all right?" asked Rudo, his waiter. When he calmed down a little, he opened the newspaper to page three, and had the same reaction. As soon as he came home, he told Tidža to pack their bags; they were going to Opatija for a vacation because his work and the patients were driving him crazy. They stayed in Opatija for three weeks. He didn't read the newspapers or listen to the news. They went for walks by the sea and went to concerts every evening, listening to hit songs, both Strausses—the older and the younger one—Russian romantic songs performed by an ensemble from Novgorod . . . But Hoffman didn't become himself again.

When he returned to the asylum, he told the head doctor, Đuro Sandić, that he thought he was starting to have mental problems and asked for permission to go visit Dr. Freud in Vienna. Đuro roared with laughter and turned as red as a tomato, fat and stocky as he was. He liked Franz, though he would get a little irritated at his innovations and all that idiocy that he picked up from the literature in Vienna and London, where they were making a philosophy of psychiatry: "It's as if mental patients, God forgive me, are smarter than mentally healthy people, who have to find ways to outsmart them."

Head doctor Đuro was a good and generous man and genuinely suffered the agony of his patients, even more than Hoffman had ever done, but he believed that there was simply no better treatment for severe mental conditions than cold water and electroshocks.

"My good Franz, you need to give your head a good shake-up, and maybe things will settle in the right places. And maybe not. But no benefit will come of all the talk and hocus-pocus that your phonies write about," he explained to Hoffman when he'd arrived in Jagomir full of enthusiasm about an article he'd read on psychoanalysis.

He tried a few more times to convince head doctor Đuro about the advantages of modern methods of treating mental illnesses, but he would always laugh at him or act as if he were angry. He made phony threats about dismissing him and turning him into the ministry in Belgrade. But when Hoffman came to him with his tale of how he was starting to have mental problems himself and that he would end up as a patient in his asylum if Đuro didn't let him go to Freud in Vienna, his boss couldn't stop laughing. He thought that he would suffer a stroke; his lungs were close to bursting, and he was already hot in his heart and belly. No one had ever said something so silly to him with such a serious expression. It was as if Franz were a small child and was imagining that he was sick only so that he would let him go to that Jewish good-for-nothing. Of course he would let him go! The young man could have his fun. There wouldn't be any harm in it, and it was better if the subordinates were content, especially Hoffman, to whom he was going to leave the clinic when he retired.

"How long do you want to stay in Vienna, you damn sniveler?" Đuro asked him, holding his belly.

"A month, if at all possible," Hoffman said, ashamed. His boss was around fifteen years his senior, but he acted as if he were his grandfather.

"Here, take three months, but come back healthy! And don't think of coming back here and pestering me with whatever that fool fills your head with because I'll pack you off into an isolation cell and electroshock that psychoanalysis out of your head. Watch out, Franz, my pops slept with wolves on Mt. Vlašić, and I'm no better! There's no touchy-feely with us peasants!"

Hoffman wouldn't understand the part about no touchy-feely until much later. It was as if Đuro hadn't let him go off to Vienna to see Freud because he was a good man and because his lies (or what he thought were lies) had made him laugh but because head doctor Đuro figured that there couldn't be too much harm in those innovations. And there might even be some benefit when later people around Sarajevo and throughout the whole kingdom told how he, Dr. Đuro Sandić, allowed the spirit of Freud into the Jagomir clinic. If it were all foolishness, as he thought, it would be easy for that spirit to head for the hills, but if there was something to that damned psychoanalysis—which Đuro wasn't going to get caught up in even if it were true—then his name would be inscribed in gilt letters in the annals of Bosnian mental health, and his frowning bust would stare out in front of the Jagomir asylum. He was already proud of that bust, regardless of the fact that its bronze head wouldn't look anything like him and that it would show generations of mental patients how lucky they were because they hadn't fallen into the hands of such a gloomy man. No matter how little he cared for earnest posturing and was always playing the clown and teddy bear as he laughed and joked with his patients, superiors, and subordinates, head doctor Đuro envisioned his posthumous role as a serious and scowling one.

But even without that, and if he'd been one hundred percent certain that

Freud was a complete idiot, he would still have let Hoffman go. One should never keep others from what makes them happy without a compelling need or reason. Head doctor Đuro didn't believe in God, but he believed that something like that would have been an unforgiveable sin.

Franz Hoffman lost seven days waiting for Freud to see him. He already had the impression that the doctor was avoiding him and had started worrying that he would be forced to try to solve the problem of his obsession with the newspaper headline of the twenty-eighth of February on his own or, maybe, get used to the fact that overnight he'd become a coward and that there was no longer any ideal that was more valuable than life.

Actually, in those days he couldn't remember a single ideal that was worth anything at all. Maybe that was one more oriental influence, he thought as he shambled through the streets of a city that had once been his. Maybe years of living in the market-square district and among its people had turned him into just another little hodja or shopkeeper, into a man who didn't want to look farther than his mosque or his shop front. But how could that happen to a Kraut who was born far from Bosnia, Islam, and everything that makes oriental Slavs so passive and obsessed solely with their own trivial human pleasures? It would have to be that this was a case of some strange neurosis, a mental disorder in the broadest sense of the term, about which Dr. Freud could certainly tell him something.

On the eighth day he saw him going into the building in which he had an unregistered practice; he ran after him: "Doctor, Doctor!"

Freud didn't turn around; he was probably lost in thought, or he was pretending not to hear. Hoffman stopped him on the steps just when Freud had ascended to the fourth step. He looked at him in surprise, trying to remember whether he knew this man, and that glance from up above—because Hoffman was standing down on the first step—was like a revelation for Hoffman. He felt as any old woman from Kraljevska Sutjeska with a tattooed cross on her arm would feel if the Pope had received her in the center of Rome.

He started babbling something incoherent, saying that he'd come from Bosnia but that he'd studied in Vienna and was a native Viennese and had been working for years in a Sarajevo mental hospital and begged the doctor for a bit of his precious time—he wanted him to give him some directions and advice and maybe some help in solving a strange mental problem.

Freud was probably in a dilemma: should he run or maybe chase this troublemaker away or talk with him regardless? An interest in various psychiatric conditions that define a person is not at all the same as an interest in street characters and troublemakers. And this guy seemed to be just that. It was hard to get rid of such types. The reason they approached you in the first place was because they felt that you were incapable of telling them off.

Hoffman told Dr. Freud what had happened to him. He listened without moving or changing his expression. He seemed tense, like someone who'd been suffering from an ulcus duodeni since the spring and would suffer from the pain for days at a time. When Hoffman finished, Freud continued his silence. Probably because he hadn't been asked a question, and Hoffman couldn't actually come up with a question for him. He squirmed like a student who had an idea of what a professor wanted to hear from him but didn't dare speak so he wouldn't blurt out something stupid.

"Are you a Jew?" Freud asked quietly.

"No, I'm an Austrian and a Catholic," he answered and immediately realized that he'd said something inappropriate. As if a Jew couldn't be an Austrian.

But Freud didn't catch that at all.

"Are you sure? Maybe some grandmother of yours is nevertheless Jewish? Or a distant ancestor?" he asked insistently.

"No, really none of my family are Jewish. My ancestors came during the time of Maria Theresa to Vienna from Swabia. They were Lutherans and converted to Catholicism. But what does that matter to you?" Hoffman asked, feeling more and more uncomfortable.

"If you're not a Jew, and it's clear that you're not a communist, I don't know why the burning of the Reichstag hit you so hard personally. And I don't know why you think that I might be able to answer your questions."

Dr. Freud continued making his way up the stairs, and the conversation was over.

Franz Hoffman left Vienna deeply disappointed. He continued to believe that the doctor was a genius, but he couldn't forgive him for that insult. Freud left him alone in the world, never again to find someone in whom he might confide his fears and weakness. After he'd lost Jesus Christ as a boy, the loss of Sigmund Freud was for Hoffman the loss of his last link to divinity, what was beyond man and served as a support for his courage. And that was his final farewell to his home city.

Before he descended from the one step that he'd ascended, he'd already forgotten his imaginary mental illness and accepted what until then had seemed to him to be completely beneath his dignity. Yes, he'd become a coward. He was frightened as old people are frightened and those without protection, rich relatives, or a secure place to call home.

He stayed in Vienna for two more days, visited a few bookstores, stood for a while in front of his childhood home and looked into the windows, behind which some strangers were living.

Head doctor Đuro was surprised by Hoffman's early return but didn't ask him any questions about it, nor did he make any jokes at his expense. He never asked him what had happened to him in Vienna, and so the story of Hoffman's mental illness that could only be helped by Sigmund Freud could be forgotten.

The months and years following the newspaper headline that had changed him were a part of the general conspiracy of fear. There was a prolonged bloody war in Ethiopia, the League of Nations ridiculed Emperor Selassie, the junta generals from the Canary Islands began their attempt to destroy the Spanish republic, Hitler annexed Austria, Vienna became a German city, and there were articles about laws that curtailed the rights of Jews in Germany. In the Belgrade assembly representatives of all three Yugoslav tribes could be heard saying that the same or similar laws should be passed in their country . . .

Franz Hoffman read all that—a mountain of leaden letters that forbade him from thinking about anything other than what he might see in the newspapers. He stopped going to Mt. Trebević, Mt. Jahorina, and Mt. Treskavica with the mountaineering society, and he refused invitations to Sunday card games in the Two Bulls tavern. And so soon he no longer had anyone to spend time with apart from his patients, head doctor Đuro, and his wife Tidža. The lax pace of oriental life, which he'd appreciated for years and in which his Viennese principles had sunk without a trace, now turned into a depression that he felt within himself and saw all around him.

In the summer of 1939 head doctor Đuro was forced to retire by law. He left Jagomir in tears, after sending several letters to the royal regent, Paul, and the presidents of the royal governments requesting that an exception be made and his retirement age be raised because his experience was necessary for the clinic, its staff, and—what was most important—its patients. Hoffman countersigned each of Đuro's letters and knew they wouldn't help. But at least he preserved his unhappy boss's faith in loyalty and friendship.

The last letter, sent three days before the decision on his retirement would arrive from Belgrade, was signed by everyone: stokers, porters, cooks, nurses and doctors, and even patients who were literate and lucid enough to sign. To no avail. No answer ever came in response to that extremely unusual petition. For two months head doctor Đuro came to his clinic as a retiree, and with the first autumn rains he disappeared. Hoffman didn't even see him at Sunday coffee in the Hotel Europa.

In the early autumn of 1940 he would learn from one of Đuro's relatives that the head doctor had died three months before and that the funeral had been as for a real pauper because according to the deceased's wishes no one had been informed of his death, nor was the news published in the newspapers. He was buried in the Orthodox cemetery in Mrkonjić Grad. After the war Hoffman went to find Đuro's grave. He thought that the clinic should have an appropriately dignified tombstone made for its long-serving director. But there was no grave, and as the registers of the dead had burned and Đuro's family had scattered all over the globe, there was no longer anyone who might know where he lay, that man who'd secretly dreamed of his bronze bust, for the sake of which he'd been ready to allow psychoanalysis into his clinic.

After Đuro left, Hoffman no longer had any superiors. No one in Sarajevo had the slightest interest in what he was doing with the mental patients, and the ministry of health traditionally did not answer letters from Jagomir because since Đuro had been there, they'd thought that there was no great difference between the doctors and the patients in the Sarajevo mental hospital. But the freedom to do as he pleased without having to answer to anyone only deepened Hoffman's fears. It was easier to be the lowest in some social hierarchy than to be outside of one. He realized this in the last days of the kingdom, when all of Sarajevo was in a lather and on the move because everyone was going to those they felt they belonged to. Communists sought out communists, Orthodox sought out the Orthodox, Muslims Muslims, and Catholics Catholics. Only the Sarajevo Jews tried to stay on good terms with everyone in town at the same time so no one would take offense or get any ideas. He watched those unhappy and frightened Jews gesture to the communists, give alms to poor Catholics, and chat with the market bosses about the good old days of the viziers and knew that they had chosen the worst possible way to protect themselves from what was coming. For completely personal and egotistical reasons the Jews used their own blood to make the only glue bonding groups that had all started going their own ways. They were the mortar in a structure threatened with collapse, and in the end they would pay for their surfeit of caution with their lives. They found themselves on the outside of the hierarchy that was set up in the city in the first days of April 1941, outside of which the only ones apart from them were Dr. Hoffman and his patients.

In the summer of 1942 he refused, with open disgust, to turn over a list of his patients that contained their religious affiliations to an Ustasha captain.

No matter how much he was afraid for his own skin and no matter how much it seemed that history had conspired against him and a few like him since that noonday of the twenty-eighth of February, 1933, he was unable to comply with the captain's request. Among the patients there were ten or so Orthodox Christians and one Jew—Sarah Nolan, a mongoloid girl who'd died in April of 1941 so that there wouldn't have been a great deal of harm had Hoffman turned over the list of patients. If the Ustashas had tried to take away the Orthodox Christians, he could have easily called Dr. Savo Besarović to intervene on their behalf, and there could be no doubt that nothing would have happened to them. Hoffman, however, couldn't accept anyone treating mental patients as anything other than patients because in that case everything would have come to nothing. Everything that he'd done at Jagomir all those years. And he'd have to accept the fact that they'd sent him from Vienna to Sarajevo as punishment, as a life sentence of hard labor. If someone had maybe thought of punishing him by sending him to the Turkish provinces and if there were those who believed that Franz Hoffman was a bad doctor—because if he'd been a good one, the Austrian emperor wouldn't have sent him so far away—he hadn't felt punished or felt himself to be professionally inferior to his colleagues.

"As far as the human soul is concerned, medicine basically gropes in the dark, and we haven't advanced far beyond treatments with spells," he would say to his colleagues. "No matter how much some future psychologists and psychiatrists will make fun of us and ridicule us—if it weren't for us, they will not have done anything either." He was proud of these words; he considered them to be witty, as if someone else had said them. If he'd given in to the captain's threats, not even those words would have meant anything any more.

But the very next day he went straight to the city leadership and to the German command post.

He told the Ustashas that he and his people were glad that the historic city of Sarajevo, the old Croatian Vrhbosna, had finally become part of the Independent State of Croatia, into whose fabric the centuries-old aspirations of this people had been woven through the efforts of their leader, Dr. Pavelić. And if the mental hospital at Jagomir, which he'd called an asylum, a clinic, or a hospital, depending on the circumstances, could assist in any way in the blossoming and defense of their precious homeland, he, Dr. Franz Hoffman, would be deeply offended if they didn't let him know.

In a ten-minute audience Hoffman told the deputy commander of all German units stationed in central Bosnia, a rather impolite Bavarian, that he felt himself to be a German and had always felt that way and would be happy if the military and civilian representatives of the Third Reich would keep in mind that people such as he had been living in this city and that for decades they'd been trying to civilize this wild country.

Neither the Croats nor the Germans were particularly taken with his declaration of loyalty. It was probably clear to them that someone who acted thus couldn't have a completely clear conscience. But they didn't check anything in his background, nor were they interested at all in the case of the head of a mental hospital. Jagomir was on the edge of the city and moreover on the side that was out of the way and where only Chetnik or partisan bandits were likely to turn up. But not even they would know where to go from the nuthouse so that Franz Hoffman was left to his own devices, alone with his fears.

The captain never came back, and it was clear that he hadn't wanted the list of patients on an order from anyone but had been out on his own hunting for a Jew to arrest so he could then brag about it in the taverns of Zagreb's old town.

But when the war neared its end and it was a matter of days until the partisans entered the city, Franz Hoffman remembered the sin he'd committed. He was sweating bullets at the prospect of the communists' finding reports of his visits to the Ustasha and German authorities among the documents they captured. Secretaries had been present in both places and had written things down, and he was certain that his name was on some paper somewhere. It was difficult to believe that they'd only been tricking him. Both the Germans and the Ustashas had taken pains to convince the cocky psychiatrist who praised Pavelić and Hitler that he'd come somewhere important and that he was getting bureaucratic attention there.

The day after the city was liberated, on the seventh of April, 1945, Franz Hoffman went to the market square and had two flags sewn for himself: one Yugoslav and one Soviet. He paid the tailor Hakija Čengić extra for the express order and because Hakija had to send his apprentice to Kreševo since there was no red fabric anywhere in the city. On the eighth of April the banners of the victors were already fluttering on the Jagomir insane asylum, but Hoffman shuddered with fear in his office for months afterward.

He rested easier when they began to bring ill partisans, both men and women, to the clinic. The ones without commissions were brought in ambulances or military jeeps, but the comrades with commissions arrived escorted by officers of the State Security Service, who would take the doctor aside and warn him that the name of Major Horvat or Colonel Šaković had to be kept strictly confidential. He was also duty bound to provide them with special treatment, not to forget the rank each had acquired in the struggle against the occupiers and collaborators, because the fact that they'd gone crazy didn't mean that anyone had forgotten their merits in the people's war of liberation and the socialist revolution. He was forbidden from giving them electroshocks under threat of the most severe punishment or from torturing them in other ways. The security service agent would then threaten to make regular inquiries about the condition of the comrade in question.

It had now been almost four years since the first mentally disturbed officers had arrived at Jagomir, and no one had taken any interest in them. No one had even made any phone calls. The families of the ill partisans didn't come to visit them either, and so Bepo Sikirić was no exception at all.

But it didn't matter. Dr. Hoffman didn't dare violate any of the orders he'd received regarding the partisans. Nor did he have any particular reasons for doing so. The thirty or so of them—twenty of whom had military commissions—could be divided into two groups. The first group consisted of those who saw the enemy at every step and stopped fighting only when they were asleep. In their battles they saved Comrade Tito and Savo Kovačević, forced the Neretva bridgehead and crossed the Sutjeska, changed their names and identities daily, and all behaved the same, without individual features.

The other group consisted of the quiet and peaceful ones. Two of them hadn't spoken a word since they'd arrived at Jagomir, and nothing apart from their silence indicated that they were mentally ill. And they gladly took part in the springtime cleanings of the park, went to fetch water, and chopped wood. At first Hoffman forbade them from working, fearing that someone might accuse him of humiliating them with menial jobs, especially Major Seid Redža. But then he realized that neither Redža nor Ivan Rukljač (the other one who never spoke and fortunately didn't have a commission) enjoyed anything besides cleaning the park and going to fetch water. Besides, Hoffman didn't even believe that either of them was mentally ill. Had it been up to him, he would have sent them home. A man could live and be useful to society even if he didn't say anything. Redža and Rukljač were living proof that this was true. Sometimes at the end of a workday during summer heat waves, he would sit down with Redža on a bench under the thick treetops, offer him a cigarette, and they would smoke in the peace and quiet, like friends who'd already said everything they had to say to one another. Hoffman didn't feel like going home because he knew that he would sweat like a pig on his way to Koševsko Brdo, where he lived. It was so pleasant under the old oaks, almost cool, and what sane person would want to go out into the sunlight? If something was bothering him or if he was caught up in all of his fears and sighed a few more times, Redža would give him a hug and smile at him with that wide, self-assured smile from placards that called for volunteers to help construct the Brčko-Banovići railway line. Who would then dare to say that Major Seid Redža was mentally ill?

Different from him and Ivan Rukljač were the Jagomir depressives and suicidal types—that is, a third group, of whom there were six or seven. One had to watch them for days at a time and keep them in isolation so they wouldn't get their hands on something that they might use to hang themselves or slit their wrists. They loved to talk, especially to Hamdija, because they were terrified of Dr. Hoffman. Because he was the supreme authority, a kind of nuthouse Tito; because he was a Kraut and acted like it; and because he was average height, which for them—mostly Montenegrins and all of them almost six feet tall—

was an obvious sign of inferiority. Hamdija made a good impression on them. They called him the "Turkish Archpriest" and didn't object when he locked all of them up in their rooms. For them he was the acceptable authority to whom they were to submit even if they were fighters and revolutionaries. If it hadn't been for him, Hoffman would have had a hard time dealing with the depressive element of his partisan unit.

There were also some who did nothing but cry, others who retold tales about the deaths of their sons and daughters, who'd never even existed, and finally there were three of them who were completely oblivious. They had no idea who or what they were; they'd forgotten both the war and their roles in it, as well as Yugoslavia and communism, and were, as Hamdija said, completely peaceful in the absence of their minds. They didn't bother anyone, nor were they of any use for anything. And you can be damned sure that nothing surprised them.

Bepo Sikirić numbered among the depressives and potential suicides, although he wasn't in fact downtrodden, nor had he previously exhibited any inclination for suicide. But that was how life was organized at Jagomir: if you weren't aggressive, then you were a depressive. The fact that you'd never actually been depressive didn't matter at all because everything revolved around the way life was organized and not around what your illness was.

Along with around twenty civilian patients, not all of whom were even civilians because Franz Hoffman had in his clinic two men who'd gone crazy during the First World War and one non-commissioned officer in the Home Guard who'd been brought to him in 1944, those thirty partisans made up for an unbelievably complex social structure, and its functioning worried the staff at Jagomir for days at a time. Thus, not even Hoffman's work had a lot to do with medicine and treatment. He could forget most of what he'd learned at the university and rely on the experience he'd gained from head doctor Đuro. Psychoanalytical writings and books, which he'd never ceased to acquire and study, were of no use to him at all. It didn't matter that after the war Freud's theories had found their way into the parlors of the most prestigious psychiatrists in Belgrade and Zagreb. He, who read and knew the most about them, didn't have his own parlor, nor was he in a position to talk at length about his favorite topic. When he would take a week's vacation, usually in August, he'd lay down his Tidža in the shade under a plum tree in the yard and would play psychoanalyst a little with her, try to hypnotize her, ask her strange questions, and made a mockery of both himself and Sigmund Freud. Actually, he would start out completely serious, and then he would start to realize how little sense any of it made if you did it under a plum tree with your own wife. But no matter how much fun those games were for him and Tidža, in his heart of hearts Hoffman realized more and more that he'd wasted his time because he wasn't even doing as much as head doctor Đuro had—he prescribed electroshocks and submersion in ice water only rarely. Nor was he utilizing what he believed in and what would tomorrow be the most important psychiatric method throughout the world. At the same time he derived no comfort from the fact that he'd believed in psychoanalysis before others had even heard about it. He had his Jagomir, his little empire that he ruled and with which he eluded all those rebellions and wars and about which no one cared a whit because it didn't stand in anyone's way.

"Drink some brandy. There's no medicine like strong brandy!" he said, trying to bring Regina around, since she couldn't calm down after seeing Bepo. Hamdija stood at the door and waited for Dr. Hoffman to think of something. He was ready for everything. Even to force-feed the uncooperative colonel, if only his boss concluded that there was no other solution.

"Have a drink, ma'am, please!" he insisted. Regina raised her eyes, and instead of one she saw two old men. He offered her a handkerchief; it smelled of roses. In that smell there was peace, family harmony, and something that had been irrevocably lost in all those wars along with the soul of her Bepo. If she thought about it even for only a moment longer, she would start crying again, and who knew how long it would take for her tears to stop. She blew her nose loudly. That noise was ugly and shameful, but at least she could be certain that she wouldn't cry any more. The first time she sighed without stopping her sobs. This doesn't make any sense, she thought, neither sobbing nor burping.

"Ma'am, please drink some brandy," Hoffman pestered her.

"No, brandy makes me burp," she lied.

She sat a little while longer with that old man and his assistant, and it seemed that no one there had anything else to do. Those two wouldn't help Bepo because they couldn't and didn't know how. They knew about as much as she did about the things that happen to people to make them go crazy. A full moon, the sirocco, nightmares, fear, decapitated human heads, ghosts, dragons, evil spirits and demons, betrayals and deceits, insomnia, inexplicable pain . . . All of this had taken its toll on Bepo. She knew this well, as did everyone, but people acted as if something else were going on, as if there were some kind of secret in the human soul. There was, in fact, no secret, but it was difficult to accept that sane people were just as close to going crazy as crazy people were to being sane. She wanted to leave this place as quickly as possible and forget her brother, who was beyond hope. But how could she do that as long as this old man was expecting something from her?

"Do you know what's going to happen now?" Hoffman asked. "Your brother will starve for about fifteen more days, and then he'll fall into a coma, and we'll feed him intravenously, and if he recovers, everything will start all over again. Until he dies." He folded his hands as if he were closing a book. She didn't answer him. She asked for her coat, and Hamdija showed her to the gate.

"Don't you want to see him again?" the doctor asked as they parted. She smiled at him and wished him all the best.

But it turned out that she hadn't seen Hamdija for the last time. Two hours later he was running after her on the railway platform; the train for Mostar was just about to pull away.

"Ma'am, wait!" he shouted. Regina had already stepped onto the iron step of the railway car when he grabbed her by the hand and said, "He's dead; please come with me! For God's sake, don't leave."

She was calm and didn't shed a tear; they went out onto the road in front of the railway station when Hamdija stopped, leaned on the wall, and started vomiting. She thought that he'd drunk too much and felt embarrassed because people were passing by and seeing her in such company. She was wearing black for her dead husband, her brother had just died, and that young man was throwing up. It would be so good to go because she couldn't make anything right now anyway.

"How did he die?" she asked Hamdija when he regained some of his composure. "A heart attack. That was his third in a year. I tried to tell him to take care of himself, but he didn't listen . . ."

"You didn't tell me that," she said in surprise.

"Tell you what?"

"That Bepo had heart problems!" she said, enraged, finally in a position to accuse someone for what had happened to her brother.

"Ma'am, I beg your pardon; it's Dr. Hoffman who's dead—not your brother!"

Soon enough it would become clear that it didn't make any sense for her to stay any longer. Hamdija had simply lost his head; after so many years of working for Dr. Hoffman, he'd probably become a little paranoid himself and thought that this woman, who was the last one to see the doctor alive, would be needed to testify that no one had killed him. But he'd had something completely different in mind, which he no longer remembered after he regained his composure and began to apologize because she'd missed all the trains that day. In the end he took Regina to his relatives in Bistrik to spend the night at their place, while he himself went off to Jagomir, where the hearse had already come for Hoffman's body and Dr. Niko Sršen had already shown up to take over the duties as head of the clinic temporarily. The police weren't there, nor did anyone ask Hamdija about the death of Dr. Franz Hoffman. He couldn't believe it. Shouldn't someone have been interested in how and why a man had died? Had they asked Hamdija, he would have told the truth: he'd died of fear because a partisan colonel was refusing his food and because the boss would have been made responsible for his death!

Horrified and disgusted, instead of going home to Bistrik, he ended up in the City Café, where he drank until dawn with strangers and cursed a world in which it was possible for such a man to die like a dog only because in that country no one trusted anything anyone said.

Thus, Hamdija sought justice and would seek it until the end of his days, becoming a greater fool with every day because there was hardly anyone who realized what it meant when he was drunk and said that Hoffman was second only to Freud. And maybe even better than him because Freud only analyzed people as if they were microbes, but Hoffman saved the little intelligence that they had left after everything. Soon the whole city would laugh at him, and his new boss would fire him because he was uneducated and drank a lot. He would end up like one of the lunatics who weren't lucky enough to have some Hoffman accept them into his clinic but instead spent their days on the streets and their nights in the city's taverns.

Regina spent the night in the home of Fuad and Begzada, peaceful and quiet people who didn't ask her anything, and she was glad that she didn't have to tell them anything about herself. They sat her down on their divan, offered her baklava and other sweets, asked her about the weather in Dubrovnik and what was blooming and what was ripening at this time of the year. He explained to her in detail how to make jam from plums and how to keep the plums from turning sour. Begzada nodded and added her comments here and there. Then she told what it had been like when the Germans had withdrawn from Sarajevo and what a sorry sight they'd been, whereas four years earlier they'd all come young, handsome, and blond, full of strength and haughtiness and thought that they would stay a hundred years. As the Russians chased Hitler's divisions across Ukraine and Poland, every German in Bosnia—or anywhere else in the world—aged and became more and more feeble. In the end the whole German people was for the old folks' home, Begzada concluded. Then the spouses fell silent for a while because each of them knew what the other was thinking. In their thoughts they were in agreement and comforted this unknown woman with their silence.

"Oh, the poor doctor! He gave his life for Jagomir," Hamdija's father said finally but didn't go on so that the woman who'd come as a guest to their house wouldn't think that she too had to say something about dead doctor Franz and then reveal why she'd come to Jagomir and whom she'd come to see. That was something that wasn't asked because it was one of those torments that one didn't talk about but kept silent. So if you knew, you knew; if you didn't, you weren't a person because you didn't realize that the same thing might happen to you.

"May the good God have mercy on him," said Hamdija's mother. Regina said nothing and drank rose juice that smelled like Hoffman's handkerchief.

"And it's hard for you too," added Fuad, judging from her black dress that those words made sense and wouldn't be misunderstood.

When they said good-bye the next morning, Begzada kissed her as if they were sisters or best friends. Regina would quickly forget her night in Bistrik and wouldn't remember those people any more when life was difficult for her. But maybe she should have. As they hadn't burdened her with anything, they could only be forgotten. If there were more such people, life would be easier and nicer. And it wouldn't last as long because it would all be forgotten.

A month later a telegram arrived from Sarajevo in which Dr. Niko Sršen informed the family that his patient, Bepo Sikirić, had passed away due to natural causes in the intensive care unit of the Clinic for Internal Medicine in Koševo, where he'd been transferred nine days before in a comatose state. The body of Comrade Sikirić, a colonel in the Yugoslav National Army, had been taken to his home city by the authorized services of the Sarajevo garrison that were responsible for his transport. The colonel's death was a loss not only for his immediate family, but also for our entire socialist society, which was left without one of its visionaries and one of the champions of its cause.

Regina got distracted thinking about what exactly *champion of its cause* was supposed to mean.

Bepo was buried in the same tomb in which Ivo Delavale had already been lying for two years. These two men, who hadn't had anything in common, so absolutely nothing that they couldn't even be one another's enemies, ended up next to one another on two concrete slabs. Bepo lay in a massive coffin of oak, with a communist star carved at the top, and Ivo in a rusted tin can with a picture of a laughing black woman with big breasts.

VIII

The news that Alphonse Capone, the greatest gangster in journalistic history and one of the main stars of the newsreels, had died on his estate in Florida was announced in Yugoslavia with a three-month delay and only in the Belgrade *Politika*, above the Mickey Mouse comic strip. Capone died in late January, when Ivo Delavale was just starting out on his last voyage, traveling in an old tin Brazilian Santos coffee can, which had been packed into the bottom of the sailor's trunk of one Milo Milidrag. As the ship sailed out of the harbor, a great Italian family was mourning its godfather, and the morning that it sailed into Gruž harbor in Dubrovnik, the Belgrade newspaper would publish the news of Capone's death.

That coincidence confirmed how far away America was from Yugoslavia in the year 1947. If America had been closer, Regina would have learned of her husband's death earlier, right after the New Year, when he didn't get up off the floor in a Chicago bar. Everyone thought he was dead drunk, but he was in fact just dead. Not even Milo Milidrag could tell Regina who'd paid for his cremation or who'd put his ashes inside a coffee can. He hadn't known Ivo Delavale and had only heard the story of his death from the man who'd given him the can and the address and passed on the request that upon his return he deliver the ashes to the deceased man's wife. Milidrag had forgotten what the man's name was, and Regina's attempts to learn anything else from the man were futile. Either this Montenegrin sailor was acting more stupid than he was because he wanted to hide something, or he really was completely oblivious. But the way that she learned of Ivo's death and the fact that the ashes in the box could be anyone's, or simply ash from someone's stove, aroused her suspicion. It could hardly have been any different. No one had provided her with a death certificate, Milo Milidrag hadn't given her Ivo's personal effects, and there wasn't really anything that would indicate the authenticity of the can with a laughing black woman on it. She put it under the sink, next to the waste basket, and decided not to say anything to anyone before she learned the whole truth. If it turned out that Ivo was alive and that a sailor had duped her, the tale would spread through the city like wildfire, and she wouldn't be able to shake it until the day she died. A woman puts on a black mourning dress, arranges for a funeral, calls in the priests and buries a box of Brazilian coffee, and then her husband comes home alive and well!

Things would have been different if Ivo Delavale hadn't had ten dollars in his wallet at the moment he died. Or if Milo Milidrag had been more honest—if there'd been any fear of God in him and he'd believed that whoever stole from the dead ended up in hell. In that case Regina's life and the life of her daughter, who was three years old at the time of her father's death, would have taken a different turn, and most of what happened would never have come to pass. One could say that a single ten-dollar bill determined the course of fate.

The man whose name Milidrag had forgotten was Petar Pognar. He was a block leader in some Croatian association in Chicago that mostly took care of arrangements for the deceased. Besides the tin box with the ashes, he'd given the sailor the dead man's wallet, in which there was in addition to the ten dollars a photograph of Dijana at three months, a Yugoslav military service booklet, and registrations of six or seven places of residence in the name of Ivo Delavale. He had also given him a worker's visor cap and two handkerchiefs, which Pognar's wife had washed so that there would be no shame for the deceased, and a small brass crucifix on a chain, of no monetary value at all.

Regina knew all those objects: she'd bought the handkerchiefs in Čapljina; he'd worn the visor cap instead of a sailor's hat; and the cross had belonged to Ivo's brother Radovan, who had been killed fighting for the Austrians on the River Soča in the summer of 1915. Had any of these objects reached Regina, she would have known that her Ivo was dead. She would have mourned and wept for him for a long time, sincerely, and would never have tried to see if any of the story checked out. But Milidrag threw those objects into the Atlantic after he found the ten dollars, convinced that it was the only way to cover up his crime. He would have thrown the tin box with the ashes overboard as well, but he was hoping for some token of gratitude after he turned it over to the widow. When she failed to show any such gratitude and got him off her doorstep more quickly than she would the postman, he regretted not having scattered the ashes into the sea. He didn't have a guilty conscience about having stolen a dead man's money.

Regina wrote the shipping company for which Ivo had been working but received no answer. Then she reported her husband's disappearance to the police, sent a letter to the Yugoslav embassy in Washington, made inquiries to émigré societies, and put notices in newspapers and on the radio. The announcer read the name Ivo Delavale every Friday on the nighttime broadcast, intended for the families of those who'd disappeared in the war. Among the thousands who hadn't returned and whose bodies hadn't been located and who'd served in various armies and were last seen in the oddest places—Dachau, Stalingrad, Berlin, Moscow, Vienna, Steinbrück, Železno, Trieste, Udin, Blagoevgrad, Bucharest, Sutjeska, Foča, Zvonimirova Street in Zagreb, Blagaj, Vis, Biokovo, and El Shatt—there was also Ivo Delavale, a ship's engineer who, according to the last reliable information, had sailed from the port of Bari in the autumn of 1944 on the American warship *Iron Star*. He'd been one of a team of sailors that would on an order from the free Yugoslav government take over the remnants of the royal merchant fleet, which had lain anchored off American harbors for three years.

Every Friday Regina listened to the radio program and waited for someone to contact her. She remembered the names of the missing and soon knew around two hundred of them, which were repeated constantly because news about them never came. Their relatives had probably memorized Ivo's name, and now it seemed like they were familiar and close, though they'd never met. Just as children remembered the names of soccer players and could recite from memory the eleven team members who would go to next year's Olympics, so the wives and daughters of missing soldiers and sailors could recite the names they heard every Friday on the radio and would read them for years, as long as there was anyone alive who didn't know the fate of their loved ones.

"I know Ivo's alive; he's boozing with blacks and chasing whores. What the hell does he care about our communism?!" Luka said to comfort her. Regina grabbed a bottle from the table that would have hit him in the head if he'd been slower in shutting the door. Dijana started wailing like a ship's siren, and creamed spinach dribbled down her chin. Her eyes were almost bulging out of their sockets, and she looked like a very strange creature—an African monkey that had been bitten by a rabid fox in the zoo. Regina took her daughter in her arms and hugged her firmly, less out of motherly concern than so she wouldn't see her like that. The green slime smeared on her white blouse, and broken glass crunched under her feet at every step. She tried to recall the words to some lullaby but couldn't from all the shouting and racket. She started singing *Sweet Little Marijana* and tried to sing louder than Dijana was crying. Since she wasn't very musical and the child wailed louder the more she sang, anyone who heard them might have concluded that Regina's mind was starting to go from grief for her husband. The windows were open, and people listened to what came out of their neighbors' windows more attentively than they listened to Radio London.

She was desperate and distraught for days. Whenever she threw potato peels and fish bones into the trash, she would see the box with the laughing black woman. Then it would hit her that her Ivo was dead, and she was overcome with sorrow in an instant. Five minutes later she would already be remembering Milo Milidrag and his dull face: that wasn't what a herald of misfortune looked like. Whoever brought such news had to be different or at least be wearing a solemn uniform. It's hard to believe that the lives of your loved ones can be taken away by bums, ne'er-do-wells, and cheats. And Milo Milidrag was all three—even a blind man could see that. Though she didn't believe in God, Regina felt that souls were nevertheless aligned in the universe according to some sort of logic that had no place for Montenegrin sailors from the Bay of Kotor and tin boxes.

She'd heard that in the Bay of Kotor relatives would get married and no one paid any attention to whether a husband and wife had the same uncles and grandfathers, so that they gave birth to children with two heads, and that there were many adult men with the brains of three-year-olds. She remembered everything she'd ever heard about people from the Bay of Kotor and was more and more certain that Milo Milidrag had made up the death of her Ivo in the hope that he would get some reward for passing on the bad news. If the sailor had been from Korčula, Hvar, or Split or was a Herzegovinian, Regina would have grabbed for other tales and legends because there is no shortage of them for anyone from anywhere, but since he was from the Bay of Kotor and nowhere else, she began to hate all people from that bay. She needed that to keep from believing that the love of her life was resting in that coffee can.

On the twelfth Friday the man on the radio announced that news had arrived from America about the sailor Ivo Delavale and asked his family to call the radio station's number in Zagreb, Belgrade, or Sarajevo, where they could receive more detailed information. Regina was beside herself with joy; what she'd barely been able to hope for had happened because in the three months that she'd been listening to the broadcast, only twice had anyone learned anything about someone who was missing. And more than that: the announcer had not said "the deceased Ivo Delavale" but only "Ivo Delavale." From this she concluded that he was alive and forgot that the word "deceased" was never used on that program. It was almost prohibited, as it were, because so many people were sitting next to their radios in the hope that they would never hear it. If they heard that one of those whose names they'd memorized was deceased, they might lose all hope and give up, and after such a big war no one should presume to give up until every one of the missing had received a plot in a cemetery. She ran through the house as if she were crazy, turning the lights on and off, hugging Dijana, saying, "Daddy's called us! Our daddy!" and the child would squeal briefly, rejecting all her mother's offers and invitations to something that wasn't sleep.

As soon as the sun came up, she took Dijana in her arms and went off to the post office, sat down on a low stone wall, and waited for it to open. Her child was sleeping on her shoulder and was as heavy as a corpse; by six o'clock her arms and legs were already numb, and she thought that it might have been better to leave Dijana at home. But who would have taken care that the little girl wouldn't suffocate in a pillow, fall out of bed, or wake unexpectedly and wander the empty house in terror? If she hadn't given birth to her so late in life, maybe she would have left her at home more easily and worried about her less. But at forty a mother's instincts probably start to wane; women no longer know what's natural, what you can and can't do with a child.

"Old mothers don't have good milk," Zajka Mujić had told her when she'd come to help her with the childbirth, "so go ahead and find yourself a young nursemaid so your child won't be scrofulous." Afterward she looked at her breasts as at buckets full of cow's milk that had either been forgotten or as if someone had abducted the milkmaid, cut her throat, and thrown her into a ditch in the woods. Black images in a black time: it was 1944, Italy was in ruins, the Ustashas were raging, the Chetniks had descended on the city, there were all kinds of terrible tales about the partisans, and Regina was giving birth at the last possible moment in the worst time in which one could have brought a new life into the world. And everything turned out all right; the child was lucky enough to make it through the war. But then Bepo had gone crazy, and Milo Milidrag had knocked on her door, as if he'd come straight out of Bepo's head.

It seemed that there was a clear connection between those two tragedies and that fifteen months hadn't passed from the time of the first piece of bad news to that of the second. The first was true; the second was a lie. But it was one of those lies that can't make anything better and continues to exist even after it has been exposed. She couldn't forget her sleepless nights, and at times she bade farewell to her husband and mourned his every tenderness but at others raged at the bearer of the news. And then her rage would spill over against Ivo, who hadn't sent word of himself for more than two years.

She knew: connections were bad, stamps were expensive, letters didn't arrive, and ships carrying the mail sank in naval battles and storms.

But other women's husbands got in touch with them while at sea. If he'd sent word to her just once, she would have known that the Montenegrin was lying and would have crammed that tin box down over his ears because her Ivo had written that he was alive and well, and it couldn't be that he'd just up and died.

And maybe Ivo had written her ten times, sent packages and messages with people, but as chance had it nothing had arrived? Maybe he was now worrying about her just like she was worrying about him, anxious about whether she was alive and well? And if not her, then the child. Every father wondered at least ten times a day how his children were. If terrible images flashed before a mother's eyes and she ran into the room to see whether her child was sleeping or dead, what must it have been like for a father who hadn't seen his child for so long? It was much harder for Ivo than for her.

Nausea rose up from her stomach. Sorrow would overcome her, and she would cry, wonder what had happened to him, believe in the truth of the tin box under the sink, and bid farewell to her love, without whom life had no meaning. Nights passed like this, and that was the reason, when the head of the post office came up to her, why it seemed that time wouldn't wash away the Montenegrin sailor's lie.

Vito, a postal clerk, tried at first to get through to Radio Zagreb. He dialed the number on the black office telephone (which had been there ever since Habsburg times) at least twenty times, but all he heard in the receiver was silence or noise and static in which it was impossible to make out a human voice. Then he tried to call Sarajevo, but no one in the radio station picked up. "Fucking Bosnia," he mumbled and tried once more. Then he called Radio Belgrade. "You've got a connection," he said and held out the receiver to Regina.

"Hello, hello, hello," she shouted, though she could hear the female voice on the other end of the line clearly. But she didn't know how to begin or what to say.

"My husband Ivo Delavale . . . ," she tried to put a question together.

"According to information that we've received from Chicago, Comrade Ivo Delavale, formerly a sailor of the merchant marine of the Socialist Federative Republic of Yugoslavia, passed away on the first of January in that city. His body was cremated, and the ashes were released to an American citizen, Diana Vichedemonni, who paid for all expenses," the female voice recited. "Please accept our condolences. Goodbye!" the voice said, and the connection went dead.

Regina stood with the receiver in her hand and nodded, repeating, "Yes, yes, yes . . ." long after the woman on the other end had hung up. "Thank you and goodbye," she said when there was no longer any doubt in her mind.

Vito, the post office clerk, waited, curious to see what would happen—when Ivo's widow would start crying and wailing, because that was what happened whenever a wife called to inquire about her husband. The times were such that all people received were telegrams of death. However, she smiled, so Ivo must not have been dead.

"How much do I owe?" she asked.

"Good news is on me," he said and pushed the money back across the counter. "If there were more such news, I'd pay for all of it out of my pocket," he said, refusing to give in when she still tried to pay.

"Oh, how lucky you are," he thought as she went out. "You have no idea how lucky you are. It's only in misfortune that a man knows how good or bad he's got it and never any time else." Vito Anaf looked at his telephone, and he was glad for that woman.

But she'd done everything in her power to hold back her tears and keep her face from betraying any burden or anguish, convinced as she was that the postal clerk would take pleasure from the truth: that Ivo was dead and that the Belgrade woman had hung up before she'd managed to ask anything . . . Everyone enjoys things like that, even when they pretend they're sorry, even if they're ready to help you.

When she got outside, her mind focused on something that had overshadowed all her reasons for sorrow and despair in a split second: who was that woman who had "paid all expenses"? It was hardly possible that she was a good soul, a rich woman who saw those who had no one of their own in America into the other world. But she might have believed that, more from a desire for belief and love that was more important than truth, if only that woman's name hadn't been Diana! If the Belgrade lady had given some other name, if the stenographer in Radio Belgrade had made a mistake, or if the connection had been worse and if Regina had heard something else instead of Diana, her life would again have taken a different course. She would have worn black for Ivo her whole life; she would have kept the photograph of him in his royal sailor's uniform on her nightstand. She wouldn't have lived to ninety-seven but would have died when her time came, reconciled with her world and her fate. No great rage at life would have been born inside her that wouldn't let her heart stop beating. All her tenderness and fear turned into rage like wine turning into vinegar.

As she was walking home, she was trying to think up a way to get to Diana Vichedemonni and to answer the question of what that woman was to Ivo. Although she was already sure she knew the answer. When Ivo had burst into their house that night a month before she gave birth, she had been terrified to see him because the city was covered in wanted posters with his name on them. And she thought he was safe and secure on Vis, in England, or wherever Tito's sailors were.

"Are you thinking about this child at all?" she asked, rebuking him as the sleep left her eyes.

"We won't see each other for a long time," he said and lay down next to her though he was fully dressed; he hugged her from behind and caressed her belly with the palm of his hand.

"They'll hammer nails under your fingernails if they catch you," she said, nestling into his embrace.

"Stay like that," he said, stopping her when she wanted to turn around to face him, "just this one more time," he said, and she laughed.

He always said that same thing—"just this one more time, just this one more time"—regardless of whether they'd been together every night or he'd just come to her bed after having been away for months or years. Ivo liked being behind her, for her to snuggle against his body and to sleep like that or do what they did. Regina thought it strange, though she didn't know how others embraced and slept. But it seemed to her that this was a little unbecoming and that women didn't agree to do it even when their men wanted them to. And men thought up all sorts of things. Men were children and demons at the same time. A woman's mind couldn't imagine the things they would do in bed. Ivo had it easy with her, but others weren't like that. Especially if they went to church every Sunday. No ass that rubbed against a male member and mounted it would sit down on a pew, just as knees that knelt before a man didn't go down onto a *prie-dieu*. She didn't like it the first time he had pushed her head down and told her to kneel down in front of the bed and kiss what lips were not supposed to kiss. Did women who went to Mass every Sunday do that?! Regina didn't think so. And it bothered her because she knew where Ivo had learned what some women were ready to do and what kinds of depravities they could commit in bed. When he told her which harbors his ship had docked in, Regina's eyes filled with a parade of all those cross-eyed, long-haired blondes and brunettes, women who looked like monkeys and had flat noses and big mouths and you didn't know how men could find them attractive. She was sure that they spread their legs for Ivo, kneeled in front of him; that they wiggled their dark asses, invited him into them, and took him in as the ground takes in a mole. And what else would sailors do in a harbor besides go to the prostitutes? He never mentioned them, but did any man talk to his wife about such things? She wouldn't have felt jealous, nor would she have been afraid of catching diseases that came into the city from distant shores and about which people spoke in low tones because every woman on the coast was afraid of her husband bringing her gonorrhea from Singapore or the clap from black Africa. So they didn't dare relish the misfortune of those sad women whose husbands, it was told, had brought them, as a gift from warm seas, the drip, which no doctor in Zagreb or Belgrade could cure. It was something else that tormented Regina: whenever Ivo came home from the sea, she was afraid of the first night that she would spend with him in bed. She was also afraid of the third and fourth because who knew when it would occur to him, or how long it would take him, to get the courage to ask her to do to him what the harbor prostitutes had taught him. Would she be able to bring herself to do it? Would she know, and would she even be able to understand what she was supposed to do? Those women studied day and night what sailors' wives were supposed to know as soon as their husbands returned home from the sea. They had accumulated knowledge about everything a man could desire. Every desire of every last man in the world. And just as people are different, so their desires are also different. Black men don't want the same thing as our men, Regina thought, just as there were certainly differences between Japanese and American men. Just as their eyes and faces were different, so they differed in those parts of their bodies that only prostitutes saw. She didn't know anything about that; they knew everything. They also knew that men were insatiable children and wanted what wasn't meant for them but for others. And then prostitutes gave it to them. Whatever they gave to them, the sailors expected it from their wives later.

No matter how much she scorned them or at least tried to think about them as the whole city did, she felt respect for the prostitutes. The respect one has for doctors, lawyers, and magicians, people who possess knowledge without which the world wouldn't come to an end, but on which the world was based. And she was afraid whenever Ivo returned from the sea, wondering whether she would be able to do what they could.

When she first took him into her mouth and tasted the salty taste of what, as she believed, the majority of women didn't know, she believed it to have been sent from Africa or Singapore. She tasted cinnamon and nutmeg, spices of decadence that had no place in any food.

That last night, while he embraced her and monitored the life of his child with his palm, Ivo didn't ask for any of what the world had taught him. He lay there dressed, but she felt him through the silk and cotton. She would have felt him if there had been a stone wall between them and felt a powerful urge to take off her clothes and do whatever he wanted. Even what no whore could have showed him, and what a woman's body wasn't made for, and what would have killed her. Regina could have done everything and wanted everything, in love as she was that night with a love greater than the city and its walls, greater than its patron saint, greater than the war and all armies combined, greater than those who would have strung up her Ivo had they known he was there. She was so proud and felt herself to be the most fulfilled woman since the beginning of time because her husband had risked his life only to come to her and slip into her bed. If she'd doubted Ivo and if she'd thought what all women thought, that she wasn't anything important in his life and that she was just there by accident—just as some other woman could have been there—now she was sure of the fact that she'd been chosen, sure of the fact that she'd been created for him and that he would never exchange her for another woman. She moved in his embrace, snuggled and wiggled like a whore, and grabbed at his hard member and was then ashamed because he asked:

"It's going to be a girl, right?"

"That's what the Gypsy women said," she said and withdrew her hand quickly, hoping that she'd done it in time.

"Dijana," he said, "That's a nice name, Dijana."

She didn't answer him but was later deathly afraid that she would have a boy. That would have been a betrayal. Fortunately, she gave birth to none other than Dijana.

Every moment of that last night went through her mind as she returned home from the post office with the child in her arms. Shame and rage mingled, and she was disgusted by everything that she'd done for him in life. Everything that he had tricked her into doing. She felt his masculinity burning and blazing and wanting to make her as miserable as possible. She had a painful sore on the tip of her tongue. As if she'd stuffed herself eating green figs. Ivo's taste was so near that it seemed to her that all she needed to do was hurry a little or shout his name and he would appear here before her, naked, sticky, and hairy. Ivo Delavale! She would ask him who Diana Vichedemonni was, and no matter what he answered, she would do the same thing: cut him up in pieces, burn his wounds with glowing hot pine logs, and drip hot sap down his scrotum and pour it into his anus, that February almond blossom that one was forbidden to touch. He hadn't let her. And now she knew why! So she wouldn't think that he'd been doing things not only with the prostitutes but also with his comrades on the ship!

He wouldn't have been able to bear such suspicion. He would have fallen apart like an old marine engine, stopped being a man. If only once she'd recognized in him Geza Mađar, whose ear the local men had cut off, marking him so the whole city knew that it shouldn't get close to him because someone had seen him under the big windlass in the shipyard while a black man, an American sailor, was thrusting his cock into his ass. They'd beaten the black man all morning until all that was left of him was a bloody mass and one wasn't sure whether that was a man or someone had tossed a rotting bull's carcass next to the rusted shipyard dumpsters in the mud, grease, and petroleum. But they didn't beat Geza Mađar; rather they sent little Đivo, the five-year-old son of the barber Karlo Karakuna, to get his dad's razor. The little boy didn't know what they wanted the razor for, but he brought it.

"Uncle Mate asked for it," he told his father, and he, foolish as he was, didn't think at all about what a child might do with a razor but gave it to him and said, "tell Uncle Mate to bring it right back." The boy was happy that he could be of use and believed that he was entering the world of adults then and there. He was a little confused when he saw Uncle Mate holding Uncle Geza Mađar by the legs and Ale Pjevač squeezing his head in a headlock.

"Hand it over, boy!" Ivanko said, who was a student in Zagreb and the best swimmer in the city; he took the razor, grabbed Geza's ear, and cut it off in one stroke. Mađar started yelling, but Ivanko shoved the ear in his mouth:

"Eat it, you fucking faggot, eat it! If you don't eat it, I'll cut off your cock! You don't need it anyway!"

And so Geza Mađar ate his own ear. Đivo watched all that and didn't say a thing; he was frozen stiff with horror and watched what happens to people who aren't like other people and what one was supposed to do to a man whose dreams and desires differed from those who were holding him.

He'd known that Geza Mađar wasn't like other people in the city, but he wasn't sure how he was different. Because he was fat and limp, because he laughed as he greeted everyone, because he talked with the women who sold fish at the market and walked across the square as if the stones were going to move out from under his feet and he had to watch how he was going to step on each one, or was he different from others only because he was all alone and there were so many of them?

Đivo wasn't sure what was going on, but he asked Ivanko to give him the razor back. His dad would kill him if he didn't bring it back.

"Spit on him, and I'll give it to you!" the student said to him.

And so little Đivo spat on Geza Mađar while blood was gushing from his head.

"Tell him, 'Fuck your shitty ass!'" the student said.

And Đivo said that too, just to get the razor back. It was bloody, and so he wiped it off on his underwear on the way, and then he remembered that his mother would bawl him out because of that and he wanted to wipe away the blood, but how can you wipe away a stain? In the end he cut his finger. A thin, bloody cut opened. It didn't hurt, but as soon as he clenched his fist the cut widened, and the blood flowed out and it hurt. He would have cried, but he didn't dare and didn't have anyone to cry to. All that was important for him was to get the razor back.

Well, Ivo was afraid of Regina seeing in him something that was in Geza Mađar, and that was why he would jump away on the bed whenever she accidentally touched his almond blossom.

"What's wrong? I didn't mean to!" she would tell him, ashamed, so he wouldn't think that she'd intentionally gone there with her fingers. And it wasn't easy to tell where a man's desire—one that the prostitutes had taught him— ended and where the forbidden parts of his body began. The parts that distinguished ordinary men from the one-eared freaks one finds in every Dalmatian town.

However, her almond blossom, as he called it when on one of those nights, all smooth, erect, and purple, he'd wanted to enter her there, wasn't a forbidden spot. He decided that it wouldn't be. But how could it be that one of those body parts that men and women shared was for him a bastion of his honor but for her was an almond blossom that was to be deflowered?

Everything that ran through Regina's head, increasing her hatred with every step, had only to do with the nights that she'd spent with Ivo. The whole world fit into her bed, so she didn't think about what happened between them during the day and outside the bedroom. Her reasons for revenge, which would become greater than any of the other reasons she had to live, originated in her sense that Ivo hadn't been sleeping with her but with some other woman in his head, on account of whom he didn't want for her to be facing him in bed. He paid money to prostitutes but just lied to her. Everything else was the same, and he didn't see any difference between her and hundreds, maybe even thousands, of women whom he'd come to know in the harbors of the world. He'd loved only one and so had wanted to give his daughter her name.

She put Dijana down on the ottoman, grabbed a piece of paper and a pencil, and wrote: "It is with sorrow in our hearts that we announce that Ivo (Etorea) Delavale has died in America. He will be buried tomorrow, on Tuesday, in the family plot of Lovre Sikirić. He is mourned by his wife Regina and his daughter Dijana."

Then she thought a little and first crossed out the bit about sorrow in their hearts, and in place of the words about mourning she wrote, "He will be returned to the earth." And then she deleted the name of her daughter. She took the piece of paper and the box with the laughing black woman and went off to a funeral home.

Only when she'd left the house did she remember that she'd left Dijana. She stopped for a moment and then continued going down the stairs. That was the first time she had left Dijana alone at home. At first the undertakers didn't want to accept the metal box, but she threatened to open it and spread the ashes on the floor and they could deal with that. She refused the idea of finding a nice urn in town, for example, one of those in an apothecary's shop that contain ingredients for medicines.

"No, I'll bury him just like they sent him!" she said, rebuffing them, and the men in black didn't think of giving her any more problems.

The funeral didn't last long; there were no eulogies or priests. Luka brought a wreath; the neighbor ladies peered into the open vault, trying to check the

condition of great-grandfather Lovro, who had died in eighteen hundred something, and the other dead relatives that had followed him, but they couldn't
have seen much because it was dark inside the vault and there was no particular smell. It stank of stone and dampness, like the flooded cellars of houses destroyed in the war. The undertaker, dressed in black, brought the box of Ivo's
ashes covered with a black kerchief.

"Get that goddamned kerchief out of here!" his widow shouted; "take it off,
dammit!" She walked up and jerked the kerchief away, as in that magic trick
with the rabbit and the hat. There were sighs of shock. Even Luka felt awkward,
though he didn't stand on graveside formalities and hated the kind of people
who went to funerals. But it had never happened that someone had been buried
in a coffee can.

"She's gone wacko!" said the old women in their headscarves as they left the
cemetery. "Isn't she afraid of God?" they said out loud when Regina could no
longer hear them.

"You picked a fine time to wet yourself, you little devil!" Regina yelled at
Dijana and slapped her on the cheek. The child squealed, and she slapped her
again.

"What's wrong with you, woman?" Luka asked. He ran up and tore the girl
out of Regina's arms. Finding herself in safe hands, Dijana began to wail at full
throttle. Her uncle picked her up in his arms and said, "Your uncle will give
you some sugar," trying to comfort the girl and to catch up with Regina, who
was hastening furiously onward. He hustled after her all the way home, and the
more he quickened his pace, the more she hurried on, keeping three or four
meters ahead of him.

She never told Luka the whole truth about why she'd acted as she did, and
Luka didn't ask too many questions. His sister was seventeen years older than
he was. She'd behaved as a mother figure toward little Luka since he'd been
young; in fact she'd largely replaced his mother after she died of heart trouble
in 1927. She rarely shouted at him and didn't get upset at his whims but would
defend him in front of his older brothers, who'd already wanted to kick him
out of the house when he was thirteen because he'd caused a scandal with the
British consul at the Pile gates, on account of which the police had been called
to their house.

Luka thought it strange that Regina lost her temper, that she hit her child
for no reason and didn't shed a tear for Ivo. He thought there must be something behind this, that she would explain it to him and tell him what he ought
to know.

"He had some whore in Chicago," she said that same evening.

"Are you sure?" he asked instead of saying that every or almost every sailor had a woman somewhere and that she shouldn't get upset about it.

Regina just looked at him and didn't answer. Dijana was sitting on the potty next to the sink and didn't dare say that she didn't need to pee or poop. She didn't say anything and looked a little at her mother and a little at her uncle, until Luka finally realized that she'd been sitting on the potty for more than an hour and hadn't let out a peep. He clapped his hands and asked:

"Are we done, Brother Socrates?" He grabbed Dijana and turned her upside down to inspect the situation. There was a completely regular and clear red circle on her bottom, the imprint of the edge of the potty.

"Nothing happened?" he asked, acting strict, smelling her bottom. She laughed like crazy and was never afraid again.

Luka asked, "Are we done, Brother Socrates?" five or six times a day. He wiped Dijana's bottom, changed her diaper when she got to playing and wet herself, and took her along into town, from café to café. And she would sit peacefully for hours while her uncle played cards. That was the rule. When uncle played cards, you had to be quiet and calm. So that no other uncles would chase them away.

"Sit still and think about me getting the best cards. If you think about it hard enough, I'll get them," he told her, and she would think as hard as she could. Although uncle hadn't said exactly how it worked, she worked out the best combinations of aunts, kings, and cops. And she always kept an ace in her heart because that was the card that her uncle liked best.

Although the image in Dijana's head didn't correspond to what Luka had in his hands (because if it had, Luka would have lost money), he began a long winning streak that would last until Dijana started going to school.

At first he thought it was luck, but he soon came to believe in Dijana's supernatural abilities. Or he believed that the child belonged to him and that he belonged to her according to some higher law of the universe. Luka wasn't just Dijana's uncle, nor was she just some little niece of his. Their being together logically produced his success at gambling. While she sat in the corner, crossed her fingers, frowned, and thought hard, he won. And whenever she stayed at home because she'd caught a cold or her mother objected to his taking her out all the time, his card game went nowhere and he would start losing.

Soon others linked her presence with his luck, and they told him not to bring the girl any more. Who ever heard of someone bringing a child to a card game?! He asked them what kind of men and gamblers were afraid of a four-year-old girl. If she could beat them, then they should forget cards and grab their hoes. In the end it was decided that Dijana could be present but not always. She could come only during the week; on the weekends they would play alone.

Thus, just like a real working man, Luka earned money on the weekdays, and on the weekends he spent what he'd earned or didn't go play cards at all but would go out on adventures with his niece. They would get into a rowboat and row—instead of an oar, she would slap the water with a big cooking spoon—to one of the little islands and play Robinson Crusoe all day long. He would catch fish on a line, light a fire by striking flint on the rocks, and they would cook the fish they'd caught and imagine how many years they'd been there and when it was that they'd seen a ship in the distance the last time. They'd usually been there for more than twenty years and seen a ship seven years before. Dijana was thrilled that in this game there was no one else in the world except them, and Luka wasn't unhappy to pretend that he was left alone with that child and no longer had to deal with people, who'd been savages for too long already.

They'd become savages not long after naked Mrs. Simpson and Edward had sunned themselves on their beaches, and he'd watched the princess, thinking how beautiful she was and how happy her queendom would be. That was the final scene of a romantic and joyful world, the one that had existed before the advent of talking movies. After Mrs. Simpson and Edward left for good, the noise of explosions began, spreading from city to city and country to country, and was followed by the rattle of daggers and knives. Italian soldiers marched through the city with plumes of rooster tail feathers on their helmets, men went to war, women baked flatbread for long trips, and it was shameful to remain outside that crazy bloodbath.

For him, however, shame was more familiar and more preferable than living the life of the brave and those who were dying. He didn't see any great politics behind what was happening or anything else that wouldn't be clear to any sane person. He wasn't interested in Germany, Croatia, or even the fight against fascism. Maybe he liked Stalin better than Hitler, and Churchill better than Mussolini, and maybe he cheered for Tito because his brother Bepo was in the partisans, but Luka was more concerned about convincing the city of his harmlessness. Playing the clown and the fool, the one who wasn't the rival of any man and didn't seek love from any woman, he was actually asking to be excepted from everything that was the lot of others by their hearts or through misfortune. However, he didn't lose his awareness of what he was doing and how hard it was to turn a whole city to his advantage and always keep it convinced of that. Nothing changed, not even with the end of the war because then the champions and the avengers came, whom he also had to convince that he wasn't standing in their way and wasn't worthy of their ire. And in 1947 and the following years that ire was terrible and at times seemed more terrible than the war.

If an adult could believe in it, and Luka believed in it without any problem, the Robinson Crusoe game was one of the best ways to get a respite from every ire.

Besides playing cards and Robinson Crusoe, they had one more adventure. Every month they went to Kuna, to the Delavale summer home. He pruned the grapevines or harvested grapes or would negotiate the olive harvest in the village. After Ivo died and the summer home was passed on to Regina, Luka toyed with the idea of moving to Kuna, weeding the grapevines, planting olive trees, and living his life like that. But that idea didn't hold him for long. He didn't have the will or intelligence for serious plans and would only make them until they left the kingdom of his imagination, after which he left them to take their own paths, farther and farther away from him. Because who would dig vineyards their whole life long, plant olive trees, and worry about peronospores, siroccos, and boras, about storms and thunderstorms and bouts of the flu that would come as soon as one had to dig or prune something? When a man plans like that, then he's figuring on a wife and children, and a wife and children would have been another source of worry for him, complications and still more serious plans in which there was no happiness. In the twenty-fifth year of his life he believed that he would never have children and was fairly certain that he wouldn't get married. Until two or three years before it had really bothered him that he'd never slept with a woman and all those who'd gone with him to school had, or at least said they had. If there had been any prostitutes left in the city, he would have certainly collected his money and gone off to one of them to open his eyes, as one used to say then. But this was in 1944 and 1945, and the prostitutes had fled in the face of all the dying and creating of states. Then his desire passed, and he realized that entry into the world of men would do him more harm than good. Sex and love between men and women were like opium—once you tried it, you had to have it for the rest of your life. And nothing that obliges a man in such a way can be pleasure. When he arrived with Dijana at the Delavale summer home, he again chose games instead of life. He felt like a rich drunk and an heir to large properties, and so he communicated with the village, paid for their wine in the village tavern, and offered to let them harvest his olive grove so cheaply that in the end they believed that he had money to burn. It suited him that they thought this and treated Dijana like a princess.

"She's not a child, you uneducated lout; she's a lady!" he yelled at the tavern keeper, who'd said that he didn't have any drinks for children. "Bring her a glass of water! The main distinction between you and her is that the lady knows that water is the most healthy drink on earth."

The tavern keeper waddled off to the kitchen while exclamation points swarmed over his head as in Disney's Mickey Mouse comic strip. He neither knew what the word "distinction" meant, nor did he understand why water should be the most healthy drink in the world, but the comment that he was "uneducated" worried him. He knew what that word meant, but no one had ever used it to describe him. That word was spoken on the radio, in tales of murderers and policemen broadcast from Belgrade. And he would hear it from ministers who held speeches at the ceremonial openings of work actions. "Our youth didn't even lack education, not even when they charged at enemy bunkers!" Comrade Boris Kidrič used to shout out. That was all the tavern keeper needed to conclude that this man had insulted him. He brought Luka his wine and Dijana her water and went back to the kitchen to get away from them. The world had been turned on its head; there could be no doubt about that, but he was in a bind about what that man was to that girl. They certainly weren't father and daughter; he would probably be something to her that there hadn't been before. He would ask around in the village.

"What are you looking at?" he yelled at old Tera, who was peeling potatoes, grabbed his hat, and went out through the back door.

"Do you know that your daddy's dead?" Luka asked the girl.

"I know," she said, looking somewhere under the table.

"And do you know what 'dead' means?" he asked.

"He won't be coming back, and mommy is mad at me," she answered.

"She isn't mad; why would she be mad?"

"Oh, yes she is; I know."

"She's not mad; she's just having a hard time."

Dijana shrugged her shoulders. It amounted to the same thing: mother was mad or she was having a hard time. There wasn't any difference between those two things.

"I'm having a good time," she said and laughed.

"And I'm having a good time, too," her uncle said and slammed his glass on the wooden table. "We've got it good!"

"Will I always have it good?" the girl asked insistently.

"Only as good as good is good! Whoever's got it good today will always have it good. That's the rule, and that's what was decided in Yalta!"

"And what's Yalta?" she asked.

"Well, you see, that's another story, and I don't think this is the time," he said and swatted with his hand as if trying to get rid of bees, knowing that this would just lead her to more questions.

"Tell me, tell me; what's Yalta?" she begged.

"But only if you listen closely and remember everything, so you can tell if someone asks you," he said, feigning a strict tone.

"I'll listen. I'll listen to the whole thing," she said, fidgeting in her chair like Lindbergh before takeoff.

"It's like this," he began. "Yalta was a cellar, or rather a stable where three uncles, or rather hooligans, met."

"Don't talk like that," she interrupted. "Don't say 'or rather.' What are hooligans?"

"Well, this is going to be hard without 'or rather.' But let's try. The three of them got together in that stable, and each one had a magic stone. Those were stones that looked like ordinary stones but weren't ordinary because you could see through them like glass, but they weren't glass but stones. Don't ask anything else about the stones because I don't know anything else myself. If I knew, I'd find one myself. You can do everything with one of those stones. You can decide how long the night will last, and how long the day will last, whether people will walk on their hands or on their legs, and whether houses will sprout up from their roofs or their foundations. Well, there was a problem because each one of those three men had one of the stones, and they had to decide how things were going to be. It wouldn't work if one of them decided the day would be sixteen hours long and the other decided it would be only five hours long and the third one said there wouldn't be any day at all. People had to know how things were going to be and what to expect," he explained.

Dijana frowned. She didn't understand why one of the uncles would want the day to last sixteen hours and the other for it to last only five hours. "But were their magic stones exactly the same?" she asked.

"I have to say that they were. Except they were slightly different colors, but everything else was just the same," Luka said.

"And each was as powerful as the others?" she asked.

"Right! That was what was worst; all three stones were equally powerful. Well, the three of them sat down at that Yalta and didn't come out for three days and three nights."

"And how long did those three days and three nights last?" Dijana asked, whereupon he got confused. He didn't know what to tell her: which one of the uncles had decided how long the days and nights in Yalta would be?

"That's a very good question, a good question," he said, trying to extricate himself, "but they shut themselves up in Yalta so they wouldn't see when it was day and when it was night but just let the sun go up and go down whenever it wanted until the three stones made an agreement. And they decided that one of the stones would tell the other two, 'You are the prettiest,' and the other one would say, 'You are the smartest,' and the third would say, 'You are the strongest.' Since there were three of them and each one was going to say something to the other two, no one knew any more which one was the prettiest, the smartest, or the strongest. So they decided to divide the world up into three equal parts, and each would decide everything in its part. That's why it's nighttime in America when it's day over here, and that's why some people are rich and others are poor. Those three men agreed on all of it in Yalta," he said, disappointed that his fable hadn't come off.

It had simply slipped away from him at one moment and turned into something that he hadn't wanted to tell her and didn't understand himself.

"Did they decide in Yalta that mother would be angry and have it bad?" Dijana asked just when the tavern keeper appeared in the doorway.

He watched them with scorn in the corners of his mouth and nodded. "I know everything," he said. "Now I understand everything! I understand everything!" he repeated and wiped unseen dust off the tables with a rag.

"Let's go," Luka whispered to Dijana.

"Just go; go and farewell!" the tavern keeper said, who'd caught Luka's words; "you don't even need to pay! Just don't ever come back here again! It'll be better for you, you old pig!"

They went toward their house in silence. Luka was ashamed because he hadn't stood up to the man in front of the little girl, and she was happy that they'd gotten out of there. That man was certainly one of the three men in Yalta, she concluded. Uncle Luka just didn't want to tell her that, and she wasn't going to ask him, so he wouldn't have to lie to her or he wouldn't have to see what she saw—that Uncle Luka was afraid of that man. For all she cared, he could be afraid; they'd be afraid of the man together. Dijana would be more afraid, just so that Uncle Luka would have it easier. Luka was worried about what the tavern keeper might have heard about him since he came back like that. And who might he have heard it from? He wouldn't get an answer, but he never went back to any of the taverns in Kuna with Dijana. He would remain like that until their last trip together.

That was the only bad thing that happened on Luka's and Dijana's adventures. Otherwise there was only tenderness and happiness, for him as much as for her. In those crazy years they were each other's guardian angels. He'd saved her from Regina's crazy obsession with that other Dijana. The girl had become the apogee of a lie, but she'd saved Luka from years of partisan revenge, love and hatred for Stalin, and everything else that might have cost him his head if he hadn't played Robinson Crusoe, hadn't had a guardian angel for his gambling, and hadn't gone off with her to Kuna. They would have continued protecting one another if Dijana hadn't gone off to school and Regina hadn't decided at that time to take Dijana's life into her own hands. As long as someone needed to feed and dress her, teach her her first words, and create images of a happy childhood for her, Regina had left her child in Luka's care, but the moment the little girl had to go out among other children and thus find herself before the eyes of the city, Regina tore her out of her brother's arms. It was enough that he wasn't like ordinary people and that he was the shame of the family. She wasn't going to let him shape and knead her daughter according to his own standards. And besides, what would a female Luka be like? A little whore that would smile at everyone and be everyone's crazy entertainment and delight. Maybe a man could be like that, but thank you very much, a woman couldn't! Especially not a woman from the Delavale line who already bore wickedness within herself.

After the first days of September in 1951 Regina never again let Dijana go play cards with her Uncle Luka or play Robinson Crusoe. It didn't matter whether it was a weekday or Sunday; she forced her to sit next to the stove and study, in the same wooden chair in which she would grow old and which would burn up along with everything else in the wartime blaze in 1991. She told Luka not to interfere with her child and not to do any harm if he couldn't be of any use. He pulled back, partly because he believed his older sister and partly because he didn't think he could save anyone besides himself. Right until he fled to Italy, he watched calmly as Dijana's mother raised her, barely saying anything and forgetting the promises that he'd made to her and about the secret brotherhood that he'd created with her. That was his only sin, but no one even remembered it.

Regina made inquiries about Diana Vichedemonni for another ten years after she'd buried the rusty can with the inscription *Santos* and the picture of a laughing black woman. She wrote the owners of the ships on which Ivo had sailed since the '30s, asking them to please send the lists of sailors. She lied, saying that she was searching for her brother, with whom she was supposed to divide a great inheritance. She promised money if they found him, made up stories about Swiss bank accounts, signed her name as the Contessa Regina Della Valle, and went to Professor Svitić to have her letters translated into Italian, French, German, and English. She ordered a stamp with her name and monogrammed stationery, until she'd spent the family gold and sold all their vineyards on Pelješac. This obsession with an unknown woman, the only person who could extinguish the fire of Regina's rage at life, was too expensive in every sense. Besides the family estate, the value of which was better expressed in memories than in the fluctuations in the price of gold on the world markets, Regina put everything else up for auction. What belonged to her and what didn't. Diana Vichedemonni became her only thought, the center of the cosmos, a black sun in her heliocentric experience of the world. Everything that did and didn't exist revolved around that name, around its own axis, and around

Diana. No one would be able to escape the gravitational pull of that black sun, nor could anything that Regina heard, saw, sniffed, touched, or felt, no matter in which way. A whole half-century later the whole family would come flying apart because of Diana Vichedemonni, and a new chain of misfortunes would begin, in which Regina's death would involve people who'd never had any prior connection to her. The heliocentric systems of misfortune repeated in cycles. They were the only living history, a history that didn't die away but was passed from generation to generation and from age to age. They existed even hundreds of years later. Just as Hitler's crimes were still alive for the wider world and caused suffering for children who were born after the collapse of the Third Reich, so for small worlds, familial microcosms, and romantic unions such small crimes, completely insignificant from the perspective of historiography, were eternal.

From time to time answers came from Lloyd's and George J. Robinson & Sons, in which they directed Regina to the Yugoslav embassies in London and Washington. A letter also came from Samuel F. Klein, a prewar shipbuilder in Trieste who was living in Haifa in 1951. He wrote her that he didn't know anything about the fate of his four ships but that all the papers had burned in the fires that had been lit by the black shirts in 1938, that he was sorry that the lady couldn't locate her brother but was surprised that she was only looking for him on account of the inheritance: "My advice to you is to look for him for some other, more noble reasons. Then the dear Lord will grant that you find him!"

She shed a tear at those words and pitied a man whom fate had led to say such things. That couldn't be anything other than fate, she thought: from some, death takes away everyone they loved and all those who never did any wrong. She didn't know that Samuel F. Klein could have told her at least part of the truth about Ivo if she'd only asked the right questions instead of asking for a list of sailors on the ship *Leonica*. And maybe Klein would have recognized who was writing to him if she'd written her surname as it was properly spelled. Or maybe he even knew and that was the reason why he was telling her to find better and more noble reasons for her search. It's a difficult claim to make, but it wasn't impossible that Samuel F. Klein might have saved Regina Delavale in more fortunate circumstances or if her rage had been a little softer and more reasonable. Maybe it would have been enough for her to have known who in fact Samuel F. Klein was.

VII

In the winter of 1942, Samuel F. Klein was a captive in the attic of the Banja Luka prep school. No one had actually captured him; even so, he didn't dare go out because he was a son of Abraham, one of those whom you could recognize by their noses, as people said. But Klein was given away by more than his big, eagle-like nose, which reached almost all the way down to his chin: he looked just like one of those Nazi character sketches. He was short and hunched, with a narrow chest and legs that were bowed as if he were riding a barrel; he had beady eyes, bushy black eyebrows, and hair that was always greasy (none of the shampoos and pomades he was able to get in good times from London and Paris had helped). Had he gone down from the prep school attic, he wouldn't have reached Gospodska Street before someone nabbed him. If not the Ustashas, then some conscientious citizens, and there were as many of those in Banja Luka as anywhere else in ordinary times and in states with no racist laws on the books. People who reported stray dogs to the city dog pound would also report Jews and Gypsies after the establishment of the great German Reich or any other *Reich*.

Klein thought about this as he lay on the dusty ottoman and played with a large school globe. He was bothered by a single memory: in 1919 he'd been sitting in his nephew Hugo's law office in Sušak, and Hugo, excited about the final establishment of authority and normal life, telephoned the local mayor and warned him of the need to establish a city dog pound because stray dogs had reproduced so much during the war years and the years of anarchy that they threatened epidemics of infectious diseases. Not only did Samuel not object, but he agreed with his nephew and was genuinely surprised by the mayor's lack of interest in the problem and the rude manner in which he got rid of the Sušak lawyer on the telephone.

Had the dogs really disturbed them? Had they been aggressive, and did their nightly barking annoy the two of them? No matter how he tried to invent positive answers, Samuel F. Klein couldn't remember a single negative experience with dogs in Sušak. Shaggy and hungry, they steered clear of people and ran when they saw a man fifty meters away. They seemed fairly disappointed by the entire race of bipeds. The dogs of Sušak, Klein thought, had reached a third evolutionary phase: from their wild ancestors and their docile forefathers there had arisen the contemporary kind of dogs: those resigned to their fate, creatures of fear, terror, and philosophical melancholy. When they were left alone, they lay on trash heaps and blinked in the sunlight. Apart from their communication with each other, that was their only interaction with the outside world. The sun alone didn't threaten them with evil.

Why then had those dogs bothered him and his nephew Hugo? He realized that the dogs hadn't bothered them. Rather, they'd transformed their euphoria at the birth of a new state into a feeling that measures needed to be taken against stray dogs. It was one of numerous hygienic imperatives. And in times when states were being built, men lived on imperatives. If they hadn't been so enthusiastic about their new state, they would have in all likelihood realized that there were much greater threats to public hygiene than dogs. Or they wouldn't have thought about public hygiene at all. Similar rules were in effect now, and because of them he didn't dare leave the attic. The only difference lay in the fact that the need for dog pounds had been replaced by the need for camps, and the elimination of stray dogs had in the contemporary world been turned into the elimination of Jews, Gypsies, and Orthodox Christians. That is, people. Men weren't the same as dogs, but the excitement that occurred when a *Reich* or another state came into being didn't recognize the difference between men and dogs.

The question that Klein pondered most, and to which there was no answer, was this: would he, if he weren't a son of Abraham, be an alert and conscientious citizen of the new state and report bipeds without pedigrees? He didn't understand how people could become wild beasts overnight, and he tried to convince himself that this couldn't ever happen to him. But then he would remember 1919, the pins with the likeness of King Petar the Liberator; anxious looks toward Rijeka, which people guessed was going to go to the Italians; and the relief that he'd felt when his nephew Hugo decided to offer their joint contribution to the birth of a new state. He took no consolation in the fact that nothing had come of the dog pound or that both of them would have been sorry had they seen people hunting down dogs. The fact that he'd felt or done something on account of the state that he otherwise wouldn't have was indisputable. Patriotism dribbled all around like honey from a silver spoon, and it sought blood with which it could mix. Whether it was the blood of dogs or men depended more on the nature of the newborn state than it did on the souls that were the source of the patriotism. The new state of 1919 left its citizens the freedom to choose their victims, and so Samuel and Hugo chose stray dogs; the state of 1941 stated clearly in its laws whose blood it sought. And this was written out on every street corner, every signboard, on the emblem and the flag. It was manifest in its military and police uniforms, their colors and cut, the death's heads and heroic songs of elite units. Patriotism was honey and blood. The living were divided into patriots and those beings whose blood was to be sacrificed. A month of staying in the prep school was enough for Samuel F. Klein to swear that he would never love another state again.

He'd come to Banja Luka in the autumn of 1941 from the village of Štivor near Prnjavor, traveling on the horse-drawn wagon of Husnija Hadžalić, under some hay that gave him allergy attacks. He'd thought that he was going to suffocate a dozen times or so in two days. But worse than that was the fact that Husnija, otherwise a gem of a person, had no idea what an allergy was. He was sticking his own neck out to save Klein's; both of them would have been executed on the spot if someone had discovered a Jew under the hay. And he was deeply disappointed in the man whom he was trying to save:

"You say the hay suffocates you. Of course it would when you're from the city. It's good it only suffocates you. It's a wonder it doesn't pinch and stick you. May thunder strike me dead if I understand anything you're saying! The Ustashas are after you. The police are chasing you. You've got the whole government after you. Oh, no more, no less than the government! But your own ass isn't as important as showing Husnija that you grew up in silk and velvet and that his hay bothers you. As if I wouldn't have wanted to roll around in silk and velvet. But, my good man, I warmed myself in cowshit! And I thought there was nothing better than that. Until I came to the city and you told me my hay bothers you. Allah Jalla Shanuhu wouldn't be able to get a grip on Himself if he saw this. But fortunately He doesn't see it. He gave up on this stuff a long time ago."

Klein tried in vain to explain the nature of his illness to the peasant.

"What kind of illness is it that doesn't pass from person to person and you only get it from hay?" Husnija asked.

"Some people get it from hay, others from flour, flowers, or berries."

"There's no such illness, and that's that! Do you know what that illness of yours is called in Bosnia?" Husnija asked him. "It's called a dog's whim! But you come down with it while you're a child, and no one's ever heard of an old fart catching it. No sir! And do you know what the only medicine is for a dog's whim? A stick, a whip, and a willow switch, right across the ass! Some need more, some less, but they're all cured of it. I fear it's too late for you."

As he listened to him, Klein didn't know whether to laugh or cry. But in any case he regretted having shown himself in such a bad light to the man who was saving his skin. When they parted, Klein wanted to give him two Franz Joseph ducats, but Husnija wouldn't take them.

"My hand would fall off if I took them," he said and vanished into the night. It would have been worth more than gold to him if the good Allah had made the world so that people didn't curse his hay.

Franjo, the school janitor, put Klein up in the attic so he could stay there for five or six days, until a contact came who would transfer him to the Italian zone of occupation. Until then Franjo would feed and attend to him. He wouldn't need a thing, but he wasn't supposed to show his face below the attic, nor should he lower his feet from the ottoman during the day, when the pupils were at school, because the ceilings were thin and someone would hear it. So during the day there was no taking a shit or a piss. If he got the urge, he'd better go in his pants! If he behaved differently and the Ustashas discovered him, Franjo would act as if he didn't know about him and would spit on him and give him a kick in the ass to boot. But if he was smart and followed the rules, there was no chance of anyone discovering him. The agreement was made: every evening the janitor would bring him food and a newspaper, and every morning he would carry away the full night pot.

"Well, I've never seen anyone who shits and pisses as much as you!" the janitor told him on the third day.

Klein blushed and began to apologize, only to realize later that Franjo liked talking about shitting, pissing, and farting. That was probably some kind of mental defect of his, but he could go on about those three things for hours, in thousands of different ways, and it really cheered him up when Klein realized this and started telling him about his experiences.

They would sit on the ottoman in complete darkness for hours and tell one another stories of their own and others' toilet experiences. Franjo was most enthusiastic when Klein told him about a Frenchman, about whom the Zagreb *Jutarnji list* had written way back in '20-something, who could fart the whole *Marseillaise* without missing a single note.

"You say not a single false note anywhere?! A perfect ear!" Franjo exclaimed, laughing like crazy. "And people bought tickets to hear him?! And women came to the concerts?! Wearing hats? And they took clothespins to plug their noses. You know what I tell you?! He was a great man! If you're not just making him up. If you are, then you're a great man. On my mother Mara, I've never heard a better tale in my life. Is the master farter still alive? Of course, how could you know whether he's alive? If he is, he must be having a hard time. Now he can play the *Marseillaise* for some Kraut and lose his hide," he said, worried about the fate of the Parisian musician.

After he traded stories with the janitor, Samuel F. Klein was left alone and he read the newspaper, in which he searched for news of a world without war.

There were few such pieces of news, and there had always been few of them. But you didn't notice until the war spread to your own backyard. It didn't take a world war for all the pages of all the world's newspapers to have nothing but stories of wars of the present and future. Only earlier he'd read newspapers without trepidation and without feeling that he of all people was affected by what they wrote about. Back then, if a mental disquiet came over him, which happened very seldom—once or twice in six months, and he felt that every tragedy was connected to every other tragedy, and that every one of them would come to his doorstep—then he simply wouldn't read the newspapers. He waited for the disquiet to pass, and when that happened, he returned to the unrest in the world, calm and collected. But now everything was different. There were no news stories that he didn't take very personally. Thus, the newspaper became a man's intimate diary for that day. The day before someone else had known how he would feel today.

Ten days passed like that, but the contact who was supposed to smuggle Klein into Italy never showed up.

"It's happened before," said Franjo, trying to comfort him. Unsuccessfully, because Samuel was already on the verge of a nervous breakdown. Soon he would either jump off the roof of the prep school or walk outside, and they could catch him and do whatever they wanted with him. There was no way he was going to stay there any longer.

"Do as you please, effendi!" the janitor said angrily. "You just go ahead and jump, and for all I care, they can quarter you and cut your throat, but why did you come here to me? Do you think I like doing this, keeping Orthodox and Jews up here in the attic? You say some keep goats and chickens, and crazy Franjo took you in so he could give you food and drink to fatten you up! It's kind of like that, except you don't lay eggs or give milk, and now you want to turn yourself in to the Ustashas to boot. Well, you know what I'd do to you if you were a chicken? I'd cut your head off! I fed you, and I'll be the one to cut it off! Since you're not a chicken, I can only say that you've screwed me good," Franjo said and left the attic without saying good-bye.

That night he didn't leave him anything to eat or drink, so Klein, hungry and thirsty, had to think hard about both his stomach and his nerves. This kind of life made no sense, and if half the world wanted to see him dead, then it was really smartest to say, "Fine, here's my head since it's worth so much to you! I don't get much use out of it." If I do that, Klein thought, nobody has the right to rebuke me for it, not those who are in the same position as me, not even God if he exists. Klein was ready to end his suffering and was, as Husnija said, done with life. His kin were condemned to disappear, over there where he was called a

Yid and here where they called him a Jew and in every corner of the globe where he was called thousands of various names, and it made no sense at all. Nor was there any way for Samuel F. Klein of all people to resist it.

If all Jews had to disappear and that was the way of the world, what factors might make him, just one of many Jews, an exception to that general rule? Hoping for that was like hoping that the force of gravity wouldn't apply to him alone. It was easy to walk on water when you were a Catholic saint and hundreds of millions of people believed that you were really walking on water, but how could he do the same thing without anyone believing in it? He could only regret that he'd been born into the sons of Abraham so late, right at the time when it was decided that they were no longer supposed to exist. Had every generation of his forefathers going back two thousand years ago married and reproduced just a month earlier, he would be living in happier times, in the seventeenth or eighteenth century or even earlier. He would have had his own little shop and synagogue and would have died like a man. From the plague, cholera, or syphilis, without suffering on account of something for which he wasn't to blame and wasn't responsible.

Klein's Jewishness, like every other group membership, was for him an unsolvable mathematical problem. There were probably people who'd figured out what it meant to be a Jew, a Catholic, a Muslim, or a Buddhist. Those were people who deserved an A-plus in arithmetic. They knew how to calculate differences in weight, height, and the depth of air. But Klein was a bad mathematician in those areas. If Jewishness was something that could be measured in register tones or monetary units, he wouldn't have had a hard time with it and certainly wouldn't have ended up in the attic of the Banja Luka prep school. True, he celebrated Hanukkah and Passover. But was that really a reason why he and the whole tribe of Abraham had to disappear from the face of the earth? He drank alcohol, worked on the Sabbath, and didn't give alms to poor Jews, and now God was punishing him. But why was he punishing him along with those who hadn't sinned against a single earthly or heavenly rule?

He couldn't figure any of it out, but during the night of fasting that the janitor had imposed on him, Klein nevertheless came to an important conclusion. Of the two worries, his and that of his feeder, the second was more powerful, and he should try to accommodate it. Jumping off the roof and thereby causing harm to Franjo was out of the question. His conscience started bothering him and he felt guilty. The less a person's circumstances offer him opportunities to be guilty, the stronger his feelings of guilt.

He could hardly wait for the next morning, the time when Franjo came for the potty. Franjo came in frowning, angry.

"I've got something to tell you," he said and grabbed Franjo by the sleeve, but he pulled away. "I've got something to tell you," he insisted. "Please, sit down!"

The janitor sat down on the ottoman, holding the chamber pot with Klein's stool on his lap, as if it were a ceremonial chalice that he was going to present to the winners of the European Czech Handball championship. But the frown didn't leave his face. Klein thought about telling him to put the potty down so the stench wouldn't bother both of them. But he was afraid that this might anger Franjo and that he would leave again, and then he would have to wait until evening. So he decided not to pay attention to the shit for now.

"Forgive me; my nerves have given out. I won't do what a chicken or a goat wouldn't do," he said.

"Are you messing with me?" Franjo asked him in an icy tone. He didn't like his mentioning animals.

"I made a mistake," Klein said.

"You made more than a mistake. You stuck a knife in my heart!" Franjo said more cheerily and raised the ceremonial chalice as if he wanted to emphasize his words.

From that morning onward there were no more misunderstandings of that kind between the two men. Klein no longer mentioned the contact who was to transfer him to Italian territory, and Franjo would only occasionally, once or twice a week, confirm that they weren't coming and that it was bad that they weren't coming. Just as it was bad when there was an unexpected snowfall or when it was cloudy when it was supposed to be sunny. He brought him food and water and took away his stools and urine. Klein lived to the rhythm of the sunrise and sunset, as the holy books of all monotheistic religions prescribe and how people had lived in distant times when they followed the changes of the day and the seasons. And so Klein lived like a chicken.

During the day he would sit on the ottoman, shifting from buttock to buttock, doze, and wait for the chickens to hatch, and at night he would sleep or go searching around the attic in the complete darkness for something that might give him a little bit of entertainment. By groping around, he recognized old school registers for the lower and higher grades of the prep school and placed them by the ottoman so that he would have something to read the next day. He had laid off the newspapers for a while, realizing that they made him more sick. And he'd already grown tired of the globe. He knew every state, city, and mountain by heart. And he'd studied the map of the Austro-Hungarian Empire so thoroughly that there wasn't a single hamlet from Bratislava to Višegrad that he hadn't visited in his fantasies.

After he learned everything there was to learn about places, he started studying people. Long-gone prep school pupils were lined up one after the other. Klein followed them from year to year, and from their grades he arrived at conclusions about their mental crises and loves, about their temperaments and characters, and about what had happened to those people after they had graduated. Could one conclude from the fact that someone had had a hard time with Latin in the first grade of prep school that he ended up a murderer? Or was it the straight-A students who became murderers? He developed a system of reading fates from school grades, according to which the consistent pupils — those who passed from start to finish with an "A" or a "C" (it didn't matter which) — became people who would turn up any time a state needed anything done. But the pupils whose grades varied would become defenders of justice who wouldn't acquiesce in a single crime. During the day he categorized them, and at night he assessed the previous day according to the results of his statistics. If the inconsistent pupils predominated, those who hadn't become murderers or accessories to murder, the day was a good one. But if the straight-A students and lowlifes took the lead, then the day was assessed as bad. Klein played and remembered: all the countries, cities, mountain peaks, villages, rivers, streams, and all the pupils of the Banja Luka prep school from its foundation to 1934, the year of the last register. He wouldn't forget a single name until his death in 1967 in Haifa, just as he wouldn't forget any of hundreds of thousands of other, equally pointless, pieces of information that he'd collected in his head. Samuel F. Klein was one of those people whose miraculous and peculiar memory was the wonder of all who knew him, but he gained no benefit from it because it absorbed only useless things and classified them in a still more useless fashion. He was incapable of remembering three telephone numbers, but he memorized the school grades of people about whom he knew nothing else. He would forget the names of his own ships but not the names of all the little rivers and streams that flow into the Drina.

Maybe this was how he remembered the name of Ivo's wife and recognized it in the contessa Regina Della Valle in her letter of 1951.

And so spring arrived in the alternation between the same morning and evening rituals, without anyone coming for Klein. He was sure that Franjo knew what was going on and why the contact had never showed up but wasn't telling him so as not to upset him. However, the janitor didn't know any more than the one he served. The letter that Husnija Hadžalić had given him along with Klein said to wait. Panther, the contact, was supposed to come in seven days at the latest. If he didn't come by that time, he should keep waiting and taking care of the friend whom he'd entrusted to him. But Panther didn't contact them, nor did he ever come, and Franjo didn't ever see him in town. Before he had run into him every other day, if not on the street, then in those two or three city bars where people played dice. On account of their conspiracy Panther acted as if he didn't know him, though over the course of six months he'd brought him fourteen men and one woman, some of whom were Jews from Sarajevo or Travnik and some of whom were communists. He always gave him money for the hotel in the attic, and Franjo would have enough left over for his own expenses.

But the money that he'd given him for Klein had run out in two weeks, and afterward Franjo had to make do however he could. Yet that wasn't what bothered Franjo the most—where there's enough for one mouth, there's enough for two, and the care of his attic guest wasn't difficult; it was easier to put up with someone he already knew well than with someone new. There was something else that prevented him from getting a wink of sleep for nights on end. And when he did fall asleep, nightmares were quick to follow him and in them—a knife to his throat. Namely, the fact that he hadn't been seeing Panther could only mean that the Ustashas had discovered and imprisoned him and were now torturing him, right until he confessed and revealed everything about his activities. Who knew what all they were doing to him, Franjo thought, and wondered whether Panther would be able to withstand it. He was a tough man and foolishly courageous—what Home Guard major would involve himself in smuggling Jews and communists into the woods or to the Italians? It was easier for Panther to do that work than it would be for anyone else because the Ustashas wouldn't suspect him. But he also needed more courage: they'd hang, shoot, or cut the throat of anyone else, but they'd cut him into pieces and cook him in boiling water. Franjo was convinced for a long time that Panther had been arrested and that it was just a matter of days before the Ustashas would find out everything. But when two months passed, he concluded that no one would be able to withstand so much torture (Panther would die or give everything away), so something else must have happened to him. Franjo had no idea what that might have been, but he slept peacefully.

It wasn't until several years after the war that Franjo the prep school janitor realized with whom he'd been dealing. He ended up holding a copy of the first edition of the monograph *National Heroes of Yugoslavia*, where on page one hundred twelve he would see Panther's photograph under the name Ivan Skočibuha—a.k.a. Kameni—and then read the following:

Comrade Kameni joined the Podgrmeč partisan units in the winter of 1942.

In the recollection of Comrade Mustafa Mulalić-Olaf, it happened like this: We were sitting around the campfire when the sentry brought before us a bumpkin in a Home Guard uniform who was carrying a mortar on his back, that heavy German one that three men can hardly lift. This is me and this is my cigarette holder, said Comrade Kameni and dropped the mortar on the ground. My comrades didn't utter a word. We looked a little at him and a little at the mortar and couldn't believe our eyes. Nobody suspected that he was an agent-provocateur, though we weren't always sure about comrades who left the Home Guard to join the people's liberation movement. But a man who walks twenty-some kilometers with a mortar on his back can't be an agent-provocateur. Comrade Kameni proved himself in the first engagement with the enemy. He grabbed the hot barrel of a German machine gun with his bare hands and tore it out of the hands of a stunned fascist. You should have seen the face of the enemy whenever Ivan Skočibuha-Kameni appeared in front of them! Around Podgrmeč his heroism has become the stuff of legend, but I can confirm that words cannot describe what Comrade Kameni was really like. No such words have been invented yet! When in the last days of the war he lost his life driving the fascists and their domestic henchmen in a panic-stricken flight across Slovenia, all of Bosnian Krajina wept for him. May his deeds be an inspiration to future generations in the struggle for socialism and a better tomorrow.

Franjo the janitor couldn't believe his eyes as he read the hagiography of Comrade Ivan Skočibuha-Kameni in the same little room in which he'd spent his whole working life, among brooms, cleaning rags, and rusty buckets. At that time one street in a suburb already bore his name, and his bronze bust had been ceremoniously uncovered in the city park. Franjo, to be sure, could have passed by it a thousand times without recognizing Panther's face underneath the worried brow and the visionary gaze. It wasn't that the bust of Comrade Kameni wasn't a likeness of Panther, especially since the famed sculptor had faithfully rendered his handsome male face. But he'd given him an expression and a seriousness that Panther had never had at any moment in his life. Good-for-nothings would say that there maybe were such moments when he looked like that: when he was sitting on the toilet. It's only on busts that one sees that an expression is a man's best disguise, far better than fake mustaches and beards.

Reading the entry in *National Heroes of Yugoslavia*, Franjo suspected that there was something dirty and smelly behind Panther's heroism — something filthy, rotten. He looked the bust over and concluded that Comrade Skočibuha was a great fraud. Even a fool could see that if he compared the dice player to the bronze head with the vision.

Franjo would learn the nature of the lie only before his death, when on one post-retirement stroll Ferid Kodžalić, formerly a teacher in the prep school as well as an Ustasha major—on account of which he'd done fifteen years of hard labor in Foča and Zenica—told him in the strictest of confidence why the Home Guard major Ivan Skočibuha had fled to the partisans. Franjo laughed so hard at that story that tears flowed from his eyes, though it showed him to be a dupe and cost him torment, misery, and fear.

The story went like this: after playing dice for months with low-ranking officers and Banja Luka's lowlifes and winning at the game, Panther went to the Christmas reception of the district prefect, and in a side hall into which only select people were admitted, he learned the basic rules of American poker from the Italian military attaché, Fernando Noa Marinetti, and lost his entire monthly salary that same evening at poker. He couldn't figure out how or why he'd lost. So he quit dice and started playing poker every day. He played with experts but also with third-rate dice players whom he himself would teach the game. He lost against both.

In three months Panther's poker debts exceeded the income of three Home Guard regiments, and since the people to whom he owed money weren't harmless or inclined to forgiveness—all the more so because he'd flayed them at dice for years—he stole a mortar from a military warehouse and fled to the partisans. He knew that gambling debts are only paid to the victors in war. If the communists won the war, he wouldn't owe anyone anything, and if they lost, the victors would kill them all anyway. He cared about saving his skin and did the most logical thing in the world and naturally didn't inform anyone that Comrade Samuel F. Klein was in mortal danger in the attic of the Banja Luka prep school. Maybe he would have told someone had Klein been a sympathizer of the people's liberation movement and not merely a ruined shipowner and a Jew. Like this he only risked his comrades finding out that he'd been charging a lot of money to save people's skin.

However, just as he didn't reveal his illegal dealings to the partisans, he also failed to inform the people in the network that had been working to save people, partly for altruistic and partly for material reasons, of his departure. Panther was the only one who knew who all made up the network. The others knew only two names in the conspiracy: the name of the one behind them and the name of the one ahead of them. And since he'd organized his people in such an ingenious manner, all kinds of people took part in the same work, or mission—communist sympathizers, friars, university professors, and humanists, along with professional smugglers, Ustasha and Chetnik cutthroats, lone murderers, and all manner of lowlifes who earned a fortune on the torment and misfortunes of others.

Unaware either of one another or of Panther's escape to the partisans, they kept working, and on one starry April night the villager Husnija Hadžalić brought Ivo Delavale to Franjo the janitor. He just dropped him off, without an accompanying letter or money for food, as packages are left at the post office. Franjo complained and held his head in his hands but to no avail. Underneath a pile of dusty placards about tuberculosis, syphilis, cholera, and the "If you wash your hands, you've cleared your conscience" campaign, one more ottoman was found in a corner of the attic. And then Franjo completed the household proto-col: "During the day keep your lips sealed because everything can be heard, and don't think anyone gives a fuck about you at night!"

He was mad as hell and convinced that all three of them would die of hunger. And he prayed to God that a fourth wouldn't be arriving soon.

At first the name Samuel F. Klein meant nothing to Ivo, although he'd read it in 1933 and 1934 at the head of the dining table of the *Leonica*, certainly the nicest and most comfortable ship on which he'd sailed. And not only did he re-member that name, written in Gothic script with red ink, but he'd also seen a photograph of the ship's owner above it at breakfast, lunch, and dinner. He'd wondered countless times what type of man he must be if he exposed his name and picture so that sailors could spit on it, swear at his mother, and curse the day that they'd set foot on the ship. And they would swear at him and curse him because they had to do it to someone, and if they feared God, the captain, and the first deck officer, they would let the first person whose picture they saw have it—the Austrian emperor, the Yugoslav king, or a naked beauty whose picture was pasted on the inside of a toolbox. They would swear at a face in old news-print, and if not even that was there because on ships pictures were few and far between, they would swear at themselves because they weren't at home catch-ing fish on a trawl line but sailing around the Tierra del Fuego and praying to God that the Pacific was as peaceful as its name suggested and not as it was ac-cording to its nature. It's always the same, on every ship and on every voyage, and everyone who has ever sailed, even as a passenger, knows it. He couldn't believe that the owner of the *Leonica* wasn't aware of that or that he was so proud of his name and personage that he would subject his name and picture to the impulses of anguished sailors. There were those who spat on him for luck and for a calm sea. Every evening, instead of prayers for calm, they would clear their throats and spit at the face of the man with the bow tie and the high top hat. Ivo didn't swear at him or spit at him but amused himself by trying to figure out what made him tick. That man might differ from other men in some way, in something that made him interesting. But hardly any of that could be learned from a single photograph. None of the crew had met the owner of the *Leonica*, nor did they know any more about him. The mystery of the photo-graph remained unsolved, if it even existed and if anyone besides Ivo Delavale saw anything more in it than a target for spittle and an icon for oaths and curses.

When the *Leonica* sailed out of his life and Ivo boarded uglier, rustier, and

more hazardous ships that had no dining halls or portraits of emperors, kings, or
Jesus Christ, Samuel F. Klein would often cross his thoughts. But there wasn't
anything at all in the appearance of the dusty little man in the attic of the Banja
Luka prep school, who sincerely rejoiced at his arrival because he would no
longer be alone for days on end, that might remind one of the spit-covered portrait on the wall of the dining hall and the name written in Gothic script. He
fit right in with the broken globes, portraits of deposed rulers. and maps with
outdated borders. It was as if he himself had been taken out of use in some educational reform and had been taken up to the attic instead of to the municipal
dump. He was nice and amusing when he spoke about his numerous ailments
or about recipes for cakes for holidays, holy days, and saints' days.

"Well, if somebody asked me now what I miss most and what I'll pine for
if I say good-bye to this life, I'd say to him—cake, nothing but cake! I've survived everything, but I can't survive without Sacher torte!" Klein said on their
first night together, and Ivo couldn't figure out whether he was complaining
or making a joke at his own expense. The same doubt would linger on until
the end of their time together. Even after they knew more about one another
than the best of friends do, Ivo wouldn't be sure when Klein was making fun
of himself or wanted to share his despair and sorrow with him. He would stay
up till dawn counting the cakes that he'd ever eaten and recalling pastry shops
and cities, and there were many of them all over the world. In an instant he
would jump from the baklava of Bitolj and Istanbul to the Kaiserschmarrn of
Vienna and then to the apple pie that he'd tried the one time he'd traveled to
America in 1921 or 1922. He told of jelly rolls he'd eaten in a Hungarian shop
in Subotica and about the difference between apricot jam and rose-hip jam—
the former was perfect for jelly rolls, but the latter tasted better in crispier cakes.
He told how there was no better drink than boza, at least to go with cakes, and
then about the Turkish delight in Prilep, the pauper's halva in Bosnian towns,
and the floating island desserts that you like only as long as you are someone's
grandchild—when your grandmas and grandpas died, your craving for floating
dessert disappeared.

Ivo listened to him and drifted off to sleep. Klein would talk for a long time
yet, even when he realized that no one was listening to him. He'd gotten a craving for tales of cakes because he couldn't talk about them with Franjo.

In the morning the janitor took away the chamber pot, which was twice as
full as it ordinarily was.

"It can't go on like this," he said. But he himself didn't know how things could
continue and what to do with the people whose care was entrusted to him.
When he'd taken on this task, Franjo believed that he was doing a good deed

and that he wouldn't come out behind on it but would also feed himself and supplement his diet on Panther's money. However, since there was no longer any money and Panther wasn't around, his good deed began to make less sense. Everyone was working for himself, only he was working to his own detriment; he was carrying other people's shit around the prep school and awaiting the day when the Ustashas would find him out.

Outside it was spring, the kind that had come only seldom during the years of peace. The hills surrounding the city sprouted, bloomed, and blossomed; buzzing and chirping drowned out the noise of German trucks. Armies prepared to move on each other. Prep school graduates prepared to leave for Stalingrad. Pavelić's speeches and songs celebrating the beauty of the homeland resounded from loudspeakers on the square . . . The world was in a season of perfect harmony; it was only Franjo's life that was topsy-turvy. In early evening one could hear the sounds of a tambouritza and a song about the sad story of two friends, Latif and Sulejman, who—for one hundred and fifty years already—had been leaving Banja Luka in the spring and asking one another the same question: "Are you sorry?" Well, how could a man not be sorry to leave such beauty behind only because he knew it couldn't last? Shouldn't you live for no other reason than you know that from the perspective of the oak trees above Šehitluci Hill you're already long dead? It's better to be born like an animal, enjoy every spring day, and have no idea that there will be something else tomorrow, something that isn't nice and might make you regret that you're alive.

"You have to get out of here, tonight! Any way you can! I can't help you any more," Franjo said, shuddering. "Here, I've brought you what I have," he said and pulled out a loaf of bread, a slab of bacon, and three onions from a shopping bag. "But you have to move on; you've got to get out before midnight!"

They each sat on their ottomans and couldn't understand what the janitor really wanted.

"Did the contact arrive?" Klein asked.

"There isn't any contact. You have to take care of yourselves. Now just go!" He said that the director had announced that the attic was to be cleaned, that he'd waved his hand and when he did, each of his fingers had caught a spider's web. Ivo wondered whether they were from one spider or whether there were more.

"But what will we do; where will we go?" Klein shilly-shallied.

"How should I know what you'll do?! You'll do just great! You'll put one foot in front of the other until you get somewhere!" the janitor insisted.

Ivo looked at him, smiled, and didn't believe anything he said. Cleaning the attic, right! No one did that in wartime. And what director would tell a janitor what was to be done the next day? Rather, the man simply wanted to be rid of the both of them and was telling lies. And in the end it didn't matter what the truth was because if the host says he's had enough of his guests, then they really have to leave.

"But they'll kill us," Klein said almost with the voice of a child.

"C'mon, dammit, didn't you yourself want to jump off the roof?! I barely held you back, and now you're blubbering that they'll kill you. They won't kill you if you watch out for yourself!" Franjo said, laying out the things he'd prepared for their trip. When that was done, he clapped his hands as if to show that their conversation was over. "I'll be here half an hour before midnight, and you'd better be ready!" he said and disappeared.

"What was that?" Klein asked, breaking the silence after about ten minutes. The ruddy light of dusk penetrated through the vents in the roof, and the muezzin's call could be heard. "I've never seen him like that," he continued when Ivo didn't answer. "He'll probably be over it by tomorrow." He wanted to see what the communist thought. He was convinced that Ivo was a communist because he looked like one of those figures on Soviet placards for spring harvests. Klein didn't want to leave the attic, and if there really was going to be a cleaning, he thought about asking Franjo to hide them in the cellar or in some other place while that was going on, anything but throwing them out into the world. Coincidentally, he'd just started to get used to the idea of living the rest of his life in the prep school's attic.

"I don't know whether he'll be over it by tomorrow, but we're going tonight. At least I'm going—you can do what you like!" Ivo said, and Klein broke out in a cold sweat. Faced with the thought that he would have to go out that night, he was overcome with fear like he hadn't felt in all of his panic-stricken life. His fear was all the greater because it had nothing to do with the reasons why he was there. He forgot about the Ustashas and their knives, about gallows and medieval methods of torture, about which he'd read as a prep school student in a French monograph with pictures that had aroused feelings of erotic excitement in him. He was no longer concerned that he was a Jew in a world that had decided that Jews could no longer be. Nor was he worried that he didn't have strength in his legs and that he would croak from fatigue if the guns and knives didn't get him. Klein was simply afraid of going into the outside world! It didn't matter what was happening or who was out there. He couldn't bear the thought of the wide sky being over his head instead of a low, slanted roof. He grew short of breath at the thought of that wide expanse and didn't know what was wrong with him.

"I can't do it," he whispered, on the verge of tears. "Don't leave me, for the love of God," he squealed. Ivo didn't know what the man wanted from him. He stared dully at him and tried to figure out if the little man was joking. He wondered whether the spiders were sorry about their demolished webs or whether they didn't care.

"Listen to me good," he said; "I don't feel like dying here, and I'm going for sure. I have no idea whether this fool is lying about the cleaning, but I don't want to find out. And as far as you're concerned, you're your own man, and you can decide for yourself. It's better for you to come with me—we'll both share the same fate. It's easier if there's two of us. Don't interrupt me, and don't fucking lose it like a bride at a wedding feast. You won't get anywhere like that with me because I don't understand it. I'm a sailor, you understand?! I'm not a city boy, and life hasn't treated me with kid gloves. I've always taken care to keep my head on my shoulders, and I've been in worse situations than this. I'm not saying this to put you at ease—it's just true. You don't know what ships are, what the sea is!" he said angrily as tears streamed down Klein's face.

"I know what ships are; I've had ships," he stammered. Ivo felt the urge to slap him like a little child because the ugly little man was also a little child, unreasonable and spoiled. Maybe he'd had a little boat and had called it a ship.

"I'll tell you a story," Ivo tried to speak as if telling a fairy tale since a slap would have been indecent. "I sailed for two years on a ship called the *Leonica . . .*"

The little man's face lit up and he stopped crying, just like a child at the beginning of Snow White.

"That was the most beautiful ship in my career—clean, powerful, and secure. The majority of merchant ships are old junk and wrecks, in worse condition than the worst fishing boats and two-masters because the owners are only trying to make a profit. They couldn't care less if the ship takes on water everywhere and the engines are falling apart . . ."

Klein nodded and folded his hands in his lap, as if he'd completely forgotten his fear.

"But the *Leonica* was something else, a ship like in the movies. Only the crew wasn't like in the movies. Sailors are a filthy lot. I haven't been in prison, but prisoners are like that. Just like sailors. They gnaw at one another and hate one another. They sail, but the only thing they care about is when they're going to moor. Instead of enjoying being on a ship from a fairy tale, the likes of which they would never sail on again, they hated the *Leonica*. They were insulted that they weren't on a rusted wreck where they could give vent to their vices. Of course, such a ship had a real dining hall, like on a rich man's passenger ship. Everything was in its place, and the furniture was in the style of Louis XIV . . ."

The little man shook his head, wanted to object—that wasn't anything like Louis XIV . . .

"Listen; let me finish my story, and then you have your say," Ivo said, unwilling to let himself be interrupted. "And on the wall of the dining hall was the ship owner's portrait, and everyone swore at that picture and spat on it. You see, I've been thinking about that man my whole life, and I can't decide whether he was the biggest fool in the world or a saint who wanted to show that people aren't content when they have it good. I wasn't content either, but I felt good on the *Leonica*. It took years before I realized that I felt good on that ship. Whenever something isn't around any longer, you realize that it made you feel good. But you see, I learned something from that man. You never know how you really feel at the time. Not when you think things are good, not when you think they're bad. Maybe it's good fortune that we're leaving tonight. Do you even understand what I've been saying, or has it all been for nothing?"

The little man grinned as if he'd lost his mind, and it seemed that nothing would come of their journey.

"Do you know what the name of the owner of the *Leonica* was?" Klein asked. "Samuel F. Klein," Ivo said, still failing to catch on.

"Yes," said the little man, scratching himself behind the ear. "And he wasn't a saint but a fool. A silly fool of a Kike. And you know that and have said it several times yourself."

He looked at his sailor, who didn't understand. Ivo frowned, and who knew what was going through his head? Certainly something about Jews. He no longer had any idea who he was dealing with. He thought that he was one of them, but now it turned out that he wasn't because if he were, how could he have said that someone was a silly fool of a Kike?

"His name was Samuel F. Klein," the little man mumbled, absorbed in thought, "and did you remember what my name is?"

Ivo Delavale didn't know whether what was happening to him was a dream or not. From that December day in 1941, when he had sailed from Florida on the tuna boat *Olaf* in the belief that he was going on a military mission to uncover German submarines in the Caribbean, he'd experienced nothing but marvels. At first the *Olaf* began to sink in front of Havana. For no reason at all, in the middle of a calm sea; it filled with water to the top in two hours, and he and three other Americans barely saved their skins. The owner of the *Olaf*, a white-bearded journalist, evidently a rich and a somewhat crazy man, said swearing that some Puerto Ricans had tricked him and that Puerto Rico should be flooded or at least burned because that was just one more sign that they supported Hitler, just as they supported Franco. That man didn't know anything about the sea or about ships either because no one with any brains would think of going to pursue German submarines in a tuna boat—but Ivo realized that too late. In Havana they parted, and each went his own way. The man with the white beard went to buy a new ship, the two sailors went in search of whores, and Ivo, without a dollar in his pocket, sought a way to get back to Florida from Cuba. And so after two days of waiting he boarded the cruiser *Zamzam*, which was sailing under a Syrian flag and transporting Jewish refugees from Spain to the United States. After having waited for two months for the people to receive American visas and after having eaten their last reserves of food (which were meager to begin with) and spent their last money, captain Sergey Prokopiev decided to sail for Miami in the hope that the coast guard would let the *Zamzam* through because there were almost a thousand people on board—Lithuanian, Polish, Ukrainian, Romanian, and German Jews who faced the threat of death in one way or another. Namely, the Americans didn't believe the tales of concentration camps or that the Germans were liquidating those people en masse in their drive eastward. Fine; it was obvious that Hitler didn't like Jews and that he'd made their elimination one of his most important political objectives. But political aims are one thing and reality is another, or so the Americans thought, convinced that Nazi ideology worked like advertisements for soft drinks. Who would really believe that sugared soda water made people happier and more potent, and who would really believe that Hitler had serious thoughts about the Jews? And if he did, that only meant he was crazy. His project would come to ruin, his state would collapse, and until then it was smarter to keep one's distance from him and not get too mixed up with those who were fleeing in all directions for real reasons or out of fear.

Prokopiev, half Jewish himself, tried in vain to explain things to Richard S. Elephant, whose response was an argument stronger than anything the captain could think up: "America has enough poor of its own and enough Jews of its own! It doesn't need European Jews or the European poor." Sergey Prokopiev had no way of knowing that he was trying exactly what hundreds and thousands of others in positions similar to his were trying and that at that moment, from the Bosporus to the Maghreb, via Portugal and Spain, all the way to the coasts of both American continents, huge masses of people found themselves in the same situation as his people.

Had he known, he never would have left for Florida and placed his hopes in the abstract humanism of the coast guard. Rather, he would have persuaded his people to swim to the coast of Cuba. Those who survived the sharks would have run all over the island, and the local authorities could search for them and send them back to Eastern Europe.

He took Ivo Delavale on board the *Zamzam* because he was already missing half the crew, and Delavale had some papers from the American army, which, the desperate captain thought, could be of general use. However, before it reached American shores, it was stopped by torpedo boats, and a gruff sergeant gave Prokopiev an ultimatum to move on in half an hour or he would give the order to sink the ship. The captain only laughed and retorted to the American that he couldn't blackmail him or the people he was transporting with their lives and that he could go ahead and torpedo them. The sergeant grew confused, and after a conversation with his superiors suggested to Prokopiev to drop anchor right where he was until someone in Washington or somewhere else decided what would happen to the *Zamzam*.

"No chance," he retorted. "My passengers are dying of starvation! Either sink us, let us through, or give us food."

The sergeant didn't do any of those things but again contacted his superiors. A motorboat with Red Cross markings arrived more quickly than he would have thought, and the *Zamzam* received a first quantity of bread and canned goods. Over the seven days that the ship would remain on that spot, surrounded by five boats of the coast guard, the Red Cross would come a few hundred times with food and medicine. The entire storage space of the *Zamzam* would be overflowing, and soon they were putting boxes with the emblem of international aid on deck. The captain waited for a decision from Washington, but he knew well what it would be. He had an in-depth understanding of the comfort of canned goods and their purpose and was ready to scuttle the *Zamzam* together with the food that had accumulated, which was enough for a year's voyage. He saw no sense in harassing people and driving them across the sea if not one shore would accept them.

When on the eighth morning the arrogant sergeant arrived with a negative answer, Sergey Prokopiev convened a ship's council, assembled on the basis of the homelands and countries from which the people had fled, and proposed collective suicide. Let history remember the Jewish *Titanic* in the Caribbean!

The people, of course, were shocked, rejected his idea, and tried to persuade him to sail back to Europe. The war would surely end before they arrived, and Hitler would of course be defeated. The captain didn't believe in a quick end to the war or in Hitler's defeat, but he didn't oppose the decision of council. Regardless, they began to spy on him and kept tabs on his every move, frightened that he would scuttle the *Zamzam*.

The drama of the thousand Jews and their captain took place at the same time as Ivo's personal drama. Namely, instead of the fact that he was taking part in a mission that had the approval of the American military helping the crew and passengers, as Prokopiev was hoping, the fact that Ivo Delavale had boarded the *Zamzam* of all ships turned out to be fatal for him. The sergeant was convinced that his papers had been forged, and he sent them as suspicious to his superiors, where they were likewise suspicious, but they couldn't investigate the authenticity of the documents and sent them further on up. No one knew how far Ivo's papers went and who all had them in their hands before they vanished in someone's drawer, but in the end it turned out that he hadn't even turned them over to the sergeant, and there was no longer any way of proving his identity. For the Americans he was just one more in the mass of European wretches who wandered the deck of the *Zamzam* and who needed to be avoided in any way possible because an encounter with them could be fatal, just as when on a rainy day you notice a little wet puppy in the mud at the side of the road and know that the little animal would stay there forever and give up its little ghost if you didn't take it with you.

Because of feelings that are awakened in such situations, it was important not to look around oneself too much and to remain indifferent to the misfortunes of people and dogs.

All during the journey to Europe the ocean was unusually calm, and everyone thought that was a good sign. The Atlantic was never so quiet, no matter what the season, and the crew and the passengers believed that the hand of fate was involved. Luck had served them, and the dark clouds over their heads had begun to clear. Maybe it was better that America hadn't accepted them, they thought, because who would ever go back home from such a distant land? And they would get back home for certain, the next day or in three months. Full and content, they were looking forward to Europe.

In the early evening entertainment was arranged on deck. A small ensemble consisting of a guitar, a violin, and an accordion played circle dances and other dances from various countries. There were polkas and mazurkas. A waltz floated out over the sea. A tango sounded like the sad horn of a dead tugboat; Balkan circle dances rumbled over the wooden deck. The hypnotic rhythms of dervish dances shimmered in the air, when a man became inured to fear and pain and it seemed to him that he was within arm's reach of God and all he had to do was reach out and accept his embrace . . . There were all kinds of music and dances, but no Jewish, Hebrew, Ashkenazi, or Sephardic songs were heard. Only once did they start playing "Der Himl Lacht," an old Klezmer song, but the audience objected. They didn't want to hear Jewish songs because they were melancholy, no one could understand them, and it wasn't good to sing and play something that differed so much from the other songs. They thought they needed to be like other people, and if their people had taken more care about fitting in, they wouldn't have ended up in a situation where they would soon cease to exist. They said things like that, and only two men knew that the truth was different and didn't have very much to do with which songs were sung and which ones weren't.

Ivo knew because he was the only one who wasn't a Jew. The captain of the ship knew, too, because he knew where they were sailing. But it would have been wrong to spoil those people's joy and take their hopes away at those moments when it didn't matter what they believed in. They had no way of influencing their fate or changing what would happen, and it was better, out in the middle of the peaceful Atlantic, in the one place where they could feel like free men, to let them live in the illusion that the war had come to an end and that their future happiness depended only on what songs they would sing.

The day before the *Zamzam* was to approach the coast of Portugal, Captain Sergey Prokopiev summoned Ivo to the bridge and asked him whether he knew how to command a ship. He was surprised, but it was clear to him what the question meant.

"If something happens to me, you'll take over the *Zamzam*," Prokopiev said. "The crew already knows."

He then saw him for the last time. The next morning the captain slipped past the watchful eyes of his spies and disappeared. They looked for him and called out to him as if he were a child and had gotten lost. The confusion lasted an hour, and everyone was on his feet; no one could hear himself think from the noise and disputes. The crew waited for the passengers to calm down a little to tell them that Ivo Delavale was taking over command of the ship. The old captain had left no message or farewell letter behind, nor did anyone know how he'd vanished or where he'd gone.

"Someone should inform the family somehow," Izak Papo, a ninety-year-old man from Bitola, said anxiously and tugged at the new captain's sleeve. They didn't know whether Sergey Prokopiev had any kin, just as they didn't know anything else about him. Except that he was born in Russia, that his mother's name was Sarah, and that on winter days she knitted socks without stopping. After she'd knitted socks for everyone in her house, she knitted some for a collie named Ataman. That was the only thing that Sergey Prokopiev had said about himself since he had taken command of the *Zamzam* a year before in the port of Marseilles. He also said that Ataman hadn't resisted, as one would expect from an animal, but had worn his red socks whenever cold weather hit or Sarah thought that cold weather had hit. Ataman didn't want to hurt her no matter how much he thought her care made no sense.

"That dog was smart—it shouldn't have been called Ataman," said Sergey Prokopiev.

The night before they were supposed to sail into port was very hard going. It was humid and muggy, as nights are for old men on their deathbeds. No one on the *Zamzam* got a wink of sleep. They roamed the deck in silence, shadows collided with a muffled sound above the blackness of the sea, and that Atlantic dream of peace faded from every one of their souls. Ivo decided to bypass Leixoes, Porto, and Lisbon and moor out in front of the fishing port of Figuera de Foz. He was counting on the element of surprise: by the time the Portuguese authorities, customs officials, and police assembled, the passengers would disembark from the *Zamzam*, and then it would be difficult to pack them back onto the ship and deport them. His plan was extremely naïve and people would probably laugh in the face of any captain who came up with something like that, but on a night when a powerful sirocco was blowing and everyone's head was filled with confusion, no idea was foolish enough to be rejected out of hand. Not long before sunrise Ivo Delavale assembled the Jewish representatives on the bridge, told them that the time of parting was near, and requested that they make a list according to which the people would disembark from the *Zamzam*.

"When you set foot on Portuguese soil, our journey will be over. From that moment onward every man answers only for himself. I advise you not to tarry in the harbor. Run as fast as your legs can carry you. The farther you get, the fewer the chances that the police will catch you. I hope you've kept a few ducats or gold rings. They'll come in handy. I wish you all luck," he said, concluding his first and last captain's address. The people dispersed in silence; the lights of a city twinkled dimly on the horizon.

The disembarkation lasted two full hours. That was how long it took for everyone to be rowed ashore in small fishing boats. Ivo Delavale was the last one to leave the *Zamzam*, as he thought that custom required it.

He bade a long farewell, not without sorrow, to that strange ship that had sailed under a holy flag and bore the name of a mythic well in the middle of the Arabian desert. When Abraham had driven out Hagar and her son Ishmael, the Zamzam well had kept them from dying of thirst. That name, written in faded letters on the rusty hull of a vessel whose history was unknown to Ivo—in the past it might have been a transport for opium, slaves, or weapons—had really protected those who'd sailed on her. He believed that at the moment when he bade farewell to the *Zamzam*.

As his boat put ashore, a terrible storm arose suddenly. It happened in thirty seconds. A wind blew up from the ocean; the wooden docks started creaking; the roofs of houses, tarps that had been covering Mediterranean fruit, the black caftans and hats of people who'd hastily fled from their homes all flew into the air. Steel drums full of oil and wooden barrels full of wine flew through the air. Earthenware pots of olive oil flew high above the sea and were then suddenly plunged into its depths. Masts of fishing boats flew through the air, as did the children of fishermen, shouting and howling; stray dogs and a few insufficiently clever cats were also seen flying through the air. A whole world flew up and away in an instant, and there could be no doubt of divine intent. Soldiers who'd waited for the passengers with their rifles at the ready began to cross themselves and then ran off to find shelter, holding their caps down on their heads. The Jews were caught all alone in the middle of the fishing port, in the crashing of masts and tree trunks, live wood and dead wood, and in the horrible droning of a wind that could only be described by someone who'd lived through the meteorology of the Old Testament.

The soldiers and policemen forgot about the Jews because in such circumstances they were of no concern to anyone. Not to General Carmona, not to his minister of finance Oliveira Salazar, nor to their Estado Novo. Far from its imperial glory, somewhere on the very fringe of Europe, it had been caught in the midst of an ordinary storm. Sensing what the storm meant, the people ran, into the wind and in all directions, and so two hours later, when the storm subsided, not a single passenger from the *Zamzam* was still in the port of Figuera de Foz. The ship was gone too because the sea had torn it apart. Or maybe it had disappeared, following the steps of its real captain. Those were the '40s, and such things were possible. People, cities, freight trains, and whole nations were disappearing, and so why wouldn't a single ship disappear too? Up into the sky, along with Chagall's fellow villagers.

Soldiers roamed the docks in vain, their rifles at the ready, and they tried in vain to figure out whether the ship full of Jews had really existed or whether it had been an apparition, another miracle à la Fátima that the Virgin uses to warn people of something they'll never comprehend anyway.

In Setúbal, after two weeks of hiding and sleeping in the cellars of abandoned houses on the seashore, Ivo Delavale boarded the Italian merchant ship *De Amicis* as a stowaway. For three days and nights he didn't emerge from a container full of oranges, and then, figuring that they could no longer send him back, he went out on deck and turned himself in. Instead of locking him in the hold, beating him up, or at least assigning him to the cook to peel potatoes, Captain Gordone and the crew split their sides laughing at a man who'd fed himself on unripe oranges for three days, and then they couldn't believe that he was fleeing to Italy from Portugal. He told them that he was going home, that he hadn't seen his wife in a long time and no longer cared how near he was to the front lines. The war was everywhere; it had engulfed the entire world, and it didn't matter whether you were in Brazil or Dalmatia. Gordone shook his head: "Oh, yes, it does matter, but if he loves his wife so much, then let him go right

ahead; let him see what real war is like." Apart from the devil having gotten him
to go on the hunt for German submarines with a gray-haired fantast, Ivo Delavale hadn't really seen war or even thought much about it. In fact, he thought
about it as much as the average American, as much as Diana, who, usually before her period or during a full moon, would fall into a fright about a Japanese
paratroop drop on Chicago. But since the coast guard sergeant had taken his
papers and he'd been continually traveling in the opposite direction from what
he wanted, not knowing whether he was dreaming or everything was really happening to him, Ivo had begun to imagine war too as one more personal stroke
of bad luck. Something that would spoil his plans for life but wouldn't cost him
his head. Here he saw a difference between himself and the Jews on the *Zam-*
zam. No matter how much he pitied those people, empathized with them, and
was ready to help them, they were still something like Martians to him. At least
as far as he was concerned, the Second World War had smashed the globe into
several planets. At the time when the war began, Ivo was in America and could
consider himself an American.

The fact that the funny little man in the prep school attic was Samuel F.
Klein, the man from the photograph at the head of the dining hall of the beautiful *Leonica*, was only one in a series of oddities that had happened to him, but
it was the first that he took to be a sign of fate.

"Don't you be afraid; I'll carry you to the sea like a sack of potatoes," he told
him and dragged him out into the night almost by force. Klein squealed like a
little animal but quit putting up a fight. Hypnotized by fear, he found himself
under a wide starry sky, on a cobbled pavement that reflected the moonlight
and looked almost like it was plated with silver. That much silver could buy up
all the souls in that country.

"Conquistadors," Klein whispered.

"What?" Ivo asked, turning around.

"Nothing," said the little man, tiptoeing, frightened and enthused. His fear
came from noises that echoed across through the market district, betraying
every living being, and his enthusiasm was made of the silver and shadows, the
gleaming cobblestones and dark upper-story porches, and the sky, which was so
vast and black that the stars gleamed brightly, like a thousand suns. He felt like
explaining all that to his sailor, first his discovery of the silver, gold, and precious
stones and the fact that riches were more valuable to people than life itself. And
why wouldn't they be when the primeval image was so beautiful, there in the
sky and on the cobblestones? And was there any living creature that would see
more in its own flesh and bone than this miracle? He also wanted to tell him
about the way that silver and gold are turned into money, securities, and checks,

into things stripped of all beauty but that still found their backing in it. And he would also have told him that there wouldn't be anything if it weren't for fear. And living creatures don't notice anything until they become very frightened and their lives hang on a thread. Klein hurried along with small steps and tried to remember everything that he had to tell the sailor if he survived that night. There was a lot, the bulk of which would be forgotten. Which wasn't a great pity because if he thought about it, it was all babbling, and he was a babbler. That was what people thought of him, and for all he cared, they could think it because they were right. And so it was enough to repeat "Conquistadors." And he'd already said enough, too much for what he was. He hadn't accepted anything in life completely, nor had he thought about anything long enough to be able to say now: Look, I've been thinking about such-and-such all my life, and I've concluded such-and-such, and there is such-and-such benefit from that! There was no benefit, he thought, as he followed Ivo's steps. Well, if that man hadn't been in front of him, he wouldn't have even known where to go. But Ivo certainly did. God forbid he didn't!

Ivo, of course, had no idea in which direction they should go. Franjo the janitor had kicked them out of the prep school without any instructions about the schedules and routes of the Ustasha patrols and the easiest way to get out of the city.

"If you're good men, you won't give me away," he said and slipped into the darkness. And from there they were on their own.

They walked through the market district for two full hours without Klein's noticing that they were going in circles and that they had passed by the Hilmina Inn twice. Ivo's hands were sweaty; his heart pounded against his breastbone. He felt panic coming over him and that with every moment he was further away from exiting that labyrinth. He silently cursed the Turks and their architectural logic, cursed Emperor Franz Joseph, who had only built his villas, mansions, shops, and ironbound storefronts to fit into it. None of them differed from any of the others at all. There was that deadly oriental need not to run afoul of your neighbor, to build a shop that wouldn't be an inch higher than his and wouldn't differ in color or form, so that one day when someone had a need to flee through the market district, he would go in circles like a caged mouse in a biology lab.

Nevertheless, they finally slipped out of the city without running into anyone, which Ivo counted among the signs of luck, whereas Klein didn't even notice. They reached the first groves and stands of willow trees along the Vrbas River and then a shed in which they would spend the day hidden in the hay. There the little man would sneeze, cough, and whine and raise a ruckus loud enough, Ivo thought, to draw the attention of three German armies and Pavelić's bodyguard. But nothing like that happened. Not the first day, nor during the next three months of their journey together. Whenever they hid in hay or walked through mowed meadows, Klein sneezed and coughed, as if he were just asking for trouble. Soon Ivo grew used to it and managed to convince himself that they weren't fated to die or fall into the hands of the army.

Two unusual men thus went through the empty Bosnian countryside, and it was a real pity that there wasn't a movie camera to film them. The tall one loped ahead; his face was already covered with a pointed beard. A short, hunched one hurried a few steps behind him. The tall one mostly kept silent, while the short one spoke for both of them. If he wasn't sneezing or moaning, then he babbled on about the meaning and meaninglessness of life, about diseases that fly through the air, and about how it was only a matter of time before you inhaled them. About international relations that had led to that terrible war, about the fact that the proximity of warm seas makes people better, so that Salazar, Franco, and Mussolini could never be like Hitler, and Hitler would have been even worse had he been born in Norway or Denmark. About Winston Churchill, who was living proof that worry and trouble make a person fat (before the war he'd been almost slender, and in the last year he'd become fat as a pig—Klein couldn't believe his eyes when he saw his picture in the newspaper). About Grandpa Pinto, who was supposed to become a Sarajevo rabbi, but the Jewish market district didn't want him because he hurried too much and they thought he would try to hurry them. About the *tarawih*, the longest Muslim prayer, and about wicked priests who, according to his grandfather, had tormented the people with frequent *tarawihs*. About the fact that he didn't know at all what kind of prayer that was (nor had his grandfather) and he'd been waiting for years for an opportunity to ask a Muslim what the *tarawih* was. About the Orthodox, who really overdid their liturgies, which were all longer than the longest Catholic and Muslim prayers. About his own people, who would barricade themselves into the temple and not come out for a whole day. About his sincere wish to be religious, but it didn't work at all because to be religious a man had to be as naïve as a child and as meticulous as an Old Testament sage (maybe he was somewhat of a child, but he didn't have anything of the sages in him). About German motors, which were the best in the world, regardless of whether they were put into automobiles, ships, or airplanes—so if Hitler won in the end, it would be because of Germany's superiority in motors. About the fact that most of the world thought that Germany's superiority lay in the spirit of Wagner and Goethe, which had nothing to do with reality because German superiority lay in motors. And he would babble on about the Ethiopian emperor Selassie, about the spears that his warriors hurled at Italian airplanes, about desert air being good for asthma, in contrast to jungle air, about his allergy that wouldn't turn into asthma (although Dr. Weber from Graz had told him that every allergy in the end turns into asthma). About the fact that professional medicine still hadn't acknowledged the existence of allergies and that you couldn't find a single word about that condition in medical textbooks (but he knew well that it was the malady of the future and that one day the whole world would suffer from allergies). He also babbled about venereal diseases and the need to have public toilets built in the vicinity of the main city squares, about homosexuals and their depravity, and about how every beauty is meaningless — but why did one have to seek meaning in everything?

Ivo would just listen to him and wonder whether that man had always been like this or whether his garrulity stemmed from nervousness. Or from fear. They say that when one is about to die, his whole life passes before his eyes and he lives his days one more time. Everything is repeated in a single second, in the blink of an eye, and so seventy years of average life fit into a tiny slice of time. It's packed and pressed like hay when it's put into bales. Likewise, when someone feels the fear of death, he feels the need to speak and repeat all the words he has ever uttered. Only Klein's fear lasted a long time. What he said was interesting, although it came in fits and starts, so that his tales couldn't be remembered, nor could anything be learned from them.

Bosnia looked like empty country all the way to Bihać. They ran into only two or three peasants, who upon meeting them were more afraid of them (probably because of their beards) than Ivo and Klein were afraid that the peasants would turn them in to the police or chop them up with axes. The going was easier at night, not because it was less dangerous — because one could never be sure of that — but because during the day they would grow weary of seeing burned houses and villages, ravaged roads, dead cattle decomposing in ditches, battered army trucks, and discarded bloody uniforms. It gave the impression that it would always be that way or only get worse and that the only thing that would grow again in this land were weeds and wild apple trees, the shoots of which they encountered at every step, as if a wind had blown untold numbers of their seeds everywhere.

But no matter how dead and destitute Bosnia was, you wouldn't starve there. Every other plant was edible. Every few kilometers there were fallow potato fields. In neglected orchards fruit grew abundantly, like wild vegetation; it bloomed out of season, not according to any calendar or changes in nature, as if it were crazed by the fact that it hadn't been picked.

"Bosnians believe that nature brings forth its fruit best in the years of the worst war," Klein said as they were picking overripe pears and swatting away wasps and wild bees at dusk on a height offering a panoramic view of Bihać.

"Bosnians believe in anything and everything," Ivo responded. "Whatever happens, it turns out they've already believed in it. I know them well. A guy named Hilmo was with me for a while, a sailor from Zvornik! He was twenty when he stuck his finger in the sea for the first time and was twenty-one when he sailed on a transoceanic ship. That Hilmo was a good guy, but nothing could happen that he didn't already know about. If a storm arose, and a storm on the Pacific is something that no living man can imagine, Hilmo would shrewdly conclude that it had been clear earlier that there would be a storm because his ring finger had been itching all day long. And as soon as your ring finger is itching, it can only mean that there's going to be a storm on the Pacific. If the sea was as smooth as a mill pond, Hilmo would say, of course, I knew it; my left eye didn't twitch for three days for nothing, and when someone's left eye twitches, that means that you'll be able to burn a candle outdoors. Hilmo could explain anything, I mean anything that happened on the ship, with his magic and omens. That annoyed me a little, and I told him it was easy: a storm arises, and he says he knew about it yesterday. So why didn't he tell us yesterday? Because you didn't ask. I told him, well, you'll be hanging from the mast the next time your ring finger itches and you don't tell me. And I waited in anticipation for the next storm, just so I could watch him squirm. Just imagine me as a sailor waiting for a storm, all for a joke and a prank. That's youth for you! And you know what happened? The next day we almost drowned. That was the biggest storm I ever experienced at sea. Not far from the shores of Australia. Men wept, prayed to St. Anthony, and no one thought we'd come out of it alive. But Hilmo, you see, knew. That's a Bosnian for you. There was nothing he hadn't believed in before it happened. And what benefit do they get from it?!" he asked, pointing with his hand at a burned, dead village, as if that village were the best confirmation that Bosnians didn't have a lick of sense. They knew their destiny in advance but didn't do anything to avoid it.

In early evening they lay down for a bit in the attic of one of the more intact houses. Their plan was to sleep until midnight and then continue the journey, bypassing Bihać and continuing on toward Kordun. Ivo found some quilts, and they used them to make beds on bare boards, and all stuffed with pears, they fell asleep like two bears as soon as they lay down.

Klein dreamed an old dream of his, which had followed him since the day he'd started school as a boy, in which he'd lost his left shoe in the middle of a street and didn't know how that had happened to him and was looking for it. Sometimes he awoke from that dream in sweat and tears, desperate because he had to return to his father and mother missing a shoe. But over the years he'd grown accustomed to his dream and accepted it as nightly entertainment and a respite from all his daily worries. He sought his lost shoe leisurely, putting off waking up and knowing that he wouldn't find it because he hadn't ever found it before, and who knew what would happen to his dream if the shoe ever turned up? Maybe he'd die then, he thought, and maybe he would really die if he found it in the dream. He knew, at least while he was asleep, that that part of the dream was far away.

And so, as Klein sought his shoe, the sound of a fiddle insinuated itself into his thoughts. It was playing a melancholy Bosnian song, and an accordion soon joined in, and when a tambourine sounded, Klein realized that something was wrong with his dream. He quit looking for the shoe and tried to remember if a song had ever been playing in these circumstances before or whether the search had proceeded in silence. He couldn't summon any kind of sound from his memory. But no silence either. Does an instrument play in dreams or not? Are there colors and odors in dreams?

So he woke up, right when the horns blared. Every hair on his arms was standing on end. He firmly clutched the edges of the quilt and caught sight of Ivo's eyes, which were bulging with fear. Though he'd already woken up at the first tone of the fiddle, he couldn't figure out what was going on either.

They stared at one another while a hoarse male voice tried to sing above the horns and the accordion. It sang, "On the far bank of the Pliva there grows a blade of grass," and then finished even louder: "And every foreign land is a sorrowful expanse."

When the song was over, someone shouted, "Play 'Zagreb Girls'!" The horns started up; one could hear squeals and male voices whooping, and a whole choir began to sing: "A young Ustasha under the banner, the battle rages on, the Ustasha banner waves, for freedom and for the home, the Croatian home."

Klein shuddered as if someone had connected him to an electric current. "Samuel won't, he won't," he whispered to himself, "he won't, Samuel won't." He repeated the formula that protected him from the dark. His grandmother had said, "He won't, Samuel won't," when he lay dying from diphtheria. She had also said, "He won't, Samuel won't," when he had fallen off a fence and broken his leg. This was the first time that Samuel told himself, "He won't, Samuel won't."

They lay at the opening between the roof and the attic floor, which in places was thirty centimeters wide and through which one could see the yard in front of the house and a campfire in the middle of it. Fifteen men in black uniforms were sitting cross-legged in a semicircle on the bare ground. On the other side of the fire were twelve musicians, unbelievably tattered, playing a song about a sweet little Marijana. At their backs were two men in black uniforms with automatic rifles across their chests. The horns gleamed in the firelight and didn't fit in with the somber scene. If it weren't for those instruments, the men would have been mere shadows—those who were sitting, the musicians, and the motionless guards. What Klein saw seemed more unreal than his dream, and the music that came from the instruments fit into this scene less than his eternal search for his shoe. It was as if someone had added music to a dead picture in the belief that they could thereby bring it to life. But instead it became more lifeless.

"Play faster!" bellowed a motionless figure next to the fire, and the orchestra started playing faster.

"Sing to me, sing, sing, o falcon, keep away, o falcon," a voice wailed hoarsely.

"Even faster; we don't have time!"

They played even faster, each musician playing for himself and in harmony with his own abilities, which were different in each of them, just as fear is different in every man, so they no longer sounded like an ensemble but like musicians who'd begun a song out of tempo with one another: one had started it the day before, another ten years ago, and there was little chance of them ever finding the same key and tempo.

"Sto-o-o-p!" The one who'd been giving orders from the beginning got up from the ground and pulled out his revolver. The others didn't move.

"And now you'll play 'Wide Is the Danube, Flat Is Srijem' slowly, but so it sounds like in the theater, without faking it. Whoever fakes it will get a bullet between the eyes."

Silence followed. Evidently no one dared to begin first. Their hands trembled in the nighttime breeze. From the northern reaches, from Pannonia and even farther, maybe even from Siberia or the dark seas of the north, there arrived a current of air that on a night like this in other circumstances might have had a sobering effect on men drinking brandy who were carried away by the lightness of the summer and led them to fall silent for a moment when each would break off a little piece of cheese from a plate painted with three red roses, put it in his mouth, and lose himself in thought about the salt in his body.

"A raid!" shouted the man with the revolver, and someone laughed.

"Look, the fiddler wet his pants," said the one who'd laughed and pointed his finger at the old man with the violin, who had a stream running down his pant leg. At the same time two other streams started running down his cheeks. Only in silent films could you see so many tears on one face. The man in black put the muzzle of his revolver to his temple.

"Play! 'Wide Is the Danube, Flat Is Srijem,'" he ordered. "Just you, and then the others will too." The old man brought the instrument to his cheek, lowered the bow onto the strings, and glanced at the man with the revolver. The round lips of the muzzle pushed into the softest bones of his head, pressing them slightly apart.

He closed his eyes and drew the bow across a string. An unsteady sound came forth, like the creaking of the door of a dollhouse. The man with the revolver swallowed and said, "I think you started the wrong song!"

Then there was a shot, not too loud, as if someone had hit a rock in a creek bed with a wet shirt. The man's head exploded, its tissue sizzled on the coals of the campfire, and he collapsed sideways and lay there.

In the flames one could clearly see an open, empty skull, like the bottom of a dirty soup bowl. Tufts of hair remained above it, and at the bottom, where there was the clear outline of a crater, as if cut out with a diamond knife, there were human lips and a black mustache, unscathed.

No one moved. The men in the uniforms sat like children watching a puppet show, with those in the back straining to get a better view. The two with the automatic rifles looked disappointed. From their perspective the scene was uninteresting. That body, as far as they were concerned, could be the body of someone sleeping. They couldn't see what the bullet had done to the man's head, and they weren't too happy about that. Ivo and Klein had the view from the gallery, from the royal box. At the base of the skull there was a gnarl; either a piece of tissue had stuck to the bone or the flames of the fire cast a shadow that made it look like there was something there when there actually wasn't.

Samuel F. Klein would never feel as protected as he did then; a small god whose immortality was unquestionable, ashamed because of everything that he could or should have felt then, everything that makes someone human. He felt an inner need to remove the remaining piece of tissue or move the body so the fire didn't cast false shadows on it and death would become a completely round piece of porcelain from the table before a Sunday lunch. That aberrant feeling would torment him to the end of his days. He would free himself of everything and forget his fear and the moments when he thought his soul was falling into a thousand rays of light that nothing could ever bring back together. But the fact that he'd seen in a murdered man only an aesthetic fact, the bottom of a pretty porcelain soup dish, gave him no peace.

"Was I crazy?" he would ask a Coptic priest in '50-something in Jerusalem. The priest would stroke his cheek as he would a boy who'd come for religious instruction and wouldn't answer. God knew what that old Copt thought or whether he understood the story at all.

"Captain, don't, for Christ's sake!" the horn player pleaded, falling to his knees. The man with the revolver grabbed him by the ears; the young man groaned in pain.

"What did you say, you Gypsy shit?" the man with the revolver asked, enraged.

"Don't in the name of Allah!" the horn player said, misunderstanding the rebuke, which enraged the man more, and he jerked on his ear. He was trying to pull it off, but it didn't work because the man's earlobe kept slipping between his index finger and his thumb; the ear struggled like an eel, and no amount of force could take firm hold of it. That brought laughter from the group of men sitting on the other side of the fire.

The man with the revolver didn't think that they were laughing at the horn player's expense, especially after his ear had slipped between the captain's fingers for the fifth or sixth time and he had covered his ears with his palms and started whining and praying at the top of his lungs. But he was no longer invoking God in any of his names, but Pavelić, the Independent State of Croatia, and his own pure Catholic origins, which were known to everyone in Pitomača and to Zovko, the canon in Novska. It was pure chance that he, a baptized Catholic, had ended up in a Gypsy ensemble.

His outcry made the captain waver for a moment. Maybe the Gypsy wasn't lying, and maybe he wasn't a Gypsy at all? His skin wasn't that dark, there were boys in the company with darker skin, and hardly anyone would see a Gypsy in that loudmouth, except maybe because of his clothes. But then he realized what a shame it would be if he yielded now. If he said, "Yeah, you're not a Gypsy, I was wrong!" and kicked him in the butt and sent him home, half the company would think that Captain Heinrich was a softy, and the other half would think he was an idiot because a Gypsy had managed to convince him that he was a Croat, and only a blind man couldn't see the difference between a Gypsy and a Croat, even if they each had an equally dark complexion. Even if the Gypsy had blue eyes.

"Well why didn't you say so, dammit? A big Croat! And I thought you were one of Pharaoh's people. Hey, no problem, we'll check that out now. C'mon over here for a bit," Captain Heinrich said, luring the horn player to get up. "Now bend down here, right, just like that, so I can see your face in the fire."

The horn player stopped a couple of feet from the fire and smiled, pleasantly assured of his salvation.

"Good; now let's see, how could I have been so mistaken?" Heinrich asked in surprise and tapped the horn player on the back of his head, as if he were petting a good hunting dog. Then he suddenly grabbed his hair and, moving like a Croatian national athlete, he knocked one of his feet out from under him, and the horn player slammed down on the ground and his face went right into the fire. Heinrich held him by the hair and pushed his head deeper into the charred oak logs. The horn player flailed with his hands and feet, trying to extricate himself.

In the dead silence the only thing that could be heard were the horn player's hands and feet pounding the ground. It sounded like a big bear crossing a dusty country road.

Heinrich was sweating from the exertion, and the fire probably singed his hand. A few times it seemed that he was going to let up and the horn player would pull his head out of the coals, but then the captain would summon a little more strength from somewhere and press his head harder. That was the strength that a man doesn't know he has until he's found himself in mortal danger or in a position to save his loved ones or, which was perhaps the strongest motive, to prove his strength before a crowd of onlookers. To keep from giving up and yielding to the fire and the desperate struggling of the victim, Captain Antun Heinrich was probably motivated most by the thought that the men in his company, at least one among them, maybe two, seven, or all of them, would be struck with wonder at his power, that they would realize what kind of a he-man they were watching through the flames of the campfire as he sweated and struggled but didn't give up. Because a real Ustasha never gave up, a real man who didn't shrink from wolves and wild animals, from hellish fires, enemies, and fear, from a heart that trembled in his chest and asked, "What is that you're doing, black Antun? You'll burn in hell for this!"

Who cared about hell?—The whole world could go to hell, but until then one had to carry out what his children and their children's children would remember and be grateful for as they prayed over their graves for the homeland and for peace.

Antun Heinrich held out longer than anyone would have thought. The horn player's body struggled and resisted for ten whole minutes. Maybe more. Or maybe it only seemed so to those who were watching. Maybe he pushed his head too deep and maybe the horn player's face extinguished the coals, but the body was alive for just as long as it takes to bake a potato. After it finally stopped moving, the captain kept holding the head in the fire a little longer so that no one would get the idea that he couldn't endure it any longer, and then he pulled it out. Klein closed his eyes.

Before a cock could crow twice, everyone in the Gypsy ensemble was killed with knives, fire, and bullets. Captain Heinrich killed nine of them with his own hands and left the men who played the accordion, the bass tambouritza, and the second horn to the guards. They performed their task without the least amount of passion. They ordered all three of them to kneel and cut their throats with hunting knives. And so, sometime around two thirty in the morning, the picnic came to an end. The men all got up off the ground complaining of pains in their knees and of the hard soldier's life in which you have neither chairs nor beds. They spread out their gray army blankets and soon fell asleep amid the scattered instruments, a few meters distant from the dead bodies. Captain Heinrich didn't assign anyone for sentry duty. He either forgot about it due to his physical exhaustion and weariness or he knew that there weren't any partisans in the area.

Samuel F. Klein and Ivo Delavale kept watching from the attic for a long time, looking at the men who were snoring and farting loudly, moaning in their sleep, and calling to their mothers, passing from a time of war to a time of peace and from their adult male bodies into the souls of children. One could hear them crying in their sleep, the way armies cry since there has been a world and wars in it, with the sadness of men who find themselves far from their wives and mothers, from their own lives and everyday civilian gentleness.

"If I were a soldier," Klein whispered, "I'd go down there, steal up to the nearest rifle, and kill all of them. If I were only a soldier," he repeated as if it were something he longed for. Ivo didn't answer. His tongue was stuck to his palate or had turned into a smooth chunk of stone, into a pillar of salt that melted in his mouth, which made him thirstier and thirstier, and he cursed himself, his stupid head, because he hadn't filled their bottles with water. It seemed to him that nothing in his mouth could make a sound any more and that he would die of thirst before the morning. He grabbed Samuel by the arm and signaled with his finger to be quiet. They remained awake until the morning. They watched the soldiers wake up, eat breakfast, pack their things, and leave. Then they watched the extinguished campfire, the horns gleaming in the sun, and the dead men. It wasn't until around ten that Ivo moved.

"Let's go!" he ordered. Klein shook the dust off his pants, wishing to act as if nothing had happened. He could walk, think about whatever he wanted. He was calm and collected and felt as he did every day. Weeks of walking and wandering around had strengthened him, and he was proud of himself. He let these thoughts roll around in his mind.

"Someone should bury these people," he said when they went outside.

"Someone should," Ivo agreed.

"We don't have anything to do it with," Klein said.

"Even if we did, it would take us three days to bury them," Ivo said.

"Maybe even longer," said Klein.

They didn't feel like going; they couldn't leave just like that. This was one of those rare occasions when both the one and the other felt the same way at the same time. They were confused and didn't know what one should do in such circumstances—as if such situations occurred at other times and there were people who knew.

"Do you know a prayer?" Klein asked.

"Don't start that," said Ivo.

"Well what should we do?"

"I don't know . . ."

"I can't just leave people like that," Klein said and paused, as if he were imagining what kind of people they were. "They were alive! We saw them while they were alive . . ."

"Yes, we sure did," Ivo said bitterly.

Then he started toward the dead men. Klein just watched him. He bent over the first one, the little bass tambouritza player, the youngest one in the ensemble, touched his hand, and whispered something to him. He touched the second one, and the third, and all of them to the last one, saying something that Klein couldn't hear.

"What did you say to them?" he asked when they had gone a couple of miles.

"Fortaleza, Natal, Joao Pessoa, Sergipe, Espirito Santo, Nova Iguacu, Vitoria, Celatina, Sao Luis, Curtiba, Sao Mateus, Santa Cruz Cabrália. That's what I said to them," Ivo answered, and with every word he felt sobs welling up in his throat.

"What kind of prayer is that?"

"It's not a prayer. Those are towns on the Brazilian coast. Beautiful places, one more beautiful than the next," Delavale said and started crying.

They stood under a huge willow tree, at the bank of a creek that was so narrow that a child could step across it but loud as little creeks seem when one hasn't taken a good drink from them. And they both wept, each from his own sorrow, for the twelve dead Gypsies. For plates of goulash eaten in the middle of a Hungarian plain in late autumn in 1930-something. For Balkan dictators with little black mustaches whose visits to Paris were reported in the yellow press. For embroidered wedding towels whipped in the wind over the Vrbas River as a bride and groom ran to get out of the rain. For a procession that saw a mayor's son off to the army while his drunken godfather poured brandy on anthills. For the battles of Kajmakčalan and Mohacs Field. For defeats and victories celebrated in song and sealed behind seven locks of the Royal Bank in Bucharest. For a dead Croatian poet in a Spanish almshouse. For Mary's Congregation of Young Women, which in 1937 at number 7 Cracow Street was celebrating its anniversary and had hired Gypsies to play the music because they were cheaper than the orchestra of the Hotel Europa. For the Majdan Hardware and Precious Metals Shop owned by Isidor A. Altarc, Klein's uncle, about whom he'd heard nothing for a year already. For the Orfelin bookstore, owned by Milutin D. Stanojević, on St. Sava Street in Belgrade, where in 1932 Ivo had bought Regina an autograph album with the title *It Is Written in My Heart, I Love You Most*, and she'd known who'd sent it to her in the mail, even though he was too shy to sign his name. For a Russian émigré who a year later jumped from the Revelin fortress and who was buried along the cemetery wall, without a name or a marker. For the clear juice of rose petals sold on the Split quay on the day the news arrived that King Aleksandar had been assassinated, when the gendarmerie had forbidden the people to drink rose juice as a sign of mourning, except for children younger than twelve. For party-colored Zagreb umbrellas that leaked drops of rain. For sea crabs on the beach in Crikvenica in late 1912, as tuberculosis patients from Prague and Požun lay dying in chaises longues with a view of the sunset. For the leather merchant Majir Alkalaj, who upholstered the command cabin of the ship *Leonica* with quality pigskin. For the Professional Association of Cinemas of Sava Province at number 6 Warsaw Street in Zagreb, which ordered reels of the newest American movies through Samuel F. Klein but whose business was ruined after a year because Rudolph Valentino died. For the copper trays and pots from the bazaar by the Old Bridge in Mostar, which Klein bought for his business partners in Hamburg and Ostend. For the Zagreb musicians who played in variety shows in Paris and London. For the blind lottery ticket vendor in the Vinkovci railway station who repeated the call, "Mouse of white, my luck's so bright!" and in a cage on his stand was an enormous gray rat. For the Albanian king, whose escort included three fierce Ottoman soldiers and whose ferocity seemed funny to the crowds in Paris because each one was more than eighty years old. For the criers who in 1935 went through the streets and lanes of Livno, Duvno, and Bugoj beating drums and advertising Bata shoes, "which make paupers feel like kings." For the ship sirens that wailed mournfully before the body of Stjepan Radić in August of 1928, while the wooden doors on the women's cabins slammed in a bitter wind and the lifeguards searched for gold on the beaches out of boredom. For the mustached revolutionaries and fighters who struggled against the tobacco monopoly and whom the gendarmerie led in chains down Stradun as children ran alongside them and spat on them. For the clockmaker Josef Kopelman of number 55 Aleksandar Street, Sarajevo, who had sold Klein a pocket watch with an engraved monogram of a Mexican prince, and for doctor Grigorij Merkulov of number 71 on the same street, to whom he'd gone after he'd gotten crabs in the Elezar & Sons hostel in Konjic. For the little boats that had drifted around in the harbor of Korčula after someone unmoored them one night as some kind of payback.

Samuel F. Klein and Ivo Delavale wept until they could weep no more, under that willow, each one for his own story, which was connected in some way (understandable to their souls) to the twelve dead Gypsies, and they didn't say anything to one another. A brotherhood of tears, which was stronger than a brotherhood of blood because it wasn't something they decided on or a matter of male friendship, brought them closer together and changed something in the way they experienced one another.

Over the next two months, the time that it took for them to reach the sea in the autumn of 1942, traveling at night and during the day and staying in one place for five or six days at a time because they would hear shooting on the next hill, Ivo told Klein the story of his two women on two continents. Of one who was his, with whom he'd gotten married and intended to spend his life and of another, whom he loved more than anyone in the world and with whom he'd become an American. She knew that he was married somewhere over there in Europe, but that place seemed so far away to her that nothing that happened there could reach her heart. If he by chance turned to look at a pretty girl on the streets of Chicago, she was jealous, but she felt nothing regarding Ivo's wife. Or he only thought she didn't, Klein thought. He didn't tell his real wife anything about the American girl because—in his exact words—she would have pulled out his fingernails and never let him go to sea again. For her, Ivo speculated, America was much closer than Europe was for the American girl. Such are our men and women. Although they live on the edge of the world, in the remotest provinces of all except maybe for those of Russia, they experience the whole world as someplace close by so that what happens in Chicago is just as shameful as what happens in Čapljina.

"So, do you love her?" Klein asked so that Ivo might quit beating around the bush.

"I love both of them," he said as they descended a mountain path overlooking Delnice. "But that's not the real question. The problem is that I don't know which continent is mine. Actually, I knew that until that gringo off the coast of Florida took my American papers and I started going backward. Like a crab, and now I'm continually going backward. I said, okay old boy, you did what you did, ran away from your wife and your house; you'll be an American, you'll die like an American, you'll never have any contact with her or your family again. It isn't human, it isn't honest, but that's how it turned out. Nobody's to blame for it, and I'm not even terribly guilty. And then what happened?—They sent me back to Europe like a crate of rotten apples. Now I'm here, and who the hell knows whether I'll ever see America again? That's how I got involved in all this. But it's a miracle I'm even alive."

In a way it was a miracle. Namely, the ship *De Amicis*, which Ivo Delavale had boarded in Portugal as a stowaway, had been attacked by Greek pirates at the Strait of Otranto. They killed most of the crew, and the only ones who got away were Ivo and two sailors. He swam and when he reached the Albanian shore, he was captured by an Italian military guard. They held him in a prison for seven days, forced him to drink castor oil, and tried to get him to confess to something. They didn't know what kind of confession they were expecting, but he was evidently the first one they'd managed to get their hands on in the middle of a thriving smuggling route, so their ambition was to promote Ivo to the level of a serious criminal. He, however, had no idea about where he'd ended up or what was being smuggled in those parts, so he couldn't even help himself with lies. Instead he endured the castor oil treatment, and in the end they threw him out on his ass. Afterward there was a journey through Albanian and Montenegrin mountains and gorges, encounters with Chetniks and partisans, and ferocious village guards who almost did him in because it seemed that village defenders had fewer problems in detecting enemies than any Balkan army. They saw an enemy in any stranger, and Ivo Delavale was probably the strangest character who'd ever set foot in the villages around Kolašin. The only reason they didn't liquidate him was probably due to the fact that not even this time around did he have any idea about what they were questioning him about. He had neither heard of Sekula Drljević, nor did he have any idea about who Pavle Đurišić was and could only shrug his shoulders like the biggest idiot on earth when they slyly tried to lure him into telling which one of them he thought was more handsome. The villagers didn't care whose beauty he preferred; they would have stuck him like a pig on account of the one or the other, but they couldn't cut his throat if all he did was hem and haw like a fool when they mentioned either Sekula or Pavle.

After he made his way through Montenegro and crossed the Drina at Višegrad, he fell into the hands of the partisans. He felt better already because he knew a little about Marx, Engels, and Lenin and the exploitation of the American proletariat. He lied that he'd left Chicago to go fight the fascist occupiers for a just society. He fascinated his comrades with his knowledge of foreign languages. They nicknamed him "Brains," dressed him in a tattered uniform of the Royal Army, stuck a garrison cap with a red star on his head, and sent him into combat. The next day he was captured by Croatian Home Guardsmen near Ustikolina. They took him to Sarajevo, where they turned him over to the Germans because someone had concluded that he was a prominent bandit, too smart and eloquent for an ordinary partisan. The Germans questioned him for two days and decided to transfer him to Slavonski Brod and later to somewhere else. Probably to a concentration camp. But near Doboj the partisans attacked the column of trucks he was in and freed him. He promptly lied and told them that he'd been captured on his way to Dubrovnik, where he'd been sent on orders from the staff of the supreme command, and requested that they immediately allow him to continue his trip. He was lucky that this was one of the more poorly integrated and organized units, in which no one knew how to establish contact with the supreme command and verify Ivo's account. But they didn't even suspect him because he made a serious impression on them. And so they decided to convey him to Dubrovnik via an illegal network, and in fact via Ivan Skočibuha—a.k.a. Panther—and his men. The first and last station on that trip was the attic of the Banja Luka prep school.

"That's how it is," said Klein instructively. "When you mess with life a lot, then life starts messing with you back." Ivo didn't know what to say to him. Samuel was right. But if everything else was leading to harm and ruin, at least he'd found a friend.

As in a romantic comedy from the early days of talking movies, they hugged and kissed one another on the Rijeka promenade, resolved to survive the war and travel their route from Banja Luka to the sea once again by car. They would stop at all the taverns, which after the war would practically line the roads. And they would drink, eat, and carouse until dawn. A dawn for every tavern. Samuel F. Klein believed in their agreement, at least until the moment he went into the cellar office of Erwin Stieglitz, who would provide him with forged papers in the name of Gustav Toehni, with which he would journey to London and on to Palestine, while Ivo Delavale knew then that he would never see Samuel again. In the catalogue of his friends, Klein would occupy an important spot, but like the others with whom he'd gone to school, drunk, sailed, or met at various ends and beginnings of the world, he too would be a man without an address, lost in a universe of faces and voices. A friend who disappears after the first parting. Ivo had never made anything of the accidental encounters he'd experienced that would last him his whole life, and those are the only kind men have. True, his friends hadn't made much of an effort themselves, in the mistaken belief that a man couldn't disappear just like that or appear randomly again, bursting through one's doorway or coming along like a random passerby in any city anywhere in the world. And they would think that it was him—that it was his handsome head appearing above a crowd of people in the bowels of the city market, in front of a mosque at the time of the *jumu'ah* prayer, or in the distance at the end of Kalelarga Street. They would run to call to him, but it wouldn't be Ivo, not even someone who looked like him. No matter how much they were disappointed, their feeling that a friendship had been spoiled by nothing would be even greater. Ivo hadn't betrayed any of those men before he disappeared from their lives.

Samuel F. Klein thought he saw Delavale's phantom ten or so times in various places in Syria, Egypt, and Israel, and he was always equally sure that it was him. The last time was in Haifa, ten days before he died. He surfaced out of a mound of oranges, in a worker's outfit, with a notebook in which he was writing something. He wasn't any older than the day they parted on the Rijeka promenade. Klein tried to walk up to him, but by the time he'd made his thirty small steps and gone ten full meters, which took several minutes, both the oranges and the worker had disappeared, and there wasn't anything but the parking lot of a construction company where cranes, bulldozers, excavators, and trench diggers waited, ready to build houses for poor Russian and Ukrainian Jews, somewhere on a rectangular desert border, within rifle shot of enemy armies or only a stone's throw away from Arab poor folk. That was the spot of the first and last hallucination of Samuel F. Klein. On that spot, if metaphysical truths make sense, there remained forever a monument to Ivo Delavale, a sailor on the *Leonica* and a brave man who valued the life of a friend as much as his own, who had compassion for all he knew and those he didn't, and who had poured tears on the grave of a Gypsy orchestra.

Because of all that it is perhaps likely that when Klein read the signature of Regina Della Valle at the end of a fairly impudent but at the same time bureaucratic and extremely private message, he recognized one of Ivo's two loves. Maybe he thought bitterly that such a woman wasn't worthy of him; maybe he was comforted by his belief that Ivo was now in America with that other, better love. But maybe he had something else in mind, something that human fantasy couldn't reach and remained hidden in documents of public and private history. Yet the fact remains that his response was too heartfelt and deep, stripped of all farcical style and frivolity, for anyone to believe that he'd sent it to someone about whom he knew nothing and who actually didn't concern him.

"My advice to you is to look for him for some other, more noble, reason. Then the dear Lord will grant that you find him!" That was what Samuel F. Klein wrote to Regina Delavale when she tried to inquire about a nonexistent brother in order to find out the truth about the lover of her deceased husband.

Behind Regina's complex formula, and the muddled reasons that led to it, were lies that were supposed to hide the blind desire for revenge. In that desire Regina was a product of her time. Because of unrequited loves, betrayals, and slanders people took revenge on one another. But instead of the real reasons, which leaders in ceremonies of collective hysteria discovered in the souls of their people, they invented lies in the face of revenge. Samuel F. Klein's answer was also typical. In it, though an atheist, he invoked the Lord and His will. That was an example of poetry after Auschwitz: God would provide what people hadn't, though it was clear that God was no longer among men.

Nor was Regina's invention of a brother for whom she was searching unusual either. Besides Luka, who was alive and well in 1951, when she was writing to

Haifa, and Bepo, who'd died two years earlier in the Sarajevo insane asylum, she had three more brothers: Lino, Đuzepe, and Đovani. All three were deceased. Lino had died from the Spanish flu during the First World War. As for Đuzepe and Đovani, there might still be something to say about the reasons why their fates weren't of great concern to their sister. Maybe. But Regina didn't see any kind of miracle in her brothers; they certainly weren't miraculous enough for her to superstitiously worry about shielding them from curses. Where there were five of them, she could invent a sixth.

VI

On the twelfth of June, 1940, someone stole Đovani Sikirić's wallet and student ID on the Place de la Concorde. It happened late in the afternoon, when, as during the entire previous week, most of the cafés and shops were closed. Few people were out on the street; everyone was behind closed windows and lowered shutters, awaiting the moment when the Germans would enter the city. A few weeks before Marshal Philippe Pétain, the victor of the Battle of Verdun, a national hero and vice president of Paul Reynaud's government, had sacrificed the homeland for peace, convinced that resistance to Hitler's troops made no sense and couldn't be effective. Aware that France had enough military victories to her credit and that this capitulation wouldn't cost her her honor, he gave the order for the army not to defend the city. Those who disagreed with Pétain had already left Paris and gone to the south. Those who guessed that the Germans threatened them with personal ruin for racial, ideological, or political reasons had also left. For days Đovani had watched them leaving the city. And he knew why many of them were leaving: they were students and professors of Jewish extraction and Russian émigrés, almost all of whom were socialists, communists, Trotskyites, social democrats, anarchists, or members of a dozen or so revolutionary organizations who'd found refuge in Paris as early as the October Revolution. And then there was the liberal citizenry, who feared the German breakthrough like the devil himself, fearing it in proportion to their previous sense of superiority over those same Germans. Painters fled, as did philosophers and writers, newcomers who had already fled from those same Germans when in 1936 Hitler had begun to expand and draw borders around the German living space. Lastly, students from East European countries left the city before the end of the fall semester—the sons of Bulgarian, Romanian, and Hungarian ministers and industrialists—in the belief that they were subject to less danger in their little metropolises, which, as the general conviction held, would not be struck by the great fury of history.

"Paris, and not London, is the main obstacle to European unification under Hitler," Trajče Bogoev told Đovani as they parted. He was an art student who boasted that his father was the chief of the Bulgarian counterintelligence service, which Đovani didn't take very seriously because if such a relational connection were true, no one in their right mind would brag about it. And by the way, wasn't it strange that all those boys were from nowhere else but Eastern Europe? Why was it that the Bulgarians, Romanians, Greeks, and Albanians were the sons of people with the wildest biographies—spies, magicians, imperial murderers, and phony stamp-cutters—and that none of them came from ordinary families, like every French, Dutch, or Swiss student in Paris?

Some uncorroborated, unsubstantiated lie accompanied their every step, and Trajče was no exception in this regard. This Bulgarian was a fairly talented portrait artist yet lacked a real artistic education and had no feel at all for beauty. He produced unbearable little kitsch paintings and would use them to develop and analyze conspiracy theories and geostrategic paradoxes. He would paint the Eiffel Tower, and above it he would brush in three black oak beams that an invisible force kept from crashing down on the city. If that force disappeared, some kind of hell would follow, probably in the same kitschy manner.

"Paris is a symbol standing in Hitler's way, and I have no intention of getting killed for a symbol," Trajče said. He downed one last vodka, paid the bill, kissed Đovani three times, and got into a Mercedes of the Bulgarian consulate that would take him to Lyons.

Half an hour later, on the Place de la Concorde, Đovani noticed that his wallet and student ID were missing. He went back to the bar in which they'd sat and talked, but it was already closed; the metal shutters had been lowered and locked with a giant padlock. He banged on the door with his fist a few times, hoping that someone was inside and that they would hear him, but there was only the metallic echo of an empty hall.

He was sure that his ID card and wallet had fallen out as he put on his blazer and that he would find them the next day with the waiter. There was almost no money in his wallet; indeed there was just enough for a metro ticket, and no one would find that worth stealing. Nor would a thief have any use for his student ID. And Đovani had to find his ID card because the university was no longer in session, and no one would be able to confirm that he was a student. There was a difference between a student and an unemployed young man from Yugoslavia, especially in a time of war and an impending German occupation.

That night he slept poorly, tossed and turned in his bed, listened to the trains in the distance, and sank into dark thoughts and a slumber in which he couldn't tell what was an illusion from what might be a real threat. For the first time he started to lose his bearings in this city and wasn't sure whether he'd been smart not to flee when they tried to get him to leave. Or when they told him that it wasn't honorable to meet the Germans upon their entrance into the city and that nothing like that would make any sense for someone who didn't have any family in Paris. But he wondered whether it was more honorable to leave the city that had taken him in and made him better and more worldly, and he stayed.

He could barely wait for the wall clock to chime seven o'clock. He got dressed and ran outside to reach that café before it opened at eight. There were no people on the street, but everywhere he heard a strange sound, like the knocking of an old, empty loom. That sound followed him all the way to Pigalle. There he realized that it wasn't a loom or any kind of machine or device but the sound of thousands of rubber soles rhythmically striking the asphalt. Those were long, eight-row columns of German soldiers moving at a leisurely pace—that is, not marching—toward the Étoile.

His throat constricted from fear. But a few moments later, he realized that the scene wasn't out of the newsreels showing military parades in Berlin and their entry into Prague and Bratislava. The Germans weren't stepping loudly and powerfully but seemed more like they were going to the theater. Now Ðovani was overcome by a new feeling. Rage grew within him, especially after he saw two women of the night following the column with laughter and squeals and immediately thereafter little groups of ten or so dark-skinned men— evidently Arabs, Algerians, Tunisians, and Moroccans—dressed in formal black suits and bow ties who were waiting, with their heads raised high and with the dignity of tribal leaders, and walking alongside the German troops. Apart from these people, no one was out on the empty Pigalle. There were no Frenchmen. Ðovani was galled—so much so that tears of fury ran down his face—by the betrayal that had just been committed by people who'd brought their faith with them into Christian Paris. They strolled through the Champs-Élysées with fezzes and turbans or wrapped in those sheets of the Bedouins; no one tried to prevent them; no one chased them or shouted anything at them. But they nevertheless greeted the Germans with their quiet enthusiasm. They'd bought formal European suits and removed the fezzes from their heads to show their respect for them. That was the moment when they became closer to Europe; their hands extended to another civilization, a gesture with which different worlds are united, fused, and permeated with one another. They'd been waiting for Hitler to remove their fezzes and turbans because without him Europe was unworthy of that act. They were betraying a city into which they didn't want to assimilate, he thought, and were taking the side of someone about whom they knew less than about Paris, but they were impressed that he'd come to quash Paris under his boot. The community of hatred and the cosmopolitanism of savagery.

He would never forget those people who were happy about the occupation, nor the closed and darkened windows behind which sat the motionless and saddened inhabitants of a city that Ðovani had thought was the strongest and most invincible. Whoever came to Paris and managed to stay there was forever spared of everything that had driven him to leave the place he'd left. He believed that from the day when he decided to go to Paris to study geology and thereby cut all his ties with home and renounced the family inheritance. So he would never again see or hear his sister, his brothers, or any one of those from whose world he was fleeing.

From Arabs who'd been arrested he heard that the entire German army was going to gather on the Place de la Concorde, and he hurried over there, less from curiosity than from the hope that something might happen in front of the Arc de Triomphe. The French had to defend that place; it was unimaginable that the occupiers could pass just like that under Napoleon's arch of glory without bloodshed and resistance. If the government had already surrendered, leaving the decaying republic to the mercy of Hitler's savagery, there would neverthe-less be Frenchmen who would defend the national pride with their lives and blood. It didn't matter how many of them there would be, three or a hundred and three; no matter how many of them there were, they wouldn't be able to stop the German troops. But one day there would be a brass plaque with their names at the base of the Arc de Triomphe. "They defended France as the world slept the slumber of the just," it would say, Đovani thought, ready to add his name to the names of the heroes of the future.

He ran breathless down the Avenue des Champs-Élysées and arrived at the triumphal arch before the column of troops. But apart from German officers, who were continually glancing at their watches, and the Islamic high dignitaries with turbans and tarbushes on their heads, there was no one at the monument itself. Fifty meters from the triumphal arch two young men stood with a young woman with long, blond hair. She wept, loudly and inconsolably, as if she were alone in a movie theater watching a sad movie in which Greta Garbo was dying on a canopy bed; the two of them stood with their hands in their pockets and didn't try to comfort her. One of those officers could approach her and ask why she was crying on such a day, he thought, and then the officer would lead all three of them away. That too was a kind of protest. However, the girl wept, and no one went up to her. The step of thousands of soldiers was heard all around; they lifted their heels and lowered them onto the asphalt in unison. Without any assonant variation, arrhythmia, or little noises that would detract from that great noise, the German army drew nearer to Napoleon's triumphal arch.

Apart from the sobbing girl and her friends, Đovani Sikirić alone experi-enced that scene as a blow to the soul, that inflated sac in his chest that Hitler's army was kicking with its boot like Ivica Bek, a Zagreb dribbler, had kicked a soccer ball around in the stadiums and soccer fields of Paris a few years before.

Đovani liked that Bek because he'd come, by some chance at the same time as he had, to seek salvation in a more elegant world.

"If she jumps in front of the troops, I'll do something too!" he thought, clenching his sweaty fists and watching the banners with the swastikas and behind them the endless formation. But when they were about fifty meters from the Arc de Triomphe and the same distance from the four onlookers, they changed direction and instead of marching under the triumphal arch, they passed alongside it.

The German command had probably decided on that action, which has been largely ignored in the history books and was unknown even to Winston Churchill as he wrote his memoirs, to avoid humiliating the French or at least avoid irritating them unnecessarily, thinking that there was an important difference between them and the Poles and Czechs. The same difference that existed between Warsaw and Paris. In a way, the Nazis looked upon that city with the same eyes as Đovani Sikirić.

Instead of entering the annals of history with a heroic act and, together with the unknown girl, becoming a part of a myth that would be the subject of books, theater pieces, and movies and lend its name to streets and schools, Đovani let the Wehrmacht troops march right on by Napoleon's triumphal arch. Ashamed and angry, since someone might think that he'd come to greet the occupiers, he missed the ceremonial formation and the speech of a German officer who told the Parisians that he was not coming like one who would subjugate France, but he and his army were there in transit, as protection for European culture from the barbarians. Đovani went off to the café where he and Trajče Bogoev had said good-bye to find his student ID and his wallet, but the café was closed. For the next five days he would go there each morning to find it closed, and only on the sixth day, when that quiet protest against the occupation no longer made sense, did the café open up again. People were reading newspapers, sitting and talking, the same faces, the same waiters, and the same manager. However, his ID and wallet weren't there. Evidently they hadn't fallen out of his pocket while he was putting on his jacket. Someone had stolen them, most likely Trajče, in order to spite him for some reason. He wondered for a long time what use the Bulgarian would have for his things, and nothing came to mind but the idea that it was a way to harass someone who'd decided to stay in the city regardless of the arrival of the occupiers. If he survived the war, Trajče Bogoev would one day tell his grandchildren about that heroic deed.

Alone, with history and a fellow student having made an ass of him, Đovani Sikirić stood in the middle of a Parisian avenue and didn't know where to go. All the reasons that kept him going and made him give up, motivated him and depressed him, also inflamed and cooled his entire generation. That was 1940, the year when half of Europe was in flames, but the war hadn't yet filled the human heart and completely covered the pages of the newspapers. In March a truce was signed between Finland and Russia, and a few months later the term Blitzkrieg entered into popular usage. A five-year-old Tibetan named Llamo Thandup became the thirteenth Dalai Lama with the holy name Tenzing Gyatso. In Rome the Palazzo della Civiltà del Lavoro was opened, and an Australian named Howard Florey and a German named Ernst Chain perfected penicillin, so its mass production began in the United States. Đovani couldn't decide which way to go.

Exactly one year later, in the spring of 1941, his older brother Đuzepe Sikirić realized his life's dream and through a fictional business transaction acquired his own tavern. He'd worked as a waiter in railway station restaurants and taverns along the Dubrovnik-Mostar-Sarajevo narrow-gauge railway. He'd made his way through Trebinje, Konjic, Jablanica, Hadžići, Blažuj, and back again from station to station, from bar to bar, living without a home and the peace of home, sleeping in warehouses and on café tables he'd pulled together, amid barrels of wine and brandy, sacks of flour, and bales of Herzegovinian tobacco.

In one waiter's career Đuzepe had covered more distance than one of Napoleon's admirals had in ten wars; in 1929 he'd gotten a bayonet between his ribs from a drunken man from Solun. Fortunately, after half a bottle of brandy the man had managed to stab it into him only halfway. A few years later a brawl broke out in the station bar in Konjic after a procession; though he was completely innocent, he ended up with a pocketknife in his belly. In the autumn of 1934 the gendarmerie beat him up because they could hear people singing in the café during the mourning period for King Aleksandar, and afterward he spent three days in jail. In April of 1941 in Čapljina a non-commissioned officer of the Royal Army put a revolver to his temple and screamed:

"Shit, you treacherous scum! If you don't shit your pants, I'll blow your brains all over the floor!"

And what could Đuzepe do? He squeezed his bowels so hard veins popped out on his forehead, and he turned as red as a beet. The whole tavern laughed and cheered, some of them for him, but most for the non-commissioned officer, telling him not to wait so long but to shoot immediately because his order hadn't been carried out as soon as it was issued. The shit, fortunately, came, and Đuzepe got out of that mess with his head on his shoulders.

But a month later, luck finally smiled on him. The owner of the largest bar in Gacko and the surrounding area, Miloš Davidović, with whom he'd been employed since he'd left Čapljina, was aware that the market square would never forget how a waiter had shit his pants, and his boss didn't want to hang on to him either because he was convinced that a waiter who'd been compromised in that way would drive away customers. So he called Đuzepe over to his house one evening, sat him down at the table, poured both of them a brandy, and said:

"The situation, if you'll pardon me, has gotten shitty. This is territory of the State of Croatia now, and I am, beg pardon, Orthodox. And let's not lie to ourselves—there's no place for Orthodox in this state. I know it, you know it. This house is my inheritance, and that café is also my inheritance. My heart would stop beating if someone burned my inheritance, and I'm not dumb as a doorknob—I won't wait in my inheritance for the Ustashas to cut my throat. So I was thinking this: I could sign both the house and the café over to you. In fact, I'd be selling them to you. We'll write up a contract that will say you paid me a thousand ducats, and all this is now yours. I'm counting on the authorities recognizing that contract because you're Catholic. But I'm also counting on this state not lasting so long. It'll disappear just like it appeared. It's created too many enemies, and there are those who'll set about tearing it down. Maybe you think differently. So be it! Everyone has the right to think what he wants. This is what I think, and you think what you want. I wouldn't want to go into that. Now take a look at how our little joint plan works out: this will be yours as long as there's a Croatia. When there's no Croatia any more, the contract will be invalid because those who come to power won't recognize business conducted with ducats. They won't recognize a deal that arose in this way. Then you'll give me back my inheritance, and I'll be grateful to my dying day. I'll take you back as a waiter if you don't earn enough to open your own tavern. And I'll help you in any way I can. If I'm not right, and this state lasts longer than I do or they do me in, everything remains yours forever. But I won't let them set fire to my inheritance. So there you have it; I've said what I have to say, and now you can have your say."

Đuzepe had to hold himself back from jumping for joy and kissing Miloš not once but twice on both cheeks. It took an enormous effort for him to click his tongue worriedly, shake his head, and turn his palms up toward the ceiling, showing with those strange gestures, which no one has believed for ages, that the trouble was not only Miloš's but everyone's together and no one could be happy as long as the life of another was at stake and the foundation of his inheritance smoldered.

That evening the contract was drawn up and signed. The very next day Miloš Davidović left Gacko with his wife and children, and Đuzepe Sikirić, Regina's older brother, the family dimwit and shame of a fine urban household, had finally become a boss. He hung a framed picture of Ante Pavelić, dressed in an admiral's uniform and gazing into the distance, on a spot on the wall where a reproduction of Predić's *Kosovo Maiden* had hung before the war. He'd ordered it from Sarajevo and taken it to be colored to Puba Weiss. And with a lot of effort and care Puba gave a reddish hue to his cheeks and managed to get a shade of blue in his eyes. He didn't have an easy time because in the photograph Pavelić's eyes were blacker than Banovići coal. Puba Weiss tried in vain to convince his client that there was no way that the Leader had blue eyes. Đuzepe insisted that they were blue, fairly firmly convinced that Puba said the opposite because he was a Jew and that was the only reason why he didn't know that Ante Pavelić's eyes had to be as blue as the Adriatic Sea and the clearest summer sky over Herzegovina.

And Đuzepe would be sorry in the autumn of the same year when they smashed the only photography shop in Gacko and Puba met his end in a ravine on the way to Nevesinje. Đuzepe would sit alone in the bar that morning, gaze at Puba's last work, the portrait of the Leader in which he had the ruddy cheeks of a young mower girl and the blue eyes of a patron saint, and try to comprehend what the world was coming to, what kind of demon was taking hold of people if Puba Weiss had perished, a man who was able to make the Leader more handsome than those who had led him off to the ravine could imagine. But Đuzepe's thoughts were short-lived. He would chase them away, telling himself that he wasn't smart enough to comprehend global politics. Because if he were, then he'd be in Zagreb, Berlin, or London making decisions about different peoples and their fates. His scale was this bar, and he shouldn't let his thoughts leap outside, out of the bar, where bigger things were at stake. Apart from the fact that God hadn't created him for that, it wasn't advisable anyway. It was hard to keep your head on your shoulders. Puba Weiss wouldn't have reproached him for keeping his head on his shoulders. Just as Đuzepe wouldn't reproach Puba if the situation were reversed and he, Đuzepe, was being led off, God forbid, as a Jew, to the ravine.

The people of Gacko, regardless of their faith and position, treated him like an idiot and a nitwit. The tavern was considered to be both his and not his, and it was clear to everyone, including the Ustashas, why Miloš Davidović had signed his property over to the waiter. What disagreement there was only concerned the ducats. The majority thought that there weren't any ducats involved, but there were those who believed that the Serb had made a lot of money when he left and that this dolt certainly had thousands more if he'd already given Miloš a thousand for the house and the café. The unfortunate Đuzepe assured some that the ducats were an inheritance from his uncle in America and that he'd paid honestly for what was now his, whereas he tried to convince the others, who actually even believed that, all of them the local Ustashas, of something else.

He himself didn't actually know of what. He smiled, shook his head, and used his index finger to trace circles above his head, made allusions concerning the Orthodox and a votive candle that burned for a long time but would, as everyone knew, burn out one day. He stubbornly tried to explain to the Ustashas that he was actually a poor man and that the tavern and the house were a miracle. More or less like the founding of the Independent State of Croatia. They didn't believe him no matter what he said, but his lies somehow settled in on the atmosphere of those troubled times, and it was as if they did everyone good: those who were on the side of evil (because they didn't question their evil deeds) and those who had only good thoughts (because they would believe that every evil deed was just as stupid as Đuzepe's).

He spent the first year of his ownership of the bar torn between two inner powers. In the morning, as soon as he went into the café, he would feel a stark, limitless happiness because he was his own boss and not someone else's servant, a wretch, and a good-for-nothing. At the sight of the clean, empty glasses and full bottles and barrels, he would fold his hands and praise God (wherever he was and whatever his name was) and the Leader, without whom God's will could not even be carried out. Without the great work of the Leader, Đuzepe would have remained a waiter to the end of his life and wouldn't have known how nice it is to have the big worries of a boss instead of the little worries of a waiter. Instead of being dumbfounded with fear because he'd forgotten whether Captain Zovko drank grape or plum brandy or whether Mr. Hamzić had paid his monthly tab or needed to be reminded, it was his place to worry about whether the wine from Konavle would arrive on Thursday or Friday and whether bandits in the woods had attacked the wagon with cheese that was supposed to arrive from Travnik, slaughtering the deliveryman and stealing the goods, which had already been paid for.

When a man is his own boss, no loss, no deficit in the cash box is too great. That was what Đuzepe Sikirić thought and was filled with joy every morning. But as the day went on and all kinds of people passed through the bar and told all kinds of jokes at his expense, most often about the thousand ducats that he'd paid to be boss, he grew more apprehensive so that by evening he was deathly afraid. It couldn't be as it seemed because this had never happened since there have been people in the world. No one acquired wealth like that, and it wasn't possible that there wasn't any price to be paid for rising from the lowest to the highest in the market square and the town. And what could his payment have been in if not in ducats? That question tormented him until he fell asleep and in his slumber he forgot the terrible answers. In the morning he would awaken happy as a child who had been allowed to begin life anew with every new day.

On the same day that he took over the café, Đuzepe took on two new waiters because Savo Ekmek, a quiet young man with whom he'd shared the wait shifts and who'd been working for Miloš since the latter had picked him up off the street as a poor ten-year-old boy, had disappeared the same morning as the Davidović family. He took the first two he came across, one Hamo Aličić, an oddball ruffian from Fazlagić Tower, and Joso Domazet, formerly the manager of the station restaurant in Jablanica. Hamo had never worked as a waiter, and Joso had suffered a brain hemorrhage six months before, so he dragged his left foot and had a hard time remembering the orders. But both fulfilled the only criterion that was important to Đuzepe. The townsfolk thought less of them than they did of him, so he believed that they wouldn't make him look stupid. And it could be said that they didn't let him down: only the two of them, of all the people who entered the café, were completely indifferent to the question of whether Đuzepe had actually paid Miloš a thousand ducats or not. No matter how poorly they did their work (Hamo was even worse than Joso, and not a day passed when there wasn't money missing from the cash box), Đuzepe was satisfied because he felt that his people saw just what he wanted to see in himself: a man who'd succeeded in life and whose success couldn't be diminished by anyone, not one bit. But one had to admit that he had a good heart and in every man looked only at what was most important: whether he was honest and honorable. If he was, then there were no problems. Then as far as boss Đuzepe was concerned, such a man was just as worthy of respect as the man in the ruddy, blue-eyed portrait that he wiped off with his sleeve every morning so it wouldn't collect dust and the filth of the terrible time they were living in.

One morning in the summer of 1942, while Đuzepe was tidying the Leader's portrait for that day, only twenty kilometers away, in a hamlet in the direction of Nevesinje, his brother Đovani crossed himself three times before a little picture of St. Panteleimon, which had by some miracle escaped destruction in a house in which the day before everything living or dead had been consumed by flames.

At that moment the brothers were the nearest they'd been to one another in the last ten years; only in terms of geographic distance, of course, because in every other sense they were more distant than brother could be from brother in one story, more distant than people who'd hardly ever met one another. They hadn't crossed each other's minds since each of them had realized for himself and for his own reasons that family ties mean little or nothing and that a man is on his own as soon as he stands out in some way. And in the Sikirić clan both Đovani and Đuzepe stood out: the older brother because of the languor of his mind, which is also called stupidity, and by his peasant's soul, which he'd inherited to the horror of his parents from some great-grandfather of his; the younger one didn't fit in because his opinion of his father, mother, brothers Luka and Bepo, and especially his sister Regina, was the same as their opinion of Đuzepe. In fact, it was for reasons similar to those that had made his older brother go work as a waiter on the railway line and never come home that the younger brother renounced his inheritance and went off to Paris. He believed that he was leaving forever. And that's the way it would have been if the command of the German army hadn't made the decision for its troops not to pass under Napolcon's triumphal arch or if there had been at least a few more Parisians to defend the city along with Đovani, the weeping girl, and her two friends. As it was, he, who until the day before had been an apostate from all faiths, a skeptic and atheist, found himself deep in the backwater of Herzegovina before a little picture of an Orthodox saint, firmly convinced that he'd seen a miracle. He crossed himself over the ashes of someone's house, over the carbonized bodies of its inhabitants, over a burned cradle in which there might have been a child (but there was nothing left of it), over Serbs, the only people who'd tried to preserve their honor, the honor of Europe, and the honor of those who sat behind tightly locked gates and windows in metropolises and cities in France and other countries, waiting for the war to end all on its own.

Strange was the path that led the student Đovani Sikirić before a picture of St. Panteleimon. He'd roamed for a year through occupied Paris and fed himself in public kitchens, even in a Jewish one that the other unfortunates avoided for fear that someone might think they were racial filth. He kept company with those few foreigners who had remained in Paris and dared to speak against the collaborationist authorities. The majority of Đovani's acquaintances and former friends fled from him and his words as from the plague. People were afraid of spies and provocateurs, or they simply didn't feel like waging war against the great German power, if only in their thoughts. The exceptions included a few Serbian students, small industrialists, former communists, and Trotskyites, mainly from Belgrade and Bosnia, who gathered in the Hilandar Tavern, which was operated by a Greek in a southern suburb of the city. In the Hilandar the erstwhile secretary of the Royal Yugoslav Consulate in Paris, Joakim Radak, called on Đovani to go with him, after the latter, thoroughly indignant, had told him how the Nazis had strolled over Pigalle.

"Where to?" Đovani asked him.

"Where the world values honor more than the heel on a Kraut rifle butt," responded Radak with pathos.

No matter how much Đovani would have laughed at such words the day before, now he waved them off and went on his way. But it was probably the fact that he didn't know where to go, or which path he was on, that made him take Radak seriously and even think positively about Radak's words.

Three weeks later he was already on Mt. Jelica, deep inside Serbia and on the other side of all the eastern borders his mind had ever reached. He sat at a rough-hewn oak table, face to face with Colonel Dragoljub Mihailović. The two of them were alone in a blockhouse, as a summer storm raged above the mountain. The Colonel's eyes blinked from behind the round glasses of a placid Jewish businessman and smiled mildly when Đovani jumped up because a thunderbolt had struck somewhere nearby. Đovani was terribly afraid of thunder, and now, you see, he had lived to see himself tremble and sweat an icy sweat in front of the leader of the only resistance movement in Europe. Instead of throwing him out and spitting on him as a coward, as Đovani thought any soldier would do, the Colonel tried to calm him down.

"Every man is afraid now and then. Only an idiot is fearless. Some fear spiders or that a horse will kick them, and you, you see, are afraid of thunder," he said. Then he told of what Paris had looked like in '20-something, when he'd gone on an excursion as a cadet. He spoke of the sun that was reflected in windowpanes in a special way and scattered over the sidewalk, ". . . before our feet, which still hadn't gotten used to anything other than pointed peasant shoes and will never walk those streets with an appropriate stride."

He spoke of the sound of street organs and French accordions that weren't any less monotonous than their own gusles but whose repetitions sounded noble.

"We sing of our bloody history like we're sawing wood, but the French have created beauty from their own, equally bloody, history. That's why the French survive every defeat, and we emerge from every defeat even bigger turds," said Colonel Dragoljub Mihailović in the midst of a summer storm in a hut on Mt. Jelica.

Đovani saw a god in him then. The first one he'd seen in his life. Or at the very least an angel of salvation. If Paris was his Jerusalem, then Mihailović was the one who was missing in Jerusalem. If he'd been there, Paris wouldn't have fallen, nor would the French have protected their honor with wooden shutters on their windows. The nation had spoiled like cream.

The very next day Đovani was wearing an English infantry uniform and a cap with a cockade. He found himself among a hundred or so fighters loyal to the king and the fatherland, who in keeping with a tradition from a time when Serbia had been reestablished on the west bank of the Drina were called Chetniks, an expression that Colonel Mihailović hadn't liked in the early days.

He wanted an army, not folklore or banditry. However, he soon realized that he would have no benefit whatsoever from what he'd learned at the military academy and had tried to implement before the war wherever he'd been assigned, despite the culture of the old veterans of the Salonika Front, which was responsible for the severity of their defeat at the hands of the Wehrmacht in April. Besides, even a cursory glance at the battalion in which Đovani found himself was enough for any intelligent man to realize the real difference between guerilla war and organized war.

Here there were illiterate villagers from central Serbia who'd never held a rifle in their hands because they'd withdrawn unarmed in 1915 through Albania in order to rush just as unarmed three years later over positions that the Krauts had already abandoned. There were reserve officers and non-commissioned officers who did indeed have some kind of training, but instead of learning military science, they'd only learned the harsh treatment of those weaker than themselves. There were overgrown boys from well-to-do Belgrade houses who arrived with two suitcases in which their mommies had packed silk pajamas and underwear. There was riffraff from towns, smugglers, swindlers, and maybe even murderers who, on the run from the gendarmerie, ended up as fighters for the king and the fatherland. There were a few Slovenes and Croats, fiery idealists who believed in the same ideal as Colonel Mihailović. They believed in Yugoslavia, the kingdom of Slavic tribes with equal rights, in one people that was united by the same origin and the same bloody history. They believed in a Yugoslavia in which there would exist one faith and one hope—in oneself and one's own origin—so that no center of spiritual or political support needed to be sought in the Vatican, Germany, or Russia.

However, the problem was that no one believed in anything like that except Colonel Mihailović and his fanatics—not even the villagers from central Serbia or the Serbian refugees from eastern Herzegovina, who were only waiting for a chance to die as heroes, because as they stood over their burned houses, it didn't occur to them to do anything else. Not even such men took the Colonel's belief seriously! They thought that it was part of a wartime strategy and that the real aim was something else. Exactly what was known only to the sages in London, the wise men surrounding the young King Petar.

Đovani felt completely lost in such company in the middle of Serbia. He couldn't abide by Colonel Mihailović's visions of the state and the people, nor did his heart favor any of the Yugoslav tribes. He was agitated by the humiliation in front of Napoleon's triumphal arch and those Mohammedan scum in the black suits who would saunter through history unpunished because they didn't belong to either of the warring sides—neither those who had crushed Paris nor those who'd seen their city crushed.

The villagers who kept bad brandy in rusty tin canteens and argued about whether Russia would help their Serb brothers or the English would send tanks to Mihailović were as distant from Ðovani as those on account of whom he'd renounced his share of the family inheritance and decided to become a Parisian. Those people, so he thought, resembled his brothers and neighbors, only they were dirtier and forever stank of onions and animal dung and were ready at any moment to die if the Colonel told them the time for dying had come. Their stench stopped bothering him when he grasped the latter. There was an erotic excitement in meeting people who didn't consider their lives more valuable than freedom, whatever that word may have meant to them. Every one of them was a little heroic death waiting to happen, and just as a lover's body stinks of sweat, so the heroes from the mountains stank of onions, dung, and bad brandy. That was the smell of sacrifice for the fatherland. Ðovani realized that great things don't smell very good.

He crossed the Drina with Lieutenant Lazar Kobilović's unit and descended into eastern Herzegovina via Kalinovik. Mihailović hadn't sent them to fight, take revenge, or sabotage railway lines and roads used by the Italian and German troops. The mission of Kobilović's group was more important, maybe even decisive for the fate of the Ravna Gora movement: propaganda and propagating ideas about the struggle against the occupiers among the unruly Serbian villagers and bands of highway robbers who'd proliferated in the territory under Ustasha control but were not under the command of the Royal Yugoslav Army in the Homeland or under the high command of the partisans. Colonel Mihailović thought it important to win those people over for two reasons: it would strengthen his position in any possible negotiations with Tito concerning their possible unification under a joint command, and he would have more arguments in seeking aid from the English, who'd already been hearing rumors that the Chetniks weren't fighting against the Germans but were only going on revengeful rampages against the Muslim and Catholic populations. Those rumors were correct, which seriously concerned the Colonel, because he would have a difficult time convincing the English that the units taking part in such revenge weren't under his control.

But on the way to Nevesinje, which was the farthest point west that Kobilović's unit would reach, the nature of the mission changed. As they passed through burned and slaughtered villages, meeting armed holdouts with all kinds of insignia on their caps, Lieutenant Kobilović concluded along with his thirty men that what was going on in Herzegovina had nothing at all to do with Mihailović's ideal Yugoslav state. Talking about one people and several tribes and about Yugoslavia as a parliamentary democracy could only get one killed.

But what was more important for Lazar was that losing one's life meant losing one's honor too. It wasn't possible to be a brother to a brother who'd renounced you; it wasn't possible to create a home with someone who was going to cut your throat. This was a time when men had only one choice: either kill or be killed. On the evening before Đovani Sikirić would cross himself three times before a miraculous picture of St. Panteleimon, Lazar Kobilović called him to his room.

"You're a good man, but you're not a Serb," Kobilović told him. "And this isn't the war of Uncle Draža's fairy tales. There's no Yugoslavia here, no King Petar, no brothers of three faiths. This, my son, is a hellish cauldron, and we're all stewing in it. And only some of us will make it out alive. Either they'll walk over our bodies, or we'll walk over theirs. There can be no mercy as long as the slaughter continues. Mercy, my Đovani, comes with peace. Then we'll forgive and be forgiven. Well, that's what I wanted to tell you. And now, listen up! I've packed you half a flatbread and all the bacon and cheese there is in this sack. There's a revolver too so that you can defend yourself if someone attacks you. Here are some civilian clothes. I can't tell you any more, and you don't need to say anything, but make up your mind yourself. Every bird flies to its flock, and it's good that way. I'll know that on the other side is someone I can say is a good man. And you'll be like a brother to me."

Đovani listened to the lieutenant, and his heart rose into his throat. He opened his mouth to say something, but the latter grabbed him by the hand: "Quiet; don't sell your honor for cheap money. Think it over till morning. And if you go, know that you've been forgiven."

That night Đovani slept peacefully, without thinking about what Lazar Kobilović had told him. In the morning they kissed each other on the cheek, and the lieutenant's eyes were full of tears.

"Brother Jovan, from today your blood is my blood," he said to Đovani.

And so on the day of St. Panteleimon began the ruin of one Parisian university student, Regina's smartest and most sophisticated brother, who'd absorbed all the scorn of the nobility for the vulgarity of the poor and the ugliness of the plebs from his home city (or from some unknown distant forefather). From that day on everyone who saw him alive would call him Jovan.

In that autumn of 1942, the partisans fled from Herzegovina, torn asunder by betrayal, and Pavelić, trying to carve out a border along the Drina, left that rocky southern wasteland to the care of the Italians ("If the sea is theirs, then let them fight for the karst too!"). So the Ustasha forces withdrew ahead of the Chetniks without putting up any resistance and left the care of the old land of Hum to the local population, which was mainly Muslim. The ravines, which were already halfway full of God's Orthodox children, were filled overnight with

Muslims and Catholics from Popovo Polje, as well as craftsmen and tradesmen with Czech, Polish, and Austrian names and surnames who were considered to be Croats, probably according to the logic of the cross.

Everything happened quickly and suddenly. Thus it happened that overnight the Ustasha sentries, city authorities, and mobile courts-martial disappeared, and when people awoke in the morning, Chetniks with fairly long beards were already to be seen herding women in shalwars, old men and children, and a few adult men who (probably because of heavy sleep) hadn't escaped through a window. ("If you're a Muslim or a Catholic—and you are, because what could you have been here until yesterday—you knew that someone would come for you like this.") They would take them to a ravine, if there was one nearby; to a gorge, if the village was on high ground; or to a remote place where the villagers tossed animal carcasses. And there the ritual would begin.

First they would pick out an old man. A Chetnik officer or squad leader, whom they often called a duke, would order the old man to remove his hat or fez and kneel down and would approach him from behind. The head of the victim would reach up to his waist. Some would lean their members and scrotums against the crown of the victim's head so they might feel the fear of the old Turks, but others would simply grab him by the hair, jerk his head backward, and cut his throat with an English army knife or a dagger. If they were at a ravine or gorge, then he would kick the victim in the back, and the latter would disappear without a sound. But if there was no ravine, then a real agony would begin before the eyes of all there who were going to kill or be killed. Namely, either there is some technical difference between slaughtering pigs and slaughtering men, or the squad leader would regularly be the least skilled in his work, but the death of the first victim usually went on longest. The old man would flop around on the ground trying to stop the blood with both hands, gurgling, gasping, and flailing with his feet in the dirt for some time, or in some not altogether rare cases, he would jump up and start running, and the Chetniks would have to get out of the way so the crimson spray wouldn't get all over them, stiff and strong as the jets of water from the hoses gentlemen use to water their gardens. Those runs, however, were short. Never more than thirty meters, when the man would fall and remain lying motionless on the ground. Dying like that was easier because it didn't take very long.

When the first victim had been finished off, the women started wailing, crying, calling for help, making the strangest pleas that any living man has ever heard. They pleaded in the name of God and all the angels, in the name of their neighbors, friendship, and the fact that someone had saved someone's life thirty years before or that one of them had breastfed an Orthodox child because its mother had no milk. They pleaded fervently, as no one ever had before. But it was no use because the eyes of the men with the knives were already full of blood. No one can know for sure, but it's likely that there were no other victims in the whole war anywhere in Europe who pleaded with their murderers like that. Maybe it was because the murderers were mostly people among whom the victims had lived and whom they'd greeted when they met at the market. Some of the women would also remember that their great-grandfathers had been forced to convert to Islam but that they had always celebrated St. Nikola's name day in the house.

And there were also those who didn't plead or implore but would use up the little life left to them casting spells, curses, and oaths that would make one's blood freeze in his veins because these would go back for nine generations and far into the future. They invoked illness, fear, itching, mange, nightmares — any and every kind of misfortune. Everything that would afflict the Chetniks, their children, and their children's children from that day on could be explained by the curses of those women. There was no point in thinking about justice or humanity or about the fact that children and grandchildren weren't guilty of the crimes of their fathers and grandfathers because the curses were uttered by women who were fated to die now. The history of family and tribal curses was even older than those who slaughtered and were slaughtered, and it didn't matter whether someone believed in them or not. They made everything happen, so it wasn't impossible that the slaughter in eastern Herzegovina in the autumn and winter was the fulfillment of some older curses that Orthodox women had cast on their Muslim neighbors into the tenth generation. Even if there hadn't been any such curse, everything unfolded according to its logic.

Men write history with knives, and women summon it with words. It was that way this time too, at the edge of every ravine, gorge, and animal dumping ground.

After the Muslim women finished pleading and cursing and their husbands, brothers, and fathers had turned into figures of terror and shame without uttering a word, only trembling and looking down at the ground under their feet, the duke would pick out the weakest of all the Chetniks — say, the one who'd wandered into the unit with the idea that the fatherland was a wheat field and the deep blue sea — grab him by the collar, drag him over to the woman who had cursed the loudest, and shove a knife into his hand if he didn't already happen to have one.

That was usually also the most exciting moment of the whole performance because it was the meeting of two souls that were disintegrating, two terrors that at first glance had nothing in common but at the same moment bade farewell to everything they'd been until then. The woman bade farewell to a lie and regretted the curses she'd uttered or because she'd been the loudest and so the weakest and least confident of all the murderers had been chosen to be her adversary, the one who hadn't even killed a chicken and didn't know how to handle a knife so that her torment would be harder and longer. And the Chetnik realized that he'd ended up beyond the point of no return, that he would cut people's throats and kill them, and that he would never again be who he'd been, not even in his own heart. If he didn't do it, he would be scorned and disinherited; his family would disown him. He would be betraying everything for which he'd been created in this world and might even end up in the woman's place. His brothers would kill him to show how there wasn't and couldn't be any forgiveness before one or the other side carried out an investigation.

And they stood face to face for a while, woman and man, while everyone around them waited to see what would happen. Bets were made, and the leader fiercely wanted for his weakest brother to become a man. This wait always lasted too long, regardless of whether it was a matter of seconds or minutes or of the way in which it was interrupted: by her spitting into the face of her foe, in the belief that this might awaken the animal in him that would, led by instinct, put her out of her misery, or by him deciding to end his own agony and rushing at her, plunging the knife into her chest or trying to cut her throat. However, that was a difficult job for someone who hadn't ever done it before or for someone who saw before him human eyes, a woman's body, nostrils that inhaled and exhaled air. It was difficult because the future murderer felt a life that existed and didn't give him any reason to snuff it out.

As soon as their weakling bloodied his knife, the performance turned into a choral orgy. The main characters disappeared; people lost their names and faces. Everyone grabbed his victim the best he knew how. Some got at those they'd been waiting to get at from the beginning—a child, a pretty girl, or an old man, according to their own impulses and passions. Most often passion doesn't arise in pure hatred, but comes from something that's distantly connected to the passion of love, which causes the male member to stiffen. God created it so that he didn't have to create man anew every time; rather, man could do that himself. But people get lost, forget their scope and the direction they've taken, and so instead of giving birth and multiplying, they start slaughtering each other. The explanation is banal but true.

In less than half an hour all their throats were cut, a few breasts, ears, and noses cut off, or people's eyes and scrotums slid down the rocks. Sometimes the duke spared the life of the youngest child, and it would run off somewhere without a sound. God probably arranged it according to his own plan. Because after every slaughter there had to remain a living image in the eyes of one of the victims.

One morning the protectors of Pavelić's picture disappeared from Gacko. They left without saying anything to Đuzepe Sikirić, who loved the Leader with the purest heart. The disturbance lasted a few moments. Someone opened all the chicken coops and stalls. The animals ran all over the lanes and the street, but the people were frozen in place. Boss Miloš Davidović came in wearing a fur hat, girdled with heavy bandoliers. He took the picture from the wall of his bar and smashed it over Đuzepe's head, as in an old silent comedy.

"Boss, don't, for Christ's sake!" said a dull visage peering from a wooden frame instead of a cattle yoke. Miloš wouldn't let him take off the picture frame all the way to the Duhovnjačka ravine, which was covered in scrub below the road to Mostar.

"We didn't agree to that," he kept repeating and kicking him in the behind with a heavy boot. Tears were streaming down Đuzepe's face, though he didn't know what he had coming. Aware that his ownership of the café had come to an end, he wasn't even thinking about what else might happen to him. Nothing was more terrible for him than the memory of the years when he'd been a nobody and nothing.

Đuzepe Sikirić became the main character in the performance above Duhovnjačka. Boss Miloš cut his throat with a large butcher knife. He did it expertly and according to the regulations, so the unfortunate wretch gave up the ghost quickly and easily. He hardly flailed about on the rocks at all. Then Miloš broke his neck with his bare hands, cut up his skin and veins, cut off his head, and threw it into the ravine. He left the body to lie at the feet of those whose turn had not yet come, amid the varnished little pieces of wood that at one time had made up the frame of a funny picture.

The news of Đuzepe's death reached Regina in late 1945. It was a sunny and unexpectedly pleasant day. She was sitting in the yard in front of the house when her neighbor Bartol came along, hugged her, and said:

"I don't know how to tell you this." He sighed and held out a piece of paper for her. "He collaborated with the occupiers," he said, thinking to comfort her and then bit his lip, realizing what he'd said.

She smiled. She rarely did that, and Bartol thought that her smile was a prelude and that at the next moment she would burst into tears. She signed the paper. He quickly put it in his pocket and hurried on, regretting his inappropriate words.

They would torment him to the end of his life. He would think that it would be good to sort it out with her, but there wasn't ever a good opportunity, nor could Bartol summon the courage. As the times changed and every human suffering, no matter how it was overcome, received its quiet rights, Bartol wouldn't be able to get over the fact that he'd called Đuzepe a collaborator with the occupiers in front of his sister. He would thereby become the only one who remembered him at all.

Everyone else—the good, the bad and the indifferent, his sister and brothers, the municipal officials, and the state board of statistics for victims of the Second World War—forgot about Đuzepe Sikirić. His name wasn't written in stone or on paper. The salt of his tears remained on some rocks in Herzegovina.

Đovani went the way of revenge twice with Lazar Kobilović, following the Drina and the towns that had grown up along it. He watched tarbushes and fezzes floating down the river and wondered what made those people, who were blond-haired and blue-eyed, cover their heads with Arab hats and worship God in a manner that was alien to that land and only unnecessarily made them different from their neighbors, to whom they were otherwise so similar. He never killed anyone; he always stood to one side as an observer. He held his hands behind his back and watched the performance unflinchingly or smoked fine Sava tobacco, while his comrades cut throats, gouged out eyes, and flayed captured partisans alive. The victims believed that he was the chief and that they needed to beg him for mercy, and Kobilović believed that someone's hands, best of all brother Jovan's, needed to remain clean and unstained by blood because only in that way would he have a witness who knew why and in the name of which justice they'd done what they'd done. He would testify before God and before men that they weren't animals and murderers but had tried to save their people and land. They had tried to do that at the highest price that living men can pay. They'd lost the peace of their souls—a man whose hands had clutched a knife would no longer caress his own child, grandchild, or a plum tree in the orchard above his house . . . They became monsters among men and could only be understood by those who'd cut throats and killed for the other side. The hatred that Kobilović had felt for the Ustashas when he saw the first burned villages and together with brother Jovan crossed himself before the miraculous little picture of St. Panteleimon, turned into a kind of understanding and in the end a kind of affection. Those on the other side had actually done the same thing as he, only in the name of their people and its right to that land. They probably didn't have it easy either and feared the nightmares that tormented the Chetniks and their leaders to the end of their lives. When they found themselves in the middle of villages and towns that Kobilović's battalion had passed through, the Ustashas felt what Lazar felt in the villages and towns that Francetić's legion had passed through. There was no great difference.

Kobilović's final belief was that the people and their nations were not to blame, but the times that had driven them to commit evil. It was probably not his alone.

That mystical temptation of blood and slaughter lasted until late 1944, when a miracle occurred, some cosmic forces turned inside out, or something happened in the outside world, the one that hardly ever came into contact with the Bosnian mountains and forests. There were no longer any undefended or unburned villages, nor were there any more tarbushes and fezzes to float down the Drina. And it seemed that there were no longer any Ustashas either. However, bloody struggles and evacuations began, and Đovani finally had to pick up a rifle. The path led across Romanija and back again a few times, through partisan positions and ambushes. There was no longer any free territory, the Orthodox villages were taken over by the communists, red banners started waving on all the towers, and Lazar Kobilović realized that the war was over and that the time had come to sell one's own skin for the highest price possible. There would be songs that would sing his name, he thought, consoling himself. And at least one living creature would remain under the vault of the heavens who would know that he, Lazar, had done good in evil. Lazar placed his hopes in brother Jovan, who'd scorned his own name, in the soft palms of the eternal student and the gleaming city of Paris, which lent his struggle a higher meaning and harmony.

He was certain that Đovani would survive the war and the partisan revenge that was being prepared without anyone knowing on behalf of which people and for which higher justice the partisans intended to seek vengeance. They wouldn't touch Đovani because he'd neither cut throats nor murdered; nor did he belong to any of the sides that had committed the slaughter and murder. He was a free man, an angel who'd seen evil with his own eyes and held his hands behind his back, to keep them from being sullied with the blood of God's creatures. He was pure, just as he'd been when he was born. He would lead these people across a river that was ten times wider than the Drina, beyond which there was something that one should believe in and in which Lazar Kobilović believed with all his heart. In Christ and his unfortunate mother, in Joseph who had worked wood and from whose hands their rifle butts had emerged, in St. Panteleimon and all the visages on church walls, whose upwardly turned eyes resembled the eyes of people whose throats had just been cut as blood filled their bowels. Blood that was bright as the sun and dark as the darkest night above Maglić.

Crazed by the changes that had occurred, Lazar Kobilović mixed the domains of heaven and earth more and more often, and it happened that in his morning prayer he sincerely prayed to Christ and Jovan, expecting salvation from both, without knowing what kind.

On Catholic Christmas in 1944 Kobilović's battalion, actually the fifteen men that were left of it after all the running, stumbled into an ambush near

Ustikolina. The battle didn't last long. After twenty minutes of bursts of partisan machine gun fire, only two men were left in a watermill surrounded by blazes. They were Lazar and Jovan.

"I'm staying, and you, brother, will surrender," Kobilović said and shot himself in the head before Đovani could say anything.

He went out of the mill with his hands raised high, a bearded apparition all dressed in black with a fur cap on his head, such that he was completely unrecognizable to those who might have recognized him otherwise. They led him to the staff, before Commissar Hurem Alaga, who briefly questioned him and then ordered him to be shot.

The high command would call Alaga to account and condemn him to death before a court in Sarajevo because he had on his own initiative killed the last surviving Chetnik of Kobilović's infamous group, whose crimes were the worst, at least in eastern Bosnia. Đovani Sikirić could have told what would forever remain a mystery because Lazar didn't leave any victims alive to testify. From Sikirić they could have gotten the names of the other butchers, of Chetnik deserters who'd maybe joined the people's liberation movement. Instead of all that, Alaga asked the prisoner only two or three questions, from which history would have no benefit:

"What's your name? Where are you from? What's going to happen to your soul?"

The news of Đovani's fate reached Regina, Luka, and Bepo in squalls, from different directions, and in the form of open threats. At first someone from the committee reported that one of the Sikirić brothers had been liquidated as a Chetnik butcher, but Regina didn't believe that, knowing who and what Đovani had been. Besides, how and why would he have left Paris and joined the Chetniks? Then in the Belgrade daily *Politika*, in a feuilleton about the Ravna Gora movement, it was announced that a few Slovenes and Croats had been in Mihailović's staff, and Đovani's name was among them. No one in the city commented on the newspaper story or—which was hardly likely—the comments didn't reach Regina's ears. The people evidently expected for a committee first to be set up concerning the shame of the Delavale-Sikirić house, and in the committee they waited for an order or directive to come from above. It was a delicate affair to challenge the honor of a family that had simultaneously produced a partisan hero, Comrade Bepo, whose heroism at Sutjeska and the Neretva was increasingly the stuff of legend. Then rumors came from Trebinje that Đovani Sikirić, a.k.a. Bloody Jovan, was one of the worst murderers of Muslims from Gacko to Bileća, and people heard that he'd gone renegade with Lazar Kobilović, for whom not even Draža Mihailović was enough, and slaughtered and burned his way across Bosnia on his own account and for his own kicks.

Regina fled from such rumors as much as she could, and when someone asked her about her brother, she said that she'd had nothing to do with him for a long time—he'd renounced his family and inheritance, and it was known for a fact that Đovani was in Paris and that coming back was the farthest thing from his mind.

"He's there because he likes to feel the male member in his ass," she said; "he's fucking Frenchmen and doing who knows what else."

And so everyone who asked anything fled as fast as their feet could carry them, knowing that Regina was capable of describing in detail what male and female mouths don't say and ears don't want to hear.

Soon the rumors quieted down, probably because there was nobody to confirm them or because people started saying that Đovani had been seen in France. The driver of the Yugoslav consul had met him and spoken with him. He was a rich and respected man, dealt in real estate, and had already forgotten their language a little. That piece of evidence was stronger than any other and stronger than the wickedness of the city. Fascinated by the fact that someone born among them had forgotten words of his native speech, people also forgot what had been written in the newspapers. Or they believed that there was another Đovani Sikirić who had less brains and luck and wasn't from their city.

V

On the sixth of May, 1937, the zeppelin *Hindenburg*, named after the glorious marshal who had handed over power to Hitler four years earlier, burst into flames as it landed in Lakehurst, New Jersey. Thirty-three of ninety-seven passengers were killed, and the tragic end of the largest and most famous zeppelin in history would be the leading story in all the newsreels the following summer.

This disaster was nothing less than the fateful end of an airborne *Titanic*, and despite all the romantic overtones, it had a more ominous effect on moviegoers than the worsening civil war in Spain, the battles for Guadalajara and Malaga, the Japanese attacks on Shanghai, and even the futuristic predictions that in ten years, at most by 1955, the majority of Europeans would fall victim to alopecia caused by frequent, prolonged undulations. The flaming crash of the zeppelin, after which the development of that kind of airship came to a complete halt, was particularly shocking to moviegoers, especially those who went in the summer because they all dreamed of flying in a zeppelin one day. The images of lounges with stylish furniture in which kings and queens, barons, lords, wealthy European gentlemen, and adventurers drank champagne and laughed at jokes that would never reach the ears of ordinary people were repeated during several summer seasons, piquing people's imaginations and producing sighs all along the Adriatic coast.

The viewers didn't notice that there were always the same pictures with the same faces and glasses because from summer to summer people forgot what they'd seen in the newsreels, and all they remembered was their enthusiasm for the luxurious palaces that hung in the air, crystal chandeliers, and string quartets that at a few thousand feet above the earth change one's image of the world. If it was true that lounges flew and that this same life, just much prettier and richer, was possible in the air, above oceans and mountains, then borders would no longer exist for people, worries would lose their meaning, and death would cease to be a certainty. One needed only to collect the fortune needed to pay for the flight, board a zeppelin, and fly off on the wings of progress with kings and queens. With those who'd be saved first from every known misfortune.

The *Hindenburg* was magnificent not only because it was announced in the newsreels to be the largest and most powerful zeppelin, but also because its name was as heavy as lead, massive as the steel mills on the Ruhr that belched forth the fires of the strongest industry in the world day in, day out. That name was as if hammered into the earth, louder and more sonorous than all other names. Not even God himself called Himself that. But then that same heavy *Hindenburg* nevertheless soared up into the clouds, lighter than a chocolate wrapper smoothed flat by a child's hand. The heaviest word that summertime moviegoers had ever heard floated off into the sky like a little feather!

When the news arrived that the *Hindenburg* had exploded in flames and that the smiling faces and hands holding glasses of champagne had disappeared in smoke and dust, the viewers were shocked to the core. They stared at the screen like children who'd woken up and found that they'd been transformed into unhappy adults.

Regina ran crying out of the Cosmos Cinema before the beginning of the movie *Gertrude's Sin*, a German love story set in the snowy Alps that had been the talk of the town. The scenes from Lakehurst were unbearable for her. People in top hats carrying gentlemen's canes watched the *Hindenburg* disappear from a polite distance, and they seemed bored. She saw their backs moving more and more quickly to the sluggish rhythm of the moving pictures and the American sky into which the ugly black smoke was billowing. And that black smoke was full of what had been people, their wealth and fame, and what had been the hope of an era. A part of her life was billowing up into the sky because she'd believed in the possibility of that flying world and that it was her future, if today was someone else's present. It's always like that, she thought; what the wealthy can have today, the whole world can have tomorrow. One only had to have enough patience and wait, and everything would end up in its place. Cities would soar up into the clouds, together with their poor folk and those who didn't even have money for bread, in some even larger zeppelins, and in the end the whole world would be free, leave Earth, and fly through spaces bigger than the sky. She imagined such a scenario watching the newsreels and didn't pay any heed to all the talk about how thirty-two was too old for a woman to be unmarried, and she was about to miss the bus. She watched the zeppelin and didn't worry. There was something to wait for up until the *Hindenburg* went down in flames.

And then it was over. At the start she looked at the screen in confusion; the speaker was excitedly speaking of people who were turning into living torches. Death came quickly, before those unlucky people managed to remember God. Luka laughed bitterly at those words and poked her with his elbow. He couldn't feel all that horror; he was only irritated at the voice that kept talking. He looked at his sister and poked her again—could she hear? She just sat with her mouth slightly agape and stared ahead, as if she were hypnotized or she could see all the stupid things that the voice was talking about.

"Wow, look at that smoke!" he whispered when the big black cloud of smoke appeared on the screen again, and Regina jumped up from her seat and began to push her way to the door.

She stepped on people's feet. A woman squealed like a mouse because Regina had stepped on her corn. The woman's husband cursed God and the blessed Virgin Mary. The rows in the cinema began to stir; the people stared at the girl who was running in sobs toward the exit. Luka couldn't figure out what was going on. It was the first time Regina had done something he couldn't explain. That was the moment, or so he thought, when her disagreement with the world began.

But it was more likely that the disagreement had occurred at least six years earlier, when Luka wasn't yet nine, and his sister had fallen in love with Aris Berberijan, a law student from Novi Sad. His rich father had sent him to the Adriatic so his tuberculosis could be treated with fresh air, though Aris actually wasn't even suffering from tuberculosis. He was suffering from something else, however, which led him to bribe doctors and pay enough money to buy a house in the center of town to a Dr. Mušicki in exchange for a confirmation that he had tuberculosis, in which two open caverns and six more months to live were mentioned rather dramatically.

"Of all the medicines in the whole world none will be better for your son than sea air, dry and warm, full of medicinal salts and fennel that the wind brings from the mainland and the sea. I can't give you a guarantee that Aris will find his cure in the sea; I don't know whether it's too late for him or how the illness will develop. There are various kinds of tuberculosis, just as various people get it, and each kind takes its own course. We can only hope that Aris's type is one of those that Adriatic winds carry away," Dr. Simeon Mušicki wrote, embellishing his story for the older Berberijan, who cried like a small child in the middle of Mušicki's office in front of the nurses, who were trying to comfort him, and his son Aris, who was coughing into a handkerchief.

But it wasn't clear why exactly the older Berberijan was crying. Was it because the best doctor in the kingdom was telling him that his only son was going to die? Or was it because his law office was going to be closed down—the oldest in Vojvodina—which had been established by his grandfather Aleksej when he came to the Austro-Hungarian Empire after leaving Erevan and studying law in Berlin?

Jovan Berberijan was a good lawyer and a "patron of the poor." His rates for those who went around town bragging that he was handling their legal affairs were exorbitant, but he represented any pauper or wretch who was accused of something by the state or a wealthy landlord for free. At the same time, that compassionate man was an unbelievably harsh father. He punished his son for anything that he thought might turn him from the path that had been laid out for him from the moment he'd been conceived.

Aris was two years old when he brought him into his office "so that the child can study and grow fond of the job that he'll do his whole life."

His mother, Saveta, tried in vain to tell Jovan that it was too early for such things and that it was better to let Aris play with the other children.

"My father Sokrat took me to the office when I was two. The first word I learned after 'mama' and 'papa' was 'law.' My father's father, Aleksej, took him to the office when he was two, and the first word he knew was 'justice,'" Jovan would answer, and at that point his mother would give up.

In the beginning he let the boy play in front of his black desk while he talked with clients. How surprised people were when in the middle of their talk a blond child would peer out and say that he had to pee or poop! Then the famed Berberijan would tap on a little bell, and Janoš, his hunchbacked, gray-haired assistant, would come running, take Aris by the hand, and lead him to the toilet. No matter how serious and dramatic the case that brought the lawyer's clients to him—and there were people who needed to save their sons and brothers from the death penalty—each one of them thought that the appearance of the child was a good sign. And when Berberijan revealed the reason why the boy didn't leave the office, they were even more confident in his expertise. Especially because it had never occurred to them to prepare their own children for their future careers in that way. That man was a little crazy and what he did with his child was abnormal, but he was a lawyer!

When Aris turned four, his father began to pose fairly simple problems to him, to test his son's intelligence, his power of reasoning, and his sense of justice.

"Who is more guilty, Laza the drunk because he stole from the cashbox of the rowing club or the treasurer Steva because he left the cashbox unlocked . . . ? Mr. Jozika's chickens kept passing through his neighbor Milka's fence for a year, and the whole time she warned Jozika about that problem, and then one day she wrung the neck of his rooster. But she didn't do it in her yard but his—who's guilty . . . ? Two men are stabbing at each other with pitchforks and they both die, and the wife of the one who started it seeks compensation. Is she in the right, and what does the other one need to do . . . ? It was raining, Mr. Ištvan's cellar flooded and all his wine was ruined, and now the tavern owners, who had paid in advance, are taking him to court. He's willing to return their money, but they aren't happy with that because they've suffered more damage than the price of the wine. What should the court decide?"

Jovan Berberijan questioned the boy, and he would answer as long as it was fun for him, and most of his answers were correct. But a boy's attention span is short. After ten or so minutes, Aris would grow tired of his father's questions. He would want to play or would give the wrong answers on purpose out of pure mischief, whereupon Jovan wouldn't stop, as anyone else would, but would keep asking newer and newer questions, with the patience of an old village horse that cannot be annoyed and provoked into tossing off its saddle and an awkward rider. It rarely happened that he even realized that the child was giving the wrong answers because it didn't enter his mind that there could be someone in this world, even a small boy, who might give frivolous answers to questions of justice and injustice.

Soon Aris began to give wrong answers from the very first question, and then Jovan Berberijan introduced a system of rewards for correct answers. For five correct answers, a soft drink; for ten correct answers, cotton candy; for fifteen, ice cream; and for fifty correct answers, a trip to the circus. In this way he captured his son's attention, or it would be better to say that he bought it, convinced that making a deal always worked. It worked for five full years, whereupon the idyll of his law office was again destroyed, and for the first time there was an open conflict between father and son. He came home completely out of sorts because Aris had told him that he was a fat old ass. Saveta tried to comfort him, but her comfort was as sincere as the Sunday confessions of Melita the prostitute. His mother knew well what was going on between the two men and what the little one had decided to do to the big one, but she'd given up on trying to explain it to Jovan.

But here's what happened: there was a long time in which Aris got the bonus for fifty correct answers once, twice, or even three times a week, and Jovan had to take him to the circus as many times. If by some chance no troupe was appearing in Novi Sad, they would go to Subotica, Sombor, Bačka Palanka, or even Vukovar or Belgrade. Wherever there was a circus. They would stay the night in a hotel and return home in the early morning. And so alongside law, the circus became the only work that Aris saw and knew something about: the names of all the elephants who set foot on the territory of the kingdom, the lions, tigers, horses, rattlesnakes, and white mice that could find their way out of a labyrinth from which a man would never emerge—he knew all of them even better than the circus owners. He also learned to tell the difference between the lions whose teeth had been removed out of caution and those that could really bite off the trainer's head when he put it between their jaws. He became an expert in acrobatic figures and magic tricks, and at seven he could already argue with authority about whether a particular clown belonged to the Russian or the French school.

For Aris, the difference between those two schools was a fact of the utmost importance, and in his eyes the French and the Russians were two bitterly inimical nations that would sooner or later, on a battlefield with hundreds of thousands of dead, decide whose clowns would rule the world. From somewhere, probably from the circus performers, he found out where the French fared better and where the Russians did. He circled cities on a map with colored pencils: blue marked cities that valued the Russian clowns, and red marked those that were inclined to the French ones, and he circled Berlin, Belgrade, and Bucharest with green because in those cities people were equally enthusiastic about both kinds of clowns.

Aris's knowledge didn't bother his father. On the contrary, he was proud of his son's good memory because it was extremely important for a real attorney. Right until the day his son announced to him his intention to become a cat trainer when he grew up, since no one except for the famous Russian Yevgeni Milinski had succeeded in inducing a cat to do anything.

His old man was horrified and insulted at the same time. Between justice and the circus, his own son had chosen the circus! And not elephants or lions, which were the wonder of every urchin in Novi Sad, but ordinary cats! Something was odd about that child, and it had to be corrected as soon as possible, he thought, and told Aris that he was a big boy already, that he'd outgrown the circus, and that in the future he could think up what the award for fifty correct answers would be himself. Aris resisted, but it was no use.

"You're a big boy now, almost a grown man," his father lied, and a feeling of enraged contempt grew in the boy that would stain their relationship for good.

When he realized that nothing could be done about this and that his father wasn't going to relent, he told him that he was a fat old ass. He'd thought up the insult with a clear head, completely aware that this would hurt and humiliate his father terribly. Namely, Jovan Berberijan never swore or even seriously raised his voice—except in the courtroom, where such theatrics were expected, and without which there were no well-placed arguments and presentations of evidence that the judges would remember. Quiet and monotonous lawyers were boring for everyone in the jury and the audience, and the judge would miss half of what they said.

When Aris screamed at him, he struck at what seemed most stable and firmest in Jovan Berberijan. Wherever he went, his good reputation went with him; people didn't dare say a vulgar word in his presence, and he commanded equal respect among the good and wicked alike. Among the beau monde as well as among ill-mannered prison guards and murderers locked in the darkest cellars of the royal casemates. Even hotel receptionists and waiters in hotels and restaurants in cities where the reputation of his legal prowess was unknown had a special kind of respect for him. There was no fear at all in that respect. That he was a fat old ass was the first serious insult that he'd suffered since his boyhood.

However, all he needed was a good night's sleep, and he appeared the next day with an unblemished aura, gentle and slow in the Vojvodina manner, and unstoppable like the English army.

"And what did you decide; what are fifty correct answers worth?"

Underneath the table the boy's knees trembled from excitement. He could repeat that his father was a fat old ass or cry or howl that he wasn't interested in anything but the circus and wanted to be a cat trainer and that his father could sell him to the circus performers for a thousand dinars so he could wake up every morning at four, feed the horses, wash the elephants, and clean animal shit! He would be grateful to him his whole life. But no matter how much he insulted him, his father would still be a fine attorney from house number 8 on Katolička Porta Square, for him and the whole world. No matter how he tried to persuade his father to sell him to the circus artists, he wouldn't do it. He wouldn't renounce his heir, his little pharaoh.

"Money," whispered Aris. His father was strict with money, and the child hoped he wouldn't agree. If he didn't agree, then the argument about the circus would become stronger, in fact infallible.

"How much?" he asked.

"Fifty answers—a tenth of your pay," the boy answered with a sense that his strength was returning. For the first time in his life, a power that made the world go round was coursing through his veins, a power that made rich men happy and drove them to become even richer. Jovan Berberijan swallowed the lump in his throat and looked up at the ceiling: above the chandelier a spider had spun a web; the cleaning women needed to be warned that they couldn't sweep and clean like a cat with its tail. He lowered his gaze to his son, who was staring fixedly ahead, just as he'd been told that he should look at a judge and jury the moment after he made a crucial point—never blink; create the illusion that you have nothing to hide; the naked truth is in your eyes, and if they want, they can take it in their hands, turn it over, and check to see whether it has been falsified. This was just how Aris was defending his first business offer; he was doing it well and hadn't blinked for half a minute already but was looking at his father like a fakir at a rattlesnake. The boy was strong; he would become something; it was just important to get that circus out of his head.

"Agreed," he said and offered the boy his hand. Aris accepted but wasn't sure whether he'd won or definitively lost. He was getting something he hadn't expected and losing something much more important to him. Was there anything in the universe more magnificent than training cats, and was there anyone more extraordinary than a man who'd subdued the world of cats?

Thereafter the questions that Jovan Berberijan asked his son were much more difficult, but they never required information from legal books or documents. He played fair, like an English gentleman playing cricket or polo, but began to make serious efforts to keep his pay and did that as if he didn't have a child in front of him and as if that boy weren't his son. He found examples from legal practice that had become legendary, verdicts and defense arguments that had made judges famous, and turned them into questions that Aris had to answer.

By the time Aris was eleven, he would spend hours justifying his position, defending it with logic, and leading his father into labyrinths from which there was no way out. The moment of victory came when his father no longer knew what to say or would start stuttering. As soon as he started stuttering, his opponent raised his hand into the air like a boxing referee, and that was a classic knockout, without counting to three. On average Aris received half his father's monthly pay. He put the money into a shoe box he kept hidden under his bed because he didn't know what to spend it on. After the circus was dropped, there was little left for Aris except his school and the office. His mother woke him up every morning at six. He would have breakfast with his father as he read the newspaper and commented on events in the world. The increase in the price of diamonds on the London exchange heralded bad days ahead; in Germany a military strike loomed; there was one workers' strike after another, one street fight between the right and the left after another; the older Berberijan worried that the major industrialists didn't realize that they were playing with a bomb that might explode at any moment.

"And when it explodes, then justice won't be served before courts but before firing squads," he said at least once a week.

After breakfast they went to the office.

"Come to the office early even when you think you don't have anything to do; it's good for the concentration."

And at twenty to eight old Janoš came and accompanied Aris to school. He met him after school, and they would go back to the office, and after an hour or two there was a lunch break. In the afternoon, father and son were again at work, until eight or nine in the evening, when he was supposed to do his homework. Such was the boy's daily routine up until he finished prep school, and there was nothing that could be changed about it. Just as Jovan Berberijan went to work even when he was sick, so his son weathered all the illnesses of childhood in the law office, pressing his forehead on the cold windowpane.

The famous attorney had to exploit all his connections and acquaintances in his efforts to get his son accepted to the law school in Belgrade. He begged and bribed his way right up to Prince Pavle Karađorđević's adjutant, but it was no use at all. For Aris had barely passed from grade to grade in prep school, always with D's, and he only got A's in Latin and history. They didn't want him in the respected school, and it was possible that his father's reputation didn't do him any good either. Rejecting Berberijan's son was a big deal, for some even the biggest success in their careers.

"If he's accepted, I'll chop up my podium with an ax! I'll shit all over honor and doctorates, and this school and this town will never see me again!" Professor Matuszewski yelled when someone arrived from the Royal Palace to intercede. The old Cracow ace couldn't fathom the idea that students could skirt the rules and regulations to enroll in a course of study that was supposed to teach justice and the law.

But in the end Aris got in, and Gregor Matuszewski was retired by a ministerial decree. He was awarded the *Karađorđe Star* for his particular achievements, those in the First World War. An article was published in the daily *Politika*, along with a photograph in which Prince Paul was pinning a star on the professor's breast and thus "crowning with the glory of immortals a man who knew when to pick up a rifle and when to pick up pen and ink to defend and build the fatherland with legal expertise." One could detect a wince in the smile on Gregor's face, as if the prince had not only pierced the lapel of a borrowed tuxedo, but also one of the nipples on his chest.

For years Petar Pardžik, the palace photographer, showed none other than this photograph from *Politika* to his assistants as an example of poor work.

"The man's face can't be seen. People's faces show their real mood for nine-tenths of a second and tell a lie for one-tenth of a second. A good artist knows when he's caught the subject in the wrong tenth of a second," he told them.

Aris's first months in Belgrade were like the discovery of a new world. He spent days and nights in the bars, spending the riches he'd earned answering questions about what was just and what wasn't. By Christmas he already had the reputation of the biggest spendthrift in the long drunken history of Skadarlija because his daily tab was as a rule greater than what everyone else spent together. He treated anyone who came to his table, and at moments of particular inspiration, or if there happened to be a pretty young lady nearby, he smashed crystal glasses one after another. The waiter would bring him ten at a time on a silver platter. In the end Aris would grab the broken glass with his hands and explain the difference between glass and crystal. You cut up your hands on glass, but crystal was like diamonds, tender and fine if handled by a gentleman's hands. The girls whom he was trying to impress with this ran away as fast as their legs could carry them. They saw in Aris either a haughty thug or someone who'd decided to kill himself and wanted to spend everything he had before doing so. And at that time at least, neither the one nor the other was a good recommendation for a suitor.

Before the end of the first semester Aris realized that nothing would come of his scholarly education. At the lectures, when he managed to go to them, he mainly dozed, sat hung-over, and tried to calm his stomach, which was raging inside him. And what the teachers were trying to teach him was uninteresting anyway. For two reasons. He was supposed to learn the basics, but as a boy he'd already passed through the advanced material. He knew how charges were brought and trials were conducted; what use would he have from learning the preliminary steps again? But the other reason why he had no desire to study was more important. He saw that he had eighteen years of torment behind him, of which he hadn't been aware while it was going on. If he continued down the path on which his father had sent him, his whole life would be miserable. Without knowing what he really wanted, because he didn't enjoy anything except Skadarlija, Aris sought a way to free himself from his father. Since nothing but death could deter Jovan Berberijan from passing on his law office to his son, Aris decided to feign tuberculosis. At first he planned on actually trying to get infected, but he gave up when people told him that that wasn't so simple. Not everyone could catch tuberculosis, and no one could know how long it would take for the illness to progress far enough to free him from his studies. He didn't have time because exams were approaching, and if he didn't pass them, his father would realize what was going on and where his son was spending his days and nights in Belgrade.

He gave all his remaining money to Dr. Mušicki for the phony diagnosis. It was worth it because Mušicki acted out his part so well that he didn't need to explain to the older Berberijan how the illness often progresses without the patient knowing he's ill, and caverns begin to open up in people who were healthy the day before. All Berberijan did was crumple the paper on which the death sentence was written. Tears flowed down his motionless face, and Simeon Mušicki felt a great need to comfort him, as one comforted the fathers whose only sons were dying on such occasions. But since that was counter to the agreement that he'd made with the young man, the doctor said nothing and sighed. For each unspoken word of comfort, a sigh.

And so Mušicki earned the biggest money in his life, and Jovan Berberijan lost his reason to live. On Monday he sent Aris to the seaside, and on Wednesday he'd already fallen onto a sick bed from which he would never arise. Saveta washed, fed, and turned him from side to side for a full three years and despaired when he died. She loved him, no matter how he treated others, but she never reproached her son, though she knew that he'd made up the story about tuberculosis and that that story had killed Jovan. If she couldn't change the situation, bawl out her husband, tell him that he was bringing misfortune upon their house, then she could at least accept and pity the both of them with that kind of tenderness that people usually call love, whereas they call the women who live in such love martyrs.

Aris Berberijan arrived in Dubrovnik in the early spring of 1931. He rented an apartment in the house of Mina Elez, an old maid who lived two houses down from the Sikirićes. Mina had a shop in her cellar for mending and darning women's stockings and pleating women's skirts. Regina often stopped by her place when a fair amount of bad stockings piled up in her house, but most often for no reason in particular, to look through fashion magazines that a nephew of Mina's sent her every week from Munich or to talk a little with someone who understood her. Whereas others badgered her—What was she waiting for? Why didn't she get married? Her time would pass!—Mina understood everything clearly. She only nodded, "Hey, dearie, I know how it is," and kept on darning a stocking while Regina would detail her bad luck with men whom she found attractive or with others who found her attractive (and things were even harder with the latter).

Who knows how much Mina actually listened to her and how much of it all she even heard, because those stories were so typical, as if they'd been copied right out of an autograph album or one of Mir-Jam's novels. Regina's problems differed from those of other girls in only one respect. Whether it was fear or exaggerated pride, it's hard to say, but she didn't dare to strike out, dive, and plunge into the waters of love for the first time. Either the cliff was too high, or the sea below was shallow or too deep; she stood up above, started, and then stopped, afterward only to discover and invent everything that wasn't right about the guy for whom she was supposed to take the plunge. The catalogue of male deficiencies was like a little picture printed in a hundred thousand copies that Regina's entire generation carried close to its heart, especially the women, as had several generations before her. What was recorded in that catalogue wasn't to be said out loud or written down because no one would believe it, and they would impute the whole affair to the wickedness and idleness of whoever was telling it. People scorn commonplaces and don't believe that there is anything under the vault of heaven that might satisfy some general criteria, so then such things are simply not said and a great deal of human history is omitted from the history books. The part that can be described and explained only with the help of commonplaces ends up being the gray area of every historiography, an apparently uninhabited and unresearched area, a mysterious outline, a warping of space in the universe, or in any case something that scientists have been making up since the beginning of the century in order to return to reality the peculiarity that existed in it while God's presence in the world was an absolute certainty. Therefore, Regina's problem is only worth pointing out, and there's no need to say any more about it.

Mina liked her company, Regina's daily lament, her litany of complaints and bellyaching filled with men's names, spoken in such a way that one would think they weren't real people but saints in whom no one believed any more. Though that was no reason not to blame them for all the sudden strong storms and squalls, for open shutters smashed against stone walls, for bedsheets torn furiously from clotheslines in a sudden northerly wind, when the only question was whether it would blow them out to sea or turn them into sails that would carry off that damned city and leave it lying in the wreckage of sunken sailboats.

Mina's head teemed with such thoughts. They were ornate, numbered, and each had a hundred little images. If anyone who wasn't Mina somehow (God forbid) entered her head, he would have gone crazy right away from all those little images. But for her they were ordinary, day-to-day occurrences.

Bedsheets and dragons; giant octopi once seen at the fish market, which Czech photographers took pictures of but the city forgot the very next day; an anthill in the unused chimney of a nobleman's villa that had been turned into a museum; pots with marigolds on a window in Begovina and men in fezzes passing underneath the window; the roar of the River Buna and the summer drone coming from the dervish tekke; Mt. Velež in the sunlight on a calm summer day, when a storm has descended on its peak, striking it with thunder and lightning; Allah's quarries; sardines that opened and closed their eyes as they waited for a quick knife to take the scales off their backs and the salt in which their last fishy thoughts reposed; the agonies of salted fish backs, their sinful souls; Christian saints caught in fishing nets; a crucifix made from a pine branch; pillows being aired in springtime in a window of someone who had died the day before; the sea as black as pitch and the smell of lavender in the pockets of men's coats; a captain's hat high on a dresser in a house where there were a lot of children; May Day bonfires; gendarmes with their swords drawn and Avram, a.k.a. Lenin, who flashed his penis at them in provocation; a condom in the palm of a Dutch sailor and his fingers, which smelled of rubber long after—which frightened her and she ran away; grains of sand under her toenails; motorboats that took foreigners to Lokrum; rowboats that took aging hunting dogs to an islet where there was no food or water; a thimble forgotten in a yard, half full of the first autumn rain; three rotten carob pods in the corner of a cellar—one winter at

the turn of the century; little Gypsies with measles running after city kids to in-
fect them; pustules full of lymph; festering sores on the flanks of an emaciated
Bosnian horse loaded with baskets of Travnik cheese; an open umbrella, fallen
into the sea and carried out into the offing. These were some of the images that
passed through Mina's mind at any moment. Whereas others thought in the
words of the language they had learned first, she thought in images and was special in that regard. Women considered Mina to be foolish, but they didn't dare
say out loud that she was crazy. They said nothing about the images in her head
in front of the men; it was better if they didn't know about her and didn't bad-
mouth her. One simply couldn't get by without Mina. Mina was the only one
in town who darned stockings and pleated skirts—and the fashion of pleated
skirts was at least ten years old, and who knew how long it was still going to be
around? Maybe it would never pass: fashion had been invented by rich people
with nothing better to do who couldn't have cared less if it took a long time to
iron pleated clothing—it was easier to iron five men's shirts than one pleated
skirt! But whoever thought highly of themselves and had a reason to go out in
public would surrender to the dictates of Paris and praise God for having created Mina. Besides, she did that work well. True, they couldn't compare her with
anyone else because she was the only one who did it, but that said something in
itself. If darning stockings were a simple task, women would darn them themselves. If anyone could pleat a skirt, there would certainly have been as many
shops for pleating as there were barbershops and beauty salons, and the world
wouldn't have depended on that one of Mina's.

"Oh, dearie, I know how it is," Mina would say, closing up her shop as she
did every afternoon and then going to the post office to get the fashion jour-
nals or little packages with special string that also arrived from Munich. Then
she would continue on to the city aquarium, where deep-sea fish languished in
watery dungeons. She'd felt a tenderness ever since she'd seen them for the first
time some fifty years before. Since then she came to visit the fish every day, except for Sundays, when the aquarium was closed. She talked to them, listened
to their grief, comforted them, and brought a little light and freedom into their
meager lives. If she believed in anything, Mina believed that God had granted
that she be the confessor of fish. She heard the confessions of their unhappiness
but not their sins because fish never sin.

Regina accompanied her as far as the steps that went down toward the city.

"I know how it is," said Mina for the third time that afternoon.

Regina went home to see whether Luka had come back from school. The
same ritual repeated itself every workday, but today it would be fateful for the
two women. As Mina waited in the post office for Vito the postal clerk to find

her packages in gray burlap bags, a stranger wearing an expensive gray suit and carrying two leather suitcases in his hands appeared in the entryway. He held the door open with his shoulder, trying to push his way inside but kept getting caught on something on one side or the other. He would have probably managed by setting down the two suitcases and opening the heavy iron door all the way and going in, if everyone's eyes hadn't been glued to him.

For Mina, Vito, and two idle city ladies, Rudolph Valentino had just appeared! Five years before women had cried for him, and men had acted like they didn't care or that a weight had fallen from their shoulders because he, the handsomest man in the world, ignited flames of outright jealousy in them from a distance of a few thousand kilometers. For the city's parish priest, also a man, his full name, Rodolpho Alphonso Guglielmi di Valentina d'Antonguolla, amounted to unambiguous proof that he was the devil. Could a Christian soul really bear such a name? In his Sunday sermon, after the city had mourned Valentino for seven full days, he warned husbands to keep their eyes on their wives, sisters, and daughters because Satan had sowed his seeds in their hearts. From every tear they shed for the American imposter, the shoots of the devil sprouted. And just as shoots eat up the tubers from which they grow so that nothing is left of a potato, nothing would be left of their wicked female hearts. That was how it was and no other way, so the men should watch out! Thereupon the female side of the church got up from the pews out of protest, and all of them, except for a few old women, walked out. It was told that on that Sunday a horrible curse had rung out in the cathedral. It had been spoken by a voice that didn't belong to any of those present.

For the believers that was unambiguous proof that the reverend father was right and that Rudolph Valentino was Satan. But Satan never died; rather, he changed the place and time of his appearance. He comes in various guises, usually contrary to his real nature. Goodness and innocence, like great physical beauty, are always a signal of danger for the faithful, so any foreigner is better off if he comes across to them as nefarious and ugly.

Seeing the stranger trying to make his way into the post office with the suitcases and recognizing in him the actor from a time when people watched films with their eyes only, whom they had mourned but never gotten over, all four of those present, even Vito the postal clerk, immediately thought it was Satan coming to their city instead of returning to America. It was hard to know who was glad about that if it were true, and whether Vito felt any of those female reasons for joy within himself, but it was a fact that they all watched him alike and that they all shared the same surprise, from one pair of eyes to the next. Mina collected herself the quickest, ran to the door, and opened it wide. The stranger

thanked her with a nod and smiled. He walked up to the counter (the two unemployed women stepped a couple of meters back from him, each in a different
direction), stopped in front of Vito, sighed deeply, and the postal clerk watched
him and waited to see which language the foreigner would speak.

"Good day, and excuse me if I'm bothering you with something that doesn't
have anything to do with the mail, but I don't know who to ask. I was in a barbershop, but they sent me to you. You see, I'm looking for an apartment! Not for a
day or two but for six months at least. So you see, if you can tell me who to go
to, I'd be very grateful to you."

Vito looked at the man in confusion. Maybe he'd been sent from the royal
palace. He would probably be some prince but surely not Prince Karađorđević:
the Karađorđevićes looked different, weren't that refined. Although it wasn't impossible, at least judging from his build, because the Karađorđevićes were also
slender and tall. Thin, but strong. Just look at him—he was thin as a matchstick,
but he could carry three sacks of cement in his arms! Vito would have taken him
in—it would be good to know such people, whatever they were and wherever
they came from, but God forbid he show him his house! That would be like trying to put him up in a doghouse or a chicken coop. Too bad, but that's what he
deserved since he always took care of others more than himself. If it were any
different, if he'd thought of himself, if he'd hoped for anything else but to be a
mailman and a postal worker all his life, he would have built a house in which
he might receive a man like this, and then everything would have gone better.
You're the same as the company you keep—people didn't say that for nothing! But now it was over; he'd missed his chance. That's too bad, really too bad,
he thought, shook his head, and seemed to the stranger to be mentally handi-
capped.

"Come over to my place," Mina spoke up. Everyone was taken aback for a
moment.

"But you . . . ," one of the other women started to say but stopped. And Mina
was almost surprised to have heard her own voice. They all laughed at the same
time, all four of them. They felt as if they were at a chance meeting of a nobleman and a noblewoman in front of the restroom in the *Hindenburg*. Someone
was inside, sitting on an ivory toilet seat and playing with the gold chain of the
water tank, and everyone had to pee.

She took him to her place, to the second-story apartment that she hadn't
gone into since the day her sister had died. Petka had been ten years older than
Mina; she hadn't ever married either, nor had she needed anyone else since she
had her sister. Petka's death was the only truly terrible event in Mina's life. She
just lay down one day after lunch, as she always did, and never woke up again.

If it had been different, if Petka had suffered, if she'd heralded her departure with any kind of sign, it would have been easier for her sister. As it was, that was the one image that dimmed her thoughts and came suddenly. When it seemed that everything was fine and that there was peace everywhere, Petka's white face would flash through her mind: her half-open lips, with a thin strand of spittle hanging from them, thinner than the finest thread, at the end of which there was a tiny globule sinking downward that would break the strand at any moment. She couldn't remember whether it actually did, whether the strand broke. Actually she couldn't remember anything because the next moment she shouted and ran from the room and out of Petka's apartment. And then she fell down the stone steps that led to the yard. She didn't know what she'd wanted then—to call for help, to escape death, which was preparing to come for her too? Or maybe she hadn't wanted anything and so fell and spent a month in the hospital, where the doctors told her that she would never walk again? They always said such things. What did doctors know about walking?! Nothing. Just as they couldn't tell her what Petka had died from. Could it have been the rancid oil that did her some harm? Or was it that the chard wasn't young? Chard had to be picked and eaten while it was still young, before it turned bitter and got to be full of poisons. Who knows what kinds of poisons kill people, where they all are, and how they are accumulated?! If people knew how to take care of themselves, they wouldn't ever die. Death wasn't something natural, like the changing of the seasons, spring, summer, fall, and winter. Rather, everyone died from some illness. And every illness came from some poison. Petka had died from some poison too. Mina knew this and didn't need anyone to tell her about it. People were unhappy, miserable creatures; people were cats that didn't know enough to run off of trolley tracks. And people didn't know what all killed them! If they knew, they would be angels! Angels were harmed by the same poisons as people, but angels knew what was poisonous and gave it a wide berth. The more poisons there were in the world, the less angels protected people. They didn't have the time or a way to do it because they had to protect themselves. And it was better that way because if angels thought more about people than about themselves, they would soon disappear. Just as Petka disappeared, and when you get old, it seems that everyone with whom you've lived is disappearing. You don't die until you're all alone. Mina was convinced that this was true. She didn't believe in God or the saints because she didn't know what God was supposed to be or what the point of being a saint was except that they were supposed to be in eternal torment. Only a sick imagination could come up with saints! But Mina did believe in angels! Angels were here and everyone saw them. Children and adults, believers and unbelievers, smart people and people with no brains at all. It was just that people didn't recognize that they were angels of all things and thought that they'd seen something else. People, just like angels, didn't have time either. That was why one should pity both of them. Almost as much as the fish. Petka might have been Mina's angel. But maybe she wasn't. Maybe she was nevertheless just her sister. Who would know any more? Time had passed; a lot had been forgotten. And how could anyone even know that someone was their older sister? You were born, and they told you that! But people tell children all kinds of things, and they believe it when they grow up.

Mina was very disturbed and didn't go into Petka's apartment. For two full years. So she wouldn't see that image or another even more terrible one.

And yet now she was unlocking the door while Rudolph Valentino stood behind her. Actually a perfect likeness of him; Mina wasn't crazy enough to believe in priests' tales! And how could Rudolph Valentino know their language? He was breathing behind her as if he were frightened too.

"He's so handsome," Mina whispered, covered her lips with her index finger, and pointed up at the ceiling.

"What's up with you?" Regina asked, confused. Her friend had never spoken first, and it had never happened that she found her just sitting amid stockings that needed darning and doing nothing. She just widened her eyes like those lizards that in summertime slip into cold bedrooms from the terraced soil outside and watch people napping in the afternoon with the gaze of elderly people when they stop in front of something pretty lying in the dirt on a road.

"He's so handsome, dearie! You can't imagine," Mina continued.

"Who are you talking about?" asked Regina. Maybe Mina had gone crazy from so much solitude. Her years weighed heavily on her, more years than you can imagine when you're a girl and only twenty-six years old, and what's more you know that even twenty-six is a lot, too old for everything you haven't begun but should have. Especially for everything that's come to pass since the day your childhood ended but couldn't stir you to act. Mina was an old turtle; her little head smiled from inside its oversized armor, and you wondered whether that was a beak in the middle of her face or maybe still a nose. Did turtles have beaks or noses? No one knew because no one cared. Too old for anything, Mina was slowly crossing from one side to the other. Something on the other side frightened Regina that morning, and it would have frightened anyone who knew Mina and loved her. There weren't very many such people, and Regina was first among them. That was what she thought. Or used to think. When Mina got old, Regina would take care of her and be the substitute for the man she'd never met. People got married mainly with thoughts of old age, their own infirmity, and death. They imagined that the other one would look after them, feed them chicken soup, and salt the earth that would cover them. No other reasons existed. That was the only one. And then you wondered whether it was selfish for every man and woman to think that they would die first. And either she or he would watch over you and rearrange the black clothes in the closets. The men's black clothes were always under the women's because that's the way the world was. One always had to please the man. However, there was justice in the fact that it was often they who died first. No one could set that up any differently; death takes us away as it sees fit and not according to the choices of men. And people who die alone are the ones who lose out. Mina wasn't going to die alone! Regina had decided that long ago, but now she was wavering. Mina was suffering from insanity, and her young friend didn't want to have anything to do with insanity. Insanity was a disgrace, and no one lost his mind by accident. With every crazy person there is a tiny decision to become insane. No one dies of his own free will; people always lose their minds of their own volition. Regina was convinced of this in the early spring of 1931. And she often thought about it. About insanity and crazy people. About Bepo Ozretić, who mumbled old Turkish curses, recognized no one, didn't turn around or twitch when children called out his name. And he smelled of urine and shit. It couldn't be that he didn't want that. He'd been the captain of a ship, had a family and a gray stone coat of arms over the entrance to his house. First he took a hammer and knocked off the coat of arms, and then he started smelling like urine and shit. That's what he wanted, that's what he deserved, and it made sense that his family and in-laws had abandoned him.

"Mina, you're frightening me. Just so you know—you're frightening me. So later you won't say that you didn't know what was happening to me," she threatened, turning serious.

"You know when Rudolph Valentino kisses the desert rose, extends it to that girl with the small mouth, but the rose slips away from her and falls into the sea, and he looks at her and it's the end? And we don't know what happened further. Well, dearie, he's upstairs now—I don't mean in heaven but right there in dead Petka's apartment. This morning I went to the post office; Vito was just looking for my packages when he appeared. He was carrying two suitcases and said he needed an apartment. And I don't know what got into me. I said I had an empty apartment. I'm not crazy. Go up and take a look."

Regina got up angrily; the chair scraped along the stone floor of the workshop. She started down the stairs, resolved not to show her face in Mina's shop for at least five days after she saw that upstairs there wasn't anyone or anything. But midway up the stairs she was seized with fear. What if there was someone up there after all? It couldn't be! Mina was toying with her nerves and knew that

Regina was sensitive to this kind of thing in particular. She would forgive anything but expected others to be serious when talking to her or at least be serious and silent. She reached out for the doorknob with her left, her weaker hand. The door of Petka's apartment was unlocked. Mina had really lost her mind if she'd unlocked it after two years. There was no one in the living room. It smelled of dust. A graveyard of bees, ants, and other household pests. The armchairs were covered with white sheets; the carpet was half eaten by moths; they were the only thing to survive in graves. In the bedroom, above the double beds hung a photograph of her father and mother. The wooden floor creaked. In the kitchen there was dry, desert air; no one had turned on the faucet for a long time. So there wasn't anyone; there was only one more door left. Just like in the tale about Bluebeard! Was it the seventh or ninth door? Here it was only the fourth or fifth, depending on where you started counting.

Regina grabbed the doorknob and gave the door a powerful push. She was angry and needed to show it—the door could slam against the wall for all she cared. And it did. And a completely naked man appeared in front of her. She didn't see his face, only his eyes. And his eyes were huge and full of darkness.

She lowered her gaze in a flash, as if fearing that those eyes might cast a spell on her. And down below his thing hung, and then shot up twice. She'd only seen one in pictures, but in real life it looked different. Like a rubber children's toy that moved and twisted all on its own. Like white blood sausage made from pig's blood, fat and greasy, with dark blue, knotted veins and a big head.

She yelled, "Mina-a-a-a! Mina-a-a-a! Mary Mother of God!" and raced down the stairs.

Either by some miracle or because it's normal, she didn't tumble down the stairs as Mina had done when her sister had died, though she wasn't any less frantic. Her heart was pounding like crazy, fear had completely consumed her, and she wished she could just hide in the cap of an acorn. It seemed to her that she couldn't move her arms, though she was waving them like a windmill. It seemed to her that her legs wouldn't move, though she ran downstairs faster than the world record holders in the long history of sprinting.

She stood in front of Mina, panting to catch her breath, and was unable to say anything. What she wanted to say was swallowed by her next thought and sentence, and those by the next ones, and on and on, so she stuttered and breathed and shook like a sparrow in the corner of a room from which it's been trying to escape all morning, and when it's finally let out, it doesn't know to fly away.

"I told you!" Mina said and grabbed the first stocking of the day. "Dearie, a spitting image of Rudolph Valentino. Rodolpho Alphonso Guglielmi di Valentina d'Antonguolla. He wanted to give her a rose, and the girl let the rose fall into the sea. Hah, damned woman. And all that just to kiss her!"

Regina really didn't go to Mina's for the next five days. Not only that, she didn't even poke her nose out of the house. She was afraid of meeting them. Him or her, it didn't matter. She probably wouldn't recognize him with his clothes on, but he would recognize her! Maybe he would come up to her, apologize for being naked, or ask her what she thought she was doing going into someone else's bathroom without knocking. Or he would begin with one of those vulgar, dirty male stories, proud that she'd seen him at his largest. Men like it when that happens—she didn't know how she knew they did, but they certainly did. And what on earth was he even thinking about and what had he told Mina and what did Mina answer him? She certainly didn't say "dearie" to him.

The moment she realized that she didn't know how Mina addressed men, or what she said to them instead of "dearie" (and she certainly said something to them because it couldn't be that she said even less to them or didn't need any crutch words and phrases), Regina was overcome with jealousy. For starters, it wasn't what she meant to him that bothered her but what he meant to her—that was what really bothered her. She and Mina were the best of friends; not a day had passed without their seeing one another, and now, you see, it was the fifth day since she hadn't seen her, and she probably hadn't crossed her mind. Why would she when Mina was probably holding that thick, greasy thing in her hand and didn't know where to stick it, the old bag?!

"Has it occurred to her that I might be sick?" she thought. "Or that I might be dead? That I climbed up in the attic, threw a rope over a beam, and have a noose around my neck, weighing whether to stay in this world or not? Or maybe a wasp stung me and I'm all swollen, and there's no one at home to bring me ice to reduce the swelling? In the end, I might have fallen down the stairs like Petka because things repeat in life. If you've ever done something really wrong, you'll do it again. If you've ever brought great misfortune on yourself, you'll do it again," Regina thought, standing at the top of the steps that went down to the city, and tried to figure out how she might get her foot to catch on something, break her neck, and fall to the account of her disloyal friend. She didn't do it. She probably would have if there had only been someone there to push her. So much rage and despair had accumulated in her because Mina had remained alone with Rodolpho Alphonso Guglielmi di Valentina d'Antonguolla, whose enormous member, like a divine scourge in the eyes of a sinner, grew bigger and bigger and turned into an obelisk that, instead of rising out of the ground, fell down toward her and almost touched that tiny crawling female being that kneeled alongside Calvary. Later, Regina would think this ridiculous. Her own torments would seem silly to her, and she would miss them because they would never come again in the same form.

On the sixth day, she opened a drawer and took out two pairs of old torn stockings that should have been thrown out and not darned, resolved to humiliate Mina. She wouldn't ask her anything; she would just throw the stockings in front of her. Mend them, girl! Mend them, you miserable dry cunt! That was what she came up with, and that's what she would say to her, so she would know what her place was or at least would realize for a moment what she'd lost when she took up with that young devil and threw her out of her house and tore apart a friendship more important than life.

She went into the shop. Mina was pleating a black skirt, one of twenty for a girls' choir that was traveling to Belgrade for the celebration of the king's birthday.

"Where have you been all these days, my poor girl? We got worried about you. He got worried!"

Regina took a look around to see what there was to smash. Should she punch the windowpane with her fist? No, that would be too much! So she kicked an old crock with all her might. It was an imitation of a Chinese vase, bought once long ago in Trieste, and her rare male customers put their canes and umbrellas in it. The crock flew over to the other end of the shop and broke into little pieces.

"You damned dry cunt!" she yelled, and the skirt fell out of Mina's hands.

That would have indeed been an effective end to a friendship and the beginning of a great lifelong jealousy if Regina hadn't overdone it a bit or the crock hadn't been such bad workmanship, made of heavy baked clay, massive like the pots holding African palms in front of the Hotel Astoria. When she tried to run out of the shop, her leg started hurting with a pain like she'd never felt, and in an instant she was aware that she wouldn't be leaving that place. She was flushed with shame because she was losing everything she'd gained over the past five days; she tried to stand on her foot again, and she got foggy in the head. She felt as if she were sinking into big bales of cotton that had been unloaded from an English ship long ago, in the first month of the Great War; the ship had left Egypt and couldn't continue its course. Regina thought she might be dying and felt a little better.

The last thing she saw were Mina's legs, white like spoiled sheep's cheese, with bluish-pink veins that had burst one after the other. When the last one burst, that woman would be dead. She thought of a bas-relief of healthy blue veins and sank into darkness.

And then she saw his face over herself. In fact, she felt his hand brushing her hair from her face. He did it carefully, so as not to touch her skin. She opened her eyes and then immediately closed them, pretending to sleep, pretending that she wasn't there. She was dead but by some miracle was breathing. That couldn't last very long because as soon as that handsome man began to slap her cheeks, which he'd certainly seen in movies about Russian counts, she could definitely see; she shot through him with eyes as wild as Hiawatha's and tried to think up a curse that would put him in the same place she'd already put her friend. But of all the ugly words, only one came to Regina's mind, the one she couldn't say because she would have died of shame. Between her lips was the word that on that day in dear departed Petka's bathroom had gone from being a swearword to a living torment.

It was Sunday when Aris Berberijan carried Regina Sikirić in his arms all the way to the city hospital. She had her arms around his neck. Mina walked beside them and every so often held up her hurt leg, as if that would help, and he hero-ically held up the heaviest burden he'd ever lifted in his life. Not once did he put her down to rest, not once did he open his mouth and say anything, nor did his hands start to shake. They went down the steps and toward the city center, and everyone who was supposed to see them did.

That afternoon women became particularly hateful toward their husbands; young women shut themselves up in their rooms, threw their quilts over their heads, and wept bitterly in the hope that they would suffocate. That evening not one husband in the houses along the way that led from the Sikirić house to the hospital got dinner. That night not a single child was conceived. The men-folk found themselves completely baffled. And only those who hid the shame-ful seeds of pederasty within themselves knew what was going on. And the womenfolk found in themselves the shared and unspoken reason for jealousy and hatred, which would accompany Regina's shadow from that day until the day she died.

Never again would the thighs of living women yearn from windows and ve-randahs for Aris Berberijan to carry them like that, but their jealousy and hatred would live on unabated.

"There are cracks in three bones," said Dr. Mikulić. "In all likelihood you'll always have a limp."

Regina shrugged her shoulders and turned her head away. She didn't know that doctors always said things like that. Aris put his hand down on her hair again, this time to touch her and comfort her. He still didn't feel anything definite for her. As often happens with men of great beauty, those small-time Apollos, he too lacked the talent or skill to see himself with the eyes of the other sex and sense when his aura met another aura.

But in that same hospital only three days later Aris would pass through

Regina's hidden lips and be where no man had been before. It happened on Sunday evening, while the doctor on call, the old Gjulio Devera, was sleeping according to his habit in the laundry room, and Hamza Begaja, the nurse, was counting the dinars that he'd received from Aris and listening in on the voices that he heard from the other side of the wall. It seemed to him that he was hearing the yelps of a bird dog that had gotten caught in a fox trap or the crying of the young Ms. Rizvanbegovica after she had miscarried her child and lost her mind. Hamza, who didn't know about the birds and the bees, was frightened by what he heard. He felt guilty and was sure that he'd lose his job on account of this if he didn't end up in prison. He was the only one who felt bad that night.

Regina didn't end up with a limp. In only three weeks she was walking normally, and the doctors again thought it had to be a miracle. Little bones heal the slowest and fuse crookedly more often than not. But, you see, her bones fused quickly, with everything in its place and in the order that God had determined. The crock that she'd smashed with her foot brought her first real love. Then she strolled through the town holding hands with the stranger and thereby confirmed what everyone already knew. Though not every woman who held hands with an unmarried man was considered an easy woman, Regina immediately became a whore. The reason lay in Aris's beauty. The old women remembered the parish priest's words on the death of Rudolph Valentino. The women who'd unleashed a scandal when they left the Mass that day had grown old full of dissatisfaction and hatred for themselves and were even harsher toward Regina. In all that she saw only a game in which she felt victorious beforehand. She wasn't bothered by the reproachful clicking of their tongues, which could be heard from the darkness of people's cellars, nor did she give a damn when women would conspicuously cross over to the other side of the street when they came across them.

"The bitch has really gotten full of herself," said Brother Dominko Miljuš, crossed himself three times, and smeared garlic on the knob on the door to the monastery. Just in case someone grabbed it whose hand had touched Regina, if only accidentally and in passing. Brother Dominko had a metaphysical hunch that the devil was soon coming to collect—crosses would be stuck in the ground upside down, people's mouths would turn inward, and the whites of their eyes would be full of blood and darkness. Generally speaking, he was right. Millions of Europeans felt the same thing, but just as Abraham's sons didn't know where the threat to them was coming from, neither was he able to recognize the face of the Evil One. Historians would later be of the view that his face was visible at every step, but Brother Dominko, a product of his time, saw it in the love of a pretty city girl and a painfully handsome stranger. He smeared garlic on the doorknob and recited the prayers that were close to his heart. Against hunger, the plague and the Evil One; against those who didn't understand anything; against baptized and unbaptized souls that consciously or subconsciously found themselves on the path to the devil. He always prayed against something, in the firm belief that the Almighty Himself knew on whom to bestow his mercy, but maybe he forgot whom all he had to send to the deepest chambers of hell in order for the world to be saved.

For nine full months (the time that the friar smeared the doorknob) the palms of the young divinity students smelled of garlic. In that year of 1931 a season of shallow and tepid contemplation lasted from spring until winter. It was revealed that in the rituals of the church the stench of garlic did more harm than the smell of incense did good. The good Lord probably would have forgotten his children without hearing the voices of their hearts if that love had lasted and if Aris Berberijan hadn't disappeared from the city as suddenly as he'd appeared. After that the bitch also lowered her tail, and her eyes filled with tears.

Why did Aris run away from Regina? She would never find an answer to that question, and as long as she sought it, it would determine the course of her life and take her in directions in which, if it hadn't been for him, she would never have gone. After the first nights they spent together in the hospital, they became everything that lovers can be for one another. She'd found the man of her life, with whom she would bear children and build a house on the coast, far from neighbors and vicious rumors outside their four walls, a man with whom she would sit on a verandah under an arbor and listen to bees buzzing above clusters of grapes that were bursting under the September sun and watch sails out on the high sea under which industrialists from Prague were enjoying their cruises; she'd found a man with whom she'd spend time while the sun set and alongside whom she would await her dying hour, on a shared bed, at the same moment, holding hands under their wedding photograph, which their grandchildren would inherit and take with them to other cities and countries.

In no time he forgot his father and the ground in which he was preparing to lie in eternal sleep, the law office that was already covered in dust, and under the door of which there was a growing pile of invitations to diplomatic balls, firemen's parties and soirées with colleagues, a gathering of criminal law specialists in Opatija, and congratulations on forgotten anniversaries and verdicts that had saved the skins of murderers. Aris didn't have an answer to the question of whether he'd really fallen in love with Regina or she'd just helped him to split with his past and flee the deceit that he'd committed. Nor did he give it any serious thought. Regardless, Aris had no doubt about it. Love was everything that didn't remind one of indifference, unhappiness, or hatred.

But the first step he took toward her was also his last. He would have agreed to live like that to the end of his life, fifty meters away from her home, receiving her every night into his bed and waking up alone because she ran home at five so no one would notice that she wasn't there. He was afraid of anything more than that. Or he couldn't endure the rhythm to which she planned their future life.

The next spring they would get married, and a year later they would have their first child. And then they already needed to be thinking about building a house! Or maybe it would be better to forget everything and leave the city immediately? To go to America? Maybe Italy? They said that New Zealand was heaven on earth, though it was far away, in the middle of the ocean. And it was better to be as far away as possible. Where those you're running away from can't reach you. And maybe Zagreb or Novi Sad? That was simpler. Building a nest among one's own people and surrounded by customs that weren't foreign.

He patiently refused Regina's offers and ideas. He would find a bad spot or a factory error in every one of them, and she would smile and say:

"Yes, I hadn't thought of that." But not half an hour later she had something new in mind, some happiness that he then found to have some defect. Instead of thinking that Aris in fact didn't want it, which any rational woman would have realized, Regina had the impression that something was wrong with her. She planned badly, silly things came to her mind, and she would have already lost her head if it hadn't been for him. Fortunately, Aris was as smart as he was handsome, so he always told her what was wrong with what she'd thought up. But he was also just as good, allowing her to keep coming up with ideas, plans, and fantasies. Another would have forced his will on her, but he wouldn't! He waited for her to discover something that would make them happy and was clever at the same time! Months passed in that imaginary waiting game, right until Aris realized that he'd jumped out of the frying pan and into the fire. Regina's plans for happiness resembled his father's questions about what was just. The time to run away again was drawing near.

Mina darned stockings, pleated skirts, and pretended not to notice and not to realize what was going on. The man who had settled into the house of fear and sadness had liberated her from Petka's death. She opened every door, went through the rooms, including the one in which the strand of spittle with the little droplet at the end had broken. She wiped away the dust and rearranged things that had been fated never to be moved from where the dead hand of her angel had placed them. On days when there was no southerly wind, when the air was like clear water, and the stars were aligned for a childlike happiness, Mina smiled at herself. She was the master of fate and fear; she mutely spread her arms and nodded, instructively as if someone were watching her. The days, months, and years when she'd avoided the empty house seemed silly. But there was no going back—it had happened once and wouldn't happen again! You're the slave of your images, and you always will be. When you emerge from bondage—which was possible with a lot of luck and if your angel was so inclined—the years you lost remained in the fetters. She could sense this on nice days as she cleaned Aris's rooms and lifted clouds of dust that could remember Petka's epithelium, hair, and fingernails. A ray of the sun is contoured best in a cloud of dust. Only then do you see its edges clearly, when it is sharply refracted in the crystalline mirror or a young woman's vanity.

Why is it that women's dressing tables are called the same thing as the futility of human endeavor? Because in city apartments young women's dressing tables are the cenotaphs of young souls. That was where Petka primped herself, combed her hair, and put on makeup for a love that never came. The mind is the place for a young woman's hope, and hope is the most a soul can have. A soul without hope is the soul of an old woman. Old age comes early, much earlier than the time when men stop turning around to look at you. Old age comes when you build bulwarks around yourself that love can't scale. Petka built them early, and Mina took after her older sister. They turned into old maids, which was the second biggest scandal in this city. The biggest would have been for people to declare them to be whores. Or even worse (and there are such cases), if people had spoken about them both as old maids and as whores. In that case there wouldn't have been any quiet compassion, according to which people draw a distinction between women without love and women who go too far in love. The change that Aris brought into Mina's life was like a belated revolution, but the harvest it produced was one of a kind of quiet happiness. At least on clear and sunny days and on nights when the stars were perfectly aligned. Then she had the temerity to do what she'd never dared before. She would talk with Petka's shadow, laugh out loud at her fears, wipe away the dust that was turning into a gray sheep's fleece under her hand. And then her heart would start pounding when she touched one of his things. A shaving brush, a razor with an ivory handle, a belt with a buckle in the shape of an eagle's head, the smooth and firm leather of his shoes. In their polished black surface she could see her own face, a wrinkled and deformed dwarf laughing silently. And then she would grow afraid of Aris's coming back unexpectedly. She skipped across the parquet floor and didn't know where to go. She was bathed in alternating waves of hot and cold sweat. Everything that the man left behind was so dangerous and attractive. She found a little red rubber pump for enemas; she could feel a handful of hazelnuts in her throat; she couldn't breathe. Poor man, if he'd told her, she'd have mixed him some tea for such problems! She quickly chased away an inappropriate thought. She squeezed the pump with her ring finger; it hissed air and there was the smell of chamomile; a few grains of dust flew up toward the sky. She ran out of the room and locked the door. If he came unexpectedly, she'd tell him that she'd grown afraid. She lay down on his bed. The pillow had absorbed the lavender in Aris's hair; her heart beat like ten galley slaves trying to escape from a sinking ship. For a few seconds she didn't know what to do and ran toward the bathroom and wet herself halfway there.

It was nice to live with a secret. Someone might say she realized that too late, but this wasn't a problem for her. It was better like this, living in love when love was something you no longer had to seek or declare. And when you didn't expect anything from it, least of all for it to be reciprocated. She was happy that Regina and he loved one another and believed it would always be that way. She was only afraid that they would leave her, go off to America or Australia, it didn't matter where, and leave her behind. Regina was surprised when Mina told her that the idea of leaving wasn't a good one, that there was no happiness to be found in an alien world. That was the first time that she was commenting on something and found a defect in an idea that Regina had come up with. Earlier she would have agreed, even if Regina had taken it into her head to attach swan's wings to herself and fly from the top of Srđ Hill. And she had to say that, though it stung her in her heart, because she couldn't take the idea of the two of them leaving, for Aris to take his little terrible objects away and for the pillow to stop smelling of his hair. Back home, she drifted off to sleep as the sounds of a mattress creaking came from Petka's apartment, distant cries that she would never recognize in their daytime voices. But now she knew them, and it seemed as if they were hers. She didn't want to lose them at all.

A month before Aris ran off, Mina realized what was going to happen. And she also knew why it would happen. Blind with love and passion, Regina clung to him ever more tightly. And she was blind and deaf to all the obvious signs of Aris's calling it quits.

"Oh, dearie, if you knew how happy you are, you'd really watch your step," Mina said, once she'd come up with what to say and seized an opportunity to tell her.

Instead of comprehending, or at least suspecting something, Regina just laughed. She laughed from sweetness, at everything people told her, or she kept quiet. She was in love in a way that was excessively rare in human beings. Like a male praying mantis. It goes off to die with full faith and a pure heart, convinced that nothing better exists. When love like that befalls them, people as a rule do survive, but something in them still dies. Every future love is filled with doubt, and every future defeat—if it is even possible in doubt—is harder for them to bear. They emerge from defeat different, worse and more unhappy in any case than they were. They start liking other colors, start hating dishes that they used to like; they become wicked in everything in which they were good; they become skilled at planning unhappiness. They become criminals.

Mina no longer visited Aris's rooms and tried in vain to reconcile herself with what was coming. She watched him leave the house upset, without saying hello to anyone, and felt relieved when he did come back. She had a harder and harder time enduring Regina's visits. Her continual babbling started to get on Mina's nerves. She missed runs in stockings; her needle pricked the tips of her fingers and underneath her fingernails.

"He's going to leave you," she yelled one Saturday in late September, "and he won't come back because you're a goat. Just so you know: you're a stupid goat. You're a goat."

She repeated it because she couldn't come up with any other insult, and all she wanted was to tell Regina the most hateful words in the world. For the first time, she was jealous of Regina's youth. No matter how much it would hurt her, Aris wouldn't be her last man. But he was the first and the last in Mina's life, though she'd never laid a hand on him.

The first time Regina fell silent, froze, and looked agape at that woman acting crazy again. That was how it began, and that was how it had to end. She'd brought him, and she would take Rudolph Valentino away. Regina ran out of the shop as soon as strength returned to her legs and heard Mina calling after her:

"Goat! Goat! Goat . . . !"

She shoved past Luka, who was about to say something, and locked herself in her room with both locks. Fear consumed the whole real world, and when she woke up a few hours later, her first thought was that she was gravely ill and couldn't get up out of bed. Nor could she say a word or call for someone to help her. And she remembered that she'd locked the door and had to get up if she didn't want to die all alone.

She no longer managed to think about Mina's fit because his letter was waiting for her on the kitchen table. She opened and read it. With every sentence she forgot the previous one. And the letter was long, ten pages of small handwriting. Evidently he'd been getting it ready for a long time. It hadn't come to him suddenly, and he certainly wouldn't be coming back. In every line he wrote that he loved her, and in every line there was one "but" that explained why he was leaving. Regina read the first part of each sentence twice and the second part only once and then forgot everything. When she read the last line of the tenth page, all she understood was that she was alone.

Aris was strolling along the promenade in Split and watching a Czech circus performer, a woman juggling bowling pins, right as Regina was hurling the last plates she found in the china closet through the window. He was traveling with that woman, whose name was Jana, as Regina theatrically tried to hang herself with a clothesline from which she'd removed wet pillowcases and thrown them into the dirt. She was running to claw out Mina's eyes with the whole neighborhood running after her when Aris kissed Jana for the first time. Regina spat before the door of Mina's shop and looked her in the eye through the display window, and that was how their acquaintance and friendship ended, while he was telling another woman that he loved her, and she was laughing at him like a tourist laughing at someone selling wooden donkeys. She was promising herself that she would never lay eyes on another man again at the moment when he thought that Jana might be the woman with whom he wanted to spend his life. She shut herself in her room and didn't go out for a month, and he woke up every morning in a different city. Trieste, Bolzano, Bologna, Milan, Turin, Florence, Rome, Naples. He bought postcards but didn't have anyone to send them to, and she was waiting for a letter of repentance—she would forgive him everything and would be his slave until the end of her life. On the day before Easter in 1932 Aris spent a crazy night with Jana and her friend Karolina, a sword swallower, and realized that his flame kissed other women as well, and not just him, but it didn't bother him for a single moment. Regina was kneading dough for walnut bread and crying bitterly when the priest Stevan Bojanić came into the house and said:

"Christ has arisen. Today or in two weeks. Don't be sad, child; you have no reason."

Before New Year's in 1933 Aris and Jana had their first fight, without even knowing what it was about. A plainclothes policeman knocked on the kitchen window, and Regina shrugged her shoulders when he told her that Mina was dead and they weren't sure whether she'd killed herself or someone had murdered her—she lay with her throat cut on the bed, whose pillow no longer smelled of lavender.

"I'm not going to that old slut's funeral!" she shouted and slammed the door, and blood started flowing from Luka's nose.

"Look at him; he could kill a lion with his fist," Jana said, admiring Mussolini, who was bawling about workers' rights from a balcony in Rome. Aris couldn't hide his jealousy.

"Fascist faggot!" he said.

That same day Luka told Regina that Adolf Hitler had become the German chancellor, and she said that it would be smarter for him to study for school than to sit listening to the radio all day long at Svetinović's, that customs guard.

"Do you love me?" Aris asked and blinked as the Reichstag burned.

Jana was practicing with twelve bowling pins and when they were all up in the air said, "You've asked me that thirty times today already. I'm not going to answer!"

Luka hit his fist on the table, and Regina slapped him, the first and last time in her life.

"You're a lunatic, a common lunatic," he shouted through his tears, and she cracked her knuckles. The joints popped like a hot pine stump in an autumn rain.

"I'll groom horses; I know everything about them," Aris told the circus owner, Tibor Timošenko.

"So you don't have any more money, huh?" the old acrobat asked and squinted at him.

"When he spends his last dinar, he'll come back to me," Regina whispered to Luka through the prison grate.

"And what if they convict me?" he asked, but the English consul didn't bring any charges.

"You fall asleep in Austria and wake up in Germany," Timošenko said and sighed as prep school students paraded through Vienna's Ringstraße shouting slogans about German unification.

"We're finished," Jana said and sighed.

"We'll fight," Aris answered. "Hitler can't conquer the world."

She looked at him sadly: "He doesn't have anything to do with you and me."

That same evening an Arab horse named Hafez struck Aris in the forehead with its hoof, and he lost consciousness briefly. The very next day he remembered everything except that he'd ever been with Regina. That detail would come back to his memory only when he died in 1940 in Paris, in the arms of Tibor Timošenko, who'd lost a bet that his trapeze artist Aris Berberijan could do a double somersault with his eyes blindfolded and without a safety net and grab onto the arms of Alija the Turk, the strongest man in the Levant. The knuckles of their middle fingers only brushed each other, and Aris fell into the abyss and broke his spine.

Two days after the Anschluss, Ivo Delavale kissed Regina for the first time.

"I'm sailing out tomorrow," he said, "and you'll wait for me if you love me."

She looked at him with yearning, as a beaver looks at a broken dam. "I won't wait for you," she said, shaking her head. "I won't, I won't, I won't." And he pressed her in his embrace and with his fingers he imitated ants climbing up her underarm. He tickled her until tears came to her eyes and then left.

The next year was the happiest in her life. She forgot one man and wasn't really waiting for the other. She didn't believe him because she'd decided not to. If you survive being in love, you can decide what you want, and you won't make a mistake or give in.

Everything went well until that May evening when she ran out of the Cosmos Cinema in tears, horrified by the *Hindenburg* disaster. She realized that she was thirty-two years old and wouldn't live to see the advances in science and technology repair what Aris had broken. What had been broken by both Aris and Mina, who'd died to pay some terrible debt, and also by her fear, which was the reason she'd waited so long and then ended up with the wrong man. Everything was wrong, and only the hope that she would fly into the clouds with kings and princes held her soul together. However, the *Hindenburg* went down in flames. And what else was left for her to do but to give herself over to the one whom she didn't believe and, when he finally came back, to create faith in him. And that faith, of course, wasn't a faith borne of love but a faith borne of fear. One of many religions that leave no holy books or stories behind. Neither holy wars nor the blood of innocents strengthen them. They have no armies of infidels arrayed against them. And no one recognized hers to be a faith because it didn't belong to anyone other than this desperate woman who'd created a new faith. Regina created hers around the *Hindenburg*, and many men of her generation created theirs around the Spanish Republic.

When years and decades would pass and the twentieth century came to an end, their grandchildren would ask what had happened to their grandfathers, what kind of romantic chaos had taken hold of their souls and led them to go thousands of kilometers away to defend something that belonged to someone else so that they died for Barcelona and Madrid and in French camps they awaited the Nazis, who then sent them to eastern Poland to death camps, gas chambers, and crematoriums, where their great illusion finally went up in smoke and ash. Their grandchildren, to be sure, wouldn't know that the old men in their families had fought for something of their own and not something that belonged to someone else! Spain fell to them as the last great hope of the world, breathing its dying breath. Hope replaced God because God didn't live to see the twentieth century. He died with the last great Requiem Masses and oratorios. Mozart still believed in him, but with Wagner faith had already become a myth. Bepo Sikirić went to defend Spain in the name of hope. And during that time his sister waited for the *Hindenburg* to land at Popovo Polje; millions of men and women all over the world hoped for hundreds of thousands of their own miracles and in doing so scorned one another because the hopes of others almost always seemed trivial. The problem came about because the majority of men believed in organized and collective miracles, those for which it was worth spilling blood. The blood of others if they were stronger and were on the attack, and their own if they were weaker and on the defensive. That was the most probable reason why revolutions broke out, stronger than all considerations of class and nationality cited in history books. In a world without God, cities, countries, and whole nations suffered on account of the hopes of men, but on account of the hopes of women no one usually suffered except the woman who hoped. Only in exceptional circumstances did whole families suffer. If a man's thinking didn't do them in with war. True, it sometimes happened that the roles were reversed and that the hopes of men became the hopes of women.

So it happened that Olga Benario, the daughter of a rich Munich lawyer, went in those years to start a revolution in Latin America. No matter whether she was disgusted at what was happening in the beer halls of her own city, or had ceased believing that Europe could become a continent of freedom and justice, or whether she was carried away by the musical melodies of the Hispanic languages, she arrived in Brazil and fell in love with Luis Carlos Prestes, a Marxist and the leader of an insurrectionist march through the jungles of Brazil. Together with him she went through a little revolution that for political reasons wasn't mentioned in the European newspapers, neither the Western ones nor the Soviet ones, and history mostly passes her over in silence because in our century the rule is that history doesn't record what the newspapers haven't already reported.

In that revolution Olga Benario saw blood, death, and villages in flames, but she also saw a flower that after her death would spread through the Mediterranean and be known by the name bougainvillea. In the Amazon jungle, where it was warm and wet, that flower was almost always a white color, but on the Adriatic coast it was blue, dark pink, and violet, depending on how much the plant lacked warmth. She liked that white flower but not because she was a woman (as one who clearly divides the world into a male and a female half might assume), but she liked it as would anyone who had a pure eye and saw something for the first time. Luis acknowledged its beauty, though he'd never noticed it before. Because he'd been looking at it all his life.

"You see, that's good. People need to mingle in order to learn to see. That's why the revolution will win," he shouted. "The Internationale is in the eye of woman and man!"

And the unfortunate Luis Carlos Prestes deceived himself. The uprising failed, and the Brazilian government extradited his Olga to Germany. She died in a concentration camp, and the date of her death, and the deaths of the majority of the camp inmates, was every date of every year for her loved ones. Olga Benario is worth remembering not only because she was guided by hope like Regina, but because one of the first bougainvilleas in the Adriatic was planted in the garden in back of the Sikirić house.

It was brought there by a Dr. Elsner, from a meeting of botanists in Padua, and he planted it there because he had no garden of his own. Elsner also died in a camp but not because of hopes and ideals but because he was a Jew. The bougainvillea grew and flourished, and its flowers were always violet. It survived the Second World War and all the misery that followed. It was still there after the bombardment in 1991, when the house burned, and lived to the end of the century, as big as the biggest pine and as old as the oldest olive tree. It outlived everyone who remembered it. It was the only constant in this story.

Regina fell asleep right before dawn, inconsolable like the country of Poland and furious at a world that felt no sympathy for what had happened in Lakehurst, New Jersey.

When she woke up, the sun was already in an afternoon hour, and she was waiting for her sailor. That was how her romance with Ivo Delavale began, which no one opposed and could have ended differently if at one moment the fates that were mutually involved hadn't crossed. Regina's, about which we know most everything, and the fate of Diana Vichedemonni, about which we won't learn anything. Such is, to be sure, the logic of life. Those who pass judgment usually don't know that they've passed judgment on someone. Just as those who are condemned don't learn anything about those passing judgment either, no matter how hard they try and no matter how sweet revenge seems. No one succeeds in taking revenge on anyone in this short life. We would have to live a thousand years, as in the Old Testament, and know more than any one person can ever know if we were going to be able to take revenge.

IV

On Christmas Eve in 1927 Kata Sikirić cursed God. Her hands clenched into fists in the black bread dough she was kneading, and she couldn't unclench them. At first a sharp pain shot through her left hand, and immediately thereafter she lost all feeling in it. She could still move the fingers on her right hand, though she couldn't free them from the dough, whereas the fingers on her left hand felt as if they'd been fused with the hard stone of the Revelin fortress. Kata wasn't overcome with fear, only with confusion perhaps. In the few seconds that the whole episode lasted, she wavered between two thoughts, two conflicting feelings: the thought about the yeast that had stopped working in the dough and, instead of making the Christmas bread rise, turned it into something sad and yeastless, a cake of pious Jews, and the thought of the curse she'd uttered aloud right before she felt the sharp pain. Rage came with the first thought and wonder with the second. Either God was taking revenge on her for the curse, which would mean that He existed after all, or she would have to take revenge on him because he was so powerless that he couldn't even give yeast any power.

Kata waited for a resolution of her dilemma: it was the longest wait in her forty-two years, and soon there was nothing left but the waiting. No hands clenched in the dough, no eyes about to pop out of their orbits, no thoughts, neither the first nor the second, no feet, and no wood floor underneath them. A moment later when Regina let out a scream, waiting was the only thing left of Kata Sikirić.

Ten minutes later the entire neighborhood was already there, even one-hundred-year-old blind Slava Tutin. The old woman's grandson, Captain Bariša, held her by the arm as she whispered, "Where's the deceased, where's she lying, are all the windows shut . . . ?"

Young people were pushing in from all sides. The women smelled of salt cod that had already been soaking in water for three days, and the men pursed their lips while their cheeks puffed out like those of forest dormice. They wheezed through their noses and turned red, careful not to let the smell of brandy escape through their mouths on a fasting day like this. The stronger and more agile ones pushed their way to the kitchen table, beyond which Kata was lying. Those behind them stood on their tiptoes trying to see something. Some were even eyeing the table, wondering whether to climb up on it and — as impolite as that may be—take a look at their deceased neighbor one last time from the best vantage in the room. True, they would see her once more at the chapel before the funeral. The casket would be open because that was the custom, and the deceased's face had not been disfigured by illness or an accident so the family would have to hide it. But that wasn't the same. People saw dead people who'd been tidied up, bathed, and dressed in good clothes at least once a week because people they knew died about that often, people whose graves one visits at the cemetery, whereas something like this only happened once in so many years. Her eyes hadn't even been closed yet; they stared up at a chandelier where a spider was busy spinning his web, and it seemed as if Kata was angry at him for doing that. She looked just like that, no different. This must have been a sign; the older women would have to know what it meant when a dead person saw a spider spinning a web. Did it mean that Kata had worked hard in her life and would now go to heaven to rest, or did it mean something else? And perhaps the sign had nothing to do with the deceased but had something to do with her home? Had fate spun a web of misfortune over this home, and was the worst yet to come? Some recoiled a little at this thought, and two women crossed themselves.

"Poor Kata, and she gave birth to five children," one said.

"Not five but six; one of them died from the Spanish flu," another corrected her.

"That wasn't her child; it was her sister's," the first retorted.

"What're you talking about? Her sister gave birth to three, and all of them are still alive," her neighbor said, ready for a fight.

"Are you both crazy, what sister? She doesn't have any sisters besides Angelina. Those are her uncle's children," a third woman said.

"Shut up, goddammit," a large man hissed at them. He was most likely the first woman's husband, and he jerked her by the arm and pushed her behind his back. There she kept grumbling for a while but eventually fell silent.

"Look, the dough on her hands still hasn't dried . . ."

"She's clenching those fists so hard they would crush a rock if she were holding one . . ."

"It was her heart, her heart, I'm telling you."

"Or a blood vessel in her brain burst."

"No, no, when a vessel bursts in the brain, the face is disfigured, and look at Kata: everything is just like it was."

"Even better than it was! All her worries have disappeared."

"Lord, she looks so beautiful."

"And young, the poor woman."

Gentle voices filled the room; one compliment and admiring remark came
after another. Kata hadn't heard this much praise lavished on her in all her life.
Regina stood hard as a stone to one side; she wanted to shout and chase the
vermin away, but her voice wouldn't do it, and her joints were as soft as cotton.
The crowd of people soon stopped noticing her; they kept coming and pushing
in front of her, and soon she found herself leaning against a wall in a corner of
the kitchen, all alone and far away from her dead mother. She would have remained like that until evening while the audience kept changing if her brothers
Đuzepe, Bepo, and Đovani hadn't arrived within five minutes of one another.

"What are you doing with my mother?!" the oldest thundered, and in
the blink of an eye the kitchen and house began to empty. Their neighbors,
ashamed, their eyes fixed on the floor, hurried out. Chairs scraped the floor and
rattled; the door slammed against the wall; one heard a muffled groan from
a squashed corn; they ran like children when someone smashes a window at
a school. Maybe not even two minutes had passed and they were alone, the
four of them, along with Kata's clenched fists. Bepo closed her eyes, Đuzepe
started quietly crying, and Đovani turned pale and started trembling. The boy
had never seen a corpse before.

A little later Aunt Angelina, Kata's sister, came running, carrying Luka in
her arms. She started wailing as soon as she reached the door. The little one said
nothing and waited for his aunt to put him on the floor, and she didn't do it for
too long. Instead she carried him around the table as she lamented, "My sister,
my dear heart, these poor orphans were born of your flesh and blood . . ."

Then she bent down over dead Kata still holding Luka in her arms, but the
child was heavy and nearly caused her to lose her balance. When she realized
what she was doing and that it made no sense, Angelina tried to extricate herself:

"Okay, dearest, kiss your mother one last time!"

Almost upside down, Luka kissed Kata on the cheek. He did that calmly and
without any fear. He knew that his mother was dead by the fact that she wasn't
moving. That's not so bad, he thought; you just stop moving and that's it. He
wouldn't remember that happening. He would forget it so completely that he
laughed when Regina tried to remind him of it much later. She also mentioned
his hysterical Aunt Angelina and the kiss on Kata's cheek on that crazy and joyful night when he returned forty years later from Trieste and was himself bidding farewell to life. But Luka only laughed and waved his hands, as if driving
away the annoying specters of invented nightmares.

"And what'll we do now?" Đuzepe asked stupidly.

"We'll wait and everything will happen by itself," Bepo said calmly and
straightened out his mother's legs and put her hands together across her breast.

Aunt Angelina sat by the stove and mumbled the two prayers that she knew at all, the *Our Father* and the *Hail Mary*. Đovani's blood returned to his head; he grinned sarcastically at his aunt and tried to get her to notice.

But Kata's sister didn't see anything any more, nor did she hear what was going on around her. She fell into that special metaphysical trance that seizes non-religious women and those free of the Holy Spirit who are inclined to fashionable shouts and submissive in the face of all folk traditions. She devotedly recited her mantra and swayed like an eastern mystic, actually enjoying everything that was happening and what was yet to happen. It would have been unfair to say that she didn't pity her sister; she loved her purely and devotedly, as do people with simple hearts and souls without a great deal of intelligence. But that was no reason at all not to give herself over to a long, attractive series of post-mortem rituals and customs. Soon everyone would come to her to express their condolences. She would buy a black hat and veil, faint behind her sister's corpse, and firm male hands would take her under the arms and lead her all the way to the grave. She would speak words of her greatest sorrow, yield to a poetic delirium, and—what was most important—everyone would listen to her. Her mourning would make their skin crawl. It would be a long time before they forgot the moment Kata Sikirić was committed to the earth, that poor woman who was the mother of five living children and a sixth that had died in her arms. Angelina would make it so that all the other funerals would be forgotten after that one greatest, most mournful, and most beautiful funeral of all. She would spill her tears before them like pearls, humiliate them with her talent for sorrow, and elevate the deceased woman to a place that she should have had while she was alive but that wasn't granted to her by these heartless people.

But Aunt Angelina was wretched in fact. She was as good as gold and dull as an ax used for chopping beechwood. Wicked Đovani was practicing his first pubescent ironies on her. Bepo was too ashamed to look at her. The simple-minded Đuzepe tried to comfort her. He put his hands on her shoulders and brushed the tears from her cheeks, as if the death of his mother were a trifle compared to the tragedy of Angelina, whose sister had died. In fact, he could have been her son because he resembled his aunt more than anyone in the family, and it was no wonder that he loved her most. She was closer to him than his mother Kata because she didn't expect anything from him, nor did she compare him to other children but let him be what he was: the odd one in the family, a kind of timid mountain creature to which civilization only caused torment and for whom school was the source of the greatest fear in his life. After the news arrived that Đuzepe had been murdered in cold blood in a Chetnik reprisal, only his Aunt Angelina would light a candle for him, shed a tear, and say a hundred *Our Fathers* and *Hail Marys*. No one else cared, or they felt relieved that he would no longer show up in the family house and remind the world that it was composed of countless oddities but that most of them cause people awkwardness and shame. The Sikirićes felt shame on their own account but also for Angelina and Đuzepe, which is also the reason they didn't like them very much.

Regina said nothing; almost all the feelings a living being can bear deep in its heart were mixing and blurring in her head. She wasn't sure whether she mourned that woman, whether it hurt her that her mother would forever be under the ground she walked on, or whether she was happy that the one according to whose standards her world also had to be tailored was gone. Kata hadn't forced her to do anything, nor did she mention marriage, though from her perspective twenty-two years was the final deadline for a woman to lie under a man and start bearing his children. But just the fact that she was as she was, that she breathed next to her and worked around the house from dawn to dusk, created awkwardness for Regina. Now that she was gone, there wouldn't be any awkwardness either. Her little fists covered with dough would never move again. Those little fists that protruded from oversized sleeves covered with countless images of camomile flowers that had faded from washing. She'd watched those sleeves and flowers from the day she was born, and they'd been getting tinier and tinier, paler and paler. She didn't remember ever having seen her in another blouse. And now she was looking at those flowers for the last time. They wouldn't fade any more; they wouldn't exist any more. They were a grievous source of sadness for Regina, a grief the size of the universe with which we see off holy women when they leave this world. Women who during their lives don't do anything to call into question the pure innocence of the sleeve of their only blouse.

The silence and calm surrounding the dead Kata lasted less than an hour. Then Father Ivan knocked on the door, a black raven that had already somehow learned about the latest deceased in his parish. Bepo let him in without a word, and Angelina readily jumped up from her chair to join the ritual, while the others pretended the priest didn't exist. Đovani cleaned his fingernails, Regina didn't take her eyes off the field of chamomile, and Đuzepe ran outside. He was afraid of priests because he didn't know what to do in their presence — when to cross himself, when to mumble something, and when to fold his hands piously. He did, however, remember that he'd gotten more thrashings from catechism instructors than from all other teachers combined. And they beat him like a rented mule because he endured it and never cried. They thought that Đuzepe was spiting them and kept to the age-old pedagogical principle according to which one should thrash a boy until his tear glands dry up.

Little Luka sat on the floor, and it seemed that not even he was particularly interested in Father Ivan's appearance. He was more interested in a lizard that ran through the kitchen and slipped under the china closet. And the priest, of course, knew his parishioners well and what kind of house he was coming into, so he didn't pay attention to those who were there. With Angelina's mute assistance he said his prayers quickly, crossed the air over dead Kata, extended his hand to everyone, and went outside hastily and without saying good-bye. It was Christmas Eve, and it was almost indecent to die on Christmas Eve.

Father Ivan had hardly left when Dara Živoderka showed up, a woman in her late fifties who ran an unregistered funeral home in the city. Stout and strong, with arms like a circus weightlifter's, she would take care of everything that a mourning family wasn't ready for or trained to do. She carried Kata into the bedroom by herself, laid her down on the floor beside the bed, and took all of the necessary equipment out of a large leather suitcase that she carried with her: a tin basin, wooden clamps for straightening out crooked joints (in case the deceased had stiffened in an irregular position), a silk kerchief for closing jaws, various pairs of scissors, and polished medical instruments that resembled gynecological ones that had no practical purpose apart from convincing families of the seriousness of Dara's work. She ordered all the men to leave the room and sent Regina to fill the basin. When she came back, she found her mother already completely naked.

"Stand here and don't ask anything," the woman ordered. She moistened a sponge and started to wash the dead body. She was agile, with a routine in her movements that one sees only in professional dishwashers in large hotels. She knew the anatomy of the human body, its folds, depressions, and bulges better than the Creator.

"Get the clothes ready that you're going to move your mother in," she said, cleaning the dough off Kata's hands. Regina didn't understand her right away. What move? Probably to avoid deluges of tears, Dara made efforts not to say death, procession, or funeral ceremony, and somewhere she'd probably heard how Muslims talked about all of that. The deceased moves to the *akhira* and continues on, according to her merits, to *jannah*, where the souls of the blessed reside, or to *jahannam*, where the sinful are subjected to the torments of hell. It was the same as with the Christians, in fact, but without words that would summon tears.

Regina got out her mother's black dress clothes from the closet—a skirt, a blouse, and a hood that Kata wore when she went to funerals. Dara dressed the deceased again without anyone's help.

"What about underwear?" the daughter asked softly.

"She won't need it," she answered firmly, placed the body on an even bed, folded the dead fingers on her chest, and said, "Okay; now don't move her any more, and you can light a candle, but be careful so nothing catches fire."

As she left the room, Dara crossed herself, just for herself and without looking any more at the result of her work. She did that as protection against curses and bad dreams. She charged a lot for her services, and left to wait and see whether death would bring sorrow to any other homes on that day before Christmas.

In those years Dara Živoderka was probably the most hated person in the city but maybe also the only woman about whom people didn't make comments when she passed. Nor was she followed by loud gossip. If anything was said about Dara, it was done under one's breath, in a whisper, and with the strictest discretion. People superstitiously feared her powers, and you never knew when you might need them. She came mostly without an invitation, after Father Ivan had finished his work, so people believed that she and the parish priest had some kind of business arrangement. The people of the city couldn't agree on whether the priest took a part of her fee or whether the agreement with Dara was a part of his curatic mission. Naturally, the pious believed in the second and the godless in the first. On the basis of such things, one could tell what kind of attitude people took toward the Almighty better than from their behavior at Mass every week.

But everyone agreed on one thing: Dara occupied a higher position in the social hierarchy than Father Ivan. Parish priests come and go, but she remained in eternal collusion with death. The world recoiled from the dead, from evil spirits and the superstition that dying was infectious. They didn't want to see the naked bodies of their parents, brothers and sisters, or dead children. Especially not withered genitalia, pudenda that had lost their last hair, members that had created them and of which all that remained was a wrinkled tobacco pouch, what you know exists but has to remain hidden. It's terrible to touch icy skin and move stiff limbs, to see those close to you turning into useless, lifeless objects. Not even the most fervent believers could accept Father Ivan's comfort completely. They too needed Dara Živoderka to liberate them from death. And everyone was glad that she came alone and uninvited because it wasn't pleasant to pass by her house, let alone knock on her door.

She lived outside the city walls, below the hospital, with a Czech woman named Jarmila who had come on vacation before the war and never gone back to Prague again. They rarely saw that woman. She never went down into the city, but in the summertime she would sun herself and swim on the hidden rocks in the direction of Trsteno. Fishermen saw her lying alone in the sun and were enchanted by her naked body. She would be wearing only men's military underwear and nothing else. But one didn't talk much about that either, out of fear of Dara. Nor did they talk about what the two women meant to one another. Four years later, in the summer of 1931, it would be shown that there exist things much worse than open gossip, when one of the most sickening crimes in the history of the city took place. Dara Živoderka found Jarmila's mutilated body, minus its head and breasts, on the hidden rocks after her friend hadn't come home for two nights. The police didn't find the murderer, nor was Jarmila's head ever found.

Until her death in the late '60s a crazed Dara searched for Jarmila's skull, and the people of the city could hardly get used to the idea of preparing the deceased for the hereafter without anyone's help. In the summer of 1931 an unspoken love was ended, and there was no longer anyone to care for the bodies of the dead.

Their neighbor Mare Laptalinka had evidently been waiting in front of their house for Dara Živoderka to finish her work so she could knock on their kitchen window. Bepo rolled his eyes and said nothing. Mare had pushed the most to get the best look possible at the deceased, and now she was there again.

"You should live, my children!" she said and held out a pan of stewed codfish. She looked around; Kata was no longer there. "Here, children, if you need anything . . . ," she mumbled and ran out.

Đuzepe had hardly opened the pan, filling the room with an aroma that gives a kitchen color and form, when someone else was already knocking on the door.

Stjepo Alar, Bartol's father and an old widower, was holding a dish full of fritters. He smiled as if to apologize, extended his hand to the two older sons, opened his mouth to say something to Regina, but couldn't remember what he wanted to say.

"My Mirica, she wasn't yet twenty, also died of heart trouble. It used to be that only men died of heart trouble. This world's gone crazy . . ."

Bepo offered him brandy, but Stjepo was in a hurry because there were already tears in his eyes. It had been fifteen years since Mirica had died. Bartol was only nine months old at the time, and his father had had to replace his mother. He changed him, cooked for him, did the washing, ironing, and everything that was a shame for men. For Stjepo it wasn't shameful, but it was sorrowful. Whatever he did, it reminded him of Mirica, and every so often tears would run down his cheeks. He cried a whole sea of tears and couldn't make his peace with it at all. People pitied him at first, but soon they started saying how Stjepo was a little flighty. A poor child with such a daddy! Because it wasn't normal to cry so much for a woman. Maybe she'd been good to him, but she certainly wasn't the only woman under the sun. He shunned company and withdrew into his house, partly because he couldn't stop crying in front of strangers and partly because of an insult that he couldn't endure. As soon as someone said that there were still good women and that he should find a mother for the child (even if they had the best of intentions), it was as if someone had driven a knife into his heart. Mirica was the only woman for him because she was his first and had departed like that. Such loves are hard to get over.

After Stjepo there came at least thirty or so neighbors to the Sikirić house—women and widowers, old ladies, unmarried girls, those who were doing penitence for having enjoyed the image of dead Kata, and those who, like Stjepo, came out of the goodness of their hearts. Each one brought a pot, pan, plate, or skillet . . . On the kitchen table were dishes of cod alla bianco and cod stews, cod alla rosso, marinated sprats, all kinds of seafood stews, shellfish, crabs, conger eels, salted sardine cakes, marinated mackerel, one monkfish stew and one bean stew, corn stew from some poor devil, and fried sardines dried in packing paper. When the holiday delights no longer fit on the table, Regina started lining them up on a festive white tablecloth that she'd spread out on the floor under a window. Here there was walnut bread and fruitcake, carob cakes and dried fig cakes, and a whole pile of fried dough and dark-flour fritters. People brought the dishes, and each one would say two or three words and leave. Outside it was dark; it was going on nine o'clock when they began to get ready for the midnight Mass, and the bustle continued.

The family members were confused, and then they were seized with a strange kind of hysterical exhilaration. Only Aunt Angelina nodded reluctantly, kept saying the *Our Father* and the *Hail Mary* halfway through, and broke off in the middle of the prayer, which no longer made sense because the spirit of mourning had been stifled in a way that was incomprehensible to her.

"I'm off to my sister," she said indignantly and went into the bedroom. Luka started after her, but Đuzepe grabbed him and pulled him up into his arms. The child's chin started to quiver, and a second later his eyes were full of tears.

"Now your brother will show you how airplane pilots fly," Đuzepe said and threw him up in the air one more time and then over and over again.

"Do it again! Do it again!" the boy cried, spread his arms, and waited for the moment when he wouldn't fall back down but would stay suspended in the air like a seagull and fly through the kitchen on his own. And he knew that it would happen sooner or later, which was why he asked his brother to throw him up every day but only when they were alone because Regina and Bepo got mad when Đuzepe did it.

When Luka was a baby, he'd thrown him up in the air like that, and once he threw him up too hard and Luka stuck to the ceiling like a pancake. Luka didn't remember that, but everyone said that was what had happened. Except Đuzepe. Đuzepe said it hadn't happened like that and would throw him up in the air whenever they were by themselves. But now they weren't alone, and no one was getting angry about it anyway. That was because their mother had died and was no longer moving. It was good when Christmastime came and mother died and everyone was in a good mood and no one thought anything bad would happen, that hot milk would spill all over the floor, that Luka would play with a knife and cut his finger, that his big brother would make him stick to the ceiling like a pancake, or that his sister would cry because that time of the month had come again. Which time of the month? Luka didn't know, but everyone always said that and giggled as if they'd farted softly and it really stank. Everyone plugged their noses except the one who did it. That one giggled, and that was how you knew that he'd farted. Most often it was Đovani who farted and giggled, and Regina never farted. Women didn't fart; Luka was sure of that.

Đuzepe threw him up in the air and caught him in his arms for a long time, up until the boy got dizzy and asked him to put him down. The floor swayed under his feet; he stumbled twice among the plates and pots. The chairs that Bepo, Đovani, and Regina were sitting on, each in a corner, rocked back and forth. Bepo laughed briefly and stopped as if he'd remembered something; Đovani slapped his knees: "Ha, ha, ha!" And then his sister started laughing like crazy.

"He shouldn't do this," Đuzepe said, laughing. "He shouldn't do this at all," he kept saying when he caught his breath. Regina couldn't get up, her eyes were tearing up, and she was already completely wet; a feeling of the coming disaster spread throughout her body. If the end of the world came, those who knew what had happened would laugh just like this.

In the bedroom lay Kata, ready for the grave. Aunt Angelina had lain down beside her and immediately fallen asleep. One could hear the murmur of thousands of people who, on the only night when the living stay up, were going to churches, calling out to one another across inlets or standing alone in the harbor, looking into the black seawater between the boats and feeling sorry for themselves. The living Sikirićes saw one more Christmas.

That night they ate and drank like never before. They talked over one another, praised the food, told each other everything they would otherwise have kept silent, everything that got lost in the dead silence of brotherly and sisterly antipathy. It was strange to be one of five children of the same father and mother and for almost nothing to tie you to the others. And then there comes a time to reassemble a disassembled world, for shared words to gush forth, and for little wonders to multiply, which give people the strength to live on long afterward.

Christmas Eve in that year of 1927 was a moment of the closest bonding—and in a strange way happiness too—in the lives of Kata's children. If history were measured in the lives of last survivors, then in the history that ended on the day Regina Delavale née Sikirić died in a delirium, there was no greater holiday. Unfortunately, no one would ever write down or tell what they said to one another, what little bits of tenderness they exchanged, or how much anguish and distrust they erased with their laughter. All five of them would fall asleep on the kitchen floor, with crusts of bread in their hands and eels' heads in their laps, and wake up hung over and with headaches, without the lesson that sudden happiness brings to the heroes of fairy tales. Nothing of that experience remained with them. The kitchen was full of trash, their dead mother lay in the other room, and Aunt Angelina stood like a statue, pressing her face with her fists, her eyes bulging, sure that she'd lost her mind and that what she was seeing couldn't be true. She couldn't remember falling asleep, but what she saw said that in the meantime something horrible had happened.

Christmas passed in silence, fear, and headaches. Đovani was kneeling in front of the toilet bowl and vomiting. That was the first time he had been drunk, and for the next fifteen years, until the apparitions of Orthodox saints and his intoxication with revenge, it would remain the only time. Đuzepe didn't dare look his aunt in the eye. He emptied pots of half-eaten codfish, and she took them and washed them without a word. Luka slept with his head on Regina's lap. She stroked his hair and thought about the time that would pass before that little boy became a man and began taking care of himself and left. When kittens lose their mothers, they totter about in yards and streets, tumble head over heels down stairways, and their meows won't let people sleep. The moment you hear them, you know that tonight or one of the following nights some sleepy man will run out of his house and break the back of the first kitten he finds. In the morning worried women will catch the other little animals, wring their necks like chickens, or drown them in shallow pools of seawater. One kitten nevertheless survives. The one that's the strongest or the luckiest. He continues the species and prolongs the suffering of the cat world. And its happiness, too, if animals know what that is. And so that's why cats have so many young. Not all of them ever survive. But children are born one by one, and someone has to care for them when they lose their mothers. She was fated to care for Luka. She would do that the best she could, as long as she had the strength, until she was overcome with despair and the boy got up on his own two feet.

Bepo went to Father Ivan to see when the funeral would be, but the priest had left for somewhere in Herzegovina to conduct a Christmas Mass. Fat Adžem, a lay friar and the priest's assistant in all affairs secular and religious, had been dead drunk since the early morning, slurred his words, and offered Bepo herbed brandy. He almost fell down the stairs when he accompanied Bepo out of his office. Antonijo the usher was spending the holiday in contemplation, somewhere on the Elaphite Islands, so there was no one to take care of funerals. The municipal building was locked; people were celebrating, some in church, others at table, still others with a bottle in their hands, each in his own way and in accordance with his own sense of God. People went from church to church, and as the Masses began at different times, their morning passed at divine services.

That evening everyone would discuss how things had been in which church and which priest had had the best Christmas sermon. They would gossip about Father Ivan because he had, as always, left his parish for the holiday and left the church to two young priests from the Bay of Kotor whose dreams of celebrating Christmas Mass in the city had come true, and he had gone off to some one-horse village near Gacko, where there were maybe twenty Catholics in all. It was there that some Andro a.k.a. Kismet had built a church all made of marble so that he might atone for his sins, which he, as was told, had racked up while working as a mine supervisor in Australia. Andro a.k.a. Kismet had killed and raped, the God-fearing people whispered, though they'd never seen Andro. And what they heard about him was so unreliable that it would have been no wonder if it turned out that no one by that name and nickname had ever existed. The story about him was important only in one respect: at the end people said that Father Ivan received a handsome sum of money for his trips to hold Christmas Mass there, and he put it all in his own pocket.

After kissing the gate to the municipal building and inquiring in vain about what to do with his dead mother, Bepo came home with the job unfinished. Aunt Angelina had washed all the dishes, Regina had swept the kitchen, and it seemed that everything was again in the best order. Indeed, just as it had been until the previous day, before Kata had stuck her fingers into the dough and couldn't get them out again alive. But no one, not even Aunt Angelina, was glad that noon had already passed and the deceased hadn't been taken away. And what was worst, Bepo couldn't say when the medical examiners would come. Luka played by rushing off toward the other room. Regina would catch him in her arms and slap his hands, but the boy wouldn't quit. He knew that his mother lay inside, that she was no longer moving, and that this was the reason why no one was letting him into the room. He didn't know what his dead mother might do, but why should he be afraid of it? He could tell that Regina was afraid, which was enough for fun. It was easy to play with adults when they were worried about you and weren't playing at all. It was harder when they wanted to play and didn't know how to do it.

"God help us, she's starting to smell!" Aunt Angelina said and crossed herself.

"It can't be; it hasn't even been twenty-four hours," Bepo said and shook his head.

"Oh, yes she has; can't you smell it? It's the south wind, damn her!" Aunt Angelina insisted.

Nothing stank of course, and least of all Kata's corpse, but the mere thought of that was enough for one's nostrils to sniff the sweetish smell of flesh through which blood no longer flowed, the smell of a slaughterhouse, an open grave, a stuffy cemetery chapel, a cave with animal remains, everything that occurs to people who have ever smelled the stench of a human corpse and imagine it to be a compound of all known unpleasant odors. Regina tried to no avail to change the subject, and it didn't even help that neighbors were coming every so often again and asking if they needed anything and taking away their plates and pots.

"The deceased is starting to smell, God forgive me, my sister!" Aunt Angelina would squeal, and any neighbors there made sure to get out as soon as possible. Thus noon passed and evening fell on Christmas Day. No one turned on the light; they each sat in their corners; Luka fell asleep in his sister's lap, and one could hear Aunt Angelina sniffing the air and announcing a catastrophe like a blind, deaf dachshund. On that night of horror everyone except for the little brother would experience moments when they hated their mother Kata with a hatred greater than any love. Kata would luckily never learn that each of her children, except the youngest and the one who'd died, had hidden her on Christmas Eve. That would have horrified her. She would have gone crazy. She would have died four times in a row, or her soul would have moved in between the covers of the holy books, where holy women, saints, and prophets endured their eternal torments together with the Son of God, who in a spectacular way had ended the history of the suffering of holy men, whereupon the history of sinners began.

By the standards of the time in which she lived, Kata Sikirić was in every respect sinful, and it wasn't unusual for her own children to renounce her when they smelled the false smell of her death in their nostrils.

Just as every whole human story starts from the end, it would be better to examine the list of Kata's sins from the last to the first. A month before her death she complained that she hadn't grown snobbish in time, that she'd fallen for the first man who looked at her, that she hadn't finished school and run far away but had instead borne him children one after another and built a tower to heaven and created six times what the Lord created only once when He created Adam and Eve. She scorned the Lord—if He even existed! But everything she thought and felt was put together and imagined as if He existed. Kata could imagine that there was no God; as more misfortunes accumulated in her life, that possibility seemed more and more probable. But she couldn't imagine that there was anything under the vault of heaven that wouldn't be in accord with the holy teachings. In short: maybe God hadn't created Adam and Eve, but there was no doubt at all that Eve had eaten the apple.

And what happened to make Kata complain about her lack of haughtiness? One morning while she was waiting for the bread dough to rise, she took Regina's magazines from the window. She liked to flip through them; they were full of the wonders of the world, photographs of big cities and famous men and women whose biographies were likewise wonders of the world. No less than saints' lives. However, these miracles weren't made of goodness and suffering but something else. Kata didn't know what, nor did she feel like thinking about that kind of thing.

Well, that morning she read about the death of a woman named Isadora Duncan in *World* magazine. She'd been a dancer, the widow of a Russian poet who'd committed suicide, and the whole world was at her feet. It's too bad that you only learn about people like that when they die, she thought, midway through the article, and by the time she'd finished it, Kata was desperate and was convinced that she herself could have saved Isadora Duncan's life. And who was the cow that had woven Isadora such a long shawl? Because if her shawl hadn't been so long, it wouldn't have gotten wound around that car tire, and she would still be alive. Why was the shawl so long? It must have dragged in the dirt before she died. Isadora must have had to take care not to step on it when she was hurrying to the theater and make sure the ends didn't end up in the mud as soon as it started raining. Otherwise she would have had to wash it all the time. And when you wash shawls like that too often, the colors fade. Maybe it would have been better for the unfortunate woman to have thrown it away after three washings; then this wouldn't have happened. Or if she'd thought twice about the witch who wove such long shawls before buying anything from her. That woman must have charged for their length. The longer the shawl, the more expensive it was. In faraway places more lace certainly cost more than less lace. That's how it was in other countries: everything came with a price and nothing was done out of love.

Love is the happiness of the poor. The happiness of the rich is made of wealth. And that's what did in the unfortunate Isadora. She was rich and didn't think as she was buying the long shawl and loved as poor folk love and wore that shawl so she would be more beautiful for the one who loved her. That's what Kata thought as she read about the tragic fate of Isadora Duncan, and then two things struck her. It was better to die like her than to live in a world in which no one admires you, in which there are no eyes that will see a miracle in you, that will look at you as at huge groupers taken by trickery, which you see only once in twenty years and whose lives are worth more than the lives of the fishermen on whose tridents they died. And the second thing: you can only be such a woman if God granted that you belong to the beautiful species. If you're a fish, then he could either create you as a lowly mackerel or sardine or give you the aspect of a heavenly being whose death is the humiliation of its killer. If you're a woman, then God let you choose for yourself whether you'd be a lowly mackerel or a beautiful grouper. At birth there was no difference between her and Isadora. Kata understood that well. The difference was created by life, which granted to some only that they would bring forth more of God's creatures, something the church cherished, but which wasn't really any more important than the work of railway porters. Life granted to other women that they would be actresses and ballerinas whose beauty would be admired by every thinking being. But in order for life to grant you something like that, you had to renounce your faith, your humility, and the *prie-dieu* that waited for your knees and made you one of hundreds of thousands. Instead of doing that, you waited on heaven even after you realized that there wasn't any heaven. Just so, out of habit or because it was too late to trade in your life for another. You didn't renounce what you didn't believe in, and that was your greatest punishment.

Until one day you read in the newspaper that the most beautiful woman of our time had died, and you realized that you could have saved her if you'd had the strength to save yourself.

She cut out Isadora's picture from the magazine and put it in the bottom of a box of papers. If there was war or the house burned, that box contained everything with which Kata could claim her right and her children's right to a new life. And now she'd put something into it that didn't belong and that in some way—never spoken and so never even molded into a clear thought—meant that she was renouncing them and that they'd become hateful to her. She would still have given her life for them, died once for each child, but she no longer loved them with that pure love of the Blessed Virgin gazing at her infant in a little painting above the altar that was already completely dark from the sighs of a hundred thousand souls that had prayed before it in the last two hundred years. Her renunciation of her own children was Kata's last and greatest sin. She'd stopped believing in the most touching of all the holy teachings.

The real truth is: Baby Jesus also made a mere mackerel of Mary.

Thus, Kata renounced her offspring, only to have her offspring soon renounce her. There were no words spoken in these renunciations. The children

couldn't have even suspected what had happened, and their mother didn't learn
of their renunciation because she was already dead. Though no one knew anything, the misfortune nevertheless mushroomed with their unspoken feelings,
and it would have been easy to follow the fates of all the Sikirićes in line with
that. If there hadn't been that shocking story about the death of Isadora Duncan, published in a Zagreb magazine, if Regina hadn't left the magazine in the
kitchen, and if Kata hadn't read it, her children would have probably lived and
died differently. At this time Darwin's theory was not yet generally accepted,
and the beliefs of the church were entering their greatest crisis in history; almost
nothing was known about psychoanalysis, and ideas about historical determin-
ism were concerned only with peoples and states—not with families. But according to all teachings, beliefs, and ideologies, the twentieth century would
have passed differently for one family if only the illusion of motherly love had
survived.

It would be better if the preceding claim could be made in a more gentle
or at least less binding manner because in that way one would avoid the false
impression not only of Kata's strength and greatness, but also the gravity of her
final sin (which was more important). But now that her previous sins have been
mentioned, it should be clear that this woman wasn't strong or great and that
her soul was full of a little of everything but not much of anything. Completely
free of malice, simpleminded, she seemed to have been born at the wrong time.
If she'd come into the world a few hundred years earlier, during the Inquisition
or the witch trials, she would have been one of those undoubted model women
who rendered the agony of the world and her own sex endurable and lent everything a sense of goodness. Maybe she would have ended up as an abbess, a care-
giver for lepers and plague victims, because the reliance on the logic and flow
of the holy teachings would have given her a strength greater than the strength
of real faith. Belief in a fable was, in her case at least but maybe also as a general rule, more powerful than belief in God. People doubt his existence sooner
or later because things don't flow according to some imagined ethical plan,
whereas no one can doubt a story. However, since she was born at a time when
miracles were no longer born in men's minds but were created by machines
without souls or hearts, there was no benefit in life from belief in a fable. Fate
had determined that she would live and die a very confused soul.

She loved her man because that was how it was supposed to be and she
didn't know anything else. Kata didn't know; maybe some did. But they weren't
her concern. She ran out when women started badmouthing their husbands:
some beat their wives; some went out whoring every Friday; some vanished
without a trace though they'd said they were just going to Herzegovina for to-

bacco . . . When they started talking like that, and they would start whenever more than two of them got together—during the grape harvest, before a wedding, or after a funeral—it seemed to Kata that every meeting of a man and a woman only brought unhappiness. But it couldn't be like that, nor should it be! If it was, we should live as if it weren't. How could those women not know that, and why didn't they feel pain at least—since they weren't ashamed—while they were talking about their men like that? She never said an unkind word about her husband. Nor did she have an unkind thought. True, he didn't beat her or leave the house more than he had to. And he didn't go to Herzegovina to get tobacco. He sat on a three-legged stool next to the chimney, sorting nails into three wooden boxes and sighing. For twenty years he'd been trying to make sure that the largest were in the first box, the smaller ones in the middle box, and the smallest in the third box. There were many of them—she could have studded her whole house all the way around with them, but even the most languid human being wouldn't have needed more than two days to put each nail in the right box. Yet he never finished the job.

Only once did she tell him to forget the nails; she would take care of that when she finished her other chores. He looked at her, and a moment—no longer than it took for a swallow to dart through the house—was enough for the thought of offering to help him not to cross her mind ever again. What did she see in those eyes? Certainly not anger. Not even fear. And it couldn't even be called sorrow. What she saw in the blue eyes of her husband was the same man who would sink when the last nail was in the right box. The man in his eyes was hardly treading water, and the one in the eye of the one in his eye even less, right down to the smallest man one could see, in whose eyes there were at least a thousand more nail collectors, all tinier than particles of flour but marked by the same horror.

Kata felt a chill around her heart, and she knew that it would never go away. He would keep going off to work at the harbor at dawn, come back home at the same time, hurry to finish lunch as quickly as possible, and sit down on the stool and sort his nails and sigh until evening. At night his trembling would wake her up, she would put her hands on his shoulders to get him to calm down, and she would change the feathers in his pillow at least three times a year because his tears made them rot and smell. She wondered why he was like that, tried to fathom his unhappiness, tried to get him to talk, and when that didn't work, she wouldn't say a word for months. If only something would happen sometime. But nothing ever did! He did the same things every day and every night, and it wasn't granted to Kata by God to get through to what he was thinking.

And how else could she love him, other than to keep up appearances and because she didn't know anything else? Kata's heart was pure but emptier and emptier so that in the end doubt crept into it. That happened a few months before Luka was born. Drop by drop, she was filling with a poison that didn't differ from the poison in those women whose husbands vanished every Friday. She began to spy on him; she would jump out of bed whenever he would go off to the toilet at night, but she couldn't catch him doing anything wrong. She didn't find out that he was secretly throwing the wrong nails in the wrong boxes so he could sort them out again the next day. Her hunch that he was deceiving her first brought rage, but when she thought that maybe he wasn't deceiving her and that there was always a fair amount of nails in the wrong box, Kata felt bad. She pitied her husband and was disgusted with herself. How could she have come up with something so wicked?! If the conscience was an organ for measuring a man's sins, then Kata's sin was terrible. The heavens were alarmed by it, and it was a miracle that in those days a thunderbolt didn't strike her in the forehead.

That was how it seemed from Kata's perspective, but from the perspective of those who would never learn of her sin or understand it if they were told about it, it was a very small one. As small as the motivations of a man's conscience relative to the whole world. It didn't matter when there was or wasn't a God above him.

Kata's other sins also involved her husband. She would blow up at him and would even shout, and once she even swore at him, standing in his face. She wanted him to hit her; she needed a slap like that more than someone under the surface of the sea needs air. Life could begin with a slap in the face. But he didn't hit her, nor did he answer her. He only mumbled something that sounded like an apology or a plea to leave him with his nails.

And so in Kata's soul the curse she'd uttered changed from its original meaning and became something inappropriate and unbearably shameful. She didn't swear any more, not even out of habit, not even in those circumstances when swearwords replaced happy and innocent words that didn't exist in the language. In this Kata was alone in a city in which it would happen that even the most timid lamb of God, the wife of a missing seaman, or a nun would let spicy words slip from their tongues at the drop of a hat. The sin of swearing was for her as hard to bear as a homecoming is for a defeated army.

In the midst of a rainy autumn, an army of desperate men covered with wounds, bitter and weary of their fate, was returning to homes that the enemy had thoroughly destroyed, to loved ones who in their own agonies had lost compassion for the agony of others. These were soldiers with no decorations for bravery and without any opportunity to substitute the heroism of the past for the life they were living.

So that was what Kata felt after she'd sworn in vain, but whether she had a vision of those defeated men who returned from captivity in the years after 1918, as late as the late '20s, it is impossible to know. Maybe she did because she saw them with her own eyes as they made their way south toward Trebinje, passing through the city and continuing over the Arslanagić Bridge, without a single one of several hundred saying a word or lifting his gaze from the dirt. With their soldiers' caps pulled down over their ears, with fezzes that seemed completely out of place (as when Emperor and King Franz Joseph II had tried to portray himself as the father of his Muslim children), with officers' epaulettes from which the gold insignias of the glorious monarchy had fallen. They walked homeward barefoot or in tattered boots, men who'd done everything to try to keep everything from being the way it was and to prevent the destruction of a state that they might not have loved but to which they were indebted, the way a wife is indebted to her husband. They owed their lives to it, and it was only that chance hadn't wanted to lay them down in the middle of Galicia, on the River Soča, Mt. Meletta, or somewhere amid nameless Albanian gorges.

It, the state, had already been very old and tired, without interest in its subjects, obsessed only with its wish to meet its end as painlessly as possible. It would have been futile to fight for it and try to rouse it from its dead slumber, but what else could those wretched soldiers do? Only what Kata kept trying to do with her own man. They couldn't understand how the empire had fallen into a stupor and how one soul had broken up into several, into as many souls as the monarchy had peoples and tribes. But they sensed that there was a diabolical plan behind it all, an insanity that would consume anyone to whom God didn't give the luxury of playing silly games in rhythm and harmony with the way states do it. Nor could Kata figure out what was wrong with her husband, why he was as he was on the inside, when on the outside everything seemed normal and according to regulations, in accordance with stories that told how the life of each of God's creatures would pass.

"Allah the Good created woman to take precautions for himself. If it weren't for her, the devil would have cast a spell on man. But He, the Great One, planned ahead for that and created woman in the image of the devil. The difference was only in the fact that He replaced the sea of the devil's wickedness with a drop of His own goodness. And now it is on each of us to charm our husbands because if we don't do it, the devil will cast his spell on them. That's the way it is, daughter, and think about how you'll do it. But remember that you don't have a lot of time. The devil is as quick as a rabbit, and you can only beat him with what you've got between your legs."

That was what a sorceress named Halima said one year in Blagaj when Kata went to her to inquire about herbs and compresses, spells and amulets, anything that might bring her man back to life. At that time she'd already given birth to two children and might have known that for him the spell of her loins was smaller than a grain of sand and slower than a turtle, but Halima was persistent and everyone said that she knew her work.

"If once isn't enough for him, then give it to him twice, give it to him a hundred times each night, until you finally wake him up. It can't be any different, and the problem isn't in him. If he's a man, and he is, and if you're a woman, and you are, then mount him, and don't stop until the devil gives up. It's a war between you and the devil. And remember: your man can't help you in this. Don't blame him, and don't curse him because God will curse you!"

Kata returned from Blagaj afraid. She knew that there was nothing to do except what the sorceress had said, even if she didn't believe a word of it. And not even the Almighty could have been sure whether she believed her or not, not even if he'd been keeping track of Kata and her sins and virtues. She herself didn't know what to do. There was no one to tell her, nor had she ever heard of a case similar to hers. So she did what was most logical.

If she'd been born a few hundred years earlier, she would have turned to her confessor; if her life had been in the time in which her great grandchildren were to live, she'd have written a letter to a women's magazine or—what was least likely given the topography of Kata's soul—gone to a psychiatrist.

As it was, she went to the most renowned sorceress in the area, one of a handful whose reputations had spread to all the cities and villages of the kingdom, among subjects whose fates needed to be redirected and who needed someone to offer them a sense of happiness and a modicum of human harmony.

At the same time she stuck to the rule that it was better to go to a sorceress of a different faith because her judgments would be more reliable and accurate. If a woman oppressed by troubles was already consenting to the sin of superstition, which was forbidden under pain of hellfire in all four faiths in the kingdom, then she'd better do it up right. No matter how sinful the sorceress was herself—much more sinful than the wretched women who sought help—it was better if both of them weren't guilty before the same temple. Because of that and for reasons of a metaphysical nature, sorceresses and prophetesses had the highest value in the predominantly Christian kingdom, and it even happened that occasionally a less popular sorceress would assume a phony Turkish name.

Thus one Persida, formerly a prostitute from the Belgrade area, was known in her new job as Fatima, but soon she had to flee before the furious people of her village. No one ever heard of her again, but it seems likely that she continued to deal in fortune-telling and spells somewhere where no one knew about who she really was. Maybe in Romania or Hungary, and it wasn't impossible that Persida or Fatima made it to the West, to Vienna, Paris, or Berlin, where sorceresses from the Balkans were already making good money. They passed themselves off as Gypsies and usually opened their studios near Jewish quarters, along promenades where prostitutes walked, or attached themselves to circuses and amusement parks. Fortune-telling, tarot cards, and exorcisms of spells became so important in the '20s that it seemed that the European continent was being seized by a kind of metaphysical panic sparked by technological progress and the consequences of the war and that the true faith and religious institutions could be saved only by a great inquisitional project or an ideological insanity that would vanquish superstition and restore religious models again. When ten years later Hitler took complete control of the German spirit and the biggest part of Europe, this assumption would be proved correct. The Nazis didn't persecute sorceresses and witches because there was no need for that. Their work had lost all its meaning. The people's fear of fate had disappeared, so they could close their studios and move to parts of Europe where the majority of people were not sympathetic to the Führer's earthly mission.

Kata's fear of what she had to do was of course unwarranted. She mounted her man as French ladies mount a horse and barely got off him until the end of their life together. He had no less stamina than a horse, and it seemed that his male member was a person in and of itself, completely different from the one that lived in his head and heart. That other one of him was somehow serene and always ready, free from somber moods, but unable to get its little head to influence the bigger one. Her man consented to nightly fucks that would have completely drained anyone else, but he would also have consented to anything else, except for her to take his boxes of nails away. Kata's tenacity didn't make him happier or unhappier, but that endless intercourse did her good. She imagined she was driving the devil out of him, played, tried to kill that devil, fell from heavenly heights into soft feathery abysses, smashed into a thousand crystals and at the next moment became whole again, wept like a flock of widows, and fell off his cock crazed with laughter as if the devil had just moved from his soul to hers.

If in the daytime life with that man was like touching her tongue to a rusty anchor, the minutes and hours spent with him at night intoxicated her with a morphinic insanity. If she had been different and inclined to drunkenness and continually taking leave of her own soul, Kata might have been able to be happy with him. As it was, she didn't know how to exchange her life for the moments of pleasure in life.

She took herself off him only in the days right before she gave birth, and her sexual desire for him would return to her as early as a week or two afterward. She would hurt awfully, cramp up, and howl when she was pierced by his white hot sword, but she didn't give up. She wanted him to ask something at least once, to tell her they shouldn't really be doing that if she'd just given birth, to show himself to be living and feel that she was living too and that she hurt. Maybe that wasn't Kata's most difficult trial or the worst agony that she'd endured in her attempts to awaken her man from his eternal slumber. But it was the greatest pain, greater than any of her six childbirths. When you give birth, you can't quit, so by virtue of that it's easier, whereas at any moment in her torment with him she could have and wanted to slip his cock out of her. Stubbornness or something else on account of which she didn't want to quit either having sex with him or living with him wouldn't let her do it. Maybe that made Kata greater and braver than we acknowledged at the start, greater and braver than any of her children would ever imagine.

They didn't actually know her, nor did she know them. She raised them calmly and without passion. She would rarely grow worried, and they didn't plague her with what mothers fear. It never occurred to her that one of her children could die in a fever. She prepared compresses with vinegar, put socks soaked in brandy on their feet, watched over their nightmares and frights, but she wasn't afraid.

When three-year-old Lino died in 1915 from the Spanish flu, she sat down at the head of his bed, caressed his hair, cried softly, and grieved it down just as softly. Neither a dead child nor five living ones could tear her away from her obsession with her attempts to make a normal man of her husband.

After the children all fell asleep, she would slip into the bedroom, lock the door, shut the windows and plug every opening with rags, and climb onto him without checking whether he was awake and begin her struggle with the devil. It didn't matter that the war was already long lost; she continued what she was doing and didn't know about anything else.

The children probably didn't wake up at night and didn't come looking for her, and if they did, the noise didn't reach Kata. How could it have when the shame felt by children is so great, greater than everything that will happen in the future, greater than the cosmos and the little histories of the people in it? If any of them heard their mother howling and crying, saying words like "cunt" and "cock," repeating "fuck me, fuck me, fuck me . . ." in the dead of the night, and at the next moment when she went crazy and everything in the room—walls, the closet, the light fixture—had a soul and the soul of everything was wet and hot, if any of them heard their mother howl "split my big fat ass, stab my cunt, devil, flood into this whore, you beast"—if any of Kata's children had heard that (and the unfortunate thing was that Regina did hear it), then Kata's futile struggle and suffering would have continued even after she was no longer among the living. And it lasted until Regina breathed her last breath.

On the morning of St. Stephen's Day in 1927 Kata lay dead on the same marriage bed, her hands folded on her breast—there was just enough space for a candle to fit between her fingers, if her family wanted that—without a pillow under her head and long since cold and stiff. Outside the sirocco was blowing; Aunt Angelina was raising a panic because her sister was starting to smell and so her soul wouldn't be able to find peace. Why? She didn't know the answer, but she sensed that there must be something written about it in the holy scriptures. Little Luka was vomiting for the third time already; something had spoiled his stomach. Đuzepe was running around after his aunt like a chicken with its head cut off, assuring her that it was the cod that smelled and not his dead mother. Bepo kept quiet and sat on a stool by the stove, smoking one cigarette after another. Đovani was passing from his stage of cynicism to a higher stage of nervous disorder and looking on and off at his older brother, wanting to whack his muzzle with the cutting board and jam his cigarette down his throat. To kill him because he wasn't doing anything. He sat and waited for something to happen, for someone to come for their mother and take her out of the house, just the way people take crocks of rotten sauerkraut out of their cellars.

"Her soul will start to smell; they won't let her into heaven like that," wailed Aunt Angelina.

Regina looked at her aunt, then at Đovani. She took Luka off her lap and stealthily started to go to her mother's room before something terrible happened.

"Don't open that door!" Đovani yelled.

Regina went in, took a blanket out of the closet, and folded it up by the door. Like that the smell wouldn't spread out of the room. Then she sat down by Kata's legs, gave a deep sigh, and put her hands down into her lap. She could feel Luka's weight in them. The tingling of a child to whom she hadn't given birth but who was hers as much as one human being can belong to another. Her little brother was the biggest worry of her life. And now he'd been left an orphan, she thought, and almost reflexively sniffled. She could smell the scent of fresh starch, which reminded her of spring and children's illnesses. Her mother had changed all their sheets once a week, and when someone would fall ill in the middle of the week, she would change their sheets once more. It was nice to be sick when you were a child, she continued thinking, and sniffled quickly once more. Or she was just sniffing the air in the room. What could one smell apart from starch? The stench of wormwood from the side panels of the bed and the distant hint of rose oil. Was that the smell of death? It probably was because there hadn't ever been any rose oil in their house. But no matter what was smelling of roses, that was the most distant smell that Regina could detect. Her mother, of course, hadn't started smelling. She knew that the whole time, but she couldn't tell them. And she didn't have anyone to tell. No one could tell Aunt Angelina anything. She was crazy, crazed by who she was and not by anything loopy in her head. She was completely clear in her head, which was why her insanity was so stubborn. She would open a fashion magazine, yell, and fall into a trance as if she'd seen Jesus walking on water. She couldn't believe that such a beautiful dress existed! She couldn't believe that there were such beautiful women, like the one wearing that dress! She couldn't believe that technology had advanced so much that a photograph looked like it had a living woman in it! Here, she was going to walk right out of that fashion magazine, that most beautiful of women in that stunning dress; she would stroll right through their kitchen and run away because we're so ugly! That was what crazy Aunt Angelina would think as soon as she opened a fashion magazine. For this reason they had to hide all the fashion magazines from her. She was unbearable. She was crazy. As she was now, while she was shouting that her sister wouldn't get into heaven because she had started stinking while waiting for them to take her away. And unfortunately it was impossible to hide their mother from Aunt Angelina. It was too late to shove her under the bed. Although maybe that was what needed to be done, Regina thought. There wouldn't be anything wicked in that. If they'd known what would happen and that over Christmas there wouldn't be a funeral, they would have shoved her under the bed and shut up about it. No one, not even their aunt, would have known that Kata had died. And it would have been easier to get through all of this. As it was, they could only wait. It wasn't easy for them, but it was nevertheless hardest for her, Regina. She alone was sure that her mother hadn't started to smell. She was the only one who hadn't been infected with her aunt's insanity. She would have gladly opened the window, jumped out, run away, and wouldn't have ever come back. It was simple to disappear in a world this big. It would have been futile to look for her. It was so easy when you were gone, she thought, when you were not where everything was yours and everything was crazy.

She got up and bent over her mother's face. Kata's skin was white as the stone on Stradun and grayish-blue like the sea before a storm. She bent closer and closer to her, with her hands behind her back, bending like a branch on which children have been hanging, until she nearly brushed her nose with the tip of her own. There she stopped. Her face broke into a phony smile; she grimaced, furrowed her brow, and stuck out her tongue, taking care not to touch Kata's lips. When her spine could no longer take the weight, Regina straightened up, got to thinking for a moment, then strained and released a long, staccato fart. "There," she whispered, and sniffed the air for a few seconds, but she could still only smell starch, wormwood, and the distant traces of rose oil. She was disappointed. She turned and went out of the room. She never saw her mother again.

III

The last thing that Rafo Sikirić saw were two swollen breasts, each one bouncing in a different direction. When the left one was up, the right one was down; when one went to the right as if it were going to tear away, the other went in its own direction, and then they went back and collided, and the sweaty skin smacked. He had to strain to make out that sound among the screams and sighs, words spoken out loud, the popping of the boards of the bed, the creaking of rusty springs, a buzzing in his ears . . . That went on for years, him trying to hear the slapping of her breasts clearly, to register the moment when they both flew in the same direction, to recognize the sign that things were finally starting to work according to some logic. And then all of a sudden his eyes went dark, the tension vanished, every muscle slackened, and he felt like he was turning into a pancake.

His wife would bounce about on the pancake that was spreading out between her knees. Soon she would stop and with a deep sigh plop down onto the other side of the bed. A few seconds later she began to breathe normally, and Rafo knew that she had dropped off.

He rubbed his eyes for a long time until his sight came back. He slowly got off the bed, taking care not to wake her up, unlocked the door, and went barefoot out of the room. Regina was sleeping in the same bed as Luka. The boy had snuggled up to her as a baby chimp does to its mother. Bepo was snoring; Đuzepe was twitching in his sleep; Đovani was sleeping on the floor by the stove. There was always one child too many, and someone had to sleep on the floor. This was one more element of Rafo's unease, proof that harmony wasn't possible, and everything he set his eyes on confirmed that it was true.

There was one too much or one too little of everything. Nothing was just right. Everything was an odd number, and nothing allowed itself to be divided into two equal parts. And if there was an even number of something, then it couldn't be divided three ways . . . He closed his eyes at lunch so he wouldn't have to count the grains of rice on his plate. He only looked up at the sky on cloudy nights.

He closed the doors behind him: first one, then another, and then a third— those that led outside. He slipped on his old shoes and started down the steps in his underwear and a shirt. It was three in the morning, mid-February, a cold year. If he met someone, that would be one more sign; then he would go back home, slip back into bed beside Kata, and take care not to touch her with his icy feet. That might wake her up and remind her what she hadn't finished that night. If he'd been filling a barrel with his male seed instead of releasing it into her, the barrel would have to be full after all those years. Where did it go in her? How was it emptied? And she'd conceived only six times. That could have happened to her three times as often. One child had died, so the number would be odd. He didn't meet anyone as far as the bottom of the steps. That was a good sign. He wouldn't go back.

It took two hours for him to reach Miladin's Cliffs on foot. If he'd put on his good shoes, it wouldn't have taken as long. But half an hour more or less didn't matter anyway. If he'd put those shoes on, he would probably have changed his mind and waited for the morning, the trip to the square, the sound of sections of railway track clanging, the maddening sensation when fingernails scratch rusted metal, and then the return home, to the boxes of nails and an attempt to calm down for once. So that's what would have happened if he'd put on his new shoes. Not only that, but he would have also had to put on pants and a clean white shirt and would have woken up half the house. She would have asked him where he had been going at that time, and what could he have said?—"To Miladin's Cliffs!"

"And what are you going to do on Miladin's Cliffs?"

"I'm going to jump from up there, that's what. I'm not going to throw out a long line!"

"You're going to jump?—I should have known right away!"

That's how the story would have ended, Rafo thought, if he'd gone in his new shoes. He would have arrived half an hour earlier and wouldn't be freezing like this. He was shaking like an aspen leaf. His teeth were chattering, his jaw wouldn't keep still; he couldn't even stop it with his hands. It was stronger than his arms, which could lift sections of railway track. He tried to press it shut with his hands and break it with his fists to no avail. It would still be convulsing after he jumped down. And down below there were reefs as sharp as the spears of aborigines; they would pierce his bowels and come out through his back. That's how they would find him, with his teeth still chattering.

That idea terrified him. The dead don't move after they die, but his teeth would chatter, bite the crumbled cliffs, create a sensation worse than the touch of a fingernail to steel. Was that possible? In his case it was. If Kata's tits never went the same direction at the same time, if one child always slept on the floor, if in the box with the big nails there were always a few small ones, if everything in the house had an odd number—and that was the rule, he'd checked it a hundred times in each case—then would his teeth chatter as they did now? And if he wasn't afraid to jump, why was he thinking about this now? He wasn't—why would he?! But if maybe he still was?

He stood on Miladin's Cliffs for about ten more minutes and then started back. In his underwear, in his nightshirt, and old shoes that clattered after him, pulled only halfway on his feet. In the city it was getting light out. The fishermen were going out to sea; Konavle women were hurrying to the square with baskets on their backs and pitchers on their heads; somewhere a donkey brayed; workers were gathering at the shipyard; milking girls were clanking tin vessels. Half the city met Rafo Sikirić and thought, "Thank God and the Blessed Virgin that he's gone ahead and gone crazy!" No one felt like watching him walk a tightrope from one side to another without falling. They admired him at first, prayed for him, and then they realized that he would never get down, that there was no saving him and that for everyone, even his poor wife, it was better for him to go ahead and go completely crazy.

"What happened?" she asked, as he lay on the bed in her lap.

"What happened, dear?" she asked, and his teeth kept chattering, and every time he wanted to answer, he bit his tongue.

"What's wrong, honey?" he asked, trying desperately to be calm.

"What is it, my sunshine?"

It would have been easier if he could have started crying, to answer her in that way. But no tears would come; there weren't any.

"Do you want me to bring you your nails, my dark angel?" she asked; he rolled his eyes and thought his heart would burst.

She thought that the nails would do him good, that they were the balm of his soul. She would have brought them to him.

That thought brought him to the verge of wishing fervently for a little more life, only half an hour, a year, or a hundred years, to tell her how sorry he was. He couldn't have done anything differently, even if he'd wanted to. Now he knew that he had to, and he wanted to; he would live, even if every day were hell. He would live for her because she'd wanted to bring him his nails. She knew about them . . .

Rafo Sikirić didn't regain his composure. He shivered until evening and couldn't say a single word. Around midnight he came down with a fever and didn't wake up again. The room smelled of vinegar and brandy. Kata ran around confusedly and changed his compresses; the children stood around and didn't realize what had happened with their papa. No one did because no one actually knew what Rafo had done the previous night and that morning. Some thought he'd gone crazy. His wife and children didn't know what to think, and in the morning Dr. Focht said that he had severe pneumonia—he must have been dragging it around for weeks—and the patient wouldn't live to see the evening.

Before dawn on the next day Rafo Sikirić died without waking. He inhaled, exhaled, and turned into a dead object, one more odd number.

That was the twelfth of February, 1924, the same day when George Gershwin and Paul Whiteman's orchestra performed "Rhapsody in Blue" for the first time. Regina read the story of "Rhapsody in Blue" three years later in the same magazine in which the story about Isadora Duncan's death appeared.

"Oh, dear papa," she whispered as her throat filled with tears. She wanted to hear the music that someone had played for the first time on the other end of the world as her father was dying.

She didn't forget her wish for ten full years, up until the day when Ivo Delavale brought home a gramophone and a single record album. "Rhapsody in Blue" was like the crackling, cold howling of wolves in the distance, random plinking on piano keys, a ghastly clattering that a stranger used to mock the death of her father. Sounds without harmony or melody, irregular like nails falling one on top of another. But Ivo had carried this music across the sea, in a wooden chest that was lined with straw so the gramophone and the record album wouldn't break, and that fact touched Regina's heart more than reason would dictate.

The Gershwin episode was unique in her life because there was a balance between two contrary feelings: love and repulsion. The gramophone occupied a place of honor in their room for a few years, but she listened to "Rhapsody in Blue" only once. That was the only gramophone record in Regina's life.

If "Rhapsody in Blue" was a mistake, an enchantment with its title or the coincidence of their dates, what kind of music had she imagined for her papa? She certainly imagined some kind of music, as he hadn't been a real father, one who sat at the head of the table, sweated as he pruned the vineyard, touched the tip of his finger to the edge of his worker's hat when a priest came along, chased children around the yard when he caught them stealing apples, called to a friend on the other side of an inlet, steered clear of underwater crags, squinted at islands in the distance to size them up, untangled long lines, and hummed Zagreb hit songs . . .

Her father Rafo was none of that, nor was there any of that in any man or father figure that she could summon from memory. He'd hardly spoken to her ten times in his life, had never asked for anything or given her any orders, but when she would come to him or called to him from the opposite side of the square, he smiled and showed that he was glad and did it in a manner that made him different from other fathers. He smiled like that only to her because she alone was his child. He barely noticed his sons at all. That was easier for him since they didn't treat him like their papa. They knew that they shouldn't bother him while he was sorting his nails, but otherwise it was as if he weren't there. If they did something wrong, they were afraid of their mother. If they wanted to get on someone's good side, again they went to her. Regina felt that that had to have hurt him and knew that he didn't dare show it. Nothing in this matter could change, except that she could show constantly that she was his child. He accepted that, her mother didn't even notice, and the brothers didn't care.

And then he died. Such an injustice couldn't have happened by chance. Someone had to be blamed for it. Who? Regina's brothers—because they didn't love him? Or her mother—because she pestered him to be like others? Or was the whole world to blame since it wasn't made according to his measure? And that measure was more honest and beautiful than any other. Still, Regina was to blame most of all: since she'd gone from being a child to a young woman (she was going on nineteen when he died), she had gone to him less and tried less to catch his attention and get him to smile. Had she done that only once or twice a day (often she would lure a smile out of him ten times in a day), maybe he wouldn't have left that night, fallen ill and died. She was the last but also the first good thing to happen in his life. So when that stopped, papa had to slip away. Whenever she was thinking like that, she would hear his music: silence produced by the fingers of a drowned man when he grabbed for a branch that wasn't there, in the middle of a sea that wasn't there. She heard a choir of island laborers on the barren ground behind a church, where illegitimate children, vagrants, and drowned men washed up by the sea were buried, the singing of sailors on a sunken galley, the poorest of the poor, drowned in a battle with the Turks. Male voices sang in harmony together, one next to another. They raised their red hats on axes, looked up at the sky, and blasphemed so terribly that the blood of the pious froze in their veins. Shallowly buried bones protruded from the ground. It was hard to tell the difference between the top of a crag that had been washed a thousand times by rain and the smooth, completely round skulls of suicides and orphans.

Rafo Sikirić was the youngest of twelve living children of his mother Matija and his father Josip. He was born far too late in the lives of his parents, a miracle about which the Viennese press reported. Namely, Matija Sikirić, née Valjan, had brought a live and healthy child into the world one month before her sixty-second birthday. Doctors from all corners of the Habsburg empire went to Trebinje, and Emperor Franz Joseph—the idolized monarch who, after occupying Bosnia the year before, was at the height of his power—sent a letter to Josip and

Matija in which he communicated to them how moved he was by the birth of their child and that he wanted to be its godparent. A special emissary from the Sarajevo military administration, Colonel Steiner, arrived with imperial gifts and explained to the father, Josip, and the mother, Matija, exactly what the emperor's godparenthood meant. Until the child's eighteenth birthday monetary support would be paid to the name of his guardians, to the amount of the salary of a second-class government official, and after the boy finished high school, he would be offered the possibility to continue his education in accordance with his talents and wishes at the emperor's expense, in Vienna, Zagreb, Budapest, Prague, or Bratislava . . .

While the Colonel listed off the cities where Rafo could study, the two elderly parents huddled together and didn't really understand anything. Josip had already reached eighty and hadn't been doing anything for a long time but was now a burden to his children. His mind was already slipping away, and he still hadn't entirely gotten used to the fact that the Turkish sultan had been replaced by the Austrian emperor. The only thing that kept him alive was his sexual desire, which had almost cost him his head. Namely, when Josip's sons had realized that their mother was pregnant in the twilight of her life and that she was going to give birth to a sister or brother of theirs, at a time when they already had children themselves, they went crazy. Mostly because of the shame they assumed would come when all of Herzegovina and half of Dalmatia heard that an old woman—their mother!—had had a baby. If it weren't for the imperial godparenthood, this would have been a great shame and an occasion for the kind of gossip that went on for more than one summer and was often a source of family nicknames. But since the emperor had intervened, it turned out that it wasn't a shame but a great, if completely incomprehensible, honor.

It was almost as if they'd become nobility when the Austrian colonel made his entry into their family home bearing gifts. At the time of Rafo's birth, his oldest sister was going on forty-five and had three grandchildren, while his youngest brother had already turned eighteen. It was this other difference that was the greatest source of amazement for the Austrian doctors. How was it possible for a woman to give birth to fifteen children—four of which were stillborn or had died in the first years of their lives—between her sixteenth and forty-fifth years and for nothing else to happen for seventeen years, only to have one more at sixty-two?! They tried to ask the flabbergasted Matija questions about her menstrual cycle. At first she didn't understand, then she started crossing herself and praying to the Virgin Mary to chase the demons out of her house. After they persisted, she called upon St. Elijah to strike the Austrian Kaiser with lightning and bring back the good sultan. In short, no matter how they tried, the doctors were unable to discover the secret of Rafo's entry into the world, and there were indeed those among them who doubted that Matija had given birth to him.

"It'll probably turn out that it's an illegitimate child of one of the old woman's daughters. These people are primitive, something between men and animals. They slip their young to one another like cuckoo birds," Dr. Gerlitzky observed to his younger colleagues. The old Bratislava bloodhound ignored the Čapljina midwife Jovanka when she swore that she'd assisted in Matija's childbirth. He was unmoved by the fact that the old woman's breasts were producing milk. "Female hysteria knows no bounds! A woman can piss gold if she convinces herself she can do it!" the doctor fumed.

But the majority still believed that this was a medical miracle, so Rafo's case entered into Austrian and German textbooks on physiology and child-birth. True, it was mentioned only as a statistical exception because it couldn't be scientifically analyzed due to Matija's refusal to cooperate. Regardless, the birth of Rafo Sikirić was the second Herzegovinian contribution to theoretical medicine in the Habsburg empire. (The first and most important was endemic syphilis.)

The boy became the family pet, partly because of the money that arrived every month from Vienna, and partly because his brothers and sisters treated him more like a Habsburg prince than like the belated offspring of their own mother. They had a feeling that if something bad happened to Rafo—if, God forbid, he fell from an apple tree or some idiot hit him in the head with a rock—they could all end up in prison. And in the terrible Beledija prison in Sarajevo to boot, a place that was the source of dark legends in Herzegovina, spun mostly by tobacco smugglers who invoked Beledija to frighten one another. To make a long story short, one of his older siblings always had the task of looking after Rafo all day long, following him wherever he went, making sure that he wasn't hungry or thirsty. In the general poverty of the Sikirić household and the wide-spread poverty of the region of Trebinje, such treatment was almost unseemly. It ended up not doing him any good.

Old Josip Sikirić died the second winter after Rafo's birth, and more people came to his funeral than would have been expected given his poverty and un-sociable nature—he was never seen in bars or at get-togethers. But the tale of Josip's fertility—worthy of the imperial blessing—grew into a legend, and the people turned that pauper into a notable. Twenty years after Josip's death the women of Trebinje still picked stones off of his grave and secretly put them in the pockets of their insufficiently potent and fertile husbands. The belief in the magical power of those little stones would wane only at the turn of the cen-tury, when the tale of the "male water" of Kladanj spread through Bosnia and

Herzegovina. That otherwise tasty and very drinkable mountain water, rich in minerals, would overshadow many local legends about fertility and would be in demand even in Vienna.

Rafo's mother Matija would depart six months after Josip. On one summer afternoon she just lay down and never got up again. Naturally, no one came to her funeral. Only the family and a few neighbors. But a letter from His Excellency did arrive in which he called Matija one of the most courageous mothers in the monarchy and a model wife of the region of Herzeg-Bosnia. That was an obvious sign, though not for Trebinje, that the emancipation of women had made great progress in Austria-Hungary, but also that there was a considerable difference between the Balkan and West European views of the mystery of human birth. The Balkan peoples were fascinated by the man who impregnated the woman, and the Westerners respected the fact that she'd brought the child into the world. The difference in these perspectives explains why the monarchy couldn't grow together along its Balkan seams. The rationalism of the Habsburgs was more repugnant than the rule of the sultan to these mystics and metaphysicians.

But in that year of 1880 it was too early for anyone to understand that the new state wouldn't come to a good end. Which state did? Not in human history has there been a state that didn't collapse and on the eve of its collapse didn't seem to its subjects to be the most ridiculous and worst of all states that had ever been created. That's simply the fate of this kind of human community: it's born in blood and dies in the realization that it was born for no reason. This banal repetition of the same old fates of countries, not favored by divine intent, was where the small lives of men began and ended. Rafo's was one of the smallest. He'd barely started walking and speaking his first words when he lost his father and mother. Not only did he not remember them, but later family stories about them would seem like legends of distant ancestors. They'd lived their lives long before his turn came. Instead of parents, he had brothers and sisters, eleven of them, who took the place of his father and mother in turns, on different days.

Until he started school, he seemed like other children. He laughed as much as they did, cried as much as they did, and endured his princely position fairly well. The fact that he received more than others didn't stir him to ask for more than he got. At the Trebinje market people told how there was no better and smarter child than Rafo and that his mother had never given birth to a child like him. Rafo was an angel but also living proof that Franz Joseph was a wise ruler.

"The emperor knows whose godparent he will be, and the eagle knows what kind of chicks are being laid in its nests," the Christians said, trying to provoke the now powerless beys of Trebinje.

"Rafo's no Mujo, and the Kaiser isn't an Istanbul fatass," they said loudly wherever Turkish ears could hear them.

And the beys wouldn't say anything in response to their remarks but slowly packed their things for the trek to the free East and mumbled among themselves that the future didn't bode well for either the German empire or that child.

There was no malice in their words, nor could there be any. Even before Turkey had renounced Bosnia, they realized that they'd clung to life by an unlikely trick of fate, though their time had passed. It was the first time in the world that someone had outlived his own age. In the next century it would happen to many. But it should be remembered that it began with the Bosnian beys and that they endured their fate (with few exceptions) with dignity and an unscathed sense that they meant something in this world.

In those days and months and in the years that followed, until they emigrated or assimilated to the citizenry, drank themselves to death, went crazy, or gave themselves over to religion, the Trebinje beys looked on everything they saw with melancholy.

They looked on the land with melancholy. And on the Viennese emperor too. They looked with melancholy on their estates, which were being invaded by common folk of all three faiths. And they looked on that child with melancholy too. Imperial grace and generosity wouldn't bring it happiness but unhappiness. A person is made happy only by what falls to his lot by God's calendar and design. Everything else loads trouble onto his back. And it can't be that a poor child, no matter which faith he was, could have any kind of ruler as a godparent and closest relative. That was what the beys thought about the fate of little Rafo.

Naturally it wasn't to their taste, and naturally there was hardly any wisdom in such apparently wise words that align the stars over men's heads, but something really did change in Rafo as soon as he started going to school. Though he was a smart boy who remembered things easily and could repeat after the teacher even more easily, none of what was taught stuck in his head. He studied what he had to, understood what was expected of him, but could get no use out of either. He would connect new things that he was learning with what he'd already learned only if someone pointed it out to him or ordered him to do it. Otherwise he would study everything as if it were for the first time. For instance, he learned all the letters of the alphabet more quickly than other children, but it took him a long time to learn to connect them into words. And even then he knew how to write certain words but without an awareness of how they were spelled.

This inexplicable disorder went hand in hand with Rafo's withdrawal into himself and the loss of any interest in being with the people around him. After he finished the fourth grade, he gave the impression of a tired, sad old man.

He would run only if he had to, he participated in children's games only when asked to, and he no longer laughed. He slipped through the children like a shadow, rarely said a word, and mostly sat under a pear tree in the schoolyard and waited for Ilijas the janitor to signal the end of recess with a cow rattle. He mastered the skill of disappearing. He wouldn't go off anywhere; people knew that he was somewhere around. But if anyone were asked at some moment where Rafo was, no one knew, though Rafo was there, two paces away from them. You had to look really hard, peel your eyes, to see that Rafo was right there. And there wasn't a child or an adult who was immune to that skill of his. If it was a skill and if some other word or explanation wasn't required.

As the Austrian empire sprawled out in Bosnia and Herzegovina and began to burden and impose on the people like every other empire, the Christians lost their desire to fill their Muslim neighbors' ears with talk about Rafo who was no Mujo and the Kaiser who was no Istanbul fatass, so the Muslims also forgot about the child. The only people for whom he continued to be important and who kept caring for him with unabated fervor were his brothers, sisters, and the office of the Austrian emperor.

Thus, regardless of Rafo's poor grades, it was decided that he should continue his schooling at the Boys' Classical Preparatory School in Sarajevo, a school that had been recently opened and enriched the pride of the city authorities because it was patterned after the best Viennese models, with a select cadre of teachers who had been brought from all ends of the monarchy.

On the thirtieth of August, 1891, Rafo went to Sarajevo. He was seen off to his secondary schooling by his whole family, which in the meantime had grown and spread, partly on his imperial appanage. Thirty some-odd Sikirićes, every-one except Rafo's niece, who was just being born, went to the newly built rail-way station in Dubrovnik, and all of them, including three illiterate brothers, were enchanted by the historical significance of the moment. The first Sikirić was going to the big city, not to be a servant but to pass through some magic whereupon others would be his servants. It was hard to imagine and harder still to describe that excitement! It was surely no less than people's excitement when man first stepped on the surface of the moon. People would start revolu-tions to experience what the Sikirićes experienced. Millions of heads would fall to the ground dead in the twentieth century due to such excitement; the con-tinent would drift out to sea; some nations would disappear and others would be born; athletic records would be broken, and humanity would be overcome with a fever on account of which not even the winters would be cold any more . . . Emperor Franz Joseph had granted the Sikirićes something that was bigger than all the valuables in all his treasuries.

Rafo was the only one who didn't feel the significance of the moment, though he knew what was going through his brothers' heads. But why was it given to him of all people to carry the burden of their happiness? There was no answer to that question, nor was there any hope that anything could be changed. Only great misery and tears that he didn't have to hide. They thought that he was crying because he was leaving home, that he felt sad because he wouldn't be seeing Trebinje for a long time, and they almost felt pride. If you were sorry when you left for paradise, that meant their town square was worth something after all. They tried to console Rafo, hugged and kissed him, and he yielded to his misfortune, certain that the imperial curse had caught up with him. He who wanted more than anything for the whole world to leave him alone.

Invisibility did the boy good; he could spend days like that without ever getting bored, happy in some inverted fashion, which was incomprehensible to others. On the way to Sarajevo he discovered the beauty of tunnels. While the wheels clattered through the darkness, Rafo could be whatever he wanted. For the first time in his life. And it didn't matter that he had no wishes and that he didn't care. He felt ashamed to his heart's content, blushed in the darkness like a carrot in the ground, and at times he felt like shouting for joy. But such shouts would have been heard; they would have risen above the grating of the steel and the coupling rods that were colliding wildly and destroying anything in their path, so he said nothing and tried to hold his breath until they emerged from the tunnel and people started interpreting the flush on his cheeks in the wrong way. The child was traveling by train for the first time, and the capillaries in his brain almost burst from fear.

Lunchtime had passed when the train arrived in Mostar, where everyone had to change to another trainset that was going to leave for Sarajevo in two hours. The dispatchers and conductors would pronounce the word *trainset* with a special dignity in their voices, as if they were speaking about Mozart or Brahms, and take every possible opportunity to mention the Sarajevo trainset.

"Please purchase tickets for the Sarajevo trainset in the station," they reminded the passengers, though most of them weren't traveling any farther than Mostar.

"The Sarajevo trainset will be brought up forty minutes prior to departure . . . The trainset is equipped with a special restaurant car, a Viennese restaurant on steel wheels—a wonder of the world . . . ! The Sarajevo trainset departs punctually and never arrives with a delay at its final destination . . . Spitting on the floor of the trainset is strictly forbidden . . . ! The trainset consists of six, seven, or nine cars. We cannot know in advance . . . ! The trainset has the strength of a thousand of the strongest horses in the empire, which stretches from the northern to the southern seas . . . ! The trainset is a marvel of human engineering; the good

Allah will have to try hard to create a greater miracle . . . ! If we nevertheless run late, it's not due to the trainset but to objective circumstances on the route . . . ! Woman, are you continuing on with the trainset . . . ? Well, you don't need the trainset; you're already crazy enough on your own!" The Herzegovinian railway workers spoke their sweet speech in rhythm and made a clear distinction between trains and trainsets. What ran from Dubrovnik to Mostar was an ordinary train, but the unprecedented marvel that would take selected passengers to Sarajevo was a *trainset*. Why? Well, you'll find out, you who'll have the luck and a reason to travel beyond Mostar! When you cross the invisible line that divides Herzegovina from Bosnia, you'll understand right away when God quit creating the world and at which moment he started making a trainset out of it. It was easy to imagine the envy that the travelers on a train felt toward those who would continue their journey on the trainset.

The name of the midget assigned to accompany Rafo from Dubrovnik to Sarajevo was Alija, and he worked in the Trebinje city administration stoking fireplaces and ovens. They chose him of all people so the boy wouldn't experience a shock as soon as he sat down in the train. There was no more ordinary or simpler person than Alija in the city administration, so the little boy would have an easier time adapting to and accepting his transition from one world to another. Even an adult would be frightened the first time he went from a carriage to a steel behemoth and a locomotive replaced horses, so how wouldn't a child?! But Alija accepted the task like a reward for his faithful service to the emperor and his homeland. He'd never dreamed of being able to see beautiful Sarajevo, and he told Rafo everything he was going to do in Sarajevo until his return to Trebinje, down to the smallest detail. He would buy roasted chickpeas and sweets for the children, buy the prettiest silk kerchief for his wife Nafa in the Bezistan Market. Then he would stroll streets where only gentlemen walked and go to the Alipaša Mosque, where the daily prayers were recited by Hafiz Sulejmanaga Ferizoglu, the most intelligent hafiz west of Damascus. Hafiz Ferizoglu knew not only the honorable Koran by heart, but also everything the Muslim mind had thought up from the beginning of time . . . And after all that Alija would go to Skenderija, which was probably some street in the middle of Sarajevo where real Vienna whores sold you-know-what! But those weren't just any whores; they weren't like Saveta and Kata in Trebinje—they were wild girls, the prettiest there were, and there were few like them even in the sultan's harem! They'd gone to school for their trade; they even have those kind of schools in Vienna, so they knew how to turn men into roosters and stallions, into Rudonja the bull, whose seed was paid for in ducats. Alija wouldn't go to bed with the Sarajevo low women, Allah forbid, because how would he look Nafa in the eye and how would he perform the abdest? He just wanted to get a look at them. He'd been hearing tales of their beauty for ten years; anyone from the city administration who went to Sarajevo was bewitched by the low women, and there were also men who wouldn't touch their own wives with a ten-foot pole after they had gone to bed with them. The file clerk Hamza had been with three low women and had lost his mind when he got back to Trebinje. When they mounted you and started singing their German songs, you forgot who you were and whom you belonged to. You turned into a winged charger, and it seemed to you that—God forgive me—the houries of paradise were spurring you onward. There was no greater sin, and Alija wasn't going to burden his soul with that, even if he didn't love his wife. But he loved her so much that even now he felt empty without her, so he would just peep into the yards with the Viennese whores, get a whiff of their fragrances—and they surely smelled of roses and jasmine. Because what could smell better than roses and jasmine? Then he would run outside so the spell wouldn't intoxicate him—God forbid—and lead him into temptation.

Alija babbled constantly and regardless of the fact that he was sitting beside a boy whose whiskers hadn't even started growing and who, in all likelihood, had no idea about any kind of female spells.

Rafo listened to him and nodded. He could have repeated everything that Alija said between Dubrovnik and Mostar, but it didn't concern him, nor did he think about what the midget was saying. He was preoccupied with his own torments and would only occasionally lower his gaze to Alija's feet, which didn't reach the floor. When Alija got completely carried away by his enthusiasm for Sarajevo and the low women, he would squirm on the bench and kick with his feet like a little boy. In that scene there was a sorrow that Rafo could easily bond with.

In Mostar they went to eat borek before the Sarajevo trainset was moved up.

"That's what Herr Heydrich ordered," Alija said darkly and irrefutably. Rafo knew that he had to eat, even though his stomach was contracting from misery, because if he didn't eat the borek Alija would probably collapse from fear before that Herr Heydrich. The midget said his name with fear, and it was very probable that he regretted that he himself wasn't of a heroic nature. Because if he were, he would have kept quiet about the borek, and then he would have had more money for the roasted chickpeas, the sweets, and the kerchief. He would have cheated the emperor and the state and gotten by better in life. That was possible, Alija thought, but God hadn't granted him to be like that. Whoever was granted this would get rich, spend his earthly days in luxury, and end up in dark *jahannam*. Alija was comforted because this was so, but again he couldn't understand why his heart filled with pain if it was true that God sees everything and thieves go to hell. Difficult questions for his little mind! He had to get them out of his head, especially on that day when he was going on this, his longest journey, with which he'd been rewarded for his faithful service to the Viennese emperor. It was true that it was an earthly recognition, but it wouldn't have come to pass without the approval of the great Allah, who sees everyone and knows everything. The emperor's will was collaborating with the will of God. It pays to be good, he thought, as he watched Rafo struggling with the borek. Herr Heydrich had reminded him to buy himself some borek too. But if he told Heydrich that he hadn't been hungry, he wouldn't ask Alija to return the money. Herr Heydrich wasn't stingy. Herr Heydrich was a gentleman.

"Hey, how about that trainset?!" Alija gaped like a fish, and Rafo wasn't indifferent when from a sideline there appeared a locomotive that was twice the size of the one from the Dubrovnik train, black as tar and gleaming like a girl's hair. It was pulling four cars, and a glance was all it took to tell that they were more luxurious than the most luxurious carriages in which Ali-pasha Rizanbegović had ridden during the time of the Turks whenever he would go to Trebinje.

"Lord have mercy! By the power of Allah!" Alija said, folding his hands and walking around the trainset in amazement. But he did so cautiously so as not to disturb or break anything and be charged for it afterward. And so the trainset wouldn't suddenly jump up and bite him on the nose.

It seemed as if Rafo smiled too. Or maybe it just seemed so. That midget was growing on him, with his little feet that swung back and forth when he was excited, as was his enthusiasm, as a mutt has when it gets excited about something but is afraid to go closer to it. Rafo had never met anyone like Alija in his life. He was small, so every mood took hold of all of him, not just half or three-quarters. If one of Rafo's moods took hold of all of him, he would burn up in a minute like a match, or he would vanish like a piece of hail that falls in a yard in the middle of the August heat. But Alija was good; he was all happy five minutes after he was all unhappy. He would have started getting on someone else's nerves, and maybe he did—Rafo would have to ask people who had known Alija longer. But Rafo came to like him. It wasn't that he didn't like other people, but Alija was the first person about whom one could say that he really liked him. It was easy to disappear in front of Alija. But when Rafo disappeared, Alija kept acting like he was there.

They'd hardly taken their places in the trainset—the car was, to be sure, half empty, but God forbid that Alija would sit in someone else's seat!—and the locomotive had hardly started pulling the cars on their way when he suggested they go to the Viennese restaurant on wheels.

He'd remembered the conductor's words verbatim, and there was no chance that he would distort something or misrepresent it. Rafo liked the game. He imagined how the midget would be surprised and everything he would say and was entertained by his happiness.

The interior of the restaurant car was all gold-plated and covered with ornaments, with a shag carpet on the floor, lounge chairs and tables of carved wood, and with strange curves. Two waiters were wearing formal railway uniforms with strange yellow fringes, ribbons, and epaulettes. If one had the impression that the imperial railway happened to be introducing military ranks, then the waiters would be generals and the conductors ordinary soldiers. Alija gently stepped back in the face of those figures, who looked at him lazily and somewhat scornfully. There was no one else in the Viennese restaurant on wheels, and the waiters didn't think that the midget and the boy looked like potential customers at all. Instead of yielding to melancholy and drawing a long face at the beauty of the car and not noticing that they were looking at him or losing his nerve and saying, "Let's get out of here!" Alija bravely stepped on in, grabbed Rafo by the hand, and with unexpected authority said, "You sit here!"

And then he went around the table and hopped up on a chair that was too high for him.

Maybe someone would think this scene was funny, but the waiters didn't even manage a smirk, nor did they think of noticing how the midget's feet hung down because Alija turned around ever so slightly, as if his neck were stiff, and with the baritone voice of a Herzegovinian aga barked:

"Young man! Some service!"

The waiters came skipping with the manners of third-class circus performers when their act goes wrong. Alija leaned on the little table with his elbow and waved in the direction of the older one with his little finger, following the rhythm of his own words: "For the boy, raspberry juice, and brandy for me. Grape brandy! No, no; bring me plum brandy, but don't let it get over twenty-five degrees. If it's over twenty-five degrees, it doesn't agree with my stomach, and I'll give it back to you. And I won't pay you because I told you nicely that it can't be more than twenty-five degrees!"

The waiters looked at him with a kind of fear that people of the twentieth century know nothing about and have a hard time understanding even when people try to conjure it up for them with images. It wasn't the fear of a weakling in the face of a bully but the fear of a Bosnian commoner before a grand vizier— fear before a grim glance behind which hides intelligence, power, confidence, tradition, and the law of heaven and earth. It was the fear that in people who are given to feel it tears away every inner and outer support. Before the vizier they were pathetic and small, even in those things that had never occurred to the vizier himself. And that's how the waiters of the restaurant car were as Alija was telling them what he wanted.

In an instant raspberry juice and brandy were on the table—it wasn't a smidgen warmer than twenty-five degrees! Rafo then saw clearly for the first time the face of that man. Earlier Alija had continually laughed, made faces, complained, frowned like a child, and changed ten expressions in five minutes, and each one was as if his face was made of rubber and created for humility of any kind. The faces of the humble are harder to remember than the words of a strange and completely incomprehensible language. But in the restaurant car the pauper turned into a grim and languid aga whose bright eyes didn't show a tepid soul but radiated fountains locked in ice in the middle of January. His face was symmetrical and typically Herzegovinian, with chiseled wrinkles wherever they are according to the rules of mature male beauty. Alija was another man. Rafo sensed that he had a protector, someone who watched over his outer and inner worlds equally. Alija knew that and was glad.

He grabbed the boy by the hand, remembered something, and started singing through his nose, softly, so the waiters wouldn't hear him: "May your repose be great, enormous, endless . . ."

As he paid the bill, Alija didn't even show with a misplaced flash of his eye that he'd just reduced by half the gifts that he meant to take home to his family. He knew that the raspberry juice and the plum brandy would cost so much; it was clear to him as soon as they stepped into the Viennese restaurant on wheels, but the price wasn't too high for him. He regretted every kreuzer that he'd paid for the borek, but the money that he'd just spent would have bought three pans of borek. He could have fed the Dubrovnik-Mostar train and the Mostar-Sarajevo trainset, but that was something else. He'd bought the borek on orders, whereas the raspberry juice and the plum brandy had nothing to do with Herr Heydrich or the radiant emperor. No one would reimburse him for the money he had spent, but was that important? And could anyone really reimburse such expenses? Honor and hospitality have no price. And it was no accident that those two words—*čast* and *čašćenje*—were so similar, though their meanings were different. The language wasn't stupid, even if the people that spoke it could be. Alija knew that well, just as he knew that Allah wouldn't hold it against him if he downed a brandy here and there. Bosnia was a land of brandy; every Turk knew it. Even those who'd never in their lives violated God's law and drunk a drop from a bottle knew it. And it was a land of brandy not only because of its plums and vineyards, but also because of the effort that it took to make brandy. Allah didn't measure every person, all of his sons and daughters, by the same ell, but took into account whether someone lived in the mountains, where the fog didn't lift until May; or lived on the seacoast, where the bora blew through a man's ribs; or lived in the desert, where it was always scorching hot and your head started to boil every so often even without brandy. Allah wouldn't reproach him even for the rage and spite that made him spend money. You couldn't look at someone you knew nothing about the way the waiters had looked at him. If someone was going to humiliate him out of the blue, then he was clearly going to humiliate them three times worse.

He sat down by the window and looked down at the Neretva, above which a canyon rose up into the sky. Gray shadows were laid softly one on top of another like layers of phyllo dough in a thick cheese borek. They wound and curved as if a giant hand were crumpling them in the borek before it let green water flow in between them. What had God had in mind when he piled them up like that? And then He planted a single pine tree on top of the highest bluff. That pine grew out of the stone; Alija saw clearly that there was no soil up there. When the wind blew, the pine clutched the cliff with its roots, and through the cliff it clung to the entire world. Anything you might touch at any spot in the whole wide world and wherever you stepped and whatever you sat down on so you could rest was a part of what that pine above the Neretva was holding on to. And there was no place on the globe that was so far away that it didn't belong to that pine. In the face of such a wonder a man had to be quiet. In the face of other wonders one was supposed to be loud and rejoice at them. The first kind were greater than the second kind. The pine growing out of that rock was a greater wonder than the trainset in which they were riding.

Rafo sat across from him but didn't notice the same sights. As he looked at Alija, his own solitude returned to him. A feeling that it was crazy to believe that it was possible not to be alone. As soon as you took a better look at something, you began to notice that it was moving away from you. If you looked at it long enough, you realized that it would soon disappear. It was the same way with Alija. And so it was better to stop watching him because he might disappear too. And that would be a pity, a great loss, the greatest that Rafo could think of before he shut his eyes, only to see Alija's feet swinging in the air a few seconds later because he'd remembered that some young men dive from the bridge in Mostar. They weren't afraid at all. And Alija had been terrified of looking down when he'd been in Mostar for his job two years before and had climbed up to the middle of the bridge. Herr Heydrich had sent him because it was his daughter's birthday, and they were baking her a cake in the Kaltz pastry shop. Herr Heydrich didn't like our desserts. He said that he thought baklava was too sweet, and Bosnian poached apples were too low class. Whoever heard of stuffing apples with walnuts?! If that were meant to be, Heydrich fumed, Eve wouldn't have bitten into the apple, but Ismo the boza maker would have brought her a poached apple. Herr Heydrich was a man of the world and knew that well. Our desserts weren't world-class; they were just ours, Bosnian. And who were we? Nobody and nothing. If we hadn't had Austria, we would have been left as orphans on the globe. Even Istanbul had washed its hands of us after a few hundred years. Why wouldn't it?! The Turks had too many headaches with Bosnia, and even more with Herzegovina. No gain at all, but the expense was tremendous! Both in blood and gold, or whatever you wanted! And then our beys went ape! They put fezzes on their heads, took their muskets out in the sun, and spread their cushions out on the dirty ground. They sunned their butts a little and started a few rebellions and uprisings! They said they weren't going to listen to what the sultan said but were going to do as they pleased. You couldn't tell them anything! Of course the Turks got up and left. Better to steer clear of lunatics; and we're lunatics and don't do ourselves any good, and so others—bigger, better, and smarter—can't do us any good either. Oh, how can Trebinje measure up to Istanbul?! That would be like little Alija challenging that acrobat from Prizren to a duel, the one who the year before had broken heavy chains with three fingers! God forbid if Austria ever gets tired of us and leaves. God pity whoever lives to see that!

Good Alija thought some of that and told some of it to Rafo while the train-set crept and crawled along Mt. Ivan, so slowly that they could have gone out and picked wild strawberries along the track. Alija might have suggested they go out, but it was dark, and if there were any strawberries, no one could have seen them. As the locomotive struggled along the last ascent before Bradina, they fell asleep one after the other. And no one knew who drifted off first while the steel wheels spun and recited their zikr, as if in the middle of a ring of dervishes.

The shouts of the railway porters awoke Rafo. Alija, coiled up, kept snoring and wouldn't have woken up until the conductors threw him out. In those years people with light sleep were rare. People fell asleep wherever they managed to, and they slept deeply and without fear of being woken up. Light sleepers are another invention of the twentieth century and a modern age in which life is easier, the body is exerted less and wasted less, and the soul has it harder and harder, so it never really gets a good night's sleep.

The platforms were as crowded as Purgatory. There were porters, people selling boza and popcorn, train dispatchers, pickpockets, town criers, people waiting for someone, policemen and spies in plainclothes, coquettes and women in black, Gypsies and cripples missing arms and legs, Krauts with disgusting expressions and their beautiful wives, travelers and clerks from provincial post offices, emigrants of all kinds, people with big butts, big eyes, or big beards, bald men, those who smelled of feces, and those who looked at everything around them more sinisterly than dogs. There were lowlifes and dolts, high-class gentlemen, traveling singers, people invited to municipal picnics, and an unfamiliar mass of people about whom no one knew which class they belonged to or what their story was. When a train arrived in the station, they all began pushing and shoving each other and sticking their fingers in others' pockets, so much that it looked just as if Noah was preparing for another voyage and everyone needed to get aboard as soon as possible to escape the flood. Alija grabbed Rafo firmly by the hand; he wasn't going to lose him now when his mission was nearing its end, and the boy trembled with fear.

Freshly awoken, he wasn't sure that he hadn't passed from one slumber to another and wasn't dreaming that he was awake when he'd really sunk deeper into sleep, into a nightmare beyond all nightmares, which he'd known had existed for a long time. Everyone knew it and awoke from bad dreams happy because they hadn't dreamed those uglier dreams. The faces of these men and women, old and young, and even of the children were without exception threatening. They laughed wickedly and shouted wickedly, and the Sarajevo speech—Rafo was hearing it for the first time—had rough and hard accents. As if those people had never felt open spaces but were all squeezed into a fit of slurring, grating their teeth, and hissing.

Grayish-yellow boza spilled on the platform; there was the fragrance of salep, intense and intoxicating like medicine given to a dying patient so his suffering might be eased with the illusion that it could be treated. Hot halva was smeared on blue packing paper and dripped down the sleeves of sweaters of undyed wool. In the distance one could hear a chorus of dogs howling and barking; the recently established dog pound was working at full force.

Beyond the high mountains, the likes of which neither Rafo nor Alija had ever seen, the red morning sky was spreading out. In a few minutes, the valley, which the city filled from one end to another, was flooded with stark colors that hurt the eye and sent a tingling up one's spine and all the way to the skull, which Goethe (who was still unknown in Sarajevo) had claimed was the last vertebra. Alija saw the minarets of a hundred mosques—did Istanbul have as many? Instead of a dusty road beneath his feet, there was a black pavement that had no end; in every direction there were buildings with five or six stories—how could their foundations hold up such big houses? Women with uncovered calves passed by—were they the low women, and were there really so many of them? Married women in headscarves passed by, but they too hurried as if their legs were naked and they didn't know how to cover them up . . .

It took time for the two of them to pull themselves together and remember the reason for their arrival in that unbelievable place, in that city, which was bigger and more powerful than what any living person could imagine a city could be. Rafo still hadn't realized that he was going to stay there, and Alija was already sorry that he was going to leave. He took a piece of paper out of his pocket. It said where he was supposed to take the boy but didn't say in whose care he was supposed to leave him. That wouldn't worry Alija, not a chance!—because the little boy was nevertheless the emperor's godchild, and no matter how big Sarajevo was, everyone here also had to know what it meant to be a bud of the soul of Franz Joseph II. He wasn't the godfather of just anyone! Because even if he were emperor a hundred times, he couldn't be a godparent ten times. Seven or eight was enough! Alija was overcome with pride, and his self-confidence returned because he'd concluded that Trebinje had what Sarajevo didn't.

On the left bank of the Miljacka, when one crossed the Latin Bridge, a three-story house had been built in the western fashion way back during the time of the Turks. Ivan Karadža had built it, an important merchant and a coach driver who maintained links with Dubrovnik and Venice that weren't broken even during the time of rebellions and wars, when all links would be broken and trading caravans had to be accompanied by strong units of the sultan's soldiers. Karadža, however, didn't need the sultan's soldiers, nor was he afraid of highway robbers. He always had agreements with all warring sides and rebels, and the highway robbers didn't touch him because he always made efforts to have a reputation worse than those escorting the robbers. Two or three times, during a time of great hunger and Karađorđe's revolts in Serbia, some wretches attacked Karadža's caravan, but neither were any of his men hurt, nor did the robbers get away with any loot. No one knew for certain what happened to those robbers, except that it was well known that none of them made it back home.

People said that Ivan Karadža would cut out their eyes, that he would tear out their fingernails, and that on the night of the big party that followed every attack he would light a fire with his own hands and build it up to a great blaze. Then he would tie the leader of the robbers to a skewer with a wire and roast him alive. And it was told on the square that he did it so that only the man's lower half, from the waist down, would be on the heat. The leader would live long enough to see when Karadža took a knife and cut a good piece of fatty meat and smeared it with a bulb of onion on the victim's eyes. That was only one of the horror stories about Karadža, and there were more. Some concerned Karadža's alleged taste for pederasty and sodomy—these contained even more horrible details, but no one knew the truth. Ivan himself never denied a single story about himself, so if anyone said anything ugly to him or accused him of anything, he just walked gentlemanly on by. He dressed in the latest bourgeois fashion, and around 1820 he was the first Sarajevan to walk the city in a top hat. He caught the eye of many a young woman, including Muslim married women, because he was handsome and strong. The Ottomans valued him, the local authorities respected him, and he allegedly had a good reputation with the merchants and diplomats of Istanbul.

When in 1878 Baron Filipović's troops were already fighting for Pašino Brdo and entering the town, Karadža got out of his sick bed, dressed up, put on his hat, and went off to the city administration, taking one step at a time.

He was already almost one hundred. People had already started gradually forgetting both him and the legends about him, but he found it proper to go to the Turkish city administration, express his condolences on the ceding of Bosnia, and tell them that it was his desire to remain on the best of terms with his Turkish friends. The administration, however, was already empty, and he didn't find anyone there except one servant, Haji Asim Brutus, the father of nine children, pious, but a savage man. Asim didn't recognize him but knocked his hat off, livid: the infidel had gotten full of himself and put on a pagan hat even before his side took the city!

Terrible Ivan Karadža only looked at him in confusion and tried to bend down to pick up his hat but couldn't do it.

"What the hell do you need a hat for if empires like this crumble?" he allegedly commented and expired the next day.

Does one need mention that he died unhappy? No, but that would fit into the legend about Karadža. It was a pity that Sarajevo wasn't a city of songwriters, as was Mostar, and that there wasn't anyone to compose a song about Karadža that would be sung accompanied by a tamboura or fiddle and preserve the memory of that unusual man.

Well, it was to that address, to Karadža's mansion, that Alija was supposed to deliver Rafo. And he took him there and turned him over to two nuns who were temporarily residing there while their convent was being constructed on Banjski Brijeg, a picturesque glade next to a mosque and cemetery in the Mejtaš district. One of the nuns was named Rozalija and was plump, ruddy, and smiling. The other was named Paulina and was tall and thin as a pole for knocking down plums.

Alija laughed as soon as he saw them and grew uneasy. He became tongue-tied in his attempts to explain what he was laughing about. The two of them, however, knew what was going on with the midget and started teasing him. It seemed that at any moment the ground under Alija would open and swallow him up and that this was the only way that Allah could save him from his shame.

"Sit down here. Here's some brandy if you drink, but if you don't drink, then may we be forgiven for offering it, just as you are forgiven for the things you ask forgiveness for," said Paulina, feigning earnestness.

Fat Rozalija showed Rafo his room: a military bunk with fine, embroidered sheets, an office cabinet, and a crucifix on the wall. Three tarps hung from wall to wall and hid the worm-eaten boards. It wasn't a place where someone would want to spend the rest of his life, but on the other hand he felt the warmth people feel when something has been allotted and furnished for them. The boy put down his bag next to the bed as the nun waited to hear what he would say. She wanted to hear the boy say that he felt good there, and then she would laugh. Rafo didn't say anything, but Rozalija still laughed. Rozalija believed that laughter couldn't hurt and that laughter hadn't ever done anyone harm and never gave up on that idea. She always laughed, as if St. Elijah had commanded her never to stop. That was the meaning of her mission and the way in which she intended to cure an unbelieving world.

After lunch, which they ate together with the masons building the convent, Alija said that he was going on a walk around town to buy a kerchief, roasted chickpeas, and sweets. He didn't mention the low women in front of Paulina and Rozalija, who were serving the hungry menfolk. He winked at Rafo conspiratorially, more to encourage himself, and skipped outside.

"Don't come back late," Paulina called after him. "This is a house of God!" Rozalija hugged the boy and laughed again. She knew that this was what one was supposed to do when someone was alone for the first time. You hug him, and he has to feel better. If you see that he doesn't, then you kiss him on the cheek. And he goes crazy because a nun kissed him on the cheek! And naturally, he feels better.

The scent of ash water on Rozalija's sleeve moved Rafo. Or was it the smell of coarse peasant soap sold by women from the Sava region in all Bosnian markets, which was the first hygienic product for mass consumption in the history of that land? What exactly he smelled wasn't important, but tears came to Rafo's eyes. He thought that he would never see Alija again.

He spent the rest of the day in bed next to the open window.

"Let the child rest; he traveled all day and night," Rozalija said.

"And will I ever get any rest?" Paulina quipped, just to spoil her older colleague's joy a bit. Rafo slept and woke up every ten minutes or so, listened to the noises outside, and then suddenly dozed off again.

"Baskets! Baskets! Buy your baskets!" called a nasal male voice. A horse-drawn wagon clattered by on the pavement. Dogs barked and horses neighed. And then the muezzin sounded from a mosque. It was loud, as if he were calling to prayer right under Rafo's window. A few moments later a second was heard, and far off in the distance a third. Church bells rang at different times. Copper pots banged as they fell off the wagon of an inattentive merchant. A child who'd been hurt playing war between believers and infidels cried for help. From a garden a woman's voice wailed: "Mustafa! Mustafaaaaa! Mujooooo! May lightning strike you dead, so help me God!"

After that he didn't wake up until he was awoken by a bright oil lamp and Rozalija's hand on his shoulder. The nun was frightened and didn't laugh.

Alija had taken care of everything in its turn, content that the prices weren't as he'd expected. He'd thought that Sarajevo would be an expensive city, and it turned out to be cheaper than Trebinje, Čapljina, and Mostar, cheaper than Dubrovnik, which had always been the essence of cheapness. Not only had he bought more roasted chickpeas and sweets than he thought he would, but he'd also bought a wooden train with a locomotive. It was a spitting image of the Mostar-Sarajevo trainset! If it had been colored black, there wouldn't have been any difference at all! That train had everything: two smokestacks, a coal car, and a restaurant car . . . If you looked hard, you might also find those two waiters, a raspberry juice and brandy . . .

The gift made him so enthusiastic that he began to fantasize about getting his three sons to work as railroaders. As soon as they saw the train, they wouldn't think of anything else.

And there were all kinds of kerchiefs, for various prices. The cheapest were the simplest: black, the ones that Christian women used to cover their heads when someone died; Muslim women used them to cover themselves when they went to a mosque during Ramadan. Colored kerchiefs were somewhat more expensive: yellow as the moon or cornbread, red as when you cut your finger, some as blue as the sky, others as blue as the sea in high summer, green as grass and flags, violet as who knows what . . . At first Alija thought he would buy a violet one because he couldn't think of anything that was so violet, but then he remembered Nafa. She certainly wouldn't put something on her head if she didn't know how it got its color. If he didn't know, then she didn't either. And then Alija saw a dizzying array of kerchiefs, and then Alija realized something that he should have known but hadn't occur to him until he saw them. To hell with kerchiefs that only have one color! There were all kinds of multicolored kerchiefs—from those with flowers, roses and carnations, to those with flourishes and decorations. The stranger the decoration and the harder it was to tell what in reality it resembled, the more expensive the kerchief.

The most expensive kerchiefs in the market had decorations that one didn't even see on mosque carpets, and they were also embroidered with gold thread.

A thread of pure gold ran ever so faintly through the middle of the kerchief and across the decorations, as if put there by accident. Such kerchiefs cost Alija's yearly pay. He looked at them and wondered: dear God, what fool would buy that for his wife? A very rich fool. But they weren't fools because they were rich but because they didn't have eyes to see that those kerchiefs were ugly. What marred them was what was the most expensive—gold! And God created gold to make each thing more beautiful.

Alija was astonished because he'd seen for the first time that gold can make something ugly. And he would have been glad if he could have been spared that knowledge. God help us from realizing that beauty can be ugly, he thought, and bought his Nafa the prettiest kerchief in the market. It had decorations that were more modest than a mosque carpet but were just right for her head, her looks, and her mind. Prettier decorations wouldn't look good on her because Nafa would look uglier in them. And he would be ashamed to be beside her. The decorations on that kerchief seemed to have been thought up for her and him. So when they strolled through Trebinje on the emperor's birthday or when he took her to Dubrovnik to see Stradun and how well the pavement was done there, everyone would say, "Now look at that fine woman, a real lady, and just look at her husband; he looks like he graduated from all the schools in Vienna!"

And all that because of the correct choice of kerchief. Alija was proud both of himself and of his choice, and of his Nafa, who was now waiting for him to return from his distant journey, from Sarajevo, the big city that was too big for viziers and so they never made it their seat of power. Or they were afraid of losing their sense of sight and their power of speech because of such beauty.

When the muezzins fell silent at dusk, Alija completed his purchases, and he still had money to return to Dubrovnik in style. Herr Heydrich wasn't stingy after all. He'd given his faithful servant enough to treat himself too and to return home with dignity. Alija was a little ashamed of the episode with the borek. Thank God he was a coward because how would he face Herr Heydrich?! Not to mention the sin that he would have committed by leaving his children hungry. Oh, the fear God gave him was good, Alija thought. The only thing that worried him a little was whether Allah counted wicked thoughts in a man's final reckoning. And how heavy were the uncommitted acts of spite on Alija's scales? No one knew that, not even Hafiz Sulejmanaga Ferizoglu of the Ali-paša Mosque, whom, you see, Alija didn't remember as he had spent so much time choosing a kerchief. He'd been enchanted by the silk and didn't think of God in time and go to the mosque. And that was a sin. But how great? He started worrying and grew sad, and in a moment all of the joy of that day turned to lead. The roasted chickpeas, the sweets, the kerchief . . . How had his mind not seen that God was tempting him all the time?! But why did he have to do it just like that? He hadn't been buying gifts for himself but was trying to make his wife and children happy.

Alija consoled himself with the thought that making them happy was the same as making Him happy, adapting and adding to the few Koranic suras that he thought he'd memorized and understood.

Still, he would go to Skenderija to see the Austrian whores, the fabled low women before whom everyone kneeled when they saw them. That would be his temptation, Alija thought, lying to himself. He would go to them, see them, and sniff the air, but he wouldn't touch them. He would show Allah how great his faith was. He would be humble, tiny as he already was, but hard as a stone in the foundation of the world. Hard as the stone that the pine above the Neretva clung to. As he went like a sleepwalker toward Skenderija, a ruffian laughed at his question of where that was and said:

"Just go straight along the Miljacka, and when you can smell women's parts, well, you're at Skenderija."

Alija mumbled the prayers that he could remember and looked up every so often at the sky, expecting that God would probably give him some sign if what he was doing wasn't good. The sweets in his breast pocket were melting, his pockets full of roasted chickpeas were about to burst, he squeezed the kerchief so hard his fingers tingled, but Alija felt nothing as his heart dragged him to the low women and his soul froze in terror.

It was almost midnight when Rozalija woke up Rafo. Alija hadn't come in for the night, and she and Paulina were worried because he too had been left in their care and because the people in Trebinje had told them that he was a good but somewhat simpleminded man who'd never been in a big city and had asked if they could keep an eye on him so he didn't get lost. Rozalija thought that this had been said in jest—would they really entrust the boy to a simpleton?—but when Alija didn't show up, both she and Paulina were seized with panic. They'd seen him as he was, and did they really not have enough sense to keep him from going into town? They asked Rafo whether Alija had happened to mention what he was going to do in Sarajevo, whom he might meet, and where they would go.

The boy repeated the story about the gifts and mentioned the wise hafiz whose prayer Alija wanted to hear, but he kept quiet about the low women. One certainly didn't talk about such things in front of nuns, but, more important, he wanted to keep Alija's secret and protect his friend. Even if the nuns didn't report to Trebinje that Alija had gone to prostitutes, they would certainly look on him with derision. And only because they didn't know the real reason why he wanted to see the low women.

On that night no one in the Karadža mansion slept. The nuns were dumb-founded with fear, and Rafo mostly kept silent and stared ahead. Rozalija and Paulina had visions of terrible stories from the time of the Turks. They remembered various cutthroats, agas, and ghazis who would draw their daggers at anyone who gave them a passing look, and the boy was tormented by an obsessive thought that Alija was dead and that he'd killed him. He'd killed him by taking a liking to him after they met—the first time he'd taken a liking to a stranger. Actually, maybe he didn't love anyone else. His brothers, sisters, nephews, relatives, cousins, aunts, his kin and relatives by marriage—all had been fated to be his, and his attitude toward them was the same as to how he breathed. With no will of his own, by an irresistible habit, with no soul in fact. He would have erased them if he could have, just as he would have stopped breathing if it were somehow possible to do so of one's own free will. Alija was the only person he'd chosen, and for that reason Alija was dead. At that moment he didn't pity him. His guilt was too great for him to be able to pity him. It was so great that that divine house would have collapsed under it if it hadn't been built by Ivan Karadža.

It's perhaps difficult to claim that there's a single day in a person's life that is the most important, but the fate of Rafo Sikirić—everything that he would become and everything on account of which his Kata would waste her life—was finished a little before noon on August 31, 1891, the second day of his stay in Sarajevo. Paulina came back from the police station all in tears, accompanied by two policemen in civilian dress, and Rozalija hurried Rafo off to his room. For no reason, because he alone knew and was certain that Alija Čuljak was no longer among the living. Someone had found him a little below Vrbanja and Skenderija, by the bank of the Miljacka, horribly beaten and with his throat cut. The policemen were unable to pry apart his hands, which were still clenching Nafa's kerchief. Roasted chickpeas were strewn all around the corpse. As he didn't have his wallet, they easily solved the motive for the crime.

However, they didn't know, nor would they ever find out, where Alija's throat had been cut. Because it hadn't happened on the Miljacka River; his dead body had only been dumped there. Whether he had seen the low women, whether he'd taken a fancy to one and thus paid with his life or kept his promise to the Good Allah, that likewise remained a secret between Alija and the Almighty. What people knew was that no one was able to take his kerchief. They tried to pry his fingers apart when they were preparing him for his funeral. But it didn't work.

Thus the silk kerchief ended in a small, open coffin, as if a child were being buried, with a body that was being committed naked back to the earth.

If Nafa didn't suspect her husband (and sorrow and pity hope that she didn't), then she knew at that time that the kerchief had been for her. Which only increased her pain and sense that the Good Allah was not accessible to the weak mind of a woman, as He ruled the world and took to himself people's loved ones.

Rafo went on living with his guilt, but in the meantime he lost the gift of invisibility. Or Sarajevo was different than Trebinje in that no one could be invisible there. A trove for those who knew how to fight, good for those with quick minds and sharp tongues, a heaven for jokesters and hotheads of all kinds, Sarajevo was a hellish place for the soft-spoken and weak souls, all of whom like to get out of the way first. In the prep school he found himself among thirty little bandits: children from upper-class Sarajevo households, children from old Muslim families, and little carpetbaggers with Czech, Austrian, Slovak, Slovene, Ashkenazi, Italian, and Hungarian names whose fathers had come in the imperial service after the occupation in 1878.

And while their families retained the manners and customs of their old countries and didn't grow accustomed to the strange humor and severe climate of their new home, their children didn't differ at all from their classmates of the Islamic faith. The latter were even a smidgen more restrained and calm — though that wasn't the rule — because they probably felt the faint traces of their bey origins, whereas all those little Aloises, Ferdinands, Josephs, and Františeks had completely adopted the harshest forms of the local mentality and moreover those of its most dangerous and most colorful residential and lumpenproletariat subtype. Their spirit, and later the spirit of the city, was not formed by the market district, which in the Turkish time had had its humor — but a humor that knew moderation, wasn't full of cynicism, and rarely threatened the integrity of the unprotected. The carpetbagger children, of which there were more in the prep school than local children, had been molded and marked by the carnivalesque debauchery of the Muslim and Christian common folk, who'd for centuries been active on the edges of the city, reveling, carousing, and starving — and who with the arrival of the Austrians had broken into Sarajevo and occupied it, in a manner of speaking. That invasion in general hadn't had a negative impact on the city itself, which was weary of the kind of oriental social symmetry that had become tiresome to Istanbul as well. But it could cost people with tender souls and lesser vigor their lives or at least their minds. Those who didn't know how to adapt, or had no opportunity to adapt, were fated never to step across their thresholds into the street with peace in their hearts. Which was again a paradox because the new Sarajevo was tuned so that most people found peace in their hearts in the street and nowhere else.

On the seventh day of school they began picking on Rafo. He tried to defend himself, but he didn't know how. He was physically stronger than Alois Schechtel, the most loathsome brat in his grade, and he could hold his own against Džemal Sirća, the son of a rich watchmaker in the market district, a hooligan who would have probably ended up among the pickpockets of Mejtaš and Bjelave if his father hadn't followed his every step and as soon as he did something wrong thrashed him with a horse whip.

However, neither Alois nor Džemal picked fights according to the rule of the world of boys, with the intention of showing their power over those who were weaker than they were and thus to gain a gang of followers. First of all, they weren't in a position to do so, and second of all, it never occurred to them. Running a gang wasn't anything that anyone in the prep school or even in the communities of Sarajevo dared to do. With the Austrians and the arrival of the common folk from the outskirts a kind of anarchy had taken hold. God forbid that someone got the idea of playing aga or vizier. Years and decades would pass before Sarajevo would receive new formal and informal leaders that would dictate what one could and dared, and what one couldn't and didn't dare, to do. At the time when Rafo Sikirić found himself between Alois and Džemal, his two enemies, there was no leader in sight. But one had to show the strength of a leader to survive in that world.

So one of them would rush at him—never both of them at the same time—and would, say, sneak up behind Rafo and stab him in his rear end with a compass. Rafo would squeal, "Don't!"

The one who did it would shrug his shoulders and say, "I didn't do it!"

As soon as Rafo turned around and started working, he would stab him with the compass again, this time really hard. Rafo could hardly hold back his tears from the pain: "Don't, you jerk!"

The third time he would jab the compass down to the adjusting screw. Rafo would turn around and grab him by the neck. A shoving match and a fight followed, but what was also more important in a physical altercation: the exchange of swearwords and insults. The enemy would withdraw strategically, avoiding a real fistfight, but would land some very precise verbal blows.

The goal was to attract the attention of as many of the grade as possible, to get a laugh, to get Rafo's eyes to tear up, to make him start stuttering and repeat one and the same swearword like a parrot because he was unable to come up with anything with which to respond. And he wasn't able not because he was stupid, and maybe even not because he was less verbally agile, but because he'd been attacked, and the one who was attacked in such fights was always at a disadvantage. The basic principle and the rule of the game was that the attacker always won, unless the one he attacked decided on a real fistfight. But even then only half a victory was in sight because more value was placed on making a fool of someone than really beating him up. Besides, fistfights were punished in the prep school but insults weren't.

After Alois and Džemal had had enough of abusing Rafo, it was the turn of the next level of bullies, who wanted to carve out a piece of the grade's respect, to test their courage and sharpen their tongues.

After two months there were only four or five boys who hadn't picked on Rafo. At the same time, he wasn't the only one they picked on. The others were cunning and resourceful, had older brothers or dangerous fathers. A boy who mostly kept quiet and stayed out of the way, and the only one who wasn't from Sarajevo and for whom two funny nuns came to the parent-teacher conferences, was fated to daily abuse. In the other grades there were miserable boys with similar fates, but never just one in a grade and never so fainthearted.

He never told Rozalija and Paulina what happened to him. They noticed when he came home muddy from school because ten or so rascals had decided to give Rafo a practical demonstration in natural history, about the Turopolje wild pigs, and would push him into the mud in the middle of the schoolyard. The nuns would see that his eyes were red from crying, and sometimes they noticed that he had bruises on his arms, but neither did they know what to do, nor did they know the logic of the world into which Rafo had been thrust. Apart from the fact that according to the nature of their calling they could have had no idea about the jungle in the schools, Rozalija and Paulina still lived in the world of Ottoman Bosnia, in which people bowed to each other when they didn't get along and people were terrified only of those who had higher appointments in the formal hierarchy. One feared the aga and the aga's men, one feared the vizier if he accidentally ran into him or ended up in his way, but that was about it. And again, the common folk, especially the Christians, thought that was too much. A free man is more afraid of fear than slavery because a slave is only afraid of his master and no one else.

Rozalija and Paulina, as well as the few nuns that there had been during Turkish rule, thought that they were living in the role of earthly slaves. They served their church, the hungry, and the unfortunate, but that was not the essence of their slavery. They slaved for the Turks and the Turkish authorities, oppressors who didn't honor Christ or his pastors and confessed a false faith. That fact upset them greatly; they prayed for the era and ways of the Ottomans to come to an end, and depending on the nature of their hearts, all of them either hated the Turks and everything Turkish or merely feared them.

Rozalija and Paulina had befriended one another by virtue of the fact that they were both unaccustomed to hatred, and the times of great upheavals always seemed to be created for hatred, and that was why those who could not stoke it in their hearts had more to fear from such times than those who were most exposed to it.

A shortcoming of that devilish gift of hatred, unworthy of reason, would in times of upheaval often be interpreted as a lack of patriotism and even a lack of faith in God. Rafo's guardians understood that in good time and made every effort to be as far as possible from everything that could summon hatred in them but also from whatever might show the world that they didn't know how to hate. Happy and content that a Christian emperor now ruled over Bosnia instead of the sultan of Istanbul, the two of them tried to be spared from further information.

"Is anyone picking on you?" Rozalija would ask him and without waiting for an answer would continue, "If they lay a hand on you, you just go ahead and get away, find some shelter; that's smarter and closer to God. You shouldn't have anything to do with fools, even if you're stronger than they are. And especially if you're weaker! If a Muslim lays a hand on you, forgive him because he's angry that our emperor is now in Bosnia. He's not hitting at you but hitting at His Highness Franz Joseph, and you should understand that and walk away. The poor boy isn't to blame because his papa and mama are of the wrong faith. He'll realize sooner or later that our emperor is a good man, and when he realizes that, he won't hit you but will be your friend. That's the way it's always been. If, on the other hand, a Christian child lays hands on you, forgive him too. The people have become wild, and hardly anyone knows what is good and what is bad. They have blood in their eyes as if there wasn't enough of it in 1878. They'd like to pay back the violence that the Turks committed for four hundred years and lash out when they can. They don't honor God or the church, nor do they honor people. Shame on them forever," Rozalija would say and grow angry, without Rafo having said a word. He would only watch the face and hands of that funny and precious woman; his gaze would pass from her eyes, which were blue and narrow like an old salamander's, to her nose, which was big like a ripe cucumber, and then on to her fingers, which moved excitedly around each word, and it seemed that they were not coordinated with one another.

The scene calmed him, but what Rozalija was saying didn't matter to him. And it didn't because one of them lived outside that world. Rafo's anguish—his inner anguish, which he'd brought with him from Trebinje, and his outer anguish, which Sarajevo had bestowed on him—had nothing to do with emperors and sultans, nor was it at any moment important which confession his tormentors professed.

The only ones for whom he was invisible were the teachers. Before the Christmas holiday and the winter vacation not one of them remembered his name and surname, nor did they recognize him by sight. His grades were a gray average: he would neither fail nor excel in any subject. Grimy, and often bloody and muddy, Rafo remained outside the teachers' field of vision, which was in and of itself unusual if only because there was a strict instruction about paying attention to the pupils' hygiene in the First Preparatory School. The Viennese teaching staff were stunned at what a dirty land they'd come to: lice, fleas, bedbugs, venereal diseases, and endemic syphilis (the most terrible thing one could imagine) . . . Still, one has to admit that they were willing to notice so much filth because they expected it. And so, more than the low level of hygiene among the local inhabitants, it was the fact that they had found a few hundred public fountains in the city and encountered the Muslim practice of washing before every prayer that surprised them. Regardless: the First Preparatory School was supposed to serve as a model of the advance of public hygiene. They looked out for dirty fingernails and lice-infested heads as one might take care of the highest strategic interest of the empire. Blood and mud and Rafo Sikirić's face cast a dark shadow on the scope of the teachers' efforts.

As he boarded the trainset to Mostar, Rafo Sikirić decided not to return to Sarajevo alive. In fact, he'd known that earlier, but now he had to review what he'd learned so he wouldn't forget, or it wouldn't seem to him that what he'd seen on the platform was true, while everything that had happened the previous months was only an illusion. Rozalija and Paulina pushed their way through the people without worrying about the dignity of their mission or about what people might think when they saw two nuns crying their eyes out while they passed a boy bags with bread, roast chicken, apples, and bottles of milk and water through the window so the little one would have everything he needed and wouldn't, God forbid, starve to death on the way to Trebinje. And people might have thought all kinds of things when Paulina began yelling to Rafo at the top of her lungs not to go to public toilets under any circumstances. All kinds of people went there, and there were all kinds of illnesses there. She shouted because they'd forgotten to warn him about that amid the dozens of other people, so now she tried in vain to outshout the locomotive.

He waved at them as long as they could see him, but he knew that his hand wasn't waving as the four of theirs were. It started hurting and would always hurt him whenever he remembered how two women of God had seen him off, how much they loved him, and with what fear they'd given him up to the wide world in the fervent belief that he would come back to them.

If mothers are known for anything and if motherhood isn't a way in which biology cheats and deceives the human mind, then they are known for that fear.

Rafo felt it in Rozalija and Paulina, but after that—never again. The fact that he was unable to give that love back to them was one of the rare sins that he would sense clearly in his life.

Another sin was that he wouldn't believe in everything that the two of them believed in. That might have saved him. And he himself would become conscious of that fact some fifteen years later, when he began to sort his nails and realized that he would now be maintaining the thread of his life more easily if he'd learned Rozalija's and Paulina's simplemindedness. But he wasn't able to drown himself and warm himself in the abundance of his family. He didn't have a sense for the comfort of the service of the Lord and the blessed, calming power of belonging to the flock of believers.

Once before bedtime Paulina told him about one day (he remembered it—January 15, 1882!) when Sarajevo had received its archbishop. In the presence of respected people, in the wooden church of St. Anthony, Josip Stadler became first among the shepherds. She described in a lively fashion the golden tassels and buttons on the uniform of the commander of the city, General Herman Dahlen, who'd come to greet the archbishop; she told Rafo what they ate afterward, what kind of soup there was, and what cuts of veal were roasted, and mentioned that white bread was served but that the general requested black bread. The hosts were surprised and a little insulted because in those days it was hard to find flour for white bread. Dahlen had completely innocently shat on their fun; that was exactly how Paulina put it, and she said just that—shat! She didn't swear or say bad words, but she didn't lie or put a false face on things. That was just the place for that word, in the story about a great day in her religious life, the day when Sarajevo became a city of Christ. Rafo was truly touched, almost as if he'd seen Alija in that woman. Until the end of the story, when she admitted that she hadn't been in the church or at the dinner that day because there had been no room for her and Rozalija. She hadn't seen anything that she was telling about with her own eyes but had only believed what others had told. And not even they had been there but had been told by those who had been. Paulina was comforted because she was able to see what wasn't happening to her as real. God hadn't given Rafo that power, so He didn't exist for Rafo.

In Trebinje he was awaited like a little emperor, as if he'd already gotten his doctorate and not spent only a half-year in the prep school. The whole family gathered at the railway station again, and all the way home they showered him with questions about the most closely guarded worldly and metaphysical secrets. They asked him about everything that had ever bothered them and for which they didn't have any answers because they hadn't finished the imperial schools:

"Are there more churches in Vienna or more mosques in Istanbul?"

"Are there more Chinamen or ants?"

"How many times a day does the Austrian emperor lunch?"

"Do people live on stars, and is it hot or cold up there?"

"How many dunams of land do the richer Sarajevans have?"

"Are there still Turks in Sarajevo, and what are people saying? — How long will our people put up with them?"

"Will Jesus return to Earth if the whole world ever believes in Him?"

"Does anything exist that is faster than the railway, or is the railway faster than a swallow?"

"Do people in Sarajevo eat baklava?"

"Is there anyone who doesn't believe in God?"

"Are there any foreign languages besides Turkish that you haven't learned?"

"How do you say *poached apples* in Latin?"

"About how much smarter is a person when they finish all their schooling?"

He had to answer all their questions, and if he didn't know the answer or the question didn't make any sense, Rafo made something up and lied. They believed everything he said — would an educated man lie? — and were content because he was clearing up things about which they'd been confused all their lives, things about which they'd racked their brains for years, and now in a second everything was becoming clear.

For seven days they treated Rafo and led him from one get-together to another. They sat him in the front pew for the midnight Mass, right next to the city elders and military representatives. Before the Christmas meal the district courier brought him a card and gifts from the emperor, and a day later a correspondent of the Vienna newspaper wanted to see him who intended to remind the forgetful public of the first Herzeg-Bosnian godchild of the Austro-Hungarian sovereign. He endured all of that and waited for a moment when he would tell Ivan, his oldest brother and the head of the family, that he wasn't going back to Sarajevo. When he had an opportunity he didn't have the courage, and when he had the courage, Ivan wasn't there, and in the end he realized that there was an easier and simpler way to save himself from the prep school and everything that oppressed and tormented him.

In the early morning before New Year's in 1892, he got out of bed before everyone else, grabbed a rope for tying up young bulls before they were castrated, climbed onto a plum tree in the yard and tied it to the lowest branch, and tied a noose in the other end. He could barely pull it down over his head; the rope was almost as thick as his arm. He looked at the windows behind which his clan was sleeping the sleep of the just, then up at the sky above the verandah, and finally at the pavement that surrounded the plum tree. At the moment when he slipped down, Rafo didn't miss anything. Nothing mattered to him for one more fraction of a second in which the visible world shot upward, and then he felt a terrible power jerk his head, his eardrums pop, his breath stop, and instead of stopping, his heart started beating like crazy . . . He forgot everything he knew and why he'd climbed up on the tree and was no longer the old Rafo; he wasn't a person but a being—maybe an animal, maybe a sinful soul in hell— that was trying to find solid ground under its feet.

No one knew how long he hung there, and no one knew how long he would have hung beside the Sikirić house if Brother Ambroz Galonja hadn't come walking by. He was a friar who suffered from insomnia and so liked to study the influence of the dawn on plant life. Brother Ambroz jumped over the low stone fence, grabbed Rafo's legs, and began to call loudly for help. His sister Slavica ran out of the house first and climbed up the tree barefoot. The friar saw her breasts full of milk fall out of her blouse—it hadn't been ten days since she'd given birth for the sixth time. He wanted not to look, but he didn't have anywhere else to turn and didn't think of closing his eyes because he was overcome with horror at the rasping coming from Rafo's throat. His breath rasped like that of old men when they died—Brother Ambroz had seen hundreds of them off to the hereafter. Slavica tried to untie the knot, but it didn't work; a man's strength was needed for that. Her breasts pressed on a rough branch of the old tree, red imprints were left on her white skin; Brother Ambroz looked at them, beside himself with fear, and for a moment it seemed that this wasn't real but that he'd lost his mind from the lack of so much sleep.

Feces were seeping down out of Rafo's underwear and slowly, like a snake on a hot rock, went down the friar's shoulder, leaving an ugly yellowish trail on his habit.

Rafo had the fortune or misfortune that the rope was too thick and didn't cinch around his neck. Instead of dying, he experienced only the pain of death; everything hurt, and he lost his voice. He lay in bed as the members of the Sikirić clan took turns at his side. Brother Ambroz held his hand and kept mumbling the *Our Father* and *Hail Mary*. He did that so no one would ask him anything, not because he thought that prayer would help the boy. Not five minutes had passed since they'd taken Rafo down from the plum tree and Ivan Sikirić was already shoving five ducats into Brother Ambroz's fist, only so he wouldn't tell anyone what had happened. Rafo's brother wanted to pay him off before he even knew whether Rafo would live or not. The friar went hazy in the head, as if someone had opened the gates of hell for a moment to air out all the stench of its sinners. It seemed to him that he wouldn't be able to come to his senses again. He shoved Ivan's hand away; the ducats jingled on the pavement. He followed the child into the house so that he wouldn't ever have to look Ivan in the eye again. There he stood, saying the prayers he could remember, waiting for the moment when he could flee that house. God had put him on earth so he could care for grass, trees, and fruit trees and not for human misfortune. That should be in the care of the monastery's brothers who more easily bore misfortune.

The very next day, of course, all of Trebinje knew that the emperor's godchild had tried to kill himself. God knows how word got out and whose mouth let out the shame, but it was certain that Brother Ambroz Galonja hadn't said anything to anyone. And since no one outside the house knew about Rafo's hanging and no outsiders had been at his bedside, there could be no doubt that it was the Sikirićes themselves—that is to say, one of them—who'd broadcast the news to everyone else. Either one of the deceased Josip's daughters, daughters-in-law, or granddaughters had taken it into her head to portray herself to the neighbor women as a martyr and babble what had happened, or one of the brothers had gotten dead drunk in Aladin's bar and told all the town drunks why he was drinking.

Ivan Sikirić went around Trebinje for days like a Turkish ghazi, yelling so everyone could hear him: "Where's that pig of a friar? I'll dig out his liver with a pocketknife! I gave him money to keep his mouth shut, may Mujo Bašaga fuck him in his filthy ass!"

Apart from the fact that Ivan had sinned by cursing the monk who'd saved his brother (and he himself knew that he was sinning), though it was easier for him to slander an innocent than rack his brains with bitterness and anger in his heart, Ivan roused the fury of hell when he invoked the name of the deceased Mujo Bašaga, an adventurer and soldier who in some battle or another had come down with syphilis and deteriorated before the eyes of the town for years, from open sores and the fact that the disease had gotten into his head. In the end his nose turned into a scab, and it was whispered that his cock had fallen off and that instead of a male organ he had a split, as when an overripe watermelon bursts or as if, God forgive me, by some punishment he'd turned into a woman. Some swore that they'd seen him in the yard behind his house digging a hole and burying his manliness and saying a prayer over the grave, but no one believed them because those were people who hated Turkish soldiers and everything Muslim and tended to make up all kinds of things about their neighbors of the other faith. The story about Mujo Bašaga's lost cock was conceived in fear of him and his disease. Violent as he was, and well aware of his condition and the way in which he'd ended up in it, Mujo didn't threaten anyone with a dagger or an axe. Stout and strong, he would tell anyone who got in his way that he would await him after dark, him or one of his people, and cram his terrible

organ into his ass, cunt, or eye socket . . . People feared him and kept out of his
way as much as they could, and only when he died did they begin mentioning
his name under their breath in various jokes and pranks.

However, no one cut loose like Ivan Sikirić; no one shouted about him on
the town square because they knew that the deceased Mujo had two sons, bigger than their papa and more excessive in their violence, to the degree that
youth is more violent than old age. His son Hamid was already in his fifth year
in the Sarajevo prison because he'd robbed and killed a French traveler, and the
younger one, Medžid, had worked in Dubrovnik as a porter. And since Ivan had
been repeating his curse for days, someone told Medžid that Sikirić was slander-
ing his deceased father on the town square.

It was Saturday when Medžid Bašaga appeared with a fishing hook for sharks
in his right hand and a string in his left hand. He didn't say anything, didn't
greet anyone; he just walked around aimlessly, and people withdrew inside their
houses and shops and knew well whom he was trying to find. No one turned up
to warn Ivan about the return of the young Bašaga, and he himself was so foolish and preoccupied with his own misery that he didn't even step back when he
appeared before him on Arslanagić Bridge.

He didn't hit him a single time. He stopped in front of Sikirić, looked him
in the eye for a long time, long enough for a shadow to pass from one end of
the string to the other, and when Ivan tried to go around him, deathly afraid
but still unsure what he'd done to cross Medžid, the giant dropped the string
and grabbed Ivan by the hinges of his jaw. He squeezed him with his thumb
and middle finger; Ivan groaned and his mouth gaped instinctively. Medžid
took the hook and ran it through his cheek. Blood streamed out, and Sikirić
fell on his knees in shock, but that didn't hold up Bašaga at all. He bent over
just enough, and just as if he were puttering about a chest with a broken lock,
he tied the string to the hook, leisurely, pedantically. When he'd tightened the
knot, he tugged the string, and Ivan thought he was going to tear his face from
his skull, but Medžid just whispered a little louder, "Let's go, dog, to lick Mujo
Bašaga's grave!"

Ivan Sikirić passed through the market square on his knees, amid people
who passed around him and acted as if they didn't see him or as if Medžid was
leading around a greyhound and not a man. He moaned because it hurt and because the hook was tearing an ever larger hole in his cheek, but he knew that no
one would help him. Nor would he have helped him if he'd been in their place.
When they arrived at the cemetery, Medžid sat down on the neighboring grave,
and Ivan licked the gravestones and the earth on Mujo's grave. When he licked
all of one side of the grave, Medžid would whisper:

"Lick the master's other leg." And Ivan would go to the other side.

"Lick his arms . . .

"Lick his hero's chest . . .

"Lick the putrid cock of Mujo Bašaga, you infidel dog!"

Medžid would shout the last command, and Ivan expected him to hit him. But he didn't hit him once, though the series of commands was repeated in the same tone and order for hours. Night came; Medžid put a bag of tobacco on his knees and started rolling one cigarette after another. Ivan would look at him askance, whereupon he would only hiss, "Lick it . . . ! Lick it . . . ! Lick it! . . . "

When he found himself on the side of the grave opposite Medžid, Ivan jumped up and started running. He clasped the hook with his hands and would step on the string, which would jerk the hook and hurt him even more; he howled, pleaded, and cried, expecting a blow to the back of his head, and couldn't even collect himself enough to realize that the giant wasn't running after him. Medžid had remained sitting on the grave opposite his father's, smoking and looking uninterestedly in the other direction. Had anyone come along and seen him like that, he would have thought that the son had grown sad and come to talk with his dead father in his thoughts.

It took time for Ivan's rage to return. He squealed and called for his mother while his sisters took out the hook. Tears came to his eyes when they tried to clean the wound with brandy and stop the bleeding. In the end they sewed up the wound with a length of fishing line because the bleeding wouldn't stop. But that wasn't enough. Every minute he spat blood into a metal basin, folded his hands as if he were at prayer, and his eyes sought someone to help him. Rafo was lying in the next room, frightened to death because he'd seen how people die and was aware that he was to blame for what had happened to his brother. It would have been nice to disappear, but people aren't snow and can't just melt away. He realized this a little too late.

He dreamed of Alija Čuljak and the two nuns. They were sitting in the dining room of Karadža's villa, eating and laughing. Before them were empty plates from which they were taking pieces of nothing, putting them into their mouths, and chewing. He tried to call to them, tell them that the plates were empty and that no matter how much they ate they would still be hungry, but they didn't hear him. The same dream went on until morning. There were five more days until his trip back to Sarajevo. Actually, until the day that they would try to take him back there.

In the morning Ivan grabbed a hunting rifle and left the house without a word. He spat blood every few steps, walked quickly, and looked grimly into the dirt. He walked around the market square three times, but didn't find the man

he was looking for. If he was even looking for him. If Ivan Sikirić had dared at all
to shoot at Medžid Bašaga. No, he wouldn't have shot at him or at anyone else!
He'd taken the rifle to make himself look frightening and to drive the anguish
from his soul. As his rage came back and he was no longer a crybaby but a man
who'd long since passed fifty, despair grew inside him. That was a frequent scene
for the market square. It happened often, especially in spring, when the blood in
people's veins went bad and their nerves frayed, that a prominent and respected
man would stroll around with a weapon in his hands. One took a rifle, another
an axe, a third a pitchfork. He would stagger around for a bit, scowl at everyone
he saw, firing looks like cannonballs meant to destroy the city, but as a rule he
wouldn't run across the one who was the cause of his misery. People would click
their tongues and sigh, ostensibly in pity, but the truth was that the majority of
them watched it with malicious pleasure because one more person's soul had
been torn asunder, his life burst before their eyes, or his mind started leaking
out, and the day would soon come when he would completely lose it, so instead
of a local bigwig, a head of a household who commanded respect, we would get
one more town idiot, fool, dolt, jackass, and wretch. Soon women would chase
him—a filthy, soiled, crazed man—with brooms out of the yards of the town.
The respected Muslims of Trebinje, those who'd withdrawn into their homes
since the arrival of the Austrians, particularly enjoyed such spectacles because
now there were incomparably more cases of imbecility and springtime insanity
than there had been in the time of the Turks, and the majority of those afflicted
were Christians or the Muslim common folk—who were all the same to them.
These people tried to convince themselves, and then the town, that such things
didn't happen in honest Muslim families, which was of course a lie. Beys, their
sons and daughters lost their minds too, only they wouldn't shamble around the
town square but would endure their mental anguish within four walls. When
Ivan Sikirić appeared with the rifle and a large wound across his cheek, no one
thought he was looking for Medžid Bašaga and that there might be trouble. The
town wrote his name down in the register of present and future idiots.

And so in two days three scandals had befallen the Sikirić family, all as bad as
could be: their youngest, Rafo, had tried to kill himself; their oldest, Ivan, had
been forced to lick the grave of Mujo Bašaga, whereupon—at least in the eyes
of the town—he'd lost his mind. The same sorrow darkened all the houses in-
habited by Matija's and Josip's offspring. They kept their eyes to the ground, said
nothing, and sighed here and there, or the women would sniffle over the pots in
which they were boiling their laundry. Someone would start coughing; a child
would squeal because someone had suddenly opened a door behind which it
was playing. A cat meowed, a dog barked, but no one said a word. In the house-

holds into which the Sikirić women had married their husbands glared grimly at their swollen ankles and calves but didn't say anything. Even their mothers-in-law, who were otherwise the first to have something to say about the family of their daughters-in-law, kept silent. But until the previous day they'd gone around with their heads held high because one of their in-laws was the emperor's godchild, and they used that to threaten a grocer who'd sold them moist salt, or they'd boasted to their neighbors how Franz Joseph would soon invite them to Vienna to show them the imperial palace. Whoever in Trebinje bore the name Sikirić and into whose house one of the Sikirić girls married began to feel a little like a Habsburg. Whenever a neighbor woman would mention her godparent Stevo from Nikšić, who was coming for Easter with three Njeguši hams, she could expect the following answer:

"Well, just what is our godparent in Vienna going to send us?! Who gives a damn about Stevo from Nikšić when your godparent is the Austrian emperor?!"

The neighbor woman would lower her gaze; rage would gather in the corner of her lips. Then the emperor's in-law would offer her another cup of coffee—solely to hear the tone in which she would refuse it. Ah, now the time had come to settle accounts! Rafo had hung himself from a plum tree, and the imperial crown had fallen from many heads.

Ivan's shame upset them less. Though he was the oldest and commanded respect not only among his younger brothers but also in the homes of their in-laws, it was easy to renounce him because he wasn't the first or the last to lose his mind and his reputation because of his own foolish behavior. If there were a curse, it would only fall on his house and the houses of his children. His sisters would lament him, his brothers would clam up and never mention him, and it wouldn't be long before the town forgot who was whose brother. Ivan understood that. He hadn't fired the rifle he'd carried through the market, and Medžid Bašaga had gone back to Dubrovnik. The oldest Sikirić had crumbled like a pillar of plaster. He had only one trump card left in his hands, but that was the strongest. The emperor's godchild was lying in his house.

"What on earth got into you, son?" he asked, watching him as an eagle watches its sick young, and he would have liked to peck out his brains.

"Nothing," said the eaglet and curled up beneath the quilt, staring at something beyond everything else upon which he might fix his gaze.

"What do you mean 'nothing'?" Ivan asked, gnashing his teeth. Rafo didn't answer; he was thinking that the whole affair would be forgotten.

"What do you mean 'nothing'?" Ivan thundered over him. "Do you know what you've done to all of us, goddammit?!"

Rafo gave no answer and didn't move. He tried not to reveal that he was breathing or that he was there. His head was empty, the fragments of the previous night's dreams were flashing through his mind, and grains of dust sank into the depth of his gaze and ended in the gleam of a ray of sunlight.

"Answer me!" Ivan yelled. "Answer me!"

The boy remembered Alija's fingers. Two of them were odd, his thumb and index finger. The fingernails on each were the same size and shape, on both his left and his right hand. He looked at his own fingers. Their nails were very different. Everyone's were like that except Alija's. His thumb and index finger were like twin brothers.

"Why did you have to be born so late, damn you?! Why did you even come out into the world, you damned bastard?! Why didn't we choke you the day you were born?!" Ivan howled with the voice of a wailing woman. Rafo laughed.

He could have killed him. It wouldn't have mattered; no one would have cared. And he probably wouldn't have served any time. He could have strangled him, and people would have said that Rafo had died of the consequences of the hanging. All of Trebinje knew that he'd tried to hang himself. There would have been a large funeral, military representatives and imperial priests would have come, and the shame would have been forgotten over time. At any rate, it belonged to the emperor every bit as much as it did to Ivan. Ivan would certainly strangle him as soon as he started laughing! He would have wrung his neck like a Christmas turkey if his head hadn't been full of what he owed Medžid Bašaga and what the town and his family were trying to take away from him. Rafo would finish school, Rafo would go off to Vienna, everybody would know about Rafo; Rafo would get an appointment at the royal court . . . And who would be the only one who'd helped, who'd saved Rafo from dying and put him on his path in life? Ivan! No one else but Ivan! Rafo hadn't been brought up by all the Sikirićes but only by him and Franz Joseph! Everyone else would have strangled Rafo as if he weren't a human child but a kitten or a puppy! They would have thrown him into the Trebišnjica River so his body would never again see the light of day.

The train left with a half-hour delay. The boy sat by the window. He was pale, and his eyes were completely empty.

"Are you sick?" asked the conductor.

"Sick—no way. He's as healthy as a horse!" Ivan answered, smiling idiotically at the uniformed man.

"Yeah, he's healthy like a horse's ass," the conductor said scornfully, evidently insulted by the difference between his uniform and Ivan's tattered suit. Since railway tickets had become cheaper, every scumbag traveled by train. Soon they'll let live pigs into the cars, just when we've started becoming upstand-

ing citizens, thought the imperial railway official, hoping that Ivan would start
to make a fuss so he could kick him off the train. But he didn't. He was mild-
mannered and frightened in the face of the fact that he was going on such a long
trip for the first time. He wouldn't if he didn't have to; he wouldn't even if his life
were on the line! He was afraid of the railroaders' uniforms; he was afraid of the
thought of arriving in Sarajevo and not being able to find his way around there,
of not knowing how to get Rafo to those nuns. The boy wouldn't be any help. It
had been three days since he'd spoken a word. You could hit him on the head,
you could spank his bare ass, you could make him kneel on corn plants and
thrash the soles of his feet with a willow switch—Ivan had tried all that—but his
face didn't twitch, nor did he make a sound. He just kept quiet; only when the
skin on his back broke did he squeal, God forgive me, as if he were an animal or
as if his soul were on one end of the globe and his ass on another. The last thing
he said was that he wasn't going back to Sarajevo.

"Well now, fool, you think you're not going back to the imperial school?!"
Ivan had never heard such nonsense. "You can shame your own brother, you
can spit all over those who gave birth to you, you can give the Lord God the
finger when he asks how you're doing, you can kill yourself, but you can't spit
all over the emperor's grace and godparenthood, my boy!" That was basically
what he told him or something like that . . . But not exactly in those words because Ivan wasn't very good with words, and he lost his nerve at that moment.
So maybe he said something else, and maybe he didn't say anything but just
sputtered something through his lips, but that was the sense of it.

"You can shame your own brother . . . ," Ivan whispered so no one could
hear him, more for himself, proud that he'd come up with such clever words.
He used these words to deflect the insult that the conductor had inflicted on
him. Listen, you horse's ass! Oh, he would make a horse's ass of him when Rafo
finished school. He would find him, give him a slap, and order for him to be
fired . . .

"Do you want some borek?" he asked him as they went across the Mostar
station to the ticket office. He was holding him by the collar—sure was sure—
but Rafo didn't answer again. And he didn't have to! He would speak up when
he got hungry. No one had ever killed themselves by refusing to eat, and he
wouldn't either, Ivan thought cleverly, and bought himself some borek. The fat
borek man held out a piece wrapped in newsprint, but the guy in front of him—
probably some Kraut—had gotten his in nice white paper. It was there for all to
see: a bunch of torn newspaper pages and a neatly arranged thin stack of clean
paper. And depending on how he sized up a customer, the borek man would
wrap the borek in the one or the other. But it cost the same for everyone! Ivan

was irritated, but again he didn't dare say anything. He knew that the world had been turned upside down, but that it had gone this far—that was too much for Ivan. He chewed his borek, the grease dripping down his chin. He bit into the imprints of gothic letters on the dough and tried to convince himself that there was no way in hell he was ever going to travel this far away from home again. Maybe we aren't such elegant people, he thought, maybe we smell of onions and brandy, but we aren't the kind of people who have one kind of paper for poor people and another for rich people.

"Now sit here," he said and made himself comfortable in a red armchair of the Sarajevo trainset and took out a bottle of brandy. The borek wasn't anything to get excited about—too much onion, and the potato was somehow rancid—and he tried to quiet the storm in his stomach with the plum brandy. He'd packed a chain and a lock in his bag, just in case, to chain Rafo to a seat in the compartment if he felt he was going to doze off, but now he felt it would be awkward with other people around. What would the conductors say if they saw him chaining up the boy? He was his child, and it was true that no one had the right to interfere in what you did with your own kin, but again—there were all kinds of people. They would laugh at him and make all kinds of comments, and Ivan would rather not have anyone talk to him any more. Hopefully they wouldn't look at him; hopefully they wouldn't know he was there.

"Don't think about making a move because I'll break your legs!" he warned the boy before he pulled his hat down over his eyes and drifted off into a slumber in which he tried to calm the sprouted onion and the spoiled Glamoč potatoes that had been frozen who knows how many times before they had ended up in Ivan's borek. The wheels of the trainset clattered in a regular rhythm, as if the unerring hand of God were tolling church bells and calling his flock to repentance. The flood was coming, and the only ones who were safe were those who had the least to lose. Ivan had less than nothing and could slumber more deeply than any of the other passengers in the trainset.

He was awakened by a painful drumming in his temples. He thought that the pain was coming from the noise of the wheels and gripped the boy firmly by the elbow. Rafo groaned softly—so he was there! And then he felt that something strange was happening in his bowels. He heard the panicked signal of his own intestines; the strength of his muscles in their attempts to contain what was forcing its way out was growing feebler and feebler. A harsh heat, greasy, painful, and viscous, was raging inside him. He didn't know what to do! Either he would jump out of the train and take a shit like a man, even if Rafo got away from him, or he would hold the fire inside him and protect the right of an eldest son, defend his honor before the Trebinje square, and save his soul . . . The only thing he couldn't do was soil his pants! People would smell it, and their scorn would devour him; they would kick him off the train and kick him in his side with their boots . . . The trainset crept up Mt. Ivan slowly; it was hardly moving. His head was about to burst and flashes of light obscured his vision. Tightening the most important muscle in his body, he took the chain out of his bag and, without saying a word, started chaining up the boy's legs and locking them. He couldn't care less whether the conductors would see him; he tightened the chain as much as he could, and then, moments before he soiled himself, he ran through the car. The passengers watched him in confusion; a lady with a hat jumped up and frowned—maybe he was a pickpocket who was running from the police! Her purse was luckily in its place because he'd already jumped out of the train. He got caught in some branches and slammed down onto the rocks. His muscle had relaxed, a little spurt streamed into his underwear, but Ivan pulled himself together quite quickly, pulled his pants down, and with an explosive whine released from himself water, fire, and the unbearable stench of digested plum brandy. His head hurt unbearably; he closed his eyes and strained to eject what was left. Then, without losing time to wipe himself, he pulled up his pants and ran toward the train. The horror of the human heart can be such that a person no longer feels pain. He ran as he'd never run in his life.

The legend of the emperor's godchild was finished all because Ivan Sikirić's intestines had started working when the Mostar-Sarajevo trainset was almost at the top of Mt. Ivan, which divided Herzegovina from Bosnia and prevented the Mediterranean climate from reaching all the way to Sarajevo, presenting a challenge for architects and designers of the railway schedule because there was no locomotive that could ascend Mt. Ivan with a speed of more than a walk. But as soon as it crossed the top of the pass at Bradina, the trainset rushed at full speed toward the golden valleys and the Sarajevo basin so that not even the swiftest Arab horses could catch up to it. Ivan Sikirić ran in vain after the last wagon. He called and swore into the night in vain. He was left alone in the middle of unfamiliar country, where all one could hear was the howling of wolves and the distant sobs of forest fairies and spirits. Luckily, that was a year with no snow and no hard frost because otherwise he would have frozen to death by morning.

They reported Rafo's disappearance, made inquiries everywhere: Had anyone seen him? Had anything been heard? Were there any children anywhere about whom it wasn't clear who their parents were? They spent all their savings on phony reports and spies, whom they sent to Bihać, Višegrad, and Brodska Vrata. But the boy seemed to have disappeared without a trace. An inquiry came from the Sarajevo prep school asking why Rafo Sikirić hadn't shown up for classes. Two nuns wrote letters every week with a request to contact them. Some people from the police also came. There was a suspicion that the family was preventing the boy from returning to school . . .

A month later a sealed letter arrived from Ivan Polak that informed the first-grade pupil Rafo Sikirić that he'd been expelled from the school due to his disregard for school discipline and unexcused absences and that the decision had been forwarded to the minister of education personally. Three weeks later instead of the imperial appanage a request came for the money from the previous month to be paid back. That was a sign to the Sikirićes that Emperor Franz Joseph had renounced his godchild and that they didn't know whether he was dead or alive. Instead of showing concern, instead of sending people to search for him across the empire, and instead of acting as godparents do in times of distress, the emperor had requested that his money be returned! In that winter of 1892, the Sikirićes were bitterly disappointed in the monarchy.

The town looked on their tragedy with malicious gloating, but regardless— the reputation of the Habsburgs sank very low in all of Trebinje! That wasn't the state that they'd been hoping for, nor did its emperor treat all his subjects in the same manner. Or didn't godparenthood mean anything in Vienna? It didn't matter what the problem was, the people didn't think it was right. No more letters arrived from the palace or from the Sarajevo government concerning the emperor's godchild. The Sikirićes paid back the money, along with the interest and the revenue stamps.

And Ivan simply shut himself out of everything. No one dared even mention Rafo in front of him: not Rafo, not Franz Joseph, not the town square, nothing of anything that had been important to him and that had ever troubled him. He rarely went down into the city. He took care of his bees, and when his memory stung him, he touched the scar on his cheek and immediately forgot everything. He lived like that for five more years, and then in the rainy spring of 1898, while he was unchaining his beehives, a swarm of hornets attacked him and stung him all over. The beasts had slipped into one of the beehives, killed the bees, and settled there. He crawled to the house and died shortly afterward. They didn't open the coffin before the funeral because his face was so disfigured that the neighbors wouldn't have believed it was him.

More than ten years would pass before Rafo Sikirić came to his hometown again, as a married man. Some didn't recognize him, and others didn't want to. He asked his brothers whether any of the estate was his. They told him none of it was and not to risk his neck and ask again! He didn't ask again, nor did he ever see any of his family afterward. He worked as a station porter in Konjic. He cleaned the Mostar railroad station and ground corn for a boza maker, slept in his cellar, and acted like he didn't feel anything when at night the fat old man touched him with a trembling hand. He loaded ships near Metković; he carried tobacco for smugglers to Split and Šibenik . . .

He grew and shot up like weeds along a railway track, listless as God had created him and always alone, with no need for friends or company. What kept him alive was the horror that he'd endured while hanging from the plum tree. He worked all day long so that afterward he could sleep free, without thoughts and dreams.

He ended up in Dubrovnik because there was no longer any work in Metković, and a lot of snow had fallen and it was impossible to make it further toward Konjic and Jablanica. He got a job in the Gruž harbor and rented an apartment from Granny Petka, an old maid and the last offspring of a once eminent captain's family. She was a drunkard who'd already gone off her rocker somewhat, from either old age or alcohol. After she'd sold the more valuable furniture, her father's maritime diaries, her grandfather's pipe collection (there were a few hundred pipes from all continents made of wood, clay, and one—a Greek one—of stone), sixteen inherited paintings (the oldest was from the period before the Hundred Years' War), countless marine and geographic maps drawn with the pens of the greatest Portuguese, English, and Bay of Kotor masters, Granny Petka no longer had any source of money for brandy, so she spent months in the harbor looking for someone to whom she could rent out part of her house. Sailors waiting to set sail, dock workers, and all manner of jobless men who gather in all harbors and railway stations of the world turned down the old woman's offer down to a man. First of all, it was expensive—she wanted a bottle of brandy every second day, which at that time cost serious money, and second of all, she didn't give the impression of someone at whose place a man would want to sleep the night if he didn't have to. Small and hunched, with an enormous witch's nose on her thin face, dressed in unbelievably dirty rags, she stank of all the most unpleasant smells that a human nose could imagine. The stench arrived first, and only afterward would she appear, shouting like a newspaper boy:

"Wanted—an honest man for an apartment, no whores, no filth!"

The harbor workers called her Granny Stinky and started chasing her away. Every time they told her to get lost, she would mope off and shrink a little more. And then one noticed that she had the pleading look of a dog that was convinced that people are beings that don't go out without bones in their pockets. She would shuffle off to the next ship at the unloading dock and would be just as surprised when they chased her off too. No matter how many times she heard a dirty word, Granny Petka never got used to it. When the workers would break for a snack around noon and decide to mess with someone for dessert, one of them would take a bottle that still had a little wine in it and shout:

"Hey, Stinky, are you still drunk?"

Granny Petka would light up like Eve when she first saw the sunrise and start for the bottle. She ran, if one could call it running, stumbled, and fell, and just as she shambled up to them, the bottle would fly off into the sea. Everyone would laugh hysterically, and the main prankster would say:

"C'mon, Stinky, jump in after the wine so you won't stink anymore!"

The same scene was repeated day in, day out, without anything changing at all. Every time the old woman raced off toward the bottle, the bottle always flew into the sea, and the workers laughed with the same enthusiasm.

Rafo refused Granny Petka when she offered him the apartment for the same reasons the others did but didn't participate in the jokes they played on her, nor did he snack with the group. However, his attempts to get away so he wouldn't see or hear anything were futile. Wherever he found a spot to break his bread and cut some salt pork, in any corner of the harbor and a hundred meters out, one could hear the laughter. And one knew that they were tormenting Granny Stinky again. That started to drive him crazy, disturbed his daily peace of mind. The daily hardship of his soul turned into a wild tension, into something that resembled the echoes of the hallways of the Sarajevo prep school. He tensely awaited the laughter, and when he heard it, he felt like beating his head on the low stone walls of the harbor. He could choose: either to flee Dubrovnik or to take up residence with Granny Stinky and buy her brandy.

The Villa Rosa Bella was the largest and most beautiful construction at the eastern edge of the city. It had been built in 1771 as an exact copy of a house in Perast in which a woman named Ruža had lived, a local beauty and the failed love of Petka's great-grandfather. As a young man, he would go on foot to Boka, sing under Ruža's windows, and in vain seek her heart, which had been promised to an old Venetian merchant. As soon as his wife died and a year of mourning had passed, the Venetian was going to come for Ruža and take her away. Petka's great-grandfather did everything to change what had been fixed in writing, and it seemed that, at least as far as Ruža and her desires were concerned, he had some success. However, as fate could not be cheated, Ruža fell ill and in a single summer month went from the most beautiful girl in Boka to dead in a cold grave. The Venetian merchant lost his money and the woman who would care for him in his old age, and the young man from Dubrovnik was left without the love of his life. He swore that he would never marry and went to sea. He was wildly courageous, worked as a captain on both merchant and navy ships—in the service of several navies and countries—resolved to leave his bones on the floor of some sea, and to be remembered in a heroic legend and not for his unfortunate love. Death, however, didn't want him, and he returned home. In his old age he was extremely wealthy, but just as faithful to Ruža's memory. He had a house built for himself that was identical to hers in every detail. He sent designers and builders to Perast and spent large sums of money to get Ruža's relatives to let him inside so he could copy and measure the inside of the house. That was how the Villa Rosa Bella was born, a perfect architectural souvenir, and he spent his final years in melancholy visits to the rooms in which Ruža had lived. He built the house so he could cross the threshold that had been forbidden to him. He sat and smoked pipes by the window under which he'd serenaded Ruža.

He violated his own vow and before his death married a seventeen-year-old peasant girl from Konavle. She wasn't particularly beautiful and even less hardworking and smart, but her name was Ruža. That girl from Konavle was Granny Petka's great-grandmother and the first owner of the Villa Rosa Bella.

On the outside the stone building had preserved its original beauty, but whoever went inside—and no one had done that for at least fifteen years before Rafo did—found something that more resembled the lower chambers of hell—where haughty French sinner women bathed not in perfume but in their own shit—than it did the house of an old family's glory and unhappy love. Granny Petka had probably never taken out any trash, nor did she recognize the value of any single thing that she couldn't sell. Expensive dresses rotted on the floor; worms laid their eggs in rolls of unused silk; ceremonial captain's uniforms disintegrated in an orgy of moths. And in that largely formless mass of everything and anything, the most terrible effect was made by scraps of food that were years old. Rafo saw a whole untouched loaf of bread, probably from a time when Granny Petka summoned pity in others, which was green like an old church bell, on which unknown creatures had spun a fine weblike fleece, in the middle of which colonies of all manner of vermin lived in Old Testament fellowship. Since they hadn't been destroyed and had no natural enemies in the Villa Rosa Bella, worms, moths, wood lice, ants, cockroaches, worms, wasps, butterflies, hornets, roly polies, ladybugs, and earwigs took on something of the habits of dignified creatures. A cockroach the size of a quail's egg lay like a lion on the top of a broken candlestick, its legs crossed and its gaze dim, and looked Rafo right in the eye. It would have asked him something, but it was too lazy.

He brought a shovel and a wheelbarrow and hauled the trash out of his room. He whitewashed the walls and poured lime in holes that teemed with living creatures and scrubbed the floor on which he spread his mattress. Along with a large military chest, that mattress would be the only thing in the room. He suggested cleaning the whole house like that to Granny Petka.

"Remember one thing—I'm the lord and master in this house," she answered indignantly and didn't speak to him for two days. "Here there's no Granny Stinky, and the Villa Rosa Bella isn't the Gruž harbor," she continued, and Rafo realized that he wasn't allowed to interfere in her life. She was no longer of this world. But if you weren't sensitive to dirt, if you didn't fear disease, and if you weren't terribly superstitious, you could live with her. In the house she was quiet and spoke only if he wanted her to. She warmed herself by the kitchen stove for days at a time, drank brandy, and chewed on a bulb of onion. Rafo didn't see her eating anything but onion. Two or three times he brought her cheese and salt pork, but the old woman refused with a look of disgust:

"I'm not a girl any more; fatty food is hard on my gut." She spent her days with onion and brandy and no longer went to the harbor.

"You can't forget the evil they do to you," she said once. "You can't be a lady among beasts."

Rafo bought brandy for the rent wherever he managed. At first he took care not to buy either the most expensive or the cheapest, but he saw that the old woman didn't care. She just wanted it to be strong and harsh; whether it was made from grapes, plums, carobs, or dung (namely, people said that the Montenegrins made brandy from sheep and goat pellets)—that didn't matter to Granny Petka. And when he brought her a bottle of wine or prosecco too, she was the happiest child in the world. Her eyes would tear up, and when she smiled, Rafo thought he could smell a field of lavender. He would sit down beside her and listen for the umpteenth time to the story of the Villa Rosa Bella and how the old woman's great-grandfather had walked on foot to Perast to sing ballads to the beautiful Ruža. Only when she was telling that story and only with the help of brandy did Petka seem to have a clear head.

"Oh, the father of my grandfather, how foolish he was, God forgive his soul," she always said after she sweetly mocked his crazy mind and how the old man sat at the window and imagined himself as a young man calling to the only love of his life.

"I've got a young daughter, and you, I see, are young," Niko Azinović said one day to Rafo as he was paying for brandy. Rafo had been buying brandy from him for months.

"Her name is Kata. My daughter. She's pretty as a picture," he told him when he came the next time.

"It's your time. Time for both you and her," Niko added two days later.

"Will you at least take a look at her?" he asked him the next time.

Rafo didn't respond to him. He acted as if he hadn't heard or wasn't interested in what he was telling him, but when he came for the brandy again, Niko wasn't there to meet him. A nervous girl was there, her hands trembling as she poured out the brandy; she looked at him askance, frowned a little, but didn't say anything.

"She likes you!" Niko said the next time. Rafo didn't answer, but her father was no longer waiting for an answer. Everything was proceeding toward its logical conclusion, and he was content.

What made Niko Azinović, a poor but respected widower, want to give his daughter to a man who wasn't from that town, didn't have roots or family there, no house, no reputation, no place under the sun? The surrounding neighborhood would wrestle with this question until that whole generation ended under stone slabs in the Boninovo cemetery. Not until they'd all died off did their wonder come to an end, and the answer—though it was simple and understandable as soon as you thought with your heart and not your head—would never occur to them. Niko sought just that kind of son-in-law because he didn't want to be left all alone. He loved Kata with the kind of love that hadn't been able to get over her deceased mother, and he was horrified at the possibility that he would have to let her go off into someone else's house. He would let his other daughter, Angelina, go, and he would also be glad if she went, but Kata was something different and had remained close to her father's heart. How was it that people couldn't understand that, and where did they get the idea that a parent treasured all his children equally? Maybe some parents did, but Niko didn't. He found a son-in-law to fit his own emotions and—or so he believed—to fit a domestic mindset: Rafo seemed to him to be a stable young man and a model pauper whom trouble had forced to live with Granny Petka (because what else would have?). He didn't have anyone of his own and gave the impression of a man who as a husband would care for his wife. What man would care more than one whose property began and ended in his marriage? That was what Niko Azinović thought and was sure that he hadn't been mistaken.

From Rafo's perspective, things looked a little different. He believed that Kata liked him, and she did, just as he would soon believe that she loved him. He wasn't exactly clear about what that attraction and love were supposed to mean to him, but why would he object? Kata tolerated his silence well. Kata's father didn't expect for the questions he asked to be answered. Neither the one nor the other disturbed his peace of mind. He couldn't have found better kin. He nodded, and that was his consent.

In the uninterrupted history of Rafo Sikirić's solitude the only exception was his daughter Regina. On the day of his death, on the twelfth of February, 1924, she was the only one who really lost anything because only Regina liked him as he was. Everyone else had washed their hands of Rafo at one time or another; they saw him differently than he was or tried to change him. And no one other than she had a bad conscience about the way that he departed.

And the conscience is a good witness to death. Better than tears and all spoken and unspoken words of mourning. The survivors feel guilt before the dead, and that guilt is the only thing that ties their children to the world of shadows. Guilt is what dead parents leave to their children and what makes them turn into adults. If there was no guilt, then there was neither father nor mother. Actually, then they weren't parents to their own children. Thus, Regina was Rafo's child, and it was with her that his lineage was continued. On the day of his death she still hadn't turned nineteen, but she accepted into her soul a great anguish that was hard to bear and by which a pure and genuine misfortune can be recognized. The nobility of misfortune depends, however, on the way it is borne through one's life.

II

It had already been raining for twenty-seven days. Rowboats that no longer had anyone to look after them were sinking one after the other in the harbor. Women in black peered from behind their curtains and hid as soon as people appeared on the street. It was better not to see soldiers because you never knew what they were looking for. And everyone else who might come along was worse than the army. For some time, starving people had been coming down from Herzegovina every so often. Hordes of crazed savages arrived from Bosnia and Montenegro, stealing everything in their path and continuing on along the coast toward Trsteno and farther in the direction of Zaostrog and Makarska. It was hard for anyone to know what was really going on at the front. Austrian propaganda spread news that Serbia was about to fall and that the army and people were fleeing toward Albania. Italian ships were allegedly on the approaches to Dubrovnik. There was no trace of the French or English. It could be said that the Austrian emperor had already won the war. But there was less and less food. The villagers had raised the prices of potatoes and grain sky high, and the government seemed to have hunkered down. Its officials sat freezing in their offices, as if they were waiting to see in which direction the wet, metal roosters on the roofs of the observation towers would turn.

Niko Azinović was sitting in the darkness of his cellar, debating with three men not unlike himself about when a child acquires a human soul. It would soon be a year since his grandson had died, and Father Ivan had refused to conduct the funeral service and didn't want to hold the Requiem Mass. The boy's name had been Angelino. They'd given him that name to protect him because he was born prematurely and was smaller than a loaf of pauper's bread. His little sister had named him Lino. He wasn't baptized on time, but not because Kata and Rafo hadn't done their part. They had; they'd gone to the rectory three times, but that same Father Ivan hadn't had time. It's true that in those days a lot of people were dying. It was true that the priest had more urgent business and that it made more sense to baptize the children of those who could feed him better, but if it was already like that and if Father Ivan's mistake was that Lino had died as an unbaptized soul, did he really dare return him to the earth like a dog?

"That's not right," the first voice in the darkness said.

"Damn right it's not," the other confirmed.

"What do priests know?! They share the same plane with both God and the devil," a third said. No one inhaled any smoke.

In a moment there was the glow of a cigarette rolled from a mixture of mint and a little wad of tobacco, and it briefly illuminated the faces of the men. One was obese, his head was planted on a body that looked like a wrecking ball for old ships, and his small, close-set eyes kept blinking. The face of the other looked abnormally elongated, with an equine jaw and an expression of surprise that was in all likelihood more a feature of his physiognomy than it was the result of his being surprised. The third face was small and barely visible under a large French hat. A ten-year-old girl sat on a three-legged stool in front of the barrel. She was pretty. Her face belonged to someone who wasn't afraid and who wanted more than anything to show that she wasn't afraid.

"If it's not baptized, that doesn't mean it wasn't without a soul but that its soul wasn't baptized," Fatso said.

"Turks are unbaptized, but people say that they have a soul," Horse Face confirmed.

"It's not that people say that, but they have souls like anyone else," objected the third.

Niko took a drag, and it could be seen that the first two were frowning and the third bristled.

"Whose side are the Turks on?" asked Fatso sarcastically.

"They're neutral, like shit from a new bride!" said Horse Face. The one in the French hat didn't say anything. A few minutes of anticipation followed in which Fatso wheezed loudly, Horse Face clicked his tongue hoping to provoke a response, and Grandpa Niko breathed. The girl would recognize his sighs among hundreds of them. She pricked up her hears to hear whether the third one was breathing, but no sound came from where he was sitting. She was amused by the fact that he wasn't there any more. And then she thought that maybe he really wasn't there. Maybe he'd died like Lino. Simply stopped breathing. It could happen to anyone. It was wartime. Grandpa Niko took a drag, but she wasn't quick enough. She didn't manage to see the head in the French hat.

"I couldn't care less about Turkey. I have no peace because I don't know what happened to that child. And where its soul has been put. That's my blood, and you're thinking about Turkey because this didn't concern your blood," said Grandpa Niko.

"Of course it did . . ." Horse Face interjected, wanting to say something.

"No it didn't. If it had, you wouldn't be thinking about Turkey," Grandpa

Niko interrupted him. If he said another word, he would throw him out, and he could think and fend for himself. And outside it was raining, now as it would forever. Or at least until the war ended.

Grandpa Niko had said a few days before that it was good that it was raining and that they should pray that it was also raining on the western front. When it rained only bombs and bullets killed, but poison gas didn't. Every raindrop saved a human life. If it rained long enough, all of them would survive. As soon as you could smell the mustard gas, soldiers died, said Admiral Sterk. He wasn't a real admiral but a common clockmaker, but since the war had broken out, his mind had gone to seed, and he told people that he was an admiral. If you believed him, he would repair your watch and pass on secret information to you from the western front. If you laughed, if you said "Jozo, you're an admiral as much as I'm St. Peter!," as Antiša Bakunin had told him, then nothing would happen to your watch and you wouldn't get any news from the front. The news didn't matter, but how could you get along if you didn't know what time it was? After Andrijica Ćurlin and Beko Albi had gone off to war and since Albi Abinun had fled to America before the war, Admiral Sterk was the only clockmaker left in town. Bakunin apologized to him, bowed down to the ground, and swore that he would personally promote him to a field marshal, but it was no use—Admiral Sterk wouldn't repair his wall clock! And now Bakunin didn't know what time it was, no matter whether it was day or night!

"He would pave over all the churches, kill anyone who wore a braid—from the emperor down to office heads; he would abolish the police, and he doesn't even know what time it is," Grandpa Niko said, mocking Bakunin, and added that he didn't know who was the bigger nutcase of the two, Admiral Sterk or Antiša Bakunin. But he listened carefully to the news from the front, believed it, and remembered even what he didn't understand. So, for instance, the fact that when one could smell the mustard gas, soldiers were dying. The girl didn't know what mustard gas was and didn't ask because she thought that this was something you were supposed to know. If you didn't, it was better not to say so. She sniffed the air and thought she would be able to recognize the smell of mustard gas if it ever stopped raining. She would be the first to know when soldiers started dying.

"There's no power greater than Russia," Fatso said to break the awkward silence.

"Like we didn't know that," the one in the French hat said, coming to life.

"In Russia the sun rises twice," Fatso persisted, "once in the west and once in the east."

Hmm, and the girl had learned in school that it rises in the east and sets in the west! She waited for Grandpa Niko to tell him that.

"That's not the reason why Russia is powerful. That's because it's a crazy country. People know very well where the sun rises," the one in the French hat quibbled.

"Great, now some of us are smart too," said Horse Face and sighed. Grandpa Niko took another drag and threw his cigarette in front of his feet. He didn't have to put it out because the water was already coming into the cellar, and the cigarette went out on its own. The girl knew what was coming. Grandpa wanted the three of them to go but didn't know how to tell them that. It had been that way for days. They came to get out of the rain and then wouldn't leave. She didn't know anything about those men, not their names or where they went. But they were always at the same place, right in front of their cellar, and thought that they would get wet. And Grandpa Niko would let them in, treat them to diluted wine vinegar, and wait for them to leave. He was interested in what had happened to Lino's soul, and the three of them argued. It didn't matter what about. But why did they have to do it in his cellar of all places, when Grandpa Niko didn't want to argue? He was always angry after they left. Not even he knew who those people were, and maybe he didn't even know their names. The girl didn't ask him about that because she didn't want to know what their names were. Those men weren't from town. Grandpa Niko said that he hadn't seen them before the war. He was in fact afraid of them. Before their first escape from the rain into his cellar, Grandpa Niko had only feared God. That was what he'd said, and she'd believed him. He could have kicked them out, but how and why? He said that he didn't know.

They left a little before it began to get dark. Every day it was the same. Fortunately, the days were getting shorter and shorter.

"God help us if they ever want to spend the night here," Grandpa Niko said to her mother. She was in the kitchen boiling the laundry, and her father was sorting nails in the little bit of light cast by the fire in the stove. Hidden from view, her brothers tussled over two stone marbles.

"God help us, God help us," he repeated and walked from one end of the room to another. Either he was looking for something, or he was trying to remember something. It had gotten dark, and now all of life was weighing down on his shoulders. It was important for his gall to pass as soon as possible, for no one to say anything rude to him, and for her brothers not to fight. If that happened, he would entertain them until they all fell asleep.

A hundred hundred years ago, when people still didn't know that wind blows sails and that the wheels on a baby carriage turn, before there were any unchristened creatures, instead of karst and quarries there were dense pine forests everywhere. And in them lived fairies and sprites; there were more of them than people in the world. In those forests there were more birds than there are today anywhere, more bears, foxes, wolves, and all kinds of creatures that one can't even imagine. Everything was tame; they ate food off of each others' heads because there were no beasts that acted wickedly to another animal. People were the only thing that wasn't in those forests. If some hardhead took courage and went off into the forest, his mother would mourn him because he would never return home. Not alive or dead, nor would they be able to make out his soul on judgment day. That was the way it was! No man thought it up, nor did the Lord God either. It was the way of fairies and sprites. They guarded the forest from everything human and divine, and you can guess for whom they did it! No, they didn't do it for the devil because this was a hundred hundred years ago, and the devil didn't exist yet. The fairies and sprites guarded the forest for the beasts, just as the beasts guarded the forest for them. And it would have stayed that way until the end of the world if this hadn't happened: Srdelica, the daughter of a fisherman named Cipolić, fell ill, and his daughter had caught the eye of the young Lubinko. The young man was as smart as a book, as good as a calm sea, and so handsome that no one could say what he was as handsome as. If someone said that anything was as handsome as Lubinko, everyone would laugh and say that that person was a nut. Lubinko sought a cure for Srdelica, his love; he searched for it from Boka all the way up to Trieste, but there was no cure anywhere. The best healers told him that the only thing that could cure her were džundžur beans. Do you know what džundžur beans are? You don't! But you'll know at the end of the story. Not even Lubinko knew what džundžur beans were, nor did the healers or anyone living by the sea a hundred hundred years ago. But people knew that one could only find them on the other side of the dense, magic forests that grew where today we have only rock and karst. So whoever fell ill and needed džundžur beans was as good as dead. But the handsome Lubinko didn't think like that. He kissed his Srdelica seven times, so the kisses would last until he came back, and set off into the forest to cross over to the other side, where the džundžur beans grew. Everyone tried to dissuade him; old Cipolić tried to dissuade him and told him that he would adopt him as his son if he didn't go. He pleaded with him in the name of his daughter's beauty, but Lubinko wouldn't be talked out of it. If there were džundžur beans in the world, he had to go find them—that's what he said and set off into the forest. He'd gone only three steps into the forest when it swallowed him up. He wouldn't have been able to go back if he'd wanted to. That was how the fairies had arranged things. Whoever went in never came out. So he walked for a day, then two, and then three; he came upon all kinds of beasts—bears with rabbits' ears, rabbits with bears' heads, winged wolves that fed on pine nuts and drank sap instead of water—but not a single beast was afraid of him because the fairies had made things so that fear would never enter the forest. On the seventh day Lubinko came to a palace that was bigger than a city and higher than the sky. The tops of its towers were so high that an eagle wouldn't be able to soar up to them. The palace wasn't made of stone but of salt. The fairies and sprites lived there. He knew that right away but didn't know how he knew. It just came to him. He stopped in front of the gate. His heart was pounding like crazy, but he remembered his Srdelica and knocked on the gate. He didn't strike it very hard, but the gate collapsed into powder right in front of him, into pure white salt, and suddenly there appeared a beautiful maiden with hair of burning gold, with the figure of a cypress tree, and wings of wind. That was Varja, the queen of the fairies.

"What are you doing here, poor man?" the queen asked him.

"I'm going to the other side; I'm going to get džundžur beans!" Lubinko answered courageously.

"No man has reached the other side," the fairy said and laughed at him.

"Has anyone ever reached your palace?" Lubinko asked her.

"No," answered the queen. "Every one of them up to now killed an animal or stepped on an ant. And here there is a rule that you turn into whatever you kill right away. The demi-beasts that you met were once people," the fairy said to him and asked him why he needed džundžur beans.

"I need them for medicine."

"And are you sick?"

"I'm not sick, but my Srdelica is."

"And you'd turn into a forest animal for her?" the queen asked, surprised.

"I'd turn into a rat if it would help her get better."

The queen fell into thought and was not happy. How could she be happy when she'd taken a fancy to such a hero?

"And is your Srdelica prettier than me?" she asked.

"It depends on who you ask," answered Lubinko. "I think she is!"

But how could poor Srdelica be prettier than the queen of the fairies?! Varja the fairy was the prettiest of all female beings in the world. But the problem was that Lubinko was the most handsome of all male beings in the world. More handsome than all the sprites put together, and Varja had fallen in love with him!

"Here's what you and I will do," she began. "I'll pick you some džundžur beans, and you'll give me your heart!"

"I can't give you my heart when my heart is locked, and my Srdelica has the keys," Lubinko said to her.

"Don't you worry about the keys," the fairy said. "If you give me your heart, I'll unlock it."

Lubinko saw that the fairy had magic powers and that she had the medicine for Srdelica, so he agreed. He waited for three days in front of the palace of salt for the queen to bring the džundžur beans, and on the fourth day there she was, with wounds on her legs, half dead because it was a long way to the other side even for her.

"Beautiful fairy, give me the džundžur beans," Lubinko said straightaway, and she clenched something in her palm and said:

"I'm not giving them. First you pluck out your heart as a pledge that you'll come back."

"How can I pluck it out? I can't live without my heart."

"You can; why wouldn't you be able to? Whoever plucks out his heart in the enchanted forest can live without his heart; he just can't love. I'll return it to you as soon as you fulfill your vow, and we'll live happily in the palace of salt."

Lubinko had no choice and plucked out his beating heart, and the fairy gave him two brightly colored marbles.

"Those are džundžur beans. Have Srdelica close her eyes, cross her middle and index fingers, and pass them over the džundžur beans like that. As soon as it seems to her that there are four of them and not two, she'll be healthy. Then you come back to me because your heart is with me. You will suffer great misfortune if you don't return."

Lubinko promised Queen Varja to come back and knew there and then that he wouldn't keep the promise. When he got back home, Srdelica was already half dead. She was bidding farewell to her mother and father, ready to lie down in her cold grave. But as soon as she passed her crossed fingers over the magic džundžur beans, her strength and health came back to her. She jumped up out of her bed, and a great celebration followed. From Boka to Trieste they celebrated for seven days and seven nights. Everyone celebrated, only Lubinko and Srdelica didn't. When he touched her, it was as if he were touching wood; when he looked at her, it was as if he were looking at a corpse; and when he wanted to kiss her, Srdelica turned her head away. He was as cold as ice to her and as disgusting as green carob. He looked like her Lubinko but was as foreign to her as a black Arab. She didn't know what was going on. He did! They were no longer for one another, but they wept together for seven days and seven nights. Being able to cry together was all that was left of their love. During that time the fairy queen realized that Lubinko wasn't coming back, that he'd deceived her, and that she held a locked heart in her hands in vain. She was unhappy; she was desperate and was ready to give her queendom for his love. The other fairies told her that she'd gotten involved in something wicked; the sprites danced and sang around her all day long, hoping that one would capture her heart and thus save the queendom, but she didn't look at any of them. The queen took the key that unlocks all hearts and said, "If you won't be mine, you won't be anyone's!"

She shoved the key into the lock of Lubinko's heart, and as soon as she did that, the palace of salt began to collapse, and the forest started withering. No one could bear looking at that horror, and all living beings on the Earth closed their eyes. After they had blinked seventeen times, in the place where the enchanted forest had been there was only a quarry and karst, and the palace had turned into a pillar of salt as high as the sky. The bora swept the salt into the sea, and ever since that time the sea has been salty, just as since that time all living creatures have blinked. They began blinking because they couldn't watch the ruin of the queendom of the fairies. When on the eighth day Lubinko went to the forest to get his heart from Varja, there was no forest, no fairies, no strange beasts.

They had disappeared because the queen had committed evil and unlocked a heart that belonged to another woman. So, you see, that's how the forest above the sea disappeared, and that's how people without hearts came into being and unhappiness took hold in the world.

As always, he finished the story in darkness and silence. No one asked any questions; the boys just gave one another their stone marbles, and every time they passed their crossed fingers over them, it seemed to them that there were four. That was proof that Grandpa Niko hadn't made anything up and that a hundred hundred years before there had been džundžur beans, a magic medicine for fatal illnesses. His little girl needed no such proof. She believed her grandpa's stories because you had to believe that something so terrible was true. One can always make up stories in which everything has a happy end. Terrible stories are true. If Grandpa Niko lied sometimes, that night he surely wasn't. The girl was cold, although she was covered with thick down quilts, between her brothers whose hot, sleeping bodies would await the dawn peacefully. She didn't sleep but tried to hear the beats of her heart as she usually heard them when she plugged her ears well or when she didn't breathe for a fairly long time. No matter what she did, now she couldn't hear her heart. She'd lived the fate of handsome Lubinko! Who knew how or why?! She hadn't deceived anyone, hadn't told a lie, but had still ended up without a heart. Something would be missing from the world; she would see it as soon as it grew light. The girl was sure and was desperate. Her brothers were sleeping peacefully. Nothing would happen to them.

It was raining for the twenty-eighth day. Rumors came that there were mud- and rockslides all around. People said that on Korčula and Hvar whole olive groves and vineyards had disappeared, along with houses and boundary stones. People stood on the shore and looked at their plots under the seas. They had no choice but to turn into fish and start cultivating seaweed. Since morning the neighborhood women had been coming to see her mother Kata, and all of them said the same thing. Just as Korčula and Hvar had fallen into the sea, so will we all—if the rains continue—fall right into the sea! They listed the names of the island towns that had disappeared; many in town had relatives there. They listed the names of the people. They did that as if reading a school roster, and horror filled their eyes. It was the first time people spoke about misfortune without any malice. The girl was sure that she had some role in all of that. She was to blame for the imminent flood. The women blinked and wrung tears of fear from their eyes. She blinked too. The whole world had started to blink while the enchanted forest was disappearing. That morning they were blinking more quickly and more often. No one was talking about the war. For the first time in the last two and a half years.

"You're crazy, you foolish women!" Grandpa Niko shouted at the group of women in their headscarves and swatted the air with his hand as if he were chasing away flies. "Which one of you started all this shit? Tell me, so I can give her what she deserves! Just how can you know that about Hvar and Korčula when not a single boat has sailed for ten days? Who told you about this? How?" he raged and in the end asked a completely rational question: Who had told them that olive groves were slipping into the sea?

No matter how panicked they were, the women were insulted by his attack. No one had actually told them about it, but if the whole town was abuzz, then it was true. It was less important how that truth had swum across the Korčula and Pelješac channels. Bad news is heard from afar, and what fool would lie and make up tales of woe? They tossed their black headscarves over their heads and went out into the rain. If there weren't any men, there wouldn't be so much misfortune in the world. The girl was on their side. That morning grandpa couldn't be believed. He was angry because he knew that the three men were coming again that day. He'd been waiting for them since he'd woken up and couldn't come up with any way of getting rid of them. Another thing that was hard to understand. If mother could chase off crazy Firgo when he came to ask for bread and she didn't have half his strength, why couldn't grandpa chase those men away? Only her father was calm that morning. He sorted his nails and sighed deeply. That was how Grandpa Niko sighed when he lost at briscola, but that only happened twice a year. Father lost at briscola every two minutes. He was calm, and he had it worst. The girl comforted herself a little. If father could get by with his sighs, then she could too. Without a heart.

At around noon someone knocked on the door. Grandpa rolled his eyes; for an instant all she could see were the whites of his eyes:

"Girl, they've come! Let's go down into the cellar!"

The girl jumped up and went toward the door, proud that grandpa always called her when it was time to go to the cellar. Never her brothers. True, they wouldn't have gone, but that wasn't important. What was important was that he never called them. They weren't up to going down into the cellar!

"Ooh, that's you!" Grandpa Niko said, full of enthusiasm. Dominko Pujdin jumped back with surprise. He didn't expect that Niko would ever receive him like that. They were the same age; they'd grown up together and fished together when they were young. Friends in any case, but not so close that they would want to see each other so much when they hadn't seen each other for a couple of days.

"It's not them; we don't have to go to the cellar! Grandpa said, keeping up his cheer. Dominko Pujdin shook off his raincoat, something made his back twitch, and Grandpa asked him why he was going out if he had the shakes. He shot him a glance, as if to say it was something important, and Grandpa gaped at him as if to ask what had happened. Dominko Pujdin raised his eyebrows almost higher than his brow, as if to say it was something very confidential.

"What?" Grandpa Niko whispered.

"Nobody can know; otherwise it's ruined," said Dominko Pujdin. "A caravan is coming. The caravan drivers are arriving . . ."

"It can't be!" Grandpa said, astonished. The girl didn't understand anything. Her mother came out of the kitchen as if she didn't like what she was hearing. Her father stopped going through his nails.

"The caravan drivers!" he repeated, surprised. There couldn't be any doubt that the caravan drivers were arriving and that this confidential information should be kept quiet. Because if people found out, the deal was ruined.

They each lit a cigarette of mint and tobacco. Good news had arrived, and it wasn't proper to be stingy with people, including oneself. They sat enjoying their cigarettes for a bit, and then Grandpa asked:

"And how will we know when they're here?"

Dominko Pujdin grinned as if he were Admiral Sterk:

"I've got it all arranged. They'll let me know!"

Since he was waiting for the caravan drivers to come, Grandpa completely forgot about the uninvited guests. The girl hadn't forgotten, but she was happy that he had. They hadn't felt so good since it had started raining. Or they hadn't felt so good since the beginning of the war. It was hard to remember good days since things had gone bad. And it had been a long time since things had started going the wrong way and against the order of the priests and the emperor. For those who had to have the sky fall on their heads to figure out that something was wrong, things had gone awry when Ferdinand had been killed in Sarajevo. That was when Dominko Pujdin had gotten the jitters. Others had already had a bad feeling during the Balkan Wars, when the underlings quartered what was once Turkish. Somewhere quite close, two or three hills away, blood would be spilled for land, and that was never good. No land was worth that, but the bigger trouble was that after the first man fell for land, the price of land began to rise to dizzying heights, and it would suddenly turn out that every inch of it sought new masters. And then blood would flow endlessly. People had to know that once doubt had been cast on what was Turkish, the same would happen with what was Austrian. Istanbul didn't have the strength to keep its land, so let's see if Vienna does! That was why Ferdinand had been killed in Sarajevo and the great war had begun. People waited for when their turn would come and their lives would be on the line. There was less and less food, and robbers and brigands again ruled the roads. The news that the caravan drivers were coming was therefore more valuable than the goods they were bringing. They would confirm that there was still justice and order in the world and that there was still respect for earthly laws, which were more important than the laws of states. And sometimes, it seemed, more important than God's laws. The caravan drivers would prove that custom was still respected! And the word for custom in Dalmatia was the Turkish *adet*, one of the few Turkish words that had remained there, on the coast and even out on the islands. It was no wonder because how could one say that the caravan drivers were coming except according to the old Turkish *adet*.

They didn't doubt that this was true at all, though it had been fifteen years since the last caravans had come. But since the war had started or since the merchant ships had become sparse and the trains stopped more often than they ran, people had been talking about caravan drivers. Someone had been to Sarajevo and had seen them. The Turks had realized that it was better to trade than to fight for someone else's benefit and had activated the Izmir connections; Austria had overrun Serbia, and there was no longer anything to prevent smuggling; Syria had an abundance of dried mutton and kid meat and was planning on transporting it to the West; there were potatoes from Anatolia, corn and wheat from somewhere, spices, sugar, wine, brandy . . . The people's fantasies ran wild, and all fantasies were connected to the East. The Turks, Arabs, matchless Jewish merchants; Damascus and Baghdad; the secrets of serpentine writing that writhed from the right to the left; the legend of Moses, who'd led his people through the wilderness; mosques facing the rising sun; incomprehensible customs and habits began to take hold of the Christian peoples who were torn between the Austrians and the Italians and whom now hunger had led to believe that salvation would come from the other side of the world, the one that didn't smell the odor of mustard gas, phosgene and diphosgene, and wasn't taking part in this war of ours that was from day to day less and less ours. As no one knew hardly anything about the East, except that caravans came from the East, their hopes for salvation came down to stories about caravan drivers.

People even knew which way they were supposed to come. It was the same way they'd been coming for centuries. The Turks would drive their goods to Ljubovija, where they would be taken over by men from Foča. Before the Smrdan watchtower near Banja Koviljača they would be reloaded.

"You don't go on a caravan without two hundred horses!" Dominko Pujdin said, sounding off and exaggerating. Then a new caravan would be formed and cross the Drina by ferry. It would have been simpler if the Turks crossed over to Bosnia before reloading, but they didn't do that, nor had they done it when Bosnia had been theirs. Their nasty beliefs drove them from that river, and those beliefs reached back to an earlier time when the sultan Mehmed el-Fatih had begun his conquest of Bosnia. At that time the river was called the Zelenka. It was high, and no one except the brave Kujundžićka, the mother of three brothers from Ustikolina, had ventured to go by ferry to fetch the sultan. More than anyone else it was that woman who had helped el-Fatih to conquer Bosnia. She arrived for him and his horse, but the beast got frightened in the middle of the water, fell into the river, and drowned. Then the sultan shouted, "Bu su derin!" which in Turkish means *This water is deep!* From the word *derin* the River Zelenka has been called the Drina ever since, and due to the death of the sultan's horse, the Turkish caravan drivers crossed it unwillingly. Well, after the Foča caravan crossed the river at the Smrdan watchtower (Dominko Pujdin knew all kinds of things about it, but there were those who knew better than he and went into more detail), it would start toward the rich Semberija town of Janja. There it would be additionally loaded with corn and wheat and start along the Drina, making its way through the canyons and high mountains along the river, and then, God willing, it would arrive in Dubrovnik five days later.

"Now it'll take them ten days," said Grandpa Niko. "These are dangerous times, and the caravan drivers have to be cautious." Dominko Pujdin nodded self-importantly. Father returned to his nails. Grandpa was evidently thinking about whether to roll three more cigarettes, but that seemed to him to be too extravagant. They still didn't know how much treasure would come along with the caravan and how much it would cost. When he realized that the smoking was over for today, Dominko Pujdin went home. He would let them know as soon as he heard that the caravan was nearing the city. They didn't need to worry; soon the house would be full of all of God's gifts.

The phantoms were evidently waiting for the guest to leave because Dominko Pujdin had hardly made it down the stairs and they were already knocking on the door.

"Help us, neighbor, the rain is killing us!" shouted the one with the French hat. Contritely and already far away from the good news, Grandpa put on his coat; Mother looked at him reproachfully and said nothing. How could you tell a man, and your own father, such things? The girl stole off after him. She took care to be as inconspicuous as possible because she was sure the day would come when her mother wouldn't let her go to the cellar with Grandfather any more. That would be her way of telling him that it wasn't good for him to be letting those men in.

He poured some diluted vinegar, and the goblet went from one mouth to another. A little light still came in from outside, and they could see one another better than they had the day before. Fatso was short, with thin, short arms. One could tell that he'd never done anything. Horse Face wasn't elongated in his face only. He was all like a reed bent at the top under the weight of its seed head. His palms were large, like shovels, but he didn't look dangerous. The small-headed one with the French hat was, however, terrible. Whether it was because of the disproportionate size of his head in relation to his body or because his body was really huge, the girl thought he was three times taller and more powerful than Grandpa Niko. The day before she could see him only in the glow of the cigarette and he hadn't been like that, but he hadn't been that way the day before that either, when they'd come around noon and there was enough light to see by. Two days before Horse Face had also been a little shorter and fatter, and Fatso hadn't had a boy's hands . . . They changed every day, she thought. Grandpa opened his mouth silently, like a red porgy when a net is lifted out of the water, because he wanted to say something, but he didn't know what. He couldn't tell them about the caravan drivers. And maybe he too saw that those men were sometimes smaller and weaker and sometimes bigger and more wicked.

"You say the priest claimed that the boy didn't have a soul," Horse Face spoke first.

"Ugh, shame on them," Fatso said, jumping up.

"Priests have no shame," said the Monster with the French hat.

"Hodjas do, thank God," said Horse Face.

"And what do you care about hodjas — do you have them in Dubrovnik . . . ?" asked French Hat.

"I don't, I'm just saying . . ." said Horse Face.

"Forget that. What was that about the soul?" Fatso interjected. Grandpa kept moving his lips without managing to say anything.

"As if they would wash their bottoms so much if they were thinking about the soul . . ." Horse Face said.

"Who do you mean? Are you talking about hodjas again?" asked the French Hat.

"No, I'm not, dammit!" Horse Face answered. "You think about hodjas as soon as I mention bottoms."

"Come on, people, get serious. The man's child died, and the priest didn't want to bury it," Fatso shouted.

"Don't talk about it now," said Grandpa Niko.

"Why not?!" Horse Face objected. "It can't be that you don't care any more?"

Grandpa didn't answer. His lower jaw quivered as if he were about to cry or he was very angry. The girl grew frightened. Her heart was beating like crazy. So it's here after all, she thought. But her fear didn't lessen.

"How can he not care?!" Fatso said and slapped his knees. "It's not like he's an animal and he doesn't care. He's a man. A baptized man! Right, old man, aren't you baptized?"

Grandpa said nothing and looked at the tips of his shoes.

"Tell us, dammit, are you baptized? Look at him; he's not saying anything. You come in to get out of the rain, and he doesn't say anything. It would have been better to stay outside. Wouldn't it have been better to stay outside?" Fatso said and raised his hands as if to say "Got me." Monster stood up and paced around the cellar; the tip of his hat nearly brushed the beams on the ceiling. He paced around and was very nervous. And he wanted everyone to see how nervous he was.

"You, little girl," he said, putting his index finger on her forehead. "Do you have a soul?"

She looked at her grandpa, but he didn't seem to notice what was going on. He sat there with his hands folded, leaning on his knees, and watched what was going on in the mud floor. Monster didn't take his finger away; he poked her to get her to answer, and she was waiting on what her grandpa would do. She waited for a very long time. Maybe hours passed, maybe even days, time that couldn't be measured by anything. He never told her what to do. The girl would forget what happened further, and by virtue of that it was as if nothing had happened. The phantoms laughed for a long time; one by one they patted Grandpa Niko on the shoulders, hit him on his back as if he were choking, embraced him, and slapped him on his cheeks, and he sat in the same position; tears were streaming down his cheeks and falling onto the mud floor of the cellar, which soon turned into a little lake.

"The old man's afraid we might spend the night at his place," said Horse Face on their way out. It was as if Grandpa couldn't hear.

That evening Grandpa Niko didn't tell a story. Mother said that he didn't feel well, so they all had to be quiet. In the light of the fire in the stove the girl watched the nails passing from one box to another. And then the fire went out. The boys hit one another and wrestled under the quilt. She knew that she would never again go down into the cellar with Grandpa. And she didn't want the caravan drivers to come, not ever. Or she wanted them to come but not to give him anything. He was in the next room, filled with bitter regret that he was too old for this war. If he'd been picked with all those in the third mobilization call, he would have met his end on the River Soča, in Galicia, Albania, or on one of hundreds of battlefields where the brave imperial army was fighting. He would have died like a man. He would have spilled his own guts in the snow; the smell of mustard gas would have sent him to hell; something ordinary and usual would have happened. He would have fared just like thousands of others. Everything is easy when you're not alone but one of many. And everything is easy when your own kin don't know what kind of misery and fear you're made of.

On the twenty-ninth day the rain was gone. No one knew when or how it had stopped raining. With the first light people came creeping out of their houses, and it was gone. Clear weather was moving in from the sea; here and there the sun broke through the clouds. Children started running around. They hadn't been let outside for days and had built up energy that they needed to release in wild play. They chased rats through the town; there were hundreds of them, and they poked their heads out of flooded cellars and basements, and when the children caught up with one, they would stomp on it, stopping it in its path and shouting, "The rat's got falcon wings!"

In the middle of all that chaos something else happened that was supposed to be a secret. Hiding from one another, the elderly went toward Rijeka Dubrovačka with baskets, burlap sacks, and all kinds of bags. If two of them who knew each other met, they made up the wildest lies about where they were going with their empty sacks and bags. All in hopes that the other one didn't know after all that the caravan drivers were coming and that it was true when the other one said that he was going to the hills to get something that he'd forgotten before the rain. They clenched a ducat or two in their pockets or a wedding band, medallions with the image of the Blessed Virgin, chains, earrings, wartime bonds and all kinds of money. Anything that might be of some value to the caravan drivers. Grandpa Niko and Dominko Pujdin were among the few that went together.

"Yeah, we're going to see whether there's any dry firewood anywhere," Dominko said to Admiral Sterk, who was carrying a wattle basket on his back that was at least twice his size.

"If somebody loaded it with spider webs, he wouldn't be able to get it back," Niko whispered.

"And I'm off to the admiralty. They've informed me that my promotion to an officer has come in," Sterk bragged. "It might be the last one because we're losing the war!" he added without fear that the wrong ears might hear.

That was the first time that Admiral Sterk mentioned the possibility of Austria's losing the war. Both Niko and Dominko felt equally awkward. The clockmaker was crazy, there was no doubt about that, but no matter how crazy he was, he'd never spoken about defeat. What could that mean? It was better to keep quiet and not jinx it, so they continued walking, each with his own dark inklings and bitter that the admiral had spoiled their excitement about the caravan drivers.

The meeting place was in Mokošica and not on the road to Trebinje. Probably out of fear of some plot, as a caution against highway robbers. And outside Mokošica there was something for them to see! A few hundred people had come there, along various paths, hiding from neighbors and friends; they'd come at various times, some even before dawn. And they kept coming. They watched each other grimly, and only rarely would they greet one another. In those glances, without words, the bonds of friendship and godfatherhood fell apart. A few chatted cheerfully and kept looking at their watches, wondering whether that caravan would finally get there. Those were people who'd come in pairs or even in small groups; if they'd antagonized someone, if they'd lied to their neighbors about where they were going, they nevertheless told the truth to those they were closest to.

The two of them selected a good spot given the direction that the caravan would be coming from. They spread out their sacks and sat down. Niko took out some cigarettes he'd rolled for the occasion; they lit up and watched the people. It had been a long time since so many people had met in one place. Maybe not since 1914 and the week after the assassination, when people had first mourned for the archduke and his pregnant wife and demonstrated against Serbia and then indeed smashed things up a bit in Serbian stores and shops.

None of them had actually done any smashing except Dominko Pujdin—he had! He had smashed the windows of Sveto Stojnić's shop; it was well known whose side Sveto was on; he practically had a Russian flag hanging out of his butt, and Serbia was always close to his heart. Later Pujdin regretted it. Not so much because he'd smashed Sveto's shop window; if he hadn't, someone else would have. But he had gone into the shop through the smashed window, stomped on all of the pipes and chibouks, torn apart the sacks of tobacco, and given the owner a good slapping. For that he couldn't forgive himself. He had slapped a man stronger than himself, and that man hadn't defended himself. So he had hit him again and then again. And nine more times. He prayed to God for Sveto to hit him back. Or at least for him to dodge. But no! Sveto had stood there like Orlando, without moving or blinking. He had looked straight ahead, somewhere over Dominko Pujdin's head, and had only mechanically flinched whenever he had hit him in the face. Finally he had fled Sveto's shop, run through the town as if he were a Serb and people were chasing him, and couldn't pull himself together for days. He lost the will to do anything that would take him to Sveto's storefront. All he wanted was never to meet Sveto Stojnić again because he didn't know how he could pass by him and live. He would completely die of shame if he ever came face to face with him, he thought. But why? Because he'd always greeted that man politely and had never been bothered by Sveto's championing of the Serbs and Russians. He hadn't thought about that as something that should concern him. If he had earned some money and wanted to treat himself to some good tobacco, he went to Sveto. Sveto would invite him to sit down and let him sniff five of the sacks. The tobacco was fantastic. He never cheated him or overcharged him. And so how could he have had something against such a man? There was no reason for it! Up until Ferdinand was killed and he'd lost his mind and then gone off and smashed up the first Serbian shop window he could think of and slapped a man stronger than himself. A man who wouldn't pay him back because he'd ended up on the wrong side through no fault of his own. Dominko Pujdin had gone through a lot of anguish on account of Sveto Stojnić, and he wasn't particularly relieved when in a couple of weeks he learned that Sveto had packed up his family and left for Serbia. This world wasn't so big; sooner or later Dominko Pujdin would run into Sveto somewhere and die of shame. Even if he didn't meet him, he wouldn't be able to forget what had happened after Ferdinand was killed in Sarajevo. Maybe Sveto would forget it one day, though that wasn't likely, but Dominko Pujdin would never be able to forget his shame. That was the kind of man he was. Screwed up and honest, as Niko would say.

They liked the fact that there were so many people. People had hardly gone outside for a month, but now the rain had stopped and everyone was going back out among people. True, those people weren't particularly talkative; it was true that they were sizing each other up like roosters before a cockfight; it was true that some might lose their lives and that there wouldn't be enough wares for everyone, but it was nevertheless somehow good. After the long, suffocating ordeals of going back and forth from the kitchen to the cellar, Niko was able to rest his mind. It stung him that his granddaughter hadn't even looked at him that morning. She hadn't said anything, even when he told her that he would bring something back for her too—the caravan drivers always brought sweets for children, kerchiefs for women, and a fine chibouk here and there, a nargileh or similar things to lure money out of your pocket. She acted as if she hadn't heard or she didn't care. But she did care! She'd cajoled him and buttered him up so many times in hopes that he would bring her something from town. He would always bring something because he knew she'd be excited. He'd spend a lot of money on a few dates, bring the first ripe rose hips, a hairpin or a fuzzy toy rabbit . . . But now she hadn't even looked at him! Regardless of the fact that he really wanted her to look at him, to be happy at seeing him, to give him a hug and ask him to take her along. Or maybe she hadn't looked at him precisely because it was so important to him. She was a child, but she already knew how to punish adults. Actually, how women punish men who love them. That was something new in the life of Niko Azinović. His wife Bare had never given him the silent treatment. She hadn't had time because she'd died too early, but he was sure that she wouldn't have done such things. Niko thought Bare was the embodiment of a real angel and so never married again.

But what if the girl was right? He hadn't lifted a finger when that jerk had frightened her, putting his finger on her forehead and looking at her the way a hunter looks at a bear cub, seeing where he would put a bullet in it so as not to damage the hide. Yes, he knew that nothing would happen and that all he needed to do was wait until those uninvited guests left, but the little girl hadn't known that. And if she had, it wouldn't have made any difference. She wanted him to defend her. But what she saw was him bowing his head before power. He didn't defend her, and that was what mattered to her. She surely thought that those robbers had spared her life and that Grandpa wouldn't have lifted a finger if they'd wanted to cut her throat.

"I'm going home!" he said, getting up and reaching for his sack.

"What's wrong, did I say something wrong?" Dominko Pujdin asked and grabbed him by the arm.

"No, but I have to go home. Now!"

"Are you crazy?—the caravan is almost here. All kinds of things to buy. What's wrong with you?"

"Nothing's wrong with me, but I'm going . . ."

"And what are you going to tell everyone at home? What will you say to them when you're feeding them bran, and whoever isn't dirt poor is eating what the caravan brought?"

Niko stopped. The old man was right. You can't come home with empty hands and an empty sack. He'd done something wrong, and now he was wanting to make that right by doing something worse. But the thought that the girl was thinking what she surely was and scorned him was unbearable.

"I insulted Regina. Terribly," he said.

"Who?" Dominko Pujdin asked; he didn't understand.

"My little girl. My granddaughter," he said and his eyes filled with tears from the sound of his words.

"Leave the child in peace," he said, holding firmly on to Niko's arm. "She'll forget about it, whatever it was."

Dominko Pujdin couldn't have done any more for him. He'd said something he didn't believe, but he thought that it was what Niko wanted to hear. He couldn't figure out what that man, who was his friend, was doing with his life. And had always been doing with it. Instead of getting over his wife and finding another, he had stayed alone. He spoke with children as if they were grown-ups. Next he would be speaking with birds and goats as if they were his equals . . .

Niko sat back down on the sack, but in his mind he was going through everything he would do when he got back home. He would tell her that for her he would . . . No, he wouldn't tell her anything. Not today. If she didn't look at him and didn't take what he was bringing her, he would act as if nothing were wrong. But the next day he would be waiting for those three with an axe — or should he borrow a hunting rifle from Dominko? Then he'd get them off his doorstep. The girl would watch that . . . No! Regina would watch it. From now on he wouldn't call her a little girl, nor a child, or a little one . . . She had her own name! If he'd thought of her as Regina, he wouldn't have acted like that. Or would he? It was no longer important. What was important was that he would chase them off his doorstep with an axe and a rifle! He would tell them off as he'd never told anyone off in his life. He'd also tell them that the only way they were coming in was over his dead body. Because they'd laid their hands on what he valued most. Regina was dearer to his heart than his two daughters. When you become a father, you fear your own children, but when you become a grandfather, you are the happiest you've ever been. He wouldn't tell his daughter that, but he had to keep it in mind! If he'd thought that then, what had happened never would have happened. And if — God forbid — they attacked him, he would shoot! That was why it was better to get the rifle from Dominko. With an axe you're never sure. He would shoot and kill! No court in the world would convict him for that. If someone tries to force their way into your home, you have the right to kill them! But what if you don't? He would do hard labor if he had to, but there was no way he could stand by and watch his kin be threatened! If he'd thought like that the day before, he wouldn't be feeling as he did today. It was better to go underground than to have your soul come apart. And his soul was coming apart!

They'd been sitting for two hours, and people kept coming. It seemed as if all of Dubrovnik had found out about the caravan. At one point it started to get on Dominko Pujdin's nerves. He was really galled when he realized that everyone had learned the same thing in confidence, maybe at the same time, in the same way that he had. Yeah, what kind of people are we? — he wondered. The worst pagan had more honor than that! And now the problem with Niko: every so often he would look at him. He would try to start a conversation, but Niko would answer curtly. It was clear that nothing mattered to him, and he kept staring at the same spot, getting wrinkles like an old oak tree—with every minute a new wrinkle appeared on his face, and one could see that great anguish had taken hold of him. Worst of all was that Dominko Pujdin was sure that his anguish was all for nothing.

"Turks have plundered the caravan! In Trebinje, at Arslanagić Bridge," said a giant of a man in a Konavle peasant outfit as he made his way through the people. "We don't have any choice but to get ready and head up there!" he said, gripping a muzzle-loading pistol (which was probably two hundred years old) to show that he was already ready to go.

"What will we do up there? If they plundered the caravan, then there won't be any stuff left. I don't feel like dying, thank you very much!"

"I'm not going!" Čare Nedoklan objected.

"Well, I'll go, by God! Are my kids supposed to go hungry just because of some Turkish thugs?" said another voice. The crowd began to stir and separate; everyone went in his own direction, swearwords flew, and people cursed God, others' mothers, and unborn Turkish children, and there were those who just gave up, grabbing their sacks and baskets to go home.

"Nobody's leaving here!" the man from Konavle shouted, jumping out in front of the dispersing crowd and waving his pistol. "Let me just see a traitor to his kind! I'll cut his throat with these hands!" he shouted. The people stepped back.

Niko and Dominko Pujdin hadn't made their decision for one side or the other but hid and waited for the fury to pass or for what had to happen in such situations. That it would come to an angry march on Trebinje seemed unlikely to them. And if they did go, they would cool down on their way there.

The man from Konavle skipped around as if he'd lost his mind, ran around the mass of people like a sheepherder around his flock, and assembled those who agreed with him. Soon there were seven men, all ne'er-do-wells: one with water on the brain (whom no one knew), another barefoot and in torn pants (he had nothing that could buy him anything except his aggressive manner), three city dandies from good houses (men who'd avoided their mobilization calls and now wanted to fight the Turks), and one more named Sreten Kozomara, a defrocked Serbian priest who'd known how to choose his side with cunning since the days of the assassination. He'd gone burning Serbian houses and smashing Serbian shops, all so no one would torch his house. Sreten was the fiercest one of them apart from the man from Konavle. He would knock a man's hat off, jerk on the mustache of someone who argued with him, threaten anyone who objected to going on the march to Trebinje.

The seventh one of this strange group was Admiral Sterk. "We should take riflemen's positions!" he said, tugging the sleeve of the man from Konavle. "And appoint a commander — I'm highest in rank!" he said, pestering the pistol-packing hero like a blowfly. Since he wasn't from Dubrovnik and didn't have a watch that might break, the man from Konavle didn't know who Admiral Sterk was. But he took an immediate dislike to him — he hated the habit that towns-folk had of touching people when talking to them. And they always wanted something. He pushed Admiral Sterk away but not too hard. As a man pushes a man away when he starts bothering him. But the admiral ended up sprawled on the ground, and as he lay on his back, he started calling for help:

"Provocateur! Provocateur! People, don't believe what he says!"

But the people moved away from him as much as the man from Konavle and his little group would allow them.

They didn't even get involved when he grabbed Admiral Sterk by the throat and started to strangle him and yell for him to shut up. And not even when the admiral wouldn't shut up but kept on saying incomprehensible, but evidently hostile, words. They didn't even do anything when Admiral Sterk started wheezing. No one dared tell the man from Konavle to let him go and explain to him that the admiral was crazy but that he was one of them and repaired their watches, right until the admiral went limp in the man's grip and lay on the ground.

"Look, the pig wet himself!" Sreten Kozomara said and laughed and then was suddenly grim. He probably expected for the others to laugh, but no one did.

The man from Konavle looked in confusion at the work of his hands, a dead man who was lying with his legs spread apart and drinking the sky with his bulging eyes. The sky had cleared without them noticing. Someone calm and collected might have asked what was bluer — the eyes of a dead man or the sky after twenty-eight days of rain?

The first victim halted the warlord and his men for a moment. No, he wasn't afraid because he'd just killed someone; rather, he was inwardly surprised at how easily the soul had flown out of the man who'd opposed him. That showed how little he was worth and how little he was actually alive. He was like an ant — step on it and it's gone. Or a moth — you make a mechanical swat at it, and it comes apart on your palm. The man from Konavle was unable to feel guilty. Had he done something unusual, something that people otherwise didn't do to others? No! It would have been different if he'd cut his throat or smashed his skull with the handle of his pistol. That would have been too much if the man hadn't done anything wrong! Maybe this one had done something wrong, maybe he hadn't. Who the hell knew? God would send his soul where it belonged. God or St. Peter. It didn't matter. The man from Konavle was not learned enough to know how those things worked.

"Did you see?! Did you see?! Take a good look! And you too. Come and see whether you want to raise a fuss; take a look at what happens to those who do!" said the one with water on the brain and went out into the crowd of people. But the people looked away; they didn't want to have anything to do with either the one with water on his brain or the man from Konavle; nor did they see or hear anything . . . And no one would be able to accuse them of anything afterward. But it chafed them that they had their ducats in their pockets. They needed to hide them somehow—sew them into the lining of their coats, keep them under their tongues, shove them up their rear ends if need be, anything but walk around obliviously with the family valuables they still had. If you didn't say anything, your life wasn't on the line. But your ducats were! Sooner or later the man from Konavle would remember their ducats, and then it was all over. The caravan wasn't coming, there were no caravan drivers, and their doorsteps were far away . . .

"Should we wait until tomorrow?" asked Čare Nedoklan slyly. "If we leave today for Trebinje, we won't arrive until evening. And it's better to arm ourselves!"

At first the proposal seemed reasonable to the man from Konavle. The people in Trebinje would be waiting for them and slaughter them all like sheep if they went like they were. But if he let his band disperse now, he would never be able to get it back together; he knew this well. They were from Dubrovnik! They always hid before it came to bloodshed. The Turks had burned everything from Gruda and Vitaljina to Cavtat and the entrance to the city, and each time they had welcomed them with open arms. They would spread out rugs for them on Stradun, treat them, grease their palms, and praise them. Seven times! Well, they wouldn't do that now!

"Fine," the man from Konavle began; "we can't go into battle like this. You speak the truth. So let's do this: whoever has a rifle, knife, or pistol at home—he can go; and whoever doesn't—he can camp here!"

Of course, it turned out that everyone had weapons and that the town was armed better than Franz Joseph's army. Angry and ready for a fight, they rushed to head home, and then they would come back armed to the teeth at dawn the next morning. All they wanted was for the man from Konavle to let them go. Among a few hundred men there wasn't a one now who wasn't ready to hit the Turks hard.

"I've got two hunting rifles!" said Dominko Pujdin, standing up on his toes so the man from Konavle could see him and Sreten Kozomara could write it down in his register.

But just when they thought they were going to make an ass of him, the man from Konavle began to speak:

"But you'll leave all the money and ducats you have on you here, and you'll get them back tomorrow when you come with your rifles!"

The crowd fell silent abruptly. Their gazes wandered, and no one felt like going home any more. Those who a few moments before had acted as if they had whole arsenals in their cellars suddenly had no weapons other than maybe some fish spears. Sreten Kozomara grinned cunningly, tapped his pencil on his black book, and awaited his leader's decision.

They'd tried to deceive him, but after seven Turkish campaigns the town of Konavle had come to its senses. There would be no more Turkish sit-down parties in Dubrovnik on the backs of those from Konavle! He was proud of himself and his intelligence and looked down on them. Just as a falcon looks down on a rabbit nibbling grass and acts as if he's not there. The rabbit thinks the bird can't see a thing. Oh, the poor thing, the man from Konavle thought, enjoying his role, and then realized that he hadn't done himself any good at all by not letting himself be outwitted. The Dubrovnikers would stay there all night long, but in the morning he wouldn't have anything he needed to head out for Trebinje. Who would bring the rifles? And there were too many people for him to shake the ducats out of their pockets and pack them off to get their weapons. They would resist if he tried it and would rather die than leave their valuables in his care. That was the only thing you didn't dare take from them—the only thing that they would give their lives for. All their honor, courage, and integrity were tied up in it! The people from Dubrovnik cared nothing about anything other than their ducats and their asses. That was why they'd come there. They waited for the Turks to send them cheese and prosciutto, to exchange valuables for valuables, to trade and kiss the Turks' asses. And they couldn't care less whether the Turks burned down everything Christian up to the city gates on their way in or out. Filth and riffraff! They multiplied among themselves, fought among themselves, spat on each other, and didn't care about anyone outside the city walls. They didn't let anyone in who didn't show them power and who wasn't one of the Turks. And if he was, they let him in and bewitched him, fawned over him, and patted his Turkish ass until he himself didn't know why he'd come. That was how the man from Konavle looked at his potential troops, and it really seemed to him that he had more in common with the Turks than with them. He and the Turks would look at each other over their gunsights; he would slaughter them and they would slaughter him; he would parade their heads on pikes as pretty village girls fainted, just as the Turks would hang his head up from a tower at the border, to warn all Christians that they'd come before a world ruled by the star and crescent. In a strange way the Turks were his brothers, and these people who clutched their ducats in their sweaty palms and tried to find a way to run off were nothing to him. It is terrible when a leader realizes that his people are below his ankles.

Just when darkness began to settle on the camp, the stamp of horses' hooves was heard.

Whispers spread through the crowd: "Here they are . . . ! The caravan drivers . . . ! The caravan!"

The man from Konavle winced—it couldn't be possible that the Trebinje beys had let the caravan through! And his group of men ducked somewhat in fear. Or it only seemed so. Sreten Kozomara stuffed his register into his bosom. He wouldn't need it any more today. But instead of the caravan, only four horsemen came around the bend.

"Where are the goods . . . ?"

"There aren't any!" . . .

"But this is only the advance party!"

"And this idiot's been telling us that the Turks plundered the caravan . . ."

"We could have committed a sin!"

"Can anyone see the caravan?"

The horsemen's hats were pulled down over their brows; one could see that they had come from afar. No one from Dubrovnik had ever seen such hats or the kind they appeared to be at that distance.

"In my day they wore fezzes," Niko said.

"Ha, not even Turks from Foča are what they used to be!" said Dominko Pujdin, cheerful that everything was now going the way it should. But his cheer was short-lived, lasting only as long as it took for the horsemen to come close enough for them to see that the men in the hats had no faces. When they came closer, they could only see the horsemen's eyes in slits in black hoods. They looked like heralds of the plague in church illuminations.

"Sit down on the ground!" ordered the rider of a black horse. He rode out into the crowd a little to scare the people. His horse neighed and reared up; its horseshoes rang on the rocks, and four army rifles with bayonets attached flashed. The mass of people fell down on the ground, groaning, sighing, and blurting out appeals to God and the Blessed Virgin. The guard of the man from Konavle disappeared into the field of bowed heads. He alone remained standing, confused and upright, with his pistol in his belt and his arms spread wide as if he were going to catch a piglet running around in a yard.

"What's wrong with you, Prince Marko?! Can't you hear?!" said the leader of the horsemen as he rode up to him. "Would you like Alija Đerzelez to ask you nicely or to skin you alive? Sit down when I tell you to!"

If tears were worth anything, the man from Konavle would have wept his whole life away at that moment. He would have flowed away like a stream and disappeared in the grass and between the rocks, never to be seen again. He hesitated for a moment, though he didn't know why, and then sat down in the grass, cautiously, as if the ground were full of sharp needles, whereupon he vanished forever from all heroic tales.

That happened on the far end of the clearing, so Niko might not have heard every word, but what he did hear seemed familiar. As did the tattered shoes of untanned leather on the horsemen's feet. He'd heard that voice once before; he knew it well, too well to be mistaken. He bent down and crouched a little more, pressing his head between his knees to be as inconspicuous as possible. He took three of his four ducats out of his pocket and pressed them into the ground. Dominko Pujdin trembled beside him and glanced around as if he were going to jump up and try to flee. There was a deathly silence, broken only by someone's sobs.

The two men on sorrel horses kept riding in a circle around the mass of people, while the fourth, the one who'd ridden up last and was obviously the least skilled on a horse, tried to dismount from his enormous mare. But each time it shifted, and he would sit back down.

"Jump down already! You're not jumping on a girl!" taunted one of the outlaws riding the sorrel horses, whereupon the fourth one simply fell off the mare and slammed onto the ground like the carcass of a calf taken off a meat hook. His hat flew off and his hood almost fell off as well. Someone giggled, but the man quickly jumped up, and then it could be seen that he was unhealthily obese. He put on his hat and spoke:

"Listen to me good because lives are at stake. And they're yours, not ours! What you're going to do is come over here one by one, empty your pockets into this sack and then go over to the other end and sit down again. Do you hear? If it turns out that anyone didn't put everything in, if he hides gold or money, he'll get a bullet in the forehead. Got it?"

There instantly arose a wailing, shouts, simultaneous curses and pleas, murmurs and yells, a cacophony that could probably be matched only by that at the lower gates of Purgatory. The leader fired into the air, and the black horse leaped. Evidently it wasn't used to gunfire.

"Use your heads, people! We're offering to let you go back to your wives and children alive and well!"

No one wanted to go first. They shoved one another, those in the rear savagely kicking those in front of them in the back, until the man with the bag finally grabbed the first one by the collar and pulled him to himself.

"Don't, for the love of God!" cried the victim, Stjepo Mašklinica, a cobbler with twelve children, one of the few God-fearing men who went to Mass twice a day and gave alms even when they didn't have enough to eat.

"Well, brother, you got it wrong; I don't love any God," the fat one with the sack retorted and opened up the sack. Stjepo looked at him the way that St. Sebastian looked at the bowmen, thrust his hand into his pocket, and pulled a neatly folded white handkerchief out of it. In it was a ducat with Napoleon's image on it. Stjepo kissed the ducat and dropped it into the sack. The fat man roared with laughter:

"And you pulled this whole stunt to trick me?"

The cobbler had to take off his coat; the fat man searched him thoroughly and tore away the thin lining of his coat but found nothing. He hurled the coat into the mass of people. Then Stjepo had to take off his pants and his shoes, and finally he had to unwrap his footcloths. The fat man searched through everything and threw all of it into the people but didn't find anything.

"You mean you thought you were going to buy something from the caravan drivers with a single ducat?"

Barefoot and wearing nothing but his shirt, which covered his private parts, Stjepo Mašklinica stood there and almost felt guilty. He'd been motivated by the same things as the others, both avarice and the lure of fancy things. Poor Stjepo didn't know what he might buy from the caravan drivers. He'd gone like the others, hidden like the others, and lied to everyone about where he was going. He sat his bare backside down on the grass and tried to cover himself with his shirttails.

The fat man pulled the next one out of the crowd. That one was a little richer, but he tried to hide two rings in his socks and as a punishment he hit him in the head with the butt of his rifle. The first time he only groaned, and then he did it again and split his forehead. Blood started flowing. People saw that this was no joke.

"The next one who tries to cheat will have to pick his brains out of the grass!" the leader called out. He was on his black horse a little to one side, watching and simultaneously keeping control of the mass of people and checking what the fat man was doing.

Niko recognized three of the four robbers. The leader on the black horse was French Hat with the little head; Horse Face was riding around them on a sorrel horse, and Fatso, who'd seemed to be their leader when they were in his cellar, was the one with the sack. The fourth rider didn't interest him, and he wouldn't have been able to recognize him because he still hadn't spoken or done anything to give himself away. Niko still couldn't figure out what the point of their daily visits had been. They'd spent hours in his cellar, and that had to have had some connection to what was happening. Had they been trying to find something out from him? If they had, he hadn't noticed. He'd been absentminded and afraid; he'd believed that all he had to do was put up with them and they would go. And they did go, but they came back. He would have knocked them on their asses if it weren't for what had happened the day before . . . He thought of Regina, who was now playing under the kitchen table while Kata was kneading bran bread. Her little house was underneath that table; she cleaned it and made order in it, looked after the children, waited for the husband to come home from work, and tied the grandfather's shoes because he could bend down only with difficulty.

Niko couldn't understand that. Why did the grandfather in her imagination have a hard time bending down so that she had to tie his shoes? Everything else in Regina's little wooden house was modeled on his house. The only difference was that the grandfather underneath the kitchen table was weak and feeble. If he was still there. If Regina hadn't kicked him out of her house.

As the minutes passed, the highwaymen became more and more nervous. They were in a hurry because it would soon be evening and someone's crazy wife might get the police to start searching for her husband. Or maybe their wives might start coming all on their own, and there would be a huge, noisy scene; soldiers would appear from somewhere, and all kinds of things could happen. The fourth one started helping the fat one with the sack and the searches. He beat people, tore open their clothes, but continued to say nothing. Niko concluded that he had to be someone from the city who had reason to be afraid of being recognized. The first thing he'd done when he jumped down from his horse was put a rag over Admiral Sterk's dead face. That meant he knew him.

Those whose turns came later could hide a few ducats or a ring without much of a risk because there was no time to dig through people's pockets thoroughly. Čare Nedoklan tried to take advantage of this and held out one ducat and a ring with a blue stone for the fat man. This might have satisfied him, but it wasn't enough for his crony. The latter whispered something to the fat man; poor Čare had to undress, and they found four more ducats, two chains, and seven rings in his pockets and socks. He shivered from fear and the cold as the gold coins disappeared one by one into the darkness of the sack.

"For this we're going to stick you exactly thirteen times," said the fat one. At that instant the quiet one unslung his rifle from his shoulder, and with an agile movement, as if he were pitching hay, he thrust his bayonet into Čare's belly. Čare groaned and doubled over, and the quiet one stabbed him next to his shoulder blade. He stabbed him exactly thirteen times, even when Čare Nedoklan was already lying on the ground. Afterward the robbery proceeded much more quickly. People threw everything they had into the sack. The fat man's voice was shaky, and it seemed that he wanted to get it all over with as soon as possible.

When the sun went down, Kata was already half-crazed with worry. Grandpa Niko hadn't come back; the boys where roughhousing all over the place; her little girl wouldn't come out from under the table and wasn't saying a word; Rafo was picking through the nails more and more nervously, sighing like a furnace, and softly farting the whole time. She could kill him now! Instead of going to meet the old man and help him carry the goods home, he was messing around at home and exercising his butt. Everyone in the house farted out loud; he was the only one who was embarrassed. He thought his farts would be quiet, but it didn't work out that way, and his backside produced a whine that made the children laugh at him. He could have just farted like a man. But that didn't matter. What had happened to Grandpa Niko? Where was Angelina? Not even she would have gone looking for him but would have wandered around all day long. She argued back and forth with herself like that and then left her bread dough unkneaded, put on her shoes, and ran out. She stopped on the top of the cliffs and didn't know in which direction to go so that she and Grandpa wouldn't miss each other. And so she gave up and went back home. The boys had just gotten into a fight, and Rafo was trying to pull them apart.

"C'mon dammit, c'mon dammit, c'mon dammit . . . ," he said trying to get them apart, but it didn't work, and he finally sat down on his chair. She swore to them that she would go get Niko's whip and thrash all of them if anyone's nose started to bleed. Luckily, that didn't happen, and they settled down all on their own.

Underneath the table Regina was burying the grandfather in her little house. He'd died from varicose veins and tuberculosis. She'd made him a coffin from an old, cracked dough tray, put together a cross from a broken wooden spoon, and softly hummed a Mass through her nose. She'd never heard a Requiem Mass or what priests said at funerals, so she made it up.

"Grandpa croaked because he was no use to anyone," the priest said in a nasal tone. "He was good, slaughtered piglets; Jesus and Mary have mercy on his soul. He spilled the cup in all four directions. A piece of shit, a cow's cunt, catgut, whore, leprosy, slobber, and holy cross, have mercy on his soul," he continued devoutly, already so carried away that he started talking too loud and forgot that others could hear him. "Grandpa croaked, for all the saints and Jesus; the diarrhea has been passed, shit, fart, leprosy, slobber," the unusual priest spoke almost in a shout from the girl's lips as she sat with her hands folded. "God let the worms eat him, in the name of the Father, Son, and Holy Ghoooooost, aaameeeen!"

As she lowered the dough tray into the imaginary grave, she felt something tugging on her ear, like hot pliers. She suddenly became afraid.

"Have you lost your mind?" her mother asked and gave her a bloodcurdling look, as if she would devour her whole then and there. Even her father was on his feet again:

"To hell with you and those women's games!" he said as harshly as he knew how. She felt like putting up a fight, to fall down on the floor and hit and kick until they kneeled down and begged her to stop. But her mother didn't let go of her ear and only held onto it more tightly. Tears started flowing down Regina's face all on their own. It hurt and burned, but even worse: she knew that she hadn't done anything wrong, and yet no one would believe her. She'd been burying the grandfather in her little house. She hadn't been thinking of theirs. Their grandfather had ceased to exist for her after that man had tried to take her soul with his finger. Or he'd done something else; it didn't matter. Their grandfather hadn't defended her, so the priest wouldn't hold a Requiem Mass for him. Her priest! There was no Requiem Mass for those who had no souls.

Darkness had fallen, and the robbers had about thirty more victims to go. On the far end of the clearing, where those who'd already been robbed were sitting, it was already apparent that the daring of the mass of people was growing in proportion to the amount of valuables that had been lost.

Someone would swear out loud: "Fuck you and your three mothers!"

Others made threats: "I'll find you wherever you hide and wind your intestines around a pole!" . . .

People were squirming, and it wasn't certain that one or two hadn't already fled, soon to return with a search party. The fat man in charge of the sack had already appealed to the leader to let them quit—the sack was already full enough; they shouldn't overdo it. But the quiet one wouldn't let him. He was determined to get the last gold-plated ring. He slapped people, tore open their shirts and pants. One could hear blows, slaps, and groans, but not a sound came out of his mouth.

"That one must be a mute, but I'm surprised he's not deaf; he can hear what the others tell him," said Dominko Pujdin, failing to understand.

"Either he's a mute or he's from town," said Niko gloomily. "The others aren't!"

"How do you know they aren't?"

"I just do," he answered. He had no desire to try to explain, and how could he explain that in recent days he'd drunk three liters of vinegar and spent more time with them than with his own children?

But that couldn't end so simply! He didn't know how it might end, but he was sure it wouldn't end like this. A ducat wasn't a big problem (though he'd stuck three into the ground as if it were sweetbread for a party); the rings of his dead wife also weren't such a problem (they should have been thrown into her grave, but people wouldn't let him, saying that the living might have need of gold); the slaps that were waiting for him weren't a problem either. If he ended up looking like an ass, he wasn't a bigger ass than all the others who also ended up looking like asses. He'd fare just like everyone else. He wasn't any better or any smarter than these people. But those three men had pestered him for days and abused and insulted him. And it was on him that they'd tested out their courage for what they were doing now. And damned if they hadn't! The finger on Regina's forehead was like the finger of God. He hadn't dared to take a stand against it.

Niko Azinović had never been a big hero. He lived precisely according to the principles that children are raised by. People told him: you shouldn't steal, you shouldn't use bad language, you shouldn't kill, you shouldn't lie. Rather you should always wait your turn, obey the laws of men and God, work hard, and life will give everything back to you. Fathers told other children the same thing, just as their children would tell it to their children, and those children to theirs, as long as there was a world, people, and children. There were few who would adhere to all that and act just as their parents taught them to. Niko, to his detriment, was one of the few who did. Everyone would say he was a coward, but he wasn't a coward; it was just that he had been told that nothing was gained by force and with curses. He could see with his own eyes a hundred times that these were lies and that brutes always got on better, but no one could change just like that and change from one thing to another. Just as thrashings and hard labor wouldn't teach a thief not to steal, what a genuinely respectful man saw with his own eyes couldn't convince him that he wasn't better off. If people insult you, steer clear of them! He kept to that because he thought it was better but also because it was easier for him like that. What property he inherited, he would also leave to his children. He never drank or gambled any money away, nor did he earn anything. He had as many grapevines as his father had left him. He had lived in his house and patched his father's boat for years, until the wood was completely worm-eaten. And then he had built a new one himself. His way of life could hardly have offered him anything more. That was the way it was in Niko's time, and who knew whether it could have ever been any different? If it could have, people couldn't remember that time.

But it's wrong to say that honest men were at a loss. They had it good because they could live their whole lives like that. Just as it was easy for murderers to kill people, it was easy for those who would never do it. It was difficult, however, when fate mixed up the roles and nothing depended any longer on how one lived.

He was standing with his arms spread wide while the quiet one dug through his pockets. The fat man held out the open sack and looked him straight in the eye. Maybe he was checking to see whether Niko recognized him, but if he did that, he quickly gave up. How couldn't he recognize him?

"I thought you were smarter!" he said with regret in his voice. "You didn't let us into your house because you were afraid that we might steal something, and yet you believed that the caravan drivers were coming. Damn—what caravan drivers?! We thought we'd fleece five idiots, but half the city came! They came, okay, but how did you end up out here?"

Niko said nothing, but he was searching for some way to show him that he wasn't afraid of him. He thought Fatso would understand if he looked him in the eye, but Fatso didn't care. It was quite clear that he didn't care. As he spoke, he began to scan the clearing again, afraid that something might happen there or that a search party would arrive.

Just then the leader on the black horse rode up. "Well, who do I see here? Our buddy! Is there any vinegar, buddy? And where's the child? See, I've collected some gold, and now it's time to find a bride, and well, I've been thinking like people do . . ."

The rider hadn't finished his sentence when Niko leaped over to the quiet one, grabbed the rifle from his shoulder, and gave it a jerk. The sling broke; the quiet one fell onto the ground, his hat flew off, and cries rang out among the people. Niko Azinović pointed the rifle at the man who'd insulted Regina and without hesitating pulled the trigger. Before the hammer struck its empty chamber, the steel of a bayonet plunged into him between his ribs. He fell with a clear and pure feeling of being cheated in life. The fat man dropped the rifle, whose bayonet remained in Niko, and he started running toward his horse. But it was too late. After one man had openly resisted, the others jumped to their feet and ran in a mad charge.

In an instant the crowd swarmed the two robbers, the one who'd wanted to run first and the one who'd wanted to stay to the end. Their revenge didn't last long because there were too many of them who wanted it. Their toes popped as they kicked into the half-dead bodies. Coarse laborers' heels smashed their temples. Someone's thumbnail remained stuck in a nostril. Their fists hit into the deep folds of the fat one's body. Someone remembered the rifle and smashed its ironbound butt into his skull; his brains popped and turned into the slush that paupers feed their piglets in wartime. It was all over in no more than two minutes. Then the crowd stopped as if on command.

"Don't kill them; they should be tried!" someone blurted out, probably so he wouldn't be held responsible.

"It's over; they're dead," said another.

The fat robber lay with his head smashed, on which the only thing left whole and recognizable was one wide open dark eye, framed by long, girlish eyelashes. However, while Fatso's hood had been torn from his head, the other robber was still in disguise. Someone had to unmask him, but for some reason the people began to hesitate and hem and haw, moving away from the corpses and withdrawing into the mass of people. Soon no one would know who'd been in the front rows, who had hit the most and broken their fingers, nor would they know whose thumbnail had remained in the nostril of the one-eyed fat highwayman.

"Hand the sack with the gold over here!" shouted the men who'd pushed their way closest to the dead men. "That's right; let's get the valuables! Everyone gets what he put in!"

Shouts and yells followed concerning what was whose and how much had been taken from whom. Whereas one could still figure out who the jewelry belonged to, Franz Joseph's and Napoleon's ducats were everyone's and no one's. Stricken with panic at the thought of being cheated or robbed once again, people forgot about the dead highwaymen. The fat mare grazed peacefully at the end of the clearing and would only raise its head and blink whenever someone shouted because someone else had stepped on their foot or already stolen their gold crucifix and their medallion of the Blessed Virgin from the robbers' sack.

Niko's head was resting in the lap of his friend, the top of the bayonet was sticking out of his chest just below his right breast. The old man looked with interest at how the hole in his shirt widened every time he sighed or exhaled, and the steel blade on which no blood was visible grew upward to the sky. That sight amused him and took his mind off other thoughts. If he concentrated enough, he no longer even felt pain. Dominko Pujdin spoke without stopping, asked him questions, and wiped the sweat from his brow with his hand. He tried to call someone over and for no good reason fidgeted continuously, like a child that couldn't calm down. Like a child that asks, "Why this? Why that? How come?" and you patiently answer it until it falls asleep. But there were no answers that could be given to him. Because Niko didn't understand a single word that he was saying. That was strange because Dominko Pujdin didn't speak any foreign languages. So what language was he speaking then? Well, who could know what happened or didn't happen in the meantime as he lay on the ground sleeping and people were stampeding all around him?! The people were hurrying somewhere; they ran like crazy but didn't bother him. He had his nap in peace and wondered at himself. Before, everything would have bothered him; he would have woken up at any rustling and felt envy for heavy sleepers. But now everything was perfectly fine for him. He had had to grow old to get real sleep. Not even crazy Dominko bothered him now. He felt that he would fall asleep again, and he was happy about it. Kata wouldn't be angry; she would mend the hole in his shirt easily. That was easy for her. She'd inherited hands of gold from her mother. What was most important was for a person to get a good night's sleep.

"People, a man has died!" Dominko Pujdin shouted as loud as he could, but no one heard him. They were wrangling over the empty sack with the gold.

"My Niko is gone, people!" he continued, more for himself than for others.

Only for an instant did he think of his ducats, but he remained sitting on the ground, with Niko's head on his lap and a feeling that with every moment there was less and less of a reason for him to tell anyone about this. Soon some women would come, the army and police would appear, Dr. Hans Eberlich would take him by the hand and lead him to a carriage, and some men in black would take his friend Niko Azinović off toward a hill.

"Why are they carrying him?" he asked Eberlich.

"Everything will be okay," the Kraut answered, as the comforting fog of veronal descended on the lights in the harbor.

Niko Azinović was one of four victims on the day after the great rains: he, Admiral Sterk, Čare Nedoklan, and—if he could be considered a victim— Antiša Bakunin!

No one was particularly surprised, not to mention moved, when it was revealed that the mute robber was actually the most notorious anarchist in the city, a dropout from the University of Vienna. Many were relieved because Antiša was not family or kin to anyone in the city. His father, Captain Ante Bartulović, was from the Bay of Kotor and had moved to Dubrovnik after he'd stopped sailing. People didn't know the real reasons, but they probably had something to do with Antiša's mother, a noblewoman from Trieste whom people in the Bay of Kotor called the Trieste Tart because of her hats and short skirts. Shortly after they bought a house in the Pile district, the captain died, and Mrs. Francesca spent all her savings on Antiša's studies in Vienna. God only knows what kind of company he fell in with there, but after wasting seven years there, Antiša was deported to his birthplace because he'd taken part in anti-imperial demonstrations and preparations for the assassination of the director of the Vienna Opera. The former might have lent him some status in his home town, but the latter (that he'd wanted to kill the director of the Vienna Opera!) only provoked mockery and scorn. Instead of settling down and waiting for people to forget about his Vienna episode, Antiša bristled and argued and tried to convince anyone and everyone that the Vienna Opera was one of the main levers in the oppression of the enslaved peoples of the Habsburg monarchy and its director an important and crucial functionary of the state as the highest means of exercising terror on the individual. He didn't notice that they were taunting him and goading him into saying the same thing over again for the hundredth time. It was too late when it finally occurred to him that they'd made him into the biggest object of ridicule in town. Then it didn't matter what he said. Sometimes they called him Antiša Carusoe, other times they called him Antiša Bakunin, but both nicknames were equally derisive.

It wasn't known whose mind was the source of the idea of the robbery or who had thought up and spread the tale of the caravan, but everything pointed to him. The other dead robber wasn't from Dubrovnik, nor did anyone recognize him, and as for the two who'd gotten away on horseback, it also seemed probable that they weren't from the city. If they had been, people would already know somehow, or people would have heard that someone was missing from someone's household. But such a robbery could have occurred only to someone who lived in the town, knew the people there, and thus knew how to set the bait for them. The main thing was to lure them outside the city, get them to gather up all the gold from their houses, and get greedy. The caravan was coming! Everyone knew about it, and everyone kept it from everyone else, so everyone thought he was the only one who knew. If it had been any different, the plan would have surely failed or the booty would have been more meager. As it was, people went with the intention of buying up the whole caravan, feeding and satisfying their families, and reselling what was left to recover their expenses. Antiša had conceived the plan perfectly, but he thought it more important to hit back at the town that had humiliated him than to get rich. That was his mistake. He wanted to leave them without a penny to their names, naked and barefoot in an empty clearing, and then watch them humbly return home as fools and asses. Maybe he would have succeeded if it hadn't been raining for nearly a whole month and his outlaws hadn't started stopping in at Niko Azinović's cellar out of sheer boredom.

Regina's grandfather and Antiša Bakunin were buried on the same day. Niko's funeral was the largest since the beginning of the war, and the town might not have seen a bigger funeral except when bishops died. Three priests saw him off; almost everyone whom he'd helped to regain their gold came to pay their respects. A lot of women and children gathered, as well as representatives of military and police authorities, plainclothes agents who were working on the case of the caravan, a large number of curious people, and wretches and misfits who came to every meeting of any historical significance. Niko Azinović became a hero and a martyr; it was said that he'd rushed at rifles with his bare hands without defending himself and his rights, consciously choosing death so others could live with dignity. He'd saved the property of his fellow citizens and the honor of the city. Only his bravery had spared Dubrovnik from the largest

robbery in its history. That was what was said by those who saw off Grandpa
Niko. And after each one read what he had to say over the open grave, he went
up to Kata and Angelina, hugged them, and comforted them, promising that
the sacrifice of their father would never be forgotten. The little girl moved away,
fleeing from the moist palms that patted her face and hair. She listened and remembered. Instead of protecting her, who'd loved him and was his, he'd tried
to defend people whom he didn't love or know.

Antiša Bakunin was buried outside the cemetery wall, in weeds and wild cabbage because people threatened that they would smash the grave of Captain
Ante Bartulović if his son was buried in his family's grave.

Father Ivan didn't want to see him off to the hereafter and explained that
Antiša had been an anarchist and an anti-Christian and that in view of this, the
sacraments that Antiša's unfortunate mother was requesting didn't mean anything. She paid two workers to dig a hole and buried him herself. If there was
anything comforting in his sad fate, it was that the town would not remember
Antiša Bakunin as an object of ridicule. His attempt at robbery would grow into
a legend that would speak for a while about the conflict between Antiša the
Antichrist and Niko the Martyr, only for Niko's character to pale soon and disappear from a story whose final version told about how in the First World War
Antiša Bakunin and three outlaws killed and robbed charitable men who were
trying to save the town from hunger.

In contrast to him, the wretched man from Konavle acquired no fame. A
few months before the fall of the Austro-Hungarian Empire he was sentenced
to death and hanged in a prison yard. How did he conduct himself under the
gallows, and did he feel any regret about the murder of the city's last clockmaker? Nothing is known about that, nor is it known where he was buried, but
it is possible that Father Ivan didn't forget his soul and that he gave his blessing
to its repose.

The corpse of the fat robber was never identified, and it was buried in a metal
coffin beyond the military shooting range. The two robbers who escaped were
never caught. However, the police worked on the case of the caravan until the
end of the war and the fall of the Habsburg monarchy. The Serbian Royal Army
was about to reach the Adriatic, the negotiations on the establishment of a state
for the South Slavs had ended, and the Habsburgs were already preoccupied
with tragedies of their family instead of tragedies of the state when plainclothes
police agents were still questioning people, listening to conversations in bars
and taverns, and trying to learn from women and children the manner in which
the story about the arrival of the caravan had spread through the town. Inspector Aldo Tomaseo, who'd been assigned to the case, didn't believe that the rob-

bery could have been organized and perfectly carried out by four men. Rather, there must have been a network of people who'd gone from house to house telling people that the caravan drivers were coming. Indeed, Tomaseo had a hard time figuring out how anyone could have believed in something that had disappeared with the departure of the Ottoman Empire from the Balkans. But that secret would be revealed, he thought, as soon as he fingered the group that had spread the rumors.

Aldo Tomaseo was retired immediately after the new liberators arrived, and the colonel of the Royal Army kicked him out of his office when he tried to explain the nature of that criminal case and the need for the case of the caravan to be solved regardless of the new international situation and relations in Europe. Bitter and confused, Tomaseo returned to his native Pula, where he wrote correspondence on his own account and to no avail at all and sent it to the Dubrovnik authorities.

"A poisonous viper is in your bosom, and the robbery of the century awaits you, sooner or later . . ."

In the house of the deceased Niko Azinović times of poverty and gloom followed. None of his savings remained, the vineyards had grown wild because there was no one to work them, and the first dusk always brought with it growing numbers of empty thoughts and boredom. The boys told one another their grandpa's tales but most often would get into a fight because of differences they had about how to interpret them, so their mother had to forbid that game. In a few months the little girl grew up, changed, and became serious. It seemed that she'd forgotten her grandpa. She hadn't, however, forgotten the džundžur beans. She would get two marbles, close her eyes, and pass her crossed fingers over them. The miracle was still there. The two marbles would become four.

I

It was late summer 1904. The grape harvest was coming up; there had been just the right amount of rain. It was the kind of year one could only wish for. At least as far as grapes and wine were concerned. August was sitting under his outside stairs with a piece of walnut wood between his knees. What was it going to be? The neck of a gusle that the French ambassador would ceremoniously present to the Montenegrin king Nikola when arriving to pay his respects? Or a model of the *Santa Maria delle Grazia* for Captain Vojko Šiškić that would adorn his house in Perast? Or would it nevertheless be the head of Prince Marko that the Sarajevo Mountaineering Club had ordered for its meetinghouse? August never knew in advance what he was going to make out of which piece of wood but sat and waited, with a chisel in one hand and a mallet in the other, for his mind to focus on what he might make that day. Some days were for making ships, and others simply weren't. And Captain Vojko had no business trying to hurry him up. He'd told him straightforwardly that the ship would be made in three days according to the plan that he'd been given. But only when the time came for working on ships! Say, when the sirocco swept down and the sea rose so no one was sailing out; well, at such time he didn't feel like doing anything but sitting somewhere out of the wind and rain and making model ships. And there were still two more months for the gusle. They were easy to make if you had the right wood, but you had to wait for it. Right until it came along among dozens of other apparently identical logs. Not every kind of walnut wood was the same; the best was that Herzegovinian walnut. A sapling that took root in rocky ground and didn't need too much water as it grew and turned into a big tree. Bosnian walnut might have produced good nuts, but in its soul it was like a man who caroused, gorged, and guzzled to excess; wasn't good with women and children; and aged before his time. Its wood rotted easily and was hard to cure. But when it did dry, it became crumbly and wasn't for making gusle. If it were up to August, he'd always say that there was no better walnut than Herzegovinian walnut!

They say it's a sin to cut down a tree that bears good fruit! Yes, and August would have admitted that too. When the barren years came without wheat, potatoes, or corn, there was nothing better to eat than walnut meat. There were those who fed on fish every day. Paupers and misers! But he'd never gotten used to fish. If God had created man to feed on fish, he would have given him fins on his back and gills to breathe under water! Those who said that Jesus had fed people with fish were lying, just as those who said there was a wood called mahogany that was better than walnut were lying. First of all, August had never held a piece of mahogany in his hands, and second, those who said that one thing was better than another should have first said what was wrong with walnut and thus how mahogany was better. Well, they couldn't do it! And they didn't know because you wouldn't be able to find a flaw in walnut wood if you sought one for a hundred years!

Since he'd moved to Trsteno from Tolma—and that was years and years ago since he'd been there for half his life—August Liščar had never touched another wood with his chisel. Those who liked oak and pine, they could just make tables, coffins, and doors for poor men's houses. They could hew and keep quiet! When God was creating the world, he had first created artists and dilettantes and then walnut and oak for each. He commanded the former to make his world more beautiful, and the latter he obligated to hew and keep quiet. They could work so the poor folk didn't rise up! But they weren't supposed to say anything! As soon as their kind started talking, August would leave the tavern, even if he left a half a bottle of wine on the table.

He knew what he was talking about because he'd traveled halfway around the world on horseback or by train, from Škofja Loka to Salonika, and all he'd ever bought was walnut. You had to travel because the wood wouldn't come walking to you on its own, and people didn't cut down their own walnut trees unless they were in deep trouble or had some compelling need. Once, when he was passing through Buna, Mostar, and Lištica and saw beautiful trees whose trunks played Mozart and Brahms when you knocked on them, it occurred to him to get a rifle, assemble a band of highwaymen, and go to the gates of those houses and tell the owners, "Your walnut or your life!" But that was just a joke; his mama Fanika and his papa Pepi hadn't raised him to be a robber, nor would he have ever taken anything against someone's will. He also understood that walnut trees were important to people; they cared about the nuts they produced and their ancestors who'd planted them. For them a walnut tree in their yard was like a coat of arms over the entryways of the houses of Dubrovnik nobles. There was no difference! Both the one and the other showed that a person had struck roots there. But those people didn't know, nor could they know, how much the soul of a felled walnut tree was worth.

There was no misfortune greater than war and pestilence! That was written in the holy scripture, so August couldn't object, but wars and epidemics were good for his work and his art. In the summer of 1878 he had cut down more than enough walnut trees in Herzegovina and Bosnia for a whole lifetime. Fortunately, he had still been young, had strength, and had been assisted by two apprentices, Feriz and Josip—who knew what they were doing now?! They'd cut trees in every village and city, and people had sold them their trees for peanuts. Embittered by their defeat and the arrival of Christian rule, they had sold their property if someone wanted to buy it and left for Turkey. August had done them a favor because they received money for something they had never even expected to be able to sell. But it didn't matter; every one of those beys, agas, or whatever they were, each one of them, wearing his turban or fez, would stand in the middle of his grove or yard with tears streaming down his face when they cut down his walnut tree. It was hard to watch a grown man cry! When that happened, the world lost something that not even God could replace. When a man cried, that was a sign that empires were collapsing, customs were changing and better times were coming for unborn children, and times of death had arrived for everyone who bowed to old banners. Only when their walnut trees were cut down did these men understand what it meant to leave the place where they'd been born. Maybe a few of them would repent and accept the Austrian emperor, but it was already too late because their walnut trees were already gone.

And then the barren years came, typhus and diphtheria reigned, and there were rebellions in Serbia and Macedonia. It was a time of lawlessness in the former Turkish provinces; the minarets in the Užica district came crashing down like rotten poplars. Misery and poverty spread more quickly than enthusiasm for the newly won freedom and the rulers who crossed themselves and went to church. August wandered around the devastated areas and cut down walnut trees, sometimes with his apprentices but often alone. At the time when his business was going strongest, he had five warehouses and as many workshops: in Šabac, Sarajevo, Mostar, Split, and Trsteno.

He made furniture for Austrian administrative buildings, churches, and mosques; carved likenesses of rulers and national heroes; made gusle for kings and highwaymen, up until times changed again. As far as others were concerned, they'd gotten better, and as far as he was concerned, they'd gotten worse than ever. Walnut wood was hard to come by, and there were fewer and fewer orders. Furniture arrived from Vienna, and dilettantes began to take over who made gusle from any kind of wood in large numbers. The world was losing its sense of esthetics. Everyone had started to entertain and celebrate things, wandering theater troupes appeared, operettas were performed, and balls and celebrations were organized and held in the Parisian and Viennese fashion. People were slowly but surely losing their minds. At first August was despondent about this, but then he began to take wicked pleasure in the coming disaster. All he had left was his house in Trsteno. He'd sold the others because he had no reason to hold on to them; he was getting up in years. More and more often he couldn't work because of his rheumatism. He was losing his strength in his hands. His children had gotten married in Zagreb and Karlovac, and all he had left was his Matilda.

Still, he didn't have it bad! August didn't complain except to his closest friends! He didn't even speak to anyone else, and friends are there for you to complain to them sometimes. He knew that they would grow tired of his whining, so when they stopped coming to his place, August was not angry but went to them. To Dubrovnik, Čapljina, Sarajevo . . . He always brought them a gift that he'd fashioned: he took a carved wooden medicine cabinet that he'd copied from pictures of a Baghdad mosque to Ilidža for Karlo Stubler, his oldest friend, a railway official. Stubler was naturally thrilled. August had been complaining of his rheumatism to him for a good seven years, and his friend had tried to comfort him and would never have thought of mentioning his heart problems. He took a figure of King Tomislav on a rearing horse to Ivo Solda in Čapljina, and it still stood there, in a special place in Solda's hotel beside a portrait of the emperor. He carved a Venetian gondolier for Mijo Ćipik and gave him Mijo's face. It took Mijo's wife Zdenka ten days to get over her astonishment at how accurate he'd made the likeness . . .

August didn't need money to live on! He'd earned enough for three lifetimes, but he couldn't come to terms with the fact that he was getting on in years—Matilda told him a hundred times a day that he needed to rest! He got upset when no one came with orders for work, and he only made gifts for friends. In those days and months he was furious at everyone—neither the authorities nor the priests were worth anything. The newspapers that his children sent from Zagreb irritated him. He would get short with Matilda. But what was worse—when there was no work, August aged more and more quickly and generally went downhill. He began to forget things; in the evening he couldn't remember what he'd said in the morning. Names slipped from his mind; he couldn't remember where he'd put his glasses; he'd leave for Dubrovnik and halfway there he didn't know why he'd gone . . . He was downcast then, but Matilda was even worse. She was afraid of losing him and that the old man would kick the bucket before his time, bite the big one, take a dirt nap—as he said in jest—and she would be left on her own. That was why it was so difficult to describe the joy in the Liščar household in Trsteno when, after six empty months, four orders came in as many days! A gusle for the king, a ship for Captain Vojko, Prince Marko for the mountain climbers, and the fourth order: toys for the unborn grandchild of someone in Dubrovnik.

That man had come to him to tell him that his daughter had conceived, and was actually in her fourth month, and that he wanted to give the child toys made of walnut wood. It didn't matter what they cost! That was what he'd said. A happy-go-lucky type, a little crazy, but August liked him. If he hadn't, he would surely have refused him. First: he'd never made children's toys in his life! Second: wasn't it an insult to the noble wood to be piddled around with for such purposes? Third: August wouldn't have admitted it, but he was a little afraid of having to make something for the first time. And fourth and most important: that man wanted toys to put next to the cradle as soon as the child was born and for the toys to work for both a male and a female child! August had never received such a difficult order. For days and nights already he'd been thinking about what the male and female worlds had in common. He started from what boys and girls would like to play with, but very quickly he raised his inquiry to a universal level, philosophizing about sexual differences, reading what scholarly books said about it, and ordered philosophical and theological treatises sent to him from Zagreb.

He went to Zaostrog for a talk with Brother Anđelo, a monastery librarian, a learned but also progressive man who reconciled the ice of the church with the fire of modern life and had read all the important books on the one and the other side. First he asked indirectly, and the monk started going on at length about how there was no difference in intelligence between men and women but that women were more sensitive and men were more rash. "Only their feelings make the world happier, whereas their rashness brings misfortune. That's the basic difference between men and women!" Brother Anđelo exclaimed, but August didn't see any great benefit from this wisdom, so he simply stated his problem to him:

"What kind of toys should I make for the child if I don't know whether it's going to be a boy or a girl?"

The monk was confused; his eyes seemed to have teared up in the face of a question that had no answer. Then he thought for a long time and looked at August on and off—some other priest or smart-ass would have certainly gotten out of it by saying that toys were a waste of time and there was nothing to think about them, but Brother Anđelo wasn't of that type. For him there were no questions of lesser importance. From how many legs an ant has to why Peter betrayed Christ, he thought every answer was important.

"I don't know what to tell you, Brother August," he said with the tone of an Old Testament penitent. "Could you make a crib instead of toys?"

No, for August that would be tantamount to admitting that there was something that he couldn't make out of walnut wood. He would have been confirming that he'd grown old, spitting on everything he had built in his life. And in the end he would have been lying to a customer! He would have been lying to the man from Dubrovnik, saying that there was something that couldn't be fashioned from walnut wood. There wasn't anything, except stoves! A stove was the only thing that you couldn't make out of walnut wood. For everything else all one needed was smarts and skill. It couldn't be that he'd lost his smarts.

August wasn't sitting under the stairs as he otherwise did when he tried to see what purpose there was in a piece of wood. He toyed around with gusle, Prince Marko, and the ship *Santa Maria delle Grazia*, but in fact all he had on his mind were toys. He hadn't done anything for hours already, and when his nerves gave out from the tension and his hands froze up, August tapped on the chisel. There were shallow cuts in the wood, but he couldn't get working. In the end he would reconcile himself to his fate—there was still time before the child was born—and he would start on what was easiest. In two days he would turn a piece of wood into the head of Prince Marko, a dark-mustached man with a low brow and lowered eyebrows under which one could sense the gaze of a bull that was about to start on a decisive run to clash with Musa Kesedžija. In thirty years August had made a few hundred Prince Markos. Every time he strove to carve the same head, without changing the expression or the shape of the nose, because there was no other way to imagine the portrait of a man when no one knew what he'd actually looked like. Every sculptor or painter, artist or dilettante, made his own Marko, and the more times he repeated the same work, the greater was the chance that people would believe that the famed hero had looked just like that. August, there was no denying it, was about to become the creator of the definitive likeness of Prince Marko. Long ago people had started copying his work and that angered him, but he was aware that in that way they were also helping him. A low brow, lowered eyebrows, and the look of a bull! If that were really Prince Marko, let it be known that he hadn't been created like that by God but by the master from Tolmin, the earl of walnut, August Liščar!

And he made one more Marko with his eyes closed! Everything in one go, with no need for any corrections and with half his power and less effort. It had to be like that. In those thirty or so years (in fact it would soon be forty, and if one counted his first carpentry projects, forty-five), August had conquered walnut wood like Napoleon's army had conquered Europe, but he had to make Prince Marko with that limit in skill and knowledge that was characteristic of a master's youth. Coarse and feigned imprecision, without the finesse with which he made other objects. Because if he made Marko with these all-knowing hands, then it wouldn't be Marko any more, and no one would recognize him. Oh, if he were to collect all the heroic heads he'd ever made and line them up one next to the other—what a series that would be! And each one was the same. And not a one of them would reveal to anyone when it was made and how he'd felt as he worked on it, whether he'd been ill or had just had a child, whether he'd been working in the middle of the hellish smithing of the Sarajevo market square, or whether it had come about in Šabac. Whom he'd been thinking of while he was working, whether he was having a difficult time . . . Nothing of that could be seen on the heads of Prince Marko. That was why they were art.

The next day he would go early in the morning to Dubrovnik. To talk with that man and hear what his grandchild was going to be like. Someone would think it stupid to ask a grandfather what his grandchild would be like, but August believed in such things. We're like people wanted us to be before we were born. Cities were full of princes and princesses, and it was easy to imagine what their grandfathers and grandmothers had thought while they were waiting for their grandchildren. In villages there were more quiet, industrious people who often resembled their own bulls. Mostly they were the seventh or eighth sons of their fathers and mothers. If they'd wanted them, their imaginations were already spent. No one imagined those people, so they came out like that.

August ruminated as another sunny day opened up over the sea and the grass-hoppers tuned their instruments. Like an opera orchestra right before a perfor-mance of a work it has played so often that each musician knows his part by heart and tunes his strings and taps his bow on them just for fun.

The grandfather-to-be was filled with cheer when he saw him.

"Who's this I see?!" he exclaimed and hugged him. None of this made any sense, neither speaking like that nor hugging someone whom you barely knew, but it didn't bother August. He hugged him back so the man wouldn't feel awk-ward when he realized how silly his actions had been. And why should one for-ever be a sourpuss? Matilda didn't tell him that for nothing. Sometimes even August had to admit that she knew what she was talking about.

He led him into his house, and the house was exactly as August expected it to be. The house of poor folk in a city, with no lineage or roots, who'd worked hard for generations, weeded their gardens and vineyards, went fishing, sold Herze-govinian tobacco, and saved little by little, ducat by ducat, brick by brick—until they got that house. It wasn't ugly or beautiful, expensive or cheap, but just as they themselves were. Good people. And his daughter wasn't some beauty, but you couldn't say that she was ugly either. A girl of real Dalmatian stock who would grow stocky and fat with the years, stand with her hands on her hips and her legs spread gently at twilight, calling her children. Now he could imagine a version of her in walnut.

"Your name is Kata? There was once a queen, and her name was Katarina Kosača. She sought justice for her queendom in Rome and died there. Her grave is in the church. They say she was beautiful," August said, and she laughed. Just as if he'd said that she was beautiful. And that made him glad.

Her husband was a placid man; he was too quiet, but as soon as he opened his mouth, he started cracking his knuckles. He really cracked them harshly. It was good that he didn't say more because if he had, he'd have lost his fingers.

"It's going to be a girl," said her grandfather, speaking in a way that was uncharacteristic for these parts.

"God only knows," said the mother. "Maybe it'll still be a boy!" And the father shrugged his shoulders, cracked his knuckles a little, and thought to himself but didn't say anything.

"I don't know what our child will be like. Intelligent and good-looking! It certainly won't be rich; there's no one for it to take after to be that. I'm worried less about what it will be like than about how people will treat it. That's what's important! Let's hope it's not worse than others. Let's hope it's not more wicked and that it doesn't want more for itself than the next one wants for itself. So, that's what I'd wish for. If it's like that, there's a greater chance it will have a happy life and take less misfortune to its grave. But you never know. You don't even determine what you yourself will be like, nor do others. Not even God does. You know what they say in Herzegovina: I got the shit end of the stick! Well, if you get the shit end of the stick too many times, then nothing else can help. Two fishermen take the same line, the same hook, and the same kind of bait, go together to the same spot, and cast out at the same time. One of them catches a forty-pound dentex, and the other doesn't catch a thing. The other one got the shit end of the stick."

That was how the grandfather-to-be spoke, mixing languages and accents as if he'd lived all over. The father and mother listened, and it seemed that they wouldn't have interrupted him if he'd kept talking until the next day. From this August was certain that the future child was his more than anyone else's and that he should make the toys according to what he said. And that was something, though the progress wasn't great.

Later they sat down in front of the house; Kata brought out some wine and salted sardines, and it was then that August first saw her belly. A small, rounded belly, as on Middle Eastern pictures, from which one still couldn't tell that she was with child. For a moment he was afraid that she might miscarry. It happened often, out of the blue, that a mother would expel an unborn child from herself. She would simply bleed it out. No, he dared not think about that. It would be horrible both for them and for him. His big job would fall by the wayside, the one that he'd been waiting for all this time, the one that many never got. How many had there been who needed only to be allowed to paint the Sistine Chapel to become the greatest artist in history! August had long ago kissed good-bye the idea that he might be the greatest in history . He wasn't the greatest, not even among these squalid people who didn't have their own artists, but there was no one better than him at carving walnut! And there was no greater commission than this one: to create a work of art for someone who wasn't born yet! It wouldn't have been good for the woman to miscarry. The old man would be unhappy, the woman would be unhappy, and the knuckle-cracking young man would be unhappy along with them. And August would be too! This discovery captivated him. He was bound to people whom he didn't know—he didn't even know their names. Except that the future mother's name was Kata.

"Oh, what a beautiful day!" August said and sighed. The sardines were a little too salty for his taste, and the wine was too bitter. But to tell the truth August didn't like fish, and in his life he drank wine only to get drunk. Now he wasn't trying to get drunk. All he wanted was for this day to last as long as possible, for nothing to change, and to stay with these people until evening.

His wish was fulfilled. He returned to Trsteno after midnight. Matilda was already asleep, and he quietly slipped into her bed feeling like an unfaithful husband. No matter how much he wandered and traveled around, August had never slept with another woman, nor had another woman caught his eye. But it often happened that he felt like an unfaithful husband. Always when something became more important to him than Matilda. And now those toys were more important to him. And not only the toys, but the child that was about to be born. He hadn't awaited his own children with such joyful trepidation.

"I know!" he shouted before he opened his eyes. He wanted to tell her, but his hand fell on an empty space on the bed—Matilda had gotten up first, as she always did. That immediately rattled him, but he decided not to get up before he told her.

"Eureka!" he howled at the top of his lungs. "Eureka! Eureka! Eureka!" he shouted until his throat was sore, but it was no use. Matilda evidently wasn't at home. He grumpily pushed away the duvet and hurled a shoe at the other end of the room. And then he thought that maybe he shouldn't have done that. An artist couldn't be angry if an ingenious idea occurred to him and at that be angry only because his wife wasn't around. He went down into the cellar, stretching himself so he could touch the beams in the ceiling, but he was still a centimeter or so too short. That was precisely how much he'd shrunk in the last few years. After he drank a glass of milk, he was going to go to the lumberyard and pick out the five most beautiful pieces of walnut there. He would need at least five for what he'd thought up. More wood would be used for a toy for a child that was yet to be born than for a small church altar. That was the way it should be!

The church served to correct and rework people who were already finished and thus incorrigible. This was for someone who still did not need an altar and, God willing, would never need one.

In a book entitled *Modern Interiors of Cities of the Future*, published by Ćelap Booksellers, he found a plan and a cutaway view of the kind of house that the majority of Europeans would live in around 1950, that is to say, in exactly forty-five years. The preface said that the book's author, an engineer named Adolf Foose, had taken into account all the current and future achievements of the technological revolution, the cultural progress of our civilization, and generally man's spiritual ascent to a higher stage of humanity, the not-too-distant future in which brotherhood and equality would reign . . . August had bought *Modern Interiors of Cities of the Future* the previous year in Zagreb, leafed through it on his way back to Trsteno, and then fallen into a deep depression and decided not to pick it up again.

If he were to live to see that year of 1950, which was downright impossible, he would be a hundred and ten years old and would be too old for all the pleasures that would be available then. He'd been born too late and lived in the twilight of a dark age full of ignorance and primitivism, wars, rebellions, and pointless bloodletting. The day before they'd still burned witches, and Turkish soldiers galloped all over the place with drawn sabers, ready to lop off the head of anyone who resisted them. That had probably gone on for around a thousand years, but then something happened: the telegraph was invented, railroad trains started rolling, gas lamps turned night into day, and the people of the world started at an accelerated pace toward happiness, welfare, and all kinds of pleasures. It killed him to know that without being able to live to see the fruits of those changes. And that was why he decided not to open that book again. He thought about taking it to Dubrovnik, to Salamon Levi, and to give it to his used bookstore for half the price. Fortunately he hadn't gotten around to it because then this ingenious idea would never have crossed his mind: to build a house that Europeans would live in in 1950! That would be a toy for a child of the future, and it didn't matter whether it was a boy or a girl. A house was the only thing in this sad world that belonged to men and women alike.

On the ground floor there was a reception room with three armchairs, a tea table, and a divan in the three colors of the French flag. In one corner there was a shoe polishing machine and a moving mirror. Here there was also a refrigerator with refreshing drinks, a movie projector, and a household telegraph. On the first floor, in addition to a toilet and a large bathroom, there was a parlor for social games, with a pool table, a piano, and Japanese bamboo furniture, that led to a kitchen with an electric stove, a refrigerator, and a series of devices whose purpose August was unable to discover. Maybe the author had placed them there just in case, without himself knowing what their function was. Here there was also a bedroom with a master bed, closets, and an electric massage table. On the second floor there were two more rooms, and in the attic, a roomy storage space in which Adolf Foose had put household objects from the past. He had done that to emphasize the contrast, but August realized that it was a precautionary measure. If the future led to ruin or the people ever had enough of it (and that was possible too!), then they would simply take down the old stuff from the attic and go back to where they had once been. The house of the future was perpetually bathed in sunlight because an electric motor rotated the house to face the sun. It had large windows and a view of an Alpine lake, above which snowy peaks rose and predatory birds flew. One day, in the distant year of 1950, cities would coexist with nature; they would be located alongside the habitats of wild animals and in the middle of forests, where there was fresh air and the colors of nature were appealing to the eye. Industrial zones would be moved to the Sahara Desert and underneath the surface of the sea, and it wasn't even impossible that they would be moved to the Moon . . . People would travel by means of electric trains, electric carriages, balloons and electric flying machines. Walking would be reduced to a minimum, and all animals would live free. No one would eat meat, the flatlands of Europe would glow golden in fields of grain, there wouldn't be states or governments, the king would change every year, and his name would be pulled out of a drum. Kingly rule would be allowed to every adult citizen who hadn't previously broken the law . . .

Okay, August didn't believe every word of it! But Foose's house was a good basis for what he'd imagined on his own, without electrical appliances, multifunctional furniture, and an excess of optimism. Besides, in 1950 the future child would be forty-five years old, which was not a time when one started to live. August would create a house that would be equally good both tomorrow and in 1950.

He sent a letter to the French ambassador in which he informed him with regret that he would be unable to make the gusle for King Nikola. He told Captain Vojko that nothing would come of the *Santa Maria delle Grazia* because it was beneath his honor to make a model of a ship that had never existed.

"You should be ashamed for trying to deceive your own children. Admit to them that you sailed the world on low ships and not on Columbus's caravels!" he wrote to him and told him that he shouldn't try to find him and talk him into it because if August Liščar decided something today, it wouldn't change for the rest of his life! He was proud of himself. He was refusing work again, as he'd done in the best of times, and had quit behaving like a frightened old man who was convinced that no one needed him any more.

For the next few months he worked from dawn until dusk making the walnut house. His back didn't ache once, his joints didn't swell, and in his arms and hands he felt the same strength that he'd had when long ago, somewhere in Bosnia, he'd lifted the trunk of a hundred-year-old walnut tree off the ground. He made the basic shape quickly, in seven or eight days. He didn't need more to divide the house into rooms and make the interior staircases, but the real work began with the doors, the furniture, and the household accessories. At first he had to fashion needles, razors, and nail scissors into tools with which he would, for example, hollow out a bathtub the size of a thumb or kneading troughs that were smaller than a fingernail. He worked on the kneading troughs for two days, working harder than he had on ten heads of Prince Marko. But in the end they looked real. It was even more difficult to decorate the period furniture, put doorknobs on the doors, and make a set of miniature kitchen knives. He adhered to the rule that there was nothing so tiny that it couldn't be made. He made kitchen rags from little pieces of silk and rugs from Matilda's formal dresses.

Every Saturday he went to the grandfather-to-be, sat with him in front of his house, and met the sunset with sardines and wine. He watched Kata's belly grow and her face swell and listened to the father-to-be crack his knuckles as he tried to say who knows what. He shared a peace with those people that he'd never felt before. He declared the toy to be a secret and a surprise and wouldn't give in for anything in the world and reveal what he was building. Kata would pester him, plead with him to tell her, poke him, and pull on his coat. She touched August, and if there was something that he couldn't stand, it was for people to touch him, remove an invisible hair from his shoulder, cheerfully pat him on the back, or grab his forearm when they wanted to tell him something important . . . But it didn't bother him when she did it. He laughed, waved her away, and said that he was an old man and that he enjoyed it when such a pretty young woman wanted something from him. Kata would blush and run off into the kitchen, and then the grandfather would jab him in the ribs with his elbow, raise his eyebrows, and flash his eyes. Just like a pimp going around and offering his girls! But there was nothing unseemly in this, nothing behind it. Only the childlike happiness of old men who, you see, became a little silly waiting for a new life.

A month before Kata gave birth, a race began between August and the child that was coming into the world. Two rooms were still unfinished, and he still had to make the future residents of the house: a man, a woman, three children, and a dog. And a doghouse, too. The residents would also be made of walnut. Rag dolls had always gotten on his nerves and wouldn't be appropriate if the child were a boy. Boys never played with rag dolls, but people and dogs made of walnut wood were as much a part of the male world as they were of the female world. Every joint on the figures needed to be movable; the people would sit, stand, walk, turn their heads, and move their fingers, and the dog would have a movable jaw so that people could see him barking. He also imagined what their faces would look like. At first he wanted the adults to look like Kata and her husband. But why would the child want to have toys that had the faces of its mother and father? He changed his mind. How had such a stupid idea crossed it?!

The last few days he had been working at night as well. Only so the house would be done on time. So then he had to give up on the dog and decide on only two children. Thus came the last Saturday, and the midwife said that Kata would have to give birth during the next week. August worked on finishing the gate of the house before dawn and then lay down for an hour before the tanner Ante came with a horse-drawn cart to take him and the toy to Dubrovnik. Everything was finished: the man and the woman were sitting in armchairs and looking at one another; the children were running around in front of the house; the clean, white kitchen was all shiny, and plates had been set on the table for breakfast. He hadn't made the plates from walnut wood but from plaster. Why? Somehow it seemed inappropriate to make plates from that noble wood. They had to break easily when it came to family arguments and times of despair. But now, when everyone loved one another and lived in the comfort of modern life, the plates on the table changed like the seasons. Some were for breakfast, others for lunch, and still others for dinner. And then it started all over again. In the small world of the walnut house time passed more quickly. Five minutes of a child's play were enough for a day to come to its end, and in half an hour a year would pass. In a year of flesh and blood, a century of wood had passed. In the world of walnut people lived longer. They lived for as many centuries as childhood lasts.

The only thing that was unfinished on the little house was the inscription over the gate. He thought about it for a long time, and all kinds of names came to mind, but none was good enough. Maybe it wouldn't be important to the child, but August wanted a name for this work of art of his. For the most beautiful thing that he'd created with his hands, for something that it had been worthwhile to labor on all these months and that justified all the years of August's life. Maybe he wasn't a great artist, maybe he'd just imagined that he was an exception among so many woodcarving dilettantes, but this little house was something that no one could deny. No one in the world. And it had been created for a single child. That made him happy—that his most important piece of walnut woodcarving was meant for a child.

He had been sleeping on an ottoman that he'd lowered into the storeroom so that he wouldn't disturb Matilda while he worked. He snored, ground his teeth, and wheezed like a woodland rodent as it slowly became light outside and the aurora illuminated the house of the happy people with its reddish glow through the open window. The glow passed over the wooden faces of the man and woman, which changed their expressions in the play of the shadows—from fatigue and thoughtfulness to a foolhardy cheer characteristic of people when they are seized by a happiness that erases any thought that ugly things might still occur in life. At the moment when they'd been most happy, Ante's head blotted out the light: "Master, it's morning, the light of day!" August jumped up from the ottoman like an eager private, and the day could begin.

They arrived at the last minute because Kata's water had already broken; the midwife was running around the house and banging metal washbasins; the knuckle-cracking father stood pale as a ghost in front of the house and barely moved when grandfather and August asked him to help them. The midwife didn't want to let them into Kata's room.

"This isn't for men!" she shouted. "You just push it in and then don't worry about anything!" she continued as August tried to make order in the walnut house. "Get out, or may St. Elijah strike you with lightning and knock some sense into you!" she shouted as August arranged the little wooden children and parents in the house: the father knelt in prayer with his hands folded in front of the room's crucifix, the children were sleeping, and the mother was looking over at Kata's bed. The midwife pushed him out of the room before he managed to check whether the children's heads were turned toward the wall. What was about to happen creates the greatest beauty in the world, but it wasn't for their eyes.

The three of them sat down in front of the house, from which they soon heard Kata's screams. She called to her mother, to Jesus and Mary, whined like a sick dog in the rain, and then screamed again and said, "Rafo, Rafo, Rafo, my good Rafo . . ." It was then that the father cracked his knuckles and August realized that he was Rafo. Rafo and Kata. That has a nice ring, and one could age well with those names, August thought. And those names were somehow homey. Life would go well for them; they would work and make something out of their lives . . . He philosophized like this so he wouldn't have to look at the other two. The old man was smoking cigarette after cigarette, as if the world was coming to an end and not a baby coming into the world. He was so afraid for his daughter that he couldn't show any happiness about his grandchild. That was normal. And August had also been worried about Matilda, and whenever she was in labor, he denied the child as Peter denied Jesus. If God had asked him then, he would have told him, "Stop this, o Lord! Don't let there ever be any more births!" Fortunately, God doesn't ask fathers or grandfathers about anything. Because if he did, children wouldn't be born or only soulless people would be able to have them, those who don't love their wives or daughters. But all would be well! It always was. Or almost always was. That day everything would be good. Rafo and Kata would have their child and be happy. One could hear that in their names. If August and Matilda could be happy, and their names were more suitable for Romanian circus performers than for married couples, why wouldn't Rafo and Kata be happy today? In the end August also started cracking his knuckles. The little bones of four men's hands popped, and it sounded like a hunter was stalking wild boar through dry brush. Grandfather smoked, clenched his fists tightly, and listened to Kata's screams and cries to God. And finally, when the contractions stopped, she again said, "Rafo, Rafo, Rafo, my good Rafo!"

On the fifth of April, 1905, at precisely four in the afternoon, a child was born. The last scream was as long as a trip to the end of the world, sharp as the saber in the hand of the world's last hero and as high as the noonday sun. At that moment nothing more important could happen under the stars. Wars stopped if they were being fought somewhere; the hunger and rage of the sailors on the battleship *Prince Potemkin-Tavrichesky* subsided for a moment; Czar Nicholas II paused, a cup of tea halfway to his lips; a Finnish fisherman with a knife that he was going to plunge into a friend of his became lost in thought; José Manitas looked at a bull and saw his brother in the beast; John Eldar Evian didn't sneeze after he took a pinch of snuff; Natasha Vassilevna looked back for the last time at a young man who would never forget her; Emperor Franz Joseph stopped in mid-sentence and no one thought it was senility; old man Boro took a little white dog onto his lap; a king's assassin removed a splinter from a boy's eye; a beaver finished its dam and rested; the Japanese emperor spit out a cherry pit . . . Everything on the Earth that walked, talked, and felt stopped for a moment when that child was born.

"That's impossible! That's impossible!" people shouted when they heard about it. But how could they know what was possible and what wasn't? How could they when they weren't there? But August knew. He wept as he waited, third in line, for the midwife to place the newborn girl in his arms. Everyone there wept, except Kata and the little walnut family.

That was the end. But it was the beginning of a life. For some reason it seemed so. A child is born, and those that receive it into the world have a sense—along with all their joy and happiness—that something has come to an end. And that, at least as far as they are concerned, something is gone forever. But that's not at all a sad feeling, and there's no fear in it. At least August didn't feel any. Neither did Grandfather. Or Rafo. Or Kata. But one of them—and it's hard now to know who because their souls have mingled with one another, and their thoughts have forgotten whose they were—thought how easy it would be to die and how death would come with no fear at all if one died on a bed on which a child was coming into the world and at the same time. Such thoughts, like dreams, are forgotten easily and quickly. And the feeling that they accompany disappears as well, and sometimes one is even ashamed of them. Or he thinks that someone was lying to someone in all of this.

August took the awl and scratched *The Walnut Mansion* in small, cursive letters above the gate of the happy house. He woke up the little wooden girl and placed her in front of the gate. She was happy forever and ever.

MILJENKO JERGOVIĆ is a Croatian writer. He is one of the most significant writers in the region of the former Yugoslavia. He was born in 1966 in Sarajevo (Bosnia and Herzegovina) and lives nowadays in Zagreb (Croatia). He is the author of more than thirty novels, short story collections, and poetry volumes and has received numerous national and international literary awards, such as the Erich-Maria Remarque Peace Award (1995), the Italian Premio Grinzane Cavour (2003), and the Angelus Literary Award for the best novel in Middle Europe (Poland, 2012). He is the most widely read writer in the region.

STEPHEN M. DICKEY was born and raised in the United States. He studied German and Russian as an undergraduate at the University of Kansas and received his MA and PhD in Slavic linguistics from Indiana University (the latter in 1997). He teaches at the University of Kansas, where he is an associate professor.

JANJA PAVETIĆ-DICKEY was born and raised in Croatia. She studied English and German at the University of Zagreb and the University of Cologne and received her MA in English literature at the University of Leiden. She was a staff translator and interpreter at the UN War Crimes Tribunal in The Hague and currently lives and works in Lawrence, Kansas.